Praise for...
MANIPULATION:

G000118167

E

Fascinating and comp lly imaginative but disturbin v's demise is an enigma within an enigma, and will's theory is as good as any I've heard. Will Cupchik is a good storyteller and *The Avro Arrow Manipulation* would make a fine movie... I hope it sells a zillion.

— *June Callwood, journalist and author*

"A compelling overview of the key issues and political dynamics of the Canadian and U.S. healthcare systems... You don't need to be a conspiracy theorist to appreciate the very distinct plot possibility of Will Cupchik's truly riveting novel."

— *Bob Couchman, Member, Canadian Federal Government's Ministerial Advisory Council on Rural Health [2005]*

I was impressed and sometimes even startled by what Will Cupchik has written. I didn't know how he could weave the Arrow story into one on healthcare in a credible manner, but he has done it... The book is worth reading if only for his comparisons, through genuine information, on the differences between U.S. and Canadian healthcare. What I found most impressive and inspiring is how Will has analyzed the various ruling "power organisms" at play in our societies... I heartily endorse *The Avro Arrow Manipulation* as a good, engrossing, and entertaining read that has a heart and a conscience.

— *Randall Whitcomb, author of <u>Avro Aircraft and Cold War Aviation</u> and former Canadian Forces CF-18 pilot*

As an American businessman whose company is deeply involved in military aircraft and aerospace projects, the premise of this novel makes a lot of sense to me.

In fact, I would be delighted to learn that Americans were involved in closing down the Avro Arrow program. Such an action would have helped prevent Canada from gaining military supremacy in an area that might have cost American corporations <u>billions</u>.

As for the notion that some HMOs and other U.S. healthcare companies might wish to sabotage the Canadian Medicare system; well, if that is happening, it's nothing personal. It's just like the Arrow thing; it is simply a matter of some of our companies working to grow their own businesses.

— *Comment summary of an American CEO*

"I think the issues in the book are very real and worrisome. Even now, the way some politicians and others in high places are acting, I sometimes wonder if a real life, covert 'bizwar' company like TAMPRR is, in actual fact, working to destroy the Canadian Medicare system... In spite of cutbacks that seem to be aimed at destroying the Canadian system, in my opinion it is still better than the one in the U.S.A.. What amazes me is the number of people who think they would be better off being bankrupted by switching to the American system."

— *A Physician in Alberta, Canada*

The Avro Arrow Manipulation: Murdering Medicare

A Novel

Will Cupchik

Tagami Communications . Toronto

Printed in Canada

National Library of Canada Cataloguing in Publication

Cupchik, Will, 1940-

The Avro Arrow Manipulation: Murdering Medicare: a novel set in 2009, involving an covert American company that conducted a covert "bizwar' spanning a half-century, aimed at first at sabotaging the CF-105 Avro Arrow fighter-interceptor program, and in more recent years, the Canadian universal Medicare program / by Will Cupchik—2nd ed.

ISBN 1-896342-19-1

I. Title.

PS8555.U63A77 2005   C813'.6   C2005-901260-9

Cover illustration by Wes Lowe
Book Design by Willy Yau

Publisher: Tagami Communications, 2528 Bayview Avenue, Box   35560, Toronto, Ontario, Canada M2L 2Y4

Distributor of Record: Hushion House
Printed in Canada by Transcontinental Printing G.P.
www.TheAvroArrowManipulationnovel.com

ACKNOWLEDGEMENTS

I thank Barbara Barash Simmons for her feedback of various drafts of this novel, and for her support of this project over the last five years. I am most grateful of all, of course, for her affection and love, and for sharing her life and loves with me, including her feisty and wonderful late mother, Esther; her caring late brother, Lance, who was my bro' for a time; also, Barbara's talented son, Matthew and his exceptional wife, Sorelle. I thank my dear sister, Nina, for her love and caring, and for sharing an enthusiasm for works of fiction of a certain genre; also, my giving and thoughtful brother-in-law, Tom.

I thank Doreen Adams for her valuable comments regarding both earlier and later renditions of this novel; T. Hardin M.D., for his helpful comments of an earlier draft; my extraordinary nephew, Howard and his remarkable and lovely wife, Lily, caring physicians both, for our conversations related to the American and Canadian healthcare systems; as well, I thank Dvora Levinson Ph.D., and Jack Birnbaum M.D., for their interest and feedback of earlier drafts.

One other person deserves special mention–and very many thanks. Denis Dean was a pilot in the Royal Air Force during World War II. Later he was an executive in the private sector, and at various other times held positions at both federal and provincial levels of government in Canada. His considerable enthusiasm for this novel was demonstrated–time and again–by generously giving of his knowledge, time, and effort in reading through the manuscript thoroughly and offering many constructive editing comments that have very much enhanced this novel's reading.

FACTS & AUTHOR'S NOTES

Although published in 2005, most of this novel has been set in the not-too-distant future, in the year 2009. Obviously, therefore, many of the events described in this novel could not possibly have yet taken place. However, *some* events and circumstances referred to in this novel actually did occur in years past. For example…

❑   There really was a fighter-interceptor aircraft, designated the CF-105 Avro Arrow, that was designed, built and flown by Avro Canada between 1955 and 1959. Two prestigious flight-related magazines of the time gave testimony to the reality of this remarkable Canadian technological achievement. <u>Aviation Week</u>, in its October 21, 1957 issue, stated that the *"Avro CF-105 Arrow has given Canada a serious contender for the top military aircraft of the next several years."* An influential British magazine, <u>Flight</u>, in its October 25, 1957 issue, referred to the Avro Arrow *as "the biggest, most powerful, most expensive and potentially the fastest fighter that the world has yet seen."*

❑   In 2005 there still existed in Canada a federal government-mandated and funded universal Medicare system providing free medical coverage for most medically related problems, for virtually every adult and child in the country. However, over many years this system has been significantly weakened by many decisions, actions, and non-actions carried out by certain powerful individuals in the federal, as well as some provincial, governments.

❑   By the early 2000s, the major healthcare companies in the United States reportedly had annual revenues of *over* $230,000,000,000, *i.e.,* <u>230 *billion* dollars</u> which, incidentally, exceeded the combined annual revenues of the major U.S. aerospace and defence companies in the same years.

❑   In 2001, the annual revenues of the largest healthcare company in the U.S. nearly matched that of the most successful computer software company in the world. The reader is encouraged to examine closely the data provided annually in certain American business publications in order to truly appreciate what is at financial stake in the intense battle to increasingly privatize the Canadian, and to preserve and expand the for-profit nature of the American, healthcare systems.

At the same time, it should hardly be necessary to state that *most* business persons, politicians, lobbyists, and healthcare workers of all sorts are generally honest and ethical; that *most* institutions and corporations (including most legislative bodies, insurance companies, hospitals, Health Management Organizations (HMOs), Preferred Provider Organizations (PPOs), and other healthcare-related organizations, operate honorably, ethically, and aboveboard, and that they consistently demonstrate that their primary concern is to serve their constituents, clients, or patients, and only *after* putting those persons *first*, do they focus at making substantial profits for their executives and shareholders.

PROLOGUE

An American President's Warning

— From Dwight D. Eisenhower's
Farewell Address, January 17, 1961

Until the latest of our world conflicts, the United States had no armaments industry. (Now) we annually spend on military security more than the net income of all United States corporations. This conjunction of an immense military establishment and a large arms industry is new in the American experience. <u>(It's) total influence–economic, political, even spiritual–is felt in every city, every state house, every office of the Federal government.</u>

"We recognize the imperative need for this development. Yet <u>we must not fail to comprehend its grave implications</u>... In the councils of government, we must guard against the acquisition of unwarranted influence, whether sought or unsought, by the military-industrial complex. The potential for the disastrous rise of misplaced power exists and will persist. <u>We must never let the weight of this (military-industrial) combination endanger our liberties or democratic processes...(or) public policy could itself become the captive of (an)... elite.</u>"

Eulogy For A Shattered Canadian Reality: Those who will not learn from their national history may be bound to repeat it.

For years, on display near the rear of the Canada Aviation Museum in Ottawa, has been the remnant of a 'cockpit and nose' section of an original Avro Arrow. This piece of torched Canadian ingenuity and aeronautical engineering excellence has been the 'highlight' of a display dealing with the Arrow, necessarily minimalist in nature and size due to the fact that all completed aircraft were ordered destroyed by the Conservative government of John Deifenbaker shortly after it cancelled the Avro Arrow program on February 20th, 1959.

To some observers the gutted remains appear reminiscent of the head and shoulders of a once beautiful and huge bird whose heart, torso, tail, and wings had been torn off with all the skill and dedication of a drunken, depressed, and surely de-listed, veterinarian.

A large notice could be found on the panel immediately behind the Arrow's remains. This notice, titled "Black Friday", articulated the fact that cancellation of the Avro Arrow program had "ended Canada's great venture into supersonic fighter aircraft design, and changed the Canadian aircraft industry's pattern of development." It went on to inform the reader that "all completed aircraft and those on the production line were destroyed and disposed of as scrap," along with other materials related to the Arrow, such as diagrams, engines, and especially designed production equipment.

The same notice also pointed out that "many of the (14,000) engineers, scientists and skilled technicians who had worked on the project left Canada to find work in the United States … "

CHAPTER 1

MAY 1962

Captain Frank Simpson was one of the most decorated U.S.A.F. veterans of the Korean conflict. He was also one of his nation's finest fighter pilots. Simpson had stayed on in the Air Force for a year after he had been repatriated from a North Korean POW camp following the armistice agreement that was declared on June 27, 1953. At the end of that time he elected to leave the air force and go to work as a test pilot for an aircraft manufacturer, flying the next generation of military planes that attested to America's stirring ingenuity and air dominance.

About the only things somewhat below average about the man were his height and weight. Handsome and charming, he made it his duty to always try to fulfill the first two thirds of Oscar Wilde's exhortation to "live hard, look good, and die young". Loving life as he did, however, he had no desire to fulfill the third element of the motto. He had satisfied virtually all of his boyhood fantasies by joining the air force as soon as he was old enough to do so without parental consent, and then stood out among his military classmates, inside and out of the classroom, on the ground as well as in the air.

Simpson was an aviator's aviator, and a genuine American hero whom the press had heralded for being one of those who did not crumble under the North Koreans' despicable attempts to break and then brainwash U.S. prisoners-of-war in an effort to get them to sign false confessions, something that several of his fellow POWs had done. Knowing firsthand what they had gone through, Frank Simpson understood, although he did not necessarily condone, their conduct.

One of the U.S.A.F.'s earliest 'top gun' flight school graduates himself, in early 1962 he was invited to give the major commencement address to its graduating class. It was an honor to be asked, and he accepted the invitation with pleasure. Although a civilian test pilot now, Frank served in the national guard, both because he believed in its mission, and also to continue to fly current-day military-issue aircraft, which in turn helped him to compare and contrast the latter with the next-generation prototypes he was paid to put through their paces. The man loved flying, cherished his country, and adored his wife and son.

It was now raining under the dark grey blanket of cloud cover as Simpson deftly manoeuvred his Air Force F-104 fighter towards a night time landing approach to the U.S.A.F.'s 'top gun' school near Colorado Springs, Colorado.

Simpson was about fifty miles away from the tarmac when he glanced momentarily at the dimly lit photograph of his small family that he always stuck on the canopy. They were his good luck charms. The man believed in God, country, the U.S.A.F, his skills, and his loved ones. As he often did whenever he thought of them, especially whenever he flew, he now murmured to himself, *Love you, Helen; love you, Ken.*

At the same instant, several alarms sounded and warning lights flashed, indicating major problems with the aircraft's fuel, engine, and altitude. The strident sounds and blinking lights all pleaded for his attention, now crashing against his eyes and ears.

What the hell...? Frank's eyes, hands, intuition, and experience instantly consulted with one another, just long enough for him to realize that either the aircraft's entire warning system had gone haywire, or the problems they were signalling to him about were imminently catastrophic and almost certainly not merely the result of ordinary systems failure. He quickly deduced that, unlikely as it seemed, somebody had somehow deliberately done some very bad things to his aircraft. One hand reached out instinctively and flipped on the 'Mayday' distress switch, while his other hand went for the 'eject' button. In the next moment *all* systems failed. In the last, long instant of his lifetime, Frank Simpson realized with certainty what was going to happen to him and his airplane, and in all likelihood, *why*.

His ejection seat exploded upwards into the still-closed canopy, his neck snapping a second before his body was incinerated in the mad fireball that was the aircraft's angry response to hitting the mountain top at more than four hundred miles an hour.

The military inquiry issued its final report on the untimely death of retired U.S.A.F. Captain Colonel Frank Simpson a little more than one year after the tragedy occurred. The crash was ruled the result of a "catastrophic systems failure of unknown origin", and that the explosion was a result of the F-104 striking the mountain. No fault was ascribed to any person or persons involved in the upkeep and maintenance of the aircraft, although "probable pilot error" was offered as the most likely explanation. A scholarship fund was established at the 'top gun' academy in the name of the deceased; the award would go to the graduating airman who demonstrated the finest qualities of leadership and dedication, together with flying skills and academic excellence.

His wife, Katherine, never truly accepted the report's conclusion. Nearly a half-century would pass before she was proved to be right.

CHAPTER 2

SEPTEMBER 11, 2001   3:00PM

On September 11, 2001, mind-searing terrorism landed on American shores. In a single day of diabolical masterstrokes drawn by a highly intelligent, hate-filled fanatic and his stunted offspring, a country and its people lost their delusion of being a safe harbor, far away from the sorts of extremists who had attacked American property and personnel in many other countries over the previous years and decades. With the speed of evil unleashed, 'over there' became 'right here', 'they' became 'us', and 'maybe, in the distant future' collapsed under the dust and devastation of 'definitely, and now'.

Almost all sectors of the U.S. economy, except for security and defence-related companies, suffered an immediate and profound body blow. Within days, certain lobbyists who usually preferred to be called 'client representatives' responded to 9/11 by making cold calls to their 'preferred' politicians to push for additional security-related R&D or equipment contracts. Their calls on that day were as well received as their coin had been previously.

A select number of these 'reps' worked for *The American Management Profit Recovery and Retention Company*, or TAMPRR Inc., a privately owned business whose clients were companies that needed their interests protected and promoted in ways beyond what most public relation firms and lobbying organizations would dare to even imagine.

In the late afternoon of September 11, 2001, the founder and president of TAMPRR, retired U.S. Air Force Colonel and ex-CIA operative Jake Marks, an aging pit bull of a man in his late seventies, with a tight mouth held in place by an even tighter jaw, held an encrypted net meeting with his senior partners. At one time Marks had been one of the youngest colonels the American military had ever produced. When he was a fighter pilot during the Korean conflict his wingman had once jokingly but not entirely inaccurately referred to Marks as 'an almost perfectly controlled and reusable thermonuclear device'.

During their encrypted meeting on the Internet, Marks's brain-trust of senior managers formulated a coordinated approach to contacting, over the next few days and weeks, their respective lists of still-wavering but potential corporate clients. Their goal was to determine whether they were now, post-9/11, somewhat keener, or, more accurately, *desperate* enough, to have their business interests represented to the highest governmental and bureaucratic levels by TAMPRR Inc.. For decades, TAMPRR's 'representatives' (*operatives* and *agents* would have been much more accurate terms) had been working the dark corridors and dank alleys of power in the U.S.A., Canada, England, France, Australia and most of the other countries making up the European Union.

It would be crass but true to say that the opportunities to capitalize on the fears and vulnerabilities of America's citizenry had never been better, at least not since at least the end of the cold war. Marks knew immediately, after the second hijacked plane hit the World Trade Center, that TAMPRR Inc. was about to go through a period of unprecedented growth.

Now, as he watched the horrors of 9/11 being replayed over and over on his office television, Jake Marks was certain that he would shortly become far richer than even *he* had ever expected. Fantasized about, of course, ever since he and his then-small team of fellow ex-prisoners of war in North Korea had pulled off, forty-one years earlier, in 1959, what among themselves they had termed 'The Avro Arrow Manipulation'.

The Arrow Manipulation 'team' had successfully, that is, totally and permanently, obliterated their northern neighbor's suddenly technologically superior military fighter-interceptor aircraft industry. Had the Avro Arrow program gone forward it could well have been economically devastating to some of its U.S. corporate competitors. By obliterating the Canadian company's program Marks's team had ensured that their own clients reacquired, and had ever since retained, their corporations' military aircraft-building supremacy on this continent, and indeed, throughout the world.

CHAPTER 3

JANUARY 17, 1961

Only a few weeks before the end of his presidential term, Ike realized–much too late to take effective corrective action–that he had been duped by some of his closest advisors into becoming, in effect, a 'front man' for what he would later label as the 'military-industrial complex', and about which he then valiantly warned his fellow citizens during his farewell address.

Through the efforts of a few key members of his administration and their shadowy cohorts in business and the military, Ike had been deliberately provided with misinformation having to do with the nation's security. He was assured that in any future war with America's main adversary at that time, the Soviet Union, the U.S.A. would need to depend, almost exclusively, upon a missile defense system to counter the threat of Soviet bombers flying over the North pole and sweeping down over Canada towards their U.S. targets. Ike was also told that the days of manned fighter-interceptor aircraft were now passé. Some advisors even dismissed any future need for such aircraft in Europe or elsewhere, and played up the notion of missiles as the answer to most of America's air and space defense needs.

By getting the President to buy and then propagate that line, the 'military-industrial complex' succeeded in turning the thinking of some prime decision makers in government to their own favored directions. This acquired attitude of the administration was then propagated amongst America's allies and led, not coincidentally, to the destruction of the technological lead, in both civilian and military aircraft design and development, of two of the United States' closest allies–Great Britain and Canada. The MIC was not prepared to tolerate any other possibility.

Meanwhile, the MIC continued to maintain and promote the further development of home-grown fighter-interceptors. Consequently, when missile defense was later determined to be inherently limited in capability (as the MIC had known all along that it would), the American military aircraft industry just happened to be ready to supply the U.S. and other NATO countries with its own, latest fighter-interceptor 'products', without having to worry about competition from the now-dead but still superior Avro Arrow.

In the waning hours of his presidency Ike realized the fallacy of his advisors' arguments and the huge influence that the MIC had acquired within his own administration. But even *he* never imagined the exponential growth that would occur over the next nearly five decades in the homegrown military-corporate threat about which he had attempted to warn the American public that frigid, lonely January evening in 1961, when he uttered the fateful lines that *"The conjunction of an immense military establishment and a large arms industry is new in the American experience. (It's) total influence -economic, political, even spiritual- is felt in every city, every state house, every office of the Federal government. We recognize the imperative need for this development. Yet we must not fail to comprehend its grave implications... **In the councils of government, we must guard against the acquisition of unwarranted influence, whether sought or unsought, by the military-industrial complex.***

CHAPTER 4

FEBRUARY 12, 2009

During his 23 years of reporting from the world's trouble spots about wars and famines, coups and crises of all kinds, Ken Simpson had steadily built a solid reputation as an exceptional investigative reporter. Looking younger, and certainly more fit than most of his early-sixties newspaper reporter contemporaries, Ken's syndicated column was read by an ever-growing legion of readers of the highly regarded *New York Era* and over three hundred other papers, large and small, across the nation.

The materials for his columns were most frequently acquired by his own first-hand observations and investigations, during the course of which, he had too often put himself directly in harm's way. Ken knew himself well enough to acknowledge, at least silently, that his tenacious approach towards his investigative work probably began with an attempt to prove himself worthy as the son of the late U.S.A.F. fighter pilot and premier test pilot, Captain Frank Simpson. This need to do his father proud was undoubtedly exacerbated when Ken resigned from active duty as a U.S.A.F. pilot after having made a horrific, lethal mistake.

In the course of reporting from the world's trouble spots Ken witnessed, again and again, the true heroism of ordinary people caught in extraordinary circumstances. Over time, his own early bravado was transformed into a respectful appreciation of those who did the deeds he merely reported upon. And as he learned how to better communicate in an increasingly articulate and personal voice about these courageous individuals and the obstacles, human and otherwise, that they had overcome, he became one of the most highly regarded syndicated journalists in the U.S.A.

Ken's still handsome, well-aging face, fit appearance, and gently authoritative yet warm, speaking voice and sense of humor had made him a popular guest on the most watched talk/news shows. His reporter's skill helped him to succinctly cover a great deal of material about a current political, military, social or business issue in one of the four-minute segments usually allotted to most guest slots on the network morning and evening shows.

Interviewers repaid Ken's showing up in the early morning or late evening by directing viewers to his syndicated articles in *The New York Era*. Often, after a particularly good interview or well-written article, Ken would think of his father, experiencing again his decades-old yearning that his dad could have heard or seen his efforts, and known how much just being the son of Captain Frank Simpson had helped him want to succeed in contributing something to the world. Ken sometimes thought that perhaps his father *did* know.

Early on in their marriage Ken told his now ex-wife, Nancy, that he had frequently sensed his father's presence beside him in the various trouble spots he had covered around the world. How else to explain that he had gotten out alive from more than a few killing zones over the past twenty years through an uncanny intuition he could neither take credit for, nor fully explain. On one occasion, a landmine exploded under his jeep during the first Gulf war, killing the driver and the other journalist and photographer traveling with him, but leaving Ken with only a broken toe and incredibly sore butt. The explosion had happened in a supposedly secure part of the desert less than a minute after he had suddenly decided to sit *on*, rather than wear, his Kevlar flak Jacket. Another time, during a period of racial conflict in the Congo, a stray bullet had traveled straight through one of his 'love handles' instead of his heart after he had 'suddenly turned around for no good reason'.

Ken was thinking of his dad a lot this particular day, and of his father's most precious military medal, awarded for actions he had taken way 'above and beyond' the call of duty. He also found himself remembering that his father had been a proud Republican who greatly admired Ike, from even prior to when he had been personally awarded the Medal of Honor by then-President Eisenhower, a few months after he took office.

There had long been a rumor in the family that a month or so before the end of Eisenhower's presidency, ex-U.S.A.F. Captain Frank Simpson had been granted a personal meeting with the

President, who had remembered the easygoing pilot with the generous smile and aura of integrity about him.

The reasons behind the rumored meeting with Ike, if it ever happened, were never disclosed to members of Frank Simpson's family. However, Ken remembered that in the weeks prior to the alleged meeting his father's mood had become increasingly distressed, and his usual even, upbeat manner was often replaced by a sad, edgy anger. When he was in 'that place', Frank would sometimes 'blow a fuse' if Ken became boisterous, telling his son to "pipe down". Then, almost immediately afterward, Frank seemed to catch himself, clutch the supposedly offending child in his strong arms, and whisper reassuring, apologetic words like "I'm sorry; I'm so sorry, Ken. Dad has things on his mind. Sorry, son; I didn't mean to speak to you so harshly; I do love you so much.". Whenever his dad's aberrant behavior reoccurred, young Ken could sense that his father was choking back a lot of emotion.

Ken's father died in 1962, about eighteen months after Ike's farewell address to the nation. His aircraft disappeared from radar screens as he was beginning his descent to the landing field at the U.S. Air Force Academy, at Colorado Springs, Colorado, from which he had graduated years earlier, and to where he was flying to deliver an invited address to the current year's graduating class.

It was a full day before the recovery team found Frank's grossly burned remains in the broken fuselage that had come to rest near the top of a mountain some fifty miles from his destination. Due to the massive destruction at the site the crash's investigators were inconclusive in their announced findings. They took note that his mangled ejection seat and canopy assembly appeared to be missing some key components, and wrote that when he had tried to eject, the canopy had not blown, thereby trapping Frank in the aircraft. The investigators' report concluded that his death was likely due to a "catastrophic systems malfunction compounded by ejecting into a jammed, closed canopy."

Ex-President Eisenhower sent his personally signed letter of regret to the Simpson family. Ken's mother had the letter framed; it now resided in Ken's boyhood home in a place of honor.

One of Ken's strongest boyhood memories was his father's oft stated, deep allegiance to the man who had been his wartime commander as well as his President. Together, Ken and his parents had watched and listened attentively to the former WWII Commander-in-Chief's presidential farewell address on that cold January evening in 1961.

Another vivid memory was of his father smiling weakly while wiping away tears, as the family listened to Ike taking leave of his office. Feeling uncomfortable yet mesmerized, young Ken had watched his father closely, thinking that he shouldn't look, yet unable to stop himself. That evening, his dad somehow seemed smaller than Ken had ever been aware of before. This impression was partly influenced by the fact that fourteen-year-old Ken's growth spurt the previous summer had suddenly made him taller than his father, although Ken could only ever recall feeling like he was always looking up at his dad.

Over the years since, Ken occasionally found himself re-running that long-ago scene on his mindscreen. He remembered feeling a little scared as he observed his father crying while listening so attentively to the President. Throughout the speech his dad rocked back and forth as he kept repeating under his breath, short, almost inaudible sentences that sounded like, "Way to go, Ike. You're telling them. You're telling them." Then, "But will they listen? Will they listen, Ike? Tell them anyway. Please. *Tell them.*"

After Ike's address was over, rocking slightly more slowly now, Frank had mumbled something like, "Thank you, Ike. Thank you, Mr. President. But, will they listen?"

These were the reveries that floated through Ken's consciousness as he sat at the hastily set up 'head table' in the newspaper's cafeteria for the celebratory gathering of the reporters and support staff of *The New York Era*. He felt somewhat embarrassed, yet at the same time, appreciative of the paper's acknowledgement of his achievement in being awarded the 2008 Paulson prize for Investigative Journalism In The Public's Interest.

All day long Ken's intuition had been telling him that something unseen and uncomfortable, related somehow to his father, was near by. His dad seemed to be close to him, now. Or, maybe it was just that, even at the age of 62, he still wished his father were alive to enjoy this moment with him.

Before the day was out Ken would be a candidate for believing even more in synchronicity and premonitions.

Ken tore away from his private musings and forced himself to focus on the kudos being directed his way by the managing editor of the paper, while slides of his award-winning, front-page series of articles were being flashed on the screen behind the head table. He felt guilty yet also proud that his award had been given for a series about human suffering and, in particular, the continuing anguish, some seven years later, of many of those who had labored at 'ground zero' on and after September 11, 2001, day after day, around the clock, for days, weeks, or months. Whatever toxic substances they had been exposed to at the savaged site had been working through their blood streams for years now, and some of them had become very ill. In fact, several had died from their illnesses, and various health officials attached to independent healthcare research centers were predicting many more chronic diseases and deaths in the years to follow.

For several months following 9/11 those working at ground zero had been reassured that the levels and kinds of toxic substances they were being subjected to were not substantial. Later it was revealed that some of those test findings may have grossly underestimated the wide variety of chemicals and substances that had been released into the air and had been finding their way into the lungs and bloodstreams of the workers and residents at and near the site.

In 2008, Ken's articles had chronicled the distress of several 9/11 workers and wondered in print whether some of those in charge had deliberately not issued sufficiently accurate health warnings about inhaling, or even touching, some of the materials near ground zero, and had also specifically not insisted upon, nor distributed, suitably effective breathing filtering devices, because they did not want to incur financial responsibility for any illnesses that might result from breathing the air at and around the World Trade Center site.

Ken had uncovered information that suggested there may have existed, in effect or in fact, a network of covert influence that had acted on behalf of certain insurance companies, as well as some HMOs and other healthcare companies. This corporate cartel appeared to have possibly influenced certain lawmakers and governmental agencies to hold up emergency legislation mandating the delivery of suitable air filtering protective gear for the World Trade Center workers. Ken's sources also indicated that a few healthcare-related companies had been routinely denying most insurance claims and submissions for coverage of medical care to assist those affected physically and/or emotionally by the horrors of 9/11.

While Ken had not uncovered all the 'smoking guns', he had found and written about so much suggestive material that a citizens' groundswell had built throughout his many weeks' long series of articles. Soon a concerted effort, driven by readers using the Internet to mobilize their efforts, became a tidal wave of public support that forced the President to establish an independent *Presidential Commission On The Health And Welfare Of The World Trade Center's 'Ground Zero' Worker-Victims And Their Families'*. The function of the commission was to root out the truths and issues relevant to its focus, and by one manner or another, to secure health coverage for those directly affected by 9/11 and its aftermath. Their report, issued on September 11, 2008, was damning of many in the previous and current administrations and healthcare 'businesses' who, it concluded, had done far less than was warranted by both the facts and effects of that horrible day, and the courageous efforts of the workers and volunteers.

Within less than two months after the commission reported its findings, both houses had passed, and the President had signed into law, a *'War Against Terrorism' Heroes-And-Their-Families Guaranteed Medical Benefits And Financial Support Act*. This legislation ensured that government funds would cover the medical costs of their resultant illnesses, including compensation for subsequently lost wages, for *all* the immediate family members of the victims of 9/11, both those who died at the time and those who came to clean up the devastation afterwards. As well, in the future, all American victims of terrorist acts would be covered by the same law, no matter where in the world these heinous events occurred.

Ken shook himself back into the present, again becoming aware of sitting at the improvised head table, listening now to the relatively new owner and publisher of *The New York Era*, billionaire Conner Gallen, praising his senior editors for "encouraging reporters like Ken to achieve and maintain the highest standards..." and so on.

After a few more minutes of actually paying attention to the speeches, Ken's thoughts again returned to his father. He was certain that his dad would have been immensely proud of his writings and of the actions they had precipitated at the governmental level.

Ken also thought of his uncle Bob, who had shared with Ken many tales of Frank's oft-expressed and exercised beliefs, while in the U.S.A.F. and afterwards, that the people who served their country should be exposed to the minimum of avoidable danger, whenever that was possible. Ken's father was particularly incensed by the actions of inadequate commanders who, without sufficiently checking beforehand, ended up too hastily ordering and then too readily condoning, what turned out to be so-called 'friendly fire' incidents. He was also vitally concerned about shoddily-made equipment, from too-often-jamming rifles and poorly made tanks to faulty military aircraft equipped with unreliable safety equipment.

Uncle Bob had told Ken that his father had made a lot of friends among those who served under him, and more than a few enemies among his peers and the more senior ranks. Those who were most peeved with his dad included officers he believed were constantly looking past the ends of their military careers to the cushy 'liaison' executive positions that frequently awaited them at some of the larger defense manufacturers. Bob and Frank had personally known some senior officers who were already having their lives made much easier through various personal 'loans', 'grants' and club memberships that certain defense contractors had arranged. "The left hand was constantly jerking off the right hand," is the way Uncle Bob had put it once when Ken was in college and better able to appreciate crude colloquialisms.

Ken had sometimes overheard Bob and his dad talking in hushed tones in the family den about dealings they were aware of among certain military and corporate personnel. Ken had heard them express disgust at the conduct of some of their superiors who had bragged that they had kept silent about their knowledge of their corporate buddies' having altered or entirely fabricated computer simulation printouts on the performance of new aircraft being proposed for sale to the military, knowing full well that the delivered equipment would never meet 'specs'.

The New York Era's other head honchos now took turns at the portable lectern, heaping praise upon Ken for having just been awarded the Paulson. They mentioned, of course, that Ken had uncovered evidence of tremendous pressures having been exerted upon some lawmakers and key people within the administration, aimed at blocking acceptance of the notion that medical coverage for any injuries or diseases incurred while working at 'ground zero' should be fully covered. The senior editor then announced that the paper was going to have a front-page editorial in the next day's edition, urging state and federal administrations to speedily pass companion bills to the *'War Against Terrorism' Heroes-And-Their-Families Guaranteed Medical Benefits And Financial Support Act'* that would extend coverage to *all* individuals directly or indirectly harmed, physically and/or emotionally, by any act of terrorism perpetrated against Americans anywhere. Follow-up editorials and special feature sections describing in detail the trials and tribulations of those who were still suffering the consequences of 9/11/01 would be published, until passage of the companion bill was assured. Ken's work would become the announced 'cause' of the socially conscious *New York Era*.

As this last announcement was being made, Ken heard his deceased father's voice saying, *"Son, I am so proud of you and the good work you are doing. I always have been, and always will."*

Ken responded silently to the memory of his father that he carried inside him; *Funny, isn't it dad, that no matter how old we get, even into our fifties, sixties, or probably until the day we die, we can still care what our own parents would think and say about us? The desire to be approved of by those who brought us into the world never dies within us, does it, dad?*

CHAPTER 5

FEBRUARY 12, 2009

Less than ten months after Ken's syndicated columns dealing with the problems of those who had toiled so solidly yet sadly at 'ground zero' began appearing in *The New York Era* and in hundreds of other papers around the USA, the groundswell of support by both ordinary and prominent citizens that poured out via phone-in talk shows, letters to the editors, and more importantly, the town hall meetings and subsequent petitions sent to state and federal legislators, had their cumulative effect. The various levels of government did indeed subsequently pass complementary legislation to mandate universal health coverage for *all* citizens and members of their families directly affected by *any* terrorist acts, no matter where they occurred. While it was obvious that some persons might want to take unfair advantage of this new coverage, the rightness of such legislation was deemed to far outweigh any such relatively minor downside. The currently most popular and prominent senior Republican war hero/senator and a Democratic colleague jointly introduced a series of bills that dealt with these matters, and not many elected officials dared to try and hold back the tide of overwhelming public sentiment. As a result, the fast-tracked bills were passed into law in near-record time.

Henceforth, whenever, wherever, and however, any citizen of the United States would become either emotionally injured, physically disabled, or deceased as a result of an act of terrorism, the U.S. government would provide financial compensation as well as all necessary and reasonable medical, psychological, and educational support for the direct victims and/or the members of their immediate families–for the rest of their lives. Also, safeguards were built in to ensure that persons who applied for such aid would not have to endure excessive delay before it was provided. The fact that the bill essentially provided universal health coverage for a potentially significant segment of the

American population that was, in essence, very similar to Canada's universal Medicare system that covered *all* citizens, *period*, went nearly entirely without mention by the major media in the USA.

From now on, the President stated when he signed the bill into law, the official government mission was *"to ask not only what our citizens have done for our country by choosing to live as free people, and thereby confronting terrorism at the risk of their own health and indeed, even their lives, but to ask what our country can, must, and shall do for them, with the true expression of our unwavering American values of fairness, gratitude and generosity"*. That line had elicited a huge positive response from editorial pages and commentators around the country.

Dr. Leo Larson, the former Surgeon General of the United States, himself once a hugely popular and outspoken figure on behalf of universal medical coverage for all Americans, but now a discarded leftover from a previous administration, was even invited to the official signing of the bills and the photo-op cabinet meeting immediately following. His invitation had been extended by the White House to show that the current administration had indeed been listening to the counsel of a broad spectrum of the people's representatives and guardians–even as it was known to despise many of them.

At the signing ceremony, in response to a direct question from a reporter for a major Washington, D.C. paper, Dr. Larson dared to take advantage of his presence on the stage to argue for similar legislation to be brought in "for the sake of the health of *all* of our people, including," he said, "the over forty-six million Americans who have no medical insurance coverage at all". Before he could say any more, he was quickly cut off by a frosty and firm presidential, "Thank you, Dr. Larson, for your well-spoken, and well-known, views."

At the in-camera expanded cabinet meeting immediately following the signing ceremony and photo-op, the former Surgeon-General was given just enough time to begin to press his case. Larson began by saying that "given that the *'War Against Terrorism' Heroes-And-Their-Families Guaranteed Medical Benefits And Financial Support Act'* has created such an outpouring of goodwill, I want to once again take the opportunity to express my fervent hope that this administration will consider extending full health coverage to *all* Americans."

Various members of the cabinet held their collective breath for what seemed like an eternally long second, and then, from all around of the table, a verbal barrage effectively drowned out Dr. Larson's words. Later, he would write in his autobiography that he could not even tell which attacker had uttered what statement, or in what order, although he did recall that at that moment he believed he had distinctly heard the sound of a million healthcare providers' cash registers ringing.

A loud, angry voice belonging to the Secretary of Commerce, shouted; "Are you frigging *crazy*, *Mr.* Surgeon General? You have no idea of the flak we've taken from some of the HMOs, and the Preferred Provider Organizations, and the other companies who were against us signing even *this* Act. They are, or at least were, some of this administration's biggest backers. Hell, they'd immediately withhold any additional funding and go out and support our opponents in the next election, that is, if they thought for one moment that we were going to seriously entertain your 'suggestion'."

Another, more measured, voice belonging to the Secretary of State, added, "Dr. Larson; if we weren't facing an election sooner than later, and there hadn't been this hysterical and overreacting public sentiment for us to do something for the victims of 9/11 and the other terrorist acts since, we would never have accepted this Act, even with the limitations that we've embedded in it."

The velvet voice of the Secretary of Health and Human Services chimed in, adding, *"Surgeon General Larson!* You should know better than any of us that Americans spend more on medical care than just about anything else. You also know that American parents will skimp on food, clothing, housing, and even transportation just so that they can get their sick kids the medical help they need. *Hell,* medical care is our country's second biggest business. It bigger than anything, anything, except the military."

The Secretary of the Treasury hastily added, "Actually, it's even *more* important than food. Everyone has to pay for it, one way or another. Damn it, Isaiah, our citizens' *illnesses* are what keeps a large part of our economy *healthy*." The Secretary of the Treasury laughed heartily at what he thought was his own clever juxtaposition of words.

The Secretary of Labor was even more pragmatic. "Christ, Isaiah, 10 of the top 100 advertisers in the whole country are drug firms. They help pay for all the newsprint and air time out there. Do you seriously think the newspapers are going to support what you are proposing? A universal healthcare scheme? *Like Canada's, for shit's sake!?*"

The head of the CIA, Martin Craig, added, in a deeply caustic tone: "Well, don't worry about Canada's healthcare system. It has been beaten up so badly for the past several years, even from the inside, that it's on *life support* itself now; and probably not for this world for much longer. It'll be dead and buried soon enough!" A few mischievous guffaws from those presumably on the inside, and a few quizzical glances from the others present, followed this remark.

It was Dr. Larson who dared to ask the obvious question. *"What do you mean, Martin?"*

Larson was old but hardly senile, let alone stupid. He had heard the scuttlebutt for years that the fix was in for the Canadian Medicare system. But no one had ever gone on record before. Perhaps Craig should not have had his three glasses of celebratory champagne on an empty stomach.

The CIA chief's face reddened, while his inner wheels ground to a gravelly halt, and futilely attempted to ram into reverse. He spoke harshly though somewhat slurred; "What I mean is, no one is going to stop our American healthcare, insurance, and drug companies' trains from rolling on into Canada. And there are more than enough right-minded Canadian politicians, media barons, and bureaucrats in positions of control of their federal and provincial healthcare systems to bring their whole damn healthcare structure crashing down. And *our* HMOs have more than enough Canadian friends in the head offices of their federal and provincial departments of health, immigration and industry, and in their print and electronic media as well, to keep on *creating* and then *complaining loudly about* the 'deficiencies' of the Canadian Medicare system. Hell, that's been going on for at least the past fifteen years. But their citizens are so stubborn that they keep holding onto their universal Medicare, almost no matter how screwed up our friends make it. One of these days, though, when they get tired or scared enough, and after even more of their nurses are let go and hospitals are closed, and when they lose enough MRI and other technical staff, *then* I am willing to bet that a majority of their own people will vote to bring in our own American system."

Dr. Larson was astounded both by what Craig had said, and at the fact that he had so nonchalantly said it. Or was it that what he was talking about was nearly a done deal anyway, so that Craig didn't much care *who* heard, at least behind the closed, and supposedly secure, doors of the White House cabinet room.

Just as Larson was about to say something else in response, Craig added in his slight southern drawl, "And in *our country*, Isaiah, the media will continue to put out editorials and articles about the sins of 'socialized medicine', just like they have done for ages, and about their long waiting times for needed tests and surgeries–which is our guys' doing, by the way. Hell, by the time we get through denigrating and demolishing the Canadians' system, that dog won't hunt–not ever again. This time we're killing it good. But don't worry. Our administration hasn't done a thing to promote the inevitable. That has been the job of American business. And they have done a bang-up job, let me tell you. I am just reporting what I know about what they are doing. It's not us, Dr. Larson. It's just American business doing business the American way. Its just 'bizwar', as they like to say nowadays."

Dr. Larson was too old to be bullied or bullshitted. But he would never be too old to stand up for what he believed was right. He understood that this meeting was closed in more ways than one and so he held his tongue. He would seek another venue to make his views known. *Somehow.*

Much sooner than he expected, he would get an opportunity to do exactly that.

CHAPTER 6

FEBRUARY 12, 2009

For the last twenty-four hours, ever since the announcement was made that he had won the Paulson, Ken had been filled with many a 'happy-sad'. Within hours he found himself on the other end of a dozen interviews requested by usually competing reporters of various publications. He quickly learned that he disliked the interview*ee* position big-time, at least when the focus was on him personally rather than on his observations or opinions, and he immediately found himself appreciating the discomfort of those upon whom the blinding light of fifteen minutes of scrutiny landed. He also somewhat embarrassingly handled congratulatory telephone calls and e-mails from a flood of colleagues, friends, and more meaningfully, dozens of soldiers, firefighters, police officers and their family members who were among the immediate beneficiaries of the newly passed legislations.

The successive waves of appreciation continued unabated all day long. For Ken the most moving calls came from some of those he had interviewed for the post-9/11 series who were residing in bare-bones, long-term institutions, or were at home being cared for by ever more elderly parents or exhausted children. These caretakers' sorrows and fears for their sons' and daughters' and parents' welfare had worsened during the past few years as they contemplated what would happen to their loved ones down the road. Their congratulatory words were delivered with voices often breaking with heart-felt gratitude. They would now be able to sleep more restfully, they said almost unanimously, knowing that the government would henceforth be compelled by law to help provide for their now chronically ill or disabled children or parents and their families.

Ken had mused about the last PowerPoint slide projected on the screen behind him during the newspaper's Paulson celebration. It was of the front page of *The New York Era* from three days earlier, with the first article of Ken's new series on the forty-six million Americans without any healthcare coverage. The long-time managing editor was speaking, and she finished up by saying, "Ken, we are so proud of your accomplishments to date, and all of us truly believe that your future articles will continue not only to inform and raise the public consciousness but will also help precipitate even more meaningful change in healthcare for the other disadvantages citizens of our nation. Your efforts, and *The New York Era*'s participation, are accomplishments of which we can all be extremely proud."

Ken nodded and smiled back at the managing editor, and then glanced at the publisher. He thought he saw for just an instant, *no...*, he *knew* he had seen a momentary, marked discomfort on the publisher's face. *Oops,* he thought. *Fame can be so frigging fleeting, like a fart in the wind.* He suddenly wondered just how supportive the top brass would be once he let them in on the content of some of the upcoming articles that were already half-formed in his mind, and in early point form, on his computer at home. Would they back him up when he was ready to reveal his sources' corroborated revelations of the extent to which some of the *Era's* major advertisers, including several of the country's largest pharmaceutical and healthcare companies, were preparing to protect themselves against even the remotest possibility that their cash cows would be corralled?

Ken had recently learned from some whistleblowing sources that these companies were ready to threaten to withdraw their advertising from any electronic or print media that they didn't already own or control that dared to seriously question their business practices. One of his sources had also said that these threats either had been, or soon would be, conveyed to the executive offices of *The New York Era* itself. He knew that the paper relied upon its usually thick 'classified' section, as well as on the ads for all manner of medications, for a substantial portion of its revenues. So what would the people upstairs do when push came to shove? *Ah, something else to fight over.*

Following Ken's brief and self-effacing words of thanks for the acknowledgement of his award, the gathering dispersed with a spontaneous round of applause and the more personal congratulations of those who chose to stay behind briefly and speak to him. The publisher was not among them.

After an additional several minutes of congratulatory mutual backslapping throughout *The New York Era*'s news department, and further glad-handing with the corporate office staff, except for most of those in the advertising division, the uncomfortable exercise was finally over. *People were, by-and-large, well meaning, but enough was enough.* Ken wanted to get back to doing some real work.

When he returned to the sanctuary of his own cubicle after the celebration Ken could barely see his desktop beneath the piles of congratulatory letters and heaps of bouquets of flowers. When he removed the top layer of flowers he first saw the shoebox-sized FedEx package that, he noted, had been sent from Miami.

Ken's antennae went up. What caught his attention as he lifted the package to read the sender's name and address were some words written with a red marker pen immediately to the right of his own name in large capital letters; ***"PLEASE OPEN IN THE PRESENCE OF CAPTAIN FRANK SIMPSON ONLY."***

For an instant Ken thought that this might be an attempt at an inside joke by his now 89-year old, feisty and irreverent mother, Katherine *with-a-K*. However, since she lived on the northwest coast near Sarasota and had not driven for years, it was most unlikely that *she* had sent the package. As well, Ken knew that his mom hated Miami, it's congestion, and its increasing violence. Also, she had lost her license after an unfortunate minor accident near her home about five years back, when she drove the front wheels over a concrete parking barrier in a shopping mall lot and badly damaged the front end of the car facing her own. Furthermore, Ken noted, it was most definitely *not* her still impeccably neat, small handwriting. Looking more closely now at the almost indecipherable, handwritten "Sender Information" box, Ken saw that a 'Mr. D.S.' had evidently sent the package.

The package did have a special holographic, time-dated, and bar-coded sticker that read, 'Cleared by Altest Senior Security'. Altest Senior Security was the company that the *Era* hired back in October of 2001 and the sticker was used to assure employees like Ken that, while their mail and couriered packages had not been opened, they had been passed through the supposedly see-all, smell-all multimillion-dollar scanning device hidden away in Altest's concrete bunker that was off-site, and rumored to be somewhere in Jersey.

Well, whomever it was that had sent the package knew Ken's father's first name and military rank, and if that were the case, probably also knew that he had been deceased for decades. As he considered whether a relative or long-time friend might have been the sender, Ken became aware of her perfume rather than actually heard her approach his chair from behind.

She stood still only a few inches behind the back of his chair, saying nothing. He didn't turn his head around, but rather leaned back just a bit and, as one might with an exotically scented flower, for just a moment dove into her fragrance. Then he leaned back just a little more, and said quietly, "Yes? Can I help you, Miss?"

Her happy, husky voice softly responded in a whisper. "Oh, yes, I believe you can indeed, kind sir. You see, I am so warm right now. Perhaps it's all the laudatory comments that were just made by so many admirers that have gotten me so... *so enthusiastic*. All I know for certain is that I need a Paulson Prize-sized man beside me pretty damn quick. However, I think I might just be willing to wait a couple of hours until I have fed and feted you and then I am going to shower you with unmistakable non-verbal expressions of the pride that I am feeling towards you at this moment."

Having by now aroused his attention in more than one way, she paused momentarily and then swiftly slipped out of her intimate mating-call voice and into her business tones as another reporter walked by, signaling 'congrats' to Ken. The colleague, a rather young and ravishing financial writer, glanced back and forth with wistful envy from Ken to the older woman standing behind him and against whose bosom the back of Ken's head almost seemed to be resting. The young thing moved on as Martha came around to the front of Ken's chair and stood in front of him, perhaps unconsciously protecting her territory. She said, "Also, and honestly, Ken. Congratulations. Everybody is... I am... really proud of you. You truly deserve the Paulson."

Martha Harrison was Ken's co-investigator and, more recently, also his lover. She said, "I have to work late tonight. See you around nine, Hon? I'll bring over a great wine with which to celebrate."

Ken replied, "Sounds super to me, Mar. Thanks. But you know as well as I do that the Paulson is yours, as well. Without your incredible help this wouldn't have happened."

"Oh, yes it would have. Honestly, Ken, sometimes you are just too damn self-effacing. Most of the work, and almost all of the writing, was yours. I was just glad to help out and contribute to a worthwhile effort."

Ken said, "Well, thanks, but I know what I know. Listen, I'm going to answer some of these phone messages and e-mails from home before you come over. See you later."

A slight swishing sound accompanied the lightest brushing of her toned thigh on his upper arm as, smiling, she nodded and walked past him, heading back to her own desk less than ten feet away. She looked back over her shoulder and smiled when she noted that his eyes were clearly coveting her still shapely behind.

Ken had definitely been aroused by Martha's verbal foreplay. *Ah, that would just have to wait.* At his age, waiting wouldn't be nearly as much of a trial as might have been the case twenty, or even ten, years earlier. *But aging has its compensations. Now, what were they again?*

Ken knew Martha as an excellent reporter, a very good friend, and a fine lover. Both of them recognized that it was mostly a matter of major loneliness and moderate lust, fed by a growing mutual respect and friendship that had led to their becoming increasingly involved in the past year. All that, and the effect of working together on the intensely moving stories of fellow Americans who had been genuine victims of terrorist acts perpetrated against various U.S. interests at home and abroad, and then were victimized again by the attitudes and bureaucracy of numerous U.S. healthcare companies and governmental departments when it came to their obtaining medical care and/or compensation for the physical injuries, emotional suffering and economic losses that the acts of terror had yielded, had also served to bring them closer.

Martha had done a first-rate job of uncovering some of the key documents involved in the deliberate dragging of heels that had gone on in regard to compensating the victims of 9/11/01 and the other, equally malevolent terrorist acts that had followed. Ken knew that Martha at least deserved to share in the money accompanying the award he had just received. He realized that she would not accept any monetary 'gift', so on his way to the office that very morning he stopped in at a Ford dealership and bought her a medium-sided SUV like the one she had been looking at longingly in recent months to replace her trusty but tired, decade-old Honda.

Ken thought admiringly about the person Martha was. Now forty-eight years old, divorced and the mother of two children both away at college, she worked hard to support the three of them doing a job that she genuinely loved and did superbly well. She had survived an increasingly awful two-decade-long marriage to a middle-level manager of a computer firm. The man became increasingly verbally abusive and alcohol-dependent as first the economy, and then his company, sank into recession. Once, in a drunken tirade over some piddling non-issue, he had actually taken a swing at Martha. In his inebriated state he had undoubtedly forgotten that his reporter-wife was also both a part-time fitness instructor and held a black belt in karate. *Big mistake, and final straw!*

Only because she still had compassion for him and knew that he would always be her children's father, Martha had acted with decisive but moderate force, countering his blow with one arm while kneeing him hard enough that he would remember his stupid, stupored behavior whenever he tried to pee over the next several weeks.

Ken acknowledged to himself that he would never have become intimately involved with anyone from work if he had not been so exhausted and in so much emotional pain following the loss of his own marriage and the geographical distancing from his young son. But he had been especially stressed and distressed by his work on the 'victims of terrorism' series, and his reporter's objectivity had been mightily tested by the gross unfairness of their plight.

In one article Ken had written, *"Had they been registered in the U.S. armed forces, these blinded or crippled or crushed Americans would have, at least, received decent medical care paid for by their government and a grateful citizenry. But what the administrations then and since were calling the 'new war on terrorism' clearly often involved the deliberate causing of civilian casualties. It is now the ordinary men, women, and children of America who are directly in the terrorists' sights. And the administration had said time and again that the now well over one thousand suspected members of al-Qaeda and the Taliban still imprisoned at Guantanamo Bay were the new, non-uniformed soldiers of the terrorist enemy. It is therefore, surely, time to also realize that all of our citizens are, and should be, considered a vital extension of our own country's new army.*

Ken wrote in a subsequent article leading off the current series on healthcare of Americans, *"If our government sees the al-Qaeda members as soldiers-without-uniforms, then it should also recognize that all Americans, including civilians, may become war-causalities-without-uniforms who deserve the same high quality of free medical care being provided by the U.S. government to those same al-Qaeda prisoners."*

Ken and Martha worked late night after night for many months on what became known as the 'terrorist act' series. The more time they spent together the more they obtained some relief from the intensity of the material they were uncovering by sharing inane comments and inside jokes. Then, the warmer Ken began to feel towards her, and vice versa.

Ken had been feeling at a loss in his personal life ever since his wife had had enough of his late nights at the paper and his inclination to fly off to cover war zones; she left Ken and moved back to her hometown, Chicago, with their young son, Brad. He didn't blame her for leaving, of course. After all, he had promised her many, many times that he would *very soon* give up reporting from places of clear and current danger. Finally, when she had had enough of his not following through with his oft-stated intention to ask to be assigned to the national news desk, she left. A few months later Ken learned that she was seriously dating an old high school flame, and that the likelihood of her changing her mind about their marriage was virtually nil.

Ken couldn't honestly say that he missed being married to Nancy, but he desperately ached over not being able to come home to eleven year old Brad.

As Ken's attention returned again to the package on his desk, the five W's of journalism–and of life–ran through his mind. Unbeknownst to Ken, pursuit of the answers to those implicit questions–*Why, When, What, Who,* and *Where*–in relation to the package from Florida, were about to take him on the most dangerous investigative ride of his professional life.

CHAPTER 7

After Martha left, Ken's eyes were drawn back to the package resting on his lap. The sender's underlined instruction to *"PLEASE OPEN IN THE PRESENCE OF CAPTAIN FRANK SIMPSON ONLY."* suggested to Ken not only that he *not* open it now, but also, that he wait until he was back in his Manhattan apartment. It was as if the sender was well aware that Ken had long ago dubbed a part of his den 'the Captain's Corner'. This is where he often sat late in the evening, occasionally gazing at his father's photographs and other memorabilia and listened to his–and his dad's–favorite jazz recordings.

Hanging on the wall above Frank's old desk were about a dozen photos of him standing in front of, or sitting in the cockpits of, various aircraft prototypes and production models of the many types of aircraft he had flown. *Had the sender really known about Captain's Corner? If so, how? Who was the sender, anyway? Did Ken know him... or her?*

One of the photos showed his father in front of what Frank had told Ken was the most exciting aircraft he had ever flown–*and it wasn't even an American plane!* It was the Canadian-built CF-105 Avro Arrow, the plane Frank once described to his young son as being at least a dozen years ahead of *anything* any U.S. airplane manufacturer was building. The youngster had even once overheard his dad talking on the phone, referring to the Arrow as "every fighter-interceptor pilot's best wet dream". Ken had startled his father when, shocked by his dad's words, he dropped the baseball and gloves his father had sent him to get from the basement a few minutes earlier. The former war ace became red-faced, Ken remembered, when he turned to see his 12-year old son standing a few feet away, staring at him with eyes and mouth wide open, shocked at hearing his dad 'talking bad'.

Ken experienced an involuntary shudder at the thought that the package before him might be from someone who had previously been in his apartment, and to whom Ken may have casually introduced 'the Captain's corner'. When he scanned his brain's Rolodex for any of his personal contacts who might go by those initials, he drew a blank. Ken was used to having straight shooters as friends, people who were disinclined to play word games when a direct approach would do just fine.

Now a premonition of concern seeped into Ken's consciousness. It came from that deeper intuition that he had relied upon countless times in various war zones or otherwise dicey situations, whether interviewing criminals in their own lairs, walking along some of the seamier streets of New York city or Saigon, or even in his personal life. It was this gift of a sixth sense that told him to go 'this way' rather than 'that way', or to avoid certain situations altogether. Ken was convinced that it was only this intuition and some dumb luck that kept him from getting his head blown off during the 2003 war in Iraq, when he was embedded with a forward convoy that was one of the first to approach Baghdad, and at the last moment, for some inexplicable reason, he asked to change vehicles when the convoy was splitting up. Ten miles further down the sandy road the Humvee he had just left, and those riding in it, were blown to smithereens by a remote-controlled landmine.

For a brief moment Ken thought of having the newspaper's security personnel re-examine the FedEx box, but he almost immediately dismissed that notion; many of Altest Security's employees were ex-cops who seemed too inclined for Ken's liking, to decide that, to be on the safe side, the box and its contents should be destroyed in order to make sure that nothing dangerous had been hidden inside. "Well, duh!" as the young people used to say a few years back. "How many important newspaper stories had ended up being incinerated and blowing in the wind as a result?" Ken asked himself. "Too damn many!" he heard himself say out loud. A couple of reporters at nearby desks turned and looked at him quizzically. Then they simply smiled at him, and turned back to their work, but only after glancing at one another with weak smiles. *Ah, the rights and privileges of being the latest 'wunderkind'. I can now talk to myself out loud, and maybe even fart loudly once or twice, and get away with it all. That dispensation should last for at least another day or two. After that, people will either think I am extremely rude or just plain nuts.*

Over the years that he had been an investigative reporter Ken frequently found that many of his best stories and 'scoops' had come from whistleblowers and others with high morality, guilty consciences, personal gripes, or some combination of the above. And not infrequently their revelations had arrived stuffed into packages with plain brown paper wrappings or couriered parcels. No, his intuition told him to keep this package out of the hands of the security boys. The invoking of his father's name on the package convinced him that this was not the gratuitous work of an ignorant weirdo. Or at least, not one who had picked Ken's name at random. So he decided to heed the package's warning and wait until he was at home before opening it.

As he would soon learn, deciding to risk dealing with the package on his own would be one of the best, but most troubling, decisions he had ever made.

CHAPTER 8

MARCH 30, 1958

The Los Angeles corporate headquarters of the MacBowan Aeronautical Corporation, one of the largest and most successful military aircraft manufacturers in the country, was nearly empty at 6:30 a.m. on most Sunday mornings. Unpeopled, that is, except for its security personnel and, of course, it's forty-eight year old workaholic (and not so secretly, alcoholic, and damned near certifiable sexaholic) founder and CEO, Sam Brannigan, and his ever-ready chauffeur and bodyguard, Dirk Logan.

Brannigan was an alpha males' alpha male; a charismatic character whose powerful, barrel-chested, 215-pound body was somehow exceptionally well matched to his five-foot, ten-inch frame. His brilliant mind had been honed through a mechanical engineering degree from USC, augmented by an MBA from Harvard. Trained to deal with both engineering and business problems by creating superb but cost-effective solutions, he had almost single-handedly made the company he had founded into one of the most innovative and successful aircraft manufacturing success stories in America. In the process he became a legend within the exotic upper echelons of American business where he had spent most of his working life. Usually, his pride in himself and his company's accomplishments kept his ego upbeat and his mood positive.

This Sunday morning, however, Sam Brannigan was in a distinctly dark and aggressive frame of mind. What was about to, what *had* to, transpire this morning in the exotic black wood-paneled, electronically secure boardroom at MacBowan, was unprecedented in his more than twenty-two years of thriving in the aviation business world. The one-way mirrored, lead-laced, double-glazed, and bulletproofed expanse of windows that stretched across the entire sixty-foot length of the westward-facing boardroom, were designed to give all those who would soon be present, a magnificent and unobstructed view of the

Pacific ocean. Sam hoped that today the view would encourage his guests to dare to peer beyond the horizon, towards that which might not yet be seen in its entirety but must nevertheless be anticipated and dealt with in a decisive manner, and immediately.

It was a room where Brannigan was truly in his glory. A bulldozer of a man in both mass and manner, he was widely known in the industry for having single-handedly saved his company from imminent ruin through a major recession and an 'accident-prone' passenger jet whose ill-conceived and poorly executed design was eventually determined by the FAA to have caused the occasional engine and odd landing gear to determine their own idiosyncratic moments and rates of descent, usually at such inopportune occasions as takeoffs and landings.

The fatal crash of the MacBowan 303 Bomber a few years earlier marked the last time that Brannigan took a hands-off stance in relation to the company's design and production facilities. Thereafter, as when he first started the company, he would appear unannounced, shaking hands with engineers and floor sweepers alike, asking questions and evaluating; frequently, shortly thereafter, some employees would be moved up, down, or even out, depending on Sam's sense of whether they were adding to, or subtracting from the divisions' needs, attitude, or output. Whether he was right or wrong in his judgments and actions, after each shuffle or firing the remaining workers got the message, and productivity in every department invariably went up, markedly.

In the rarified world of California-based CEOs, Brannigan was infamous for his trademark pacing back and forth from one end of his boardroom's expanse of windows to the other, glaring into the daylight-bathed faces of those fortunate or unfortunate enough to be present. As he moved, his audience could usually only make out a hulking, backlit, agitated 'energy field', rather like a great white in a glass tank that is much too small and too thin-walled to contain its life force for much longer. It was in this boardroom where he was known to gather his company's 'critical few' for weekly 'update sessions', alternately berating and encouraging them with his own inimitable mixture of vigor and invective.

This early morning Brannigan was not entirely alone on the executive floor while waiting for his six guests. Two armed and uniformed security personnel were present; it was their responsibility to double-check the guest list names and mug shots with the actual bodies that soon would be emerging from the elevators. Not surprisingly, virtually every new arrival had a face, body and bearing that suggested he could easily have at least a supporting role, if not the lead, in what at the time, Hollywood was referring to as the 'gangsta movie' genre. Ordinarily, this morning's guests would seldom allow themselves to be found in the same room as the others, except, of course, when competing for the government's bountiful aircraft contracts, or if they had to come together under some sort of duress. Today's circumstances appeared to suggest the latter scenario.

This buttressed boardroom would soon be tested as an ego container, perhaps as never before.

It was more than a *hint* of duress that brought them out at such an ungodly hour as seven in the morning on the Lord's–and not coincidentally their own–day of rest. But nearly every man coming knew Sam Brannigan as a mentor as much as a competitor, and… well, if *he* didn't care what hour or day it was, or how their own plans to grab an extra hour's shuteye or an early morning quickie had been thwarted, then so be it.

The crisp message they had received from Brannigan's secretary less than twenty-four hours earlier was that this meeting would be of "priority importance". The two who initially objected to the time and date of the proposed meeting received a terse, "I am sorry, but *no!* In Mr. Brannigan's opinion, it *cannot* wait another day". With the exception of these two CEOs, everyone else agreed immediately. The two king-of-the-pride contenders took only an extra few minutes during which to flex their autonomy. After a minor amount of such reflexive posturing, however, they too agreed to attend.

The single most seemingly out-of-place person on the executive floor this morning was a most sensual–and only–representative of her gender. With a face and body that had occasionally caused her to be mistaken for Marilyn Monroe (at the time, all the rage) more than a few times, Barbara Masson, had been Sam Brannigan's 'executive secretary' for about 18 months.

A couple of those on the way to the meeting had heard through the gripevine that Miss Masson was originally hired as one of the 'pool girls' who did the secretarial work for lower-level executives at MacBowan. However, once 'Mr. B' had laid his eyes on her, he had her promoted to the suddenly created position of 'executive personal assistant', thereby bypassing–and offpissing–his long-time secretary, Louise. The latter was a middle-aged, obese but highly competent woman whom Sam's wife, for some reason, had handpicked to be her own eminently suitable replacement. But that was ten years (and multiple affairs on both their parts) ago. Now Amy Brannigan, an attractive forty-something, hardly cared what–or who–her over-sexed husband was into; for her own part, she was mainly interested in enjoying the fruits of her laboring at MacBowan and under Sam, and restricted her extracurricular activities to non-involving flings with 'boy toy' tennis pros and others of that ilk.

Barbara Masson's trial period as an executive personal assistant had been just long enough for her and Mr. B to discover that they had compatible appetites for steak, sailing and sex. Their openly rumored liaison gave her more access, and a hell of a lot more clout, than that to which she would have otherwise been entitled. At her boss's insistence, MacBowan's head of security, Kurt Ramsey, had ensured with all dispatch that Miss Masson was vetted for the requisite 'top secret' security clearance designation.

Barbara Masson greeted each CEO as he got off the elevator with a smile almost as wide and welcoming as her bosom, the latter currently having some problem just staying inside her benevolently stretched blouse. Like imprinted newborn, these masters of industry gladly waddled along behind her too tightly fitting skirt as they were led briskly but hardly unhappily along the walnut-paneled hallway of the executive floor. All felt at least somewhat compensated for having risen so early this Sabbath morning by the currently involuntary stirring of their not-so-conservative loins.

The walls of the executive floor hallway were lined with photographs of the MacBowan Aeronautical Corporation's most financially successful airplanes. Some of the CEOs who managed to glance away momentarily from Miss Masson's hypnotic hip motion almost instantly experienced some corporate envy as they viewed the fighters, bombers, and commercial aircraft for which MacBowan had acquired many lucrative contracts, usually to these onlookers' companies' bitter disappointment. And yet, they reminded themselves, that was why they had agreed to come to this meeting, or whatever the hell it was going to be; as they could all personally attest, Sam Brannigan certainly knew how to win—one way or another.

As they arrived, they congregated at one end of the boardroom, schmoozing stiffly while gulping coffee and passing on most of the pastries. There was no alcohol, a sure sign that Brannigan was on the wagon again.

They milled around in the manner that people who are used to being in charge sometimes display when they *don't* occupy the power position; just *pretend* this is your home and the others present are your guests. That way, at least, you could present yourself as superior and in charge, whether or not you were.

In the style of the late 1950s there were some stage-whispered and sometimes clever but generally inane comments to one another about the fortunes of various L.A. sports teams and of course, Miss Masson's substantial endowments. One comment brought forth unanimous guffaws: "That Sam, at least we know why *he* doesn't mind getting up early on a Sunday morning and coming to the office".

Their forced frivolity would end soon enough, just as soon as Sam Brannigan would begin to show them another image of bountiful beauty, one that would be displayed in all its glory through a series of stills and corporate-made movies that had arrived overnight from Malton, Ontario, Canada. Once they were viewed, the effect would undoubtedly be to wipe away those king-of-the-hill smirks, short-circuit their wise-ass comments, and leave them gasping for air and grasping at straws, in collective traumatic shock.

Their host suddenly appeared in the boardroom, emerging from behind a camouflaged door that looked like all the other wall panels of exotic wood. Stepping into the room, Brannigan greeted each of his guests in an extraverted yet business-like fashion, as he made his way promptly to the lectern set up in front of the panoramic window, about midway along the lengthy boardroom table. Looking around from this blatant power position, Sam Brannigan officially welcomed them all as they quickly took their seats at marked places on the other side of the magnificently lacquered, Sequoia stump-supported, glass-topped boardroom table. He smiled slightly as he thanked them for sacrificing their beds, boats, golf courses, or "whatever undoubtedly well-deserved pleasures" they might have otherwise been indulging in on this, their universally Christian day of rest.

Then, without any further introductory comments, Brannigan said, "I have asked you here on such short notice because, while you and I have been sleeping soundly in our beds, the very existence of *all* of our companies have been placed in grave jeopardy."

His words had their intended effects. The looks on the others' faces molted from pseudo-smiles through curiosity to outright anxiety. These marked changes were largely due to the fact that Brannigan was known as a man who chose his words deliberately–and accurately. He was not known to be prone to exaggeration.

"*Perhaps* all of us can be excused for being preoccupied for the past five months, ever since October 4th last year to be exact, when we and the rest of the Western world got kicked in the nuts by the Russians when they put their Sputnik into orbit. Our media was so filled with that event and its implications that perhaps few of us read or heard that on the same day, Avro Aircraft up in Canada rolled out their new fighter-interceptor. And when we finally did learn of the Arrow's rollout, we were probably still too busy shitting in our pants about the missile threat to pay much attention.

"And God knows *this* has been an exciting week all by itself, what with some of us being on hand to watch Sugar Ray win his fifth middleweight boxing championship, and with the implications to our companies of the formation of the European

Economic Community and West Germany's parliament finally getting off its ass and approving the deployment of our nuclear weapons in their country. But, gentlemen, we have not been paying enough attention to our bread-and-butter issues."

He watched their faces dim as he used the controls at his lectern to simultaneously lower the boardroom's overhead lights and shutter the expanse of window behind him, with walnut-veneered, metal curtains. At the same time, a movie screen descended from behind a valence on the left side of the room. Almost immediately it was painted with images thrown upon it from some unseen projection equipment.

Brannigan now began to speak more slowly than his usual rapid pace. His voice was ever so slightly subdued but as forceful as ever. He explained that the exciting but disturbing photographs they were viewing were copies that had been made surreptitiously in Avro's own darkroom by a worker who recognized that it would not be to his advantage to have his daily marijuana use reported to anyone in a position to have his security clearance revoked. The five hundred dollars he received for his extra efforts had provided an additional incentive.

Sam explained that the first 'movie' on the screen at the moment was a public relations introduction to the plane's builder, Avro Canada, whose name and winged logo appeared above the entrance to its headquarters, located, Sam said, close to Toronto. More interesting, but also more anxiety provoking, were the drawings and models of the awesome looking aircraft that everyone in the room recognized as *not* one of theirs. Next, the 'movie' became downright scary as it showed an apparently fully operational aircraft assembly line with a high proportion of 'suits', probably engineers, talking enthusiastically with various technicians in what appeared to be great collaborative intensity. Then, as the end of the assembly line came into view, first increasingly large segments, and then seemingly completed, huge and visually magnificent, delta-winged aircraft were seen. Each one had black trim outlining the white wing segments, with large numbers and letters painted on their sides. The numbers ranged from 201 through 208. The CF designation before the numbers proclaimed that these were Canadian-built aircraft. *The arrogant bastards had not only designed the bloody thing; they appeared to be building their prototypes on a fully working assembly line!*

The film sequence was an aeronautical engineer's best fantasy or, if it wasn't one of *his* company's creations, then his worst nightmare. The problem, as all those present immediately recognized, was that these images were not mere fantasy, but only too real.

Another image now showed a close-up of a completed two-seat, twin-engine aircraft at the end of the assembly line that appeared, even while standing still, and then even more so as it was now shown being towed away from the assembly building, like some giant, mechanized, prehistoric bird, its head and chest raised, as if already straining to rise into the air. The viewers' corporate hearts alternately raced and skipped beats, again and again.

Momentarily they were stunned into silence. Then, the air in the boardroom was instantly filled with invectives and pleadings careening around the boardroom table.

"What the hell?"

"For Christ's sake!"

"God help us."

"Holy shit."

"We have to stop them."

Even before this round of alpha noise-making had finished, the screen began to show one of the majestic monsters beginning to taxi down the runway. *Not ready to fly, surely.* And then, *now*, suddenly airborne, followed on either side by current production versions of American and Canadian fighter planes likely photographing the new aircraft, and looking rather puny and passé alongside it.

The film continued rolling over the cascading murmuring in the room, now showing the new plane banking to the left, then right, and left again, revealing more views of its amazingly clean lines.

The screening of the production lines and test flights continued as the viewers became starkly silent. Like boxers temporarily knocked off balance by a surprise blow, their dazed and wounded egos began to angrily pick themselves up off the mat. Jeff Winslow, of Marinik Aircraft Corporation, a former aircraft designer and the newest and youngest CEO present, spoke first. "Where the hell are they going to place the armaments? Those wings are too damn thin to hold much weaponry."

An instant later, the flying phenom banked and moved away from the airborne camera now filming it, and the belly of the beast opened. What appeared to be a multiple-missile carrying cartridge dropped down, right out of the fuselage, like a mechanical mother quickly birthing her lethal offspring.

"What a frigging great idea!" shouted an excited voice from elsewhere around the table.

"Shit, what a brilliant design," mumbled the slumping Winslow.

Over the next few minutes, both admiring and anxious comments emanated from inside the ever-worsening cigar smoke haze that even at this early hour was challenging the boardroom's air conditioning equipment.

"Holy Christ! Look at that baby," uttered another anxious voice, followed by someone else's, "Hell, most of us in this country don't have anything close to that *on our drawing boards*, never mind ready to roll down the goddamn runway *and take off.*"

The comments now became increasingly more strident. Winslow pleaded, "How could such a minor company, in such a unimportant country, accomplish so much in such a short time?"

Brett Gorsan, the legendary founder of Gorsan Aircraft, a 'good old boy' from the south, former top quarterback in his college days, and still an extremely fit, forty-three year old former WWII pilot, spoke up in his smooth southern drawl. "Now, just lets not go gettin' our knickers awl in a knot. Probably awl of us here have known and read about the Arrow in *Aviation Week*, and such. Why, ah personally even went up there, to Tor-on-to myself, and saw them tooling up to build the darn things. Those boys knew what they are doing. And our boys knew that. Hell, they even asked *our* Air Force for input, and darn near asked for our 'by-your-leave' to go ahead and build them thar planes. And we said, *"Be our guests."* Hell, if they wanted to solve the damn engineering problems involved in making an aircraft thet would go thet fast with all the ridiculously stringent specs they were given by the Canadian Air

Force, well, thet was all right with us. Let *them* design *and* develop *and* then test, *and* spend all the R&D money they want *and* even build the bloody things. *That doesn't mean they would ever get to sell them, now does it?!* And it sure don't mean our government or the American people would tolerate the USA buying them foreign aircraft. And where *we* go, most of our allies will damn well go, thet is, if they ever want to do business again with these here United States of America!"

Concurring comments and hurrahs massaged Gorsan's ego.

Considering the relatively refined WASP-infected environs of the boardroom, Hormont Aeronautical Corporation's CEO Anthony Grosso guttural and menacing voice, still sounding like the New York City, Mafia-controlled subculture from whence it came, issued what sounded like more of an order than a question. *"Who the hell do those Avro people and their puny country think they are?* We can't, and we won't let them get away with this. They have to be taught a lesson that they won't ever forget. You don't intrude into a territory where you don't belong. And it ain't good enough to stop them for this time only. We have to make sure that they *don't ever again dare* to create something that could threaten our companies, *eh*, I mean, of course, our country."

Everyone laughed at his presumably, hopefully deliberate, 'slip of the tongue'.

Agreeable comments like "Damn right!" and 'Right on.' greeted Grosso's comments. Most of the others present were probably giving silent thanks that they were on his side in the usually gentlemanly business of aircraft building. None would want to be on the other side of Tony Grosso in any kind of dirty turf war, such as the one in which they were probably about to be invited to enlist in.

Tony Grosso, it was widely rumored, had become the head of Hormont Aeronautical Corporation three years earlier, after his previously little known Las Vegas real estate company, Barter-Steel Real Estate, had acquired a privately held but highly successful helicopter manufacturer. The latter's former owner was evidently a compulsive gambler who, for years, would race his red Jag convertible from L.A. to Vegas nearly every weekend to try his luck at the tables. After initially making a bundle and becoming increasingly risk-taking, the guy's luck inexplicably turned south and his debts quickly grew until they were reportedly into the seven figures, a horrifying sum in the 'fifties. After an apparently terrifying confrontation with Grosso, who had a not inconsequential interest in the casino concerned and personally held the CEO's IOUs, the unlucky gambler was persuaded to accept a low-ball, buyout bid from Grosso's real estate company that, coincidentally, also exactly forgave the moneys owed.

The principal partners at Barter-Steel R.E. had bought into Las Vegas twenty years earlier when the place was about ready to take off in value, and more recently its owners had wanted to invest their profits in other kinds of companies that did a lot of business with various levels of government, including especially the feds. Hormont Aeronautical got them that access. Mucho access.

Grosso said, more menacing now; "Those bloody Canadian hotshits. They *dare* to think that they can push their way into *our* businesses. A country–and a company–has to know its limitations."

The others became very quiet as the pot continued to bitch about a kettle.

Grosso was now, so to speak, on a roll. "We need to show them that they are only allowed to make and sell to us and the rest of the world all the hockey pucks they can make." Grosso roared at his cleverness; the others mostly chuckled to signal their appreciation. "The Canadians need to leave the more sophisticated stuff to the big boys."

Some more concurring comments wisely made their courteous way around the table.

A new, more polished voice now spoke for the first time since the audio-video show started. "And *we* need the people who designed and built that baby, working for us!" The speaker was Harvey deCourt, of Colossus Aircraft, a tall and emaciated looking man of about fifty, who had long ago perfected the art of raiding his competitors and stealing away their best people. There was no love lost between deCourt and the others present, most of whom had become personally familiar with deCourt's corporate raiding behavior. The universally accepted assumption by the others present was that ever since his wife had left him for his supposedly best friend (and former business partner) a decade earlier, deCourt's mission in life had become that of screwing *everyone else*. The idea of sabotaging or otherwise decimating a competitor's prime project, thereby possibly destroying that company's very existence (all in the name of business and/or patriotism), and then hiring away dozens of first-rate employees, was simply too glorious an opportunity for him to let pass. Although he was detested by most everyone else at the table, and was most certainly not to be trusted, on this occasion they could only concur that it was more than okay to bring down and raid a company who was not 'one of their own'.

"EXACTLY!" boomed Brannigan, who had been scrutinizing his guests through the escalating din of smoke and bravado. Now that the initial small-talk bullshit had been sent scurrying by the downright fear of what they had been viewing, Sam's assessment was that they were ready to behave like typical male gorillas, who having suddenly realized that an uninvited silverback was about to make a move on their harems, had concluded that the *only sane and reasonable response was for them to gang up and kill the bastard.* Now, thought Sam, the boys were beginning to sound like the sons-of-bitches they surely were, or were at least capable of becoming, under the right conditions and with the appropriate direction.

The voices had been silenced by the roar of Sam's one word exclamation, and he again started to narrate as the screen showed more amazing test flight movies and still photos. There were only a few more verbal farts as the screen showed apparently *fully built aircraft emerging from fully functioning mass production lines, for Pete's sake! Not simply chaotic collections of equipment assembled for the making of a few prototypes.*

Sam said, "Those conceited Avro bastards were so confident that they could accomplish the technological advances in military aviation that would be required to produce the Arrow that they built the mass production lines into the very beginning of the plane's development. What a magnificent and ballsy move that was. And by building the prototypes on an up-and-running production line, Avro has saved itself at least an additional year or two of pre-full production downtime."

Sam's narration seemed to add to the intensifying aura of determination of the others present, quite like team members' utterances in response to a pep talk by a college football coach who uses the opponent's accomplishments to stir up his own athletes' determination.

Brett Gorsan, the still-stuck-in-the-old-south good ol' boy, knew better than to say out loud exactly what he was thinking about some of these oh-so-superficially politically correct *Californ-i-a-n-s*. He knew better, alright, but he was just so incensed that he let fly anyway. "This *is* 1958, after all! Those uppity Canadians are acting just like some of the colored folk back home. They are forgetting just who they are and where they belong! Do they really think that *we* will let *them* play in our league just because a few of them can run faster, or pass or catch better, than some of our boys?"

The others exchanged furtive glances in response to Gorsan's racist comments. Sam then said in a cool, level voice, "Many of us, of course, have been aware of the Avro Arrow project virtually since its inception, and have received updates from our friends in the departments of defense and the U.S.A.F. about Avro's progress. However, more than a couple of us, myself included I will admit, had been damn sure that our supposedly militarily insignificant neighbor to the north had bitten off a hell of a lot more than it could possibly chew, let alone swallow. Perhaps we were even somewhat arrogant in believing that that they wouldn't be able to make their dream plane fly. We probably blindsided ourselves on this, just like we did by thinking that the Soviet space program couldn't hit the broad side of a barn, let alone build and fire a satellite through the 'gravitational window' and into orbit."

Sam's voice hardened as he made the turn towards home plate. "It now turns out that Avro has gone from specs to mass production assembly line *in under five years*, much less than the time it usually has taken *our* companies to achieve the same state of readiness. And the Arrow can fly higher, faster, and is more maneuverable than anything most of us even have on the drawing board, let alone in the pipeline. I should also tell you that Avro's sales force is gearing up, right now, to go out and get contracts from *our* military as well as those of our allies, who up to now have often relied on American-built aircraft."

Sam paused, and looked around the smoke filled, dimly lit room. He could smell their collective fear. He would wait just a little longer to play his ace.

"Well, Sam! What do *you* suggest we do about the Arrow?" inquired young Jeff Winslow.

The detested DeCourt, spat out *his* answer with mad-dog ferociousness. *"I've already told you all. We have to damn well kill it. We've got to frigging destroy it, like it never existed!* Like I said, after we kill both the Arrow *and* maybe Avro itself, the Canadians won't dare try such a thing again. And I'll gladly take the best of their design and production engineers Stateside to build some real *American* airplanes. I'll even leave some of you guys some!"

DeCourt guffawed at his own remark. Alone. Seeking to crawl out of the quicksand he had just jumped into, he hastily added, "Well, look, it'll be like when we all got the rocket scientists we wanted, after 1945. I mean, we will each get at least some of those bright Avro boys. *All of us."*

No one in the room threw deCourt a lifeline.

The lights came back on and Sam Brannigan's voice boomed, "That's right, Harvey," as he pushed the button beneath the lectern's surface. The camouflaged door to the boardroom opened abruptly again and a hard-bodied, uniformed military essence entered the room. Its owner carried a cold-forged smile signaling an attitude that the others present instinctively knew better than to mess with. It was virtually the same look that some of these CEOs had previously seen on war-seasoned senior officers who had attended the military-corporate briefings-and-bullshit sessions that had become increasingly popular over the past few years.

This officer's strangely handsome yet almost cruel-looking face was immediately recognizable to most of those present. Younger than most of them in the room, *this* alpha male's mere presence somehow transmitted an unmistakable explosive energy no one present would be inclined to challenge, especially not now, not with their business pants down around their ankles, and their corporate genitalia flaccidly resting on miniature guillotines, put there by the damned airplane still appearing on the screen in front of them. Small wonder they found themselves spontaneously standing and applauding in response to the military man's presence among them.

"Gentlemen," said Sam Brannigan, as if he were introducing their savior, "it is my great honor and considerable personal pleasure to introduce to you U.S.A.F. Colonel Jake Marks."

Each person present enthusiastically uttered his respectful greetings to Colonel Marks, again applauding beyond the time sufficient to signal respect.

For months now the L.A. Daily Journal had been in a fearsome battle for readers with its main rival. The latter had chosen to boost circulation by first featuring photos of puppies–a different type every day, on page three. After a few weeks of apparently lessening interest, the paper then began placing full-page photographs of Hollywood starlets in what passed, that year, as provocative poses. In response to the escalating circulation wars, the more upscale, conservative Daily Journal did a series on U.S. military heroes, of which there were plenty since the Korean War had ended only a couple of years earlier. The impressive figure now before them, just days earlier, had received the paper's full hero treatment, with a commanding photograph and accompanying story chronicling his patriotic exploits in the Korean conflict, first as a fighter pilot and then as a natural leader in North Korean POW camps.

Sam Brannigan said, "Some of you, I am sure, have been reading and hearing about Colonel Marks in the press". Most of the CEOs nodded enthusiastically, leading to another, much briefer round of applause.

Sam said, "Most of you, however, are probably not aware that you have also seen photos of Colonel Marks earlier this morning." His guests exchanged quizzical looks as Sam added, "In a few of the slides and scenes in the films you have just viewed, if you happened to be looking at the right place on the screen at the right moment, you would have seen Colonel Marks, first talking to some Avro engineers on the production line, and then to a couple of his Canadian opposite numbers while the Avro Arrow was being rolled out of its hanger for the first time."

Those present were now even more openly appreciative of the presence of this genuine American military hero *and* Avro Arrow insider. And, sensing that the Colonel might also somehow now become their own redeemer, another brief round of applause made its way around the table. Colonel Marks allowed a smile to acknowledge the expressions of appreciation from those present, and in a tightly leashed voice, issued the words, "Thank you."

Sam Brannigan went on. "Colonel Marks is here today at my request, and as a favor to us all, in recognition of the fact that keeping America's military aircraft manufacturing capabilities in control of America's aviation future is in *all* of our best interests. In order to ensure that matters work out the way we all would like, the Colonel and I are going to now be asking for," Sam said, slowing down his rate of speech and releasing each word with threatening deliberateness, "your corporate cooperation."

A chorus of sphincter muscles almost audibly tightened.

"At the least," Sam went on, "regardless of what you may hear before this meeting is adjourned, you are all requested ('commanded' is what absolutely everyone present knew he meant) to kindly forget that this meeting–and the presence of Colonel Marks and your colleagues–ever happened. If anyone here has a problem with what I have said thus far, I would ask that you leave–right now–with no hard feelings."

No one got up from his seat. In fact, no one moved.

To seal their collective agreement, Sam Brannigan made unmistakable contract-securing eye contact with each person at the table, one at a time, his eyes moving on only when the recipient of his piercing glare unquestionably signaled agreement.

For a full, socially awkward minute *no one said anything*, and no one dared look anywhere other than directly at Sam Brannigan. When he was absolutely certain his message had been clearly received *and* agreed to, Sam continued, his voice as measured as before.

"Excellent. Well then, gentlemen, the Colonel is here today as a personal and professional courtesy to all of us, because he loves and wishes to protect this country, as a soldier, as a concerned citizen, and a patriot. As he will shortly explain, he believes–and I think we all concur–that the continued development and probable sale of Avro Arrow to our allies, and possibly even to the U.S.A.F. as well, constitutes a clear and immediate danger to this country's industrial and military future generally, and even to the continued existence of at least a few of the companies that you and I are privileged to lead, and duty bound to make flourish."

The collective anxieties of the CEOs escalated. Sam now administered a well-timed antidote to their fears when he said, "The good news is that Colonel Marks is here to share with you his views on how the threat of the Avro Arrow to our–and our companies'–continued health and well-being can be removed relatively quickly and absolutely permanently."

The sudden reduction in sphincter muscle tension was almost dangerous. DeCourt uttered an audible, "Thank God."

Colonel," said Sam as he yielded the lectern, "would you care to say a few words?"

The assembled guests collectively locked their eyes and ears onto Marks.

Colonel Jake Marks moved to the power position of the lectern, acknowledged Brannigan's words and invitation with a nod, a steely smile, and a firm handshake, and then gazed slowly around the room and into the hopeful hearts and minds of the assembled CEOs. His impatient, crisp manner made it appear that, while he was agreeable to speaking *to* them, he was likely not interested in entering into much discussion *with* them.

"Good morning." said Colonel Marks coldly, as if addressing a class of brand new pilot-trainees on their first day of flight school. "Nothing personal, gentlemen, but I am *not* especially pleased to be here this morning." His words were said in a dismissive tone that triggered some raised eyebrows and narrowed gazes.

Marks, if he noticed the reactions, gave no sign of doing so. "There is simply *no excuse,*" he said forcefully, "for Avro Canada to have gotten this far in the development of an exceptional aircraft like the Arrow. In fact, *your* companies should have been the ones to come up with the specs, design, technological breakthroughs, and super-efficient assembly and production lines for a fighter-interceptor that would have been every bit as advanced, and as successful, a design as the Avro Arrow would likely be, if only it were to be given the chance to continue to fly. But, and I am certain that you will be relieved to hear this, it won't be, *if* you are willing to back up your desires with the means necessary to kill it dead on the tarmac. To put the matter succinctly, if you mean what I heard earlier from the other room, then with your help, I am certain that I can make that frigging airplane go away."

A couple of guests unconsciously made sure that their wallets were still in their back pockets, for somewhat the same reason that many men will automatically double-check that their pants zippers are still in the 'locked up' position when they are about to enter a room.

"As to *why* your companies have not developed an aircraft as fine as the Arrow, well, that is something that our government, our military, and you and I could argue about for years and still never come to any consensus."

Hearing no firm objection, Marks shifted into a higher gear, now almost shouting. *"I mean, Jesus H. Christ!* The Canadians even came to *us*, years ago, before they had given the go-ahead for their project, and asked whether our government or military had any problems with them going ahead with their plans. And everyone Stateside said, "Oh, no!" Not only did we say 'no'; we even loaned them *our* own wind tunnel facilities at Langley for *their* tests of the optimal fuselage design for their damned aircraft."

Colonel Jake Marks paused, and then said, "*Shit, gentlemen.* Obviously some of our people decided that if they wanted to go ahead and try to solve a lot of technical problems for the next generation of aircraft design, why not let them? The reasoning seemed to be that it would save us a lot of money, time and manpower down the line to let our little brother to the north try to act like a big man. Of course, most of our guys were sure that it would all be a waste of time and money anyway, and that they wouldn't be able to meet the seemingly impossible specs for this new fighter-interceptor. Anyway, we could always see and keep tabs on what they were up to. They even accepted the notion of a U.S.A.F. liaison group. That was how some patriotic Americans, including myself, managed to occasionally check in and see how the bloody Canadians were doing.

"Well, gentlemen, we got snookered. Our own arrogance blinded us; we never really believed that they would be, or even that they *could* be, successful. Just like we got fooled when the first goddamn Sputnik went up the same bloody day. Who the hell thought *any* other country, let alone the damned *Russians*, could possibly beat *us* into space? We told one another that they were just a backward bunch of commies who couldn't possibly build a rocket and all the accompanying mechanics and electronics required to get the job done. We bragged to one another that they couldn't hit the orbit 'window' unless someone stuck their head through it.

"And then, what happened when we learned that a Sputnik went up? *We shit ourselves, that's what!* And now we have to work like hell just to play 'catch up'. Well, my friends, we can't afford to, at the same time, be playing 'catch-up' in the realm of military aircraft with the damn Canadians. *Can we?*

"Taking the Russians out may prove the more difficult in the long run, but as all of us in this room know, we are going to be working damned hard on the problem, and the arms and space race will undoubtedly be on the front pages every single bloody day for the next several years, lighting fires under our government's, the military's, and our own asses. It's a damn shame that it has come to this. We could have had the jump on the Russkies and then we would never have let *them* catch up to *us*."

His audience was listening, absolutely silent, with only occasional grimaces and head nodding offering any sign that they were capable of independent motion.

"Thankfully, taking out the Canadians *should* be a hell of a lot easier. All we need is the right pressure applied in the right places to certain key figures in their government and military, backed by the right amounts of good old American greenbacks and horseshit. Let's just say that some of my colleagues have been spending the last few months nurturing a significant number of Canadian politicians and other citizens whose interests can be aligned with our own. I like to call these good folks, '*Ca*mericans'."

Marks issued what passed for a cold chuckle, thereby giving permission for the others to relieve their tension momentarily by a loud but brief burst of laughter that rose up and then died down just as quickly.

Marks hit his stride. "I don't want you fellas to be bothered with the details. Well, *actually*, I have no intention of discussing *any* details with you, for obvious reasons. But I can tell you that to be victorious this situation now requires an assault that must be quick and overpowering in order to be decisive. There must be a 'take no prisoners' approach. Come to think of it, *actually*," chuckled Marks, "those of you who choose to participate in this venture will be free to take all the 'prisoners', that is Avro engineers and technicians, that you can get your hands on."

Looking at the relief flowing across his guests' faces, Brannigan could tell that the Colonel was handily winning the battle of the boardroom. The others looked like they could hardly wait to surrender.

Marks said, "And if enough of you, hopefully *all* of you, concur, then within a year, with your financial support and cooperation, you can be assured that the problem of the Avro Arrow will just disappear."

Marks paused momentarily to scrutinize the faces of the men around the table, and then concluded with a tone befitting the military commander he was, challenging them with the words, *"That is, if you really want it enough, and have the balls and bucks to back this fight."*

Marks stopped talking and sat down in a chair beside Sam Brannigan. No one said a word. The CEOs present all seemingly understood that they had just been offered, at some as yet unspecified price, total victory against an awesome competitor, thereby ensuring their companies'–and as or more importantly, their own–continued prosperity. Who could argue with that?

Sam Brannigan stood up and said, smiling, "Thank you so much, Colonel Marks, I am certain that it is now clear to us all how you unfailingly gain the respect of those under your command."

The others present applauded as Colonel Marks stood and shook Sam's hand.

Turning back to his guests, Sam Brannigan became serious once again. He said, "To achieve the swift success that Colonel Marks has described will require *all* of our companies' good will and cooperation, including some considerable financial resources. The alternative, without a doubt, may well cost some, or perhaps all, of our companies' futures in the long term, especially if the Brits and the damn French get as cocksure and then become as successful as, the Canadians. So I am sure that the funds being requested–a minimum of $15,000,000 from each of your companies, by the way–will be a bargain. Certainly far less than the R&D costs of developing a brand new airplane from scratch, since that won't be necessary, given the experience of the Avro Arrow engineers who will be offered jobs Stateside. Their knowledge, incidentally, will be shared amongst all those companies who will be fully backing the Colonel's future efforts on our behalf."

The assembled guests showed a host of expressions in common–principally worry, shock, and anger–as they tried to digest the financial number Brannigan had just given them.

Before anyone could even begin to mount any opposition, Brannigan said, "I am sure the funds necessary to carry out our project can be justifiably acquired from your respective research and development budgets and/or your companies' contingency funds. And by the way, the monies are to be provided within 48 hours, via wire transfers to the Swiss account numbers on the documents that will now be passed out to you by Miss Masson."

The men sitting on the 'receiving' side of the table did not normally take kindly to being told what to do. A couple of them, for the briefest of moments, glared at Brannigan and then looked quizzically at Marks as if they were actually having difficulty comprehending the corner into which they had now been painted. Sam sensed that a few wanted to ask questions, to find out more about *what* and *where* and *how* and *how much* in regard to the actions being proposed. He moved quickly to cut off any such dialogue.

"Gentlemen, you do not, I am sure, wish to be bothered with the details of *how* your wishes will be made to come true. In fact, it may be decidedly to your advantage to *not* be privy to such… *umm*… sensitive information. Not to put too much of a fine point on it, but almost all of us in this room have fucked up. Let's just face the facts, and be done with it. No excuses, please. We have had our heads stuck up our own fat, arrogant asses for too damn long. Too many of us are still looking down our noses at Japanese camera manufacturers, for Christ's sake. I am sure that all of you will agree with me that the Japanese are changing the phrase 'Made in Japan' from a bad joke into a value-added label. And now the Japanese are making cars that are proving to be a hell of a lot bigger problem than a mere pimple on the Big Three's noses."

Brannigan acknowledged to himself the lack of foresight (or as he sometimes called it, the lack of 'guts' for failing to be honest about one's own deficiencies) of some of the men sitting in front of him. Until recently, he had been one of them. His first-hand investigation of the progress of the Avro Arrow project had shaken him out of his own complacency. And he believed that these CEOs would not move decisively unless their feet were put to the fire, both as business people and personally. He knew where and how he had to lead them next.

Sam softened his tone. "Alright. Look! So the Russians caught us with our pants down taking a leisurely crap while they jumped into the lead in the space race. But I'll be damned if I am going to allow us to be bested by a military pipsqueak, a country with less than ten percent of our population, and without the responsibility that *we* in the USA have to shoulder every single day, in order to keep the Western world safe from the commies. We simply cannot, we *must* not, permit a technologically and militarily third-rate country like Canada, even if it is an ally, to gain military supremacy over us *in any area of military defense–or offense!*"

Brannigan could see that the troops were stirred up, although it was difficult to say if they were getting angry with him for suggesting that America's failure to be first into space had anything to do with failures of their own. Sam knew only too well that some CEOs, especially the ones doomed to crash and burn because of their rigid thinking and overblown egos, did not take kindly to being told anything, by anybody, at any time, that inferred a possible deficiency on their part. *Well, too bad.* This was no time to be 'sensitive'. It was, damn it, a time to be bloody smart and grow giant gonads.

As he peered at their frightened and confused faces, Sam reminded himself of a true story about an especially arrogant and defensive CEO he knew who, as he was about to step onto the stage at the company's annual general meeting, was told by one of his vice-presidents (who was simply trying to do him a favor) that he had not zipped up his fly, after having just come out of the men's room. The CEO's response to this information was to glare at the messenger and announce proudly as he corrected the problem, *"I knew that!"*

Sam gave another strong yet compassionate look around the table, somewhat like a physician who really wanted his long-time patients to accept some necessary but distasteful medicine. His voice was conciliatory. "We are not speaking only of American pride here, my friends: we're talking about the very survival of our companies and the security of our nation. Let's not make the same mistake that our so-called 'intelligence community' made in underestimating the capabilities and threat of the Russian space program. Remember that the Avro Arrow has been built by the same company that built the first jet transport that flew in North America *seven years ago.*"

Sam pushed a button and a slide of a New York City newspaper, dated April 19th, 1950 appeared on the screen, showing a jet aircraft flying over New York City. The caption below the picture read, "This should give our nation a good healthful kick in its placidity." The fact that our massive-in-size but grossly under-populated good neighbor to the north has a product that licks anything of ours is just what the doctor ordered for our over-developed egos. The Canadian plane's feats should now accelerate a growing realization that Uncle Sam has no God-given monopoly on technological genius."

"With apologies to Colonel Marks here, and with our acknowledgement and compassion for all he and his fellow prisoners-of-war went through in those damn POW camps, we were fortunate in at least one way," Sam said, his face momentarily displaying a mischievous–edging toward malevolent–grin, "that the Korean war came along when it did, and that we were able to convince Avro Aircraft that, instead of building commercial airliners they should really be focusing on smaller, military aircraft, like their then-on-the-drawing board, CF-100 interceptors. The CF-100s kept them so busy that they had to drop the Jetliner, *and*," now Sam's face was pure grin, "some of our American designers were able to catch up and get our own commercial jets built and sold! The Avro people never tried to build a commercial jetliner again. Now the same company has to learn the same lesson again, only this time about building *military* aircraft. And this time, the lesson must be unforgettable–in fact, *final*!"

There were no wisecracks, no false bravado from the others present. They just sat silently on their tails.

"I am certain that Colonel Marks and I have convinced you to support our endeavor to shoot down the Arrow, and Avro, once and for all. Doing so is not merely an option; *it is an absolute necessity.* However, to accomplish this goal requires that those who would benefit most by the downing of the Arrow also contribute to the mission."

Now a stronger, more somber and even somewhat threatening voice emanated from Sam's body. "Of course, it will be essential that the technological gains made by our colleagues at Avro be preserved, and that their best people should be encouraged to move Stateside and work for some of us. To deal with the Avro Arrow matter, therefore, we have to act immediately–and massively. And it will cost plenty to purchase all the... eh, *support* that we will need from the right parties in Canada to make that happen–hopefully within a matter of a few months.

"There are currently at least eight Avro Arrows in various stages of completion. The Canadians have also been working on a new jet engine for the Arrow that will be far more powerful than anything we here in the U.S.A. have, and it is just months from testing readiness. What we need to do–peaceably, you understand–to the Canadians, is what we did militarily to the Germans. They–Avro–must be conquered and crushed."

Silent nods greeted these last comments.

"In the folders that Miss Masson has placed in front of you are the bottom-line figures for putting the Colonel's plan into action. Since time is of the essence it is essential that you agree to this proposal and forward the requested funds within forty-eight hours, by this coming Tuesday morning at 8 am, to be precise. Regardless of whether or not you intend to contribute towards our goal, you are asked to please sign the confidentiality agreement that you will find on the last page. I invite you to take a few minutes to review the information contained in these documents; I think you will agree that it is appropriate and advisable to comply, at least, with the terms of the confidentiality agreement. Hopefully, as well, you will agree to sign the contributory agreement."

Sam's guests sat silently, wearing expressions of naked vulnerability. As they examined their dossiers in detail, most looked like they had just been stripped butt-naked and then asked to cough by a sadistic physician.

Sam spoke again and the CEOs looked up. He said, "Those who sign the contributory agreement, and who follow up by ensuring that the funds are deposited in the mentioned accounts by Tuesday morning, will get first dibs on the engineers, technicians and hardware of the Avro Arrow. These assets of personnel and technology should allow the participants to this agreement to leapfrog, by years, over those who don't wish to take part."

Brannigan watched as the CEOs peeled their eyes away from his stare again and once more focused on the materials in front of them. Each of his guests almost immediately understood why Brannigan was so confident that they would comply with his requests. Each dossier included a personal greeting from their host, an individualized one-page letter that had neither letterhead nor handwriting, and ended with the typed words, "Thank you for your anticipated cooperation." Each letter contained at least one oblique but recognizable reference to that CEO's personal IOU to

Sam as well as the specific "minimally acceptable" dollar amount expected of that particular CEO's company. Another letter indicated that Brannigan had developed the equivalent of a college players' athletic draft system. In return for the specified payment, each company was assured of getting first dibs on at least one former major engineer or scientist of the Avro Arrow project and some relevant R&D documents. It was made clear that the more a company contributed to the 'project', the higher would be that company's position in the draft rotation and/or the more frequent would be its turn at selection.

On the other pages of the dossiers were photos and other personal information of such a nature that every CEO in the room, were the personal information contained therein to become public knowledge, might be immediately charged with embezzlement and/or accused of infidelity, or worse. One way or another, the individual might conceivably be left high, dry, and dead broke after what would surely become front-page business news and/or tabloid fodder. At the least, the appearance of these materials clearly guaranteed that there would be no leaks about this morning's meeting.

In one case, where a substantially proportionately greater contribution had been 'requested' from a particular CEO, the photographed 'other person' was of the same sex; in another CEO's dossier, it was difficult to tell the gender of the child in the photo upon whom an 'indecent act' was being performed.

The merciless nature of the dossiers made it evident to everyone present that Sam Brannigan considered the threat of the Avro Arrow to be of the greatest magnitude, and that he was prepared to force and enforce immediate and total compliance from everyone present.

What happened next was likely due to a combination of the too-early hour, the cigar-smoke filled air, the sickeningly accurate dossiers, the 'no nonsense–take no prisoners' re-appearance of the armed security personnel who were now stationed at diagonally opposite corners of the room, and the too aptly named 'Arrow' aimed directly at the hearts of their companies' and, in most cases, their own personal future prosperity, family tranquility, and/or freedom.

Whatever the 'reasons', within less than twenty minutes all the guests had signed the confidential agreements along with the 'contributory' documents committing their companies to provide the financial sums requested "within forty-eight hours".

None of them would ever trust one another, or Sam Brannigan again. And that was just fine with Sam. The situation, about which he had been informed by Colonel Jake Marks just days earlier, was just as dire as he had described, if not more so. This was not the time for niceties. He had done what the situation required, no more but no less. So, if any of his guests' sensibilities didn't heal pretty damn quickly, well, *screw 'em*!

As the meeting finished, Sam Brannigan and Colonel Marks shook the noticeably sweatier hands of the guests who took turns quickly excusing themselves to their host for their inability to stay behind and chat. Seemingly, they all needed to get on with their Sunday morning activities. No doubt some would be praying extra hard in church later this very morning, that their days at their companies and in their expensive homes with their families, would be long, and that their families, the FBI, and the IRS would remain blissfully ignorant of any past indiscretions.

After the last CEO had left, the two 'hosts' stood looking at each other, neither speaking immediately, yet both saying plenty with their satisfied, nodding expressions.

"Colonel," said Brannigan finally, "you laid the matter out just right. We not only have to kill the Avro Arrow, we have to bury it. And not only bury it, but frigging incinerate it. Until only ashes and charred bits of bent metal remain. This is one business battle none of us in this room this morning can afford to lose. Hell, this is bizwar for aircraft manufacturing *supremacy* of the whole goddamn western world."

Colonel Marks said, "Not to worry, Sam. With the access we have up in Canada and the additional clout these *donations* will provide, by the time we are through with our Canadian friends, they'll not only stop production on the Arrow, they'll bloody well apologize for their misguided arrogance in starting the project in the first place. Then, to punish them further, we will arrange for them to do us the favor of destroying the planes they have already built with blowtorches and sledge hammers and say, in their irritating and ingratiating way, "Sorry," while doing it."

Marks laughed heartily. "As you know, Sam, Canadians are always saying, "Sorry", even if it's the other guy's fault! Kiss-ass types, most of them."

"Colonel, do you really think you can get them to actually destroy the aircraft they have already built?"

"All except one plane, absolutely," Marks replied. "Just as you and I have discussed already. Once we have gotten to the right people, they will see to it that the entire Avro Arrow program is obliterated like it never existed. Within a few years no one in Canada will even remember that there *was* an aircraft called the Avro Arrow."

They both smiled in warm anticipation of their success.

Then Sam shook his head, and said, "Christ, Colonel! Can you imagine, in your wildest dreams, that an American President, or the American media, or the American people, would ever tolerate an *American* aircraft company taking its finest technological achievement—the best in its field that the world had ever seen, that had been already paid for with taxpayers' money, and that had already demonstrated that it works, even better than the specs require—*and actually going ahead and destroying it, blueprints and all?!"*

Colonel Marks replied, "Of course not! Not a chance. Never happened; never will. Americans are always proud of what we have accomplished; damn proud! No one would ever make *us* hide our light under some goddamn bushel basket. And God help those that would ever even try."

Brannigan concurred. "Anyone who would try to pull that stunt in this country would be strung up by the short and curlies."

"So, how the hell will you pull it off, Colonel?" As soon as the words were out of his mouth, Brannigan was trying to reel them back in. "Oops! Forget I asked that. I, of all people, know better than to ask. None of my business."

The colonel smiled, rock hard; "Its better that way, Sam. Let's just say that we'll get it handled. The right people will do what needs to be done, or at least influence those who need to do it. And then they will all shut up about it. And we'll make sure they shred and burn all their blueprints—except, of course, for *our* copies. Then they will destroy their production line equipment–again, everything, that we don't need. And we will ensure that it will appear to the Canadian public that the Avro Arrow program was shut down because it cost too much, or that no one would buy it, or that it really didn't meet specs. Whatever bullshit it takes to get their citizens to swallow the pill and justify killing the program."

Sam asked, "And you really think they will buy those stories?"

Marks was ice cold. "Of course. Look, Sam, I learned a lot in those POW camps about all kinds of techniques that can be used in breaking people's minds and bodies. And companies and even countries are just like people in a lot of ways. Anyway, it will be all over before there can be any opportunity for opposing voices to have any effect. The Arrow will be long gone. And the *way* in which we will do it will destroy their military's credibility and break their aircraft industry's back. And we will make sure that their air force will 'buy American' in the future, and give up entirely the idea of 'building Canadian' ever again. We just have to punish them psychologically, so that *they will never even think about conceiving* another program that could seriously challenge America's military might or our corporations' bottom lines. We'll tell them to concentrate on building bush planes or short haul domestic aircraft or something along those lines. Maybe we will even let them build a piece of a tail or a part of a wing of one of *our* aircraft, just so their government can claim a token victory of some sort. It won't mean anything but we probably will throw them a scrap or two. After all, by the time we get through with them, they'll literally be in tremendous economic and manufacturing distress and pain that they ever started the Avro Arrow program; it will hurt that much. So, we probably will throw them a few bones."

Listening to the colonel's strategic thinking, Brannigan knew he had found the right man for the job.

"Besides, which," said Marks, "we plan to fight the next war with the Russians over Canadian airspace, so it's probably in our interest to throw them a few crumbs by letting them build a couple of airplane components."

Brannigan was mildly shocked yet, truth be told, mostly impressed by the Colonel's pychopathic-like non-caring. He almost couldn't believe his good fortune in having found a man like Colonel Marks whose ways of thinking so nearly mirrored his own. "So, Colonel, you really think that we can actually get away with this? But won't it create so many problems with their own business people that the Canadian party in power will be reluctant to completely terminate the Avro Arrow?"

Jake Marks sighed. He was used to fools, but didn't suffer them gladly. However, Brannigan was a brilliant man, a legendary figure in the business, and was about to be the source of more money than the colonel had ever seriously believed he would accumulate in his lifetime. So he smiled and said, almost kindly, "Sam, don't worry about it. The media will be taken care of; we will just give them some *other* stories to write about. Invite some of their reporters down to California next winter, all expenses paid, for some bullshit 'conference' that you and your colleagues can throw together in Palm Desert or wherever. It'll be cold as hell up there then; they'll love coming south to get warm. And also invite some of their reluctant politicians down as well, for a 'fact-finding' mission on 'The Future Of Military Supremacy' or some impressive bullshit title like that."

Marks paused and smiled tightly again. "And as far as the Canadian 'citizens', as you put it, they are so busy with their lousy economy that they will be happy to drop what we will make sure they will think of as just another futile, costly, government-funded, pork barrel-type program that can't go anywhere, producing an inadequate plane that wouldn't ever be bought by any other NATO countries."

Brannigan nodded, signifying his satisfaction with Mark's responses to his questions. Sam said, "Strange, isn't it? If they only had the balls to stay the course, they could probably sell those Arrows to most of our Western allies and perhaps even the U.S.A.F., and then their country could probably *fly* their way out of their recession."

Marks nodded but said nothing. He was already mentally reviewing which politicians, military, and media people whom he had met and whose acquaintanceships and friendships he had cultivated, that he could get to quickly, and turn the way he wanted–fast. He felt comforted as he reassured himself that accomplishing his goal was eminently 'doable'. This invasion would be swift and devastating; the victory lucrative. And not even all that costly to accomplish. Hell, there would be enough money left over for him to put into some Swiss bank account and allow him to live in luxury, with enough left over to buy himself the home and office building in Florida he had already picked out for the next part of his surely illustrious life.

Both Brannigan and his new friend gazed out at the Pacific briefly, basking in the pleasure of their plans and the profits they had just assured themselves of making over the days and years ahead.

CHAPTER 9

1958–2009

'TAMPRR' was a multiple-meaning moniker for The American Management Profit Recovery and Retention Company, a seemingly legitimate consulting organization that carried out overt public relations and lobbying work on its corporate clients' behalf. These efforts TAMPRR was only reasonably successful at, most likely because the mind, heart and energy of its owner was usually focused elsewhere, on TAMPRR's far more profitable and much less overt services for a more select segment of its clientele. Nevertheless, TAMPRR's more public efforts served their main purpose, which was to explain away the company's existence and its obviously substantial income, while at the same time covering its far more profitable 'black black' operations.

TAMPRR didn't actually *win* many contracts through an open bidding process; nor did it gain business through aggressive marketing via 'dog and pony' shows. In fact, TAMPRR had what constituted, in effect, an *anti*-PR department, to which most inquiries, including potentially nosy media requests for information and interviews, were directed. After learning how boring was its routine work and how seemingly inconsequential its clients, most business reporters looking for a meatier story usually got the message that wasting either ink or air on TAMPRR could not possibly be of any interest to their audiences.

If only they knew the truth.

The occasional reporter who did think there was a story to be had at TAMPRR usually backed off rather quickly when faced with what passed for 'press releases' announcing a new flavor of a corporate client's toothpaste or the latest 'improved wet weather tread pattern' by a tire manufacturer. Surely, here in Miami Beach, where TAMPRR's headquarters occupied several thousand square feet on the top two floors of a low-rise office building the company owned near the bottom of Alton Road, not too far from Paul's Stone Crab restaurant, there were other, far more interesting business stories to uncover.

Thankfully also, no media people had ever inquired as to the purposes of the various antennae located on the roof of the office building in which TAMPRR carried on business. And no one who worked for the American Management Profit Recovery and Retention Company, ever referred to the company by its initialed acronym. That, and the inside joke it represented, was openly shared mostly among the six senior members who had started with the company at its beginnings.

The media at large were only somewhat aware that virtually all of TAMPRR's corporate clients were large U.S. aircraft, high-tech, pharmaceutical and healthcare related corporations; usually these companies gave TAMPRR some minor PR or lobbying work to do, most often in response to an informal directive from their CEOs. These corporate Zeuses were often the only ones in their organizations who had any idea about the true nature of TAMPRR's specialized capabilities, and they occasionally used their companies' so-called discretionary funds to acquire TAMPRR's more unique services, such as whenever they needed a congressman or a senator sent scurrying in the direction of voting for or against some bill in the House or Senate, or, as was occasionally the case in recent years, whenever they needed something even more sinister to be carried out.

By 2009 TAMPRR had been around for over fifty years. It was the brainchild of retired U.S.A.F. Colonel Jake Marks, and originally it's sole mission was to carry out covert corporate surveillance and, if required, surreptitious sabotage of either friendly or unfriendly countries' civilian and military aircraft industries. These assignments arose as word was leaked about Mark's original, and his greatest, success, the so-called Avro Arrow Manipulation. As a result of the efforts of Marks and his team, according to the rendition that made its way into aircraft manufacturing folklore, nothing less than the complete and utter destruction of a state-of-the-art airplane and the company that had designed and built it, as well as Canada's entire independent military aircraft industry, had suffered a lethal blow. The rumor was that the entire operation had been carried out on behalf of a few military aircraft companies who had subsequently never been allowed to forget that they in no small part owed the last half-century of American military air supremacy, as well as their financial success, to the actions undertaken by the forerunner of TAMPRR between the years of 1958 through 1959. In any case, the scuttlebutt was that the TAM in TAMPRR really stood for *The Arrow Manipulation.*

Now, in February of 2009, after decades in which the company that Jake Marks built made fortunes for himself and his senior principals, TAMPRR was on the verge of finally accomplishing an even more lucrative and audacious goal, the complete undermining and collapse of Canada's publicly-funded, government-run, universal Medicare system. And this goal, which TAMPRR had been pursuing for over a decade and a half, would provide the company a substantial end-of-project bonus of over three hundred million dollars, and yield to Marks himself, a final retirement gift of over 250 million dollars. The word inside TAMPRR was that the old man would then take his leave of the daily grind of presiding over TAMPRR, Inc, and would thereafter focus on his only other love, the hunting and killing of every kind of wild animal worthy of his attention. After each one of his invariably pleasurable hunting expeditions, Marks would return to his Miami Beach home and relax by going on biweekly marlin fishing excursions on his yacht in the Florida keys.

Killing of any kind had always felt just so darn good to the man!

CHAPTER 10

2009

Over the nearly half-century since the Avro Arrow program was shot down by 'friendly fire', so to speak, shortly after it had taken off, Jake Marks occasionally learned from various of his Canadian operatives that the bitter memories of the tortured demise of the Canadian-designed and built CF-105 Avro Arrow, and what it had meant to that country's manufacturing industry, still remained an open sore to a sizable segment of Canadians, growing rather than diminishing to this day.

In the 1990s Marks was told that a number of ex-employees of Avro Canada, many of whom had *not* taken the road most easily traveled to California after the program had been closed down by the Canadian government, along with some dedicated technical types and history buffs, some of whom had not even been born until after the Avro Arrow program had been killed, had been volunteering their expertise and energies to construct a number of scale models and even full-size mockups of the damned plane, at various places across Canada.

These metallic apparitions were being touted as tributes to that country's once blossoming military aircraft industry and its then-unsurpassed technological capabilities. Marks also knew that some of these Arrow ghosts were scheduled to be unveiled in various Canadian provinces within a few weeks of February 20th, 2009, the 50th anniversary of the cancellation of the Avro Arrow project.

Another disturbing fact about the upcoming 50th anniversary, of course, was that it also meant that Jake Marks's most brilliant business triumph had happened nearly a half-century earlier. Marks was determined to have at least one more major success that would dwarf even 'The Arrow Manipulation'. All of this *stuff* that he was being continually updated about regarding the damned Arrow, he conceded reluctantly to himself, was probably at least partly responsible for his markedly disturbed sleep patterns of the last several months. He kept waking up from dreams in which whole bloody *squadrons* of Avro Arrows were attacking the houses and office buildings where he and others involved in the demise of that aircraft had been living and working back then, or were living in currently. *Stupid bloody bullshit dreams! Never believed in their having some deep meaning. 'Just some psychoshit,'* is how he usually referred to so-called 'dream interpretation'. *Never had time for that crap!*

Some other repetitive and upsetting dreams were filled with poison-tipped arrows or spears and various sharp implements appearing out of nowhere and then, at supersonic speed, they would begin penetrating his body. They always seemed to be aimed towards his head, heart or genitalia, and frequently found their targets. He really wished these attack-dreams would stop so that he could have a decent night's sleep. Unfortunately, that seldom happened.

Marks told himself that erasing the Avro Arrow from Canadian consciousness should have become easier in recent years, given as how the survivors of Black Friday, now mostly in their seventies and eighties, had been dying off at an increasingly gratifying rate. However, the *idea* of the Avro Arrow and the issues surrounding its birth, its life, and especially its death, had *not* abated, but rather, had continued to be a strong–and even growing–force. That fact was attested to, and undoubtedly fed by, some books, plays, documentaries and docudramas that had been produced over the past few decades. Marks found this interest in the Arrow almost morbid. *Get over it, guys. You lost out. You didn't have the balls to match either our bats or our bucks. Just accept the fact and move along.*

It disturbed Marks mightily to read in a recent report prepared by one of TAMPRR's operatives working in Ottawa, that the National Flight Museum of Canada's gift shop, while offering a wide variety of books, airplane models, etc… pertaining to many military *and* commercial (mostly American) aircraft, past *and* present, was to this day continuing to find a seemingly unabated appetite on the part of many of the museum's visitors for Arrow-related paraphernalia. *Fifty years after it's demise, for Christ's sake!* Furthermore, and completely unfathomable to Marks, was the fact that the buyers of this Arrow crap were both Canadian *and American* visitors. Apparently, sales of the Avro Arrow items accounted for more than those for all the other aircrafts *combined. Go figure.*

The most recent operative's report, written after the thirty-something, ex-marine and now TAMPRR operative, had succeeded in taking one of gift shop's employees out for dinner, included the curious fact that some museum visitors were evidently returning to the pitiful Avro Arrow exhibit again and again, as if they were seeking some greater understanding of an apparently senseless act, or were paying their respects to a loved one cut off in his or her youth, perhaps as a result of a fatal accident or even murder. *Screw them all!* thought Marks. *Killing the Arrow was a goddamn tour de force. Why the hell can't they just forget about it?* He had actually viewed the paltry Avro Arrow display with great pleasure a few years back during a business trip to Ottawa. He thought it resembled nothing so much as an ill-conceived and poorly executed, above-ground gravesite.

Another, probably more relevant reason Marks was so pissed off about the near cult status of the Arrow, was that it was seemingly stuck in the Canadian psyche, and was probably one of the main factors making his more recent project of destroying the Canadian government-run universal Medicare system all that much harder to finally accomplish. All this continuing fuss about a so-called 'national dream' of a Canadian-designed and built 'world-best accomplishment' having been destroyed nearly fifty years ago had already cost TAMPRR an extraordinary amount of time and effort, and its clients a hell of a lot more money than Marks had originally estimated.

"Well," he told his American healthcare corporate clients, year after frustrating year, whenever he came back for additional funding with which to pay off currently, as well as newly corrupted, Canadian politicians, bureaucrats, medical administrators, and physicians, "just put the additional expenses down on your books as 'unforeseen cost overruns' or 'exceptional research and development' expenses."

Sure, some of our American healthcare providers and insurance companies are outstanding, but as for some of the others... shit! As of last year, in 2008, some of the biggest American healthcare providers already have annual revenues greater than either Microsoft or Ford, for Christ's sake, so they shouldn't be bitching so much about how long it has been taking to get them into position to take over the Canadian healthcare system. After all, once they have their customers locked up in a health insurance plan, most of the suckers probably stay with them forever, being too scared to be without coverage, or afraid that other HMOs or insurers will refuse to insure them, or will charge them even higher rates, or give even lousier service. And to keep on raking in the dough, all they have to do is buy off some more politicians while they continue to deny service and keep their hands on one of the most lucrative scams before and since the Enron debacle. Talk about creative accounting practices, all the while stonewalling the delivery of possibly life-saving services in a timely manner. Hell, what a business! Now the big automakers annually spend more on healthcare-related expenses for their employees than they do on the goddamn steel for their cars and trucks. No wonder it is so hard to convince Canadians that they should ditch their healthcare system for ours.

The Canadians' memories of what happened to the only other 'world-best' creation they ever came up with, the bloody Avro Arrow, as far as Marks was concerned, was just making his current project that much harder. *Not impossible,* he reassured himself. *Just damn harder!* It was almost as if Canadians' 'collective unconscious' (as his thankfully-long-gone psychologist/first wife would have labeled the phenomenon) had realized that they had been screwed out of the Avro Arrow, and they weren't going to allow themselves to be beaten out again of their precious government-run healthcare system.

Marks viewed the tenacity of the Canadian public in wanting to hold onto their system as plain bullheaded. Polls showed that they continued to give their Medicare system high marks in spite of the fact that, with TAMPRR's urging (meaning 'bribing and coercing') some of the best-bought politicians and bureaucrats in Canada (Marks still called them 'Camericans') had shut down entire wards and hospitals, laid off thousands of nurses, and deliberately misspent moneys supposedly earmarked for healthcare, on golf courses and road pavings instead. Also, many provinces still allowed physicians to charge for 'professional services' such as psychotherapy, for which they were often, hardly sufficiently professionally trained and qualified. TAMPRR had pressed to have such questionable services tolerated so that there would be fewer doctors available to carry out physical medicine. This redirected use of funds helped ensure that many Canadians were faced with increasingly long waiting lines for critical diagnostic assessments and surgeries, thereby providing plausible rationales for introducing American-style medical clinics. *You would think the Canadian public would have been crying 'Uncle Sam' by now and be begging for some enterprising U.S. companies to open up across Canada and offer good old fee-for-service hospital and diagnostic services. And some had opened, but not enough. Not nearly enough!*

Well, so be it. Why the hell should they have anything better than we do in the U.S.A.? And what right do they have to keep my corporate clients from doing to the Canadians what they have been doing to Americans for decades? After all, business is business. And everything is a commodity. Everything is business. Even a child's healthcare. Hell, especially a child's healthcare. Christ, after all, parents will sell anything and everything, to save their child. That's where the money is.

Marks felt a twinge... of something... as he found himself thinking about his own grand-daughter having died while giving birth some twelve years earlier because some asinine gatekeeper-clerk at her HMO had refused permission for the obstetrician to employ an extra procedure in order to ensure that, after a difficult third trimester, the delivery would be more likely to go smoothly. But that was ancient history; Marks wrenched his focus back to the problem at hand. *Regardless, we just have to kill their Medicare system, pure and simple.*

CHAPTER 11

FEBRUARY 2009

TAMPRR's Miami Beach headquarters was walking distance from its owner's waterfront home on Pine Tree Road. Jake Marks had purchased both his home and office building with some of the moneys gained from the Arrow triumph which, he was well aware from the time he awoke this morning, had occurred fifty years ago this very day. Like a big game hunter's trophy, Marks kept an enamel-painted, wooden model of the Avro Arrow on his office credenza, right next to the models of certain other airplanes, all U.S.-built, that owed their own existence and success in no small measure to the Avro engineers who needed jobs after the Arrow's demise.

TAMPRR's headquarters' location was in large part strategic. In order to conduct their business, TAMPRR's 'associates' were themselves frequently put up in hotels or office buildings near their 'targets', close enough to headquarters that the audio and video recordings being made could be transmitted, in encrypted form, for immediate downloading onto the company's massive memory databanks.

TAMPRR's associates, both men and women, were mostly ex-special forces and intelligence types. They had been trained to be adept in employing the latest generation of electronic surveillance tools, including those that had been developed in TAMPRR's own research laboratories, assisted through the generous support provided by a variety of U.S. military and CIA contracts.

Over the previous decade some of the largest healthcare and pharmaceutical companies had acquired major investment interests in certain print and electronic media. Now, not only were some media outlets dependent on these companies for a major chunk of their advertising revenue, but these same advertisers now either directly owned, or indirectly controlled,

71

the media outlets themselves. *Dare to bite the hand that feeds you and you could well lose your head as well as your hand.*

'Convergence' provided these companies with preferred advertising rates plus nearly endless free 'name placements' by the overly paid 'talking heads' whose forced joking with one another on their programs allowed for the opportunity to drop a product's name several times a week, with such inane comments like, *"Boy, could I use an UpsunAD now!!!"* The latest and wonderfully financially successful major anti-depressant, UpsunAD, was a much-advertised product of the Medsoar Corporation. Medsoar and a consortium of other pharmaceutical and healthcare companies now jointly owned and tightly controlled the newspaper/magazine/radio/television/Internet/ news service, Liberty United News Cable Hookup [LUNCH], and UpsunAD was currently being blitz-advertised using the same sorts of supersaturated colors, upbeat music and happy, smiling actors as those used to sell candy bars. *"Feeling blue? Take two."* was UpsunAD's blazing tag line.

On this blissfully warm, February afternoon seagulls were surfing the warm Florida updrafts past the balcony of the hotel suite occupied by the Honorable Raymond Clease, M.P., Member of Parliament for the Omberta Northeast district of his province. Sixty-one years old, markedly overweight but still reasonably handsome, he had been re-elected to three consecutive terms as a Member of Parliament, largely on the basis of his 'family values' and born-again electoral platform that played well throughout his huge, mostly rural constituency. He was also, currently, the chairperson of the Twentieth Federal Commission On The Revitalization Of The Canadian Healthcare System, constituted in 2008. He was in Miami on an official four-day information-gathering junket, ostensibly to consider the 'hypothetical integrative compatibility features' of the U.S. and Canada healthcare systems.

The conference was sponsored and paid for by the academic-sounding International Research College of Medical and

Healthcare Services Providers (IRC/MHSP), a purportedly non-partisan organization that regularly put on 'professional development' courses for medical practitioners, healthcare system university researchers, and especially politicians in a position to influence healthcare policies in their own countries.

In actual fact, IRC/MHSP was largely financed by TAMPRR on behalf of certain HMO-clients, including for-profit hospitals, insurance, and pharmaceutical companies who had, in the early 1990s, brilliantly short-circuited the Clinton administration's attempts to develop a government-run, universal healthcare program along the lines of the Canadian system.

Incredible advances in advertising research now allowed those with the financial means and motivations, to hire firms that used, among other tools, MRIs and CAT scans to measure the positive and negative responses of samples of the public to any audio and/or visual material presented to them. A couple of these PR firms claimed that they had succeeded in decoding the 'DNA' of attitude-shaping that was effective for about eighty percent of the population; the huge increases in profits for some soap and sundries companies suggested that the eighty percent claim was probably understated.

The Honorable Raymond Clease's own most honored member was presently upright, assisted by an incredibly attractive thirty-something, a special assistant to a key member of the new U.S. administration. He had met her the previous evening at the opening cocktail party of the Research College's conference, and they had agreed to meet the following morning to discuss various healthcare-related topics in which the young lady had expressed a keen interest. They had been going at it, or to be fair, *she* had been going at *him,* for most of the morning, since an hour or so after they had finished what was supposed to be an information-exchange meeting in the hotel's coffee shop.

She had come right up to him the previous evening, accompanied and introduced by Senator Sam Hendry's almost equally vivacious 'junior executive assistant', Charlene somebody or other. This blessed child's name was Mary Super, and ever since she had come to his room, supposedly to receive a copy of the paper he was going to deliver on the last day of the meeting, she had been living up to her surname. Possessed of an incredible body, a most kissable face (if he had only allowed himself to think it, he would have recognized that she was about the same age and had the same fresh looks–high cheekbones, long, wavy black hair, hazel eyes–as his own daughter, Amy), and lips that telegraphed their talents with her every smile or pout.

In between their innings in bed they drank and toked. Clease presently felt like he was trying to pitch in the top of the 8th and wasn't sure he could make it to the mound again with anything left to deliver, even though she had clearly been expending most of the effort. When the young vision intuitively called 'time' while she went to the bathroom to 'freshen up', Clease managed to make an extremely brief, reassuring 'wish-you-were-here-and-you-didn't-have-to-look-after-my-Alzeimer-afflicted dad' phone call to his wife.

Harriet Clease, a dutiful political wife of the 'old school', reported to her husband that she was busy having *her* ass frozen off in the typically stormy Canadian winter weather. She had already spent much of the day in their SUV doing her meals-on-wheels number for senior shut-ins in their constituency, in between schlepping her husband's eighty-seven year old father around to his various medical visits. Quickly excusing himself to his wife as the muffled sound of a toilet flush reached his ears, he said that he had to hurry as he was late for a meeting with his American opposite number, and just managed to get off the phone when the bathroom door opened.

Thankfully, the best lay he had had in a long, *long* time announced that she was now ready to "just snuggle". He was out of strikes anyway. *Hell*, he joked to himself, *thanks to the best of Ms. Super, I think I am even out of balls.*

The young thing, in her blessed nakedness, came around to his side of the bed. Clease was impressed by Mary's proud comfort in her beauty and sensuality. When she touched his arm and slid back into bed she heard him mumble, seemingly to himself, "Oh my God. *I can't believe this.* " as he became aroused yet again.

Settled into room 310, an efficiency unit at the much lower cost West-By-Eastern Ocean Resort just a few blocks further south on the beach, and taking in all of the action in the suite at the Civilar Bal Harbor, was Chad Warwick, himself an exceptionally earnest and extremely busy 30-something. Warwick was an ex-CIA operative who had expertly installed the remotely operated digital camcorders in the Canadian parliamentarian's room a bare twenty minutes before the Honorable Raymond Clease had first entered his hotel room the previous afternoon.

The monitoring suite at the West-By-Eastern Ocean Resort had been reserved by TAMPRR as soon as Clease's reservation was confirmed, because it was ideally located well within the requisite maximum one mile transmitting range of the equipment that Warwick had planted. In fact, TAMPRR frequently rented that particular unit for its operatives, since it faced north towards the convention-friendly Civalor Bal Harbor Hotel and because its potted palm-lined balcony could shield the receiving antennae from passersby who religiously walked up and down the beach from dawn to dusk.

TAMPRR Inc. had many paid informants among the desk clerks, taxi and limo drivers, and housekeeping and maintenance staff that serviced the major convention-oriented hotels in Miami Beach, New York, Chicago, San Francisco and Los Angeles, as well as in selected foreign capitals, including Ottawa, Paris, London, and Berlin. Most of the low-level operatives believed that they were being paid by a shadowy government intelligence agency, primarily to be on the lookout for prospective terrorist-types. And in certain cases that was true enough. However, many of them were also asked to provide information about the movements of some quite reputable business and political leaders, as well.

By the time Raymond Clease had finished attending the four-day International Research College of Medical and Healthcare Services Providers conference, he had been audio and videotaped screwing, smoking, snorting, and accepting offers of share options from various healthcare and pharmaceutical companies for himself and members of his family. As a bonus he was also the recipient of promises of jobs for his newly university-graduated daughter and nephew at a prominent HMO's future

Canadian head office, which would be located in Edmonton, the provincial capital of Alberta.

During the conference at the Civalor Bal Harbor, Chad Warwick and a few other TAMPRR operatives had collected enough digitized ammunition to sink any opposition that Raymond Clease or other members of his delegation might be inclined to mount to TAMPRR's clients' plans in regard to partially, if not entirely, privatizing and taking charge of the Canadian healthcare system.

It didn't hurt the cause that Clease had also received assurances during the conference that his own father would be placed in one of the finest full-time medical care facilities in Scottsdale, Arizona, whenever his Alzheimer's progressed to the point that he could not be cared for in a home environment. Clease had also been given the keys to a nearby three-bedroom villa that would be made available immediately and for an indefinite time period, for the use of any members of the Clease family. The home away from home was located just three blocks away from his father's future –and presumably last– place of residence.

In his own mind Raymond Clease was comforted by the knowledge that he had fought the good fight on behalf of his constituents for over twenty-eight years at no small cost to himself and his family. He believed that he now deserved to have his family and beloved father, a former federal politician himself, looked after in ways that his own salary, even with all its perks and generous pension plan, simply would not allow. His family surely deserved the best of everything, now and in the future, to compensate them for all his loyal efforts on his constituents' behalf for so many years. And Raymond Clease was damned proud to be able to announce these newly promised perks to his family when he returned home.

He knew, of course, that he would not run for re-election but instead would retire just as soon as the new privatized healthcare facilities currently being fought for, were running full-tilt, probably within a couple of years from now, if he had anything to do with it. *And he surely would.* He had also received assurances that a man of his experience, prestige and integrity would be a shoe-in as a member of the board of directors of the future Canadian subsidiary of an American company that specialized in building and operating for-profit hospitals.

As soon as the conference was over and his target had departed, Chad Warwick packed up his equipment and checked out, paying for the stay in cash. TAMPRR employees always paid with cash so that there was no direct paper or electronic corporate trail leading to TAMPRR Inc.. Warwick didn't mind at all; TAMPRR always paid a 5% bonus on items paid for in cash or put on the employee's personal credit card whenever they were needed to conduct company business. Expenses related to such purposes were always reimbursed promptly.

"And so it goes," thought Chad. Conference after conference, or more correctly 'junket' after 'junket', more and more greedy and horny politicians, ex-Prime Ministers, co-opted media types, and assorted bureaucratic and corporate schmucks would end up in TAMPRR's back pocket for whenever the need arose. And in the case of finishing off the government-run Canadian Medicare System, Chad had heard through the TAMPRR grapevine that crunch-time was coming soon.

"With these suckers," mused Warwick to himself, "it would likely be much sooner than later." Warwick viewed himself as a quick study and he was pretty well up on Canadian issues of interest to the U.S. generally, and to TAMPRR in particular. As it was, with its large 'snowbird' influx of Canadians every winter, Florida had as much Canada-oriented news as any state in the union, and probably more, especially from November through April. In recent weeks, for example, the Miami Chronicle had published several articles about the fact that the Canadian government was preparing to finally introduce major modifications to its Canada Health Act. He even saw Raymond Clease's name among those mentioned in the article as being an influential politician who was known for his apparently oft-stated public position that while he wanted to preserve a government run, definitely non-U.S. type of healthcare system, he was, nevertheless, as he had put it so well in a recent speech, "open to considering more efficient transformative alternative ways of servicing patients."

Under his breath Chad Warwick said to himself, *Oh, yeah. Right. Asshole! You're just a dirty old man who has sold out in order to line your own and your family's pockets. With 'loyal' politicians like you, Canada doesn't need any foreign enemies.*

Not that Warwick really cared. Since he left the CIA less than three years ago and came to work for TAMPRR, his income had doubled and he got a kick out of carrying out nearly the same kinds of covert intelligence operations his country had taught him to do so well while he was a government employee. *Mind you, TAMPRR Inc. is even ahead of the CIA in some areas of surveillance.* He also appreciated that the company's fringe benefits included paying for items like thoroughly releasing massages for tired, achy operatives. And they really didn't care what 'extras' came along with the 'therapeutic' massages.

Chad was also thoroughly enjoying having his own modestly upscale apartment in SoBe, or South Beach. Miami Beach's trendy and easy-to-blend-into area definitely worked well for an attractive, clean-cut, thirty-something like himself. Except, of course, for the fags.

Not that he was really prejudiced, or anything like that. Like, hey, he had video-taped politicians who were closet chicken hawks who preyed on the young 'un, juveniles who hung (and he really meant 'hung') around some of the gay bars in SoBe, as well as the regular fare of New York business types who visited South Beach for the relief and pleasure of crawling out from beneath their macho married covers to let loose a little.

Anyway, none of the homos ever repeated the mistake of thinking he was one of them. Within a month of his moving into his apartment, the word was out in the neighborhood that the great-looking guy living at #10009AB Ocean Beach Drive, unit 3704, was most definitely either not interested, downright loco, or plain homophobic.

CHAPTER 12

Jake Marks's reputation at TAMPRR was that of a hard-nosed but fair business owner, as long as his employees did their best. Everyone working for him sooner than later heard the legendary stories about Marks, the daring–some said "reckless"–pilot of F-86 Sabres, the U.S.A.F.'s first swept-wing fighter and the U.S.'s aerial mainstay in the Korean conflict that began in June of 1950 and ended three years later, in July of 1953. They had also heard all manner of stories, mostly only somewhat exaggerated, about his charismatic leadership qualities that saved the lives of a lot of American soldiers during his sixteen-month stay in a North Korean POW camp.

Although he was a 'natural' fighter pilot and most of his military buddies had expected him to make flying his career after his POW exploits became widely publicized, he made several rapid promotions up to Colonel, after which he mostly flew his desk around the inner sanctum of the Pentagon. Paradoxically, he had become just too valuable a symbol of all that was supposedly good about the United States Air Force to let him keep flying. From his Pentagon perch, Marks had gotten into his post-military line of 'business consultation' effortlessly.

During the Korean conflict, as both a fighter pilot and member of the U.S.A.F. special forces trained in intelligence and infiltration, he had organized and led a number of highly effective sabotage forays into the enemy's back yard, some of which helped cripple North Korean military capabilities. He found that he loved that kind of work from the get-go. He was without either fear or mercy. Deception, outright lies, killing, gaining strategic advantage and winning at all costs, just felt 'right' to him. Not only were deceit and corruption among his military special-ops duties, he was awarded medals and promotions for such services to his country, 'above and beyond the call', etc…

The truth was that he *preferred* lying. Telling the truth was never as satisfying as deception. He never understood and frankly didn't care why that was so; it was just his way. He made a great covert warrior.

As a boy growing up on a farm with a brutal father and sickly mother outside the town of Kanesti, in upper New York State, Jake discovered that he could fool just about all of his peers and most of the adults around, including his teachers and his old man (especially when the latter was drunk), nearly all of the time. Sometimes, of course, he was found out. But even then, with his devilish grin he had the most charming ways of getting out of trouble. He was convinced that the expression, 'bullshit baffles brains' was made up by someone who knew him personally. And even if that wasn't the case, well, it could have been.

While he got away with his shenanigans most of the time as a young boy, his ex-marine sergeant father occasionally caught him out. Then the old man took obvious pleasure in lecturing young Jake on the errors of his ways, especially if he wanted to be saved by the baby Jesus. These lectures were frequently alcohol-fueled, and the slurred speeches nearly always ended the same way, with his father saying that he had the somber (though decidedly not sober) responsibility of teaching his son to respect others and to tell the truth. So, of course, he then proceeded to carry out his God-given duty and parental privilege of beating the crap out of the kid. That happened too many times over too many years for Jake to remember a great deal about the assaults years later.

When he was twelve Jake was provided with a broken collarbone and ribs, courtesy of one particularly violent parental 'lecture'. Under threat of further beatings Jake told the family doctor that his mother insisted his father take him to see, that he had been injured when he was gang-tackled during a school pick-up football game. Dr. Benson, whose son usually played in these same games, looked closely at the damage that had been inflicted upon the boy's body and a highly skeptical expression creased his face. However, that look was submerged quickly when he glanced at the terrified eyes of his young patient who was obviously staring over Benson's shoulder towards his father.

Dr. Benson taped the lad's ribs and shoulder, and prescribed some medication to alleviate his pain in spite of Jake's father's objections that surely the boy "wasn't hurt that bad, was he, Doc?" As they left the doctor's building, his father dropped the crumpled paper bearing the prescription into the gutter. No further help was ever sought, nor did any ever arrive to save the boy from additional agony at the hands, feet, and vicious mouth of his sadistic drunken father.

Dr. Benson apparently didn't follow up with young Jake, nor evidently, did he contact any child protection agency. Not surprising, then, that in later years, Colonel Jake Marks never had much time, let alone respect, for any of the so-called *helping* professions. Or most other authority figures, generally, for that matter.

Whenever his father was having his way with him, frequently with a belt on the Jake's bare bum or back as he was held bent across his old man's knee, the sadistic sonofabitch sat, appropriately enough, on the 'throne' beside the old Thor washing machine in the bathroom. The young, increasingly defiant Jake used these occasions to pretend he was a brave soldier running through a battlefield, and that the belt's blows were really stings from the shrapnel of the bullets smashing into his imaginary hero-soldier persona. His fantasies had the desired effect of providing some mental distance from the immediacy of the excruciating present and the constant reminder of being a nearly helpless child subjected to the alcoholic whims of a sadist adult. Eventually, Jake just didn't give a shit about anything his marine father did to him.

The lectures and beatings continued until the fall that Jake turned fifteen. It seems the old man hadn't entirely realized, until it was too late, that his son had experienced a large growth spurt that summer while he had been working down at the foundry to help pay for his school supplies for the coming year. One late Friday evening in early autumn his father staggered home from the bar where he and his cronies usually spent the bulk of their paychecks. No more than five minutes after he had barged through the front door, the drunken bully reached back to take a roundhouse swing at his wife after she started to complain that he wasn't behaving like a decent father and husband. It turned out to be the last time he ever raised a hand to anyone. In fact, it was the last time he ever moved either his hands or his feet without assistance.

A still young but now much stronger lad, Jake reached out from behind just as his father hauled back to slug his mom. The momentum his father had built up during the back-swing that he was intending to let loose at his wife's right cheek, plus the additional torque created by Jake grabbing his father's still-backwards moving arm and pulling him even further backwards, caused the old man to do two wobbly 360s, right at the head of the staircase. As he tumbled and crumpled his way down the stairs from the second floor, head over tail over heels, Jake heard what turned out to be his father's back, thigh, and hip bones breaking, one after the other, until the old man finally landed in a contorted heap at the foyer just inside the front door.

After more than twenty-two months recovering in the veteran's hospital, the old man was spoon-fed by Jake's mother for the remaining eight years of his life. And it was surely amazing how much that flight down the stairs had done for the old man's disposition. He immediately stopped his drinking (of course, he couldn't move to get the bottle; couldn't have drunk from it once he had it sitting in front of him, and wasn't going to be given any, anyway), and became so scared of being left high and dry to wipe his own ass (a task that was also now impossible) that he became almost a sweetie-pie to his wife. After the 'accident' [that his mother had attested to for the police record], Jake knew it would be safe, by comparison, to leave home and join the Air Force.

He never saw his father alive again.

Whenever he was on leave, Jake would meet his mom at the coffee shop in town for a couple of hours, where they would get caught up and he could assess the toll her caregiving was taking. She died five years after the old man, five relatively peaceful and quiet years in their modest house on the wrong side of town. After his mother died, Jake buried her next to her parents in Albany, settled her affairs, and swore that he would never again go back to his hometown.

During the Korean conflict Jake made the acquaintance of literally hundreds of soldiers in the U.S, British, and Canadian forces. He recognized the many who had come to fight for right and their country's honor. Some of the others, he knew, found the whole thing to be an adventure that they undertook so that they could face themselves later, or to compete for bragging rights with the guys back home after it was all over. A few were politically motivated; they wanted to bring 'freedom and democracy' to the inferior, yellow races. He had little in common with *any* of these servicemen.

There also were, however, a small number of comrades who had the balls to acknowledge to themselves and one another that they simply loved the job of seeking out and killing others. They were the ones who were interested in the 'business' of killing, and of doing this particular job extremely well. All of these characters interested him very much and Jake Marks made a point of reading their files as part of his duties, and tried to pick those pilots to fly in his squadron. Almost as an intellectual curiosity, Jake thought about what it was that made him and these men enjoy doing their wartime jobs. "A man has to love what he does," his father, who had hated just about everything and everybody, including himself and his job at the mill, had always said. Jake believed that was about the only thing that his father had gotten right. Too bad he never found any true callings of his own except for the bottle and the beatings.

But Jake Marks had. In July of 1953 he was released from the North Korean prisoner of war camp where he had spent the last months of that campaign after his F-86 was shot down. During those cruel months he suffered the most terrible torture and attempts at brainwashing. His captors and tormentors couldn't fathom how a man could smirk and laugh even as he was screaming and squirming in agony. Paradoxically, every day and every night Jake cursed and thanked his old man, whose meaningless brutality had prepared him so well for these sadists. It is true that, on a few occasions while in captivity, Jake bent a little: *but he sure as hell didn't break!*

Once back in the U.S.A., and after many months in a V.A. hospital where some deliberately broken bones were reset and a few brutally extracted teeth were replaced by enameled bridges, Jake Marks returned to duty. Jake would actually have been proud to know that the few POWs he kept in contact with sometimes whispered to one another that, while in the camps, Jake had gotten progressively meaner and less tolerant of those of them who broke under the North Koreans' torture and brainwashing efforts. They also agreed virtually unanimously that Jake Marks was the most resilient POW of them all.

After his stay in the VA hospital, Marks was multi-medalled and quickly promoted through the ranks. Then, in January of 1958 he made Colonel. Two weeks later he contacted his old military commander, two-star General Todd Bogart, as he had been instructed to do.

General Bogart was a massive entity; 6 foot 6 inches tall, with a 48-inch chest set above the rest of his former competitive bodybuilder's frame. His personnel file, which Jake surreptitiously checked before meeting with him, had a note indicating that Bogart had been voted 'the best proportioned body in the Northeastern United States' at some competition back in his twenties. Now in his early fifties, the relatively recently taken photograph in his file suggested that the man remained a daunting presence.

When Jake was let into the General's office, Bogart got up from behind his larger than the usual military issue desk and extended his massive mitt, saying warmly, "Colonel Marks, thanks for coming. How are you?"

"Just fine, sir." Bogart was one of the few senior officers to whom Marks willingly showed any respect.

"Good, Jake, good. I wanted to tell you personally how proud I am of you and what you did over in Korea. From what I heard, you kept your guys together, and prevented even more of them from breaking down and signing those treasonous, bullshit, so-called 'confessions'." Bogart spat out the last words.

Quickly adopting a much softer tone, Bogart said, "Jake, one of the jobs that you and I have, now that the Korean crap is behind us and we are dealing with a much more serious Soviet threat, is to make damn sure that our allies get into line behind our lead, and don't do anything that might threaten either our pre-eminent military position or the industrial powerhouse that nowadays *is* these United States of America. Too many of our NATO 'friends' think that *they* should be the most influential nation in the alliance, or at least, that *we* shouldn't be. But we don't trust the French, and we will probably always rightly resent the British. And, needless to say," and even the notion contributed a chuckle to his ridicule, "we sure as hell don't ever think about the Canadians, except insofar as making sure that we get to use *their* airspace in which to attack any incoming Russian bombers, and that we bring their planes and bombs down over Canadian instead of American territory. *Right?*"

"Absolutely." Marks sincerely agreed.

Seemingly satisfied with positive tone of Marks's response, Todd went on, venturing into territory that was a tad touchy.

"Jake, there are just too many 'lefties' for our satisfaction in some of those other countries; even outright commies, or commie sympathizers. I happen to be one of those that think that Senator McCarthy had that right. Now, I know that we have our own but we know how to take care of our own. However, we can't have foreigners with their goddamn left-leaning governments having *their* fingers in *our* military 'pie'. And we must make absolutely certain that none of their military projects could ever seriously threaten American fighting supremacy in any way. And if they do, then we have to make damn sure that they aren't successful. If any of our allies' *potentially* superior offensive or defensive weaponry ever comes even close to being operational, then either we have to take them over or get rid of them, somehow, one way or another."

Bogart paused again, waiting for any verbal reaction.

Jake knew when and how to kiss ass, and for how long, as long as it was in his best interest. Thankfully, since he agreed with the General entirely to this point, indicating his concurrence was not a problem. He said, "No question about it, sir. Our forces and the companies that supply us with our military equipment have to be American, and number one!"

Bogart nodded with pleasure. "To tell you the truth, Jake, there are some pansies in the current administration, including even among our joint chiefs of staff. But most of the military men that I know and respect are agreed on this one point; we want our U.S. military forces and our American corporations to work closely together. So we have a proposition for you, Jake."

Bogard focused his radar on Colonel Marks to detect even the slightest incoming negative reaction. He saw nothing to cause him the slightest concern, so he continued. "Jake, some of us, among the top brass, well... Jake, we would like you to *retire* from the Air Force in a couple of months–with a full pension of course."

Jake, reacting as if in shock, exploded. *"What? What the hell are you talking about, sir?"* Catching himself, Jake lowered his voice a little, but the next words were squeezed through a tight, reddened throat as he choked back his fury. "Excuse me, General, but you can't be serious."

For one of the few times in his adult life, he had been taken completely by surprise. He had no idea any of this was in the works, although he now remembered that one of his friends at headquarters had said there had been some intense questions being asked about him in recent weeks, and that his personnel file had been examined on at least a couple of occasions by different departments within the military. When Marks heard that, he speculated to himself that either he was about to receive another promotion or the little Asia-to-America smuggling business he had been growing had been uncovered.

Well, if they want to take me out, they had better have something big, or at least goddamn profitable, in mind. Or else, screw the big wigs! I like it in the military and they will have to throw me out. They wouldn't dare.

For a soldier with so much rage in him, the only down side of his job in the military, as far as Marks was concerned, was when, early on in his career, after he had gotten into some bar brawls that might easily have turned deadly, he had been told by his commanding officer in no uncertain terms that "You don't go around killing your allies... at least, *almost* never."

General Bogart paused, and as if he were reading Marks's mind, he said, "Jake, hear me out first, before you close your mind to what I have to say."

Marks was still seething. *How dare they do this to me!*

"Jake, listen. You know as well as I do that there are damned few excuses for the occurrence of friendly fire fatalities. Reasons, yes. But excuses, never. Right?"

Marks nodded his agreement, but didn't know where Bogart was going with this seemingly new and seemingly unrelated topic.

Bogart said, in a dead cold voice, "That is, of course, unless you really have no choice." He continued, probably not wanting to give Marks an opportunity to begin to work up a head of steam. "Look here, Jake. We want you to work on behalf of our country's military and corporate interests, *but at arm's length*, in case, frankly, anything or anybody screws up. We can't afford to be associated with what we are going to ask you to do."

Jake Marks was still hot, but was also intrigued. "What exactly do you have in mind, sir?" The usual tactics that military intelligence people used at will were those Marks was admittedly already expert in: lying, spying, disinformation, bribes, blackmail, and collecting IOUs left over for favors done or services rendered. And, of course, if the above failed, then outright threats, or even deadly force was sometimes permissible, as the situation required. Jake had always liked the job description.

Bogart said, "We know your loyalties lay with the military, Jake, and we appreciate that–more than you know. You are a fine soldier, and have what it takes to eventually rise to the very top of the command structure. But, some of the senior staff, including myself, have talked matters over carefully for the past few weeks, and we now recognize that while we wouldn't hesitate to invade an enemy's country with our own armed forces, we simply can't protect some of our country's vital business and military interests among so-called 'friendly' nations by using the usual frontline military resources. And we have decided that we need and want a man we can trust completely, a military man, one who understands the need to look after the interests of our armed forces in any way that might work best; we want that man to be in charge of a *new* organization that is presently being set up and funded by a joint task force of the CIA and the Joint Chiefs, but under the CIA's bureaucratic umbrella. It will not be acknowledged as a part of any official government agency or department, however. And we need this new group to oversee and carry out covert incursions into, and where necessary, interference with, certain allied governments, their military or businesses, even if they are some of our nation's 'best friends'. There is no other way that we can make sure that America stays at the top of the heap among our allies. And we have decided, Jake, that you are just the man for this mission."

Bogart noted that Marks seemed to be listening with increasing interest so he decided to push ahead with laying out his proposal. "This new section will have to use more genteel tactics than we are currently using in South America, for example. That shit is going to blow up in our faces, big-time, sooner or later. And after all, the countries we are talking about really *are* our friends–sort of. We just want to make sure that their activities are, and remain, compatible with the interests of the USA, and that they don't get ahead of themselves, or us, on the world stage or in any potentially damaging area. Anyway, Jake, we want *you* to run the section. You will get to retire from the U.S.A.F. with a full pension, and will receive a ten-year long, ironclad but top secret consulting contract that will give you more than triple your current pay, to boot. You will have access to nearly all of the research and development that the CIA is carrying out, and you will also have your own substantial R&D budget to develop whatever kinds of specialized surveillance and intrusion devices you may need to carry on your work. So, Jake, what do you say?"

Marks was already evaluating the proposal. He certainly believed in the stated goals of the mission as outlined by Bogart and he had already begun to think of ways that he might possibly manipulate the proposed organization to his liking, while at the same time giving himself an initially modest personal slice of the action. His North Korean interrogators had taught him some tricks that he had seen work on some of his fellow POWs, and he had fried *their* experts' brains with some of *his* own counter-attacks. After all, strategizing, bullshit, and brutality were his forte, too.

Marks's mind began to appreciate the huge potential of the proposed change in careers and missions. He would still be making war; he just wasn't going to be killing a lot of people–directly anyway. And he foresaw what a few years of working for the military, corporations, and the CIA in his new capacity might yield, especially in terms of the extremely lucrative business known as commercial warfare.

Marks looked at General Bogart, smiled a shark's worth, and shook hands to seal the deal. Bogart responded with his own charming grin, and told him that a contract, marked TOP SECRET, would be forwarded to him within days by a CIA courier.

Within two weeks of meeting with General Bogart, Colonel Jake Marks retired on full pension. A few days later he was introduced to some of the top brass within the CIA. Jake Marks understood immediately why Bogart had said that he needed to work at arm's length from any official military or other governmental agency. If his group screwed up, or was exposed somehow, their activities must never be traced back to official government policy. Yes, Marks concluded, this new venture might be much more interesting, and a hell of a lot more profitable, than pushing little model tanks, aircraft and boats around a war games table. And his desire for killing could be satisfied in other ways–hunting came to mind immediately. He would buy himself a new shotgun and promised himself that he would go on at least three hunting trips a year. And who knows, maybe there might even be room for some human killing in the new job.

But that would have to come later, if at all. First, General Bogart explained, there was a matter of a new Canadian built, fighter-interceptor aircraft, the CF-105 Avro Arrow to be dealt with. It had to be made to disappear–permanently. In his heart of hearts, destroying any such threat to American military supremacy had to be 'Job One'.

CHAPTER 13

2009

In his first meeting with his CIA contacts back in 1958, Jake Marks was offered a couple of their agents to help him get started. He was also told to recruit a few good ex-military types, especially those with Air Force backgrounds, since at that time, it was generally believed in the halls of power that whichever country was capable of controlling the skies and space would rule everything else. He needed men who appreciated the Soviet threat and could apply that understanding to their work.

Among the best people he had found more than a half-century ago, were the three men who were expected at his TAMPRR Inc. office at 11 a.m. this morning. True, two of them were no longer in the best of health, but they all still loved the action. Only now they were more like old warriors who preferred strategizing by moving the pieces around the battlefield board. When he first brought them together all those years ago, they had all worked diligently and brilliantly to effect the shooting down of the Canadian Avro Arrow program. And they had, of course, been completely successful.

Now they were all old farts in their late seventies and early eighties. But they still loved the game, and more importantly, were still fully capable of developing timely means and methods of accomplishing TAMPRR Inc.'s goals. These days, however, as had been true for the last couple of decades, they usually restricted themselves to overseeing those who controlled the 'grunt' operatives who, in turn, actually carried out their designated hands-on missions.

The four of them were still capable of getting some of the same kind of deep satisfaction that they had felt when they had successfully brought down the Arrow. Granted that nowadays most of their targets were civilian rather than military, and their adrenalin rushes, like most of their bodily experiences, were not quite of the same intensity as in earlier times. But no matter. This sad fact of aging was at least partly compensated for by the fact that their remunerations had increased exponentially over the years, as TAMPRR became increasingly recognized among the upper echelons of government and certain segments of the corporate elite as the go-to organization for virtually guaranteed solutions to crucial problems and situations.

Patience was never one of TAMPRR's virtues. Its operatives had now worked behind the scenes for over fifteen years on the task of bringing down the Canadian government's surprisingly stubborn Medicare system. This job had proven to be far more difficult than the Arrow thing. Finally, however, they were on the verge of achieving their goal. This would be one of their greatest–and certainly their most lucrative–coup, and probably their joint swan song; Marks had told them of his intention to turn the day-to-day running of TAMPRR over to the next generation of already thoroughly groomed senior associates.

Jake's secretary rang to let him know that the three senior vice-presidents had arrived. Marks asked her to have them come in. As the door opened, Marks boomed, *"Just in time, too, goddamn it!"* As the three men entered his office he dramatically flung down the morning's *New York Era* onto his massive walnut desktop. None of his senior VPs were frightened by Marks's huffing and puffing. Truth be told, they rather relished the 'piss and vinegar' fight of the old guy; it made them all feel younger, like college football old-timers bitching about the current coach or some loudmouth running back screwing up big time during a crucial game. Loud barks had replaced their bites long ago.

Marks shouted, "Something has to be done about this asshole, this Ken Simpson guy at *The New York Era,* right now, before he stumbles onto anything that could *really* upset the entire cart." Having got off his opening salvo, Jake and his arrivals exchanged their white-haired, moderated-macho greetings while taking turns glancing over at the paper. Marks had hastily called this meeting personally and, as per his direction, all had already read the paper on the way to his office.

On the front page of *The New York Era* was an article entitled, "Enron-ing Healthcare Subscribers", the latest article in reporter

Ken Simpson's investigative series on healthcare. This piece focused upon regular citizens who were suffering all manner of moderate to major physical and mental problems for which they were having trouble getting coverage, either because their medical insurers or HMOs were stonewalling them, or because they didn't have any medical coverage at all. Simpson had cleverly placed alongside the article a sidebar showing the salaries and bonuses of the major executives of several major healthcare companies.

Simpson had drawn the analogy between what he referred to as "the ever-increasing U.S. healthcare fiasco" and what happened at now-bankrupted companies in the energy and electronic fields not too many years previously, when a few executives at the top made so much money while so many employees and shareholders were left holding decimated pension funds and worthless shares.

Jake said, "That damned columnist, Simpson, is now on another bloody crusade, drumming up support among his readers, and gentlemen, there are actually hundreds of thousands of readers of this guy. He is going to make such a loud fuss that voters are going to pressure the government to force healthcare companies to ante up with more timely medical coverage, and with less stonewalling by their clerical 'gatekeepers'." Marks pointed accusingly at the sub-headline, which dared to assert, *"Too many Americans suffer and die due to lack of health coverage: What is wrong with our values?"*

Jake Marks almost shouted again, even though the others were standing only a few feet away from him. "I have been hearing from our healthcare corporate clients all morning. If this guy, Simpson, won't stop writing these sorts of articles," said Jake, "then we may have to put that traitor's *son* out of commission, too." His visitors looked alternately at Jake, the paper and one another, with some confusion written across their faces. Marks gave them the facts.

Marks said, "This reporter is the son of Frank Simpson. Remember him, boys? The sonofabitch who ratted on us to Eisenhower?"

Now it was clear to them all why Marks was so pissed today. *Captain Frank Simpson's son. Shit!*

The senior vice-presidents of TAMPRR Inc. now nodded both their understanding and agreement about what Marks would undoubtedly say next. They had all been down this road many times over the last fifty years. Marks didn't really have to spell things out, but just to be certain there was no doubt in their minds, he did anyway. "We have to somehow get through to this guy. He is an ex-U.S.A.F. pilot, so we know that he has balls–that's for sure. But my sources tell me he got soft over some 'friendly fire' accident and checked out of flight crew. Or was turfed out. So maybe the guy has a guilty conscience or something. And now he has been awarded the damned Paulson Prize for Investigative Journalism. So we are going to have to be extra careful. But we have to stop him."

The others seemed to all be on the same wavelength, so Jake added, "I think I have a way of getting the job done, but we have to move quickly. Like, I mean *right now!*"

After an hour of intense brainstorming, Bill Montage, the acknowledged top strategist amongst them said, "Alright, Jake, if that is what has to be done, let's get on with it." Bill was designated to be the one overseeing their efforts to control, and if necessary, close down the crusading reporter.

After they left, Jake Marks reflected briefly upon the fact that he had definitely selected the right men, back in '58, to do the jobs that needed doing; there was not a bleeding heart among them and they had never let him down. Together over the years, they had mapped out and executed some of the most brilliant covert activities in American business life, including deep-sixing President Clinton's proposed Medicare program. Of course, in that instance they had the benefit of decades of media led-and-fed conditioning of a large portion of the usually reasonable and intelligent American public who had been programmed to respond to certain words with a reflex-like rejection of any ideas associated with them. The two words that worked best as killers of progressive ideas were the words 'liberal' and 'socialized'. Whenever *they* were used, whatever notions were being put forward could be relied upon to be killed off by millions of miniature 'Manchurian candidates'. The irony was that such outright conditioning was supposed to be the domain of socialist states or those led by cruel dictators, and that the USA was supposed to stand for freedom and embracing independent thinking.

TAMPRR's most oft-used strategies included involving themselves in the elections of senior politicians, including a few American presidents, as well as the presidents, premiers, and Prime Ministers of countries that were supposedly, or at least potentially, 'close allies' of America.

The unofficial mission statement of TAMPRR Inc. was, "We can get to anyone, and will do whatever needs to be done on behalf of our clients, one way or another, whenever we are given enough resources." And TAMPRR had lived up to its mission statement time and again over the past fifty years, making everyone in Marks's office multimillionaires. Now they did the work for the fun of it, and getting to Ken Simpson shouldn't be that difficult.

If only that were true!

CHAPTER 14

AFTER *THE NEW YORK ERA'S* TRIBUTE

As he entered his Fifth Avenue condominium apartment Ken checked the condition of his own low-cost security device to make sure it had not been tampered with. Every time he left his apartment he was in the habit of wetting a three inch length of thread and putting it in place across the like-colored front door and the door frame about three feet above floor level. In the past he used to harvest his own hairs, à la James Bond, but as he had become increasingly follicle-challenged, he decided that discretion was better than bravado. The thread, on this as on all previous occasions, was thankfully still in place. For the last few months, for backup purposes, Ken had been keeping copies of his most important, and all of his confidential, files at home. While official newspaper policy was still to *not* make copies of sensitive materials and to leave the originals at the office, as more and more reporters were increasingly working from home and using e-mail and faxes to communicate with the office, that policy had not been rigorously enforced in recent years.

A year earlier, one of his closest friends and mentors, Harvey Boyd, the renowned senior reporter at a competing newspaper, had had his office file cabinet broken into and the files of his investigations into organized crime in New York City, stolen. In response, Harvey, Ken and many of their other colleagues had increasingly taken the precaution of keeping a complete duplicate set of data at home. Ken believed that it was simply the prudent thing to do, and when it came to safeguarding his sources, he would make no apologies. His reputation and years on the job had given him the luxury of an extra level of security by limiting the persons who were on his must-share list at the paper. Even the people he reported to at *The New York Era*, including his editor, Rusty Elliot, no longer asked for his sources' identities until and unless they–and Ken–were ready to use their names in a forthcoming article.

Ever since Nancy had taken their son, Brad, back to Chicago, Ken had lived in a decent 'two bedroom plus den' apartment on the sixteenth floor of a forty-story Fifth Avenue condo building that had admittedly seen better days. Fortunately it also was very well kept, had some style, a modest workout room, and 24-hour concierge service. Given that this was New York City, the price had been quite reasonable because it was located in what was now a somewhat 'less desirable' address on Fifth Avenue. Since Nancy had worked as a senior corporate litigation lawyer with an income several times his *New York Era* salary, their divorce settlement meant that she owed Ken a substantial sum, which she almost embarrassingly easily and readily paid. Ken was not so proud that he didn't accept the exceedingly generous terms Nancy had offered in spite of her own divorce lawyer's almost apoplectic opposition. There was a mother's reasoning to her settlement offer, given that on those occasions (holidays, mostly) when Brad visited his father, Nancy wanted to be sure that if Ken was tied up getting a story in for the late edition (something that had happened far too often during their fiery marriage, and which had been a major contributing factor in their deteriorating relationship), at least she would be reassured that their son was in a safe, secure and comfortable environment.

The apartment was tidy and clean, thanks to Ken's and Nancy's long-time cleaning lady, Teresa, whom Ken, in effect, got 'custody' of as an informal part of the divorce settlement, and who had been there just the day before, Tuesdays being her bi-weekly 'day'. "God bless all the Teresas of the world," said Ken under his breath as he entered the apartment and noted with pride that he had not, in less than twenty-four hours, completely deconstructed her good works.

When they were married Nancy and Ken lived just a few blocks further up Fifth Avenue. Teresa was now able to get to Ken's current apartment more easily, given that it was substantially closer to her own modest almost-tenement housing, where she lived with her "alcoholic-bum husband and dope-head kids", as she not so lovingly referred to them. Teresa was scrupulously honest and had a good and pure soul that had been bruised mightily by her marriage and the guilt associated with some lustful decisions she had made while still much too young and much too 'good' a Catholic girl back in her native Portugal.

Ken's apartment was about fifteen hundred square feet in size. On the left side of the long entry hallway was a coat closet next to a small washroom. Next on the left was the entry to a compact kitchen connected to a reasonable sized dining room/living room with a quite spectacular view of the Empire State building. Off the right side of the hallway was his den, with 'the Captain's corner', and furnished with a worn but comfortable two-seater leather couch and an easy chair.

The main bathroom was located between the two bedrooms. Ken's bedroom also had a small desk and piles of banker's boxes containing innumerable files filled with the fodder of his recent and upcoming articles. The en-suite locker held shelves filled with older files containing once crucial notes. Ken thought they should be kept indefinitely just in case some ancient stories were resuscitated or, more likely, in case the paper was sued at a later date. He trusted his own apartment's en-suite locker over the paper's 'sources and materials lockup' that was largely under the control of some surly and poorly paid menial workers of questionable citizenry.

Ken walked into the den still holding the FedEx package, and sat in the Norwegian built, so-called 'de-stressing' chair and ottoman that constituted the one genuine luxury item in his entire apartment. He swiveled around to face the old desk that had been his father's and that was positioned in the middle of what Ken called the 'Captain's Corner'.

On his father's small desk were two airplane models. One model was that of an F-86 Sabre, the plane Frank Simpson had flown during the Korean War, and the one in which he had earned his ace-pilot label.

The other model was that of the still futuristic-looking, delta-winged CF-105 Avro Arrow. His father had told Ken a few details about this plane, articulating them with such fondness that Ken knew that it was, hands down, his dad's favorite. Frank Simpson had told his son that the company that built the Arrow was the same company that had built the CF-100, also a two engine, two-seat, all-weather interceptor. The CF-100, he said, was the world's first straight-wing combat aircraft to exceed Mach 1, and many hundreds were built and had seen service in Canada and several European countries. His dad shared with Ken that he had been invited to test fly the CF-100 on several occasions, had done so, and found it to be a satisfactory, if not exceptional, aircraft.

But test pilot Frank Simpson told his son that the CF-105, the so-called Arrow, was another species of airplane altogether! Ken never heard his dad talk with as much enthusiasm about any other aircraft, even the ones that he flight-tested after he left the Air Force. He recalled the day his father returned from observing, first hand, a test flight of an Arrow near Toronto, and then told his wife and son that he sure hoped the U.S.A.F. would soon order some of them. He added that the aircraft had flown as great as it looked, and that it had met or exceeded virtually all of the flight requirements established at the start of the program. He also said he was certain that the Arrow would almost certainly give America and its allies true fighter-interceptor superiority for at least another couple of decades.

A few months later, at the dinner table, an unusually moody Frank Simpson told his small family that the Avro Arrow program had been cancelled. He had said it quietly, but with evident restraint, as Ken recalled the scene. His father's voice was unusually tight and his facial features taunt when he spoke. Ken didn't know why it bothered his father *so* much, since it wasn't even an American airplane.

Wanting to appear 'grown up', while at the same time being definitely curious, Ken asked his father, "But if it is such a super airplane, dad, then why did they cancel the program after they've already built it?"

The answer Ken received to his question was delivered by a voice of such intensity that Ken momentarily became rather frightened. Looking sharply at his son, but unable to contain his disgust about the matter, Captain Frank Simpson said, "What? Why they did it? Because, son... because, ... because..." stammered his father, until he spit out the rest; "because some people have suddenly become either unbelievably stupid or damned rich–or both."

No one at the table spoke for the next couple of minutes while everyone attended to their dinner. Finally breaking the silence, a shaken Ken said, "But dad, I don't understand".

"Neither do I, son, neither do I." mumbled his father, talking more to himself than Ken. "Here we are in the shadow of a Soviet nuclear threat that is bound to come at us via their bombers flying down over Canada to the USA, and our government seems to be telling everyone, and especially the Canadians, that they–and we–won't need any interceptor aircraft to knock them down. I just don't get it. And I sure as hell don't like it because... because... *it's bullshit!*" Banging his fist down on the dining room table, Ken's father got up abruptly and left the room.

Ken had almost never heard his father swear in the home nor seen him so angry. Ken and his mom exchanged glances; Ken's look was one of shock and fear in response to his father's outburst; his mother offered a reassuring smile and gentle shrug of her shoulders. There was also clear warning in his mother's look that told Ken he should let his father be for a while. Ken nervously nodded that he had gotten the message.

Frank Simpson never again mentioned the Avro Arrow in his son's presence.

Ken once read in one of his late father's military aviation magazines that in 1962, less than three years after the Arrow program was cancelled, Canada had bought a number of what the article referred to as "a relatively altitude-limited, American-built fighter-interceptor" from the United States to semi-fulfill the role for which the Avro Arrow had been designed and would have been eminently capable of carrying out.

The desk and wall in the 'Captain's corner' were covered with a pot pourri of framed photos of Frank Simpson in either military uniform or a flight suit, and of Ken and/or his mom and/or dad, in every combination, from his parents' wedding day nearly up to the time of his father's death. Framed letters of commendation were bordered by pictures of Frank either standing in front of, climbing into, out of, or simply sitting in the cockpits of more than fifteen different test and production models of the various aircraft he had either flown in the U.S.A.F. or test-flown after he left military service. There was also a cluster of three framed photos, including one from the front page of the Toronto Examiner, dated January 7, 1959, of Captain Frank Simpson standing with some other military and civilian personnel in front of Avro Arrow number 208.

Ken's eyes moved from the items on the desk and wall back to the FedEx package now resting in his lap. Again he looked closely at the admonition written on the package in large letters beside the recipient's address: **"PLEASE OPEN IN THE PRESENCE OF CAPTAIN FRANK SIMPSON ONLY"**.

"Weird," he said aloud to himself.

Perplexed and curious, Ken began to carefully open the package. After he removed the plain brown paper it had come wrapped in, he lifted the lid off of what turned out to be a boot box. As he did so, his eyes widened and he felt the hairs on the back of his neck stand on end.

On top of whatever other contents lay underneath, was a single sheet of paper with the following words printed in red, 18-point font, capital letters; **"KEN: YOU CANNOT TRUST ANYONE IN REGARD TO THE ENCLOSED MATERIAL EXCEPT THIS SENDER, AND AS LONG AS YOU ARE WORKING ON THE HEALTHCARE SERIES I URGE YOU TO *NOT* OPEN, WITHOUT TAKING THE UPMOST PRECAUTIONS, ANY MORE DELIVERIES FROM UNKNOWN SOURCES THAT DO NOT HAVE THE CODE, "AARP-208", WRITTEN ON THE UPPER LEFT HAND CORNER OF THE PACKAGE."** Ken looked again at the discarded cover paper, and sure enough, in what had been the upper left hand corner of the package's wrapping, was written, 'AARP-208'.

Ken knew that the letters AARP usually stood for the American Association of Retired Persons, and therefore such a code would appear to be an innocuous enough notation to any unsuspecting observer. The meaning of the designation '208', if any, escaped him.

Clipped to the sheet with the warning was a faded photograph of his father standing in front of a large, delta-winged airplane together with seven other men–five military and two civilians. Some of the military types were wearing what Ken knew to be

Canadian Air Force uniforms. Ken recognized that the airplane in the enclosed photo was an Avro Arrow.

As he examined the photo more closely his gaze was suddenly drawn back to one on the wall of Captain's Corner that appeared to be identical, except for the fact that the two 'suits' did not appear in the newspaper photograph on the wall. He repeatedly gazed up at the Toronto Examiner picture hanging on the wall, and then back to the one in his hands. Getting up from his now-not-so-stressless chair, Ken's adrenalin was pumping. He approached the photo on the wall and looked alternately at both photographs several times more.

When he turned over the newly arrived photograph, Ken read a handwritten note that said: "To answer the obvious question, let me mention that the men in civvies did not wish their photographs to appear in any newspaper. They therefore prevailed upon the free-lance photographer who took the shot to make certain that he would have them cropped out of the negative he turned over to the newspaper. Before he had agreed, however, he had unfortunately suffered a broken telephoto lens–in fact, the one that he had used to take this picture before he was spotted and chased down as he tried to run away across the tarmac. The photographer was easily convinced that to make an entirely unnecessary fuss about such a small matter as their request could result in much more than a lens being broken. After he agreed to crop the photo for the newspaper and send us the original negative, we let him keep his other camera equipment —and his fingers — intact. And as you can see from the Examiner photograph on your wall, it is clear that their request was granted."

"What the hell!" Ken said out loud. "The sonofabitch has been in my apartment!"

How? When? Ken turned and looked around behind him, half-expecting to see his latest 'informant' standing there. He wasn't, however. Ken went back to reading the note.

"As a matter of interest, the two 'suits' were American 'special forces' types who explained that they, that is, *we*, had no problem with, and in fact welcomed, photos of *some* of our military personnel being printed in American and Canadian newspapers posing in front of an Avro Arrow, but a couple of us preferred that our own pictures did not appear. We didn't want to raise too much of a fuss with the photographer. After all, America and Canada were neighbors, and more importantly, allies.

"Ken, I am one of the 'suits'."

Ken shook his head, more in confusion than criticality. He did not recognize anyone else in the photo other than his father. The newspaper's version had the following caption: "Ex-U.S.A.F. Captain Frank Simpson, center, now a senior test pilot for a major airframe manufacturer in California and a consultant to the U.S.A.F., is seen standing with some members of the Canadian and U.S. evaluation teams, after a highly successful test flight of the CF-105 Avro Arrow, Canada's newest fighter-interceptor aircraft."

Which of the men in suits was the sender of these materials, Ken wondered? One looked like a high-priced lawyer or accountant; the other, significantly taller, had the bearing and chiseled facial features of a military type. Although Ken could only recognize his own father in the picture, the taller 'suit', whose hand was on his father's shoulder, seemed vaguely familiar. From where? When? His boyhood days? One of his father's friends or fellow flyboys?

Ken looked back into the box again. Underneath the photo and its attached note, were a VHS videotape, a copy of Ken's most recently published article (the first of his series on the state of healthcare in America), and a regular-sized envelope. There was no written label on the tape.

Ken picked up the copy of his article. Written across the top of the page were the following words; *"Do you really know whereof you are writing, Ken, or are you just blowing smoke?"*

Ken reread the article, noting that some of his words had been underlined.

Are Some American HMOs Making Us Sick?

Nearly five decades ago, the U.S. government convinced our Canadian neighbors that manned fighter-interceptors would be of no further use to our Western defense strategies, given the advent of missile technologies and the then existing threat of Soviet bombers flying down across the top of Canada towards their U.S. targets. In recent years _it has been suggested by some that in the 1950s certain unnamed persons in the U.S. as well as others in Canada's own government and military circles, had pressured colleagues and parliamentarians to kill off their most sophisticated and successful military technological accomplishment–and the most advanced aircraft of its type then under development anywhere in the west, the CF-105 Avro Arrow._ Not coincidentally, it has been suggested, the dumped Arrow also happened to be many years ahead of anything American aircraft designers even had on their drawing boards, and was therefore a major threat to certain American aircraft manufacturers.

It was recorded by several media sources at the time that immediately after the Avro Arrow project was shut down, American military contractors swooped down on Toronto and Avro Aircraft, where the Arrow had been designed and built, and proceeded to hire away many of the key engineers and scientists who were among the more than 10,000 workers let go by Avro the day the Arrow was cancelled.

Since the Arrow program was shut down, American air supremacy has been unquestioned virtually anywhere in the world. Some informed observers, including this writer's own father, who was a test pilot for MacBowan Aircraft on loan to the U.S.A.F. as an observer during the Avro Arrow project, believed that _certain civilian, military and political forces in our country and theirs did not want the Canadians to succeed, lest it threaten American military-industrial supremacy._

Could it be that there are currently, in 2009, a full fifty years after the Avro Arrow program was shot down, certain parties both in and outside of our government who, for their own reasons, would like nothing better than to ensure that what has been, arguably, one of Canada's other finest developments, namely the Canadian government-run, not-for-profit, taxpayer-funded, universal Medicare system (that covers all Canadian citizens, rich and poor, employed and on welfare) should meet the same fate as the Arrow?

There are some indications that indeed efforts may be underway to ensure that eventuality. Some academics and political personnel with whom this reporter has spoken, have said that a few of our least scrupulous—and most greedy— HMOs, for-profit hospitals, PPOs, and pharmaceutical companies want to 'protect' Americans from ever realizing that there is a viable, far less expensive, (we spend fifty percent more than do the Canadians, per capita), and all-inclusive alternative to their own financially crippling ways of servicing the health issues of only some Americans. These interviewees also pointed to the far too frequent refusal on the part of certain healthcare providers and insurers to authorize needed services or pay for treatment.

The same sources have told this reporter that some of these so-called healthcare providers' primary function, according to their unofficial mission statements, is to continue making huge profits by denying many necessary or desirable medical services and/or overcharging for same, in order to continue their runaway commercial success. One frequently mentioned company, MagnusEast Healthcare, is reported to have made double-digit percentage increases in its net profit every year for the past ten years. At the same time this HMO has been allowing a smaller and smaller percentage of requests for tests or treatment, and taking more and more time to process claims that it has allowed. This reporter's sources have stated that many similar organizations have managed to wrest more and more control for patient care away from the doctors and nurses who are the most knowledgeable front-line medical caregivers.

<u>Surely the question must be asked; to what lengths would some American businesses go to convince our Canadian neighbors that their healthcare system is broken and can only be fixed by adopting our own, for-profit system</u>? Incontrovertible statistics already indicate that, on average, Canadians live longer than Americans by nearly two years, that they experience 14% fewer childhood deaths per 1000 live births, and that virtually 100% of their citizens are covered by their Canadian Medicare system, while over 46,000,000 Americans, or fully over 15% of us, have no healthcare coverage whatever, even though

we spend nearly 50% more of GDP on healthcare than do our northern neighbors.

It is argued by some informed individuals in our country that the real issue is not that some greedy healthcare providers in the U.S. are out to sabotage the Canadian Medicare System merely to add Canadian subscribers to their own businesses, thereby increasing the size of their revenues by a paltry ten percent (given that Canada's population is only one-tenth the size of our own).

No. According to two of this reporter's sources, the real issue is that if enough of the American public were ever to discover the untruths, distortions, and worse that certain of our media, at the behest of some of their best HMO and PPO advertisers and/or owners, have been perpetrating and endlessly chanting about the Canadian Medicare System, then a sizable voting segment of our fellow Americans might begin to demand that we should finally adopt something similar to the Canadian system. Then these healthcare providers could conceivably stand to lose one hundred percent of their businesses.

No self-respecting, or at least, self-serving U.S. company can stand by and allow itself to be put out of business, even if its product is decidedly inferior and much more expensive than other alternatives. No, Sir. No, Mam! Such a company would rather destroy the better system, if at all possible, so that it remains the only game in town. This, then, is the classic Avro Arrow type of scenario, and there may well be forces afoot aimed at bringing down the Canadian healthcare system just as surely as the Avro Arrow program was destroyed all those years ago. And surely some American businesses have become far more voracious and vicious in their practices over the intervening years.

Some academics, including Dr. Simon Lacey of Heaford Franklin University, a physician and medical ethics specialist, have suggested that it is time to consider changing our American Bill of Rights to read that every citizen of these United States is entitled to life, liberty, <u>healthcare</u>, and the pursuit of happiness. After all, they argue, what kind of Life, Liberty or Happiness can one have if one's children and/or oneself don't have, and cannot afford, healthcare.

In upcoming articles in this series we shall compare and contrast the American, Canadian and other countries' healthcare systems. We will also examine the efforts by certain forces in American business to defeat and destroy our northern neighbor's healthcare system (considered by the United Nations to be a model for the world) while gaining increased control over the health of their -and our own- citizens, as well".

Ken Simpson, senior investigative reporter, The New York Era

In his usual writer's self-critiquing mode, an occupational habit and hazard, Ken rewrote the article in his imagination even as he read it. While it was not a 'smoking gun' piece it was definitely provocative and had already shaken someone out of the shadows. The aim of the first article had been, at the least, to provoke his readers' interest, and at best, to invite insiders, potential whistleblowers, and genuine victims of the healthcare system in the U.S. to come forward with information that would help drive the series even deeper into the belly of the U.S. healthcare system.

The advent of the Internet, and especially of e-mail, had turned out to be an investigative reporter's dream tool. Readers tended to believe that the reporter whose e-mail address they wrote to would personally read, and could instantaneously reply, to anyone who might have something worthwhile to say. Ken and his colleagues had often commented to one another that, since its advent, the convenience, ease and immediacy of e-mail had prompted countless readers who previously might not have taken the time to engage in snail mail, to actually write and send off their electronic letters to their most trusted or despised reporters.

True, some e-mails were less than kind. In fact, reporters not infrequently received vicious missives from furious readers. Therefore, the immediacy of modern communication was a double-edged sword. So far, though, it had served Ken exceedingly well.

His attention now turned to the other items in the box. He picked up the unlabelled videotape, walked over to the stack of audio/video equipment in his wall unit, and placed it in his VCR. Almost immediately a written warning appeared on the television screen. It read, "This tape is for the viewing of only one individual, Ken Simpson, of The New York Era. Ken, do not play this tape in the presence of anyone else, or our relationship will end immediately, but not without grave risk to either myself, yourself, or perhaps even the other party or parties who have viewed the tape."

Was this a threat or well-meant warning? Or both? What relationship will end? We don't have any relationship!

After the taped warning dissolved, the screen was filled with several old, black-and-white still photos, interspersed with some mostly washed-out color stills and movies, probably of similar vintage, most seemingly involving the Avro Arrow. But Ken's heart skipped beats when he watched a piece of film showing a close-up of his father smiling broadly from underneath his flight helmet. As the camera pulled back, Frank Simpson and another aviator, both in full flight suits, were climbing *out* of the cockpit of an Arrow! When his feet touched the tarmac Ken's dad began enthusiastically shaking hands and hamming it up with several other uniformed and plain-clothed personnel milling about in front of the aircraft.

Ken had never seen these pictures before. He choked up as he saw the images of his father, looking healthy and fit, and in obvious good humor, smiling, laughing and talking animatedly to the other, obviously keenly interested men, using his hands and body to show what appeared to be descriptions of some flight manoeuvres, occasionally pointing or nodding approvingly in the direction of the Arrow behind them. Watching his father's body movements Ken recalled the way, after a little league game in which Ken had played, his father would use body language to describe to his mother, who didn't attend Ken's sports activities as often as his dad, some of his son's best plays during the game.

So dad had actually flown in the Arrow and perhaps even piloted the aircraft. Ken rewound the tape a bit and then replayed the scene of the two men in flight suits climbing down the ladder from the aircraft. His father had definitely climbed out of what was likely the pilot's seat. Ken could not recall his father telling him that he had ever flown *in* an Avro Arrow, let alone that he had piloted the aircraft.

Ken paused the tape and didn't move for a minute; he just sat and thought and then felt almost overwhelming tiredness. Seeing movies of his father–happy, vibrant, and alive–was both thrilling and terribly sad. He really didn't want to see more, to know any more; not just yet. Yet he felt compelled to know it all, including why he was sent this tape and the photos, and so he pressed the 'pause' button again, and the tape began moving once more.

On the screen there now appeared a series of photographs that had evidently been extracted from old newspaper articles or newer books on the Avro Arrow. One was a photograph of plane 208 on the assembly line at Avro with its number already appearing in black on its white fuselage. Beside that photograph was another one of apparently the cockpit section of the same plane with its number 208 also clearly visible on its now torn and truncated fuselage. The words *'National Flight Museum of Canada: April 2003'* appeared below the newer photo. The number 208 was circled in red ink.

A resonant, commanding, older male's voice now emerged from the television set. It said, "Ken, look closely at the numbers on the aircraft in these pictures. What do you see?"

I don't see anything.

The voice said, "Look closely at the number "8" in each photograph."

Ken exclaimed aloud, "Hey, they are different. What the hell is going on?"

After several seconds the voice said, "Ken, the pieces of the Avro Arrow in the National Flight Museum of Canada in Ottawa are not that of #208. The number was altered before they got their hands on it so that the remains of the plane would *appear* to be that of '08'."

Why would someone have bothered to do that, Ken wondered.

Other photographs now followed, showing the broken remains of several Avro Arrows. The voice said, "These are the only published pictures of the Arrow aircraft that were destroyed after the program was shut down. If you look carefully, you will see that there are only pieces of seven aircraft. We got '208', Ken, and we flew that baby away before the demolition derby started."

Is what he is saying true? If so, where was '208' taken? And whom did he mean by 'we'?

The voice anticipated his questions. "Actually, Ken, *your father* flew '208' out of there. He flew it, under cover of night, to MacBowan Aircraft's BlackBlack division located in the infamous Area 51 of the Nevada desert."

On the television screen now appeared a grainy black and white movie sequence, probably taken by an old 16mm film camera, of an unmistakable Avro Arrow aircraft being towed into a hanger. The number on the side of the fuselage was '208'.

Ken was struck speechless. He watched wide-eyed and slack-jawed as the aircraft slowed and stopped. Then the canopy opened and the pilot emerged from the cockpit, waving and smiling that unmistakable smile; it was without a doubt, Ken's father. A large, hand-painted sign above and behind the Arrow announced, "Welcome To MacBowan's BlackBlack Foulworks. Ha-Ha."

The voice knew with whom he was dealing. Ken could hardly believe what he had just heard and seen.

My father had flown one of the Avro Arrows out of Canada. Without telling anyone. My mother. Me. ... Why?

The voice on the tape started speaking again. "I am now confident that you realize that what I have been saying is the truth. However, this information could get you killed, Ken, if you were to write about it prematurely in one of your columns, because that would be interpreted by those who arranged it, to mean that you likely knew who was behind the taking of '208', and they would do anything to stop you from revealing your suspicions. It would also mean that *I* would probably be killed as well because I am already considered to be the possibly 'weakest link' by those who were behind the taking of the Avro Arrow. How do I know that? Ken, I am one of *them*."

When the voice spoke the last words, it seemed to quiver just a little bit. *Was the person experiencing regret, or fear, when he said them?*

The voice started again. "Look, Ken, that bird is now long gone. But you have another one by the tail now; so don't get distracted. I have shown you these photos and provided you with this information so that you will realize that you have come upon more truth than you probably ever imagined when you wrote your first article on the healthcare issue.

The screen, that had been blank while the voice spoke these last words, lit up again with only too familiar images that had long ago seared themselves into Ken's brain and heart. "Ken, you are now watching the film that I took of your father's plane getting shot down, and that the North Koreans confiscated when I was caught. They later released the film to the world as their own. I had landed safely a few minutes earlier during a paratroop drop and was supposed to acquire some intelligence about certain bridges and ammo storage depots. I was captured while taking these pictures from what I had thought was a safe place. As you probably know, this film was played, first on North Korean television, and then here in the U.S. weeks later."

Not a year had gone by ever since Ken had first seen, as a boy, that terrible film footage, without him having at least one nightmare involving some fanciful version of the film he had just seen again, in all its fiery near-finality. In these repetitive dreams Ken was usually a commando, dare-devil or conjurer who kept trying to intervene in the situation before the plane was actually hit by enemy fire, or before it broke apart in that clear blue sky, or before his father's chute semi-opened, or just afterwards, somehow in time to prevent his dad being captured or beaten. Sometimes, in the dreams, he was successful in preventing a tragedy; more often than not, he just got to watch helplessly as the sequence unfolded pretty much as it had in reality. He invariably awoke from these night-time terrors shaken and sad.

Sometimes Ken thought that it was this singular filmed event that had produced two driving interests in the very fibre of his being; one, to become an air force pilot like his father, and somehow symbolically undo these awful events; the second interest was in seeking a career where he might prevent, or at least, expose the unfair treatment of the defenceless. At the least he would bear honest witness to such events, recording and reporting, if not repairing them.

The voice on the tape started speaking again while old films of American POWs were running. "Ken, your father and I were close friends who ended up being sent to the same North Korean prisoner-of-war camp. We became even closer friends during that horrible time, and, when the truce was signed, we were repatriated together. A few years later we were both invited to look at the Canadians' new fighter-interceptor. Their air force and their government wanted the blessing of the United States for their project. We gave it to them and even helped out by loaning them the use of one of our wind tunnels during the R&D phase, when they were looking for the optimum fuselage shape. We were even going to sell them our Sparrow air-to-air missiles with which to arm their planes. Later, when the Arrows were coming off the line, your father sweet-talked his way onto at least two Avro Arrow test flights. As you probably know, your father was a quick study. He got to pilot Arrow number 208 on a half-hour flight shortly before the project was shut down."

"Ken, I want you to know that your father was one of the bravest men I've ever known, and one of best friends I've ever had. I admired him greatly; he helped keep some of us sane in the POW camp with his uproarious imitations of the guards, and his all-around optimistic take on most aspects of life in spite of, and even including, our predicament. When the North Koreans tried to have us sign false confessions your father refused right to the very end of our imprisonment. At the same time he protected those soldiers who had broken under the brainwashing and torture from being beaten or worse by some of our own guys."

Up to this point the voice had sounded authoritative yet kind. Now it changed so dramatically that Ken was shaken from his semi-reverie recalling bits of visual memories and snippets of dialogue between his mom and dad. The voice on the tape suddenly seemed sombre and severe.

The next image on the screen was of Arlington National Cemetery. Slowly the camera zoomed in on some of the tombstones. Ken guessed where it was going but couldn't anticipate why.

The voice continued. "Unfortunately for many of us, including me and, of course, yourself and your mother most of all, your father made a huge miscalculation in choosing to meet and talk with President Eisenhower. He evidently believed he had first-hand evidence of what he considered to be the irresponsible actions of certain military and defence industry personnel whom Ike had been trusting to help him make the best decisions for our military and our nation.

So the rumors were true. Dad did see Ike!

"Ken, your father was brought into our plans less than a week before the Avro Arrow program was shut down. He was told to fly the plane overnight to MacBowan Aircraft's BlackBlack facility in Area 51. He was told that the flight had been cleared at the highest level to bring the Arrow Stateside. He actually thought he was bringing the plane in for specialized tests by some of our best designers in order to help the Canadians perfect their plane's surface and instrumentation design.

"Ken, your dad was shocked when he learned the program had been terminated. He told me personally that, after that flight, he became privy to information that indicated that some of our senior military commanders and some of our aircraft manufacturers were more interested in pushing their own corporate agendas than in making sure that our servicemen got the very best equipment at a fair price, no matter which company in which friendly country built the things. Your father's one failing, Ken, was that he was a too much of a trusting boy scout."

The camera continued zooming in until it showed only one cross–the one belonging to Captain Frank Simpson, U.S.A.F., retired. After many seconds the colors began to change, until the cross digitally turned crimson red and stayed that way as the voice softened and saddened.

"Actually, Ken, your father had unwittingly become part of a plan that only myself and a few others had conceived and organized, code-named TAMPRR, which stood for 'The Arrow Manipulation, Patriotic Reconnaissance and Recovery'. He was entirely in the dark as to what our real plans were. He was a test pilot and the only American who had actually flown an Arrow. Before his flight he never knew that certain power groups both in and out of our military, our aircraft industry, and the administration, were determined that the Canadians would never be allowed to bring the Avro Arrow into full production."

Ken's head was overloaded with mounting questions and intensifying fury.

The voice on the videotape continued. "The Canadians had wanted to build the best fighter-interceptor in the world, and build it to what at the time were seemingly impossible specifications. So our guys decided, 'Okay, let *them* solve the problems inherent in designing an airplane to do what their preposterous design specs demanded. No one else had yet figured out what new materials, new designs, and new equipment, would be required to actually meet those specifications, let alone actually working out how to produce them. We honestly never figured that a country with less than one-tenth our population and resources could ever get such a project off the ground, let alone make it successful. Who could know that?

"I hope you will believe me, Ken. I had never realized what some in the working group were willing to do about your father if talking to him wouldn't work, or if he was known to have spoken to the wrong people. To *any* of the wrong people–people like the press, for example, never mind the President of these United States. Perhaps I should have known. If I had, I would have tried harder to get him to change his mind, or maybe I would have even warned him of the possible consequences. But he didn't, and I didn't, and so he died."

As those terrible words sank into the soupy fog that was Ken's state of mind at this moment, his lips formed words that were barely audible. *My father was murdered. You bastards killed him.*

Images of times and experiences needlessly missed, no, *deliberately stolen* from his father and himself, tumbled across Ken's mindscreen in random order; ball games, family vacations, meals together, a grandfather knowing about his grandson, a father taking pride in his son's accomplishments and vice versa, just times spent quietly together. The quasi-peace that Ken had made with the hand he had been dealt in life was suddenly shattered. Now Ken vowed that it would only be restored when the score was settled.

Ken suddenly became aware of his shaking and his tears. A man's fury: a son's tears.

So my father's plane was sabotaged before he took off for the Air Force Academy. And it happened right here, in America, perpetrated by Americans. After all the risky combat missions and test flights he had flown! Bastards! ... Who the hell is this guy who sent me all this... this stuff... and who says that he was involved in the mission that led to my father's death?

The tape had gone blank while Ken scanned his angry-sad thoughts. Now, abruptly, on the TV was a photograph of Ken at about eleven years old, lying between his parents on a blanket at some beach.

Ken recognized the photo and remembered the scene immediately. It represented some of his fondest memories. Plattsburg Beach, near Plattsburgh, New York, a short distance from the Strategic Air Command bomber base located just a few miles from the U.S.-Canada border. His dad was lying on his side, shading his eyes from the sun with his right hand, talking to someone in uniform whose back was turned to the camera. The next picture was taken from about ten feet further back and showed two other people in the scene in uniform, standing, looking down at his father. The picture quality was poor, and Ken had only a vague recollection of the presence of these men and a notion that they had been engaged in an animated discussion. Ken recalled that he had taken the pictures with the new Brownie Hawkeye camera his parents had bought him for his just-past June birthday.

The rich voice on the tape was saying, "As I said, Ken, your dad and I were friends. I am the person in uniform standing directly in front of your father. I and the other men speaking with your dad would all become involved in what we would later simply call the 'Avro Arrow Manipulation'."

There was a pause and then the voice said, seemingly choking a little, "And one more thing, Ken. You should know that your father saved my life".

Ken was taken aback once again. He also had a vague sense that the man's voice was somewhat familiar, but couldn't place him.

Another long pause, then the television's now plainly emotional voice said, "We learned from our sources that your father had met with President Eisenhower. I didn't think they would do more than be really pissed with him, as I was, and maybe scare him a little. But instead, the head of TAMPRR had him killed."

Ken was drowning in despair now. He felt dazed under cascading feelings of hurt, sadness, and seething anger.

And then, as if an insight 'switch' had been thrown somewhere deep within his psyche, Ken became coldly unemotional and totally focused. He understood that the voice on the tape was warning him that he was in danger. He just didn't know the names of those who represented that threat, or for certain why they were now turning their guns, figuratively and perhaps literally, on *him*. He hoped the voice would tell him.

The voice had stopped, probably so that Ken could have the time to cope with the flood of information in which he was now drowning, being aware of getting dragged under again and again as he tried to swim to the surface against the data rip, so that he could finally breathe again. While the voice on the tape paused, the screen displayed a photograph of Captain Frank Simpson in full military dress, looking his most athletic, handsome, healthy self.

Then the voice continued. "They said afterwards that they could not risk having your father disclosing TAMPRR's existence, which they think he would have, had he appeared as he was scheduled to, after talking to Ike, at the Armed Services Subcommittee hearing on the equipment deficiencies affecting our country's fighting forces. Your father was going to expose our part in getting the Avro Arrow project killed, as an example of American companies putting greed and self-interest ahead of our fighting men's need for the best equipment possible.

"I was told that your father was warned by someone from TAMPRR not to appear at the hearing, or to appear but not say anything about our existence, and his unsuspecting part in the project, but he apparently refused to make such a promise. Some of us had been in the POW camps in North Korea with him, and he probably thought that our shared experience would save him from serious harm. I didn't quite believe it myself, that the others were prepared to go all the way to protect our group from discovery. I tried to warn him one more time and maybe scare him enough so that he would back off. But he just told me to go to hell!"

The voice on the tape slowed and then became more ominous. "And now, Ken, they are after you. I won't... I can't let that happen; I will do whatever I can to stop them. They won't listen to me, even though my position is still quite senior in the organization. The only way I can help is to feed you enough information that you, through your articles, can put them enough on the defensive that they will back off."

Ken felt only slightly reassured.

"You probably won't remember, Ken, but I had been in your parents' home once, and had even played with you when you were just a boy. You were a great kid, and a really good little leaguer as I recall.

"I admired and loved your dad, Ken, and I know that he adored you. That is why I am contacting you in as clear a language as I can at this point, before it's too late."

The screen darkened momentarily and then the visuals changed to a new topic, showing a succession of photos of the corporate headquarters of some American HMOs, PPOs and other insurance companies, as well as of some major U.S. pharmaceutical companies.

This slide show was followed by a series of sometimes low-light and somewhat grainy videos involving certain congressmen and senators, including a few especially prominent ones. Off-camera voices, including at times possibly the same voice as the one narrating the rest of the video, repeatedly used the phrase, "We are pleased to be able to make a substantial contribution to your next re-election campaign". Again and again the pictures showed a hand holding a bulky envelope reaching across to recipients who invariably accepted the envelope. As this play was repeated over and over again, the recipients' faces changed, their 'thank you's' morphing into a chaotic intermingling of southern drawls, New England nasals, fractured Brooklynese, and west coast pseudo-sweetness. There were representatives of every party, as well. Most could be seen and heard acknowledging and thanking the giver of the gift, whose own voice repeatedly replied, "You're welcome. I'm sure you will put it to good use," in a 'nudge-nudge, wink-wink' tone.

The miniaturized device that took the videos probably used a necktie clip-lens with a cable going under the shirt to a recorder possibly hidden in a pants pocket. The audio and video were less than perfect in quality, but certainly good enough to make the actions of those present entirely clear to a grand jury. *Chutzpah, thy name is political power.*

The video darkened again, and then became pornographic in nature. Ken watched a bedside view of a well-known senior Canadian politician, one that even some Americans would recognize, being given what looked like, at first, a regular massage, and then more energetically and obviously, a 'happy ending'. Ken knew the man as a law-and-order, 'family values' standard bearer who had spoken recently at a Senate Foreign Relations subcommittee hearing on 'Extending Democracy By Healing Families in Needy Countries Through Healthcare.'

Ken knew that there were now several extremely powerful state and federal politicians in the U.S. with close ties to private healthcare facilities and/or pharmaceutical manufacturers, and that they were helping to drive a highly aggressive foreign aid-through-building-privatized-health-care-organizations in several third world countries, where relatively poor people could get access to decent healthcare using the barter system. Essentially that meant that families could get their ill loved ones healed by either signing over their deeds to their homes or land or, at least, the mineral rights underneath their properties. Actually, the idea was not too foreign, given that, as Ken well knew from his research, over 1,000,000 individuals were losing their homes and going into bankruptcy in the U.S. every year, in order to pay for their own or their loved ones' healthcare.

And the Canadian politician shown on the tape being given relief, a former Prime Minister, was one of Canada's most vocal advocates of bringing everything American into his own country. Ken recalled reading on one of the more reputable online news sites that he was recently voted the most despised politician in his country, and that the oh-so-smooth-talking guy had never met an

American company's ass he wouldn't lick for a seat on its board of directors. The same online news source said that in his home province his nickname was something like 'le plus gros cachon', which evidently meant "the biggest pig," or words to that effect. No doubt the bestowing of that title had something to do with reports that he particularly appreciated being paid for his 'services' via plain brown paper bags filled with tens–or even, sometimes, hundreds–of thousands of dollars in cash delivered to him personally at previously-agreed-upon spots in underground parking lots. *Where does style cease and sheer chutzpah begin?*

Ken mentally reviewed what he had just heard and seen. The most devastating news by far, of course, was that the narrator–someone who had known his father and who had once had been in Ken's home when he was a child–had said that his father had been murdered by people the tape's narrator knew and still worked for. Ken wanted to meet him as soon as possible, and *… and… do what?* Ken couldn't get there yet; he needed time to process everything he had just learned.

The man to whom the taped voice belonged had also said that he tried to get Frank Simpson to back off, to no avail. *Dad, back off? I don't think so.*

Ken remembered that the storyline the public had been given of his father's plane crash never made sense to those who knew him. The official report, released more than a year following his father's death, had spoken of "catastrophic systems failure" and "probable pilot error". Family members knew that Frank had flown into the Top Gun facility at least a dozen times over the previous few years on various guest lecturer and flight demonstration contracts; they had decided among themselves that his father had likely been flying a defective aircraft, and that the 'pilot error' comment was intended to get the government, the airplane manufacturer and/or the U.S. Air force got off the hook.

So now Ken had been told that neither the original official rendition nor the relatives' versions were true. His father's death had been planned in advance and it–and he–had been executed. Frank Simpson had been murdered. Ken repeated the word "murdered" to himself several more times, as if to let its meaning and implications sink in more fully.

The investigative reporter in Ken kicked in again. He wanted to uncover the *whole* truth, including the identities of the perpetrators. He just didn't know what he would do when he had the answers to his questions.

Somehow, he wanted to meet the person who sent him the package, ASAP. This was a murder case; he had doggedly investigated many unusual murder cases, including some decades old, in his years on the city beat. On two previous occasions his efforts had directly influenced the course of cases that he had followed up on and written about. One case led to a conviction of the victim's sister and the other to the release of a wrongfully convicted husband. In both instances Ken's reporting had garnered national attention, at which point his editors kicked him upstairs into the national news department.

Ken decided that he would uncover the names and seek the convictions of the bastards that were responsible for his father's death. But if convictions were not forthcoming, then… the truth was, he wasn't sure what other actions he might take.

Ken knew that it was in large part his fresh objectivity that had won the day in the other cases. He had not been biased for or against any alleged or suspected perpetrator. He had only been interested in seeing to it that the real killers were apprehended and received their day in court.

Now, however, for the very first time in his life, he thought that if the courts wouldn't handle the job once those responsible had been found, if they were to get off on a technicality or received a sentence that was only a slap on the wrist, then he could well understand an overwhelming desire to see to it that his father's killers didn't avoid the punishment they surely deserved.

Ken recognized that he was in territory that was new to him. Personal vengeance was something that he had never sought for anything in his life. He never, until this moment, fully appreciated at a gut level what that desire felt like. Now it was stuck in his gut and he felt a rush of revulsion even as he embraced his vengeful rage and malevolent intention.

He shuddered as his memory banks replayed an occasion when, even though he was merely an embedded reporter on patrol with American troops, he himself had killed. The victim was an armed fighter in Somalia. A team of U.S. marines were chasing down a warlord who they knew hated all Americans from the get-go and who had sworn publicly to kill as many of them as possible. Ken had been traveling with the patrol when he saw someone, mostly hidden behind the side of a building, raise what looked like an AK-47. The figure aimed it at the soldiers in the Humvee just ahead of the one in which he was riding. Ken dropped the reporter's notepad in which he had been writing and grabbed the M-16 rifle that had been resting, barrel end up, on the floor between himself and the soldier to whom it belonged. He had immediately realized that by the time he had gotten the soldier's attention and the latter had seen where Ken would be pointing and understood the immediacy of the need to pick up his gun, aim and fire, it would be much too late.

Ken felt completely justified in grabbing the gun, releasing the safety and shooting the semi-hidden fighter. He had later written of his personal/professional conflict at having broken the code of being a non-combatant reporter in order to save some American soldiers' lives–and possibly his own. His article evoked virtually unanimous understanding from his readers, and not entirely muted derision from many of his colleagues. Meanwhile, he and the members of the patrol had returned to their base safely. It was easy, Ken mused, to argue ethics when your own testicles are, in effect, safely tucked inside a Kevlar athletic cup an ocean away from the bullets and the blood filling a foreign landscape.

Ken had pushed the 'pause' button on the VCR when his thoughts and reminiscences had taken over. He again pushed the 'play' button.

The voice on the tape began again: "Ken, you are currently up against most of the original team that killed the Arrow program–and your father. Only now they are in charge of a much bigger operation, and *they* are not the operatives. For such activities they now hire ex-intelligence and ex-military personnel, which is what they… what we… were, back in the Avro Arrow days. You have to understand what you are up against. They are not going to let you get your series on healthcare published, not if you get too close to the truth or if your articles garner so much attention that you threaten their corporate clients' goals."

The taped voice continued. "They intend to neutralize your impact, Ken, one way or another. Your winning the Paulson has merely put their plans on a temporary hold; any attempt on your life at this time would bring too much attention and possibly jeopardize their mission. If this were Russia, killing off a nosey reporter could be done with impunity. But not here. Not yet. At least, not usually.

"Ken, your articles on our healthcare system could potentially cost their clients billions of dollars or even put them out of business entirely, long-term. The 'Arrow Manipulation' people have been working behind the scenes for several years now on behalf of a few major HMOs and pharmaceutical companies in this country, who have so far paid out well over two *billion* dollars over the past decade and a half to help ensure that their companies would grow unhindered. The 'Arrow manipulation' group would lose five hundred million dollars themselves if their clients got taken down.

"People kill for peanuts, nowadays, Ken; you of all people surely know that. But your efforts, if you are not stopped, might just end up getting rid of a whole damn elephant! Well, they won't let you do that. They *will* stop you, Ken, just as soon as they can work out a way that is foolproof, and after the interest in your winning the Paulson has wound down. I don't want that to happen: I can't allow that to happen. That is why I have sent you all this material. I hope you will believe that what I am saying is true."

Ken experienced a raging torrent of conflicting emotions as he listened to the voice and watched more early photos of his father, mother and himself emanating from the television set. Feelings of loss, disgust, fear and fury took turns zapping his consciousness.

He recalled the case of a brave reporter who several years previously had written a series of articles about biker gangs, and then had been shot four times in the back the day after one of his most revealing articles on the criminal activities of the bikers had appeared in his newspaper. Staying the course could be deadly.

His investigations of American healthcare apparently might become so. He shuddered involuntarily. His instincts told him that the voice on the tape was telling the truth.

In the case of the reporter who had been shot, his subjects, the bikers, were allegedly in it for many millions, but the healthcare 'establishment's' profits were in the *billions every year* and growing faster than any other sector of the economy. And the voice on the tape had said that some of the healthcare companies, a rogue handful perhaps, had hired those responsible for downing the Avro Arrow... and for killing his father. Bizarre as it was to think it, continuing the healthcare series might turn out to be as dangerous as a conventional war zone where, usually, individual reporters were not singled out for killing. Then Ken recalled what happened to the Wall Street Journal reporter, Daniel Pearl. Maybe it was more accurate to say that *any* investigative reporter risks a brush with death when he or she gets too close to the truth where questionable issues related to money and/or power are involved.

After a few moments of weighing the idea, Ken knew that he couldn't drop the series he was working on and simply walk away. Especially, not now. If he dropped his investigations and the series on healthcare, then the 'Arrow Manipulation' people could disappear back into the corporate-underworld caverns they had constructed for themselves and then could continue to manipulate who-knew-what other major events and situations from behind the scenes.

Now, in fact, he had *two* subjects to investigate and write about–the healthcare situation and a newly revealed sort of 'corporate underworld'. Ken was certain that if he kept on coming after them, they would eventually show themselves, and he might be able to learn a great deal more about them and their operations. Exposing them would be a public service, and help to avenge his father's death.

The TV screen began showing the infamous North Korean propaganda film, the one that Ken had seen as a boy and that had been played over and over again on television over the decades–the film showing his father at the same table as another prisoner-of-war, both being yelled at and berated by several

North Korean officers. Both men were emaciated and Ken's father looked frighteningly older than when he had seen him just a few months earlier, before he shipped out to Korea. The other POW was speaking; he was admitting that he had committed germ warfare, and had been instructed by his superiors to deliberately bomb buildings that were clearly marked as hospitals, in order to breed such discontent that the citizenry would revolt against their north Korean leaders. Both soldiers, Ken now noted, looked exhausted and/or drugged.

The other soldier was going on and on, reading from a prepared script, admitting to all kinds of outrageous atrocities. Ken's father looked straight ahead the entire time they were being filmed. He only said a few words, stating that he had never committed any such mayhem. The response of the North Korean soldiers was to ridicule and scream invectives at U.S.A.F. Captain Frank Simpson. The hollowness and sadness in his eyes could be perceived as guilt-ridden; indeed, that was the interpretation put on his facial expression by the English-speaking Korean narrator.

When he was repatriated Ken learned that, at the time of the filming, his father had not slept in over three days, had been beaten and starved, and that at the time he was filmed he had been obsessively thinking of the distressing effects on his wife and son of seeing him in such a debilitated state.

After his release from the prisoner-of war camp Frank Simpson spoke at length with his wife, and briefly with his son, about his experiences in the POW camps. Both men in the video, he said, had their waists, one hand and both feet chained to their chairs. The man who was speaking later committed suicide, after he was charged with treason by the U.S. government, but before his military court martial could begin. Such trials eventually exonerated most of the soldiers who had 'confessed' to having committed illegal and inhumane acts against the North Korean populace, on the grounds that the enemy had used brainwashing tactics for which the U.S. military had failed to prepare them, in order to break the men psychologically to the point that they would readily confess to virtually anything their captors wished them to admit.

The voice on the tape started speaking again. "How else can you know that what I have been saying is the truth, Ken? Only your father, myself and our wives knew the signal that we would use, in case we were captured and not able to speak the truth, that would let our loved ones know that we were being forced to lie. Ask your mother about the signal. And look at your father's fingers on his left hand during the next piece of tape. Notice the crossed third and fourth fingers. Your father was signalling that what was being said was a lie. Your mother knew that. And the signal that he would be telling the truth is if he stuck his thumb between his first two fingers." Ken had known about the true/false signal code for years. But if his father really had been through so much with this man, how could the latter later betray him?

Now his father's face and voice emanated from the TV. It was another of the propaganda films released by the North Koreans. He heard his father, who was fidgeting a lot while he spoke, say that he was alright (thumb between fingers: true), and that his captors were treating everyone well (crossed fingers: false); and he was looking after himself (thumb through his fingers again). As the camera now zoomed back to show other POWs sitting at the table and saying other things, it was clear that his father, who appeared to be fidgeting with his one free hand, was changing the position of his fingers and/or thumb frequently. At first it appeared that Frank Simpson was simply nervous. Only after Ken replayed this section of the tape once more did it become obvious that his father was indeed continuously signalling which statements being made by the other POWs were true and which were falsehoods.

Ken choked up. He had known for many years of the signals for true and false. After the propaganda films were shown around the world his mother had explained to him that she knew her husband was okay from the hand signals he had given, according to the code they had established together.

Ken only half-heard what the electronic voice said next, but when he realized that it was important he quickly replayed the first several words. "Ken, be careful. Check your sources, double-check your colleagues, and above all, watch your backside. I cannot put it more plainly. If and as you continue with the healthcare series your life will be in increased jeopardy. I will be in touch with you again soon. Perhaps I can help you stop them from harming you if they think that you may be onto the 'Arrow Manipulation' group. They may not want more blood on their hands if they think that you are onto them and especially if you had secured proof that would expose them, should any harm come to you. Put this tape away someplace safe, but not in your apartment. *It* is most definitely not safe. I was able to easily enter it last month. By the way, the 'thread across the door' thing is just too amateurish; all of us have seen the same James Bond flicks. You had better find a new gimmick.

"If you want us to meet, Ken, but only if you are willing to keep me and my name out of your articles, then sign your next article 'Ken F. Simpson'". Ken smiled weakly. The man behind the voice probably knew full well that Ken had no middle name.

The screen went blank as the tape ended. Ken was stunned by all the information, by the words and the images, and the import of both. He slumped down onto the carpeted floor in front of the television, as tears began finding their way down his face. His father had been killed, murdered. By... by these people, and with the knowledge of the person who had sent him the package containing the tape he had just viewed. Ken accepted as distinctly likely that he could become their next victim.

The emotions associated with the award he had received earlier in the day had now faded into the distant past. The present held only pain and longing, and the foreseeable future was already filling with fear and fury.

CHAPTER 15

An hour had gone by since Ken had removed the tape from the VCR, an hour in which he sat, almost motionless, the tape cassette in his lap, venting silent tears and icy anger. The only sound emanating from Ken was a single word that he repeated over and over, like an anti-mantra: "Bastards. *Bastards. BASTARDS!*"

The celebrations of earlier in the day were distant, indistinct memories now. There was only this… this *thing* that was suddenly his to take in, come to terms and then deal with, by whatever means he would determine were most appropriate.

And he knew he *would* act. Decisively! Yet just now, he continued to sit, slowly coming back to this room, now aware of the uncomfortable hardwood floor. The words and images that had been hurled towards him from the television felt like metal shards that were embedding themselves in the parts of his brain that held memories, evoked emotions, and precipitated action.

"Take back control!" he told himself, just as he had said to himself umpteen times when he was just about shitting in his shorts on the front lines of the many war zones he had covered, repeating these same three words over and over while hot, flaming hell came a-calling.

Over the years he had interviewed thousands of witnesses to horror, usually without entirely losing his sanity-saving professional detachment. But then he had a job to do, being a witness to the suffering. Get the information, taste it, smell it, sort it, send it, and get the hell out of harm's way. So they, the public, would know. About hell. About life. About death. About the prices paid for tiny but magnificent moments of bravery or horrible bad luck. Or karma. Who knows, really?

Now, though, he began to interview himself. What was now nearly instinct to him started slowly to kick back in.

Who? When? How? What? Why? *Who? When? How? What?*

Why? What was the 'Arrow Manipulation team', exactly? Who were their members? How did they work? Who did they work for; for which corporate clients, and for whom in the military? Who and where are they now? Are they still a renegade organization that almost no one knows about? Obviously some people know about them; so why haven't they been exposed and stopped before now? How to get to them? What else have they been up to for the past half-century? What other areas of American life have they influenced over all this time? Which Presidents? Which States? Whom have they bought? How much money did the trick? What threats or promises were made? What did they 'accomplish'? Who else, if anyone, did they eliminate?

These were the easier questions. They were the same ones that he had asked himself time and again over the years when he was stationed in places like Panama, Argentina, Chile, Columbia, Russia, China, Africa, and the Middle East. To be asking the same sorts of questions about elements in the USA was simultaneously sad and infuriating.

Next came the nearly unspeakable questions that nevertheless had to be articulated and answered. *Who, specifically, killed my father? I want the names. Who ordered the killing? How and where do I find them and get to them? How best to pay them back? Where, how, do I start?*

Ken desperately wanted to meet the person who sent him the package. And he wanted to meet him quickly. He was sure that the FedEx package had been deposited at a drop-off site, and that the required return address would be a fake. He probably couldn't find out what account number or credit card was used to pay for the FedEx. And besides, of course, the man almost certainly paid by cash.

The business line in the den rang. He got up from the floor and walked over to answer it. It was his long-time editor, Rusty Elliot, one of the few 'old school' types still around; a crusty, supportive, lovable, tough and exacting boss who insisted that the truth be told, told well, and with no errors that could come back and tarnish either his or the paper's reputation. "Simpson!" the too familiar voice bellowed. "Congratulations again, guy! Great award. You deserve it. You've really got people hopping around

127

now. And changes are already in the wind to help you move ahead with your healthcare series in a big way."

"What are you talking about, Rusty? What changes?" Ken responded.

"Your comely part-time researcher, Ms. Martha-got-the-hots-for-you is off your part-time support team. And, you're going to get a brand new, *full-time* investigative researcher, Ken."

"*What?* Who's stupid idea was that? You know damn well that Martha does first-rate work. Just let *her* work on the series with me full-time."

"Look, Ken, it all came down after you left the office. I got a call from the new publisher, and he says that questions have been raised in certain quarters about the accuracy of some of the supposed facts stated in the article."

"What? By who, specifically? Which facts?" Ken inquired, angrily.

"I can't tell you, Ken. He didn't tell me. And that's not all. There are also some rumors about your objectivity. There have also been suggestions that you may be losing some of your edge to a sexual distraction, one that is screwing up your usual compulsive attention to the truth and to balanced reportage. One of the mistakes on the stats already has been verified; I checked on it myself and they're right."

"Which stat?" inquired Ken.

Rusty didn't answer his question. Instead, he said, "I'll go over it with you tomorrow in my office. Anyway, Martha is off the series. And I am surprised at you, Ken. I only just found out that you two have been doing more than flirting over the past several I don't-know-how-many months. Keep your peter in your pants on the job, will you? If they can smear your reputation, or mine, or this newspaper's, they will."

"Who's 'they'?" asked Ken, insistently. .

"Ken, whoever 'they' are, is irrelevant for the moment. 'They' could be any individual or group or company that can find an error in what you write. All that really matters is that the job gets done well, with no foul-ups. Either Martha, or you, or the both of you, screwed up a little. That's it. But it can't happen again, Ken. Paulson prize or not, you are taking on the biggest guys now, and they don't take kindly to anything that comes between them and their money. A few of their corporate friends have apparently already threatened to pull their advertising from the paper if it happens again. The words I got were, "We are all for freedom of the press as long as the press is accurate, fair and balanced, in it's reporting."

Ken recoiled from the phone as he listened. Rusty sounded anxious, and he was not the sort to scare easily. In fact, Ken never had received anything but complete support from him up to this point. Who's toes had Ken stepped on in his last piece, he wondered?

Ken was pissed off. "This is horseshit, Rusty. You know Martha and I double-check our sources and their information."

Now Rusty got a little testy and came down hard. "Look, Ken, I called the public relations department of MagnusEast Healthcare myself. They say that the numbers they gave you about their revenues over the past few years are not the numbers you used. The message I've gotten from upstairs is that they don't care if you did win the Paulson, your judgment may be clouded because you were mixing business with pleasure by screwing your research assistant. You messed up, Ken. And don't you understand that as far as 'upstairs' is concerned it's the same old, 'Never mind yesterday and whatever award you just received. Just tell me, what have you done for us today?'"

Neither of them said a word for several seconds and then Rusty, perhaps embarrassed by his role in crapping on his top reporter's finest day, abruptly ended the conversation saying, "Hey, don't worry. Everything will work out. I promise. Just be in my office tomorrow morning at 9:30. We will go over the stats and everything. I'm sorry to have to call you at home on this, especially at the end of what, I'm sure, has been a really great day for you. And I meant it when I said that you do deserve the Paulson. Look, get a good night's sleep, will you? And congratulations, again." Rusty hung up before Ken could respond.

An angry and confused Martha arrived at Ken's apartment a half-hour later. She told Ken that she was called into Rusty's office about twenty minutes after he had left the building. Their editor then informed her that she was being reassigned to cover for an almost full-term pregnant colleague for the next several months "at the *Ottawa* desk, for Christ's sake!", or what *The New York Era's* reporters not so jokingly referred to as 'Stalag DeepFreeze'.

After brainstorming about who might have been behind the complaints regarding the supposed inaccuracies in their reporting (they each had some good guesses, but no conclusive ideas), and after each became clear that the other had not played a deliberate role in creating whatever was going on, they went over their respective notes from the MagnusEast Healthcare part of their investigation, including those Martha had grabbed from her desk as she left the office in a fury. Ken concurred with the numbers and other information that she had. So it wasn't faulty data that was the problem. After another hour of intense discussion, there were more tears (Martha's) and expressions of regrets (both), about not being able to continue working together, or even be in the same country for the next whatever number of months. Then they both just stopped talking, exhausted.

Martha sighed and said she was all talked out. From the manner in which Rusty had spoken with her, as much as what he had said, she was certain the matter was a done deal. She said she was going back into the newsroom over the next two days to clear out her desk, and then she intended to go home and pack her skis (a joke–she hated snow and cold). She would begin her drive north to Ottawa in the next day or so.

Martha led Ken to his own bedroom where they came at one another with a vengeance. Quickly undressing one another, they fell into bed and made love like there was no tomorrow. Maybe both knew something they didn't know that they knew.

CHAPTER 16

THE NEXT DAY

The next morning Ken and Martha left his apartment separately, as usual, and arrived a few minutes apart, undoubtedly not fooling anyone important any longer. Both were tired from several rounds of last-night-on-earth lovemaking, and each apprehensive about their new respective work situations. The weather in the newsroom had turned decidedly chilly overnight, and yesterday's eager handshakes and 'hail fellow, well met' backslaps had been replaced by sideways glances and mumbled, nervous 'good mornings'.

Ah, fame is not only fleeting, but fickle as hell, reflected Ken, as he walked past obviously remarkably too-busy-to-really-look-up colleagues. *Well,* Ken thought, *the tom-toms have certainly been working overtime. Yesterday I had the Midas touch; today I've got leprosy.*

As he walked toward his desk Ken glanced at the large glass wall into his editor's office and saw three people talking with Rusty in what appeared to be a highly animated but amicable conversation, what with smiling heads bobbing up and down and shaking about like dashboard bobblehead dolls. One of those conversing had her back to the window; Ken found himself appreciating the closely fitting business suit of a shapely female.

Horny bastards. Be ashamed of yourselves! Ken silently chastised his overly worked-up hormones.

Rusty, who was standing in front of his desk, saw Ken and directed an overly expansive smile towards him, along with an exaggerated 'come on in' circular arm and hand gesture. Ken got the giant hint and after putting his L. L. Bean knapsack down on his desktop, walked toward his editor's office.

Upon entering, Ken saw that the others present included the managing editor and the relatively new publisher of *The New York Era*. Compared with yesterday's gushingly congratulatory greetings of the paper's newest Paulson Prize winner, today Ken was met by a muted warmth by the three people he knew. At least Mr. Gallen, the managing editor, extended his hand, and with a semi-warm, half-smile, said stiffly, "Good morning, Ken. And congratulations again; we are all really proud of you."

Ken said, "Thank you," and turned towards the shapely thirty-something.

Rusty did the introductions. The young woman smiled widely and purred, "Hello, Ken. I am so happy to meet you," as she extended her hand to him. "And congratulations on your award. What a wonderful honor."

As he shook her sensual yet strong hand, Ken found himself gazing into the eyes of one of the most gorgeous women he had ever seen, never mind met. She offered him a direct, open, but hardly innocent look, her beautiful face framed by a shimmering wavy black mane that happily cascaded over her shoulders, seemingly effortlessly wafting one way or the other whenever she moved her head. For just an instant Ken felt like he had become part of a television hair color commercial.

Rusty's introduction replayed in Ken's mind. "Ken, I would like you to meet Sylkeen Bowry. Ms. Bowry was the top graduate of the Barkley School of Journalism three years ago and has just joined us from the Chicago Sentry." Then, in a semi-veiled tone that made it clear to Ken that he was not merely making a request but rather, was most certainly issuing an order, Rusty said, "Sylkeen is your new research assistant... an excellent choice, I am sure you will find."

Ken stared at the young woman; if she had not been so attractive and amiable, Ken later reflected, he might have been more inclined to tell Rusty what to do with himself right then and there, and then stormed out of the bastard's office. Instead, he just issued an inane smile in her direction, and said to Rusty, "Er..., right. Okay. Wel... welcome aboard, Sylkeen."

Rusty kept talking, recognizing that Ken was momentarily off guard, but also knowing that he would probably soon recover. He had a narrow window and so he launched into his selling spiel. "Over the past several months Sylkeen has been working on an upcoming series in the healthcare area for the Chicago Sentry. She has already been successful in gaining access to certain senior personnel in both government and in the healthcare industry that no one else, including yourself and Miss Harrison, have been able to get to agree to an interview. Since her undergraduate degree is in mathematics, specializing in economic statistical analysis, any number crunching you acquire can be vetted through her. That way we won't have any more doubts cast on the figures we may publish in the future."

Ken flushed with fury but deliberately didn't bother to look at, or respond to, Rusty. Instead, he looked at the vibrant young woman with increasing interest. *Well, all right.* Maybe Rusty did know what he was doing, since neither Ken nor Martha had more than a rudimentary understanding of the healthcare data they were looking at when it was first received from their various sources. And there *were* problems getting to talk to the evasive senior executives of the HMOs, PPOs and insurance companies he was interested in knowing more about. Obviously, Sylkeen (*What kind of name is that, anyway, even though it somehow suits her?*) with her undeniable charms, might well find it easier get some of those alpha male CEO-types to find the time, sit down and open up. Ken could come along to future interviews and ask some of the more probing questions.

Ken realized that he was feeling mildly sexually aroused. *Good sex is like a good novel; it satisfies, but leaves a strongly felt desire for more authored by the same hand, so to speak.* In an attempt to cool his late middle-aged jets–not usually that difficult to accomplish–he redirected his attention to the very tasteful, probably very expensive jewellery his new assistant was wearing around her neck and wrist.

From his investigations a few years back into some high end jewellery stores' use of what amounted to 'price fixing' and their occasional inclination to sell good quality knockoffs of famous watch makers' and other jewellery companies' products, Ken recognized the young lady's watch: a limited edition, museum quality, diamond encircled gold watch, weighing in at about $20,000 US. Also, the string of pearls gracing her elegantly long neck was almost certainly not a costume jewellery knockoff of Jacqueline Kennedy's but was the genuine article and worth a small mint in its own right.

The lady came loaded in more ways than one.

Looking at her (*her* eyes had not left *him* since they were introduced) Ken was beginning to feel as if he was in the gunsight of a master 'marksperson'. He silently laughed at himself as he, recognizing an at least twenty... *alright, thirty-five*-year-age-difference between them, found himself wanting to impress her by even *thinking* in a politically correct fashion. *Horny fart!* He had to admit that he was simultaneously feeling both his age and his oats, something he hadn't recalled experiencing quite that way before. *Is this what being a seriously middle-aged man is about?* And was silky Sylkeen really such a great package or was he still feeling sexy because of the intense lovemaking with Martha that ended less than two hours earlier?

Ken was rescued from his musty musing by Rusty, who was now suggesting that Ken bring Sylkeen up to speed on the angles he was working on for the healthcare series. Ken replied, just a bit hesitantly, suddenly wanting to get away from them both, "Oh, for sure! Hey, look, Sylkeen, let's meet later this afternoon and we can go over the files together then. All right?"

Smiling to himself, and undoubtedly looking ridiculous to the others present, Ken now recalled his series on sexual offenders, when he interviewed some major researchers working in the area of male sexual response. Ken remembered learning that, when connected to the sexual researchers' testing equipment that measured what they liked to refer to as the 'PVC', which stood (so to speak) for 'penile volume change', *even so-called normal men exhibit some engorging of the penis in response to almost anything, including pictures of landscapes! Granted that many men claim to like the great outdoors, but gimme a break!*

Thereafter he had occasionally wondered, whenever he felt himself attracted to anything, including a new model car, some piece of electronic equipment, or whatever, whether he was having a PVC. *We men are weird,* he told himself, not so reassuringly. In this instance, however, Ken was reasonably confident that any physiological change that he might be undergoing in the presence of this '10-plus' was at least happening for a heterosexually-related reason.

Turning her head just a little to the side while continuing to look at him with laughing eyes (and, could it be, a self-congratulatory smile), Ken had the distinct impression that the gorgeous Ms. Bowry was reading his mind.

She probably is, damn her. Ah, the blissful power of a beautiful woman who accepts and is comfortable with her attractiveness.

Sylkeen, in a strongly determined voice, said, "That's extremely kind of you, Ken. I would like to get started right away. I just have to see the people in personnel next, and get myself straightened away at my desk. So shall I see you in a few hours, then, say around 4:00pm?"

Ken said, "Sure."

With that exchange, she turned her body in a way that took momentary remote control of Ken's eyeballs and forced them to closely follow her egress from Rusty's office.

Once she disappeared from view Ken regained command of his physical self, and before Rusty could say another word, he said "Later!" and hurried out the office, nodding to the paper's publisher as he went.

Ken walked quickly to his desk, picked up a fresh writing pad, and then moved briskly towards the elevator, as if to avoid any other encounters from impeding his progress any longer.

Ken left *The New York Era* building, hailed a cab, and headed to his appointment with the former U.S. Surgeon General, Dr. Leo Larson. He was still shaking his head over the realization that he had just become more turned on than at any time in years. All it had required was a woman about half his age, with movie star looks, a big brain, and big... Ah, well, maybe the first three were the main requirements. He admitted to himself that he appreciated the fact that this young woman evidently had the smarts to complement her physical beauty. The latter got her through the doors she wanted; the former would get her into the psyches of her subjects.

Or, maybe it was the other way around. Shit! Here he was, a 63-year old man, divorced, a father, and a hard-nosed newspaper reporter to boot, and at this moment all he really knew was that he had gotten a semi-boner in his boss's office, while encountering a magnificent woman who was young enough to be his daughter, had he had one.

In his time Ken had been with his share of terrific women with great bodies and big brains. But that had been when he was twenty years younger and at least ten pounds lighter. He had aged well enough, mostly, and still had enough of his hair, sort of. But he wasn't given to fooling himself about his decreasing attractiveness to younger women.

As he got his head around to the upcoming interview with a once-powerful member of the former president's administration, his cab headed towards a predominantly black middle-class suburb of New York City. He wanted to learn whatever Dr. Larson might be privy to that could help him with the healthcare series.

Reflecting upon the information communicated through the contents of the FedExed package he had gone through only the day before, his intuition told him that he might not have the luxury of much time to uncover and deal with the subject of healthcare issues in the USA and elsewhere.

As usual, his hunch was correct.

CHAPTER 17

As he settled into his seat in the back of the cab, Ken turned his attention to his next interviewee, Dr. Leo Larson. It was two days earlier that he had arranged an appointment with the retired African-American, former Surgeon General. Dr. Larson was a widely known figure and highly controversial for having publicly taken on many of the largest and worst environmental polluters in America, including industrial powerhouses and waste disposal companies. He had also clashed mightily with some especially greedy so-called managed healthcare companies who had systematically stonewalled many of their subscribers-in-need seeking compensation or permission to have medical procedures performed.

The previous year another newspaper's chief business writer had written that Dr. Larson had repeatedly resisted lending his good name to a variety of healthcare business suitors, young and middle-aged men with brash ideas about making a financial killing in the growing healthcare market. A devoted family man with three grown children and a large number of grandchildren, he had apparently listened to these entrepreneurs, especially the younger ones, in large part because of their clear eagerness to make something of themselves. A couple of them had been his grandchildren's ages.

In fact, one of the companies that pursued him had a young black woman about the same age as one of his granddaughters, with the impressive title of Senior Vice-President. Some time after he had politely considered her and her associates' proposal and then declined their offer, he learned that she had been immediately demoted from her V-P position down to a glorified 'administrative assistant' role. That particularly sour piece of work reminded Larson why he had refused to join some of the biggest companies in the healthcare field who wanted a public relations coup by getting a former U.S. Surgeon General on board; he recognized that they could immediately turn his token presence into an otherwise unwarranted profit by signing up a greater number of black-owned businesses for whom Dr. Leo Larson's name was a seal of approval.

Ken recalled that one article from a major paper in the 'new' but still deep south also mentioned that Dr. Larson had recently been referred to as "that old boy who still didn't know his place," in a leaked memo from one of the healthcare companies whose overtures Larson had rejected shortly after retiring from the S-G position.

During the forty-minute drive from the canyons of Manhattan, Ken felt himself begin to unwind. He was admiring the four and five bedroom homes they was driving past, set back as they were about fifty feet from the quasi-country, suburban streets that had deliberately been kept sidewalk-less. Ken's cab presently pulled into the short, tree-lined driveway of one of the smaller, well-kept homes on a less graceful side street.

The cabbie turned off his engine, picked up a newspaper from the front passenger seat, and settled in to wait as Ken had requested.

Ken got out of the cab, walked past the neatly trimmed hedge and climbed the four steps to the front door. He rang the bell; a moment later the front door opened, and he introduced himself to a large, warmly smiling black woman in her mid-fifties who was wearing a crisply pressed nurse's uniform. She directly led Ken into a large den and said that she was sure Dr. Larson would join him shortly. Ken deduced that she was probably a day-nurse who was helping to look after the elderly former S-G now that his own health was reportedly failing badly.

Ken studied the framed photos and letters of commendation on the wall; they reminded him of the 'Captain's corner' in his own home. There were pictures of Dr. Larson shaking hands with four different American presidents as well as a number of Secretaries-General of the United Nations. Larson's name appeared on the numerous plaques bearing words of appreciation from various medical societies, hospitals, as well as some state, federal, and even some foreign, health-related agencies.

A couple of the photographs revealed Larson's imposing

physique from his college football-playing days. Ken smiled as he clearly saw in the photos a physical presence well matched to an unforgettably resonant, deep voice that used to thunder at those in the healthcare arena whom Larson believed cared much more about their shareholders' profits than their subscribers' well-being.

Ken sensed, rather than heard from behind him, the entrance of his host into the room. Dressed in a bathrobe and slippers, and looking fitter than Ken had expected from the various news bulletins that had been issued over the past few months regarding the old man's state of health, Dr. Larson slowly shuffle-walked towards Ken and greeted him with a warm smile and a still firm handshake.

"Good afternoon, Mr. Simpson," said the gentle, deep voice emanating from the still six-foot, four-inch, but somewhat emaciated presence. Ken observed his hand disappearing into the XXX-sized mitt that received it mercifully. He must have stared at Dr. Larson's hand longer than would be considered good manners, because the latter released a surprisingly hearty laugh, and said, "Young man, you now know why I became a general practitioner in the military, rather than a surgeon. I just couldn't get my fingers to move delicately enough among those tiny little blood vessels and hard-to-reach organs. On the other hand," he said, now roaring and obviously enjoying himself, "when I told our inductees at their initial physical to cough, they damn well all coughed the very first time I asked."

Ken shared in the joke, and gave silent thanks that he had not met this former giant during their shared times in the military. At least, not for that part of the induction process.

"What can I do for you, Mr. Simpson?" asked Dr. Larson in a more serious tone. He motioned to Ken to take a seat on the sofa, while he took up residence in what was probably his favorite, massage-capable, easy chair, one that Ken believed he had seen pictures of, and that had been especially built for–and presented to–Dr. Larson as a gift by a grateful departmental staff, when he retired as Surgeon-General.

Ken said, "As I told your secretary on the phone, I am writing a series on the problems with healthcare in this country, and I would very much like to know your views on this subject. I am especially interested to hear what you think about the possible influence of American healthcare businesses and the pharmaceutical industry on our government's policies in general and, in particular, towards the more than forty-six million Americans who don't have any significant healthcare or prescription coverage at all."

Larson looked at Ken without saying anything, and slowly nodding to himself. Finally he said, "Mr. Simpson, truth be told, I am a sick and dying old man. The only reason I agreed to this interview is that I have been a faithful reader of your columns the last number of years, and I was genuinely moved by your articles on the Gulf War veterans' medical problems, as well as the September 11th victims' difficulties in getting proper medical care. You, sir, have done a good deal to help motivate our citizens and their legislators to do the right thing and look after these heroes and their families."

"Thank you, Dr. Larson." replied Ken, genuinely embarrassed.

"In fact, Mr. Simpson, I may have had some small hand," here Larson chuckled at his choice of words, "in encouraging some of your recent sources for those articles to come forward."

Ken was surprised and wondered, *which* sources?

Before Ken could ask, Dr. Larson added, "I want you to know how much I appreciate what you accomplished through your writings in the healthcare field. Your columns, and the public response they triggered, thankfully forced our politicians, at long last, to take serious legislative action to help look after our wounded soldiers and civilians who have been harmed merely because they are Americans. That is far more than I was able to do during my entire tenure as Surgeon General."

Ken replied, "I would like you to know, sir, that your own publicized efforts to put these matters on the table were, in large part, what led me to do that series of articles in the first place. So, I thank *you*, as well."

Dr. Larson paused momentarily, and Ken noted Larson's moistening eyes and slightly quivering chin. Ken surmised that Larson's labors during his many years of battling to help protect and heal his national flock had cost him a great deal more than he usually let on.

Larson gathered himself again and said, "When I read your first article on the new series the other day, the one in which you said that you intended to explore, in depth, the *real* problems in providing the best healthcare for our citizens, no matter where your series took you, I decided then and there that if you didn't call me pretty damn soon, then I would get in touch with you. There are things I want to say, and want you and your readers to know and think about, and I probably don't have the luxury of taking my good time about getting around to saying that stuff."

Ken got out his pad and tape recorder, placed them on the coffee table between them, and leaned slightly forward in his chair. He frequently had to finesse interviewees until they were ready to talk about whatever they knew on a particular topic. With such an obviously primed subject Ken could begin by asking direct questions. He said, "That is generous of you, Dr. Larson. What would you like my readers to know?"

Dr. Larson seemed to hesitate again and Ken suddenly realized that the old man was having trouble breathing. The older man had flinched, as if reacting to some suddenly heightened bodily distress. Ken recalled a rumor that Larson was now dealing with some form of terminal cancer. A premonition told Ken that the end of his suffering was not far off.

After another moment Dr. Larson said, "Mr. Simpson, you were probably too young or were much more interested in baseball at the time, to recall much about President Eisenhower or his farewell address."

Ken's eyes snapped up from his writing pad and stared at his subject. The images of his father rocking, nodding, and choking up, intruded themselves once more into his consciousness. He swallowed hard and said, "Actually, sir, I *do* remember. Very well, in fact. I was just a teenager at the time, but I recall that my entire family watched it on television that night. What about his speech, Dr. Larson?"

"Mr. Simpson, Ike's farewell address was delivered on January 17, 1961. The president said some things that night that most people at the time either didn't pay much attention to, or have long since forgotten. I have replayed his speech over and over again these past many years. I believe that he tried his best then to warn our fellow Americans about what he saw coming down the 'pike, but most of them probably didn't get it. Let me show you what has been disturbing me so much these past few years."

With that, Dr. Larson stood up with some difficulty and slowly walked over to the built-in bookcase against the far wall. He said, "I have all of Ike's major speeches.," He took a DVD out of its plastic case, put it into a player and, after a few moments of exploration of the remote with his glasses shoved up over his bald dome and the device close to his face so that he could read the now too small and indistinct lettering, he finally found and pushed a button he liked, and said, with some satisfaction, "There."

The screen on his television went bright blue, and then the insignia of the President of the United States appeared, and then President Dwight D. Eisenhower. The only time Ken had heard the speech before was when he had been a teenager, but at the time his attention had been almost totally focused upon his ex-U.S.A.F. father's unmilitary-like response to his , former commander-in-chief's words. Ken had not really paid much attention to what the president actually said.

Now, as he watched and heard the speech being replayed on Dr. Larson's television, the investigative reporter in Ken really listened to the messages being conveyed. Without question the brief farewell address was moving, but what pulled Ken to the edge of his seat were the foreboding sentences Ike delivered towards the end of his speech: *"The conjunction of an immense military establishment and a large arms industry is new in the American experience. Its total influence–economic, political, even spiritual–is felt in every city, every state house, every office of the Federal government. We recognize the imperative need for this development. Yet we must not fail to comprehend its grave implications..."*

Dr. Larson paused the machine, turned to Ken and said, emphatically, "Now listen to what he says next. He pushed the pause button again. Ike said, *"In the councils of government, we must guard against the acquisition of unwarranted influence, whether sought or unsought, by the military-industrial complex. The potential for the disastrous rise of misplaced power exists and will persist. We must never let the weight of this combination endanger our liberties or democratic processes. ... Public policy could itself become the captive of a scientific-technological elite."*

Neither Ken nor Dr. Larson spoke for several moments after the tape ended. Then, Ken said, as much to himself as to the doctor: "So he knew, didn't he?"

The doctor nodded, smiling a little that Ken had evidently heard what he had hoped he would.

Ken said, "He saw it all. Imagine how those influences must have already been impinging upon his government, and perhaps himself."

Dr. Larson again nodded his head in agreement.

Ken said, "I recall reading that you served under him, Dr. Larson, as an army physician on the front lines and then, later, for the General himself. What do you think? Was he given at all to exaggeration or fear-mongering?"

The old man drew himself up so that he sat forward and tall in his special chair. For just a moment he appeared to project a fighting stance, even though he was still sitting. "Mr. Simpson, that man always called things the way he saw them. And he cared more about the fighting man on the front lines than any senior officer, let alone President, that I have ever known. He wanted his men to have the very best equipment, and have it as soon as humanly possible! But some of his advisors and senior staff had other ideas. I knew some of them: slimy, power-hungry, short-sighted types they were. Some of us called them 'P-I-Ws, or 'Promotions-in-Waiting'. These were men who were infinitely more interested in their next promotion than they were in either their men or even their country. They couldn't wait to destroy whoever or whatever got in the way of their next stripe or star. And there were credible rumors of some of them double-dipping, in other words–considering the expensive cars and homes they owned–it appeared that some were already on the payroll of the corporations that they could only join officially *after* they retired from the military."

Ken nodded, hearing his father's words echoing through this legend.

Larson added, "And now you can add the words 'healthcare'

and 'pharmaceutical' and 'media' to the words 'military-industrial'. Their influence on our government, and especially on our elected officials, right up to and including the White House, is immense, Mr. Simpson, and affects everything to do with the delivery of healthcare services and prescription drugs in this country."

Ken asked, "Would you care to elaborate, Dr. Larson?"

"Gladly. By keeping healthcare services spending in check, which means short-changing their subscribers, some of the HMOs are making unconscionable profits while these same subscribers are facing ever-increasing premiums, and higher co-pays. It is also obvious to many Americans that their healthcare providers, if they can afford to have one, too often stonewall them whenever they or their physicians apply for coverage of service. As for the pharmaceutical companies; by keeping the costs of prescription drugs much higher here than it is in Canada and most other countries, too many Americans, including our seniors and children, are going without needed medication, or on welfare or even into bankruptcy paying for them. The entire healthcare-related area is simply another money-making business to the management of those companies."

Dr. Larson was becoming increasingly agitated as he spoke. He had to pause to catch his breath before he could continue.

Ken was concerned about the state of health of his interviewee, and whether the discussion was taking too much of a toll. *Why was it that so many of the good ones, like Larson, suffer for what they couldn't accomplish despite their best efforts, while the ones who couldn't care less, sleep like babies while doing their worst? Tobacco executives come to mind.*

Dr. Larson continued. "I also know, Mr. Simpson, as do you, I am sure, that for many years now, Americans have been paying far more than most countries, per capita, for healthcare, according to GNP figures. Just look it up in your own newspaper's yearly almanac. And the health of our citizens is certainly no better in many ways than that of those who live in most modern countries. In fact, longevity data tells us that we are actually worse off than many, and that our for-profit-uber-alles system is damaging to our citizens' health. For example, the latest statistics show that life expectancies for both men and women is actually *less* in the U.S than in Canada, the UK, Germany or even Israel!

"Also, consider the fact that in Canada, their male population now expects to live over 76 years, on average. Here in the United States it is less than 73 years. That's three years more life for the average man, just across our border. And our females' lives, on average, are about two years shorter than theirs, as well. And their infant mortality is lower. Meanwhile, as a percent of GNP, we spend 45% more than our Canadian neighbors on our health expenditures. If these numbers don't tell us that there is something wrong with the way we deal with healthcare in these United States of America, then I don't know what will!"

Dr. Larson took another moment to get his wind back. "Now, sir, what is the story behind these statistics? Is it that we don't have enough doctors? In fact, we have more doctors than the Canadians, on a per capita basis. We just don't make their expertise available to enough of our people, enough of the time, and at sufficiently reasonable cost. Our people are terrified of getting sick, afraid that they will have to go into bankruptcy to save their own or a loved one's life. Do you know that over a million people went into bankruptcy last year alone, just because they could not afford to purchase the required healthcare for their loved ones? And that once they were bankrupt they weren't able to afford to purchase the needed healthcare for much longer?"

As Ken watched and listened, Dr. Larson's face looked increasingly distressed, his powerful voice quivered, and then his entire body began to shake with fury. Ken considered asking a question just to interrupt his interviewee's obviously highly distressed state. But the man seemed determined to complete his comments, so Ken simply nodded his head and wrote as fast as he could.

Larson continued, his tone just a touch less distraught. "And, meanwhile, Mr. Simpson, some of the companies in the healthcare field are little more than Enrons. They don't necessarily produce anything themselves; they just contractually tie up both the producers, that is, the doctors and the hospitals, and the purchasers of their products, that is, their consumers, our

145

fellow Americans. Basically they sell practitioners' services to their own patients. But they tightly control what the physicians can and cannot do, so that major medical decisions are too often made by clerks, for heaven's sake, some of whom receive cash bonuses, or at the least, secure their own jobs, by routinely refusing doctors' requests to carry out tests and procedures. And they refuse these requests, not necessarily for medical reasons, but because they would cost money to do and would therefore reduce the profits of the so-called healthcare companies.

Larson's weathered face and voice now seemed to express both anger and sadness simultaneously. He said, "And people with health insurance are hesitant or downright terrified to change–or worse, *lose*–their jobs for fear that they might also lose whatever medical coverage they still have. That's plain wrong, sir. And furthermore, in my opinion, it is immoral and unethical in a supposedly modern society where freedom is to be cherished."

The doctor stopped again, just long enough to catch his breath. "Now, if you would like to, Mr. Simpson, there are some colleagues and friends of mine, here and in Canada, who I believe you would find most interesting persons to interview, and who could give you their own first-hand experiences in dealing with the healthcare systems in our respective countries. That would, I believe, and I hope you don't mind me saying, add even greater depth and perspective to your current series."

Ken replied, "On the contrary, Dr. Larson, I would be appreciative of any and all leads that you might share with me, especially those that could give me additional insights into the impact of our respective healthcare structures–both *our* for-profit, and *Canada's* government-funded model–on the doctor-patient, delivery-of-service level."

Dr. Larson nodded, then sighed, and said, "I am sure that even Ike would not have guessed that, more than forty-eight years later, the problems he foresaw and warned us about, would have been ignored to such an degree and for so long that *now* the main threat to the health and well-being of the citizens of this country may well be from what has become part of this 'military-industrial-healthcare-pharmaceutical-media' complex. And woe be unto those who attempt to stop them, sir, because *they* are on a roll now. They and their lobbyists and their in-place people high up in the administration, with their massive amounts of money, have a whole host of politicians and bureaucrats on their side. And believe me, they won't stop until they bleed our people dry."

The doctor stopped speaking suddenly, and Ken looked up from his notepad. He saw an exhausted and critically ill-looking face staring at him.

Dr. Larson, in his now suddenly weakened voice, said, "They won't allow anyone else–not me, and not you–to stop them if they can help it. If they think that a person or a newspaper, for example, is getting too oppositional or influential, well, if they can do anything about that, they will try. Believe me, son, they will try. They tried, and they succeeded, for example, in getting me put out to pasture."

Dr. Larson said, "Please be careful, Mr. Simpson. Take good care of yourself."

Ken nodded, shocked at the second warning in less than twenty-four hours intimating that he might be in some kind of danger. He decided, however, to challenge the doctor just a little.

"I appreciate your concern, sir. I will heed your words and your warning, and I certainly will stay alert. But, may I ask without appearing insulting, how would *you* respond, doctor, to those who might say that your comments, however well-intended, are overly exaggerated, if not downright paranoid?"

Larson instinctively sat back in his chair, surprised by Ken's challenge, but almost immediately seemed to recognize that Ken had to do his job as a professional. Dr. Larson's facial expression became kind once again and his voice softened. "I would ask them to what extent they believe that some of the executives at *End-run* had the public's, as opposed to their own, well-being in mind, when they made hundreds of millions of dollars by selling their stock while their shareholders' investments were about to go down the tubes. And, to what extent do they think that the management at their accounting firm were looking after the public's interests rather than their own, when they advised *End-run* as they apparently did, and then even shredded documents they should have known the government would want them to retain pertaining to that debacle?"

Larson was back in full stride. "Furthermore, I would ask them if any one of them believes that our tobacco companies are serving the public health interest, including especially that of the youth of America, by promoting and selling cigarettes; or, if the administration's watering down of the previously legislated pollution control requirements for automobiles in upcoming years, was really in the public's, as opposed to the polluters' best interests."

Dr. Larson's face became fearsome. "I would also ask them if they think that the senior citizens of this country are being treated fairly or are being fleeced by pharmaceutical companies who are charging them a great deal more for the very same medications than they are charging our Canadian neighbors, and why they think the companies are able to get away with doing so. If one looks at the accounting statements of those same companies, they are among the most profitable in the entire country."

Ken was writing as quickly as he could. He was hearing confirmation by the former top doctor in the land, of what other physicians had told him only in confidence because they were afraid of being dropped by some HMOs and PPOs from their lists of 'preferred providers', should their identities be revealed. And Ken understood that they knew that the word 'preferred' meant, among other things, someone who presumably would simply shut up and not rock the boat.

Ken had been monitoring Dr. Larson's agitated state for several minutes, and was getting increasingly concerned about the elderly man's condition. He asked softly, "Dr. Larson, should we go on with this interview any longer?"

"Why? What do you mean?" replied Larson, somewhat coldly.

"Well, I truly appreciate you seeing me today and what you have told me has been both informative and insightful. Yet I find myself concerned about you, sir, since you are obviously becoming quite upset, and I just now reminded myself that there has been a publicized rumor that your heart may also not be in as great condition as it once was: I don't want you to become too distressed by all this... conversation."

Larson's expression, which had momentarily been as severe as Ken remembered seeing in old footage of the Surgeon General responding to some reporter's inane questioning, softened once he understood that Ken was concerned about his problematic physical state.

The doctor slowly nodded and was silent for what seemed more than a full minute, though it was much less. Then he quietly said, "Mr. Simpson, as I am certain you well know yourself, most of the print and electronic media are controlled by conglomerates that have in their stable, all manner of companies, often including healthcare and pharmaceutical companies. For that reason alone, my views are seldom sought, and even less often printed or aired.

"At least, your paper is still independent, or so I have been led to believe. In reading your first article in what you referred to as your 'State of the Nation's Healthcare' series, I became convinced that you and your paper were one of the few representatives of the 'fifth estate' that seemed to be willing to risk tweaking the bull's balls. I respect that, sir, and want to help you and our fellow American citizens as much as I can. But," he sighed wearily, "perhaps you have a point. I do get riled up once I get going. And my heart is *not* in the shape it used to be."

Again Larson stopped talking, and he seemed to be weighing what to do or say next. Finally, looking directly into Ken's eyes with his own now watering, giant orbs, the ex-Surgeon General's face suddenly seemed like a young boy's, and when he began speaking, it was in such a soft voice that Ken found himself leaning forward to catch his words. But there was no mistaking the pain that now layered Larson's face. He said, slowly, "Mr. Simpson, may I... tell you something 'off the record'?"

Ken said, "Certainly," and turned off his tape recorder and put down his writing pad.

"When I was Surgeon-General, my own daughter's oldest child, a wonderful young woman with a fine husband and three beautiful young children, in the early stages of her career as a young doctor, became seriously depressed. She was having a lot of trouble coping with her various responsibilities at home and at work. And she began making distraught statements, such as saying that the world was not a fit place to bring up children and that therefore it was the duty of parents to prevent children from growing up in such an awful place."

Dr. Larson's voice trembled as he continued. "Even though her own family doctor and her psychiatrist tried desperately to have her hospitalized, the case worker at the healthcare company with whom the family was registered, said that she was only experiencing a typical postpartum depression, and for that reason the case worker refused to authorize the admission. Instead, she was put on a major antidepressant and sent home with an appointment to see her psychiatrist for follow-up."

More than a full minute passed in silence, and Ken sensed that Dr. Larson had gone someplace too dark for a person to be left alone for too long. He gently asked, "What happened to her, Dr. Larson?"

Tears began tumbling down his crag-filled face as Dr. Larson struggled to get the words out. "What happened... Mr. Simpson, is that... after being on the antidepressant for less than two days, she drowned her babies and then tried to take her own life. Her husband came home just after she had swallowed the remaining antidepressant pills, using a bathroom cleanser as a chaser."

He stopped talking again and Ken felt he was witnessing a grandfather's caring collapsing under the weight of unrelenting guilt and anger.

After a long while Larson's eyes seemed to run dry, his chin stopped quivering, and the once famous steely resolve re-emerged, guided back by that rich, deep, God-given voice. Ken found it amazing to hear such a powerful voice now being offered so gently. "My granddaughter couldn't get the psychiatric hospitalization that she needed from her healthcare provider, because, as we learned later, that company gave bonuses to its workers in proportion to the percentage of medical claims that they denied. So, instead of putting her medical needs first, they simply OK'd a refill prescription for her antidepressant, a product that was already under review because of its apparent association with the precipitation of suicidal and homicidal behavior. A few days later she succeeded in killing her children and herself."

"I am so sorry, Dr. Larson."

The older man said, "Without our physical and mental health,

Mr. Simpson, the quality of life and liberty of a human being is obviously grossly diminished, and the attainment of happiness is that much more difficult. Genuine living, real freedom and genuine joy are grounded in, and can only grow from, the health of our minds and bodies. Isn't it amazing that most governments, including ours, permit tobacco corporations to produce and promote products, the consumption of which often leads directly to lung cancer, heart attacks, and the destruction of the health of millions upon millions of our citizens? And that these same governmental and corporate powers make sure that our pharmaceutical and so-called healthcare-related corporations are allowed to put profit before service? Is there not madness in their methods?"

He was back in full stride again, and Ken continued his note-taking, processing what Dr. Larson was saying while at the same time deciding to end this interview very soon, as his subject was beginning to pause and gulp for almost each breath.

"Mr. Simpson, are you aware of a study carried out a few years ago by Bradford Hayford University's School of Public Health, which showed that, over a one-year period, about one-half of adults younger than 65 reported having had a problem in dealing with their health plan? Can you imagine? About one in two people who *did* have health insurance had difficulty getting coverage for the treatment that they and their doctors believed they needed. And that study received only passing reference in the media, and was mostly buried on the inside pages of the few newspapers in which it was mentioned. Now, why was that, do you suppose?"

Before Ken could respond, Dr. Larson added, "And why is it that we have even had a couple of movies dealing with the problems of the likes of some managed care companies, like that "John Q" back a few years ago, movies that many audiences have responded to with loud applause at the end of the films? You and I know why; these few films have voiced ordinary folk's concerns by pointing out what too many healthcare and insurance companies have been doing to their policyholders, and still almost nothing has been done at the legislative levels of government to change things? Why is that, would you say?"

Ken offered his answer. He said, "Soft and hard money to politicians, plus lobbying to control a large chunk of the media, especially since back in 2003, when the Federal Communications Commission allowed the same company to own even larger shares of the media pie in this country."

"Exactly!" said Dr. Larson. "And the influence of big business generally, and of the healthcare, insurance and pharmaceutical companies in particular, has been building for decades. When I was a young doctor and one of President Eisenhower's on-call physicians while he was traveling around the U.S., I was, on occasion, privy to conversations he had with certain advisors. Ike absolutely saw that there was forming in these United States, certain military and business alliances that were gathering together and increasing exponentially in power and influence, even during his brief time in office."

Larson paused to catch his breath yet again, and when he started to speak once more, he seemed to be in warrior mode. "Now, here we are, more than four decades and thousands and thousands of mergers and acquisitions later, and with what they now call inter-industry 'convergence' that has been going on at a furious rate during the past several years in the health, pharmaceutical, and media fields. These conglomerates already have in place alliances with, or ownership of, the means of influencing both the politicians *and* the public through the media outlets they hold or control, to an extent that was hardly dreamt of previously. Now all of this is a reality. The combination of both their open and hidden efforts pose, I believe, one of the greatest threats to the health and welfare of the citizens of this country."

Larson frowned, shook his head, and continued. "Among the things that I learned, particularly in the 1990s, was that these companies were expert 'gardeners'. They realized that to keep and grow their market share, they had to be continually planting the seeds of the next phase of their expansion. They continually set up bogeymen to scare the American public, as they have done by continually referring to what they refer to as the perils of 'state-controlled, state-funded' healthcare. They repeatedly spoke, for example, of the long waiting lists for certain surgeries in Canada, neglecting to mention, of course, the forty-six million Americans without any health insurance at all, most of whom can't afford needed medical treatment at all, which is one major reason why those who can may find they get faster service. And they also never mention that most Canadians report being satisfied with the quality of medical service they do receive.

"Which is not to say, by the way, that the Canadians shouldn't have their waiting times shortened where they are too long. But by repeating the 'worst case scenario' mantras over and over in the media, our so-called healthcare companies scared enough people so as to pan the entire idea of President Clinton's attempts at a healthcare initiative, and instead paved–and paid–their way towards building opposition to the President's plan in the public's mind and well as in the House and the Senate, and in recent years, of course, in the White House itself.'

Ken asked, "So would you say that the odds of real reform of our for-profit healthcare system remain slim for the foreseeable future?"

"Well, Mr. Simpson, there are those in the current administration who know full well that, especially since September 11, 2001, each time we have reports of another terrorist threat against Americans, they are then in a position to ask for more and more military spending. Then they are able to get away with spending less and less on Medicare coverage and other social services. At the same time, many of the chief executives of the administration-friendly corporations that have received billions in untendered and/or tendered contracts since our so-called 'war on terror' began, well, while they may not exactly hope for the next terrorist act to occur, they may not cry too much when it happens, knowing that their companies', their own, and their shareholders' profits, are about to go way up.

"Just think about it: the acts of that single brilliant, ruthless and fanatical Osama bin Laden have prompted trillions of dollars in increased military spending over the last eight years, mostly for the development and deployment of weapons that are primarily suitable for full scale attacks of entire countries, when what may have been needed was a combination of a greater use of diplomacy coupled with the training of more superbly trained, surgically effective, strike forces so that the terrorists could be eliminated and the states that protect and support them could be stopped from developing and deploying weapons of mass destruction."

"Dr. Larson, may I quote you on what you have been telling me today?"

Dr. Larson said nothing but Ken had the distinct impression that he was exercising the carpenter's rule of 'nine times measure and the tenth time cut'. He surely did not want his good name being used in some sensationalistic fashion, and undoubtedly had been evaluating Ken throughout the time they had spent together.

Dr. Larson alternated a couple of times between gazing quizzically at Ken and then looking thoughtfully inward. Finally he said in a firm voice, "Mr. Simpson, the fact is that my heart problems are the least of my health concerns. I have only a few weeks, or at most, a couple of months. Cancer has been making itself at home in more and more of my body for some time now and I know only too well how these things go."

Ken said, "I'm truly sorry."

The dying man said, "It has been my fate that I outlived my wonderful wife of forty years, by over a decade. I have lived a long and full life. I don't owe anyone anything except the truth, as I see it. You may quote me on anything I have spoken of today, except what I told you about my daughter's child. I would prefer that those sorrows not be spilt across the pages of a newspaper."

"Of course, Dr. Larson. Thank you."

Ken thought of the battles that his editor, Rusty, had been required to fight over the years with various managing editors of the paper in order to get particular articles published. Business was not Ken's bag, but he had heard the same stories from other reporters both within *The New York Era* and other media, about the pressures applied to editors who dared to try and print or air any of the many complaints or horror stories of ordinary Americans having been denied coverage for medical care that their own physicians had told them was imperative.

Ken flashed on the memory of the managing editor of a competing paper who, over drinks, told him that she had been reprimanded by the paper's owner when she had expressed a reluctance to slant editorials, editorial cartoons, and 'letters to the editor' so as to infer that most health insurance complaints were being made by chronic malcontents.

Larson spoke again. "One of my medical colleagues writes a syndicated health column for a prominent weekly magazine. He told me that some of his more probing articles had led to his paper being warned that advertisements for all manner of products, from baby formula to birth control to allergy medications and cough medicines, might be pulled if his articles continued to raise questions about the pharmaceutical business, including the excessive delay in pulling certain dangerous medications off the shelves of drugstores."

Ken inquired, "How far do you think those companies are prepared to go to stifle genuine discussion and reporting by the press?"

Larson answered, "Well, I saw them at work when I was the Surgeon-General. I was approached time and again by registered lobbyists to go easy on criticizing certain drug companies for their questionable ways of conducting and reporting clinical trials, and for advertising their powerful drugs on television in the same manner as aspirin or cough drops. I once stated outright at a press conference that some pharmaceutical companies might be burying unfavorable clinical trial findings or pressuring physicians to rewrite or withdraw unfavorable comments about some of the medications they were reviewing for professional journals. Well, sir, even though these matters potentially affected every man, woman, and child in our country, the reporting in the news media of what I had to say on these matters was most noticeable by its brevity or outright absence.

Ken inquired, "And what, might I inquire, was the cumulative effect on you of this lobbying pressure and lack of coverage?"

"Well, some of the lobbyists who sought meetings with me on behalf of their healthcare or pharmaceutical companies, reminded me mostly of viruses, the types that attempt to enter any orifice, infect any organ they can, in order to try and bring down the entire body. They can often seem so innocent and their offers of campaign support so appealing, that it is easy to see why some usually conscientious and previously ethical politicians might fall victim to their overtures, and thereafter be reconstituted as mouthpieces of the corporations that now control them. I like to call them 'the Stepford Senators', although some are in the House as well."

They both laughed. Then Ken asked, "Could you provide me with a specific example?"

Dr. Larson replied, "Of course. Just look at OurHealthyUS HMO. It is one of the largest Managed Healthcare corporations in this country, and has recently bought LibertyDemocracy Media, which owns outright, or is a major shareholder in–and therefore controls–over two hundred media outlets of various kinds across the U.S. You can easily guess what kinds of books, television and radio news items, and magazine and newspaper articles will be coming out of the LibertyDemocracy 'media stable' about our healthcare system? Why, the public will be told that managed healthcare is the best thing since penicillin."

Ken asked, "What, then, doctor, in your opinion, is the solution to the problems you have been describing?"

The old man narrowed his eyes, took a long, deep breath, and his strong, clear response hit Ken full force. "The only way to obtain affordable and sustainable healthcare for the poor and middle class in our society is for the few remaining independent politicians, business leaders, and media organizations like yours to finally have the balls to take a stand for what is right and in the best interests of your readers and viewers. And your paper and the other independent media will have to fight like hell, and probably even risk your working lives, in order to help save the health of perhaps millions of Americans.

"Look at the financial data, Mr. Simpson. HMOs have become among the wealthiest companies in the country. Put them all together with the medical devices companies and the pharmaceutical industries, and they represent many times more revenue dollars, annually, than all the U.S. defense *and* software *and* computer companies' revenues combined. Do you think for one moment that they will voluntarily let go of their grip on their flock of golden geese? Hell, they are almost printing their own money, and giving most of it to their executives, first and foremost, and they still have enough left over to make their shareholders money on the backs of their customers' miseries.

The huge piles of profits certainly are not being made by the doctors, or being put into providing the best treatments for the sick and the needy."

Now, as if he was suddenly aware of the heightened state of agitation he had worked himself into, and its possible consequences for a man in his medical condition, Dr. Larson appeared to be struggling to calm himself down again.

After a few moments Larson's huge fists, which had been pumping while he was having his say, started to unclench and finally came to rest in his lap. He said in an almost relaxed tone, "Mr. Simpson, I will put you in touch with a few of the best damn doctors in this country and you can talk to *them* about the effects of the HMOs and PPOs on their profession. I believe you will find some awfully frustrated, disillusioned and angry physicians who have lost control of their practices to a bunch of clerks and what I call 'Health-rons', companies that are little more than crooked toll-collecting gatekeepers that don't provide any direct service to those that need it, but have cornered the market and control the folks that do, or at least *should*, provide needed medical services. "

"I would very much like to speak to those people, Dr. Larson. That would be much appreciated."

Ken stopped writing and considered what Dr. Larson had told him to this point. The issue of the mainstream media's limited coverage of poor medical treatment and the questionable practices by HMOs and insurance companies was undoubtedly accurate. And the advertising dollars spent by drug companies, he knew, were among the highest of all categories of businesses in the United States.

Ken recalled Martha's comments after she had dug out the figures for advertising and campaign contributions by drug companies. She had said to him, with wonder in her voice, "Ken, get this! As far back as a decade ago, in 1999, the U.S. drug and remedy companies were spending *over four billion dollars on advertising alone*? That was more than was spent on advertising by the food, travel, hotels, real estate, sporting goods, audio-video equipment, or gasoline companies in this country! No wonder they have a stranglehold on the media! I guess, when you have them by their economic 'balls', their news and editorial pages and programs will fall in line." Martha had a way with words.

Ken also knew that, even though his column was syndicated in hundreds of newspapers and that they paid a pretty penny for the privilege of printing his words, some of his articles on healthcare had been buried in the most unlikely parts of many newspapers or did not appear in them at all.

Ken had also heard rumors in the past few weeks about the venerable *New York Era* being a take-over target, and that it was being pursued by a conglomerate that had made an exceptionally generous offer. After Dr. Larson's comments, Ken now better understood why. Once the few remaining major independent newspaper and other media voices were silenced in their criticism of what they saw as wrong in government and/or business circles, the public would be almost entirely without any independent sources of information. The 'fifth estate' was now prime *real estate* and representatives of certain corporate buyers were making cold calls offering obscene amounts for the equivalent of what sometimes could be termed 'tear-down' properties. In the past few years, in fact, newspapers, radio and TV outlets had been bought up at an unprecedented rate, and even merged with huge Internet and other 'new economy' companies.

While Ken was reflecting on these matters Dr. Larson took out and swallowed some pills in conditioned response to his watch's beeping. The doctor's visage was once again transformed into that of a tired, extremely sick, old man. Ken knew that this rich resource of integrity and information would not be around much longer.

Dr. Larson inquired, "Is there anything else you would like to ask me?"

Ken said, "You have already been extremely helpful. But there is just one last question that I do have. If you could direct our country's leaders towards a healthcare plan that you personally believe would be the most beneficial *for* Americans and run *by* Americans, what would you recommend?"

"That's an easy one to answer," responded Dr. Larson. "I have been a career military man, a physician in private practice, and was Surgeon General for several years, long enough to have met with my counterparts in many countries in the world. At my direction a few years ago, my department conducted a comparative study whose summary never saw the light of day, because its findings were not compatible with the philosophy of the then administration."

"I understand."

"Well, to begin with, we noted that year that Americans spent over 14% of GNP on healthcare. That was nearly 40% more than the Germans, the Swiss, or the French and 55% more than the Canadians. Yet we have no health insurance for over 15% of our people, including that same percentage of our children under the age of eighteen. And that year twice as many Blacks as Whites were not covered because they were relatively poorer and couldn't afford insurance."

Ken had heard some of these numbers before from other sources but they never failed to both embarrass and infuriate him.

"Meanwhile, our northern neighbors up in Canada cover virtually 100%, that is, *all* of their citizens, at *45% less cost* per capita. My colleagues in that country just shake their heads at us in dismay, if not downright disgust. And meanwhile our politicians make self-congratulatory claims about America being the most generous and the best democracy that ever there was. My God," said Dr. Larson, his voice and his chin quivering, "have we no insight into ourselves, and no shame?"

Dr. Larson continued. "What we are is the greatest *capitalistic* nation in the world, *not* the greatest democracy! Mr. Simpson, for all our sakes, you have to help our American brothers and sisters come to their senses." Dr. Larson was pleading by the time he had finished speaking.

Neither man said anything for a bit. Then, with his emotions obviously much aroused, Dr. Larson spoke in almost a whisper, asking, "Mr. Simpson, have you ever heard of the Underground Railroad?"

Ken nodded. "Do you mean the escape routes used by African Americans to get to Canada during the years of slavery?"

"Exactly. In the 1800s, you may recall then, thousands of black folks in the United States fled to Canada and Mexico to escape the horrors and injustices of slavery. Canada had abolished slavery years before we in the U.S. did, and some 30,000 blacks made it to Canada."

Dr. Larson's face exhibited a cascade of expressions as he spoke. Anger, fear, pride and, finally, a wide smile of pure pleasure captured his entire face as he said, proudly and yet another burst of energy, "Some of my own relatives made it to Canada, Mr. Simpson. They became free men and women years before the rest of us. My people traveled the 'underground railroad' all the way to Nova Scotia, on Canada's east coast. Well, some of us descendents of those brave folk still stay in touch. They are, by and large, lower or middle class socio-economically, as we might say, but many of them are of the highest order as human beings."

The doctor paused, looking inward again, nodding and smiling, as if he were watching an inner film of his ancestors successfully making their way up north, risking their lives and those of their children in order to taste freedom.

Then he came back to this room, and continued. "Mr. Simpson, my third cousin, Alfayus, is about my age. He is not well off; in fact, he was not blessed with much beyond a marvelous kindness and simple tastes. Which is just as well, because neither he nor his children or grandchildren have been able to do much more than run the family farm just well enough to be able to put food on the table and a warm fire in the fireplace with which to hold out the cold and damp in their modest home during the freezing winters and early springs and wet autumns. A couple of his kids work in the nearby town at a hardware store and the one small, so-called supermarket. Well, about six years ago, Alfayus needed a heart bypass operation, and one of his kids needs regular dialysis treatment. A year later his wife had to have surgery and treatment for breast cancer.

Ken was listening closely.

Dr. Larson continued. "Why, if those folks had lived on the U.S. side of the border, they would be bankrupt today and it is most likely that Alfayus' child, his wife, and himself would not have been able to have the medical attention that they needed, and perhaps all three would be dead. Well, they *all* did have *all* the treatments they needed, and it cost them *nothing* out of pocket. And they found out who the best doctors were up there and got into see them, and had their surgeries and treatments done by the surgeons *they* wanted and then received very competent nursing care. And it cost them nothing more to have the best. Nothing! Their Medicare system is paid for out of all their citizens' taxes. And the universal health coverage they have up there treats everyone the same. Not anything at all like we have here in America." And," Larson added with great emphasis, "they were in the same hospitals, the same wards, and had the same doctors as the more financially well off people did who also happened to be undergoing similar treatments at the same time!"

Larson was out-and-out beaming. "Sounds too good to be true, doesn't it?"

Ken asked, "But aren't Canadians restricted as to *which* doctors they can see?"

Larson went from pleasure to indignation in one second flat, *"Horsefeathers!* That is absolutely and entirely baloney, my boy. Most Canadians have no restriction whatsoever as to whom they can see in their own province, and their doctors don't have to get permission from anyone else, and certainly no glorified clerk or bean counter, before he or she can determine that tests or procedures be carried out, although it is true that it may well take more time before they can be carried out. It's *we* Americans who are restricted as to which doctors we can see, and then those doctors have to get permission from a glorified clerk, for goodness' sake, before they can be assured they will be paid for any tests or procedures they want to do."

"If what you are saying is true, Dr. Larson, and I believe you, then why do so many Americans have the clear impression that it's the Canadians who are the ones who are restricted, and that *we* are the ones who have freedom of choice?"

"I have already told you, Mr. Simpson. Some of the so-called healthcare companies have been waging a disinformation campaign for years now. It's like the 'weapons of mass destruction in Iraq' notion that former President Bush and his cronies perpetrated. If enough people repeat outright lies enough times, a surprisingly large proportion of people will believe it, especially if you can squelch or attack almost any message to the contrary."

Ken wrote, and ideas started forming furiously as to where he wanted to go next with his series on healthcare. The doctor was a treasure trove of information.

"And shall I tell you another thing, Mr. Simpson? We in the U.S. have some of the most 'socialized industries' in the world, businesses that are primarily or completely dependent upon government contracts and funding for their income. They create, design and build according to government needs and specifications. Our military and its equipment procurements, including our 'star wars' anti-missile defense system, and the like are all effectively dependent upon our government paying the shot. All of these areas are funded directly by our government, yet we, or rather our politicians, business types and the media, apply the term, 'socialized' only to medicine and any other ideas that we want people to reject. Such nonsense. Such chutzpah!"

The doctor shook his head, laughing bitterly. And then, suddenly, his head dropped slowly towards his chest and his shoulders slumped. The man had completely exhausted himself. He looked up and smiled weakly at Ken.

Ken knew that it was time to bring the interview to an end and leave a dying old man to find some peace. As he started to close his reporter's writing pad and retrieved his tape recorder, Dr. Larson said, "I'm afraid I have tired myself out. How unfortunate that when we finally gain enough wisdom and courage, we are sometimes too exhausted to fight for the changes that we know are so desperately needed."

Ken wished his own father had had the opportunity to get old. Dr. Larson provided a wonderful example of valor in aging. Looking into the moist, kind, but tired eyes of the sick man, Ken said, "Well, you have fought *today*, Doctor Larson, as I am sure you have during much of your life. And I assure you, sir, that I will make full use of your insights, and I will attempt to relate your views as accurately as I possibly can."

Larson smiled and said, "Thank you, son; I am sure you will! And tomorrow I will mail you a list of physicians and others to contact. Now you will need to excuse me because I have to... I need to... *pee*!" Laughing heartily, the dying ex-Surgeon General of the United States excused himself and, as if in slow motion, got up, turned and walked towards the door on the far side of the room.

Ken stood, and talking to the doctor's back, said, "Thank you, Doctor Larson."

The doctor's left hand raised up weakly and waved a shaky goodbye as he quickly disappeared behind the closing door of a washroom. He said, "God bless."

Ken quietly let himself out, moved by the effort the old man had made to respond to his questions during the interview. Suddenly, Ken felt a wave of sadness in response to the realization of the imminent loss of another good 'father figure'.

It's strange but the older I get the more I appreciate good 'fathers'. I had thought they would have mattered less once I became one myself. The lump in his throat told him otherwise. He silently promised Dr. Larson again that he would make appropriate use of the information to which he was now privy.

As he descended the steps off the generous front porch, Ken felt an unexpected shudder. He knew that his intuition was warning him that he was entering a territory of uncontrolled, yet undefined, danger.

He had not noticed the car that had followed him from *The New York Era* building to Dr. Larson's home–nor the one that tailed him all the way back to Manhattan.

CHAPTER 18

The cabbie had been happily waiting for his fare, marking time and the crossword puzzle that always appeared on the page opposite to the daily dose of nubile flesh that was hardly restrained by some too-small thong. His meter, meanwhile, had equally happily measured the passage of time and the earning of easy money.

As he emerged from Dr. Larson's home, Ken felt a momentary apprehension about what might have already happened to his own position at the paper. He was also concerned for Martha. And he wondered about the real reasons behind the insertion of the bountiful Ms. Bowry, in her place. He decided to find out a lot more, and quickly, about the young reporter who had been so abruptly, although not entirely unpleasantly, dropped onto his lap and into his investigations of healthcare in America.

As he walked briskly to the cab parked in the driveway Ken glanced at his watch. He had been with Dr. Larson for nearly an hour. He needed time to complete his note-taking, sift through what Dr. Larson had told him, and think further about the relevancy of what President Eisenhower said in his farewell address back in 1961 to what was going on now, in 2009.

He was already dialing his cellphone as he settled into the back seat of the cab. While he waited for his call to be answered, he told the driver to take him back to *The New York Era's* building.

On the third ring the unmistakable throaty voice said, "Hello. This is Sylkeen Bowry. How may I help you?"

Ken's mind instantly thought of a couple of ways, neither of which were one of the reasons he was calling. *Or were they?* A beat later his own mouth finally shifted into gear: "Hello. Sylkeen. It's Ken Simpson."

"Oh, hello, Ken. I am so glad you called. I hope this doesn't sound presumptuous, but I have some ideas for the series that I would love to go over with you, whenever you might have the time."

"Of course. That's why I called, actually. Listen, if we are still on for four this afternoon I can bring you up to speed on the state of the healthcare series and you can tell me what you have in mind. I really want to move forward on this as quickly as possible."

There was just a brief gap of time before her not-quite-embarrassed response. "Well, I hope you don't mind, Ken, but actually, Rusty was kind enough to go into your desk and pull out some of the files related to the series."

Ken's teeth gritted and his whole head began to ache.

"He said he wanted me 'plugged in' to where you were at, right away. I hope that was okay with you."

Had she imparted this bit of news in person, Sylkeen would have seen Ken's face turn flaming red. *Damn Rusty; he had no right to do that. Well, okay, so maybe he did have a right, as the editor. But thankfully, I keep most of the really important material on the memory 'key' that I carry around to use on my home computer, my laptop, or the desktop at the office.* He had decided over three years earlier to not network the three computers together, just in case someone at work decided to poke around to see everything he had written. He also changed his password nearly every few weeks, often 'forgetting' to inform Rusty of the latest one.

Ken issued a just slightly cooler, "No, of course not, Sylkeen. Good idea. I should of thought of it myself."

"Great. Well, Ken, I've been reading over the material since you left and think that I could help you get answers to some of the questions you had written down in the margins of your notes."

Damn! You're already 'in like flint', aren't you?

"As far as us meeting later on today, the problem is, Ken, that my appointment with HR is at five-fifteen. Then I would really like to go for my workout. My thighs desperately need the Stairmaster today; I have been sitting on my butt for hours. Would you mind?"

Animal, don't dare say a word. But methinks she is flirting with me. Maybe. Once upon a time, a comment like that which Sylkeen had just uttered might have led to Ken to say something that nowadays could get him accused of sexual harassment–or worse. But Sylkeen can get away with talking about her thighs needing a workout and then claim that she was simply making a factual comment. *But when I did that article on the influences of advertising the key researchers all agreed that it is nearly impossible to hear a word we understand without triggering a visual image of the thing the word represents. Pink elephant, anyone? Hello? Is there something wrong with this picture? If she talks about her thighs or her butt, then I can't help but see thighs or butts with my mind's eye. Christ, will my mind always work that way? Or are all men horny forever, even when we get so old and down and out that we can't even get 'it' up anywhere near as easily–or as often–as in the old days?*

Having had this micro-reverie, Ken said, after just missing a single beat, "Of course, Sylkeen, go ahead. We'll go over everything tomorrow."

That so feminine voice once again stroked his ear, saying, "But, hey, Ken, if you wouldn't mind, and if you don't think it inappropriate, then how about meeting later over a drink; or even better, if you would not be taking yourself away from anything terribly important (*Did she also know about Martha?*) how about coming over to my place later on this evening and I'll even manage to do something quasi-domestic and make us something to eat before we work?"

Taken aback by her invitation, Ken stumbled just slightly and then said, "Oh, um, if you're are alright with that. I wouldn't want you to get all worn out your first day." *Take that! Two can play the same game.*

She quickly reassured him, "No problem. I am just really excited about getting to work on this series with you, and can hardly wait to get into the material."

It wasn't a question of *whether* she was trying to get close to him as quickly as she could. The only question was, *why?* To discredit him? To have him drop his guard in response to being flattered that a 30-something might be interested in him, or at least, in working with him? Or, perhaps she was just naturally eager and playful.

Ken replied, "All right, then. Dinner it is. What's your

address?" She gave it to him, and Ken, duly impressed but for some reason not entirely surprised, wrote it down in the back of his hand, underlining the apartment number, "PH 2".

She asked, "Is around seven-thirty a good time for you?"

"Fine. See you then. Bye, Sylkeen." Ken hung up, somewhat bemused and, in spite of that inner voice telling him to be careful, definitely *en*thused.

He had recognized her address, of course, as one of the most prestigious condo towers in Manhattan, near Central Park, and close to where he used to live with his ex-wife and son.

She hadn't paid for that place on a reporter's salary. What gives with this young lady? And why has she landed on my doorstep? Obviously she wants me to know that she is someone who has the financial means, and maybe the connections, to get in to see the CEOs who had proven so elusive for me to interview. Can she really help open those doors? Or is this a show for some other reason? If so, what?

He would find out soon enough. He gave the cabbie new directions, having now decided to go home first, work on his notes there, and then shower and change. He next called Martha and told her he would be working late. He chose not to tell her *where* he would be working late; she had had enough upsetting news for one day. He would see her later, he told her, if he finished work at a reasonable hour.

He felt slightly embarrassed when he realized he was excited at the prospect of what might happen later in the evening.

CHAPTER 19

When he left his apartment at about 7:15pm Ken took along a couple of interesting pieces of information for articles he was working on in the healthcare series. However, neither came from any particularly sensitive sources. He was not yet prepared to reveal to anyone, including and especially Ms. Sylkeen Bowry, most of what he had uncovered, including anything about his just completed interview with Dr. Larson and certainly not even the fact of the existence of the package he had received.

The ride to Sylkeen's building took less than ten minutes during non-rush hour. When he got out of the cab he glanced up at the impressive façade of one of *the* prestige addresses in New York City. As he approached the front entrance, a famous, or more correctly, an infamous cable television news-talk host emerged. The man nodded slightly and smiled, as if he either recognized Ken, or thought he should. The icon quickly got into a limo, and Ken presumed that he was off to the television studio to host his nightly show. Ms. Bowry had definitely settled herself in amongst the 'rich and famous'.

But where did *her* money come from? Since she was in her early thirties she could not have worked long enough after university to be able to afford such luxurious digs. Ken had noticed the jeweled pin attached to her suit jacket as well as the other jewelry she was displaying when they met in Rusty's office. Together the pieces were likely worth at least $40,000, if his recollections from the research he had done a few years earlier were reasonably accurate. Therefore, young Sylkeen was either one of the multitude of 'born rich' or 'divorced rich' who inhabited the condo heights of Manhattan's canyons. Or both. And if she was not wealthy, then who was footing the bill for this place? On a reporter's salary she probably wouldn't be able to afford a broom closet at this prestigious address.

A doorman eased Ken's entry into the building. Quick as you

could say 'show me the money', the concierge greeted him, and once given Ken's name he said, "Ms. Bowry has asked that you go right up, Mr. Simpson. Please take the second elevator on your right, and it will bring you directly to her suite".

Ken entered the marble-and-glass lined elevator, which could more correctly be referred to as a 'mobile room', since it was almost the size of his den and had a leather loveseat and easy chair resting on a Persian rug, and what looked like expensive modern paintings hanging from the two non-mirrored walls.

Ken noticed immediately that, except for the red emergency button, the elevator had no others to push. Where one would expect buttons to be, there was, instead, a computer-like numeric keypad that, he guessed, could be programmed from either the concierge's desk, the condo unit, or from onboard by someone who knew the correct code.

The elevator doors closed, and the 'room' began to move swiftly and smoothly upwards with no vibration to be felt by its human cargo. When the doors finally opened Ken stepped directly into his hostess's foyer. Waiting for him was an even more ravishing Ms. Bowry wearing a black silken (*really!*) pants suit that did both her and the fabric gentle favors.

There was a drink on the glass entry table, which she offered to Ken as she greeted him with an inviting smile and dancing eyes. "Thanks *so much* for coming over, Ken. Come on into the dining room. I do hope that you're ready to eat something delicious."

Ken took the drink, somehow only slightly surprised that it was his favorite brand of scotch. Had she already stereotyped him as the scotch-drinking, hard-nosed investigative reporter, guessing at his preferred 'poison', or did she actually know that for decades now he drank Glenmorangie single malt whisky, just as his dad had done?

Ken followed her into the dining room where he was genuinely impressed by the magnificent nighttime views of the Empire State Building, the Chrysler building and a fair portion of the New York City skyline that filled the floor-to-ceiling windows making up two walls of the room. He noticed that the apartment had hallways that led off in at three directions; the suite probably took up a substantial portion of what she told him was the 47th and top floor. He guessed he was walking through over $8,000,000 of sky-high real estate. A junior reporter's entire annual salary probably wouldn't even cover more than a couple of months of the condominium's maintenance fees. *What the hell was this lady about, and up to?*

Sylkeen followed his gaze and seemingly read his mind. Laughing lustily, she said, "You are the first person I could call a kind of co-worker that I have ever had up here, Ken. In case you were wondering, the apartment is about 2300 square feet, excluding the terrace, which is another 1000 square feet off the master bedroom." She paused, and then toyed with his mind and hormones again. "Perhaps you would like a tour of the entire suite later. The view from the master bedroom is really fabulous." She was smiling. "Meanwhile, shall we have something to eat... in the dining room?"

They ate and talked, starting with what passed for reporters' small talk; about newspapers in general, the *Era's* mission statement of being the social conscience of the city, standing up for the little guy, and so on. Halfway through the second glass of wine she began disclosing some of her own personal history, telling him that she had been a rather wild teenager in Jackson, New Hampshire who had rejected what, at that time, she perceived as her parents' ancient ways.

When she was eighteen, she told Ken, she took the entire three thousand dollars she had saved while doing part-time work at a local sporting goods outlet store over the previous four years, and had gone off to New York City, to "stop suffocating". Within a few weeks she met, and shortly afterwards began living with, a man in his late thirties, ending up spending a lot of her time "wasted" on drugs and liquor.

Her uncle, her father's brother, somehow located her in New York City several months later and informed her that both her parents had been killed in an accident at a cottage two weeks earlier. Hearing the news, a drugged out Sylkeen described feeling more pain than she thought possible. After a turbulent hour or so, during which her drug-pushing lover, foolishly as it turned out, had threatened to hurt the old man, her ex-military uncle made him a hands-on offer that lover-boy apparently couldn't dare refuse, something about giving him the choice of keeping his genitalia attached to his body—or not!

The next thing she knew, her roommate broke out in a wide-eyed sweat, and was soon helping pack her things in spite of her loud protests. He even carried her boxes and suitcases to a waiting limo, whose driver bore a striking resemblance to photos she had seen of Al Capone. Her uncle, driver 'Al', and herself then drove to a private airport an hour outside of New York City. There she and her uncle boarded a private eight-seater business jet and flew non-stop to Miami, where he lived in a palatial home on the intracoastal.

Uncle Jake was kind yet firm with her, Sylkeen said, confining her to a room for a few foggy days, while she 'dried out'. He had a registered nurse as well as one of his female employees baby-sit her for the next several days. When they were convinced she was dried out and ready, and in her presence, he gave her 'guardians' twenty thousand dollars in cash and sent them off shopping with 'driver Al' to the Bal Harbor shops at Collins and 96th. Their mission was to outfit her in clothes her uncle had specified should be 'presentable' to his friends and clients.

Sylkeen told Ken that she had never seen such stores in her life before, expect when she had occasionally roamed New York City's ritzier areas in one of her stupors. Now sober, the salespeople fell over one another to treat her like royalty. Within a few hours she was multi-outfitted and ready to help out her uncle in his business in as yet undetermined ways. After a visit to a beauty salon, Sylkeen returned to her uncle's house. When he arrived home after work, she greeted him in one of her most enticing leisure outfits. He complimented her taste and her looks, and said that he wanted to hire her to work for his company at a salary that most starting employees would seriously envy.

Uncle Jake spent dozens of after-business hours with her over the next weeks, introducing her to a number of the trendiest places in South Beach. Sylkeen had never seen such affluence, nor been given so much one-on-one attention by a 'parent figure' before; both her parents had worked hard and never seemed to have much money, time, or energy left over for either their children or themselves.

Sylkeen told Ken that after a few weeks of training by her uncle she had gotten 'it', and suddenly understood there were genuine opportunities awaiting her by meeting well-connected people, the likes of whom she previously hadn't even fantasized about. She said that she soon made a deep-down decision to not waste her time, talents, or temperament in ways that wouldn't help her fulfill whatever goals *she* would decide to work towards.

Within months Jake became her surrogate parent in a full sense, supporting her financially and otherwise as she worked hard over the next three years to complete her Bachelors degree at the University of Miami. During reading week in her senior year, at one of Uncle Jake's house parties, she met and then, after a whirlwind romance, married Martin Bowry, a handsome, jock-type 'alpha male' who, at the time, was president of a Canadian Internet security software dotcom startup company that had set up its U.S. headquarters in Miami. The company IPO'd about a year later, and overnight Marty and Sylkeen were paper multimillionaires, worth over $300 million. Marty was courted by a major American 'old economy' company that wanted to get in on the new economy by taking over a promising 'turnkey' Internet company. When he sold the company, barely three months before the high tech 'bubble' burst, Martin Bowry walked away with over half a billion dollars and change.

Sylkeen and her husband moved back to Canada where they lived in a high-tech mansion in an area of Ottawa called Rockcliffe, which she described as the toniest section of Canada's capital city. She told Ken, "We lived surrounded by hundreds of 'movers and shakers' in the high tech, government and diplomatic circles. It was great fun, at least at first."

Ken easily imagined this ravishing young woman strutting her stuff at 'A-level' embassy parties, bringing her husband's newest business concept in proximity to potentially lucrative business contacts through various countries' ambassadors and their corporate leaders. That was probably where and when Sylkeen honed her style of stimulating and stroking hungry yet shaky male egos that needed continual reassurance that they were indeed still virile and attractive enough to draw the attention and keep the interest of such a beauty. Just at that moment Ken glanced past Sylkeen and saw one such man's reflection looking back at him from the sliding glass door to the terrace. *Honesty is a bitch.*

Looking at Ken with a matter-of-fact expression Sylkeen said, "After two years and endless embassy and 'new economy' parties, about two or three nearly every week at that time, I realized that I was little more than a bored, tired trophy bride. My husband had 'won' me, just like he and his company 'won' contracts. Once the 'deal', whatever it was, was made, he would be after the *next* new thing. Anyway, his company was taking up about 24/7 of his mind, time, and energies. Finally, it was all too much–and too little–for me. A couple of particularly drunken–him, and stoned–me, spats later and we were on our way to an amiable separation and divorce, eased by an exceedingly reasonable settlement. And best of all, I was out of that cold, back-biting, small-minded town."

Her voice abruptly switched tempo from dirge to disco. "Anyway, then I came back Stateside, took a post-graduate journalism program, et voila! Here I am." Silken signaled the end of her personal history lesson by batting her eyes and slightly nodding her head in a 'so there' fashion.

Ken had been listening intently while eating the delicious poached salmon entrée she had offered. Like the good reporter she probably was, she had just delivered a summarized version of the five W's; the Who, What, When, Where and Why, of the past fifteen years or so of her life. At the same time, however, Ken suspected that she had left out some information crucial to his understanding of how she came to land her job as his assistant on what was turning out to be one of the most important assignments he had ever undertaken. Well, he would let it go for now; something told him that it would be revealed to him soon enough. Or, if not, then he would raise the matter in the near future.

While listening, Ken was supplementing the information Sylkeen was offering with his first-hand observations. If her manner since he had arrived at her home was any indication, Ms. Bowry was obviously an excellent cook, very witty, definitely flirtatious, extremely bright, and outrageously gorgeous. He could easily see the plausibility of her just-completed rendition of events.

Halfway through dessert Ken found himself having a high-speed fantasy of having great sex with this lady, falling in love, and then, when they were both ready, moving in together, probably into her place, since it was so... so damn fantastic.

Ah, the mind, the mind! What a fool's game. Is it immature optimism, neurotic delusion, or what psychology types and pro athletes refer to as 'imagery rehearsal' that makes a person fantasize about what it would be like to settle down with another within moments of meeting and talking with that person? Do most people mentally test-drive new persons as life-partners in their imagination?

"Why work at all?" Ken found himself asking, without having thought about the possible perceived impudence of such a personal question during an initial collegial conversation. Being an investigative reporter made for the occupational hazard of having a fast brain hard-wired to a big mouth.

He tried softening his question. "What I mean to say is, I presume that you don't really have to work. So why not just travel the world, ski at Vail, tour the Amazon, backpack through Australia, or just kick back for a few decades?"

She smiled at his question but Ken sensed that her back was up.

She said, strongly, "I doubt you would have asked a man in the same situation the same question."

Touché.

"Anyway, I did try that route. So, been there, done that! The Amazon, twice; Australia once. The Austrian Alps a few times. Remember, I grew up skiing around Mount Washington back home. But that isn't really the point of living, is it, Ken? I mean there are still the issues of accomplishment and contribution." Her face changed; in a much quieter voice, she added, "at least, that seems to be the issue for me. You have won awards for writing, Ken, so I am sure you can relate. Like yourself, I am sure, I really would like to do something that will make a difference."

"Very commendable," said Ken, meaning it. He felt momentarily disarmed by her story, especially the loss of her parents and her response to his last query. *The lady has clearly known pain and seemingly acquired priorities.*

"But why become a reporter?"

"Because I love words–and writing. I enjoy meeting people and finding out about them, what they have to say, and how they react in different, and especially trying, situations. I love the challenge of relating my experiences to others via the written word. I have always found that people, young and old, seem to *want* to talk to me. And I like listening to them. Perhaps, as a therapist once suggested, I am looking for my parents in different people. I don't know if that is true but I *do* know that I like the intense, if limited, no-bullshit conversations we can have with people, in our line of work. I like the challenge of getting facts and impressions down on paper in such a way that people who read what I have written have an awareness of having learned something, and of having, in some sense, 'been there' with me. I especially enjoy working on a story that I think *should* be told. I want to get so good at it that, in time, I will be able to uncover and report on ever bigger and more important stories. And one day," she said a little embarrassingly, "I would like to write on important subjects well enough that *my* work might be worthy of at least *being considered* for an award like a Paulson."

Now she blushed with what Ken took to be an indication of rather endearing humility.

Sylkeen quickly regained her composure and said, almost matter-of-factly, "That's the plan, anyway. Now, what about you, Ken? Did you pick journalism or was it the other way around? And if you don't mind saying, what does it mean to you to have been awarded the Paulson?"

Before responding to her questions, Ken hesitated. Perhaps it was the wine from dinner now having its fuzzying effects, modulating the glow of a beautiful young woman expressing enthusiasm and interest. Or perhaps he sensed that Sylkeen, whatever else she had going on, seemed a quite substantial young woman. He admired her openness about her background, her wealth, and her ambition.

Ken decided to give her a reasonably full answer to her first question. "How I got into journalism? Easy. My ticket in was killing some children." Sylkeen, who had been leaning forward towards him, eyes and face open and warm, recoiled as if by some sudden, invisible, repellant force. Which she had, in a manner of speaking.

Ken was actually pleased to see her negative reaction. He said, "I was a helicopter pilot in Vietnam; I was a kid, really, but I had always intended to make the military my career. I flew Hueys into the North…"

Barely recovered from her initial revulsion, Sylkeen said, in a monotone, "I once had a boyfriend who flew helicopters… he was killed in Iraq." Momentarily she looked sad, and then seemed sorry that she had interrupted him.

Ken continued. "Well, I loved it. I was a really good pilot. Top sky jockey in my graduating class in flight school." His rate of speech speeded up now. He was seeing it again.

"One late afternoon we were sent to attack a convoy of trucks that the Vietcong were supposedly using to bring in some heavy artillery and munitions that they couldn't easily take through their systems of tunnels. We wanted to make sure they wouldn't get an opportunity to use their weapons, which our so-called intelligence said was going to be used to attack some of our bases. It was late in the evening by the time we located them and the sun was going down in front of us, making it harder to see our targets clearly. We came in low. Then, just as I was firing my machine gun, I saw what looked like large bags of potatoes come tumbling out of the back of the lead truck. I kept firing all the way in… The bags turned out to be blankets that had been wrapped around people to keep them warm on a cold evening. When they landed on the ground the 'bags' suddenly opened and their contents started to run away. We… I… assumed they were all soldiers."

"When the bullets hit them, their bodies looked like they were flailing and falling apart, collapsing in ways that people normally can't. When I was almost on top of them I saw there were more hiding behind and under the trucks. So I fired again. Several times. I thought that I got almost all of them. Then the gas tank of the truck blew up. The few on the ground nearby who were still alive turned and starting to run away, way too late. My chopper was no more than thirty or forty feet away from them by that time, almost at ground level, and closing fast. One of the runners turned and looked back in my direction; I think at that moment we looked right into each other's souls."

Ken paused as he forcibly moved his diaphragm to make room for his lungs to fill. He took a gulping breath, then said, "The person running away... was a child. She couldn't have been more than 10 or 11 years old. They were all... the runners were all... *children*!"

Ken's voice began to crack; his eyes watered. "My co-pilot and I were on 'go' pills and my finger reflex was faster than my thought processing. Our eyes met again just as I fired instinctively, just as we had been programmed to do."

Ken's chin quivered as he relived it all yet again. He said, slowly, "I saw in her eyes... not hate, but instead, just wide-eyed fear and questioning. The child just seemed to be asking... *'Why?'* That was all she was asking. *'Why?'*"

Sylkeen leaned forward in her chair. Ken said, "I heard myself shouting, screaming my answer at her, "I don't *know* why," just as her torso seemed to separate from her legs. Then, just a fraction of a second later, her sweet face exploded in blood and brains and bone, almost like the grotesque cartoon figures in the war games simulators we used to practice our eye-hand coordination in flight training."

Ken couldn't stop his tears. He said, very quietly, "There was nothing wrong with my eye-hand coordination. I was an excellent killing machine and I killed them all, all ten or twelve or more of those lovely children. And a part of me, a deep, dark part of me, was glad that I had carried out my mission, regardless of who I had killed. Within minutes though, I wanted to kill that part of me, too. I turned and headed the chopper towards a nearby mountain. At the last moment, my co-pilot realized what I was going to do and took over to keep us from crashing into the rock face. We flew back to base all right, but my fighting career was over."

Neither Sylkeen nor Ken said anything for a time. Sylkeen's

face had softened completely while Ken was recounting the incident. Now she displayed only compassion and sadness.

Ken said, "That attack finished me as a military pilot. On the way back to our base I began to throw up into my oxygen mask and I had to take it off. Then I still felt claustrophobic so I took off my helmet and I just sat there, shaking and pissing into my flight suit. My co-pilot brought us back home. I just remember him repeating, over and over, "It was just a mistake, man. That's all it was. Just a goddamn mistake! Get over it; shit happens."

Ken paused again, and then began speaking in a voice filled with resignation. He decided that he might as well let it all out. The military shrink had said it would serve to retell the story again and again, although Ken sometimes had his doubts. But why did he want to tell this young woman whom he didn't even know if he could trust, about the worst moment in his adult life, when his first career died alongside those sweet, massacred children.

"Right there in the copter, I felt completely shattered; I kept seeing that child's eyes and her questioning look. We flew back to base with my co-pilot at the controls and him continuing to scream in my ear that it wasn't my fault. He kept shouting, "They could have been soldiers." He kept shouting the same words over and over and over again. And all the time I kept seeing that young girl asking *"Why?"* as the bullets first sliced her body in two and then made her head explode.

"When I got back to base and filed my report they took me off of flight crew–temporarily, they said. That was when I told everybody in sight, including the base commander who came screaming at me, demanding to know, "What the hell happened out there?" to *"FUCK OFF!"*

Ken realized that he was yelling at the table. He raised his eyes to Sylkeen's, and saw that tears were streaming down her face.

"Sorry, Sylkeen. I didn't mean to..."

"I'm not upset for me, Ken. I am just very moved by what you're saying. My tears are for that girl, for those children, and... and for *this* man." She reached out and lightly touched his trembling hand.

Ken suddenly felt exposed and embarrassed. The Air Force shrink he had been ordered to see after the 'incident' had been more compassionate than the military probably would have liked. That may have been partly due to the fact that the framed family photograph on his desk included two pre-teen girls, presumably his daughters. One of them looked about twelve years old or so.

Ken hadn't talked about the entire incident in a while, not since he had told Martha about it more than two years earlier. Probably, it had been time that the recurring boil was pierced again. So he finished his tale.

"Anyway, they couldn't wait to get me out of flight crew permanently, and honestly, I couldn't wait to get out. I still had a year to serve; we agreed that I would be temporarily transferred to the communications section. I thought perhaps I could at least write about flying. So that was it. I never went back to flight crew. I waited out my time in the communications branch, got out with an honorable discharge, took a journalism program at NYU and then started working at the *Era*."

"Did you ever feel sorry that you didn't go back to being an air force pilot?"

"Well, I miss flying, having the sense of seeing 'the big picture' in all its clarity, from horizon to horizon. But I loved my work as a reporter from the first day so I am not really sorry. In a way, flying brought me to what I do now."

Ken was aware of feeling just too damn vulnerable and small. That was not how he wanted to be at this point. He shook his head, as if to say "No," to any further revelations on his part. And he shifted conscious state, out of the past. He wanted to focus on the present, the point of Ms. Bowry's presence at the paper, and why they were here in her apartment having dinner. He actually felt like making love to this beautiful woman he hardly knew, as if that would somehow soothe the rawness he had exposed and felt.

He didn't know what to say next, so he changed the subject. Or at least he started to.

Sylkeen reached across the table again and put her hand on his cheek; then she got partway out of her chair, and leaning across the table, gently kissed his lips. It was clearly a *com*passionate, rather than a passionate, kiss, but her remarkably full, soft lips, and her sweet perfumed aura had their effects instantly. As he started to stir, she softly broke off the kiss and sat back down again.

Neither of them said anything for a bit, and Ken found himself not knowing what to make of, and unsure what to do about, what had just happened. She saved him the trouble, smiling and saying gently, "Shall we go over the files you brought, Ken?"

Ken gratefully said, "Good idea."

And with that, Sylkeen got up again, quickly gathered up their dishes, and walked towards the kitchen. She paused, half-turned, and said, "Why don't we work here at the table? I will be right back with some coffee." She paused, and this time perhaps just mildly teasing, she smiled and asked sweetly, "Or would you prefer that tour of the apartment now?"

Having regained his professional composure, and after thinking better than offering a provocative response that might have tested the waters further, Ken caught himself, thinking that they had each uncovered more than enough for a first private meeting, and besides, he finally remembered why he was supposed to be there in the first place. Instead he said, "Coffee is fine... *for now*; thanks." He watched for her response, and saw, or at least he thought he saw, just the slightest suggestive widening of her warm smile.

She tossed her hair back as she said, disappearing into the kitchen, "I'll be right back then, and I promise that I will be 'all ears'."

They spent the next forty-five minutes going over the files of some possible leads Ken was working on for the healthcare series. Sylkeen asked a few perceptive questions that suggested she understood the territory, and offered a couple of credible ideas about how she might be of assistance. Ken thought, *This might work out all right, after all.*

Ken noted that Sylkeen was careful not to inquire as to his sources, or how he had arrived at the conclusions that some HMOs might have certain legislators in their pockets. Sylkeen offered to arrange an interview for Ken and herself, if he wished, with the CEO of one of the HMOs he had mentioned, Bill Braxton of HealthLifeUSA, a prominent and charismatic industry bigwig with more clout than most.

When Ken asked her how she thought she could be of assistance in this particular case, she said that she had met the man socially, having gone to college with his wife. She had even played doubles tennis with the two of them on a couple of occasions. Ken was tempted to ask her who her doubles partner had been, and how many other healthcare heavy hitters she knew, but he decided to let those questions ride for a while.

Ken already knew that the CEO in question, Bill Braxton, had been a major contributor to the U.S President's election campaign, and that Braxton's cousin was a prominent senator and part of the President's inner circle of advisors on health matters. Ken asked Sylkeen how much influence she thought Braxton might be able to exert during the anticipated upcoming battle over the proposed corporate-favorable amendments to the U.S healthcare legislation that was expected to be brought forward sometime in the next year.

"He is a very powerful, very attractive man, Ken. He comes across as a nice guy, but he is definitely a 'take no prisoners' kind of businessperson."

Ken was also interested in the man's closest contacts in the Senate and Congress. He believed that whatever legislation would be put forward, to the extent that it might in any way threaten the increasingly larger territories that HMOs were continuing to carve out for themselves, Braxton would likely play a major part in making sure the offending clauses were killed.

Sylkeen said that, if Ken wanted, she could phone Braxton the next day, inform him of her new job and her interest in finding out his opinion of the proposed legislation. She would then suggest that the three of them meet, perhaps over lunch, for an off-the-record conversation, at which time they could make inquiries about Braxton's involvement in the process leading up to the legislation being put forward.

The lady definitely seemed genuinely eager and willing to help wherever she could. But could she truly be trusted? Ken thought back to a column he had written a few years earlier about studies into the question of which categories of professionals could tell with accuracy whether a person was being deceitful. A number of psychologists, criminal lawyers, preachers, high school teachers, newspaper reporters, and FBI and Secret Service agents, were shown videos of people lying or telling the truth. Only the Secret Service agents, probably because they had to hone their skills in analyzing people's intentions on the basis of very little information, were able to judge with reasonable precision, when the people shown on the videos were being deceitful and when they were being honest.

The findings of that study had been very sobering to Ken. They meant that, in all likelihood, no matter how experienced a journalist he or most of his colleagues ever became, and no matter how many thousands of people they interviewed, their judgments as to whether a person was telling the truth or not were likely to remain quite fallible. So he knew that he could *not* know with certainty whether or when Sylkeen Bowry –or anyone else for that matter–was being on the level. Hence the invariable need for corroborative evidence.

Ken glanced at his watch and was shocked to see that it was nearly eleven. They had talked, first about personal matters, and then about business, for more than three hours and he was now very aware of feeling tired. *Getting older was great! Not.* He put away his lingering fantasies for the night, and suggested to Sylkeen that he should be on his way.

In her nodding acknowledgement her body language, including the tilt of her head that caused her long, dark hair to trace sweetly across her face and bosom, suggested that she was sorry to have him leave. Ken realized that he was not ready for anything more, not right now; besides which, he began to think that he could be way off as to what the young woman actually wanted or was about. Perhaps she really was a straight shooter. Or not. Anyway, he realized that, after having spent the evening with her, he wanted her to be innocent of the indefinite charges he had in his mind. A handshake at the door, a last shared lingering look, and he turned and he stepped into the elevator. As he gently descended to the ground floor he thought about the fact that he had initially wanted to get rid of her. Now, *well*... he would see how she did with the Braxton interview, and would watch her very closely over the next while. He had taken on far more onerous tasks over the years.

After Ken left, Sylkeen made a lengthy long distance phone call during which she described the entire evening in detail to the person on the other end. The latter listened intently, asked a couple of questions, and then signed off, saying "Excellent work, dear. Now, do call every day or so and let me know what Mr. Hotshot Reporter is up to. ... Alright, then. Good night, now."

CHAPTER 20

Ken returned to his apartment shortly after eleven-thirty. During the brief cab ride he decided that he wanted meet the sender of the FedEx package he had received, ASAP. He especially wanted to find out what else his mysterious source knew about his father–both his life and his death–so he decided to comply with his demand that he remain a confidential source. The signal that he wanted to meet and that he was willing to assure him of anonymity, was that Ken use the byline 'Ken *F.* Simpson' in his next column.

Ken called in the paper on his way home from Sylkeen's and had them insert the middle initial into his byline for the article that was to be published in the next day's edition, about his reaction to winning the Paulson.

In the article Ken wrote of his appreciation of the honor of being the recipient of the Paulson Prize for Excellence in Investigative Print Journalism for material published in 2008. He also restated his commitment to providing the readers of his syndicated columns with all of the truth that he would unearth about the goings on behind the scenes in regard to the U.S. healthcare-related companies.

Ken had been told that an editorial would appear *The New York Era* the same day, praising him for his well-deserved award, and then, blowing the paper's own horn, mentioning some of the other reporters over the years who had also won major awards. Ken didn't mind in the least that the paper tried to make hay with his award; newspapers were in unprecedented competition with one another and all of the other types of media. The expanding elephant, the Internet, was daily providing more and better websites that offered to search all sources of news reporting, 24/7, for items related to whatever topics individual readers specified they wanted to know about, and then delivering them via e-mail, to wherever the readers preferred–their computers, cellphones, or PDAs. The IINCSN, the Individualized Internet News Clipping Service Network put a latest edition search engine and delivery system to work, full-time, on any subscriber's request for the latest information on virtually any target topics.

Four hours after the paper appeared on the streets in New York City the following morning, Ken received an e-mail that read, "Very pleased to learn that you are interested in meeting. I'll be in New York City later this evening. I suggest we meet for a drink at a restaurant I know called The Very Last Bistro, just off Times Square across from the Millennium Hotel. Let's say at eight. Kindly confirm by e-mail and please come on your own. I have already made a reservation, in your name, for table number 12, which affords us the most privacy."

Ken immediately e-mailed his acknowledgement and acceptance of time and place for their meeting. He thought of attempting to have someone else from the paper take photos surreptitiously of his mysterious correspondent, and/or possibly secretly wearing his miniaturized digital audio recorder or using his video-streaming cellphone to transmit their conversation to his own recording equipment at home. Each thought was quickly negated by the likely possibility that if he tried any such maneuvers, then their first meeting would likely be their last. Normally Ken would not be so conniving; but then again, this interview was personal. After weighing the pros and cons, he decided to forget the sneaky stuff. Bottom line: he didn't want to turn off a possible major source of important information at their very first meeting.

Before he left Sylkeen's apartment the previous evening, Ken gave her the assignment of double-checking the stats regarding costs of healthcare in the U.S, Canada and western European countries, since that was supposed to be her expertise and it wouldn't involve giving her any personal names of his present or prospective sources of information. He also asked her to check the annual corporate reports and balance sheets of a number of HMOs, pharmaceutical, and biomedical companies, since it was clear that the healthcare sector was now the biggest and most profitable sector of the economy. He wanted to know which of these companies owned outright, or had major stakes in, any media outlets. Since he had already covered a large part of the same territory himself, whatever she reported back to him might give him some idea of whether she really did have the goods–professionally speaking.

While Sylkeen was thus occupied, Ken busied himself with other matters, including making appointments to speak to the doctors who Dr. Larson had said he would contact for him. A voice mail from Dr. Larson left the previous evening had provided the names and phone numbers of several such individuals. The old doc also said that he had spoken of Ken to them and had let them know that Ken would treat their views and information respectfully. One of the things Ken wanted to discuss with the doctors was the effects of HMOs and PPOs on their practices.

Ken was not looking forward to being part of the news department's goodbye lunch for Martha, who was going to be leaving later in the afternoon for Ottawa.

After the group lunch that was attended by several of Martha's long-time colleagues, she and Ken walked over to a nearby favorite coffee shop to chat and have a more personal goodbye. Ken asked Martha to contact a couple of key people in healthcare in Canada when she arrived, which she promised to do. She also said 'yes', without question, to Ken's request that she henceforth e-mail him at his private Yahoo address, rather than using his e-mail address at the newspaper. Martha was just happy to oblige. After all, she didn't want Sylkeen leaning over Ken's shoulder reading her messages to him. Hell, she didn't want the young thing leaning over his shoulder–period!

She was initially somewhat more reluctant to comply with his other request, however, which was that, for the next several days, that she *not* report the contents of her upcoming interviews to anyone else at *The New York Era*, at least not until she had discussed them with Ken and he had made a determination of whether he wanted the information she uncovered to be sent on to the paper. After Ken had briefed her on his conversations with Dr. Larson and his concerns about the true motivations of Ms.

Bowry, however, she acceded to this request, also. If he is suspicious of Ms. Bowry's intentions, she thought, then he would be more likely to keep his distance. *Yeah, right!*

Ken passed across the table towards Martha a small gift box, which surprised and clearly touched Martha. She opened it to find an attractive and rather expensive watch, on the back of which was engraved, "For M. With affection, K."

She laughed warmly at his gesture, and then lustily said, "*Well*, Mr. Simpson! You? Sentimental? I thought that your motto was "Lay 'em and leave 'em."

Ken smiled but said nothing. He merely took another small box out of other coat pocket and passed *it* along to her. When Martha opened this second small box her expression registered confusion. The tiny attached card said that the enclosed key was to a 2009 Honda SUV. The card also said, "Drive safely. Love, Ken."

Martha was taken aback. She said, "What is…?"

Ken interrupted, smiling. "Your new car, I suppose."

"What the heck are you talking about, Ken?"

"It's my present to you, with thanks for helping me win the Paulson and for keeping me much happier these many months than I probably had a right to be."

The fifteen minute long conversation that followed, with its protestations from Martha and reassuringly appreciative comments from Ken, left them both momentarily drained. Finally, Ken won, clinching her acceptance of his gift giving by saying, "Martha, I really care about you. I wouldn't let you drive that old jalopy to Ottawa, let alone around it in one of their lousy winters."

Martha looked admiringly at Ken, gently shook her head, sighed and said, "You know, Hon, you have been my best friend over the past few years and, I might add, my best lover *ever*." She seemed a little flustered, and for the first time, Ken realized that Martha might just have fallen for him more than he had ever suspected. Or, maybe it was just that they would now be hundreds of miles apart, and each thought the other might not choose to be 'faithful', especially since, except in the midst of passion, they had never used the "L" word with one another.

"Listen," she said, her face beet red, "I've got to run. Thank you, thank you, thank you. I'll accept your gift, on condition that you visit me in Ottawa very soon."

"Deal."

"Alright. I should get to Ottawa tomorrow evening, and I'll be staying at the newspaper's apartment. And I'll contact these people you have asked me to. They're pretty high up, so it may take me a few days to get to see them. I'll try to interview them as soon as I can."

Ken stood as she got up from the table and they hugged and friend-kissed just a little longer and more intimately than business types at that restaurant were probably used to seeing. Or, maybe not.

Ken walked with Martha to get her new car, which Ken had parked at a nearby underground garage. They then went back to her apartment, loaded up her things, and rather excitedly now because of her new 'wheels', Martha began her luxurious ride through upper New York state towards the U.S.-Canada border. Ken drove her old car to the dealership that had agreed to take it as a meager, 'mercy' trade-in, and then took a cab back to the office in the mid-afternoon, where he worked until after seven.

Ken left for the restaurant about 7:30pm, feeling torn up about Martha, turned on about Sylkeen, and curious as hell about his dinner date.

CHAPTER 21

Ken arrived at The Very Last Bistro a few minutes before eight. An upscale neighborhood restaurant ten minutes cab ride from his apartment, it appeared that several of the young families with their generally well-behaved children in tow were just leaving, and the later diners, primarily older singles and even older empty-nesters, were starting to take their places. When he gave his name, the maitre d' checked the reservation book and then deferentially showed Ken to a table near the rear that was set apart from nearby tables behind a partition with plants lining its top, and isolated from the line of sight of most of the other diners, and from the front door.

He began to think about the FedEx package again, its contents and what the person he was going to meet had to do with all of this business. He recalled the nostalgia and poignancy evoked by the videotape he had viewed in his apartment, the horrific statement about his father's death having not been an accident, and the admittedly distressing comments about the potential threat to his own safety and well-being.

Ken started to feel his anger building again. He was about to meet one of his father's supposedly close friends, who had said on the tape that he somehow had a hand in the circumstances leading to his dad's death.

"Mr. Simpson." said the commanding yet surprisingly humane-sounding voice from the videotape.

Ken looked up to see a tall, somewhat filled out, white crew-cut-and-bearded man in his late seventies or early eighties, with an imposing bearing that Ken immediately recognized as military. The older man's somewhat sad but still energetic eyes looked intently at him, obviously measuring. As Ken extended his hand to shake the large and surprisingly warm one being offered, he said, "Hello, whatever your name is; what is it, anyway?"

"We will get to that shortly, Mr. Simpson… Ken."

The stranger sat back down and began to speak authoritatively. "Ken, I have some things to tell you that are extremely important, so please listen carefully. Before I start, however, you must agree to only report what I specifically tell you that you can. You may take notes but no recordings of what I have to say. By the way, are you carrying any sort of audio or video recording device or cellphone?"

Since reaching his sixties Ken seldom felt intimidated, but he did now. He didn't much like being on the receiving end of piercing questions. He recalled guiltily that he had thought of possibly secretly recording their conversation but had decided against it, predicting that this initial contact might be merely introductory and include some sort of test of his trustworthiness. He was relieved to be able to honestly say, "No, I don't have my recorder with me, although I would like to tape some of our conversations in the future, if you wouldn't mind."

The older man said, "Only *if* and *when* I tell you—*in advance, mind you*—that you may do so. Is that agreed?"

The 'question' was clearly of a non-negotiable nature, and Ken nodded his head in the affirmative, agreeing to a condition that he had seldom accepted in all of his years of interviewing. But this time was undoubtedly different. Before the next obvious question could be asked, he took out his cellphone and placed it on the table, face up, so that it could be easily seen to be 'off'.

His new acquaintance said, "Ken, my name is Lieutenant Colonel Dan Stevens, U.S.A.F., retired. Around fifty-two years ago I was one of our Air Force's liaison officers for the Avro Arrow project. With what I am going to tell you now, and if you do things my way, with what else I can add later, you are likely to end up with *several* stories that may just lead to a couple of other Paulsons, and more importantly, certain other results that I am sure will be far more meaningful to you. But, if you reveal prematurely any of what I have to say, or my identity, *to anyone*, then not only will you *not* get the most important material that I might offer, but you will put me, yourself and," now he paused, looked sharply at Ken, and then continued, "possibly your son, Brad, as well, in deep jeopardy."

Ken reacted as if he had just received to a 220-volt electrical shock. His head and spine had been leaning forward to better hear Stevens, and suddenly snapped back as if he were coming to attention.

Ken was livid; when he spoke his voice was loud enough for people at the nearest tables to turn towards him and stare in fear. "Now just one goddamn minute! If you're threatening my son then I say you can go to hell." Ken began to get up out of his seat.

The older man's tone became reassuring, while still maintaining its authority. "Hold on now, Ken. Please. *Sit down!* I don't think that you understand. *I* am not the one who is threatening you or your son. I am simply warning you about what might happen, at the hands of others, if you aren't very careful about how you use whatever information I choose to share with you. You have no idea what or who you would be dealing with. If they find out that you know what I am about to share with you, and how you came to know it, and that you may be about to print it, before you and I are both ready for you to do so, then *you*, not I, will be the one to have put your son's well being, and both of ours, at risk."

"But why would 'they' want to hurt him or me… or you, for that matter?"

Lieutenant Colonel Stevens stared at Ken, seemingly measuring him again. After some consideration, Stevens asked, "Ken, do you really not appreciate what a potentially lethal can of worms you have opened up with this new series of yours on the state of healthcare in our country?"

Ken said, "Stevens, some people are always getting pissed at me. I know that. But what makes you think that this series is any riskier for me, or anyone else, than others I have done in the past?"

Stevens frowned and shook his head, evidently disappointed with Ken's naiveté. "Because, Ken, 'before', you were just another reporter looking for a sensational story. But now, with the Paulson crown on your head, you can't be so easily dismissed. You have been all over the media for days; hell, you're the media flavor-of-the-month. And a hell of a lot of people read your columns. Right now you have a temporary titanium-strength mantle of credibility that makes you much harder to discount as either an incompetent reporter or another 'bleeding heart liberal'. And it is this blanket of legitimacy that your words will now come wrapped up in that potentially makes you a serious threat to too many people in high places, both in business and in government. I mean, look what you have already done to change the way the 9/11 and other American terrorist victims are going to be looked after from here on in, all because of the powerful reaction that you, deliberately or not, whipped up in your readers through your articles.

"And, Ken, you surely know that healthcare is our country's greatest growth industry, even bigger than the military, one that can only expand through both good times and bad. Heart attacks don't wait for economic recovery; in fact, they may increase in times of financial distress. And in good times, the type A's literally make themselves sick through overwork. Cancer cells don't much care which direction the stock market is moving. Diabetes doesn't depend upon on the health of the economy or whether we are at war, either. The people who run some of the major healthcare-related companies make fabulous profits out of both childhood and adult illnesses. Your series, however, if you are successful in digging too deep and writing too much, could threaten the health of those businesses."

Ken asked, "Are you talking about particular Managed Health Organizations, Preferred Providers Organizations, or pharmaceutical companies? Are you really suggesting that they would *dare* do anything physical to me, or those close to me? That's rather far-fetched, don't you think?"

Lieutenant Colonel Stevens's voice dropped an octave and now came from a previously unleashed and terribly foreboding place. "Ken, you really still don't get it, do you? It's not *all* of them that would do something; they don't have to. It just takes a few companies whose very continued existence or profit base is threatened, and they don't have to do anything in-house, either. They can simply outsource the work; in other words, they can hire people, or companies, whose job it is to do something, anything, to make a possible threat to their corporate interests go away."

Ken's heart rate ramped up. "And you are suggesting that is what might happen in the future, is that right? Or has it already happened? Is that what you are saying; that one, or some, companies have actually hired someone, or some other individuals or organizations, to cause me or those I care about, harm?"

Stevens's impatience surfaced. Although they were less than twenty years apart in age, and Ken was already past his middle years, the Lieutenant Colonel said, "Young man, I am not simply suggesting it. I am telling you directly what I know has already happened."

"And how would you know that? That I, or my son, or yourself for that matter, are in danger?"

Stevens did not respond immediately. His eyes seemed to be focused at some point at the back of Ken's head. It was as if he were trying to peer deeply into Ken's psyche, carefully sifting through and weighing whatever he found there, in order to reach a decision.

Finally, after at least a minute that to Ken seemed to last an hour, Stevens blinked, refocused, and now engaged Ken directly. "I know it because I am still a senior partner in the organization that has been hired to stop you–by whatever means necessary!"

The background music emanating from the loudspeakers and the din of the other diners helped keep what Ken said next clearly audible to only the couple of tables about five or six feet from their own.

"Fuck you, Stevens. You and whomever you work for can go to hell. You people are nuts if you think you can frighten me into keeping quiet. Now, if you will excuse me…" Ken began to get out of his chair again.

When Lieutenant Colonel Dan Stevens issued an order, no one usually dared disobey it without the utmost consideration being given to the severe consequences implied in the deadly cold tone of his voice. *"Sit… down… Mr. Simpson!"*

Ken froze in position halfway out of his chair. His mouth still moved however, and he spat out the words, "Why the hell should I?"

Stevens's next words tasered him and he fell back into his seat. "Because," Stevens said, "I am here to help you stop them from getting to you. I believe that I can hold them off for a while, and perhaps give you enough information so that you might be able to expose enough of their entire operation to get them to back off permanently."

"Why would you do that for me?"

"Because I owe you that much."

Ken asked, "What do you mean?"

"I mean I owe you, or more to the point, I owe it to your father to try and protect you. And I owe it to myself. I am an old man who wants to finally be able to sleep without dreaming of sabotaged airplanes falling out of the sky, with their pilots screaming at me all the way down, "You traitor, Stevens! You bloody bastard!" Now, Ken, are you beginning to get the picture?"

Ken didn't reply. He stared at Stevens, whose fluid face was succumbing to a chaotic procession of emotions; sadness, anger, guilt, and disgust kept tumbling over one another in seemingly random sequence.

Stevens said, "Ken, you have already threatened and pissed off some of the most powerful healthcare business people in the country. And TAMPRR has been hired by them to stop you, one way or another."

Ken said, "You talked about TAMPRR on the tape you sent me. "Who, or what, the hell *is* TAMPRR, anyway? And what exactly do you mean by 'one way or another'?

Stevens's voice softened and slowed. "TAMPRR Inc. Spelled T-A-M-P-R-R. Anyone who asks is told that the letters stands for 'The American Management Profit Recovery and Retention company'. But those initials stood for something else entirely when the core group was formed back in 1958. Back then TAMPRR stood for 'The Arrow Manipulation, Profit, Rescue and Recovery mission'.

Ken impatiently said, "Say more, please."

Stevens said, "Sure. The original organization that constituted TAMPRR did such a near-perfect job that it continued in business even after it successfully killed the Avro Arrow program, and it has grown over the years into what you would call a semi-covert organization responsible for making sure, for one thing, that the kind of bad press you might produce about some of our clients, doesn't happen. Or, if it does happen once, then we see to it that it doesn't occur again."

Ken caught the chink in Stevens's comments, and asked, "Why did you say your group's job was only 'near-perfect'?

Stevens responded with some irritation, like a military commander who cannot stand even partial failure. "We never counted on the blind dedication of so many people in that country to never let the politicians or the public forget about the demise of the Avro Arrow program. Over the years, there have been more than a dozen books published about the Avro Arrow, in addition to some TV 'specials', a made-for-television movie, and even at least one goddamn play. At this very moment, in fact, there are actually groups of civilian volunteers in Canada who are building scale, and even full-size, models of that fifty year old aircraft, and they intend to parade and even fly some of them around Canada later this year.

"Some of these Canadian Avro Arrow fans keep pointing in the direction of the U.S., but without any conclusive proof as to *who* in our country might have done *what* to kill their beloved airplane–and their military aircraft industry. And no matter how much bullshit TAMPRR feeds to their media, some of those guys have enough brains to see through what we are still trying to do to discredit them and their hunches. Anyway, some of our original clients are still paying us a sizable yearly retainer to keep a lid on the rabble-rousers up there, and TAMPRR Inc. is happy to continue to take their money and do whatever we can to make sure they don't get too much publicity about what they are doing. As far as I am concerned, who really gives a shit about what those Arrow fanatics say or do. All they can do is write books and produce plays and model airplanes and such. Meanwhile, fifty years ago *we* ended up with the breakthroughs in technology that they had made, as well as many of their best designers and engineers, and ever since, the U.S.A. has made some fantastic planes to protect our country–and theirs, I might add.

"Of course, their major military aircraft building ambitions went down the tubes, permanently. So they griped. But we didn't control their media then as well as we control theirs–and our's–now, so it is not surprising that there would be some continuing 'leakage' long after we deep-sixed their ambitions. Hell, most of the guys who built that plane are either dead or in their seventies and eighties now, so the whole issue should finally die down in a few years, as the few remaining ones bite the dust." Having finished his summary Stevens settled back into his chair with a satisfied smile.

At that moment a somewhat nervous but pleasant-looking young waitress appeared. It occurred to Ken that she had probably seen, if not heard, some of the animated conversation that had been going on at their table. Sometimes reading from the little piece of paper that she held in her slightly trembling hand, and only occasionally glancing directly into the faces of the two intense men at her table, she earnestly described the 'specials' of the evening. Stevens and Ken quickly put her out of her misery when they said that they would decide on their entrees later, but each ordered a glass of an Italian wine that she hesitently recommended. Undoubtedly relieved, she turned and sped off to carry out their orders.

Ken had been watching and listening very intently while Stevens talked about TAMPRR and its various reprehensible deeds. Stevens was a proud man who, in spite of what happened to his friend, Frank Simpson, seemed satisfied with at least the outcome of TAMPRR's original handiwork. The Canadian Avro Arrow aircraft program had been killed, and that country had successfully been permanently taken out of the whole military aircraft production game.

Ken decided that, while Stevens might be willing to help him, probably out of a sizable amount of guilt, the old soldier was still a proud man. He helped defeat a neighboring country's military efforts in a major area and that counted for a lot in his book, even if the country was an ally of the United States. Ken decided that he would have to watch Stevens very carefully; the man might be guilt-ridden but was hardly a totally disillusioned part of TAMPRR.

Ken asked, "So, since you say that you want to help me, tell me how TAMPRR plans to stop me and my column?"

"Stopping bad press is one of our company's specialties. Look, TAMPRR has two divisions. One is involved in lawful business activities, especially public relations and lobbying. You can even find us listed on various registries of legitimate lobbyists, and on the paid consultancy staff of the highest levels of politicians in America, Canada, and a number of our other allies, for that matter. The other division of TAMPRR is the rather 'darker' side of the company, and is the main reason why most organizations really hire us. This second division doesn't play nice. It makes up its own rules, and it does whatever it needs to do to get the job accomplished."

Ken was incredulous. "Like what?"

Stevens replied, "Oh, come on, Ken. I know that business reporting has never been your beat. But remember that most of the wars that American corporations have fought have taken place on foreign soil. And, believe it or not, relatively few of the biggest business battles ever receive much notice in our media, and that is the way we like things, and we want to make sure that things stay that way. Any business reporter who gets too nosey finds that his business sources dry up really quickly and he is soon out of a job. So, they play along, just as most of them did before the Internet bubble burst. They sucked up to the 'new economy' people so hard that the only real companies that made any money for a time were those who sold lip balm.

"You know very well, Ken, if you are honest with yourself, that most of our media provide just different flavors of corporate-controlled junk food, for Christ's sake. A very few entrepreneurial reporters like yourself, and a select number of non-conformist media outlets like *The New York Era*, dare to be devoted to actually getting the truth out, no matter who might get hurt by being exposed for their wrongdoing. But most other media in this country are owned by one or other of a few conglomerates, and so their stables of various print and electronic outlets just piggyback on one another's skewed reporting. Like television programs promoting the films the Hollywood studios that are owned by the same conglomerate are busy churning out.

"Furthermore, even the media that are owned by different companies often prefer to chase each others' stories rather than spend time and money to go digging for their own newsworthy items. You know full well, Ken, that when media outlet A sends out a reporter, and the story gets printed or aired, then competing media go and interview the same people about the same events. These people tell everyone the same stories, and all the reporters end up putting essentially the same stuff on air and into their papers. Its not as if, with over three hundred million people in our own country, and billions more around the world, that there aren't enough *original* stories of interest for everyone to go and find their own. Most of our media aren't even that interested in reporting on what is actually going on out there in the world; they just want to look like they are. And TAMPRR helps make sure that they stay that way, chasing each others' tails and staying away from stories our clients don't want publicized."

Ken felt his own defenses rising, even though he basically agreed with Stevens. He knew that too few reporters searched out original stories; most just did their own versions of those that had already been covered by their competitors. Watching the evening television news programs, it didn't much matter, most of the time, which channel or network a person watched. Of course, that was comforting, in a way. For most people it meant that they didn't feel like they were missing anything by watching one so-called news source instead of another. In actual fact, though, Ken knew that most of them were missing *most* of the news out there because too many media organizations really didn't view that as their primary job. Their main goal was to sell commercial time to promote cleansers, cars and pharmaceuticals. Only programs like '60 Minutes' still did any real news investigative reporting, and on occasion, various groups and organizations had even gotten them to kill stories.

Ken also knew that it was not the reporters' faults, mostly. Too often the word came from on high to cut costs, use 'feeds' from other sources as much as possible, and piggyback on the momentarily 'in' story. Conglomerates viewed their media businesses as 'delivery systems' for their advertisers and for skewed articles that kept certain political parties in or out of power, and certain companies' products from becoming the focus of potentially embarrassing or damaging news. The ink devoted to Internet start-ups and their overblown IPOs being a particularly painful case in point for most small-time American investors. At the very least, when newspapers did report negative news about any of their sacred cows, they were prone to bury them in very brief articles on the inside pages, or wherever they would do the least damage.

Ken said, "So, now you are saying that news outlets *should* be more independent and that they should be digging up and reporting on their own original stories? But wouldn't that work against what TAMPRR wants?"

Stevens laughed. "Of course it would, and you and I both know it. But imagine if the General leading the First army kept on sending his troops to fight on a front that is already being handled by the Third army. Unless that many armed forces personnel are actually required, they each should be fighting on different fronts. And you know I am dead on, Ken."

Ken was getting a little exasperated since their conversation had become something other than what he was seeking when he had first signaled a desire to meet the sender of the FedEx package. He said, "Alright, I get your point. And I basically agree with you. But what does that have to do with why we are here? What is the *point* of your point?"

"My *point*, Ken, is that there are a whole bunch of wars going on, right now, including the battle over control of healthcare in this and other countries. Meanwhile, most of our media pretend much of the time that it isn't even happening. Either they don't know or want to know, or they do know but don't want to investigate and report on it because that would mean less healthcare-related, 'help wanted' advertisements and less drug advertising in their newspapers. Meanwhile, ordinary Americans continue to suffer and to pay for the *dis*-service they are receiving."

"Hell," hissed Stevens, "I, and you too, can remember when our American newspapers used to have real balls. But then, you just have to look at the various 'patriotic' vanilla flavors that our embedded reporters and their kiss-ass networks have churned out about Iraq to see that they and their masters were almost entirely under the control of our military and the administration. Of course, that time I was really happy that all you guys were suckling at our teats; that gave us virtually complete editorial influence over what you people reported."

Ken replied, "I don't know why you are so upset, then. After all, you just told me that you approved of the 'embedding' program in Iraq, and in the other places we have invaded since. So what are you so hot about?"

Stevens glared at him, and said, "What pisses me off so much, Ken, is that even I have finally just come to hate the *abuse* of power. And, of course, I am guilty of it myself, so I know that I also hate myself. I am like a goddamn tobacco executive, for Christ's sake. How do those guys sleep at night? Maybe like I do: goddamn poorly! That's why I am here. I am getting very old and I am fed up with the bullshit. This is not what your father and I were fighting for, back when we had our youth, our ideals and our gonads. But look at what we have turned into. Why is it that so many in the media were so surprised and shocked by what had been going on at Enron or Anderson, or in the whole damn energy, high tech, and accounting industries a few years back? Why was it that so many major newspapers, news magazines, talk radio, and television news programs pumped, or should I say 'pimped' for the whores on Wall Street and in Silicon Valley who screwed so many people, what with the 'rah-rah' pieces on how everyone was going to become rich by investing in the 'new economy'? Why was it that so few voices in the media expressed any doubt about what was happening, until most of these companies went belly up. And by then, of course, it was too late to save the millions of schnooks who got stuck with hundreds of *billions* of dollars of worthless stock. Only then did a lot of your media buddies express shock, laid low for a while, and then crawled out of their well-padded caves and went right on to promoting the next 'hot new thing'."

Ken wanted to reply but didn't get past inhaling. Lieutenant Colonel Stevens was on a roll and Ken wasn't going to get to interrupt him. Not yet, anyway. "Why is it, Ken, that the public doesn't trust that their newspapers and the other media will make it their business to find out what the hell is really going on, and then damn well expose the deceits and the impending disasters before they occur?"

Ken said nothing. He was guilty by association, and he knew it. He had invested early in the 'new economy' and had gotten out of some high-flying Internet stocks at the personal suggestion of one of his close friends, the paper's top business writer. Ken was not sure why, but sometimes his friend gave Ken investing tips several days or weeks before he offered the same advice to his readers. So Ken lived in his own darkened home of glass–and Lieutenant Colonel Stevens was simply shining an angry light through it. Truth be told, there were precious few innocents left in the media or anywhere else in positions of influence, for that matter, and he was certainly not one of them. He always knew that, in part, his investigative articles were his own mea culpa, and the Paulson prize simply told him that he was practicing his penance well.

Thankfully, Stevens continued in a somewhat softer vein. "I will tell you why people now have trouble trusting the so-called 'business news' channels and newspaper writers. Where the hell were they while the 'new economy' balloon was getting ready to blow up? They all had their mouths on the balloon, using their every breath and written word to help it make it bigger. And all the millionaire hosts of their own business shows and their business writer-friends were making a hell of a lot of money, being given first dibs at IPOs, interviewing and promoting companies they were all too often greedily invested in themselves. Why are there fewer and fewer newspapers and television networks that dare to hire guys like you to ferret out what is really going on, and then make that public?"

Ken didn't reply. Aside from his own minor part in bailing out of the stock market's 'irrational exuberance' near the beginning of the millennium, he was for the most part a Boy Scout type who was fortunate enough to have the right editor at the right paper. He had, of course, heard from many other reporters over the years, who told him either straight out or in so many words, how much they envied his working situation because their own editors and publishers had time and again given them SASA, or 'safe and superficial assignments', while stopping them from pursuing valuable leads that had been phoned or e-mailed or couriered in from whistleblowers and contrarians with a conscience to contend with or, sometimes, an axe to grind.

At this point the waitress suddenly reappeared, deposited a small breadboard bearing some freshly baked multigrain bread, the two glasses of wine and two glasses of ice water. Just as quickly, she was gone.

Stevens cut to the chase. "And more relevant to our meeting today, Ken, why do you think there has been so very little of an investigative nature in our media up until now, as far as healthcare is concerned? Almost everyone in the know or in power is silent. Meanwhile, the most reputable, advertisement-free consumer-oriented magazine in the country writes about the problems inherent in our healthcare system, describes the comparatively considerable advantages of the Canadian Medicare system, and almost none of the other major magazines or newspapers even report or comment on these findings and conclusions. Their position is, 'Honor thy advertisers that thy days in print or on the air shall be long, and thy pockets shall be filled with coin…' "

The waitress's reappearance beside them interrupted Stevens's riff. They both ordered light, and the disappointed order-taker turned in a semi-huff and walked toward the kitchen.

Ken asked, "Why are you bothering to tell me all this? It seems you have gone along with TAMPRR's actions for fifty bloody years. So who are you to talk?"

"Ken, you are right, of course. And I will tell you why. Aside from the fact that I owe it to your father, and to you, I am talking to you because I am truly sick and tired of all the games, and the real cost of this corruption, which is the killing of Americans. I could handle it in wartime; in a just war the loss of life is regrettable and, of course, terrible. But it might be justifiable. But when the loss of American lives is the result of 'the way of doing business', then that is where I have to finally get off. "

"Look, Ken, about two years ago, in order to gear up to help some of our corporate clients, we were invited to one of the biggest HMOs in this country. They had us watching TV monitors and listening in to the two-way conversations of some of their frontline people, the ones who handle the requests from doctors and patients about having tests, diagnostic assessments, and even surgeries, done. Our 'guide' was the company's CEO himself. He had this entire room filled with closed-circuit television monitors and people, the ones he called his 'field observers and remote coaches', listening in to the calls to see how well the frontline folks handled them, and coaching them through their earpieces.

"Anyway, this CEO guy loved football and used football terms the whole time. He said the frontline people were the defensive frontline, whose job it was to keep those calling in away from the company's end zone –meaning the company's profit. He said that the job of the 'frontline' was to keep the other side away from the company's pocketbook by doing things like repeatedly asking for more information on the patient, the doctor, the request, anything to delay the decision–which he referred to as 'taking a defensive time out'; anything that might work in delaying, or far preferably, denying service altogether. And the people in the 'observation booth upstairs' had direct audio contact with the frontline workers at all times, so that they could coach them on tactics, just like a football coach can call in plays to his team through his quarterback's or defensive linebacker's earpiece. A complete rejection of a request to do exploratory surgery was referred to as 'saving a field goal'; refusal to allow heart bypass or other major surgery was called 'saving a touchdown'.

"At the same time, the guy talked about his 'offensive team'. His team could score by signing up more companies and their employees, raising premiums, increasing co-pays, and de-listing certain procedures altogether. He even bragged that some senior executives' remunerations were directly tied to a complicated formula that took into account how much net profit the HMO made and what percentage of claims and services they had disallowed that year."

Ken was disgusted at what he was hearing, but kept his voice level. He said, "But I repeat, you have gone along with them for so long, why are you ready to do something about it now when you haven't before now?"

Stevens replied softly, "Because two years ago I wasn't also dying from colon cancer."

Ken's head had been down while he was making notes. Now he looked up and said, "I am sorry."

"Don't be."

Ken said, "You can help me now to expose these companies and their practices. And help me to understand what and whom I am up against as I move ahead with my investigations. Point me in the right direction. You can tell me more about TAMPRR; how it operates; who the other principal members are, and so on."

Stevens nodded, seemingly to himself. His expression slowly transmuted from what initially looked like despair into determination. He spoke thoughtfully: "I already told you that T.A.M. stands for 'The Arrow Manipulation'. They... we, the five of us who originally came together, handled the whole business of getting the Avro Arrow project killed off. We had a very substantial budget that included a hefty bonus that we collected on February 21,1959, the day after the program was killed.

"In order to achieve that ultimate result, we spent millions to blackmail and bribe whichever politicians and bureaucrats we needed to, in order to ensure that the Arrow program would be shut down completely. And when it was killed we refused to let them give their baby, that bloody magnificent plane, a decent burial."

Ken asked, "Who do you mean by 'them'?"

"'Them' is Avro Aircraft, the company that built the Arrow. By 'them' I also mean a few of the members of their parliament who had fought to preserve at least the prototypes, if not the program, and 'them' is also the Canadian public who had paid for its development and production. After all, they had the best aircraft of its type in the world by far, already flying, and at least ten years ahead of anything our own aircraft companies had in the works! Your father and I couldn't believe what Avro had accomplished in four tiny frigging years! From seemingly impossible specs to fundamental scientific breakthroughs to successful flight testing, with a full *production line* already in place, in four little years? Unheard of at that time; unmatched since. They built their prototypes right on the production line they created. They were 'good to go' in four years, and we shot their baby down, right out of the sky. And if we hadn't destroyed their program when we did, within weeks they would have had an even more powerful, all-Canadian designed and built *engine* installed in the next Arrows coming off their assembly line. Then they would have set even more impressive altitude and speed records. We just couldn't take that chance."

Ken asked, "And who were 'we'?"

"'We' were our American corporate clients, our military... hell, our whole country. American aircraft manufacturers had everything to lose. Most of our allies–the French, the British, and some other NATO countries–had already declared interest in possibly purchasing some Arrows. The flyboys who went to Toronto to see them built and flown, just about got heart attacks and hard-ons as they watched the bloody Arrows just taxiing down the tarmac. They looked like smaller Concordes. Hell, some of the guys who built the Arrow went on to help design and build the Concorde. That's how good that plane and its designers were.

"Anyway, by the time our operatives got through with some of the key people in their government, air force, and federal bureaucracy, not only did we get them to kill the project, we bloody well convinced them, for security's sake, you understand, that they had to take blowtorches–*blowtorches*–to most of the prototypes. They maimed and killed their own babies, and then sold their parts off for scrap. *For scrap, for Christ's sake!*

"We also 'accidentally' let the media get photos of the disassembled Arrows, and let it be known that *all* of the blueprints and tooling, and *all* of the completed prototypes, had been destroyed. In the process we basically destroyed the company that built that plane. And then we swooped in within hours and hired away some of their best engineers and technicians, for McBowan Aircraft and our other clients. In short, we raped Avro Aircraft, burned most of her babies, stole one of them, and spirited away a lot of their mothers, those who had given birth to the Arrow in the first place."

Ken responded. "But why force them to destroy even their prototypes? Why obliterate everything?"

Lieutenant Colonel Stevens leaned menacingly close to Ken, and with a defiant smirk, said, "Because we wanted to punish those Canadian bastards, to scar them for a lifetime, for daring to best our best. We wanted them to hurt so badly, that they and their country would never, ever, *dare* to try to do such a thing again! For the Avro people, for their military, for their whole damn nation, the message was so purposefully brutally painful, it provided 'a genuine trauma to their national psyche', as I once heard a military shrink describe it. It totally demoralized and de-energized their scientific and technical aircraft community. And they never got over it, and still haven't to this day.

"And they probably never will. Their military aircraft ambitions died with the Arrow. Oh, we let them build the odd tail or wing section of some of our American aircraft, but mostly just for show."

Stevens sat back in his chair as the waitress delivered their light meals. Then he said, "Why, even my own Canadian cousin, Ronnie, who went into engineering at the University of Toronto in 1956, one year after the Arrow project was started, ended up being burnt professionally. I still remember the pride he took in being in engineering in Canada back then. He and his classmates believed, with all the publicity surrounding the Avro Arrow's promise, that when they graduated in 1961, they were going to go on and make the greatest military and commercial airplanes in the world. They were planning to work for Avro in Toronto, Canadair in Montreal, or Computing Devices near Ottawa. They were going to be the cocks of the walk. Instead, by the time they graduated the Avro Arrow program had been dead and buried for a couple of years. Of course, I knew he and his classmates would never get a chance to work on the project themselves, but I couldn't tell him what was going to happen to the Arrow. He still doesn't know that his cousin helped screw his country's best military product ever, and left him without a chance to do much real engineering. He became a science high school teacher instead."

Ken decided to push for a fuller answer to his earlier question, so he repeated it. "But I am still not entirely clear; why destroy *everything* to do with the Avro Arrow, at least as far as the Canadians knew?"

Stevens said, "Don't you get it? We wanted to, we needed to... to break the Canadians' *spirit*. They were a real threat to our corporate clients. Also, we wanted their best brains down here in America. We didn't want them to build anything else that would challenge us. As it was, Avro was already building a frigging 'flying saucer' that they called the Avrocar. They had been at it since 1953 and even had it flying up and down the tarmac at their main airport, although it only ever got a few feet off the ground. Our guys eventually took over that program as well."

Lieutenant Colonel Stevens laughed loudly and shook his head with what Ken couldn't decide was admiration or astonishment. "Honestly, Ken, these guys were incorrigible." Stevens laughed and shook his head again. "Our clients just had to get those guys and their projects Stateside. We convinced the Canadian government to stop building the Avrocar, and our guys took over the design and development outright. That's the honest truth."

An early memory in the recesses of Ken's mind dislodged from its subterranean perch and popped up into his consciousness. He was a teenager at the time, and had been 'bugging' his father about reports on the local news of flying saucers, or as they were being termed, 'unidentified flying objects'. His father responded on one of these occasions of his child's endless questioning by showing Ken a newspaper photo of Canada's 'flying saucer', with a caption that referred to the picture having been taken at the commercial airport just outside of Toronto. His dad had howled at the idea of commercial passengers looking out their aircraft's window and seeing the saucer-shaped object, which was about twenty feet across and had a bubble canopy off-center where the pilot flying it could be seen. Frank Simpson added, with a warm chuckle aimed at his wide-eyed son who was now gazing at the picture of the Avrocar, "Well, son, here is one '*identified* flying object'!"

Stevens was speaking. "And by the time my cousin finished engineering in 1961, the Arrow program had been dead for two years, and he was one of the few guys to get a *real* engineering job. I remember him telling me about when one of the Canadian aircraft companies came to the major Canadian universities for the graduating engineering students' career recruitment days. After taking up an hour of Ronnie's precious time when he could have been interviewing other companies, this Canadian aircraft company's recruiter says to Ron that *if* his company *were* hiring engineers, he would certainly have been offered a job. It turned out that the company had no jobs at all to offer; it had just come to the 'career fair' to fly the company flag. Killing the Avro Arrow program had killed virtually their entire military aircraft industry."

Ken asked, "Stevens, are you confessing or bragging about what you and TAMPRR did to those companies and those Canadian engineers?"

The older man's eyes narrowed, and his lower lip grabbed his upper one, as if to hold himself back from saying something uncharitable. He gradually took a deep breath, and said, "Ken, we destroyed a lot of those young graduates' futures. At this point in my life I am not proud of that, although at the time I took it as another measure of TAMPRR's success that a lot of those Avro guys who hadn't come down here to work, had left engineering altogether. We kept tabs on them, just in case they decided to resurrect the Arrow or design and build some other world-beating technological marvel. A lot of the ones who left the profession went into teaching science or math or metallurgy, or changed fields altogether and became dentists, physicians, or something where no one could again take away their successes. Several of them had physical and/or mental breakdowns. The message we had wanted to deliver had been received loud and clear.

"And as for the engineering students in Canada, I recall Ronnie telling me about one of the other guys in his class. This guy, he said, was an even more talented electrical engineer than Ronnie believed he would ever be. Anyway, this other guy called him a few months after Ronnie had started his first real engineering job. The other guy was crying over the phone, for Pete's sake; he had been working for a Canadian subsidiary of one of our large American companies, and ended up at a job in Montreal working for the division of that company that made kitchen stoves.

"It seems that in the three months since they had graduated, my cousin had designed three different guidance systems for the next generation of our military aircraft at one of the few Canadian defense companies still standing, maybe because it had already been bought out by a much larger American company. Meanwhile, his classmate had designed just one element control knob for one model of household stove. *One bloody stove knob!* He told Ronnie that the Canadian plant was using the same blueprints as they did in the U.S., but to make the product officially 'Canadian', they had to change something in the design. So they changed the bloody knobs. The guy was sobbing with frustration and humiliation over the telephone when he asked Ronnie if *his* company might be hiring any other engineers. My cousin felt so sorry for him, and when he told me that story so did I. In America in the sixties, preserving the best jobs for our guys had been 'job one'."

Once again, somewhat less timidly than previously, their waitress appeared with their meals. She flashed a quick smile, deposited their plates, and as she began to turn away, mumbled a less than hearty, "Enjoy." Benevolently, they let her depart without any demands or requests.

While he began to play with, rather than enthusiastically eat, his meal, Ken would not be deterred from ferreting out the information he wanted. He asked, "Is there anything else specific you could tell me more about what you and TAMPRR did in relation to the Avro Arrow project?"

Stevens leaned forward in his chair again, pointing his fork at Ken as he spoke. "You know your father was a liaison officer attached to the Avro Arrow project. What I am about to tell you *no one else*, outside of the people involved in it at the time, knows. But you have to agree to not report on this until I say that you can. If you were to write about it prematurely, then others will figure out that it must have been me that told you, and the number of my remaining days in this life form will be reduced even further overnight, and then I wouldn't be able to pass along any other, more currently pressing, information to you."

Ken's sense was that Stevens was a virtual mother lode of information, and that he would only let out a bit at a time, in a sequence and timing that he would control. The fact was that it was in their mutual interest to be able to trust one another, at least as far as not precipitously divulging any information to others, was concerned. Ken nodded his agreement to keep confidential what he was told, until the Lieutenant Colonel had given his okay. *Unless, of course, some regrettable circumstances occurred: like Brad being hurt, for instance, or perhaps, this source's untimely demise.*

Stevens acknowledged Ken's nod with one of his own, and went on. "Look, the Canadians actually completed eight Avro Arrows before the program was cancelled. Your father had already flown in two of them. And on the night of February 27, 1959, just one week after what their media called 'Black Friday', the day when the project was officially cancelled by the Canadian government, he got into number 208 at two o'clock in the middle of the night, and under cover of darkness, flew out of Malton, Ontario where the Avro plant was located, to a secret site in the American southwest. He made two pit stops on the way down, shadowed throughout by a CIA-seconded American pilot in a 'borrowed' CF-100, an older model Canadian twin-engine fighter-interceptor aircraft, that was equipped with a U.S. military aircraft-recognition system.

I was the liaison between your father and TAMPRR, although he had no idea that our organization even existed. He thought I was working for a consulting company that did occasional work for our military—which, of course, was partly true. Your father was told about the flight less than twenty-four hours before he took off. He was also told that Avro had authorized the flight, which, of course, was bullshit. Actually, no one, aside from the TAMPRR team, a few key military personnel, and a couple of Avro employees we had promised jobs to in the U.S., knew about the flight.

"The CF-100 shadowed and directed your father, its pilot telling ground controls at various commercial airports that he was flying alone on a top-secret equipment-testing mission. When some traffic controllers replied that their equipment was telling them that there were two airplanes clearly visible on their screens, he told them that they must be picking up radar-confusing defenses that he was testing that sent out multiple false images on purpose. Air Defense Command radar operators were told that our test equipment deliberately sent out erroneous signals so that any potential future enemy would be confused as to how many planes were coming at them, and which ones to fire their missiles at. The guys in the control towers were to see if they could detect which of the two signals was the phony one. In fact, of course, there were actually two valid signals, the Avro Arrow's being substantially larger, by the way, but we didn't want anyone scrambling fighters to check out the real source of the second signal, and then see and possibly photograph the Arrow. And the officers in charge of air traffic control tower duty had been told in advance about the test of a 'multiple image generator' by certain higher-ups in the Air Force, so the ruse worked great."

Ken asked, "Why not just tell everyone that you were taking one of the Avro Arrows for further testing?"

"The whole point, Ken, was that the public not know about the U.S.A. getting one of the Arrows. The Canadian governing party was terrified that their media would go ballistic, claiming that their national pride and sovereignty had been compromised, and that if the aircraft was really not necessary or worthwhile continuing to fund, then why the hell were Americans interested in having one of them?

"Your father actually thought that the flight was okayed by both Avro and the Canadian Air Force. A couple of security guys on duty at the Avro plant that night were bought off with offers of new jobs Stateside. Unfortunately, one of them met with a most unfortunate accident on the way home one night, a day after he called the wrong person at a Canadian newspaper to try to sell his story."

The more Ken heard as he listened to Stevens, the more concerned he was getting for his son's safety. He was also becoming impatient and angry again, and his feelings seeped into his voice.

Ken barked, "And just who exactly were TAMPRR's clients?"

"I've told you. We were contracted by a few of the major military aircraft manufacturers as well as some key senior military types, all of whom had a direct interest in seeing to it that the Arrow never got into production, especially once the prototypes flew and they realized that the darn thing would actually exceed, let alone meet, specs! These clients, naturally, also wanted an Arrow delivered to their own facilities, to help them figure out, up close, just what made the bloody thing so damn good. They wanted Avro's technology, their key personnel, and all the profits that would have gone to Avro and Canada.

"Your father got sucked into the scheme by our telling him what we wanted. We knew he was too much of a straight shooter for what we had in mind, so he was told it was okay with Avro, and so on. When he found out, after he had delivered the plane, that it had not been an Avro-authorized mission, he was furious, not only with the powers that arranged the Arrow 'acquisition', but with me in particular, because I was supposedly one of his best friends, and he knew that I had lied to him. He was so damned ethical about it all, claiming that we had screwed both our closest ally *and* our own American pilots out of having the most advanced plane as soon as they could and should have had them."

Stevens's face looked both sad and bewildered. He said, "Your father simply didn't want to acknowledge the 'big picture'."

Lights began turning on in Ken's mind, illuminating that which had been unsaid. "Christ, Stevens, you guys knew you weren't going to let the Canadians bring the Avro Arrow program into full production from the very beginning, didn't you?"

"Of course. We couldn't afford to."

"You even kept our own air force, our own pilots, from getting the best aircraft under them for the years that it took to try and duplicate what the Canadians had already accomplished by 1959."

Stevens pushed back. "It was a necessary sacrifice. It only took us about a decade to catch up to and nearly duplicate the Canadian technology."

"Meanwhile, our guys were left with second-rate equipment at a time that the Soviets were building better and better MIGs."

"It was worth it."

"*For whom?* For you? For TAMPRR? For U.S. airplane manufacturers? Not for our pilots, that's for sure. Hell, this was happening in the middle of the cold war, right? Canada was a full partner in NORAD and NATO, right? We should have had the best weapons at the earliest time that they could have been available. You people prevented that."

"True. But in the long term it was for our own country's sake."

"You mean it was in your corporate clients' best interests. And in TAMPRR's best interests as well, I am sure"

"Things turned out fine, *mister*!" Stevens was not accustomed to being talked back to. His voice was louder than he intended as he hurled the next words at Ken. "Anyway, it's done with; it happened five decades ago, for Christ's sake. Let it go."

Ken was not about to let the matter of his father's death 'go'. "In the materials you sent me, you said that my father's involvement cost him his life. *That means it's not over, it can't be over, for me.*"

Stevens slumped back in his chair. The fire in his eyes had been doused with water that was now threatening to overflow his lower eyelids. And he had gone somewhere else.

Ken caught his breath and waited. After a while Stevens came back to the restaurant, back to their table, and back to Ken's last comments. The fire would not come back again at this meeting.

With what seemed to be deep remorse, Stevens glanced at Ken, and then looked down and far away. When he resumed speaking his voice was much quieter and his tone softer. "Ken, I tried to talk your father into accepting reality. He kept saying that he felt betrayed, especially by me, and that he had been made out to betray his Canadian colleagues, and his fellow American pilots. We told him that no one would ever know what happened to the Arrow he had flown. Everybody had been told through the media that all the finished aircraft had been destroyed. Most people bought the story we put out, that the Arrow, the one seemed to be missing from the photo that appeared in some Canadian newspapers of the time that showed broken-up Arrows on the tarmac outside Avro's manufacturing building, had been cut up *inside* the hanger where it was being built."

Stevens shook his head in amazement. He said, "And yet, after all these years, after nearly five decades, would you believe that there are still some Canadians who never bought the story we put out, and who have continued to try to find out what really happened. But no one still around dares tell them, and most of the people who haven't let the whole Avro Arrow thing go are dying off of old age, anyway. So, at least, soon those who were around back in 1959, won't be for much longer."

"Well," replied Ken, "*you* know, and now you have told *me*. But *why* have you told me all of this? What the hell is this meeting really about? Is our meeting supposed to be your confessional? Do you want my forgiveness? Is that it?"

Stevens stared at Ken, his weary, baggy-rimmed eyes scouring the terrain of the younger man's face, as if looking for... *what*? For signs of compassion or absolution?

Finally, Stevens said, "Ken, I have reached even *my* limits of deception and self-disgust, because now TAMPRR has targeted my dead friend's son and perhaps even his grandson, for elimination. And I won't, I can't go there."

Ken held his anger and his fear for Brad's safety in check. He said, "Go on."

"Ken, TAMPRR is at it again, and this time it has the mandate, the money, and the means to go after another whole economic enchilada in both our country and in Canada, namely our healthcare systems–and TAMPRR's corporate clients want it all! They want to control the healthcare and pharmaceutical programs in *both* our country and Canada, plus as much of the media as they can buy, bribe or, if need be, bury, in order to help them gain that control. These corporations have already become so rich, with their double-digit annual profit growth rate that they have emerged, arguably, as one of the most powerful economic influences on our respective governments. TAMPRR's healthcare and pharmaceutical clients want us to do for them now what we did for our military aircraft companies fifty years ago this year. So if TAMPRR succeeds, Canadians will get screwed again, by some of the same people–or their successors–and in largely the same ways as before. Hell, they already have America nearly sewn up;

Canada is the last bastion of resistance on the continent."

Ken was reeling. Since opening the FedEx package in his apartment he had learned things he had not known or fully appreciated about his father's life and his death, about the Avro Arrow, and about the organized threat to the very fabric of two of the world's supposedly most democratic countries. He now realized why he or anyone else who dared to get in the way of TAMPRR and its clients, might be considered mere impediments to be eliminated without a second thought.

Even Ken's lifelong image of a heroic, almost larger-than-life father who did only good, was now a little tarnished. Even though Stevens said his father had been duped into flying an Arrow from the place it had been built in Canada down to the U.S. southwest, the fact is he *had* done it. And surely he must have had some awareness that all was not right with this flight. Maybe he did it because he knew full well the Avro Arrow program was doomed and he wanted to save what he could of it. He may not have known that the real intention was to steal the technology and hire away the personnel. But such a portrait of innocence was rather a hard sell, at this point.

Ken recalled how, immediately after WWII ended, both the Russians and Americans made off with as many of the German rocket scientists and engineers as could be caught and bought. Now it turns out, only 14 years later, in February 1959, some of his countrymen had done it again, this time defeating a *corporate* enemy of a sovereign government and political ally, and making off with *its* scientists and engineers. Maybe all is fair in business, as well as love and war. Maybe… but Ken wasn't buying it.

Lieutenant Colonel Stevens interrupted his thoughts. "Look, they… *we*… did whatever we had to do to kill the Arrow. That's true. But TAMPRR is now employing virtually the same kinds of tricks that we used to down the Arrow, to kill the universal Medicare system in Canada, and to complete the final takeover of the healthcare system here in the U.S.. If TAMPRR doesn't succeed in killing the Canadian system, then, sooner or later, we risk the possibility that just too many Americans will lose their blinkers and eventually demand that *their* politicians provide them with a government-run, non-profit healthcare system along the lines of the Canadian one."

Ken asked, "Why do you think that might happen if it hasn't happened in all these years?"

Stevens said, "Well, remember what happened around the beginning of the millennium? First, when they realized they could save twenty to fifty percent on their prescription drugs, a lot of our senior citizens living in the northern states started going across the border into Canada, *by the busload, for Christ's sake*, to get their prescriptions filled. Then a whole lot of Canadian Internet sites started handling prescriptions from individual Americans. Then whole American cities and states started to order drugs for their employees and retirees from Canada. Remember the fight that went on to buy the votes of senators and members of congress, and the direction of the White House, to prevent our government from sanctioning the importation of drugs made by U.S. companies into America, so that some of these same pharmaceutical companies could continue making billions in extra profit by gouging our own citizens. And to make sure that the drug flow from Canada was stopped, TAMPRR infiltrated and/or paid off an awful lot of Canadian politicians and lobby groups who were scared shitless that their own drug supply was at risk–which it was, thanks to some of our pharmaceutical companies restricting the sale of their most popular drugs to those Canadian pharmacies that hadn't agreed to play along with stopping to sell to American customers.

"Granted that not all pharmaceutical companies were involved in the buying of votes and the turning off of the drug availability taps. Most of those companies were way too ethical for that. However, there were a few who were willing to play dirty to further their bottom lines. Well, these cowboys and their HMO and PPO buddies, with all the people they own, are now virtually in charge of whole sections of our government, including the FDA–and Canada's too, I might add."

The old military man's white mane shook as he laughed loudly. The gullibility of even many of the most intelligent and educated people who should know better, never ceased to astound him. The malleability of the middle class was one of the main factors that had allowed TAMPRR to accomplish so much, so much of the time. "Of course, when TAMPRR first got into the act, one of the first things we did was to have some U.S. legislators suggest that perhaps the drugs being imported from Canada weren't as safe as our own."

Ken said, "But Canadians got the same drugs that were produced at the same facilities as the ones provided to U.S. consumers. So that argument made no sense, for the most part."

Stevens nodded, smiling. "That's true; of course. We simply did our own version of the old line used by that husband who protested his innocence when his wife found him and his secretary fornicating on his office desk. Remember? He said, "Who are you going to believe, me or your own eyes?" Anyway, that ploy was one of our few failures. Pretty well everyone knew by then that most of the meds came from the same factories as those sold Stateside, and that the drugs had merely been shipped across the border to Canada where their federal government controlled the prices on prescription drugs. So all that the folks up north were doing was shipping us medications that had been made in this country, or in our companies' own offshore manufacturing plants in the first place. Well, as more and more of our citizens woke up to the fact that Canadians pay much less for the very same meds, more and more Americans began thinking that maybe the folks up north really were getting a better deal in other aspects of healthcare, as well. So it made our work that much harder."

"What do you mean?"

"Well, we realized that we should have done with regard pharmaceuticals the same as we did with the Avro Arrow. We simply started pumping money into some powerful people up in Canada who were in a position to influence those in the government and private organizations to back the stopping of exporting drugs from Canada to the U.S., by convincing them that there were not going to be enough drugs to go around. In other words, we put it out there that Canadians would be soon be running out of drugs for their own use if they continued to allow their supply to be shipped to Americans. That scared the crap out of enough of them to get the practice stopped."

Ken said, "But the argument you put out there was completely bogus. Who ever heard of a major company not being able to find some way of boosting production to fill all the demand out there in order to make more money?"

"Ah, but that was just the point. Because drug manufacturers make two to four times as much profit–*or even more*–for every prescription filled Stateside, why should they have supplied so much to Canada when, after they have been purchased up there by Americans, would bring the manufacturers so much less profit?"

Ken said, "I obviously have a lot more faith in Americans than you do, if only they get access to the truth. And I think a lot of folks in America *are* waking up, partly because too many people in this country are having to sell their homes or are going bankrupt just trying to provide medical care for themselves and their families, and because those who don't even have enough assets to go bankrupt, are out and out dying for lack of the medical help that they so desperately need. And so many are terrified to lose their jobs because then they would lose whatever medical coverage they have, and all the while so many of their companies are cutting back on what their medical coverage actually pays for, anyway. Meanwhile, just like with prescription medicine, there are the Canadians, still stubbornly holding on to their universal healthcare coverage, albeit by their fingernails. So what you are saying is that TAMPRR is working to chop off their fingers, so to speak."

Stevens nodded and semi-smirked, almost in spite of himself. Affecting an English accent, Stevens said, "By Jove, I've think you've got it!"

Ken smiled, shook his head, and then asked, "Are there any other reasons you have come to me with this material? Are you attempting to get back at some of the other principals at TAMPRR? Or is this your version of some kind of last minute religious conversion that you are having, because you don't want to die and go to hell?"

If he resented the way Ken formed his questions, Stevens didn't show it. Instead, he said, "Maybe I *am* trying to undo some of the harm I have done, Ken. And just maybe *this* time there are just too many parallels to the Arrow situation for me to ignore them. Look, here again Canada has what everyone who has examined these things knows full well is *one* of the best, if not in fact the *very best,* healthcare system in any major democratic country, and at its foundation, it is infinitely better than the hodgepodge, profit-making, service-obstructing systems that we have in so many parts of America. And as in the Arrow situation, we have clients who can't afford to allow their system to continue to exist because they believe that pressures will continue to build Stateside and they could eventually be put out of business. So for the past decade and a half we have been using a lot of the same tricks we developed to kill the Arrow. And some brand new ones."

Ken asked, "Would you care to elaborate?"

After a slight pause, Stevens said, "Sure. Just as in the case of the Arrow program, we have used disinformation, blackmail, and bribery, and have taken advantage of the habitual political pissing wars over power that go on almost continually between some of their provincial governments and their federal government.

"On the other hand, one difference with the Avro Arrow situation is that in that case, the federal party that killed the Avro Arrow program had been in opposition at the time their rival party had started the project–the baby they killed wasn't their own, in other words. The problem is that this time the party in power is the party that introduced their healthcare system. So this time we are going after getting some of the governing party's members to help kill their own program. That has made it somewhat harder–but hardly an insurmountable problem."

Ken said, "I'm listening. I am especially interested in the comparative details, especially if I am going to be able to write about this at some point."

Stevens took another deep breath. He was keenly aware of the possible personal cost of divulging the specific information Ken was seeking. But he had come too far to turn back. And, in truth, he didn't really want to stop. So he said, "First of all, we have used similar kinds of disinformation. With the Avro Arrow, we told the Canadians and our other allies that the chief threat was going to be from Soviet bombers coming over the North Pole and sweeping down over Canada's north, and that only missiles could do the job of knocking them down. We said that fighter-interceptor aircraft were passé."

Ken said, "But that wasn't true."

Stevens said, "Not only that, but don't you think we knew damn well that we also needed fighter-interceptors to protect us from the Soviet threat in Europe? Of course we did!

"Anyway, the too-innocent-for-their-own-good Canadians bought the line we sold them. Just like many of them buy it when we have our paid-for politicians, think tanks and newspapers tell them that they can't afford their health care system. We just don't tell them that the so-called 'administration costs' of our system is many times their own. And we also don't advertise the fact that one of the main reasons that people in the states can get access to doctors so much more readily is that so relatively few of us can actually afford to see them."

Ken was not quite ready to let go of what Stevens had called 'the Avro Arrow manipulation'. He said, "To go back to what you were saying before, was it really that easy to get Canada to kill the Avro Arrow?"

"Pretty well. Actually, we even got them to buy the next-to-useless Bomarc missiles that our military knew damn well wouldn't do the job, but wanted to get rid of them for the sake of public optics and to justify paying so much for their development costs. Then, a couple of years later, our government said, in effect, "Oops, sorry, you Canadians. Shucks, guess what? It turns out that the Bomarc won't do the job and there really is a need for aircraft like the Arrow, after all. Too bad you folks destroyed all the prototypes, the drawings, the assembly line, and now you don't even have the personnel to built another aircraft like the Arrow, even if you wanted to!" So we sold them some of *our* relatively inferior planes. Ah, but we let them build some of those airplanes' *parts* in Canada, so their government could say they were at least *partly*, home built. What a crock!" Stevens roared at the brazenness of it all.

"Of course, we also used blackmail, to great effect if I say so myself. We had dozens of still photographs and hours of 16-mm film and, later videotape, of some of their key elected politicians, military brass, and higher-ups in various government circles, screwing around with the opposite sex, the same sex, or children, even; the whole nine yards, as they used to say up there.

"Through our intelligence agents we were able to find and buy enough key voices and parliamentary votes. We used outright bribes; we even offered to fund and/or run several Canadian politicians' re-election campaigns and, it goes without saying, we added substantially to their trust funds. In certain cases, we upgraded their homes, issued several of them timeshares in Florida and Arizona at fire-sale prices; whatever the hell it was that they wanted; whatever it took. They could even sit on some Boards of Directors of American companies after they retired, if that was what they wanted."

Ken was fighting his own revulsion but kept his cool. He said, in a reasonably modulated voice, "But surely some of those whom TAMPRR approached were unreachable and threatened to expose you."

"Ha! You are undoubtedly a fine investigative reporter, Simpson, but you really are a boy scout in your heart of hearts, aren't you? Don't be so bloody blind. We only approached the ones who were ripe and ready, and who wouldn't dare to expose us or else we could threaten to expose *them* for the philanderers or pedophiles or whatever the hell they were. In fact, most of the ones we approached, and remember that we picked very carefully, actually loved what we offered. The promise of lots of greenbacks and goodies bought us plenty of ink and air in their media about how the heavy costs to little Canada taking on such an expensive project like the Arrow could possibly bankrupt the country, even though *we* knew damn well that that damned fantastic plane would be bought by a lot of our allies in NATO–even if *our* country didn't–and it would end up being a financial cash cow for the Canadians and they would make billions. And then, God help us, they would probably get even more ambitious and decide that they could build bombers next. We couldn't take that chance. We just knew that we couldn't afford to allow the Arrow to go into full production. So, with our money and our promises of key jobs, stock shares and cash, we bought more than enough voices in their political and military back rooms, to have all the influence we needed.

"Remember, Ken," added Stevens, in a possible allusion to what happened to Ken's father, "one rogue aircraft mechanic can bring down a whole aircraft. How many heavy-duty politicians and government bureaucrats do you think it really takes to bring down an entire airplane program? Not nearly as many as you might imagine, I can tell you that. TAMPRR has done the same kind of thing in a number of other countries ever since–including our supposedly close ally, England."

Ken's mind was flooding with questions. Stevens was describing the covert actions of a private sector company with intimate ties to the U.S. military and business interests. How close these relations were, and what other parties were involved, were questions that Ken wanted answered. For instance, how could such conduct have gone on unchecked for so long, without appearing on the radar screens of either the FBI or CIA? Or was it that those two agencies tacitly ignored such actions? Was TAMPRR a private company that might even, on occasion, have been doing the FBI's or CIA's bidding is some kind of perverse 'outsourcing', in some kind of scary P3, or 'public-private partnership', arrangement. And were there perhaps even *other* companies out there like TAMPRR that also carried out sophisticated covert activities that benefited American corporate and/or private interests, unbeknownst to the American public?

Ken realized that he had just perceived an entirely new, previously unheard of, business sector, one that could hardly openly advertise its products or purposes. What he had suddenly imagined, or at least had been led to by Lieutenant Colonel Dan Stevens, was somewhat akin to a kind of corporate business mafia. It was also a logical if diabolical extension of the more usual and expected corporate spying scenario. The latter was more of a receptive function devoted primarily to merely collecting information. Corporate-driven sabotage would have to be a much more aggressive activity, one that would probably come more easily to ex-military types.

Ken felt a shiver pass through his entire body. His intuition signaled danger, but not merely a personal kind. The apprehension he was experiencing, he sensed, was also for his country and the direction, with the guidance of the likes of

TAMPRR Inc. and Lieutenant Colonel Dan Stevens, into which it seemed to be sliding. At that moment he believed that he truly understood what President Eisenhower might have been feeling and thinking when he made his Presidential farewell address.

CHAPTER 22

"Well, why the hell doesn't he pick up the goddamn cellphone?"

While Ken and Stevens were in the middle of their conversation in the restaurant in New York City, Jake Marks was at home in Miami Beach, yelling into the phone at the head of TAMPRR Inc.'s research lab, Ivan Fordish. "Is there something wrong with the damn thing, Ivan? Do you think he knows that it puts out a location signal whether the phone is 'on' or 'off'?"

"I don't know, sir. As far as I can tell, the phone is working fine. And no one aside from you, me, and my man in the lab that installed it, knows that it transmits continually."

"And you're saying that the full-time GPS is transmitting its location accurately?"

"I can only tell you, Colonel Marks, that it is transmitting Lieutenant Colonel Stevens's location as being in and around his Palm Desert condo. The one thing that doesn't quite compute is that it seems that he is only going out of his home two to three times a day, for anywhere from five minutes to a half-hour. Then he comes right back in."

"So, otherwise, he is just sitting around at home?"

"He seems to be sitting or laying down in the same place for up to an hour at a time; then he gets up and moves around for a minute or two, and then stays put again for another length of time."

"Ivan, Can you tell where he goes when he is out?"

"He goes into his back yard, or jogs for a couple of minutes, kind of erratically, kind of like he is zigzagging his way along the streets in his gated community. But he always comes back home in a pretty straight line."

"Ivan, how long has it been since you 'serviced' his phone, and put in the 24/7 always-on, GPS transmitter?"

"Sir, I had the same service job done on all of TAMPRR's

senior executives' phones over a period of about two hours, nearly six months ago now, while you were all meeting in your office."

"Ever had any other problems with any of our other phones that you 'fixed'?"

"No, sir."

"Well, we have a problem here, right?"

"Seems so, sir."

"Look, get one of our L.A. techies to drive out to Palm Desert first thing in the morning with a new 'fixed' phone. And have him bring in the old one and check it out, all right? And, since Mr. Stevens just seems to be hanging around his place goofing off and not taking my calls, let the guy gently remind him that he has a responsibility to keep the phone turned on to receive calls. I don't know what the hell he is up to, but I don't like it. I don't like having one of my top guys unavailable to me, for any reason, even if he is shacked up with Miss America for the weekend."

"Yes, sir."

At Lieutenant Colonel Stevens's spacious three bedroom condo that backed onto one of the three golf courses in the development, his cleaning lady/dog walker was getting ready to take Chewy, Stevens's increasingly arthritic eleven-year-old German Sheppard, out for another one of his thrice-a-day constitutionals along the streets in the development. Chewy happily came when she called him into the foyer in order to attach the bulky collar with a small, locked pocket attached, rather like a smaller version of what a ski-patrolling Saint Bernard might carry.

Chewy loved going for quiet walks, meeting neighbors who readily recognized the friendliest ex-police dog one might ever hope to encounter. In spite of the heart murmur that resulted in his being dropped from K-9 unit training, Dan Stevens relied upon Chewy for security as well as companionship. At the moment, however, the dog was functioning as a decoy, helping to give the impression that his master was still in Palm Desert instead of in New York City divulging some of TAMPRR's most vital secrets.

CHAPTER 23

Ken sat staring in the general direction of Lieutenant Colonel Stevens: his appetite was long gone and he pushed his food around its plate while he thought. He finally said, "TAMPRR has to be stopped, Stevens! You people are like a bloody virus that can infect a whole nation."

Stevens said, "Good analogy, Ken. How many excellent hackers and computer nerds does it take to sabotage an entire, worldwide Internet system with a virus? Very few; I know. TAMPRR has used them more than once."

"What? When did you do that?" asked Ken.

Stevens responded, "That's for another day, Ken. Lets just say that a certain software security company wanted to raise its share price by showing how quickly it could respond to a 'new' virus, but couldn't very well make and distribute a virus on its own. If such an activity were ever uncovered they would go down the tubes. So they outsourced the job to TAMPRR.

"But, Ken, we don't have time right now to go into depth about any of the other sorts of covert actions we have been involved in over the past fifty years. If we did you could well end up with an entire apartment full of Paulsons. The point I want to make clear to you is that we didn't need to buy off *everyone* to have all the votes we needed in the Canadian parliament to kill the Avro Arrow. After all, a very few rotten apples really *can* spoil an entire barrel. Anyway it never even had to come to any kind of public vote. They did it in caucus, with just a few of the members of parliament and their Canadian military on our payroll casting the key votes. Hell, even a lot of their genuinely ethical politicians and pundits were so bullshitted by the people we used, that they voluntarily killed their own goose, leaving us pretty well all the golden eggs in the military aircraft nest, from that point on to today.

"Anyway, the Arrow project had been started by the previous

government which was led by another party so when the new guys got to control their parliament a lot of them were more than happy to shit on the old party from on high by destroying what would have been one of their crowning achievements–a world-class, best-selling, homegrown military marvel. We simply gave the new guys a lot of baloney excuses to use with the press and they, in turn, buried the entire Avro Arrow issue onto the back pages soon enough."

Ken could tell that Stevens, in spite of himself perhaps, seemed to be reveling in the telling of what he had referred to as 'the Arrow manipulation'.

Ken reminded himself that people were generally proud of their accomplishments, whether they were ethical or diabolical. Mafia dons and research scientists both admired their own successes, regardless of the potential or actual consequences to others. Ken momentarily thought back to most of his fellow air force pilots who bragged about the tonnage of bombs they had laid down on their peopled targets. So it was for people involved in all manner of questionable projects–manufacturing bombs or cigarettes came to mind. Babies, no matter how ugly, are almost always beautiful to those who conceive and birth them.

Stevens wasn't quite finished in the telling. "Now look, Ken, we simply played on the Canadians own general feelings of insecurity and inadequacy." Stevens shook his head in amazement. "We got the word out that the plane wouldn't live up to specs, that it would cost too much, and that it wouldn't be purchased by other countries' armed forces, especially and including our own U.S.A.F.. Scared the Canadians shitless. Not enough of them, from the top down, believed in themselves; not enough of them dared to stand up and take us on and tell us how full of shit all that crap that we had made up really was! So they contributed to their own loss, big-time."

Ken said, "But the plane actually exceeded specs, even with the original, less powerful engine that was installed in the first few that came off the line."

Stevens nodded his head enthusiastically. "Of course. But surely you get it. You media people tell your readers and viewers what you call 'facts', and then tell them what to think about those 'facts'. Anyways, we had *their* media bamboozled, blindfolded, blackmailed or bought. It was so very easy! Like shooting at ducks with their feet frozen to the ice on a Canadian lake during one of their winters." Stevens laughed.

"And I repeat, Ken, it wasn't *entirely* our fault. A lot of those Canadians didn't think that a small country like theirs could–or should–have produced such a first-rate aircraft. Deep in their psyches they didn't even think that they deserved to. A lot of Canadians, even now in 2009, still say the same thing about other items they produce, from wine to feature films and back. They will even say to one another, almost apologetically and in their typical Canadian, 'I'm sorry' kind of way, "Oh, I see, its *Canadian*!" as if it had a built-in second class quality."

Stevens shook his head in seeming amazement again. "Honestly, you should hear them when they talk about what movie they are thinking of going to see on the weekend. They will happily see a crappy so-called 'American movie', even if it was filmed completely in Toronto or Montreal or Vancouver, using an entirely Canadian crew and some homegrown actors. But if the same film was made by a recognizably Canadian film company, they will say things like, 'Not bad for a Canadian movie, eh?' A lot of them talk that way, even if the film had just won an Oscar, for Christ's sake."

Stevens was chuckling to himself again. "Hell, Ken, if you fart in their faces, they are the ones who say, 'I'm sorry'. How lame is that?"

Ken recalled reading a few years earlier that it had taken many months to even get a decent theatre distribution deal for a 'Canadian movie' made by and about Eskimos, even after it had already won first prize at several major film festival awards, including at Cannes.

He asked, "Did what happen to them with the Avro Arrow program help *give* them their feelings of inferiority?"

In spite of himself Stevens sounded irritatingly boastful as he said, "We at TAMPRR certainly like to think so. It's rather hard to feel good about yourself when you have been told that your best work just isn't good enough, and when it is totally destroyed before your eyes. And that is, in effect, the message we got across to them by insisting that their prototypes be broken up and displayed that way, in broad daylight, and then sold for a few cents on the dollar, for bloody scrap. And that is what happened.

"Now, on the other hand, with the healthcare system attack we have been perpetrating on them for years, our job has actually been harder, because their population has been using their Medicare system for over three decades, and they intuitively know how bloody good they have it. Unfortunately, TAMPRR wasn't even hired until their entire system had been in place for many years. So, even now, in spite of all we have done to slow down, dumb down, and generally screw up their healthcare system, polls still tell us that most Canadians are basically satisfied with their system. So we have had to work extra hard with our Canadian provincial and federal politician friends and media types to get them to cripple their system. We have, shall we say, 'encouraged' them to cut back on services, on doctors and nurses, and on hospital beds. Some of our best friends, who just happened to be provincial and federal Ministers of Health, have forced the closing of entire hospitals, limited the availability and use of hospital equipment like MRIs and CAT scans, and then allowed some U.S.-style private clinics to perform the services that they wouldn't let their healthcare system's own personnel and equipment perform. So our plan's been working, but slowly.

"Also, for the past few years we have essentially controlled a right wing-oriented Canadian media conglomerate that was going to go belly up before we propped it up financially, and now it happily spews out our messages at every opportunity so that more and more Canadians have gradually become accepting of a for-profit healthcare system. And it has certainly helped that, by killing off the Avro Arrow, TAMPRR helped instill the idea that "If it is Canadian, how bloody good can it be, anyway?" So our techniques are gradually having their effect."

Ken was getting hot again. He said, "But you are saying that TAMPRR has bribed and blackmailed and bought key people of a sovereign country—our closest neighbor and an ally, for Christ's sake! Are you guys nuts?

Lieutenant Colonel Stevens couldn't stop himself from bragging. "Its a bitch, isn't it? Actually, it was a piece of cake.

Remember, Simpson, the closer you get to the guy at the helm and to the ones with their hands on the triggers, the fewer people you need to instigate a mutiny. And by the way, do you seriously think that we've pulled off a kind of 'Avro Arrow Manipulation' number, only in Canada? Grow up, for Pete's sake!" Stevens chuckled again.

Ken started to reply but the words got stuck somewhere as the import of General Dan Stevens's last comments sunk in. He asked, "What other countries have you and TAMPRR screwed out of their best minds and/or their finest accomplishments?"

Stevens's headshaking suggested he was getting increasingly exasperated with what Ken guessed he saw as the latter's 'boy scout'-ness. Ken reminded himself that, truth be told, there was a large part of him that still clung to an increasingly precarious belief in the inherent goodness and honesty of people generally, and of the democratic principles of the founding fathers. By extension, he was also inclined to extend the notion of 'innocent until proved guilty' to the mavens of American industry, Enron, WorldCom, and the others. Ironically, as an investigative reporter, his work involved repeatedly testing–and all too often finding exceptions to–his personally-held philosophy.

Stevens's entire body seemed to soften somewhat. He sighed deeply and said, "Look, I will tell you something else that you cannot write about, at least not yet. The fact is that we no longer need to 'screw other companies or countries out of their best minds and finest accomplishments', as you so graciously put it. We now have a much more efficient way to access both their minds and their accomplishments than bothering to buy people and bribe politicians."

Ken asked, "And what might that be?"

Stevens replied, "TAMPRR worked for two years with a major software company to develop our own spyware program, called Subvertor. Subvertor is a microprogram patch that has been inserted by our own operatives into the latest versions of some of the most popular computer programs, a few of which are even installed at the computer manufacturers' factories. Another version is inserted into a target computer's hard drive when the user accesses the Net. So, whenever the user first fires up a new computer, or the latest upgrades of some of the most popular programs, or whenever that computer is used to access the Internet, Subvertor sends its own e-mails from the computer it now resides in, to specified e-mail addresses, transmitting as hidden attachments, the contents of all files then resident on the computer. Thereafter, whenever the same computer is again used to access the Internet, Subvertor sends only the updates; in other words, it uploads and transmits only the work that has been done on various files since the last transmission. That way, we and/or our corporate customers can have direct access to the latest thinking of the 'finest minds' as you put it, without either them or their companies even knowing about it. Our customers can then view these files–for a very sizable fee, mind you–and then use the materials they have acquired in order to leap-frog ahead of their competitors, developing their own versions of similar products more quickly and getting them to the market sooner."

Ken was astounded. He immediately thought of the computer files that he had at work and at home, and wondered if his own security had been breeched. He asked, "Does TAMPRR have access to my files?"

Stevens said, "I honestly don't know for sure, but I would suggest that you not use your own computers to access the 'net if they have any sensitive material on it. And that will only work for a while. Subvertor 2010 is about to be rolled out of our labs, and it will be able to access your computer even when it is off, as long as it is plugged into an AC outlet or has the capability for wireless connectivity."

"*You bastards!*"

"Look, Ken, we haven't got time for your indignation. In fact, you have much less time than you think, to take advantage of my assistance."

Ken recoiled. "Are you threatening me?"

"Not at all. I am simply *warning* you. The Paulson just bought you a little slack, probably no more than a few weeks. The company would be hesitant to use deadly force against you or yours, right now. Too few would believe that it was just a random occurrence, and all hell might break loose if the wrong people started poking around the right places."

Ken regarded Stevens with dismay. Before he could say a word, however, Stevens said, "Now, look, you are not dealing with anything the likes of which you have ever encountered before. *Ever.* Believe me."

Ken asked, "What do you mean?"

"I mean, TAMPRR subcontracts, too."

"Are you bloody psychotic? And now whom are you threatening? Me? My son? Do you really think you can get away with this? I *will* get my findings published, Stevens. If my paper or the other media outlets won't let me, then I will put it out on my own web site. I will unravel the whole sordid, sick story of TAMPRR. All confidentiality agreements between you and me are hereby cancelled. They were gone the moment you threatened my son."

Lieutenant Colonel Stevens smiled. "Good for you, Ken. TAMPRR should be afraid of *you*! But they aren't. Don't threaten *me*, though; I really am on your side. Now, do you want the biggest story of your career, or not? Are you interested in helping ordinary Americans–and their doctors, for that matter–get back control of their own healthcare?"

Ken glared at Stevens, and then said: "Of course I want the story. But I also want to know who the senior people at TAMPRR are, in addition to yourself. And who is acting on their orders. Of course I want it all. And I want to get them all. And that will most definitely include you, Lieutenant Colonel, if you are bullshitting me in any way right now. Now, will you help me?"

"Of course."

"Then start telling me what you know damn well that I need to know."

Stevens nodded, admiringly. "You are definitely your father's son, Ken; I am very glad to see that. You have the same 'go fuck yourself' attitude as your dad had when he believed someone was jerking him around. Well, I am not doing that to you. And I won't."

"And how can I know that?"

"I'll tell you how. Do you remember, when you were just a young lad about ten or twelve, playing with my own son? Do you remember a boy named Ben?"

Ken abruptly had a recollection of a tall, pale, somewhat older playmate whom he had met once or twice, when someone, presumably Stevens, had come to his home to visit his dad.

Stevens continued. "My son, who was born a couple of years before you, Ken, died in Vietnam in a so-called 'friendly fire' incident. When that happened I was completely devastated. Nothing meant anything to me any more, so I just piled myself into my work. It has taken me all this time to find something else, some*one* else, worth fighting for, in an area where I know I can help *save* lives instead of destroying them. The lives of young children as well as those of older folks.

"But if you and I have a falling out right now, or if you reveal the confidences I have shared with you, then an awful lot of Americans will lose out, especially those who are currently uninsured for healthcare. That's over forty-six million people in our country including, I happen to know, over eleven million kids under the age of eighteen. Those folks are going to remain at risk if they need medical attention, and may well live entirely unnecessarily shitty physical lives, and die a whole lot of years before they should.

"Ken, I am an old man who has seen too many young people die. So this old soldier still has one last battle to fight, and one last war I very much want to win. And you, Ken, will be my army. Are you willing to enlist, or shall I take my intelligence and weapons elsewhere?

Ken said nothing. He had noted the choking sound the old man made when he mentioned his son, and again when he talked about American kids. Ken was an experienced investigative reporter but he also knew he could be fooled, just the same. It was a crapshoot but he was inclined to believe that Stevens was being straight with him. If he walked away and tried to continue his investigations without Stevens's help, then his son and himself, according to Stevens's comments, might be in greater danger. On the other hand, if he played along, perhaps he could find a way to protect them both. Ken hoped that, sooner or later, Lieutenant Colonel Stevens might slip up, *if* he was trying to string him along in order to set him up for a fall.

"I'll enlist, but please, I want to caution you that I have

already put everything you FedExed to me in a safe place. I will do the same with my notes on what you have told me today, and may tell me in the future. But, if something happens to me or to my son, then that material will be released to friends in the media and others who *won't* be deterred by anything you or the thugs from TAMPRR might do. And I have arranged that they will also activate a new website I have been developing that will contain hundreds of pages of material taken from my notes and various documents I have uncovered. With that understanding in mind, do we have an agreement?"

Stevens smiled. "Sounds fair to me, Ken. I have no problem with that. Now, here is the 'good stuff'. TAMPRR has been using the same techniques today that we used with the Avro Arrow problem and some of the same guys who helped kill the Arrow are in charge of this program. And you can be assured that they are just as dedicated to killing off what TAMPRR's healthcare, pharmaceutical, and insurance clients think is the biggest threat to their existence since Clinton tried to push for a universal health scheme similar to the Canadian model. So, if you bring TAMPRR down, you will be taking down some of those behind the downing of your father's aircraft."

Ken choked back his anger as his motivation escalated.

Stevens said, "Listen. TAMPRR is very similar to the FBI and the CIA. In fact, many of our employees picked up their basic skills while working for those organizations before leaving to join TAMPRR, at multiples of their former income.

"We also have one of their provincial premiers, an arrogant asshole by the name of George P. Linden, sewn up. That cigar-chomping, alcoholic, former television news announcer and tennis pro, has done everything we've asked of him, and more. We have one of our people on his short list of major consultants. And at our consultant's suggestions a couple of years ago, and in the name of 'fiscal responsibility', he closed a bunch of hospitals, laid off thousands of nurses, farmed out what had previously been governmental testing of his province's food and water supply, and made sure that their remaining hospitals couldn't handle the needs of the people that needed their services by, for example, refusing to allow their MRIs and CAT scans to be used for more than eight hours a day, five days a week, even though the hospitals' employees were willing–and the equipment was actually built–to be used 24/7, and he did all kinds of other things to get the local citizenry upset with their healthcare delivery system. The only problem was that he went too far too fast and shot his wad; he cut services back so far that a lot of people in several communities got sick and several of them died from contaminated food and water. We tried to get him to slow down but the overeager son of a bitch was just too brutal and crude, and caused a major, but hopefully temporary, backlash against the direction in which we want things to go."

"So we worked behind the scenes in our usual style to get him re-elected. It wasn't easy. But we dug up and/or invented enough dirt about the opposition, put enough millions into our guy's political advertisements, and planted enough false stories in their media, that the other guys went from a 'sure thing' when the election was called, to a distant second."

Ken was appalled, but impressed at the same time, by Stevens's bragging rant.

"Anyway," Stevens continued, "we got Linden back in power, and he and his cronies will do whatever needs to be done to cripple the healthcare system in their province. Give me a few more of those amoral, greedy, and power-hungry types and we could rule the whole world. Hey wait, *we already do!"* Stevens laughed.

Ken didn't know how the man could claim to want to help him yet be so obviously filled with pleasure and pride at what TAMPRR had done. Pride is often a bizarre attribute, he had long ago decided. *At least those soldiers who killed and maimed hundreds of thousands of Iraqi children and old people were our soldiers. My country, right or wrong. Right?*

"What else did you do to get Linden re-elected, and what will his people do now to help TAMPRR bring down their healthcare system?"

"It was simple. We told them that to get re-elected they had to promise to hire *more* nurses, open *more* hospitals, cover *more* services. In other words, we told them to say they were going to undo the damage that they and their predecessors had done previously. Now that they are back in power, they will simply reverse their positions again, claiming the need to lower taxes, create less government interference, and so on. The same bullshit cycle of promising whatever gets you into power and then ignoring the wishes of the people who voted for you and acting in the contrary way once you are in. Just like most political parties in most so-called democratic countries do most of the time.

"Anyway, with all the destruction that has already been carried out over the past few years, TAMPRR thinks that Canadians should, by now, be begging for 'the American alternative' healthcare model. Unfortunately, our polling continues to indicate that over seventy-five percent of Canadians still say they are satisfied with their system, and too many of them think that free healthcare is some kind of inherent 'right'."

"Well, isn't it?"

What do you mean?"

"I mean," Ken said, "they have had their system for decades now, where everyone in their country is covered by the government-run Medicare system. So isn't it natural that they have come to expect that it is their 'right'?"

"Have you tried drinking from your local river lately, Ken? Americans used to think clean water in their lakes and streams was their God-given right, too. But people can't get clean surface water almost anywhere any more, can they? They've even gotten used to toxins in their water, their air, and their food, while our government has continued to cut back on regular testing of such essential 'consumables'. We just tell them that it's the price of progress, and that 'the American way' means that every single thing is, or at least should be, a saleable commodity. And we should all have to pay for it. And that sure as hell includes healthcare."

Ken asked, "Do you really mean what you are saying?"

"*Of course not!* But that is the prevailing thinking at the top of most of our businesses and in government circles here in the U.S.. That is why we refused to go along with the Kyoto agreement. No one is going to stop *us* from polluting, not if we can save some bucks by dumping waste into the air and water, and onto the ground. No, sir. If anybody wants any of that stuff to be clean then they will have to purchase it along with their milk and cookies."

Ken said, "I still don't get it. You obviously seem to think along the lines of TAMPRR. Your pride in TAMPRR's accomplishments is very apparent. So, honestly, why are you doing this? I mean, why are you telling me *any* of this? Is it all really because of my father's or your son's deaths? You've been part of TAMPRR, you say, since it started. You must have taken part in dozens, if not hundreds, of covert actions on behalf of your corporate 'clients' over the past fifty bloody years. And frankly, you seem to be enjoying telling me what TAMPRR has been up to. So where does this guilty conscience come from? Why now? You could just stop doing these things, and 'fade away' like the old saying goes. So what's really happening here?

Stevens glanced sharply at Ken and then looked away. He was quiet for a moment, and then looked back and said, "Ken. I told you what happened to your father. What I didn't tell you is that after I failed to talk him out of speaking to the Senate subcommittee I phoned my colleagues at TAMPRR and told them that I was having trouble getting through to him. I said I would... keep trying... Up to that point TAMPRR Inc. hadn't kil..."

Stevens's voice became almost inaudible as Ken strained to hear. Then, steeling himself, he began to speak again. "Up to that point, Ken, TAMPRR hadn't yet killed anybody." He stopped talking and waited for what he knew had to come.

Ken's face was crimson as he reached across the table and with his left hand grabbed Stevens's tie and expertly began using it as a tourniquet. Through clenched teeth he said, "You bastard. All you crazy bastards! You're all nuts!"

Ken was almost shouting; people turned from their mealtime conversations and stared, wide-eyed and seemingly paralyzed, at the man at the corner table of the restaurant throttling his companion with one hand while raising his other arm in a fist.

To Ken, everything in the restaurant was simultaneously whirling about at different speeds and in all directions while he was somehow stuck out in space, his fist accelerating towards Stevens's temple.

Stevens's eyes were open wide as he waited for the blow to land. Ken's accelerating fist was stopped by the sight of an elderly man, staring wide-eyed and stoically awaiting the inevitable. Ken froze.

Stevens, realizing that he was not going to be hit, at least not now, said, "Please, Ken, let me finish telling the whole story."

Ken slowly let go of the old man's tie, and his whole body slackened slowly, like an exhausted priest who heard yet one more parishioner pleading to have him hear just one last confession. Ken slumped back into his chair.

Stevens looked directly at Ken and began to speak, tears streaming down his craggily face. "They decided to have your father killed. I thought I had convinced them that we should simply discredit him, say that he was using drugs, or that beat his wife, or had been chasing under-aged girls or diddling little boys. The usual kind of shit that puts people off and makes them not want to hear or believe anything the supposed offender might say. But the others were afraid that your father's war hero status would give him too much clout. So they just went ahead without telling me, and they had his plane sabotaged and got rid of their 'problem' that way."

Ken's entire body started shaking, as if flu had suddenly hit him full force. He looked around the restaurant as if he wanted to hit somebody... or something. *Not yet. Not yet.*

He wanted them all, not just Stevens, but *all* those who were responsible for their unforgivable act. He would bring TAMPRR down, and all the people who were in it from the beginning who did away with the one good man who wouldn't stay silent about what they did, and who couldn't tolerate the fact that they used him to do it.

Stevens used a softer tone. "Ken, as I have told you, the stakes are just as high, or even higher, this time around, as they were with the Avro Arrow situation. And make no mistake; the others at TAMPRR will see to it that if you don't back off, then you and/or your son will get hurt—or worse."

Ken's face became stone, and his voice, ice. "How are they going to get me to back off? Or are *you* supposed to do that? Is your story about what happened to my father, and your threats about my son's safety and my own, supposed to do that? Is all this 'mea culpa' a show, to leave me with an impression that you people are deadly serious, and that since you did it at least once before, you could just as easily do it again?"

Stevens shook his head vigorously from side to side, his white mane waving like a washed out flag in a tempest. "That's not it at all, Ken. My contacting and meeting with you is all my own doing. They would never have had me tell you about TAMPRR. And they haven't told me yet exactly what they have in mind for you, or for when. They've already heard my objection to their doing anything to harm you or your son, so they may have already cut me out of the loop on this one.

"After your father was killed, Ken, I went kind of berserk. I threatened to expose all of them, all of *us*. I was warned that I should remember that I had a son; they didn't have to say anything more. Then a few years later, after my son died in Vietnam, I again thought of doing something... but I didn't.

"They probably took me off this job, too, right after I said that you were Captain Frank Simpson's son. So I don't know what plans they now have to get to you. I am not, this meeting is not, and the things I have told you are not, part of their plan. In fact, if they find out that I have established contact with you, my own health will in immediate jeopardy."

Ken asked, "Have you told me everything you know about them wanting to get me to shut up?"

"Almost everything."

"What else is there?

"Well, they also know about you and Martha Harrison. They know that she matters to you. They could choose to take advantage of that weakness. Look, I may still have ways of finding out some of what they are up to, and if I learn anything I will try to warn you. But the information that I can get will likely be at least a few beats behind most of the others dealing directly with this... situation. So I may not be able to warn you in time."

Stevens paused and then said, "Be very careful, Ken. ... Tell me, has anything unusual happened around you or Martha in the last few days?"

Ken told him about the changes at the office, Sylkeen's coming and Martha's going.

Stevens said, "I don't know about her. You say she seems qualified. Maybe she is legit. Or, it could be that she works for TAMPRR. Just watch out what you tell her, Ken. We have a policy at TAMPRR that we don't reveal, even to one another, the names or identities of the operatives involved in any case, except on a need-to-know basis. So I don't know if she is one of ours. Just stay very alert."

"Is there anything else I should know?"

"Well, I can tell you that TAMPRR has gotten wind that something may be about to happen in Canada that could be pivotal as far as the long-term future of their healthcare system is concerned, and that it might well have repercussions on this side of the border. Our people have just heard in the last couple of days that someone in Prime Minister Perry's party is seriously considering introducing a private member's bill in the Canadian parliament within a matter of weeks, if not days, that would *permanently* enshrine into their Canadian Charter of Rights and Freedoms the right to what is apparently going to be referred to as *'free, expert, and timely, publicly run and funded universal medical healthcare'* for all legal residents of Canada."

Ken softly whistled his exclamation.

Stevens said, "Up until this rumor started circulating TAMPRR had believed that Prime Minister Perry and most of his governing party's members were all sewn up. He had been doing our bidding, getting Canadians softened up for the introduction of U.S.-style, for-profit healthcare by talking about preserving the Canadian Medicare system but improving it by what he has been repeatedly referring to as "transformative constructive changes", which was the phrase that our guys had developed that, like the term, 'compassionate conservativism', sounds vague but positive, yet could open the door to just about any kind of action.

"So now there is this idea that has apparently been spreading like wildfire across Canada over the past few weeks, that could lock up their not-for-profit healthcare within the virtually bulletproofed Charter of Rights and Freedoms. As you can imagine, TAMPRR's corporate clients will go apeshit when they find out! If the Canadians were to actually do that, if they put free Medicare into one of their lockbox documents, then it will be virtually impossible to get it out again, and that will challenge what happens down here like nothing else. It will make it a hell of a lot more difficult for our media to ignore such a Canadian development. If it happens, there will be great fear among our clients that, even with our largely corporately controlled media, there will still be a hell of a lot of unfortunate coverage of such a significant development, and that would threaten our clients' healthcare 'golden goose'.

Ken asked, "So what is TAMPRR going to try to do about it?"

"Well, the pointperson on the proposed bill is a woman. In fact, she is their 'golden girl', an up-and-coming member of the Prime Minister's party who has spent the last ten months or so going around Canada holding televised town hall meetings on the subject of the status and future of healthcare in Canada. At first, it was no big deal. But this woman, whose name is Trish Markridge M.D., by the way, is also a medical doctor in her early forties who just happens to be *gorgeous*–a former Miss Canada or something–and is charismatic as hell, bloody independent-minded, and as far as TAMPRR has been able to find out so far, almost obscenely squeaky clean. And, she is a genuine war hero to boot."

Ken said, sarcastically, "She shouldn't be too difficult a problem for your guys at TAMPRR. You know how to kill off war heroes."

Stevens acknowledged the dig with a fleeting pained expression but otherwise let it pass. He said, "Anyway, Markridge has an online petition with nearly three-quarters of a million authenticated signatures from Canadians from all across the country, endorsing what she is trying to do. And an awful lot of the politicians whose campaigns we helped to finance, are terrified that TAMPRR will expose them for the corrupt phonies they are if they fail to stop her from getting her motion through parliament. At the same time, they know that the great majority of their constituents back Markridge and that they would likely be thrown out of office if they dared to vote against the motion."

Ken said, "The woman sounds really interesting."

Stevens said, "Well, she certainly is going to be putting her fellow politicians between a rock and a hard place. Apparently even though Perry is one of our guys he is very reluctant to try to stop her in any official way. His own party's history has been officially pro-Medicare and he, like all of their former Prime Ministers, has this desire to 'leave a legacy', as they say, that would give him a distinct and positive place in his country's history books which, given his track record so far, is hardly a foregone result. And the man is so wealthy himself that he can't be bought; at least, not by offering any *financial* reward down the road if he plays ball with us. The problem is that neither Perry nor the people we have in his party have yet settled on how to deal with Markridge. So right now there is a very hush-hush team at TAMPRR working on a solution."

Ken asked, "What sort of solution?"

"I don't know yet. TAMPRR is operating more and more like a bunch of terrorist cells. You can only get information if you are part of that particular team. Anyway, I'm trying to find out."

"Anything else I should know?"

"Ken, I've told you just about everything I know, right now. Our current healthcare corporate clients care about what is happening north of our border *now* for some of the same reasons our airplane manufacturer clients cared about the Avro Arrow back in the nineteen fifties. It isn't just that we want the Canadians' Medicare business, although that would be nice. But it would only add about ten percent to these companies' gross income. They just don't want to be facing a tsunami Stateside that could threaten one hundred percent of their business here in the U.S.A..

Ken had observed ex-Lieutenant Colonel Dan Stevens express a very wide variety of emotions over the time they had been talking in the restaurant. At different times the old fellow appeared alternately sad, angry, hurt, larger than life, shriveled up, proud and humiliated. Ken looked into the tired eyes of the old warrior and said, gently, "You are one complicated man."

Ken almost felt sorry for Stevens. He had to make a judgment call, and he did. He said, "I appreciate the risks you may be taking in talking to me. But for me to make the best use of what you have told me today, I need to get corroborating statements. I need you to tell me whom I should interview. And I promise you that, whatever independent information I dig up and can confirm, if I think the material is warranted, I will write about it, but if I can, not before I get back to you and get your off-the-record comments first."

Stevens nodded weakly. He slowly reached into his inside jacket pocket, withdrew a single page of paper. He unfolded it and handed it over to Ken. Ken saw written on the page a list of fifteen or so names along with their respective contact information. Beside each name were also written a few words indicating why that individual was on the list.

Ken noted that several of the people on the list were living in Canada. One name that caught his attention had also been provided by Dr. Larson; a psychiatrist by the name of Dr. William McTavish. According to the notes next to his name, he had previously been an electronics engineer who worked on the Avro Arrow, and who was living in Toronto.

Also on the list were two other persons, one a former, another a current, politician, both of whom were apparently currently living in Ottawa. *There are two good reasons for visiting Ottawa, and seeing Martha.* There was also another apparently former Avro engineer who, a note stated, had gone to work for McBowan after the Arrow program was shut down, and who now lived in San Francisco. Some of the others were spread around the continent, in places like San Diego, Washington, D.C., and Florida. Ken would have several busy days ahead of him.

The lengthy dinner meeting and confessional was abruptly over. Before they got up to leave, Stevens reached into his jacket pocket and handed Ken an otherwise blank business card with his cellphone number written on it. He also gave Ken a CD, saying that it could be used to set up a special software tool within Ken's e-mail program, one that would allow encrypted 'comments' to be embedded in and/or extracted from, seemingly innocuous e-mail attachments. Stevens said that if Ken wanted to contact him with sensitive information he should do so by sending an e-mail with "'Update" in the subject line and an innocuous-sounding travelogue-type statement in the body of the e-mail. The real message would be buried in encrypted form in the spaces between the seventh and eighth words in the text attachment. Messages that Stevens might send to Ken would begin with

"Have a relaxing holiday".

It hardly required his uncanny intuition for Ken to conclude that the next few days would hardly be that.

CHAPTER 24

When Ken returned home he immediately loaded onto his laptop the software 'patch' from the CD that Stevens had given him, and committed the access password to memory. He was flooded with feelings relating to both his personal and professional lives. He wanted to nail the people at TAMPRR for his dad's death, including probably Lieutenant Colonel Dan Stevens, especially if he was in any way deceiving Ken at this point. Tracking the Avro Arrow program's demise might well lead him to some of the key people on both sides of the border who had a hand it killing it, and therefore directly or indirectly, his own father as well.

He also wanted to look into the Canadian Medicare system situation and what efforts were also keeping American citizens from getting their own 'free, expert and timely' healthcare.

Ken had concluded that if the Canadian parliament dared to pass a law making Medicare for all residents a part of that country's Charter of Rights and Freedoms, then the pressure on American politicians to do something similar might grow rapidly. Ken recalled that Americans paid much more than Canadians for healthcare on a per capita basis, even though more than thirteen percent of his fellow citizens didn't have any healthcare coverage, and that many HMOs' and PPOs' premiums had been rising at more than twelve percent every year for the last few years.

The companies who had hired TAMPRR were enormously powerful moneymaking machines for their senior executives and investors. He knew that several were notorious for keeping their costs down by refusing coverage for what were frequently considered medically appropriate tests, procedures and even surgeries by their subscribers' doctors. Ken had read that in Canada, with the 'for-profit' element out of the equation, if a test needed to be done, or was merely advisable, it was most often done. Of course, the media had made certain that everyone knew about the waiting lists for some tests and procedures in Canada. But he had heard from Stevens that these delays were largely due to a variety of real and fabricated problems. At least, however, a Canadian patient's doctor did not have to make a case of the need for the test or procedure to a non-physician, gate-keeping clerk. It was simply a patient-doctor decision. If the waiting list issue was resolved, which system would probably better suit most citizens in America? Talk about a no-brainer!

The next morning Ken made several phone calls, including one to Martha who, at the moment she answered her ringing cellphone, was approaching the outskirts of Canada's capital, Ottawa, in her new SUV.

Martha was excited to hear from Ken and thanked him repeatedly for her new 'wheels'. She was even more thrilled to hear that he was going to be coming to Ottawa in a few days. After he had explained why he was coming, the tone in her voice changed ever so slightly, giving away the fact that she was more than a little disappointed that his primary motivation for the trip had not been because he was already missing her desperately. However, the professional that she was, she readily agreed to arrange interviews for Ken with the people from a list that he would be faxing to her within a couple of hours. While he told her that Dr. Larson had provided many of the names, he deliberately did not mention anything related to Lieutenant Colonel Dan Stevens—including even his existence. Martha would later report to Ken that everyone on Dr. Larson's list had already received a positive call from the former Surgeon-General, and they had all readily agreed to be interviewed.

Next, Ken made an airline reservation leaving LaGuardia for Toronto the following day.

Ken decided that he simultaneously hated, appreciated, and felt sorry for Stevens. However, he was determined to use him in order to get to the people who were involved in sabotaging his father's aircraft. The fact that they were also some of the same individuals who were actively attempting to sabotage the Canadian—and possibly the American—healthcare systems, was a bonus; it meant that he could justify devoting time, effort, and the paper's money to digging into the web of deceit and corruption woven by TAMPRR Inc. on behalf of its corporate clients. He just wished he could get rid of the nagging feeling that it might be himself who was going to get caught in it.

CHAPTER 25

Within 48 hours after having first been contacted by ex-Lieutenant Colonel Stevens, and less than 24 hours after meeting with him in New York City, Air Canada's Boeing 737 crossed the U.S.-Canada border over Lake Ontario and touched down at Pearson International Airport. By eleven in the morning Ken was in the back of a taxi heading to the downtown Holiday Inn, a hotel he had stayed at once before, on a weekend getaway with his then intact small family. Dropping his bags off at the hotel, he took another cab to his appointment, one that he had arranged over the phone with the secretary of one of the first names on the list that Dr.Larson provided him. Stevens had said that Ken would find Dr. William McTavish a particularly interesting individual with whom to speak, since he had the unique qualifications of being both a medical doctor, and an experienced psychiatrist at that, who had worked, almost a half-century earlier, as an electrical engineer on the Avro Arrow's navigational guidance system.

Dr. McTavish's office was in a well-to-do residential area of mid-Toronto, on St. Clair Avenue West, a wide and once stately street lined by many large, 'typically Canadian', three-story brick houses.

The street was clearly a sort of 'angst alley'. Ken noted dozens of psychiatrists, psychologists, and clinical social workers had their shingles proudly displayed on 'St. Clair'. They undoubtedly drew many of their patients from the obviously well-heeled surrounding neighborhood, probably peopled by what Ken had heard a New York City psychologist-friend refer to as his 3N folks, for 'Nice Normal Neurotics'. Here, Ken thought hopefully, at least some of the consumers who found their way to St. Clair Avenue West felt better for their efforts and monies expended during their truncated 'clinical hours'.

Ken admitted to being slightly skeptical... all right, *very* skeptical, of what its practitioners referred to as 'psychotherapy'. Which is not to say that he doubted that there were some very skilled practitioners of that art-science who actually benefited their charges. Perhaps he was simply still a little sore after his own experience with a so-called marriage therapist who his then-wife had insisted they see, but who seemed far more attentive to the clock on her desk than to the couple in front of her who were obviously teetering on the brink of their undoubtedly self-created disaster.

Ken arrived a mere two minutes before the appointed time of 3:10 p.m. that had been merrily assigned to him by the pleasant-sounding, older Scottish woman who had answered Dr. McTavish's number the previous day, and who had been given to understand that Dr. Leo Larson had suggested to Dr. McTavish that Ken was someone he would like to meet.

Ken wondered whether most shrinks kept such precise starting times for their clients. The military shrink Ken was pressured to see after his traumatic experience with an exploding child during his last bombing attack had been positively 'anal' in his compulsive timing at the start of sessions. His door always opened right on time; Ken could set his watch by his therapist's punctuality. In fact, on one occasion he actually did.

To give the guy his due, though, after first wondering aloud whether Ken had simply given in to fear during combat, at least he had taken the time to 'kick Ken's tires' for a few sessions. Sharing his clinical findings with his patient, he told Ken that the fact he was having trouble "repressing his revulsion" over what he had done in killing those innocent children, while probably making him unsuitable as a combat pilot of the U.S. Air Force, not only did not mean that he was nuts, but on the contrary, most likely indicated a mature moral sensibility. However, this admirable quality probably better suited him to be an asset in a field that more directly promoted individual and societal well-being. In short, the shrink indicated that Ken was, in that area anyway, an emotionally healthy person.

Ken appreciated the doc's diagnosis, which was also a factor in his deciding to take an honorable discharge from the air force and then 'enlist' in journalism school, even though he doubted that his newly chosen profession would be one where 'emotionally healthy persons' would be more likely to be found in great abundance.

Dr. McTavish's waiting room was small and sparsely furnished, except for three simple straight back wooden chairs, a side table covered with weeks-old newspapers, months-old magazines and a small clock radio tuned to an all-jazz station. The volume of the music was presumably set just high enough to effectively mask any sounds short of outright screeching that might emanate from the doctor's main office. The waiting room was far more functional than formal. *Good.* And, with the wall holding framed cartoons poking fun–gently–at a variety of human foibles, definitely more laid back than Ken had expected.

The inner office's door opened, sure enough, at 3:10pm. A still powerfully built, six foot two, bearded, balding and distinguished-looking gentleman in his late seventies, wearing a handsome tweed Jacket, slacks, and open shirt, greeted Ken. With a warm smile, firm handshake, and a rich Scottish brogue tinged with some reserve, he said, "Mr. Simpson, I presume. Please, come in."

Ken entered the psychiatrist's office and took the well-worn leather chair across the plain desk from an even more worn out, but somewhat more impressive, high back leather office chair. Quickly glancing around the office Ken was rather surprised to see what appeared to be a combination of a classical therapist's office, a veritable storeroom of file cabinets, and a compact video studio, complete with camcorder, playback monitor, VHS recorder, and a DVD recorder/player.

Ken noted the old laptop on the doctor's desk, along with other assorted electronic paraphernalia, including a compact but modestly expensive stereo with a pair of audiophile-appealing speakers bracketing the desk. Above a bookcase behind and to the right of the doctor's chair was a collection of about ten still and movie cameras; Ken recognized a couple as being about sixty years old, including a Kodak Brownie Hawkeye, similar to the one that his dad had given him for his tenth birthday.

In an even, somewhat guarded voice, the psychiatrist said, "The message that you left with my secretary indicated that you wanted to ask me some questions regarding both the Avro Arrow and the Canadian Medicare system. A novel request, to be sure. Might I ask why you are interested in both of these matters?"

"Well, Dr. McTavish, I have been doing some research for a series of articles on the healthcare situations in our two countries for *The New York Era*, in the course of which I came upon some disturbing information about the termination of the CF-105 Avro Arrow program."

McTavish cocked his head in interest.

"To put matters succinctly, I have come to believe that the manner of–and the men behind–the termination of the Avro Arrow may be related to certain current political and corporate goings-on in the healthcare fields in our respective countries. You are possibly aware that you have been mentioned in at least two books about the Arrow as one of the most talented engineers involved in that project. I would have therefore expected to find that you would have moved to the United States and worked for one of our American aircraft companies, as I understand a lot of others from the Avro Arrow program did. So I was surprised to learn that you had left the field of engineering entirely."

Dr. McTavish gave Ken a sharp look and inquired, "And why does that either surprise or interest you, Mr. Simpson?"

"Well, of course I wondered about your experiences working on the Arrow program, and why you left engineering entirely after that project was terminated. I am also interested in what, as a psychiatrist, your thoughts are about the possible effects of the cancellation of the Avro Arrow program on the other individuals directly involved, and on Canada's aviation and engineering companies generally. And I wonder what your thoughts are about the *way* in which the program was terminated."

McTavish leaned forward almost menacingly in his chair, resting his elbows on either side of his laptop. "You mean, Mr. Simpson, do I think that the Avro Arrow program was not just cancelled but raped, pillaged and murdered?" McTavish did not care to be coy about the matter.

"Something like that, if that is how you see it, yes, sir."

"I see," said McTavish slowly. "And may I ask what you might do with this material? After all, it is now five decades since the Arrow was cancelled, and never, not once, in all the years since, have I had any reporter–American, or even Canadian for that matter–ask me about my views on the closing down of that program."

Before Ken could respond, the man's countenance grew darker, and he added, "And why now? What the hell for?" The doctor's Scottish accent was more pronounced when his voice was raised; the man's dander was definitely on the way up!

"Well, Dr. McTavish, I have received information that suggests that the motivations behind the cancellation of the Avro Arrow program may have been more sinister than they were made out to be at the time."

"Oh? You don't say!" responded McTavish sharply and sarcastically. "And *why*, may I ask, do you think so?" McTavish's eyes had somehow become halogens.

Ken was not going to be deterred, however; in fact, he had hoped for a strong response to his statement.

"Because, Dr. McTavish, I have recently learned that back in 1958, a covert operation had been hatched and operated from the U.S., involving both civilians and politicians, and most likely, some key military and governmental personnel in both our countries. This operation was dedicated to bringing down the Avro Arrow program–completely and permanently. And I now also have reason to believe that the some of the same methods employed to kill the Arrow have been used much more recently, by a few of the very same people, with the goal of taking down, and then taking over–and privatizing–the entire healthcare system in your country.

McTavish did not express surprise at Ken's revelation. He said, "Well, Mr. Simpson, for the sake of argument, let's say you are right. That would hardly surprise me or most of my colleagues. Some of us in this country have suspected as much for a long time, although we haven't had definitive proof. What we have known is that the goings on in healthcare in Canada among our various levels of government often look, walk, and squawk like a flock of privatization ducks. So all right, then; suppose you go ahead and ask me specific questions, and I will do my best to answer them, if I can."

Recalling the notes he had downloaded the previous evening to prepare himself for this meeting Ken said, "Thank you. Well, I understand from some of what I have read that you were a key member of the team looking into the high performance demand requirements that could expected to be placed upon the aircraft's navigational and fire control system. Yet after it was cancelled, when I am sure that you must have received substantial offers from some American aircraft manufacturers to continue in your field, you chose to leave engineering altogether and change careers. Why was that?"

McTavish's eyes bored into Ken. "And why does *that* interest you, Mr. Simpson?"

"Well," said Ken, "actually what interests me isn't only your own personal experiences and your decision to leave engineering, but also what insights your training and experience as a psychiatrist might have given you into what were the real costs of the Arrow's demise–in human, business, and national terms. Also, why do you think the prototypes were destroyed with blowtorches and sledge hammers, and what do you think were the effects of those actions upon the folks involved in the project and on Canadians generally, for that matter?"

McTavish sighed, temporarily bit his lower lip, and then slowly nodded his head as he spoke. "Quite a lot to answer, Mr. Simpson. Well, the effects of that desecration were indeed massive in this country. If I might put it in terms that my friends in engineering might be more inclined to use I would say that 'they', whoever *they* were, tried to break our business 'balls', our confidence in our own technological abilities, and our national pride. And in many ways, and with a large number of people in the business, engineering, and aviation worlds of this country, they succeeded."

McTavish paused, sighed again, and then asked, "And if I tell you what else I think about this subject, how will that help you with your series on our countries' healthcare systems? Most people would think that to be rather a stretch, if you don't mind my saying so."

"Dr. McTavish, as I have said, I have reason to believe that some of the same people behind the destruction of the Arrow program are currently working to wreck our countries' healthcare systems. If I can understand more about how they did their work back then, perhaps I can alert my readers on both sides of our border about what to be on the lookout for now."

Dr. McTavish said nothing for a full half-minute. He seemed to be thinking hard and long as he stroked his goatee with the back of his hand. Ken wondered if he was actually considering his questions, or just deciding how to get him out of his office. He decided he had better give the engineer-cum-psychiatrist more information to weigh, just in case he was considering the latter.

"Dr. McTavish, my father was an ex-U.S. Air Force officer and civilian test pilot attached to the Avro Arrow project. His name was Captain Frank Simpson."

Ken observed the man's defensive expression transmute into what looked, at first, like surprise, then relief, and finally, understanding and thoughtful satisfaction. When McTavish focused on Ken again, he seemed to regard the younger man in a fresh, more welcoming way.

Dr. McTavish said, "I believe that I may have met your father a couple of times. A good man, and an outstanding pilot, I remember. He died a few years after the Avro Arrow program was canceled, didn't he?"

Ken said, quietly, "Yes, sir, he did. I was only a teenager at the time, but I remember him telling me how impressed he was with the Arrow and how much he respected the people who had designed and built her. I know he was very upset by its cancellation."

"As were we all," McTavish replied, mostly to himself. "All right, then. Let me tell you what I know and also what I speculate to be true. I know that the way they killed the Arrow program was dramatic, *traumatic*, and cruel if not outright criminal, and based upon decades of reflection, it seems clear to me to have been aimed at causing the maximum psychological, as well as economic, injury to all parties concerned."

Ken asked, "Why would anyone want to do that?"

McTavish's right eyebrow shot up as a scowl started to mask his face. He calmed himself, and then said, "What happened to the Arrow program was the political and corporate equivalent of a sadistic rape and murder. There was, if I may continue the analogy, an unwanted intrusion into a young industry and company and the utter rape and pillage of the same. The victim was beaten, mutilated, her body burned and blowtorched until one could barely tell who or what she had been, originally. Most of her body was lost, leaving only a few body parts–you can see them on infamous display at the ass-end of the National Flight Museum of Canada, in Ottawa. Just think of it. You Americans put *your* Spirit of St. Louis at the *entrance* to the National Aviation and Space Museum in Washington, while the few pieces of an Avro Arrow that remain are located all at the rear of *our* national flight museum."

He continued, "Shortly after the program was ended and almost all of the employees were let go, all on the same black bloody Friday, by the way, February 20th, 1959, our newspapers carried photos of the pieces of the broken prototypes there on the ground outside the building where they had been built, to let everyone in this country see with their own eyes that our aeronautical and technological Camelot had been decimated. Those photos were, to some extent at least, the Canadian aeronautical equivalent of the Zapruder film frames of your president's assassination that occurred four years later. Both sets of photographs told their stories in unforgettable–and surely intolerable–detail. Both Camelots, yours and ours, were blown apart in front of the whole world. In the case of the Arrow, well, that glorious product of some of the best and brightest brains in this country, was literally and figuratively splattered all over the tarmac. And like the Zapruder film, we have our grainy equivalent of a puff of smoke on the grassy knoll in the form of a few telling documents and photos, to have made us wonder, for these past five decades, what the hell *really* happened to the Avro Arrow project? But at least you had a state funeral and the Warren Commission. We didn't even give the Arrow either a proper burial or a reasonable investigation. This year is the fiftieth anniversary of the death of the Arrow, and a few private, non-governmental organizations are again bringing the attention of the public to the unsettling question of what really happened back then, although it is undoubtedly far too late for a Royal Commission to be set up to thoroughly investigate the matter."

Dr. McTavish looked alternatively ferocious and melancholy as he continued. "I don't know if you remember this, but when President Kennedy was killed in Dallas, his wife, Jackie, refused to change out of her blood-and-brains splattered clothes. She said, "I want them to see what they did to him," or words to that effect.

"Well, our aeronautical equivalent version of her clothes now reside in the National Flight Museum of Canada and at a few other locations across this country, where the terrible things done that day in 1959, are still remembered. All that remains of the Avro Arrow at Ottawa's museum is one limb in the form of a single nose-wheel assembly and the cockpit and nose of Arrow number 208. And if you walk to the back of that murderous memento of a fuselage you will see, I kid you not, the blowtorched hind end of the cockpit, that section having been brutally severed from the rest of the fuselage to which it had been attached. Then, some seventy-five or so feet away to the right, nearly entirely hidden behind a lot of other far less noble bits and pieces of other less important airplanes, at least as of the last time I was there, are the two wing tips of an Arrow. And, mind you," McTavish said, "those are the *tips* of the wings; not the whole wings, you understand; that would be too damned much to have expected the powers that were, to save."

The elderly psychiatrist certainly didn't lack for either energy or emotion. McTavish's eyes watered somewhat and his chin quivered slightly as he struggled to stiffen his jaw. Then he said, sadly but defiantly, "Damn them all, those bastards. Our military aviation industry never recovered from the actions of those gutless thugs who were the so-called military and political 'leaders' of this country.

"I can tell you, speaking as an engineer, a medical doctor and a psychiatrist, that the hearts, minds and souls of too many of the fine men and women who worked on that marvelous dream that became a momentary, shining reality, were utterly shattered. In the days after the program was cancelled there were vans outside

Avro's gates filled with American recruiters from NASA and some of your aircraft companies, a few of whom apparently were already in town because, it seemed clear, they had advance warning that the program was going to be shut down. It was like a 'sitting duck' shooting gallery for them. The workers were lined up outside the hiring companies' trailers, in a state of shock, and many of the best of them were easily picked off."

Ken asked, "What happened to the others, the ones who either weren't hired, or didn't want to go south?"

"Believe it or not, some of the engineers who didn't want to leave this country found themselves being treated as pariahs as far as many other Canadian companies and American subsidiaries were concerned. Of course, many of them tried to get engineering jobs with other companies. But the publicity surrounding the killing of the Arrow tainted many of the guys who had worked on her. Some of them told me during their therapy sessions years later that they were most unwelcome to join other companies in this country, either because they were seen as too much competition for the engineers already working for the companies doing the hiring, or because the companies thought that these Arrow guys wouldn't last; after all, how do you keep some of the finest engineers in the world happy if all you have to offer them are jobs designing light fixtures or toilet bowls?

"A few of the engineers I knew who did go to the U.S. found jobs at the so-called 'big three' automakers. The work was hardly inspiring, however, designing cosmetic tail fins for family automobiles that would be changed the next year, instead of dynamically critical wing surfaces for the top fighter-interceptor in the world. I can tell you, without exaggeration, that some of these men's souls were crushed. Others did what I did. They decided, somewhere deep down in their psyches, to get the hell out of engineering all together. After all, as many of us thought, "If they can kill your job for being successful, and if you have already tasted tremendous success and, in effect, won 'gold' at the aeronautical engineering equivalent of the Olympics, then why would you settle for designing toasters? Why sell yourself short? And who ever wants to give anyone else that kind of power over you again?" Not a lot of my friends at Avro, I can tell you. *And not me, that was for certain!"*

Dr. McTavish stopped talking, and as Ken watched the doctor's eyes darting about, he guessed the former superb engineer was recalling some of those decades-old events.

Dr. McTavish shook himself out of his reverie. Ken gently inquired, "Where did some of the other Avro engineers who left the profession, end up?"

The psychiatrist's voice took on a proud tone. "A number of the lads went back to university, either to teach engineering or to get higher degrees in the same field. Others of them, *of us*, became teachers, doctors, lawyers, dentists, anything... *anything* that served as outlets for our creativity and our energies but would allow us more control over what happened to us from that point onward."

McTavish then said, in almost a whisper, as if he was being deliberately respectful, "A few never worked again. *They* were the *worst* casualties. They were truly broken, lost to themselves, and often, to those who loved them. Deep depressions got many; breakdowns took others. Look, Mr. Simpson, people's identities are often so tied to what they *do*; they think that is who they *are*! And for most people who have not cultivated many other interests outside their work, when they stop working they feel lost. They feel like nobodies; like nothings. And far too often, they may kill themselves off with one sort of illness or another."

Ken asked, "Did you personally know any Avro workers who died within a short time after the Arrow program was shut down?"

McTavish said, "Of course. One was my good friend, Lewis, a wonderful systems design engineer who was in his late thirties. He was possessed when it came to his work, and to his credit, he did some of the best work on the Arrow. When the program was cancelled he felt like *he* had been cancelled. It was like being caught at the top of Mount St. Helene when it erupted. He had been at the top of the engineering 'mountain', so to speak, loving every minute, totally exhilarated. Moments later he was blasted off its–and his–peak, his career instantly blown to bits, and his fractured ego fell into an abyss. He became a drunk in an attempt to anesthetize himself to the pain of the loss and disappointment.

That didn't quite do it for him, though, so he became a womanizer, probably to reassure himself that he was still essentially a man, because with the cancellation of the Arrow he felt as if he had personally been castrated."

Ken understood that this was not a mere story he was being told, but a eulogy being recited. He put down his pen and paid his respects.

McTavish was almost done the telling. "Then everything really went to shit. Lewis's antics were intolerable to those who loved him. He lost his house, his wife, and his children. Nothing seemed to matter to him any more; he gave away whatever else materially that he had left. It was as if he didn't want to ever again be in a position to lose something of value to him by someone else's hand. So, of course, he lost everything that mattered. They broke his mind, his heart, and his soul.

"He ended up a psychiatric chronic-care ward, where he spent the rest of his shortened life not even trying to find himself. Unfortunately, the therapists he had didn't understand that. They tried to help him find his way back to living his life. When they thought they had very nearly succeeded, he panicked at the prospect of regaining success and then losing it all again. He ran away from the hospital, and threw himself off an overpass onto the freeway below."

The eulogy ended, Dr. William McTavish looked up at Ken. Their eyes met; Ken saw that the halogens were out, and in their place a soft and intolerably sad candlelight gently illuminated an old man's face and tears.

Without a doubt, when the Avro Arrow program was shot down, the debris-field destroyed many peoples' lives—including, Ken hardly needed to be reminded, the life belonging to Captain Frank Simpson, U.S.A.F., retired.

CHAPTER 26

Neither Dr. McTavish nor Ken said anything for a while. Finally, the older man stood up wearily and walked across the room. He opened a door behind which were a small fridge and cupboard. On a shelf above the fridge was a single-element, table-top burner. He turned on the element and within a minute the kettle he had placed on it signaled that the water was at a boil.

"Tea or coffee, Mr. Simpson?"

"Tea, please," said Ken, mostly in deference to his host.

McTavish made a fresh pot of tea, and then lightly lifted a tray bearing a few cookies, two cups and saucers and a teapot, plus accessories, back to the low table that separated their two chairs.

"Dr. McTavish, may I ask you something more about the Avro Arrow?"

"Of course," he replied in his strong, deep Scottish brogue, all signs of his personal anguish having vanished. *The doctor was in.*

"Well, I have read that the powers that were said that it was necessary to destroy the prototypes for the sake of national security. Did you, and/or do you now, believe that?"

"Almost nobody believes that bullshit!" the ex-Avro engineer roared. "Listen, they could have ripped all the sensitive equipment out of every one of those prototypes, if they were really concerned about security, and still could have left the fuselages intact. Hell, that was all we had up to Black Friday anyway, the day they shut the program down. We didn't even have the complete firing instrumentation on board because they had just made up their minds as to which air-to-air missiles would be used. But leaving the shell of an Avro Arrow intact, *no*, that would be too kind. They wanted to make a truly unforgettable statement, a huge 'Fuck You' declaration, to those of us in Canada who didn't know our place, so to speak." He was Mighty McTavish now. *"National security, my arse!"*

"Look, Mr. Simpson, the psychology is straightforward

wartime Psyc-Ops. By completely flattening your competitor's factories and destroying everything in it, *including even his bloody blueprints, for God's sake,* and making off with his scientists, you are ensuring that your enemy won't threaten your supremacy for a long, long time, if ever. Dr. McTavish was shaking with fury.

With some trepidation, Ken asked, "Why then, feeling as strongly as you did, and obviously still do, about the importance of engineering in Canada, why would you leave the profession?"

McTavish flashed a smile of remembrance. "When I was a young teenager, a mere sixty-plus years ago, I couldn't make up my mind whether to be an engineer or a psychiatrist. I thought that engineering was probably so tough that it likely had to be done through full-time university studies. I had always thought that one day I would go back to university and take up psychology, probably part-time. When the Arrow program was cancelled, though, I knew that I had already helped create something far more important and innovative in the previous few years than I had ever thought that I might. Or than I ever thought I would have a chance to do again, unless I went to the U.S., which at the time I had no interest in doing. So I was done, 'like toast', as we used to say."

McTavish semi-smiled, and then continued. "Besides, a lot of the guys from Avro were disgusted with both our government and yours. The lame excuses our politicians gave for canceling the program—that it was too expensive, that the Russian missile threat at the time had made fighter-interceptors obsolete, that no one would buy the airplane, that it would never meet specs. All of the above was bullshit!

"Why do you say that?"

"Hell, the Arrow was at least a whole decade ahead of the competition. It had a fly-by-wire system, carried its weapons in an undercarriage internally, and would soon have had the more powerful, Canadian-built Iroquois engine. And it had already exceeded many of its design specs with the smaller engine.

"They also said, *'Oh, the Avro Arrow has technical problems.'* Well, like all high performance aircraft, or any new aircraft, in its early stages, it had a few technical matters that had to be solved.

Big deal! The biggest technical hurdles of fuselage design had already been overcome. The remainder would have been dealt with completely within a few more months. And none that the Arrow design team came across were 'show-stoppers'.

"Then our magnificent government said that the Arrow was too costly. *Also crap!* The costs were similar to those of U.S. aircraft, and the likelihood was that we would be able to sell an awful lot of Arrows to other NATO countries, including perhaps even the U.S.A.F., thereby bringing the cost-per-plane down even further. So, instead, we spent a fortune, *after* the Arrow was cancelled, for completely useless U.S.-made Bomarc missiles and some lower-rated U.S. aircraft. If only we had been allowed to continue to develop and produce the Arrow, the costs would have been far less than the costs of buying their replacements, your F-101B Voodoos, and those bloody stupid, useless Bomarcs."

Ken asked, "So you sincerely believe the Avro Arrow was canceled because it was *too* good."

McTavish did not suffer baiting or foolishness lightly. He said, sharply, "Look here; *your* American aircraft companies *never* stopped designing fighter-interceptors; not for a minute. Their aim was simply to stop their competitors, *us*, from producing any *competing* aircraft."

His words now began to emerge more slowly. "Anyway, a decade or so after the Avro Arrow program was shut down, I finished my medical degree at the University of Ontario, and then took my specialty training in psychiatry. Over time, largely through word of mouth, some of the men and women who had worked on the program became clients of mine. They knew that I 'knew', which always trumps being merely 'understanding'. The blows to their egos, the trauma of what they had experienced, was something many of them—and myself—were still trying to get past.

"One patient, a former senior executive at Avro, used to come into my office, look at the Avro Arrow model over there," the doctor said, nodding towards a beautiful, painted, twenty inch long model of the aircraft that Ken had first noticed when he entered the office, "and he would say nothing; that went on for three sessions. At the end of each session he seemed he was about to cry but before that could happen he would quickly leave my office. Then, halfway through the fourth session, he started to cry. He sobbed like a baby after that, session after session, making such grief-stricken, keening sounds that I nearly lost my own composure more than a few times. Whenever he would try to speak to me, no words came out. Then one day, he came in and told me that after he was let go by Avro he spent every single day of the next two years just walking the streets of Toronto. He said that he couldn't even bring himself to look for another job because he had felt somehow personally guilty that the program had been shut down. He thought that perhaps, if only he had done more, provided more cogent arguments in favor of the Arrow, gotten the plane traveling faster sooner, that his efforts might have helped to convince the government to keep the program going."

Ken said, firmly, "I can share with you, Dr. McTavish, that it wouldn't matter what your patient had done or said. The 'fix' was in–absolutely. It was threatening the military aircraft industry of the United States. That *is* why it was killed. The only thing wrong with the Arrow was that there *wasn't* anything wrong with it!"

McTavish seemed surprised to hear such a firm concurring statement. "Mr. Simpson, do you have some inside knowledge of what really happened to the Arrow? If so, would you care to share what else you know?"

Ken said, "I promise that I will, Dr. McTavish, just as soon as I can."

From the dark expression that traveled across the psychiatrist's face, Ken surmised that McTavish was about to say something that was unlikely to be complimentary; he cut him off at the in-breath.

"Doctor McTavish, as soon as it is *safe* to do so, I assure you that I will tell you everything that I have learned about this matter."

The older man took some moments to ponder the implications of Ken's last statement and his hesitation to be more forthcoming. Then McTavish changed direction. "You also asked what other effects the killing of the Avro Arrow program had on the

Canadian psyche. As I said, it made some of our best and brightest business and scientific people stop believing in themselves. Others thought, why bother building up something special, unless you wanted an American company to either buy it or wipe you out? Over time, in fact, that became the goal of many Canadian entrepreneurs; and too often still is today. *'Build something that an American company will like so much that it will buy your company'.*"

Ken asked, "Has it really been that bad?"

"You are a reporter, Mr. Simpson. Check it out in the business section archives of our major papers. Our newspapers celebrate each new sale of a Canadian company to a Microsoft or a Boeing, and make much more of a 'to-do' about it than if one Canadian company buys out another Canadian company, even if the same dollar amounts are involved. We have come to view ourselves as the 'farm team' to American business–their 'B' team. So, is this what you came to find out from me, Mr. Simpson?"

Ken said, "Yes, in part, Dr. McTavish. And I want to say to you that I am sorrier than you can possibly know for the loss of the Avro Arrow program. I recently received probably accurate information that my father was involved in the way in which the Avro Arrow program was terminated. And because he was determined to correct, or at least, compensate for the loss of the Arrow, he was... *he was*... he was killed. He apparently knew too much about what really happened to the Avro Arrow. In fact, *he* personally flew one of them, number 208, from Avro's plant in Malton to its final destination in the American southwest a few days after the program was cancelled. The remnants of the Arrow on display at the museum in Ottawa are not that of 208."

Ken thought that McTavish's halogens were going to burn out due to over-heating, but not before they had baked Ken's brain. Successive microexpressions of shock and anger flickered across McTavish's aged face.

Ken quickly added, "As I said previously, I have reason to believe that some of the very same key people involved in killing the Arrow are at it again. This time they have their sights set on killing another thing that you Canadians have designed and built that is decades ahead of what we have in America. And, just as with the Avro Arrow, there are again people in my country who believe that if what you have created here is not destroyed, then within the next few years, dozens or even hundreds of American HMOs, PPOs, and pharmaceutical companies, many in the multi-*billion* annual revenue category, will face financial disaster. Some of these companies are *so* terrified by what you have created here that they have been actively working for over a dozen years to kill off the Canadian Medicare system and then privatize it. And it so happens that this moment in time is 'crunch time' for their efforts."

Dr. McTavish appeared to be mulling over Ken's comments. He then said, "That would certainly explain certain rumors I have been hearing for some time now from some of my friends in Ottawa."

Ken asked, "What sorts of rumors?"

McTavish said, "Well, as nearly every Canadian knows through media reports galore, there have been some very strange goings-on in this country in regard to our health care system for many years now. For example, somehow we have too few radiation, MRI and CT scan machines available, and some of them are so old and unreliable that when some hospitals out in western Canada tried to give them away to so-called third world countries, even *they* wouldn't take them. For Pete's sake, even *veterinarians have refused to take them–for free*–because they couldn't do the jobs well enough to even be used on animals."

"Really?"

"Not only that, Mr. Simpson, but when some of the most up-to-date versions of these machines were bought in the past few years for hundreds of millions of dollars, the people in charge somehow didn't bother to make sure that there were nearly enough qualified radiation technicians to operate them. For that reason, among others, these hi-tech tools, which are built to be used around the clock, were not able to be operated for more than eight hours a day.

"Also, our federal government's immigration department takes an exceptionally long time before they allow appropriately trained technicians to be admitted into Canada to work the devices. On the other hand, they fast-track and basically rubberstamp immigration for professional athletes from the U.S. and elsewhere in a matter of mere weeks after they had been hired by one of our Canadian professional sports teams.

"As well, a few of the provincial governments who had been given money by the feds specifically earmarked to help them acquire more MRIs and CAT scans and properly trained technicians to operate them, claimed that they would not allow themselves to be bossed around by the feds or told what to do with the money they received. So they used the money instead to build indoor hockey arenas and, in a couple of cases, to help some farmers establish more ecologically dangerous, humungous pig farms near some of our biggest cities."

Ken shook his head in dismay, but to bring some lightness to an otherwise distressing conversation, said, "Sounds like when your politicians, like some of ours, think of 'pork barrels', they take the term literally as well as figuratively."

McTavish smiled pleasantly, nodded, and said, "It gets worse. The government in Ottawa cut back on its health dollars, and then, in turn, Premier Linden's provincial Minister of Health went ahead and fired thousands of nurses. Then, when we were faced with the SARS outbreak a few years back, there were not enough nurses to handle the job, and so a lot of them burned out; that lack of human resources may well have helped the disease to spread unnecessarily. Not providing enough people to do a job properly virtually guarantees that they will fail at it. It is as if the federal, and some provincial, governments have been bent on destroying our Medicare system.

"As another example, a few years ago the ruling parties in some provinces closed down entire hospitals and shut down emergency wards in some of the ones that were still open, so that many ambulances ended up on redirect, and people died unnecessarily while being bounced from one hospital to another. On occasion some had to be driven to other cities more than a hundred miles away just to get admitted to a hospital. The problems made headlines for a while, and some bigwigs were quoted in the media as complaining that those problems 'proved' that our Medicare system wasn't working, and that we should adopt the American system as soon as possible. The 'fix', as you called it, has undoubtedly been in for quite some time, Mr. Simpson."

Ken said, "What you have been saying is filling out some of the details of what I have been hearing about in general terms."

McTavish said, "Oh, there is much more, I assure you. For example, some years back, we even had to send hundreds of our cancer patients to the U.S. *every month*, because the provincial government refused to run its radiation equipment more than eight hours a day, and then announced that it would be forced to allow private companies to run the very same equipment in their hospitals after-hours. It's like sending our people to the U.S. for gas for their cars after we have deliberately closed down some of our gas stations, and the ones that are left are operated only a few hours a day, and then in the evenings are run by U.S. operators. The entire situation stinks, and begs for answers, doesn't it, Mr. Simpson, as to why we have these problems, and who is behind them?"

Ken nodded while writing furiously.

"And consider this," said the doctor. "During our last several elections, healthcare has been one of the top items of interest to Canadians, and has had a central place in the political promise platforms of all the political parties. All the while, our Medicare system has been considered among the best in the world by the United Nations and a whole host of different countries' healthcare commissions. And yet here we are, talking about destroying it, and setting up what is euphemistically being called a two-tier, public-private system. Why? And now there have even been rumors, ever since the last federal and provincial elections, that the same governments that came in last time on a 'keep and strengthen Medicare' platform, are about to either bring in legislation to do the very opposite or are simply not going to enforce the legislation that already exists to prevent Medicare being weakened."

Ken said, "That is interesting. Meanwhile, in the U.S., surveys done over the past several years ago by some of the Ivy League universities, have found that nearly one-half of subscribers to HMOs in the States had complaints about the ways in which they were treated."

Dr. McTavish said, "Well, that is certainly no surprise. By

contrast, polls in this country indicate that between seventy and eighty percent of Canadians are somewhat to very satisfied with Medicare in our country. Yet, to listen to many in the media, you would think the entire system is falling apart and not worth saving.

"When some of our endless committees and so-called royal commissions wanted our provinces to report on where in the health system, the money that the feds gave to them actually went, many of the provinces stonewalled. They don't want the public to see how they are *mis*using funds earmarked for Medicare, for other purposes."

Ken said, "Well, I want to find out what is going on behind the scenes here in Canada, by whom, and why. Do you think that I'm likely to be able to get any politicians or others in a position to know, to allow me to interview them for the series I am doing?"

"You might, but you will have to be very careful. Most Canadians don't trust their politicians to tell the truth or to act in their constituents'–as opposed to some special interest group's–best interests. In Ontario, for instance, when the government moved to privatize the hydroelectric production and delivery systems, it was widely believed that the party in power had received financial contributions from American companies who wanted to move in on our energy markets. The bloody beggars were so greedy, however, that the next thing people knew, their hydro rates skyrocketed, and the government, facing a re-election, had to back off the sale of the provincially-owned producer of electricity.

"So with that caution, I will tell you what I *will* do for you. I have a good and dear friend in Ottawa who is an ex-politician, a physician, and was the former Minister of Health in a previous federal government. Dr. Judith Brown probably knows more than almost anyone in the country about the behind-the-scenes goings-on in Ottawa in regard to our Medicare system."

"Do you think that Dr. Brown would speak with me?" Ken asked.

Dr. McTavish chuckled. "I will ask her myself. I did some checking up on you after you called yesterday and asked to see me. I read your articles about Gulf wars One and Two, and the ways in which various levels of your government dropped the ball in looking after the workers who were lost or involved in the cleanup in New York City after 9/11. I agreed to see you for longer than a very few minutes because I admire your work. And about the Paulson, by the way–congratulations.

"Thank you," responded Ken.

"You are, just maybe, one of the few reporters who has the balls–and from what you have told me, also the motivation–to look into what is going on in this country and yours in regard to healthcare. So I will clear the way for you to meet Judith... Dr. Brown, if you would like me to do that."

Ken's head-nodding signaled that he would like that very much.

McTavish's voice now took on a markedly sterner tone. "Just don't take up her time unless you are willing to follow through with this, and treat her fairly in your reporting."

"I will do the best I can, Doctor McTavish. That I can promise you."

Getting up to leave Ken extended his hand. "I am very grateful for your time, sir, and for your insights. I would appreciate it very much if I could get to see Dr. Brown in the next couple of days, if you think that would be possible."

"I will call her and get back to you later today."

"Thank you very much."

Momentarily McTavish got lost in some seemingly sad thoughts. He caught himself quickly though, and asked Ken, "Where are you staying?"

"At the downtown Holiday Inn," replied Ken, offering his business card with the hotel's phone number and his room number written on the back.

"Good. Well, then," said the doctor, his voice warm again, "if you like fish or seafood, let me suggest that you try the Filet of Halibut restaurant around the corner from your hotel."

Ken accepted this advice with appreciation. "I do, and I will; thanks for the suggestion. And I will look forward to hearing from you later."

"I will call your cellphone number and let you know."

As he shook Ken's hand, the elderly psychiatrist held it a tad longer than necessary in a vise-like grip. "Again, *please,* Mr.

Simpson, just don't waste Dr. Brown's time."

Ken retrieved his hand from a grasp that left no illusions as to the message behind the doctor's rib steak-sized admonition. And then, McTavish added, "One always keeps up hope for the genuine article, Mr. Simpson, and to not be let down by it. After many of our experiences in this country, as for example with the Arrow, you can appreciate that no one cursed by that traitorous ending can ever be sure of how far anyone will be willing to look into and fairly report what is going on at the upper echelon levels of business or politics."

Ken nodded and took his leave, testily moving each finger, one at a time, to make sure they were all still functioning. For several reasons, Ken knew that he did not want to disappoint Dr. McTavish and the others, including his own father, who deserved to have the truths that shaped, or even ended their lives, finally revealed.

CHAPTER 27

Ken had a delicious early dinner at the fish restaurant that Dr. McTavish suggested, choosing the wild pacific salmon served on a cedar shake; an excellent choice, as it turned out. From their attire and instructions to their waiters, it seemed that most of the other diners were headed to one of the plays being staged nearby at some of the city's major theatres.

While at the restaurant, Ken called the paper and spoke to his editor. Rusty Elliot was more than a little perturbed to learn that Ken had gone off on 'some fishing expedition' to Canada, without letting either himself or his new assistant reporter know that he had intended to make the trip. Rusty became even more irritated when his inquiry as to why Ken had gone to Canada's largest city was met with the vague response of "just checking out a few leads".

Ken told Rusty that it was vital that he keep his sources entirely confidential at this time, in order to make sure that they didn't get skittish. Rusty was not pleased by Ken's stonewalling, even though the two of them had a long-standing agreement that, because they recognized that *The New York Era* had too many big ears and even bigger mouths, Ken could keep the identities of sources to himself until he was ready to put them into one of his articles. At that point Rusty, the managing editor, and the paper's lawyers, had the right–and in fact–the obligation to know, at least the veracity of his sources' identities and information.

Over Rusty's mid-sentence objection, Ken said, "Got to go, Russ. My next contact has just come into the restaurant. I'll call you later."

Rusty's "Just a min…" was truncated by Ken's cellphone's 'end' button. Ken didn't like lying to Rusty; he reassured himself with one of Winston Churchill's pithy comments that "It is a very good thing to be honest, but it is also very important to be right." In Ken's mind, the right thing to do at that moment was to get off the phone so that Rusty wouldn't be able to badger him any further about who, why, where, when and what. He only wished that he knew why he was now feeling that old intuitive sense of warning, this time with regard to Rusty.

Half-way through his meal, his cellphone rang. Ignoring disapproving looks from a couple of nearby diners, he looked at the name and number on the screen, and answered the call. He scribbled some information down on the paper place mat and thanked Dr. McTavish. Ken next called the airline's reservation line and booked a seat on a flight to Ottawa leaving early the next morning. Then he read his e-mail on his Blackberry and learned that Martha was already ensconced at the paper's rented apartment in Canada's capital and missing him terribly. He sent his reply, letting her know what time he would be in Ottawa the next morning.

As he had coffee and dessert Ken read a local Toronto paper. There were a few articles about healthcare issues but they appeared to be mostly negative in tone, referring a couple of times to "the sorry state of Canadian universal Medicare system" or words to that effect. When he turned to the 'careers wanted' section he noted that there were only a few ads for jobs in the healthcare field from all over the country. Why, he wondered? Was it a matter of job cutbacks, or were most workers in the healthcare field, people like medical doctors and nurses, happy to stay where they were? Or were there some other reasons that he couldn't think of right now, what with a full stomach and a couple ounces of scotch in him? Ken abruptly realized he was both physically and mentally exhausted, and decided to call it a day as far as work was concerned.

Ken paid for his meal, and walked back to the hotel. It was a pleasant evening and the women heading to the plays looked gorgeous in their 'big night out' outfits. He, meanwhile, was ready to turn in early.

He had a premonition that tomorrow things would start to get more difficult. *Much more difficult.*

CHAPTER 28

Ken slid the plastic passkey through his hotel room's door lock, and realized that, in addition to being tired, he was feeling quite uneasy, but without knowing why. He decided to telephone Lieutenant Colonel Dan Stevens. When Stevens answered Ken said, "Lieutenant Colonel, my journalist's nose is telling me that something just doesn't smell right about what you've told me. What did you leave out when we spoke at the restaurant?"

"Well, good evening to you, too, Kenneth. I am well, thank you."

Ken said, "Sorry, but I am getting very involved in my work here, and I don't like being kept in the dark by a supposedly reliable source."

Stevens asked, "What makes you think that I left something out?"

Ken said, "My intuition is kind of like that. It not only helps me decide whether the people I have interviewed were telling the truth or not, but also, and sometimes this can be even more important, whether they are telling me the *whole* truth."

At first Ken didn't know whether the phone had gone dead. There was no sound, nada, for nearly a full minute. Ken listened for the sounds of someone breathing, but heard nothing.

A deep, repentant-sounding voice finally said, "When we took the Arrow to our facility in the southwest, *I* was the navigator for your father. We flew the Arrow number 208 down from Canada together. Hell, from the time we took off from Toronto, we were over Lake Ontario and into U.S. air territory in less than two minutes. It was a piece of cake." Stevens added that his father was easily duped because he was falsely given to understand that Avro and the Canadian government had agreed to one of the Arrows being saved from demolition in order to further test some of its technology and remarkable flying characteristics once it was back Stateside. His father had been taken in, and he subsequently paid for his naiveté and misplaced trust of Stevens and his cohorts with his life.

Upon receiving this salvo Ken suddenly didn't want to talk any more lest he say something that would most likely alienate Stevens permanently. Right now, he needed to sort things out in his own mind. Ken simply said, "Look, next time I ask you questions, you need to tell me *everything* I need to know."

Stevens started to respond but Ken, who now felt nauseous, began to choke up. "We'll get to this another time. Goodbye." Ken hung up. He felt angry, disappointed, and hurt–all at the same time. Over the next few days these feelings would become only too familiar.

CHAPTER 29

Retired Air Force Colonel Jake Marks, the seventy-nine year old President and CEO of TAMPRR Inc., was thoroughly enjoying the view from his first class window seat as the huge Boeing 747-400, American flight 2302, from Paris via Miami to San Francisco, banked left over the Bay bridge, flew almost due south for a few minutes, and then banked hard right until it was heading due north. The pilot lined up the behemoth's approach to the runway that ran straight in from the bay and directly toward the terminal at San Francisco International Airport. Marks was on the port side, and just before touchdown he spotted the cluster of hotels in Burlingame where he usually stayed, about a mile from the airport, all backing onto the man-made jogging and walking park. In past years, when he was much more active in the day-to-day running of TAMPRR's operations, he preferred staying overnight close to the airport at either the Embassy Suites or Crowne Plaza hotels in Burlingame, partly because he usually enjoyed taking an invigorating early morning walk around the jogging path that served the guests of those hotels.

Jake Marks always enjoyed watching the big birds coming in for their landings onto what, from the path, looked like a very long pier stretching out to meet them. While he always admired good air jockeys, he reminded himself that these guys had it easy compared to the tight airfields *he* had flown in and out of during the Korean conflict. These commercial pilots earned their dough, though, as long as they didn't board their aircraft too much under the influence. Any employee of TAMPRR who would have been similarly negligent in his or her duty, unless drinking was part of their particular job assignment, was immediately turfed. Marks reserved the word 'terminated' for another way of getting rid of some people, traitorous employees included.

There was no excuse for irresponsibility on the job, as far as Marks was concerned. 'Loose lips sink ships', was one of his favorite sayings when speaking to newly minted recruits who were about to be sent on their first missions for TAMPRR. In fact, he pointed out that it was part of their function to catch *other* people making verbal slip-ups while in *their* company.

On this occasion Marks gave his 747 pilot an 'A' for bringing the plane in expertly through the rainy and windy, 'flight soup' foggy conditions. Only ten minutes behind schedule, too; more than acceptable in these days of high-tech checks for cargo-hold bound baggage and lengthy passenger line-ups for security checks.

Marks was feeling hungry by 11:55 a.m. Pacific time as he steered his Hertz rental onto 101 North, past Monster Park on his right, and followed the hectic traffic flow as it jammed up coming into South San Francisco. Once inside San Francisco city limits he took the off-ramp for 101North that led onto busy Van Ness boulevard, a six-lane main drag lined on either side by block after block of car dealerships, restaurants, bookstores and low- and mid-rise office buildings, providing a commercial pit-stop and nearly direct link to the Golden Gate bridge that for so long had been the primary–and most magnificent–means of getting across the bay from San Francisco to Sausalito and Marin county.

He undoubtedly would have been in more of a hurry in his pre-bypass days but, as his doc had told him, "One of the advantages of getting older, and maybe the only one, is that you get better at deciding what is really worthwhile worrying–and hurrying–about." Still, Marks found himself thinking, *Some of these alternately laid-back and aggressive west coast drivers, really piss me off. Why don't they make up their damn minds?*

He stayed in the middle lane proceeding up Van Ness until he got to Lombard Street and the Fisherman's Wharf area. There he continued straight ahead when 101N turned left. He soon found the parking lot was still there, immediately across from his favorite restaurant, Fisherman's Cave, where he had been coming for well over forty-five years for his favorite meal-restaurant combination in the world.

Another glance at his military-issue watch informed the head of TAMPRR Inc. that it was now 13.05 hours; he had more than enough time for a brief walk, followed by a leisurely lunch. Then he would make the short ride to the Terragance Hotel in lots of time to get ready for his meeting at 1700 hours. He wandered around the moderately busy Wharf area for about twenty minutes, partly in order to get the circulation flowing in his extremities after having spent most of the previous six hours or so mostly sitting. He checked out the retail 'spy equipment store' nearby to see the latest in what the commercial guys were currently selling, just on the unlikely chance that they had in a new piece of equipment with which he was not personally familiar. As usual, the answer was 'nada'. TAMPRR's R&D department was far ahead in most areas of covert, especially electronic, surveillance.

Deciding it was time, and now feeling rather hungry, he made his way past the touristy, end-to-end, Dungeness crab and sourdough bread outdoor stalls to the door with the blue neon sign above it that announced 'Fisherman's Cave'. Marks entered the restaurant, and climbed the wide, well-worn oak staircase immediately to his right. At the top of the stairs a presumably new maitre d', dressed in the obligatory tuxedo, led him to the table that Marks indicated he preferred. From here he could look out the window to his left and down at the commercial fishing boat dock a mere thirty feet away. The boats were already back from their early morning expeditions, and he watched as they heaved their bins of succulent crab onto the dock.

Marks nodded and shook his head in acknowledgment to chutzpah as he gazed down upon the California governor's definitely non-fishing boat, the one that had caused all the commotion in the national media when the gov had done a political piggy-grab, taking over a docking space for what clearly was, with its stubby, forty-five foot long teak deck, ample shiny brass railings, and Chris Craft insignia on the back, definitely not a commercial fishing boat. When word got out to the press that he had obtained the prime mooring spot by somehow making sure that a local fisherman didn't get his dock space license renewed over some technicality, and that he had acquired the newly-available spot for the meager sum of $500 yearly, an awful lot of folks were really pissed. The offender's response had been that he frequently conducted *official* business on the yacht, thereby saving taxpayers mucho bucks since they didn't have to repeatedly rent banquet rooms at one of the expensive waterfront hotels or eateries to impress foreign investors and dignitaries. Californians in general, and the fishers in particular, were not amused. One bumper sticker that quickly became an 'in' item read, *"The fishers crab; the gov' grabs."*

Ahhh, politicians, mused Marks. *They're all the same. With the occasional exceptions, and most of those are ex-military types, they're after whatever they can get from the public and private purses, plus all the power and influence they can seize. They really are the personification of that old joke whose punch line was, "Well, we all know what you are; now, we are merely haggling over your price." Whores, just whores! If we simply put the right amount of money into your official and unofficial campaign chests, we could even get you to sell your young. And we have, and you have!*

His attention turned to the reason he was in San Francisco. He thought, *Well, the Canadians we are going to talk about later today are at least as bad as our own politicians. TAMPRR easily got to them the first time out.*

We got you Canucks to sell out your brightest technical people, and to kill your country's military aviation future–for peanuts. Schmucks! You guys could have sold your Avro Arrow to the world, including maybe even our own military, but you didn't have the balls to tell us that you knew damn well that we were bullshitting you when we gave you twenty different 'reasons' to get rid of that plane. You should have told us to go fuck ourselves. No wonder your own people don't respect you. Of course, most Americans don't respect our politicians much, either...

"May I take your order, Colonel?"

Marks was startled by the intrusion into his internal rant. His head turned back from looking down in the direction of the fishing boats. He looked up and to his right to see the same waiter who had served him so well for at least the last thirty years now smiling at him as he set down a wooden plate atop of which was an inviting loaf of freshly baked sourdough bread.

Smiling his widest CEO smile, Marks said, in the 'hail fellow, well met' voice and manner he reserved for those who had earned his regard, "Hello, Henry. How the hell are you?"

"I am fine, Colonel, thank you. Good to see you, sir. And how are you, sir?"

"Hey, I'm pushing eighty, Henry, so all things considered, since I am here, and I can still walk and eat and piss and crap reasonably well, I'm excellent, thank you. I'll have a Chivas, straight up."

"Of course. Will there be anyone joining you?"

"Not today, Henry. But, you know me, I always like to come here whenever I am in town, just to have my favorite meal, look out at the wharf and the city," he said, cocking his head to the left and then, turning his head to one o'clock he glanced towards the now empty, bay-facing window and added somberly, "and also, of course, to look out at the Golden Gate bridge. That's how I could tell that I am in San Fran."

"I understand, Colonel. 'The Cave' had the best view in town. Maybe in the entire country. Until those *goddamned* terrorist bastards... sorry, sir."

"That's alright, Henry. You're right."

Neither man said anything more for a couple of beats, as if observing a moment of silence to honor the fallen bridge. Then Henry asked, gently, "Would you like me to take your order now?"

"Sure, Henry. I'll have the usual: my Dungeness."

Henry smiled. "Same as always, right, Colonel? Cold, with extra tomato-based seafood sauce, and not the creamy one, right, sir?"

Marks's smile momentarily became genuine. "Exactly, Henry. Thank you for remembering."

"Of course, Colonel. I'll be right back with the Chivas, sir."

"Thank you."

In the good old days, before he slowed down following his bypass, whenever he had visited San Francisco, Jake would come to this same restaurant, have his Dungeness, and then drive over to the visitors' parking area at the south end of the bridge. There he would leave his car, bundle up, and walk the full length of the

Golden Gate and back, relishing the sharp winds that almost always came in from the ocean, as if God was using the bridge as a reed as he blew air across it, above and below its six lanes of vehicular traffic and its pedestrian walkway. The bridge issued a continually variable, low frequency, audible groan while unmistakably vibrating beneath his feet.

The sound that the bridge made wasn't what most people would call a *musical* note. But to Marks the vibrations created as the winds blew and the vehicles rushed across, produced as melodic a non-musical note as ever there was. The bridge always felt *alive*, moving, vibrating, sometimes even momentarily shaking, and never, ever staying entirely still. Marks thought of those walking, rollerblading, cycling or just driving across what had been the most beautiful bridge in the world as dancing on the reed of one of mankind's greatest instruments.

Unfortunately, everything he had liked and loved about the bridge had also made it one of al-Qaeda's prime targets in America.

Marks was not emotionally moved by many things, or people for that matter. Human beings, with their inevitable 'stuff' and bullshit, no longer mattered to him very much, aside from their usefulness. But planes, boats, buildings and bridges were things that he would appreciate, could deal with, and perhaps, truth be told, could identify with at some deeper level. If he were ever asked what bridge reminded him most of himself, after giving the questioner shit for asking such a touchy-feely question, he would say that he was more like the double-decker Bay bridge that joined San Francisco to Oakland: massive, multifunctional, stronger after each successive earthquake or other tragedy, and ugly as hell, in some kind of almost attractive way.

But that had never stopped him from appreciating the awesome achievement of the Golden Gate, just like so many millions of visitors over the years. In fact, he recalled that he had unsuccessfully attempted to schedule a business meeting back in May of 1987 when, for the fiftieth anniversary of the bridge's opening, it was closed to vehicular traffic, and over 300,000 people showed up to walk across the Golden Gate in celebration. He would have loved to have taken part in that event but just couldn't get away. He remembered that, as a precaution, the bridge had to be closed to any additional pedestrians at one point because it had sagged so much in the middle under the weight of all those people that the engineers thought it might be unsafe to stress the structure any further.

Uncharacteristically, Marks mused further. Maybe it was the fact that he had just recently stopped seeing another pretty, relatively young thing who had actually *almost* meant something to him that was making him—God forbid—somewhat less impervious than usual. He found himself playfully wishing he could find a woman who was like the Golden Gate bridge in some ways: elegant and beautiful, with a great rack that seemed to hold the rest of her up, of classic proportions, and with a keen sense of drama and mystery, the kind of woman who could also be a magnet for a lot of people. A real siren. He chuckled out loud as he acknowledged to himself that that description fitted his ex-wife, Valerie. Too bad she was also a 'nutberg'. Of course, a lot of charismatic women of his acquaintance had turned out to be precisely that—*nutbergs*!

To give Valerie some credit, however, she did possess an awful lot of sometimes interesting information about people, and why they do the things they do. Marks thought of some research she had told him about while on one of their visits to San Francisco. If he remembered correctly, some psychology type who had studied human relationships for several years had concluded that *ropes* and *bridges* were two material items that often represented relationships in dreams. Apparently, this guy's studies had determined that every word or phrase that people use to describe the characteristics of a relationship—long or short, strong or weak, colorful or bland, rigid or flexible, simple or complex, and so on— could also be applied to human relationships. The psychologist had concluded that the Golden Gate bridge, which was, after all, the ultimate rope-bridge, had a natural pull for those who wanted to end their relationships to this world. Hence, so many hundreds of people over the years who had decided to cut all ties to this world, were drawn to jumping off that beautiful, but apparently deeply symbolic, structure. Probably, Marks mused, such reasoning had also helped make the bridge such an appealing target for terrorists.

Anyway, he liked structure–and structures. He appreciated them, enjoyed, and even 'felt' for them. He had become genuinely sad, not so much for the human beings who had died, but for the manmade structures themselves, when the Concorde crashed, the World Trade Center towers collapsed, and the space shuttle Challenger came apart. He choked up even thinking about the tragedies that befell those inanimate 'beings'. He also felt anger over the loss of those and other magnificent technological marvels that burned or collapsed or crashed through no inherent faults of their own, but rather, because of deliberate sabotage or the stupidity or carelessness of the people who were supposed to look out for them. The fact that TAMPRR Inc. had played a hand in bringing about some of those catastrophes did not lessen the sense of empathetic loss he felt.

Marks's cellphone rang and broke his reverie just as his second drink arrived. He nodded 'thanks' to Henry as he reached into his inside jacket pocket and retrieved the phone. Recognizing the number displayed, he gave what for him passed as a cheery and almost warm tone when he took the call. "Hi, dear. How are things going?"

He listened intently, frowning ever more deeply as he heard the lengthy response. Then, his voice hardening just enough, he said, "Look, this is very important. Somehow get and stay close to him. Find out where he went, whom he has seen, and why. I have to know who he talks to, and especially, if at all possible, what they told him."

Marks nodded slightly when he heard the reply. He then said, "I don't care *how*; whatever floats his boat. Just get to him… All right, then. Call me when you have anything. Good. Goodbye, dear."

The old warrior was already thinking of his options in dealing with the new potential problem he had just heard about, even as he ended the call.

Henry arrived carrying a plate with a large, succulent Dungeness crab resting atop it. Marks smirked. *Henry understands that size matters, especially when it comes to getting a substantial tip.*

"Here you are, Colonel. Enjoy." Smiling, the waiter set the crab plate down and walked away, leaving Jake Marks alone.

One of the largest crabs Marks had ever seen lay on his plate, along with an extra pair of claws. He didn't like to talk business at meals. He believed that food was to be enjoyed, without a stomach made tense by conflict or concern. Which is why he minimized problematic business meetings over meals, or at least, *he* didn't eat much until after any potentially contentious issues had been dealt with. *People shouldn't suck in food and blow out hot air at the same time. Interferes with tasting and digestion.*

After the main course plus only two or (with apologies to his cardiologist) perhaps three forks-full of the restaurant's 'famous cheese cake', Marks paid his bill, left the restaurant and retrieved his rental car. He headed in the direction of the elegant Terragance Hotel.

It was time to prepare for this afternoon's business meeting, the one that would surely cap his career, netting him more money than the sum total of all he had previously earned over his lifetime, up to this moment. That warm thought made his meal go down just fine.

CHAPTER 30

On the same morning that Jake Marks was winging his way to San Francisco from Miami, Martha picked Ken up at Ottawa International airport, as they had arranged when he called her the previous night. On the way out of the terminal Martha teased him, saying that she hoped he would find the local accommodations satisfactory, since the paper's apartment had only one functioning bedroom plus a den, with the latter set up as an office, with a computer, copier, fax machine, and file cabinets galore. She added that, if need be, the couch in the den could fold out into a double size bed.

Ken responded, "Oh, I wouldn't enjoy sleeping on a sofa." They both laughed and held hands as they walked to the short-term parking zone and retrieved Martha's SUV.

Martha again told Ken how much she was enjoying her new car, and how delighted she had been to get his phone call of the previous day. She teasingly told him that she could hardly wait to express her appreciation, in private.

They brought Ken's bags up to the apartment and after an hour or so of thoroughly enjoyable lovemaking, they got caught up on the status of his investigations. Ken told Martha about his interview with Dr. McTavish, and that he hoped to learn a great deal over the next few days about the Canadian healthcare system, from politicians and physicians alike.

Ken also said that he wanted to check out the National Flight Museum of Canada. This desire surprised Martha until Ken explained that he had reason to believe that there were Americans who were involved in attempts to manipulate the Canadian Medicare system, and that some of them had probably also had something to do with events that happened decades earlier that decimated the Canadian's military aircraft building sector. He didn't go into further detail about how he had made this connection, but Martha knew that Ken would likely tell her in his own good time. That had always been good enough for her. He gave her general directions from the Mapquest printout he had acquired from the hotel's Internet business depot the night before. Martha happily drove while they commiserated about his agenda while in town.

As reporters with both national and international experience, Martha and Ken were well aware that most Americans knew little, and cared even less, about Canada, its politics or its people, until and unless its government didn't dance to Washington's tune, such as happened during the Iraq invasion in 2003. In the intervening years the U.S. had alternately pressured and bribed Canada to join its gradually dissipating so-called 'coalition of the willing', either as frontline troops, or at least as support forces. The Canadians had stubbornly resisted such efforts, for the most part, and probably would continue to do so, at least until it elected a more U.S.-leaning, right wing government.

Martha reminded Ken of the comments of Pierre Elliot Trudeau, arguably Canada's most charismatic and best-known Prime Minister in recent memory, who had said that living next to the United States was akin to sleeping in bed next to an elephant. Trudeau appreciated the risks inherent in ignoring or pissing off the elephant; nevertheless, he went to China before the U.S. government was ready to recognize that country, and did a number of other things that upset American administrations, big-time. An aristocratic intellectual with a creative thinker's bent, Trudeau and President Richard Nixon had very little in common, including especially their political leanings.

Ken pointed out that during the so-called 'cold war', when the U.S. persuaded the Canadian government that any battles with Soviet bombers sweeping down over the arctic should happen over the northernmost parts of their two countries, i.e., Alaska and Canada, Canada was again–temporarily–on the U.S.'s radar screen. The terrorist attack of 9/11 had put the less populated country back on the administration's 'to be used' list. There were some semi-justified concerns about a seemingly loony Canadian immigration and refugee policy that sometimes allowed ex-Nazis as well as Islamic and other potential terrorists to apply for Canadian citizenship, or at least, avoid extradition back to their own countries of origin, for decades. Having such people close by a largely porous, four thousand mile long common border was highly disconcerting.

Pushing forward with its Star Wars anti-missile defense system against substantial scientific and political criticisms, the U.S. was again giving Canada some not entirely welcome attention and 'face time'. The pressure being placed upon the Canadian government had been unrelenting for years as the U.S. was very intent on using Canada as what was referred to by their strategic war games think tanks as a 'PFDF', or 'Preferred Field for Debris and Fallout', over which to shoot down any missiles or satellites of whose intentions, or mere existence, they disapproved.

Ken briefly told Martha about his interview with Dr. Larson. He also said that he had used some of his time at the Toronto airport waiting to board his flight to Ottawa as an opportunity to again speak to former U.S. Surgeon-General. Dr. Larson had appeared genuinely happy to hear from him, and asked if there was anything further he could do to help with Ken's investigation into health care. Ken replied that he was on his way to Ottawa, and that he wanted to learn as much as he could about what was going on in healthcare in that country.

Dr. Larson told Ken that currently the staunchest advocate of the Canadian government-run healthcare system was one of that country's most up-and-coming federal politicians, Dr. Trish Markridge, a physician who had consulted with him in the past. Keeping his prior knowledge of Trish Markridge M.D. to himself so as not to compromise Lieutenant Colonel Stevens, Ken asked Dr. Larson to tell him more about Markridge.

Ken matter-of-factly told Martha what he had learned about Dr. Markridge, specifically, that she was "a former Miss Canada or something" while in her early twenties; that in one online article he had found she had been described (and in order to protect Martha's sensitivities, in a neutral voice he read directly from the printout) "a striking five-foot, nine-inch blue-eyed blonde, a fitness advocate who had been a Rhodes scholar, graduated in medicine from the University of Toronto and then earned an MBA from Harvard Business School. She later took a leave of absence from her position as Dean of Medicine at one of the country's most prestigious medical schools and ran successfully in the last federal election, getting elected by a huge majority as a member of parliament."

Martha said, "Is that why does her name sounds familiar to me?"

Ken said, "Probably, or because of what I was about to add; the woman also was part of an all-female international team a couple of years back that reached the North pole on skis."

"Wow!" was all Martha managed to say.

"I know. She really is something, isn't she? There's more. Listen to some of the other things she has accomplished."

As Ken carried on enumerating some of Dr. Markridge's other exploits and achievements, he noticed that Martha kept glancing at him, seemingly looking for signs of *something*. He finally concluded that, in spite of her upbeat manner, Martha was probably feeling quite vulnerable. After all, only a few days had passed since she had been replaced as his assistant by the lovely Sylkeen Bowry, and Ken feared she was already more than a little sensitive about what he thought she was guessing would be the outcome of such a liaison.

Ken decided to briefly and matter-of-factly relate some of his other Internet-derived information about Dr. Markridge. He told Martha that Markridge had once taken a leave of absence from her academic duties to serve as a medical-coordinator specialist in Afghanistan, after the invasion of that country and the defeat of the Taliban by Americans, British and Canadian forces, following 9/11. Her own frontline heroics became front-page news when it was reported that she had risked her own life in tending to wounded Canadian soldiers in yet another 'friendly fire' incident caused by a U.S. helicopter pilot on 'go pills' who, in a possibly sleep-deprived and stress-induced psychotic state, decided that his fighting comrades' bodies had been taken over by enemy insurgents and that it was his duty to wipe them all out. Which he damn well nearly did. Dr. Markridge was also credited with talking the crazed airman, via a quickly improvised battlefield communications hookup, into surrendering following the multiple-casualty episode.

Markridge's actions led to media interviews with most of the major networks, newspapers and magazines in Canada once she was back home, soon after the Canadian government and defense department officials ordered her return for her own protection and their own aggrandizement.

When Markridge returned to her duties at the university, her obvious energy, integrity, and outright sex appeal kept bringing her more and more offers of speaking engagements. She was described by one senior political pundit as a possible future Trudeau-type public personality; in other words, way smarter, sexier, and more exciting a potential political force than most of the rest of her colleagues combined. And what set her apart even more, evidently, was that she appeared to be extremely principled, highly ethical *and* very courageous.

Listening to all this 'information', Martha gave him one of those piercing looks she could still manage to issue on occasion.

Ken went on just a little more, hoping that the next bit would make Martha more sympathetic to Markridge. "In an opp-ed article that she wrote for Canada's self-proclaimed most prominent newspaper she mentioned that while in Afghanistan she used the meager time she had for herself to contact some of the previously oppressed female intellectuals of that sad country. What she took away from her experiences, she said, was much more than she gave. She reflected upon the needs of ordinary people, and what *should* be considered their inalienable rights. She said that Americans had come very close to the crux of the matter when they spoke of the rights of every citizen to "life, liberty, and the pursuit of happiness." But her experiences as a physician had led her to what she considered the unavoidable conclusion that, since genuine happiness is made most difficult to find in the absence of good health, a *"constitutional guarantee of a government-run, not-for-profit, free, public Medicare system"* should be added to the basic rights offered, if not by America, then at least in her home country of Canada."

Without any apparent envy this time Martha issued a 'whew' sound and then said, "Some woman! Some human being!"

Ken nodded his agreement. Now he read; *"In the months that followed her return from Afghanistan she publicly announced that she had joined a group of prominent Canadian physicians, writers, entertainers, politicos, and other citizens who had formed a committee whose sole stated purpose was to work towards the enshrining of free and universal Medicare coverage in the Canadian Bill of Rights and Freedoms.*

"Markridge's advocacy efforts apparently put her directly at odds with certain colleagues at the medical school where she was Dean of Medicine, including, and in particular, some members of its Board of Governors who, coincidentally, were also the heads of the Canadian subsidiaries of American pharmaceutical and other healthcare-related companies. Rumors were that two huge pharmaceutical companies who were in the process of endowing large grants for new medical buildings and high-tech equipment at her university threatened to withdraw their proposed funding for these much needed projects unless something was done immediately to silence her. Since she had tenure, Markridge couldn't be fired or threatened in any other major way that would make her 'more amenable' to changing her views. However, it was apparently made abundantly clear to her that if she did not cease her vocalizations on behalf of what were gratuitously referred to as her 'pet peeves' of free and guaranteed universal health coverage, then she might be removed from her position as Dean of Medicine and might find it exceedingly difficult to continue to obtain grants for her own medical research into non-invasive means of ensuring women's heart health."

At hearing these revelations Martha uttered only a single word. "Bastards!"

Ken continued reading. *"At about the same time, Dr. Markridge had apparently become impatient with, and increasingly distressed by, what she called the "financial vice" being applied to universities in attempts to control how they studied medical procedures and drug usage, including the restrictions put on the publication of contrary findings.*

"She decided to take the sabbatical due her the following year, and to try her hand at politics. In previous years she had served on various public commissions and inquiries sponsored by various governmental agencies regarding healthcare. All the major political parties now wooed her, and it was conjectured

that she rather reluctantly joined the party that was least repugnant to her.

"Dr. Markridge's general aims could be found on the pages of the position statements of the ruling political party she finally joined but, unfortunately, hardly evidenced themselves in the party's practices. While spouting phrases that clearly suggested they wanted to preserve and enhance free Medicare for all residents of Canada, their manner of running various components of the government frequently acted in ways that virtually guaranteed that this model of healthcare would be defeated. Nevertheless, the senior executive of her party apparently concluded that they could not afford to lose a prospect with Markridge's Trudeau-ish lustre, and so, at least until after the next general election, they were willing to let Markridge speak out as she wished. It would reflect well on them, they concluded, and besides, they could always dump her proposals–or her, for that matter–afterwards.

"The party's inner circle was reported to have even briefly considered adopting her proposals as official party policy, and then, after they were hopefully elected to form a majority government, as one unidentified source put it succinctly, "they could do whatever the hell they wanted to afterwards, just as provincial premier George P. Linden and his party had done after the last election, after having been elected on a 'no healthcare cuts' platform."

"Hey," Martha laughed, "they sound just like our 'read my lips' and 'axis of evil' guys. Tell the electorate anything to get and hold onto power, and then screw them afterwards."

A couple of beats later, Martha became more serious, and perhaps slightly defensive. "And I suppose, Ken, you would like to meet with Dr. Ms. Perfect while you're in town."

"Yes, actually I would. But the lady is in England, apparently, at a Rhodes scholars' reunion or some such thing. She'll be back the day after tomorrow. I used the in-flight phone on the way here this morning to schedule an appointment, for *us* if you must know, to see her when she is back."

Martha responded, unabashedly relieved. "Good idea." Her voice instantly became much lighter. "Oh, and by the way, Hon, how long will you be staying in Ottawa?"

"I'm not sure yet. A few days–three or four, maybe."

Martha decided to be optimistic. "Great. I'll scope out a couple good restaurants for us. ... Hey, we're here."

They had been driving along a manicured two-lane street named Tarmac Trail, with a great expanse of carefully manicured lawns on either side of the road. They turned right, went under an overpass and drove a couple of hundred feet further along a wide green expanse to the parking lot in front of a factory-sized, single story, rather plain looking building with a relatively impressive, wing-shaped entryway clearly designed to add some sort of architectural interest to what would otherwise look like the short side of a very long hanger. A long neon sign showing aircraft shapes simulating takeoffs and landings ran across the entire front of the building above silver lettering that told them they had arrived at the National Flight Museum of Canada.

Parked along the longest side of the building, were four or five large older planes, including a four-engine prop design that Ken recognized as a Super Constellation, a popular aircraft used in the commercial field for transoceanic flights in the early 1960s.

When they entered the museum the former Air Force pilot in Ken was immediately impressed by what he recognized as a varied array of vintage aircraft. To their immediate left as they entered was a F-104 Starfighter, the American-built fighter plane that Ken remembered his father referring to, when talking to one of his pilot buddies, as 'a missile with a man in it'. He shared with Martha that his dad had told him of the other, even less appealing moniker that pilots used when referring to the F-104; they had unofficially dubbed it 'the Widowmaker'.

The word in military circles at the time, Ken informed Martha, as they gazed at the seemingly so small, ultra-thin winged jet, was that in the 1960s German Air Force pilots were reputed to have had the worst crash and mortality rate of all the NATO pilots who flew the Starfighter. The main reason for their difficulties allegedly was because it had been a very difficult aircraft to control, what with its stubby but razor edge-sharp little wings. Apparently its pilots had to use their seat-of-the-pants sensory *intuition* to an even greater extent than was required with most other military aircraft of the period. The consensus among the U.S. flyers was that German pilots were typically so rigidly trained, a mere fifteen or so years after the end of World War II, that they only knew how to fly 'by the book'. Apparently, that could get one killed damned quick in this on-the-edge aircraft.

As they made their way to what Ken knew was the primary subject of their visit, they passed a North American Aviation F-86 Sabre, a major fighter aircraft of the Korean conflict in the early 1950s, and the model of the plane Ken's father was flying when he was shot down over North Korea. Ken felt a painful twinge as he stared hard at the aircraft, and was again reminded that he was here on a personal, as well as professional, mission.

A little further along they came upon a Soviet-built MIG 'on loan' to the museum that might have been a variation on the type of plane that his father had had several dogfights with over North Korean airspace. One had launched the attack that had hit his dad's Sabre, forcing him to eject and leading to his having been captured and interred in the North Korean prisoner-of-war camp.

At this moment Ken felt closer to his dad than he had in some time. He paused briefly several times as he took in the myriad of mostly military planes of various periods all assembled under the museum's roof. At times he shared with Martha some of his own knowledge of the apparently intact aircraft they were viewing. When he saw an example of the helicopter he had flown, Ken experienced a flood of emotions: first nostalgia, and then almost instantaneously afterwards, the too-familiar nausea, as he momentarily and for the ten thousandth time, saw the disbelieving and questioning expression on the face of the young girl he had vivisected. He quickly moved away from that aircraft without mentioning its relevance to Martha.

Ken attempted to turn off his mind's re-running of horrific images as he and Martha looked at some of the other aircraft. They gradually made their way towards the rear of the museum, past seemingly ready-for-takeoff aircraft, to where the layout guide they had received at the front desk indicated they would find the Avro Arrow display. On the way Martha stopped and remarked upon the World War II vintage, B-29 bomber, standing proudly where they and a small number of other museum visitors now gazed at it.

An elderly gentleman standing nearby said to the teenager with him, "I suppose that it is quite shocking, isn't it, Jeffrey, in your age of the B-2 bomber, to think that the B-29 did such a valiant job for us, back then?"

The wide-eyed boy responded admiringly, "Gee, gramps, it sure is; that plane isn't much bigger than a medium-sized corporate jet."

Martha said quietly, "This looks like a remarkable collection of aircraft to my mostly uneducated eyes. What do you think, Ken?"

Ken replied, "Well, I must say that they have done a really good job of collecting and displaying some very interesting aircraft. I give them a lot of credit."

As they continued walking and gazing at the displays Martha was aware that Ken had become not merely quiet, but silent. His running commentary had dissipated and then was cut off entirely by what she assumed were memories having to do with the poignant experiences he had shared with her in the past, about his own time as a U.S.A.F. pilot. She was sure that he was also thinking of his own father, about whom he had shared a little when, on one of her earliest visits to his apartment, she inquired about the photos and models of aircraft that respectfully adorned what Ken referred to as 'Captain's corner'. Walking several feet behind Ken, Martha gave him the space he seemed to need at the moment.

For another few minutes they wandered, stopping and looking at a wide variety of well-preserved flying machines from various countries of origin, including some that Ken recognized as being of strictly Canadian design, such as the De Havilland Twin Otter, one of the world's best and most reliable 'bush' planes, and the long-retired workhorse of the Canadian Air Force, the Avro Canada CF-100 fighter-interceptor, the much older and much less technologically advanced predecessor of the Arrow.

Ken was stopped dead in his tracks by a sight that struck him as so illogical and grotesque that he violently shook his head from side to side as if to force himself to wake up and refocus.

These actions did not help.

Near the very back of the museum was a sorry sight for any pilot or airplane aficionado to view, especially in the midst of dozens of apparently intact, younger *and* older aircraft. Supported on metal struts was a crippled front nosewheel assembly along with an approximately twenty-five foot long, front section of the fuselage of an Avro Arrow. The rest of the plane was simply *gone*, seemingly cut away by some welder's blowtorch; the erratic 'burn' marks of the acetylene torch clearly showed on the rump end of the partial-fuselage. It was as if the remainder of the plane had been rudely ripped away by giant pliers, the burnt, bent and twisted metal shards at the back end of the cockpit bearing witness to the apparent fury that carried out the dirty deed. Only the cockpit, nose and nosewheel were left to display. The 'plane' was missing most of the length of its fuselage, both engines, both wings, and its entire tail.

Here, Ken mused, *hoisted up on a bare-bones support, is all that is left of a superb technological accomplishment that, fifty years earlier, was the pride of an entire nation.* What made the sparse spectacle even more poignant was the number '208' painted on its side. Ken immediately realized, of course, that he was one of only a select few who knew that the number did not belong to *that* fuselage. He immediately surmised that it had been ordered put there, perhaps a half-century earlier, in order to squash any lingering doubts that not all eight initial aircraft had been destroyed.

Ken was astounded as he circled the pitiful pieces of what was left of the Arrow. He knew instinctively and immediately that no U.S. President or Houses of Congress would *dare* to destroy all examples of such a crowning measure of America's industrial and technological prowess. It would have been like chopping up every single one of the space shuttles or stealth fighters and not allowing people to see a single complete model of what their taxes had paid for and what their skilled workers and professionals had achieved.

We Americans sure know how to honor and celebrate our successes. And, yes, maybe even glorify them. But this… this piece of junk is a national disgrace.

It was as if the Canadians had been ashamed of their crowning accomplishment. Americans wouldn't have stood for it. Witness the proud displays at the Kennedy space center in Florida and at the National Air and Space Museum in Washington, D.C..

Ken was becoming furious, partly in response to seeing a great aircraft destroyed by the very country that had designed and built it in the first place, partly because of the vengeful effectiveness that Lieutenant Colonel Stevens had told him was behind getting the Arrow program killed, and yes, also because he identified this aircraft so closely with his own father, and knew they had both met the same fate by the same bloodied hands.

Martha had wandered away again to give Ken time to reflect on what he had found, but now she rejoined him near the 'front' of the Arrow. She said, "A sign way over there says that there are two Avro Arrow wing tips over behind some of the other aircraft." She pointed in the general direction of an area about seventy feet away, chock-a-block full of various aircraft of various vintages crammed in together. "I could just make out the tops of the wing tips back there; they are mostly hidden from view by those other planes."

"What the hell are they doing over there, for Christ's sake?" Ken asked sharply.

Martha was literally rocked backwards on her heels by the angry energy of his question.

"Well, I didn't do it!" she responded heatedly, almost in the same tone Ken had used.

Ken looked at her with curiosity for a moment and then said, "What? Oh. Sorry, Martha. I didn't mean to bite your head off."

Martha replied in mock anger and a sly smile, "At least it wasn't the other way around!"

Ken said, "Thank goodness," and smiled back at her. Then he turned serious again, and added, "I just can't believe the extent of the deliberate desecra…, I mean, I'm just ticked off by this… this *disrespect,* by whomever is responsible for what has happened here, and for what should have been their prize exhibit. That's why I am so pissed."

Martha said, "It's alright, Ken. Since you told me about your father having been particularly fond of the Arrow, I thought you might find this display a disturbing experience. Anyway, I asked one of the workers who was doing something with one of the exhibits over by the Arrow wing tips, why they weren't with the remains of the fuselage, and he said the reason was what he termed "a space management problem".

"A 'space management problem? What a load of crap! That's bullshit!" responded Ken angrily again, and this time loudly enough that the members of a young family standing about fifteen feet away all turned away from the exhibit they were viewing and stared at him, the parents with sharp disapproval and the children with their mouths and eyes wide open, in shock. The family then scurried off, the parents' body language suggesting that Ken should have known better than to talk that way with children around. He felt sorrier for his outburst when he saw one of the children, a girl about six years old, looking back at him while walking away hand-in-hand with her parents, mimicking her mother's disapproving eye-rolling and head shaking.

Somewhat chagrined and now speaking much more quietly, Ken said, "Martha, perhaps some people don't really want visitors to the museum to get a solid idea of how damn big the Arrow really was compared to how pitiful little of it still remains. Look," he said, pointing behind and over her shoulder, "to give some idea of the actual size of the Arrow, all they have is that two-dimensional schematic side view painted up there on that back wall. And all they have to tell the story of the plane are a few audio and video displays over there," Ken said, pointing at a short display wall about twenty feet behind and to the left of the Avro Arrow cockpit, "with a bunch of words and pictures."

Martha turned and saw an approximately thirty-foot long panel covered with enlarged photos and large printed commentaries all over it. Followed by Martha, Ken walked directly over towards it.

The words, "**BLACK FRIDAY**" were written in large type on the center panel. He moved closer and read aloud a paragraph that he speculated was possibly placed there only after one hell of a bureaucratic battle. It read, *"On February 20, 1959, Prime Minister John Diefenbaker's Conservative* *majority government cancelled production of the Avro Arrow, an aircraft that had become a symbol of pride, sovereignty and accomplishment for many Canadians. And so ended Canada's attempts at supersonic fighter aircraft design. The government's action forever terminated Canadian military aircraft design and production."*

The next sentence Ken now knew to be false, and his knowing that had now put Ken and his son, Brad, directly in harm's way.

"All completed aircraft were destroyed and disposed of as scrap, along with all related drawings. Only the nose section of the eighth Arrow and a few other components survive in the Museum's collection."

Ken turned away, disgusted, from the shameful words on the wall. Now knowing the truth of what actually happened, were he Canadian rather than American, after seeing such a sorry excuse of a display standing in for something so magnificent, he would want to shout about the betrayal of the many by a few cowards and their accomplices.

Ken thought about Black Friday, about the deceit and covert actions that Stevens had described to him, about how certain members of the U.S. military, industry and government had perpetrated their lies and bribes upon their counterparts in Canada. He felt the weight of guilt by association because of what Stevens had revealed to him about his own father's part in spiriting away the last, surviving Avro Arrow. And knowing now *where* the eighth was taken, as well as *when*, *why*, and *by whom*, he was even more distressed by the devastation that TAMPRR had perpetrated.

"Bastards! Bastards. Bastards!" Ken repeated out loud, seemingly to himself.

When he looked again at Martha, who was facing him, he was surprised to see that she had an 'Oh-oh, look out!' sort of expression on her face. An instant later Ken sensed a very large presence behind him. As he turned around, a thankfully kind voice emerged from an elderly gentleman who exclaimed, nodding in the direction of the Arrow display, "She was the best of us!"

Ken found himself staring into the bright eyes and broad face of a barrel-chested, tall man in his late seventies. From the look of his wrinkled, Marlboro man's grandfather's face and physique, Ken quickly associated his presence to that of either a long-retired professional wrestler or football lineman, but with the manner and smile of a kindly professor. The man warmly offered his hand, which Ken took.

"Hello. Couldn't quite help but overhear your succinct comment, sir. Let me introduce myself. I am Dr. Jonathon Timberlaine, professor emeritus of aerospace engineering at Rideau University here in Ottawa. The administration of the museum has been good enough to provide me with a small office in this building in which to do my writing about the history of military aviation in Canada. I frequently just stretch my legs and walk around the museum partly, if truth be told, so that I can eavesdrop on visitors' reactions to the displays as I just did on yours. I am always keen to learn of our visitors' responses in order to help improve the quality of the museum's displays. You would seem to have some strong opinions, sir, which as a rule, are of extra special interest to me. I wonder if there is there any way that I can be of assistance?"

Ken noted the old fellow was smiling especially warmly as he gazed in Martha's direction, and her slightly flushed smile back told Ken that old Dr. Timberlaine likely used to be, and obviously still was, quite the charmer with the ladies. He also realized that Timberlaine had possibly overheard several of his harsh utterances, and had come over to check out whether there was going to be some sort of problem.

Ken said, "Dr. Timberlaine, my name is Ken Simpson. I am a reporter with *The New York Era*, and this is my associate, Martha Harrison, who is also a reporter with the paper. I was just trying to get my head around the story of the Avro Arrow, and how the supposedly most advanced military flying machine of its time met such a sad fate." Ken nodded towards the 'Black Friday' statement on the wall behind the Avro Arrow's truncated cockpit and front landing gear.

"Well," responded Dr. Timberlaine without any sign of defensiveness, "I worked on the Arrow, so perhaps I can help."

"Really?" replied Ken, happy to meet another Arrow insider.

He wondered whether McTavish and Timberlaine knew each other, but preferred to keep his sources as independent from one another as he could. "That would be much appreciated, Dr. Timberlaine. What part of the project were you involved in, if you don't mind my asking? And I wonder if you might shed some light on why you believe the project was cancelled?"

"Not at all. I was a professor of aeronautical engineering at Rideau University in the 1950s, and was part of the team that helped design the Arrow's fuselage–its body's shape." He looked approvingly at Martha.

Ken followed his gaze. *You old dog!*

"A few of us old timers have reunions now and then, and we ask each other the very question you just asked. It has taken us decades to piece things together, but we now think that we know a great deal about what may have happened to the program."

"Well, sir, my father was one of the U.S.A.F.-affiliated folks that liaisoned with your people and I am *very* interested in the views of you and your associates."

When Ken said 'U.S.A.F.', Professor Dr. Timberlaine flinched, as if he had just been given a mild shock. A look of what Ken interpreted to be sudden suspicion passed across Dr. Timberlaine's face.

Ken pretended he had not noticed the signs of Dr. Timberlaine starting to shut down, and quickly added, lest he lose the opportunity to learn more, "My father was ex-U.S.A.F.; he was a test pilot who greatly admired the Arrow, Dr. Timberlaine. He thought our Air Force should have purchased squadrons of Arrows from Avro. He also was convinced that the Arrow would have been bought by several NATO countries, as well. In fact, he intended to say that to a Senate subcommittee on military preparedness, except he was killed in an air crash."

Timberlaine scrutinized Ken closely, as if making an executive decision whether to continue the conversation or immediately end it. Finally, Timberlaine said, "Ah, yes. I think I do remember that there were a couple of American flyers who pressed for the Arrow program to be continued, and for your country to acquire a number of squadrons of Arrows. So one of them was your father, then?"

Ken nodded, and said with pride, "Yes, sir."

Timberlaine softened considerably. He said, "Well, your father spoke a truth that too few of your people–*and ours*–seemed ready or willing to hear."

Dr. Timberlaine regarded Ken and Martha both for a moment and then said while looking directly at Martha, "I was just finishing my afternoon walkabout, so to speak, and was about to return to my office. Would you care to join me and we can chat a little more about all this? Perhaps I might be able to provide you with some additional background that you would find useful."

Ken and Martha replied in the affirmative. As they made their way past the museum's bookstore, Dr. Timberlaine said, "Ms. Harrison, you may be interested in knowing that the many Americans who visit this museum are a good portion of the reason that our museum survives. And many of them are quite knowledgeable about aviation and frequently show particular interest in the Avro Arrow display."

Martha said, "And why do you think there is still so much interest shown in the Avro Arrow, especially by Americans?"

"Because," said Dr. Timberlaine, possibly more forcefully than he had intended, "whenever there is an unsolved, high profile and nonsensical death, especially a particularly gruesome and brutal murder, folks always take an interest. And the people who have learned about the Avro Arrow seem to understand this." Timberlaine's face flushed, seemingly first with anger and then, perhaps with some embarrassment. He quickly added, "I am truly sorry, Ms. Harrison, for perhaps sounding more severe than I should have."

Martha gently patted his arm with her hand and said warmly, "Please, call me Martha. And no apology is necessary, believe me."

"Yes, all right. And thank you."

Dr. Timberlaine's said, "I am afraid it is just that I have felt like one of the last 'immediate family members' who will be able to act as custodian of the Avro Arrow's memory here at the museum. And I can tell you that many times I have had to resist, along with a few of my colleagues, some very strong efforts from certain quarters to make the final, meager physical remnants of that magnificent flying machine disappear completely from the museum."

As they walked the length of the display area towards his office, Dr. Timberlaine turned towards Ken, and added, "Perhaps your father would understand how I feel."

"I am sure he would."

Ken looked at Martha, then at the Arrow's custodian, and said, "Dr. Timberlaine, we should tell you that we are here, in part, to investigate and perhaps do an article on the Avro Arrow, and what really happened to it."

Martha gave him as sideways glance, since Ken had not put the matter to her quite that way when he said he wanted to come to the museum.

Timberlaine's face showed surprise but no apprehension. "Ah-ha! Well, that's very good. And would you kindly tell me, seeing as you are both *American* reporters, and aside from your own personal interest pertaining to your father, Mr. Simpson, why you might have a professional interest in this story?"

Ken replied quickly. "Gladly. We are developing a series of articles having to do with how and why certain major programs, in the U.S. and Canada, that may have benefited our respective populations, and were in place and operational, have been curtailed or cut off from the financial and political support they deserved and required. From my father's stories about the Avro Arrow, it seemed like a natural for an investigative article on this topic."

Dr. Timberlaine's face began to show some signs of recognition as his mind now put Ken's name, that of his newspaper's, and his reference to 'investigative reporting' together. "I see. Of course! *You* are the young fellow who just recently won that Paulson prize."

Ken nodded, adding with a smile "Well, no and yes, Dr. Timberlaine. Perhaps 'no' to the *young* fellow, but 'yes' to the *award*."

Dr. Timberlaine took Ken's comments good-naturedly. "Well, to someone of *my* age you *are* a young man, and I *did* read one of your articles, after someone drew my attention to a brief reference to the Arrow in it. So, now that it is clearer to me who you are and why you are interested, I would be more than pleased to tell you anything you want to know about Avro and its Arrow."

At that moment Dr. Timberlaine stopped and pointed to some photographs on the wall and a glass-encased, foot-wide model of what looked like a flying saucer in a display case beneath the photos.

"By the way," he said to Ken, "your government took over another of Avro's projects, the Avrocar. That design was Avro's attempt to build and explore possible propulsion systems for use in an actual flying saucer-shaped vehicle. I was there when it was flown out at the old Malton airport, near Toronto. Dozens of us just stood transfixed as this 'flying saucer' emerged from its hanger, and then flew along a runway about two or three feet above the ground. Have you ever seen a whole bunch of adults struck speechless at the same moment, and then suddenly starting jumping and hooting for joy like six year olds? It was all rather amazing."

Ken gazed at the model and photographs; he was fascinated by the saucer-shaped craft, apparently about twenty feet across, with twin glass domes atop it and a pilot clearly visible sitting in one, as it was either hovering or moving, a few feet above a runway. It was like a futuristic-looking hovercraft, except you could see daylight under the thing as it flew along. Ken was impressed by the depth and breadth of Arvo's research and development capabilities.

Martha asked, "Did the Avrocar really fly like that, like a flying saucer?" She found the whole notion quite astonishing.

Dr. Timberlaine said, "Well, it got off the ground all right and made it a hundred feet or so along the tarmac. But no, as far as I know, it never did 'fly like a flying saucer', as you put it, at least, not at any serious altitude. Of course, once your country's military took it over, it went under wraps. So I don't know if *they* ever got it to fly higher. There were sightings of remarkably similar-looking UFOs that occurred several years after the Americans took over the project. Whether they had made much progress with some kind of airborne nuclear propulsion system, for instance, I have no way of knowing."

Dr. Timberlaine said, "Lets get some coffee or tea in the hardly adequate coffee shop near the entrance; then we can sit in my office and I'll be very happy to respond to any other questions you may have."

"Yes, thank you," both Ken and Martha said, almost in unison. It was as true in the world of reporting as in the rest of life that chance meetings and events sometimes provided far more of value than those that had been arranged far in advance.

CHAPTER 31

Once they had their coffees and muffins in hand, they climbed up one flight of stairs, and were soon all seated in their new acquaintance's second floor office with its two picture windows, one facing the parking lot and the other set into the wall opposite, providing a generous view of the aircraft on display. The two visitors noted a foot-high cluttering of papers and newspaper clippings threatening to cascade in on the small wooden desk bearing up an older model desktop computer.

Dr. Timberlaine asked, "Now, what would you like to know?"

Martha spoke first, which was fine with Ken, especially since she and their host had observably struck up an instant camaraderie. "Well, Dr. Timberlaine, would you mind briefly reviewing for us how the Avro Arrow project came into being, how far it progressed, how you recall it being terminated, and what you believe was really going on behind the scenes to kill off the project and leave so little of the Arrow behind to even display?

Ken nodded his approval of Martha's succinct inquiry.

Dr. Timberlaine began his reply eagerly, saying that he hoped that this rendering might acquaint many more people, specifically Ken's American readers, with this pinnacle of Canadian technological achievement.

Timberlaine said, "As you know, the Arrow was designed and built by Avro Canada. That company came into being after World War II; it was the peacetime manifestation of Victory Aircraft, which itself had built the Lancaster bomber in Canada, one of the major weapons that enabled the Allies to emerge victorious in that war. Avro Canada was created to design, develop and then produce new aircraft. Two aircraft operations were established, one called Avro Aircraft and the other called Orenda Engines.

"Avro's first project was the CF-100, a twin-engine, two seat, high altitude, all weather interceptor. You may have seen one as you walked around the museum. Nearly 700 of these aircraft were built and the CF-100 flew here in Canada and in Europe with NATO for nearly three decades.

"In the early 1950s, the Canadian military establishment and Canadian government decided to develop a replacement for the CF-100. This new aircraft was to be ready to go into service in the early 1960s. At that time the main threat to North America was considered to be Soviet supersonic bombers that, in any attack, were expected to fly down over Canada from the Arctic on their way to striking their targets in the USA. To meet this threat the demand specifications for the new aircraft were daunting, indeed. Is this the kind of information you want?" asked Dr. Timberlaine.

"Yes, sir. Definitely, " replied Martha. She was happy to have more background information so that she could converse with Ken about it later in a more informed way. Ken nodded his agreement, as well.

"Alright, then. Well, the specs for the new aircraft stated that it had to be able to operate at Mach 1.5 at an altitude of 50,000 feet, and also be capable of a 2 G maneuver capability with no loss whatever of either speed or altitude. It was to have a mission radius of a minimum of 200 nautical miles for supersonic intercept, and was to get from 'starting engines' to 50,000 feet at Mach 1.5 in under than five minutes. And its turnaround time on the ground was to be less than ten minutes.

"Those were the demand specifications, and extremely demanding–if not downright impossible–they seemed. In actual fact, however, one of the early Arrows, fitted with less powerful engines than it would have had in place within weeks of the program being terminated, actually exceeded the demand specs when it reached a speed in level flight of over Mach 1.9."

At this point Dr. Timberlaine pointed to a framed photograph on the wall behind Ken and Martha. It was a poster-sized blowup of the cover of one of the U.S.'s major military aviation magazines, Aviation Week, the October 21, 1957 issue. The photo on the cover was unmistakable: it was the Arrow. Next to the photograph, also blown up to poster size, was a portion of the article on the Arrow that appeared in that issue, which read:

"(The) Avro CF-105 Arrow has given Canada a serious contender for the top military aircraft of the next several years."

Ken made notes about both cover and comment.

Dr. Timberlaine continued. "The design of the Arrow included many unique features. It was so exciting to be designing and building such a remarkable aircraft, from scratch. It had to have a removable armament pack, one that fitted within the shape of the fuselage, so that it could be removed and replaced within minutes, allowing for reloading with either more of the same or some other kinds of armaments. And because it was held within the fuselage, the armament pack wouldn't offer any additional wind resistance that might affect the speed of the aircraft.

"As well, in designing the Arrow, there were to be no prototypes as we had known of them to that point. Even before the aircraft flew, the testing and design of the fuselage and all systems were to be developed and checked out using computers or scale models. The fact that eight Arrows were successfully flown more than seventy hours in total using this approach demonstrated that this way of designing and building an aircraft from scratch on what was essentially an already-in-place assembly line, worked exceptionally well. The Arrow, whose main role was as a high altitude, high speed interceptor, and whose other roles included carrying bombs or reconnaissance equipment, was all in all, a hugely successful project."

Ken asked innocently, "If it was such a great design, if it met and passed all of the specifications that had been laid out for it, then why do you think it was cancelled? Some of the stories I read suggested that it was too costly. Was that it?"

Dr. Timberlaine shook his head so violently Ken was momentarily concerned lest the man gave himself a massive headache, if not a stroke.

"Not at all, compared to the costs of alternate systems, including the U.S. aircraft that our country eventually bought, and which, I might add, were decidedly inferior to the Avro Arrow. They cost us more, and did not allow for the development of a home based, 'built here, buy here' aircraft industry, the very philosophy that, of course, your country has had for decades."

"The decision to cancel the Arrow was supposedly made in cabinet meetings by the party in power. There was no significant public or parliamentary debate. Our then Minister of Defense apparently presented the cabinet with an American proposal that Canada purchase your Bomarc anti-aircraft missile program, which we did at about the same time that the American military itself had expressed major reservations about the same missile system. In fact, the Bomarcs became operational in Canada in 1962, only two years before your military had such serious second thoughts about the equipment that they were soon dismantling your own Bomarcs."

Martha asked. "But if the Avro Arrow was such a great aircraft, why didn't the United States simply buy them from Canada?"

Dr. Timberlaine paused, looked intently at Martha, decided she genuinely wanted to know, and replied, "Quite frankly, Ms Harrison, I and many of my colleagues in Canadian research and development circles of the time have long concluded that there was simply no way that certain elements in your country would have allowed so much expertise, and the production of what would have been the most sophisticated airplane in your air force, to reside outside the U.S."

Ken noticed, as Dr. Timberlaine paused again, that the retired professor-turned-historian appeared to be struggling to keep his emotions in check. Clearly many of the people involved in the Avro Arrow project had never entirely gotten over the pain of having their greatest professional success destroyed.

Timberlaine gathered himself together. He said, "Over the years a few of my fellow engineers and I have acquired a considerable amount of information, including Cabinet documents that were released after the thirty year secrecy time period expired in 1989, and arrived at the virtually inescapable conclusion that the Arrow program was most likely killed because it was *too good* an aircraft. Not only was it suitable for Canada's extreme weather and its air defense requirements, but it was also likely to be the weapon-of-choice for several of our other allies. It could fly farther, faster, higher and operate more effectively than any other allied aircraft.

"But it wasn't American! And that was the main problem;

there was no problem with the airplane itself. It could beat the pants off of anything your own country had. It would have made little Canada the most advanced fighter-interceptor aircraft manufacturing country in the world. And that was entirely unacceptable to elements of the then U.S. government, its corporations, and many in your military. The Arrow had to be killed in order to save and secure your own military aircraft manufacturing supremacy."

Timerlaine stopped talking and, gradually, the redness in his face faded away. He looked intently from Martha to Ken and back.

Ken pushed the envelope some more. He said, "But the U.S. and Canada used to boast that they were the closest of friendly nations. We had what we both bragged about as the longest undefended border in the world, at least until 9/11. Do you really believe that our country was so filled with power and/or money hungry elements that we would do such a thing to an ally's program? And that there were enough people in your country that would have gone along with doing such a thing?"

The old man smiled slightly and slowly shook his head. "I see that you are still an idealist, Mr. Simpson. However, think about it. Does General Motors not spend hundreds of millions of dollars a year on advertising to beat Ford and Daimler-Chrysler, to say nothing of Toyota and Honda and the rest of its competitors? And do these other companies not reciprocate in kind? Whether they buy out or bankrupt their competitors–think American Motors, Jeep, Mazda, Rover–the business way of the world is to kill off and/or take over the competition."

Ken nodded.

"And, Mr. Simpson, what about the battles between Boeing and Airbus? Would either of them mind if their competitor went belly up?"

Ken again nodded his concurrence.

"Also, folks, remember, we are talking about a period that was just fourteen years or so after World War II. When the war ended the Russians and the Americans descended upon the German missile-building scientists and engineers like ravenous dogs. The Americans made the better offers in some cases, and got some of the very finest of the Germans scientists who were responsible for designing and building the missiles that had attacked London. Americans have perfected the art-science of defeating an enemy and then swooping down and carrying off its best and brightest, for the greater good and power of the U.S.. Well, many of us believe that is the very thing that happened in the case of the Arrow. Whether it was your government, your military, your aircraft manufacturers, or a mixture of some or all of them, *that* I have no way of knowing.

"What I do firmly believe is that on February 20, 1959 some vested interests in America succeeded in securing, permanently, the defeat of Canada's burgeoning military airplane building industry. Keep in mind that there were American military liaison officers and engineering personnel who we had invited to sit in on nearly every phase of the building of the Arrow. Your people even facilitated the use of wind tunnel testing in the USA since we didn't have sufficiently powerful equipment here in Canada. Your people were thereby continuously monitoring the plane's progress. Then, when the first few Arrows showed that they would not only meet, but would actually exceed their design specs, it was probably decided that it was time to shut down the program and take over the people and the technology.

"The killing off of the Arrow program also meant the total elimination of over 14,000 highly skilled jobs in my country. But it was obvious to many of us, in retrospect, that the actions taken had likely been planned months before, although we still don't know how many people were involved in bringing it about. We also don't know precisely *who* was involved, although we have our ideas. But the facts of the invasion of U.S. interests into our decision-making process, and the subsequent capitulation of vital segments of our Canadian military and government in regard to the Avro Arrow program, seems to us a virtual certainty."

Martha asked, "So you have no doubt in your mind as to what happened, and why?"

Dr. Timberlaine said, "Please understand, Ms Harrison, I am not saying that it was a great big, vast conspiracy that involved all of the then American administration, military, or U.S. aircraft manufacturers. I wouldn't suggest any such thing. But it doesn't take a lot of people to influence or even completely destroy a project of any kind, if they set their mind to it and have the resources to back up their intentions. Think 9/11. In fact, all of us understand full well that it takes compromising or turning only a very few well-positioned individuals to sabotage an entire system–your Robert Philip Hanssen, the FBI agent who spied for the Soviets, being a case in point. And remember, it also takes only a single inebriated person at the helm of a supertanker to steer it onto a reef, thereby causing billions of dollars and incalculable ecological damage. And a single rogue trader can bring down an entire bank."

Ken was feeling increasingly uncomfortable as he realized that Timberlaine was only missing a few pieces to complete the rest of the puzzle. Ken held these pieces on the tip of his tongue, but had given his word he would not divulge what Lieutenant Colonel Stevens had told him. At least, not yet. He would write Dr. Timberlaine a personal note once he had the go-ahead from Stevens to make public what he had told him. Ken said, "Your points are convincingly made, sir."

Timerlaine replied, "Mr. Simpson, many of my engineering colleagues and I do not have a very high opinion of certain people in high places. We have learned that some folks are far more easily corruptible than most of us would like to believe, especially we too often, too naïve Canadians. We have come to the virtually inescapable conclusion that Canada, Canadians and the Avro Arrow program were sold out by an enterprising but undoubtedly small number of morally reprehensible people. And the people whom *they* convinced to terminate the program were either extremely gullible, easily corruptible, or both. There was, essentially, a domino effect that knocked down the Avro Arrow program.

Ken asked, "Since you and your friends are so convinced of what happened, have you ever brought your conclusions to the attention of the media?"

Timberlaine cocked his head, squinted, and smiled in the manner of a loving parent whose young child has just unknowingly said something rather silly.

"As a matter of fact, Mr. Simpson, there are several books, videos, articles and web sites devoted to the theories behind the rise and fall of the Arrow program. Hell, we even had a made-for-TV movie, a number of documentary television programs, and at least one full-length play on the subject. Many of these productions intimate at what I am saying, or even provide documentation that is highly suggestive of what we think happened."

Martha asked, incredulously, "So even a half-century after the Avro Arrow program was shut down, the matter continues to exist in the consciousness of Canadians?"

"Absolutely, Ms. Harrison!"

Martha said, "That is really amazing."

Timberlaine replied, "Not really. Treachery and betrayal bequeath lengthy memories."

Ken asked, "Very well put, sir. But after all, we are now a full half-century on. With apologies, if I may put the question in a New York City reporter's skeptical and perhaps insensitive manner, why haven't your citizens gotten over the Arrow thing already? Have you not accomplished anything else of significance in this country in the last fifty years?"

Timberlaine seemed momentarily stunned by Ken's crassly put question. Then, recovering his composure, he said in an even tone, "The Arrow means something, in fact a great deal, to many of us, both to people who know the story and to most of those learning about it. I can tell you, as an amateur military and aeronautical historian who is still learning his avocation, that acts of glory and infamy are seldom forgotten. Neil Armstrong's landing on the moon was a glorious achievement. The terrorist attack and destruction of the World Trade Center obviously is an example of the worse infamy. The building and the sinking of Titanic, like the Avro Arrow story, combines both elements, that is, great achievement and the worst destruction, and was therefore a tragedy of heroic proportions. People remember these events. Successive generations pay attention. They seek to get closer to something important to their own history, perhaps as a way of coming to understand their current lives just a little better. A historian's job, then, is to bring people into contact with their own past, as a means of providing a context to their present, and hopefully, some direction for their future."

Ken and Martha both nodded.

Ken thought of MacBeth. *'Murder most foul', is not easily forgiven, or forgotten.*

Dr. Timberlaine saw his new acquaintances were both making notes. He waited until they were finished writing, then continued. "There have been questions raised in the public domain now and then about what was really behind the demise of the program and how it came about. But aside from a very few editorial and opp-ed pieces, the capitulation of our then government, and the destruction of the Arrow program was planned, one might say, with military-like precision. By the time we knew we were being raped, we had been plucked, fucked, and, ..., *oh, please excuse me,* Ms Harrison..."

Martha laughed and said, "That's quite alright. My father was a mechanical engineer and irrepressible inventor. Throughout my childhood I was used to hearing some very colorful language emanating from his basement workshop."

"Well, all the same... anyway, thank you for being understanding. I do get quite worked up, sometimes. Not an ideal attribute for a historian, I am afraid. Anyway, you have already seen the cockpit of an Arrow, at least all that remains of that original aircraft, at the *rear* of this museum. Of course, your Spirit of St. Louis, at least the last time I was there, was just inside the entrance to your National Aviation and Space Museum. Yet, if certain forces in Ottawa have their way, and they might yet, the Avro Arrow program might not be represented at all in the museum in the not-too-distant future. About the only major item to have a less prominent location is way over there," he said, pointing to the corner furthest from where they sat, and from the entrance to the museum. He said, "There is the bloody shameful Bomarc missile, which was supposed to replace the Arrow. *Hah*!"

Ken, Martha and Dr. Timberlaine sat quietly for a little while drinking their coffees. The old engineer seemed lost in his private thoughts. Ken guessed that he was perhaps momentarily back at Avro, that fateful Friday morning, either at his desk or maybe on the production line, speaking with some other engineers about how to interface the new weapons package with the flight control system within the fuselage in a manner similar to the way a kangaroo holds its joey, when the public address system made its clicking 'on' sound, and those awful words poured out from the loudspeakers and spread throughout the plant like a poisonous vapor, instantly killing the hopes, dreams, and realities of some of the proudest fourteen thousand workers in the entire country.

Timberlaine said, "I should tell you the only current, good news that I know relating to the Arrow."

Ken said, "Please."

Timberlaine offered a very broad smile. "Well, this being the fiftieth anniversary of its termination, you may be interested to learn that all across Canada the Arrow is being remembered with displays, at least one full-scale model, and a smaller version that will actually take off later in the year. And some of us are lobbying to have a full-scale Arrow mockup placed *at the front* of the museum, in take-off attitude. All of these projects should help remind us of what was, what could have and should have been, and also invite us to dream of soaring again, in all areas of creative endeavor."

Martha said, "That sounds wonderful. Since I have just recently taken over the Ottawa bureau of the newspaper, I would love to come to any celebrations planned around the Arrow."

Ken thought he saw her eyes flash when she said those words. He definitely saw old Timberlaine come to attention.

"Lovely." the old guy said. "You will be my special guest."

Martha smiled even more broadly at Timberlaine.

Ken was not entirely amused at this little byplay. *Or was it social foreplay? Do men ever really stop their macho competitiveness? Will I?*

Timberlaine inquired, "Will you be able to make use of what I have told you?"

Ken said, "You can count on it, sir. You have just corroborated and elaborated upon information that I have received from some other sources. And I believe that your hypothesis about what may have actually happened to the Arrow program, and why, may be right on."

Dr. Timberlaine looked quizzically at Ken, but seemed to recognize that it was probably best to ask nothing.

Ken and Martha handed him their respective business cards. Dr. Timberlaine returned the courtesy. He then walked them to the front door of the museum. They said their goodbyes, Timberlaine shaking Ken's hand and then gently holding Martha's. As the two of them walked toward their car Timberlaine stood at the entrance and waved goodbye.

They waved back as they drove off. Then Ken and Martha briefly shared their impressions of their museum experience, and while Martha drove back towards the center of the city Ken filled her in on his interview with Dr. McTavish.

Martha asked, "Why didn't you inquire if Timberlaine knew McTavish?

Ken replied, "I didn't want to interrupt his flow, or let their connection, if any, affect what he had to say."

"How did their comments compare?"

"They were pretty well right on."

"And what do you make of it all?"

Ken replied, "Whatever did go on back in 1959 *still* stinks. And some of our own government and/or military and/or business people were likely involved up to their necks in it."

Martha nodded in agreement, and added, "Well, I suppose that most of our readers Stateside will think that it was okay to do what was done; after all, the American airplane business, military and civilian, *has* been the dominant force in the air in the whole world, for at least the last four or five decades."

"True," Ken replied. "I suppose some people think that all's fair in love, war, and business. But we'll see what our readers think when they learn that *they* are the major current target when it comes to health care."

Martha glanced at Ken. He had a serious expression, and was nodding his head very slightly, up and down, as if he was concurring with whatever it is that he was thinking. Martha had seen that look before. It usually meant that Ken was very much in play and it was probably best to leave him to his own musing for a while. And that probably meant that some of the potential subjects of his investigative pieces would soon likely become very uncomfortable, indeed.

CHAPTER 32

Ken and Martha had left the museum just before closing, at 5:25p.m..

Riding along in silence back the way they had come they turned up Sussex Drive past the Prime Minister's official residence on their right, number 24. A minute or so later they came upon a tragic scene that had been etched in many Americans' minds by endless re-runnings of the videotape of the U.S. embassy explosion that had taken its infamous place alongside the horrors of the World Trade Center's collapsing towers and the missing façade of the building attacked by Timothy McVeigh in Oklahoma. They were driving past the just recently excavated hole in the ground where the American embassy had formerly stood. It had, several months earlier, been the target of a devastating terrorist attack that had also caused major collateral damage to Canada's parliament buildings and National Art Gallery.

Ken recalled reading several articles, following 9/11, that quoted, among others, a retired U.S. Army General, a former senior CIA official, and at least two former Canadian security czars who openly and repeatedly referred to what they had termed the 'sheer arrogance, lunacy and/or stupidity' of placing the narrow but one long, full block in length, multi-storied and much glassed U.S. embassy, literally across a small park from the seat of the host country's federal government, Parliament Hill, and bordered on each long side by the most heavily trafficked, multi-lane, one-way streets in downtown Ottawa, Sussex Drive and Mackenzie Avenue. Now, one brief look at the location of the former embassy made Ken realize the obvious, that securing the embassy from a terrorist attack had been entirely impossible from the get-go.

What made the matter even more astonishing was that several years earlier the U.S. Secret Service had prompted the District of

Columbia to take the entirely sensible–though sad–measure of removing the White House, the Capitol building, and several other major governmental official offices in Washington, D.C. from such easy access to potential ground-based terrorist actions. This was achieved by closing off and/or rerouting Pennsylvania Avenue traffic, and by ensuring that a perimeter of fences and defenses of various kinds prevented either vehicles or pedestrians from getting any closer than two hundred feet from these potential targets. And yet, even years later, people in potentially bomb-laden cars and trucks were able to drive by a mere thirty feet from the sides of the U.S. embassy in Ottawa. The only barriers protecting the embassy from attack had been four-foot-high concrete traffic dividers.

The stubborn refusal on the part of those responsible for locating, building, and maintaining the embassy, to acknowledge the obviously prime target they had created for terrorists, and the unnecessary risk at which they put their own employees, their host's seat of government, and the local citizenry, was surely unconscionable. The virtual inevitability had happened in all its completely predictable–and predicted–horror.

The previous spring, at the height of the usual bumper-to-bumper morning rush hour, two explosive-laden trucks had driven along in the lanes closest to the embassy building, one on MacKenzie and the other on Sussex, at the same time. When they were both close to the middle of their respective long sides of the building, the bombs were detonated at virtually the same instant by the trucks' drivers, who had been relaying their positions via coded comments over their cellphones.

The embassy building was massively imploded on both sides, effectively collapsing and destroying the entire structure along with numerous historical and renovated residential and retail buildings in the SoHo style 'market' area of downtown Ottawa, and damaging sections of their host country's parliament buildings and its National Art Gallery.

How could so many supposedly brilliant minds be so collectively dumb? Could anyone seriously claim, as was done re 9/11, that no one had ever conceived of such an attack happening? Or was the whole idea to have a reminder, 24/7, for

Canadian politicians, that our two countries are in the same boat, terrorist-wise, and therefore, whatever affects the security of the U.S. could–and in this instance, certainly did–*impact the United States' closest ally and most important trading partner.*

Ken had read that various Canadian government buildings in the vicinity of the U.S. embassy had a virtually invisible protective coating of some sort applied to their windows. The National Art Gallery of Canada, literally a stone's throw away from the embassy, had a similar lamination applied to *its* hundreds of windows in order to try and protect its art collection from any flying glass or debris in case the U.S. Embassy was attacked. The protective coating had done a minimal job. Mind you, the coatings were only applied after the U.S. embassies in Tanzania and Kenya were bombed in 2000, and only after hundreds were killed and thousands injured from glass fragments on those earlier occasions.

In 2003, reports surfaced that al-Qaeda linked terrorists had considered bombing the U.S. embassy in Ottawa, but the plan didn't take place for unreported reasons. Now, Ken understood that the target had simply been too damned accessible for such an attack to have been resisted indefinitely. As well, since al-Qaeda had listed Canada along with the U.S., Australia, and several other countries as "infidel nations", attacking the U.S. embassy in Canada and the Canadian parliament at the very same time was a 2-4-1 opportunity that was simply too convenient to have taken a pass on.

Ken felt disgusted as he recalled the obsessive focus of George W. Bush in regard to invading the country of Iraq as a supposed response to 9/11 and to the supposed threat of what turned out to be non-existent weapons of mass destruction, thereby diverting so much attention and resources from the real war on terrorism. That war would have focused upon tracking and eliminating al-Qaeda's and the other terrorist organizations' principals and their disciples, while at the same time securing the safety of American property and citizenry at home and around the world. Instead, his administration's actions had occupied literally hundreds of thousands of American soldiers thousands of miles away from home and therefore unavailable to help protect

American ports. The Bush-propagated disaster was a self-inflicted, uncontrollable chaos that had bogged down the U.S. for the previous eight years at a cost of many *trillions* of dollars and the lives of thousands of American soldiers and hundreds of thousands of ordinary citizens in Iraq and other countries.

Over the past few years the folly of Bush's warring actions had become only too painfully clear. Ken knew that it was not only the American media that had become mute in the face of reprisals by Bush's supporters. As well, probably most mental health professionals, including prominent psychiatrists and psychologists, had so feared for their professional lives (perhaps by possibly losing their licenses and 'preferred provider' status with various HMOs and insurance companies) that they too were almost entirely absent from the sorts of discussions that only in the latter part of the Bush presidency had come so much into vogue. Only when the man was nearly out of power did a plethora of articles emerge in certain professional journals that hypothesized about the president's intellectual abilities and conjectured about whether he had almost unbearable feelings of inadequacy when compared to his father, a genuine war hero. These feelings of inadequacy, it was hypothesized in some writings, had been compensated for by presenting himself–to himself and the world–as a mighty warrior. How much pain had the world been subjected to while the emperor freely walked about naked, all the while proclaiming the importance of decency and modesty?

Only after the U.S. embassy was attacked did the White House accept the long-standing unofficial offer of the Canadian government to provide, gratis, a several-acre piece of prime land located a few minutes drive away from Parliament Hill, where the new, much less vulnerable embassy was currently being built, set back from the nearest road and buildings by three hundred feet of more easily protected real estate.

Ken thought some more about the fiduciary responsibilities of those who had participated in the decision to destroy the Arrows that had already been built, and the closing down of the entire program. One could argue, he thought, that his country's business and military people had done the right thing in initiating terminating a program that would have made relatively thinly populated Canada a world powerhouse in military aviation. But he also felt sad for the Canadian engineers and technicians who were technological Olympians, but who nevertheless had their participation in the 'games' cancelled by their bosses' bosses' bosses.

And underlying all his thoughts was the notion that the same people who had killed the Arrow had also murdered his father.

Ken was now very anxious to meet Dr. Judith Brown, the former parliamentarian and ex-Minister of Health who was apparently the current head of a medical clinic in Ottawa, and whom Dr. McTavish had described as a close friend and an extremely knowledgeable person about the political goings-on in regard to the Canadian Medicare system. Ken had a hunch that their friendship either was now, or had been in the past, something more than platonic. He had called her office while flying into Ottawa and arranged his appointment with Dr. Brown for the next morning.

Ken speculated that Dr. Brown might know more about what was going on behind the scenes to kill the Canadian Medicare system than just about anyone else he might gain access to, except perhaps Dr. Trish Markridge, M.P.. And he wanted to know what they knew.

Martha was driving in the direction of the company's apartment. Acknowledging to one another that they were both famished, on the way they stopped at an Italian restaurant with a crooked-looking sign above its front window announcing '*The Peace-a Tower*.' Ken chuckled, sharing with Martha that the clock tower in the middle of the so-called 'center block' of the Canadian parliament buildings was called the Peace Tower. *Very cute!*

Martha said that a note she had read in the briefing binder at the apartment indicated that the restaurant was known by the local media wags to be a favorite haunt of some members of parliament and foreign embassy types. From the number of limos and Mercedes in the valet parking lot it seemed likely that some of the reputed patrons were already on site.

Once they were seated at a table from which vantage point they easily made out some likely heavy hitters having intense but whispered exchanges, their own conversation oscillated between being alternately easy and forced. As long as they were talking business or superficialities they did well.

Martha answered Ken's inquiry about her early impressions of Ottawa, saying, "I like it okay; "it's just like New York City or Washington, D.C., but smaller-minded, and without the slums, the violence, or the excitement."

They briefly discussed their reactions to Dr. Timberlaine (very impressed), the National Flight Museum of Canada (quite well done), and the Avro Arrow display in particular (miniscule, tragic, and infuriating).

They also chatted about the current newsroom gossip back at *The New York Era*. As long as they stayed on such topics they were on generally safe ground. However, whenever Martha even indirectly approached the subject of Ken's new "little helper", as she referred to Sylkeen, his stumbling responses were probably less than reassuring.

Ken believed that Martha was sure that nothing had happened between himself and Sylkeen–at least not *yet*–but she also knew that a recipe of time, familiarity, opportunity, and working closely together under the pressure of deadlines, could conveniently meld into a sexual stew only waiting to tasted. After all, it had happened with her and Ken, hadn't it?

But at least Ken was here, now, with her, and away from the home office and that little...

Ken thought that it was obvious to Martha that he was not entirely comfortable talking about Sylkeen. He knew that although Martha was emotionally as well as sexually drawn to him, she was also practical. Tonight she would probably take out her muted frustration and simmering jealousy through their lovemaking. *Worse things could happen.*

When they finally arrived at the *Era's* apartment just past eight in the evening, Ken made out a list of questions he wanted researched and answered, if possible, by the next morning. Martha dutifully called a local researcher that the 'familiarity binder' indicated the *Era's* reporters often used to dig into Canadian subjects and personalities. The researcher, a Ph.D. student in political science who supported herself by doing this sort of work while working on her thesis, answered Martha's call on the first ring of her cellphone, received the questions via e-mail a few minutes later, and replied that she would fax back whatever material she could uncover before eight the next morning. Since she had planned to pull an all-nighter, it just meant shifting subject focus. While Martha was shutting down the computer, Ken took a shower, got into bed to watch the early television news, and fell fast asleep.

Martha took a long, luxurious bath. By 10:30 pm, she finished in the bathroom, turned off the lights and television in the bedroom, and lay down beside the most attractive and decent man she knew. Once under the covers, Martha proceeded to wake up Ken in the fashion that most men never cease to fantasize about. It was not long before enough of the rest of him was also awake that she could take out her frustrations and insecurities in a mutually acceptable–and satisfying–fashion.

Afterwards, they both slept soundly, spooning most of the night. That would be the last sense of peace they would have together for some time.

CHAPTER 33

Whatever the reason, Ken was feeling quite relaxed as he lay awake at dawn, having been woken up by the sound of the fax machine in the adjoining room spewing out what were probably the researcher's findings. He knew that he very much cared for–and about–Martha. He also loved her, even though he was experienced enough to realize that he was not *in* love with her. *It is what it is.*

Ken was also in a very good mood this morning. He had learned a great deal in the past few days. His information had come from reputable and well-placed sources: from Drs. Larson, McTavish, Timberlaine, and Lieutenant Colonel Stevens. From being at the museum and seeing the sorry Avro Arrow display firsthand. And he sensed that he was going to be learning a great deal more over the next few days. While he had been somewhat embarrassed as well as proud about having been the recipient of the Paulson Prize, he acknowledged to himself that it definitely added more credibility to his name and more weight to his requests for interviews.

Too often, he well knew, columnists pushed their own agendas, including when their so-called 'facts' were quite at odds with reality. Those writers often believed that their *versions* of the truth were more valid, or at least made for more interesting reading, than the unpolished truth, and therefore wrote their skewed stories by neglecting significant contrary information, shaping and squeezing their biases into 850-word columns and 1000-word features. Too many columnists he knew personally had sold their souls for the sake of seeing their signatures continuing to appear as a byline, reduced to applying their own writing styles to promoting their publishers' agendas. *Just look at what happened to the press during Bush's presidency. The man usually only called upon certain reporters, by name, to ask their pre-planted, or at least predictably politically safe questions.*

Ken knew that just as live sitcom TV audiences had so often been replaced by canned, or at least partially canned, laughter tracks, so it was that many reporters were reduced to tamely barking out their masters' tunes.

Ken thought of some of the pro-American-style healthcare articles he had read over the past few days in one of the supposedly major Canadian newspapers. That organization, he knew, also owned or controlled a significant number of Canadian radio and television outlets as well as a substantial stable of smaller, local newspapers and had just blanketed their listeners/viewers/readers with some of the most skewed reporting Ken had encountered in some time.

The fact was that Ken already knew that some American investors had been welcomed on board a couple of years earlier to help shore up the newspaper chain's sagging fortunes. In the context of what Stevens had told him, deliberately making such a seemingly poor investment now made complete sense; such actions were likely part of keeping TAMPRR's plans on track. The U.S. investors didn't expect to make money from the newspaper's success; they had already been paid, by TAMPRR, for providing its American healthcare clients with a 'Canadian' mouthpiece.

Ken read one article in which the reporter had written about deaths that had occurred in some Canadian hospitals because some kidney patients had received injections of potassium chloride instead of sodium chloride during their dialysis treatments. The writer of the piece stated that, if only there were hospitals competing with one another for patients via a Canadian version of the good old American-style free enterprise system, then competition would have kept them all on their toes and such a mix-up would not have been as likely to occur.

Ken had actually laughed out loud at the audacity of the writer for having entirely ignored the voluminous number of similar reports of drug administration mix-ups that occurred regularly in American hospitals by overworked and understaffed medical personnel. The same writer had also failed to point out that, too often, prospective American patients find it difficult to get even moderately expensive medical tests or treatments unless they and their doctors were willing to get into long, drawn-out fights with their so-called healthcare providers. The article also did not bother to mention, of course, the fifteen percent of Americans had no health insurance whatsoever, or that most of *them* would never get to even *see* the inside of a hospital so that their illnesses could be treated. *Ah, the power of the press to propagate selective bullshit was amazing.*

Ken was pleasantly surprised when he realized that he hadn't thought much about Sylkeen throughout the previous couple of days. Over dinner the previous evening he had deflected Martha's queries about the professional capabilities of, as she had put it, "the *so* very beautiful and *so* much younger" reporter who had taken her place, "at least as far as the paper's agenda was concerned." Ken had replied in generalities until the entrée mercifully arrived, at which point Martha dropped the subject. Thereafter Ken had an enjoyable meal, and later, a delightful snooze, delicious sex, and finally, much needed, deeper REM sleep.

It was a clear, cold Ottawa winter's morning at minus ten degrees Celsius, which Ken translated into something close to fourteen degrees Fahrenheit for his mind and body to comprehend. Meanwhile, the weatherwoman on the local television station called the day "rather warm"; Ken was glad that Martha had been out of the room at the time—he knew that she detested the cold and the weather report might have set her off into a poor mood, which was not where he had left her when he got out of bed a half-hour earlier.

Their researcher's efforts had paid off quite well. Ken and Martha had decided the previous evening that it was best for them to split up and attend to different tasks for the series on healthcare. Martha would attempt to determine which lobbying firms were representing which U.S. healthcare interests to which politicians and government bureaucrats in Canada's Medicare and pharmaceutical overseeing departments. Meanwhile, Ken would go see Dr. Brown on his own.

By 9:00 a.m., the taxi he had called was making its way

through Ottawa's insane morning rush-hour drive to the meeting with Dr. Judith Brown. Ken's mind was very much in play, jumping about from topic to topic, preparing for the interview. He wasn't quite sure what he expected to learn from Dr. Brown, except that, from what Dr. McTavish had said about his colleague, she had been a fierce defender of the country's Medicare health care system while she was Minister of Health. This meant that she most likely could provide Ken with insights into the way the Canadian healthcare system had been managed during her time in government, and possibly even before, and perhaps after, she had left politics.

Interesting material about Dr. Brown had come through on their fax machine in the morning from the undoubtedly sleep-deprived researcher Martha had called the night before. Ken read over several articles describing Dr. Brown's exceptional reputation as a physician, woman's rights advocate, and universal Medicare protector. She was clearly recognized as that rare breed of independent-minded politician who invariably put moral and ethical principles above party politics, to the point that she apparently made many enemies during her relatively brief tenure in parliament.

While her forthright manner had made the late middle-aged maven a media darling, it also had brought forth a great deal of opposition from other cabinet members who were much more inclined to operate in quite the opposite fashion. According to one newspaper article written about three years back, Dr. Brown had finally had enough of the back-stabbing and political pressures, and since, at the time, she was also caring for a terminally ill spouse, she decided to relieve herself of additional burdens and to leave politics altogether.

She therefore resigned both her cabinet position and her seat in the House of Commons, and after two years devoted to making her husband's final days as peaceful and loving as she could, she left her home for several months and spent most of that time abroad at the empty home of long-time friends. The article, written in a crisp yet compassionate style that Ken admired, also stated that Dr. Brown evidently used the peace and solitude she had found, to recharge her batteries and rethink her priorities.

When she came back home to Canada she returned to the work she truly loved most, that of tending to patients who needed and wanted her medical expertise, and whom she could actually help and–sometimes, at least–even cure.

While the taxi wove its way towards Dr. Brown's clinic, Ken occasionally glanced up from reading the most recently written article. Ken could vouch for the piece's accuracy insofar as the description of Dr. Brown's workplace's catchment area was concerned.

The Ottawa East Urban Hospital was located in a rather shabby part of town surrounded by small houses in serious need of repair, many with rusted pickup trucks and good-for-parts-only cars parked in their driveways and on their lawns. There were also some ancient, low-rise apartment buildings and small stores with barred windows located on several streets. On her way to work at the clinic Dr. Brown would undoubtedly see children from many cultures playing in the tiny, barely equipped playgrounds. One article mentioned that after only a year back at work she had personally called upon enough individual donors to acquire several hundred thousand dollars that were immediately used to help create a number of large, modernly equipped playgrounds in the hospital's more downtrodden service areas.

As the taxi drove through the open gates of the hospital, Ken noted that most of the buildings looked relatively new or, at least, recently renovated. There were dramatically reshaped buildings with renovated modern facades, linked together via aboveground, futuristic, glassed-in pedestrian walkways. Doctors, staff, gurneys, and people pushing stand-alone drip-poles on wheels could be seen making their way either slowly or hurriedly from one building to another through these oversized transparent arteries.

As per the instructions Ken repeated to the Sikh driver, the cab drew up in front of the hospital's maternity ward's main entrance, under a marquee that announced it was *The Dr. Judith Brown Pre-Natal And Newborn Healthcare Unit*. Ken paid the driver, got out, and walked into the building.

At the reception desk he gave a pleasant-looking black woman his name. A moment after she made a brief phone call, she directed Ken, in charming, French-accented (possibly Haitian) English, to follow the green line on the floor to the first green elevator, and to get off on the second floor. There he was to follow a yellow line all the way to the third set of doors on his right, and then walk along the red-striped corridor until he came to the door marked 2-R194. She mercifully highlighted the directions on a color-coded map she then gave to him.

Ken wondered what *blind* people did to find their way, with no color code to keep them on the right path until he noticed the raised Braille lettering placed at strategic points along the walls of the corridors.

Ken found the doctor's office, and as he was introducing himself to the secretary, a spry, cheerful woman wearing a lab coat, and about the same age as Dr. McTavish, came out of an adjoining room and warmly took Ken's hand. "So very good to meet you, Mr. Simpson. I am Dr. Judith Brown," said the lovely Scottish voice.

Dr. Brown's greeting seemed very genuine and generous; evidently, McTavish had said some nice enough things about Ken after *their* interview.

"Dr. Brown, thank you so much for seeing me," Ken replied.

"Of course. Well, we had a couple of emergency C-sections overnight, and I am anxious to learn how the mothers and babies are doing. Would you mind accompanying me on my rounds?"

"With pleasure," Ken said, not exactly meaning it. He had never really understood what women went through in childbirth, and his usual bounding curiosity did not generally extend to things physiologically medical. Nevertheless, Ken walked alongside gynecologist/obstetrician Dr. Judith Brown as she made her way along the corridor to the maternity ward's ICU. While Ken waited on the other side of the glass, the doctor entered the unit and spoke to some of the nursing and medical staff on duty. Ken observed the obviously warm respect that Dr. Brown was given. A young woman doctor, two nurses and Dr. Brown huddled around one incubator, and discussed in evidently hushed tones, what the current issues were that needed addressing with the hours-old and problematic infant who was now in their charge.

Having apparently agreed on the best measures for the newborn's care, Dr. Brown looked in on a few other babies, and, then, gazing up at Ken with obvious pride and joy, she pointed to three incubators that seemed to be somewhat closer to each other than the others. She then raised her left hand, with the three middle fingers raised, as she pointed at the triplets with her right hand. At that moment of apparent pride and wonder she seemed to have taken on the appearance of a white-garbed, senior guardian angel, who had probably just parked her wings under her ample lab coat.

When she came out of the windowed nursery she said, "I, along with two other specialists on my staff, delivered those triplets yesterday evening. It was an awesome experience. Imagine, over forty-five years as a pediatrician and I have only delivered triplets twice before.   It was a great evening, last evening. Fabulous!" The consummate professional was grinning from ear to ear with pride. Ken felt surprisingly moved, as well.

Ken always enjoyed making the acquaintance of those souls who were fortunate enough to truly love the work they did. And Dr. Judith Brown clearly belonged to that group.

They made their way back to her office, past a ward of women in various stages of their pregnancies who sat chatting together, a few with their husbands in tow. Dr. Brown explained that many of the women in this ward were having trouble in carrying their fetuses to full term and so considerable efforts were being directed to utilizing all possible means, including group therapy, meditation and other stress reduction techniques, to help the parents-in-waiting make it through this period with the least distress.

When they had first entered the ward, Ken noticed a plaque on the wall that announced that this part of the clinic had been named the Dr. Judith Brown Neo-natal ICU. Ken noted that the date on the plaque preceded the doctor's time period as an elected member of parliament. Ken reflected that she had received this honor the old-fashioned way; she earned it.

When they arrived back at her office Ken was motioned to a chair in front of which, on the coffee table, rested a pot of steaming tea with a few cookies beside it on a tray.

"I appreciate your patience in joining me on my early rounds, Mr. Simpson."

"Not at all, Dr. Brown. I enjoyed it."

She nodded, her facial expression suggesting that she had picked up on Ken's initial discomfort. She said, "So, now. What can I do for you? I understand that you are doing a series for *The New York Era* on your medical care system, and perhaps our own. Are you here for background, then?"

"Actually, Dr. Brown, I am very interested in your opinion about what you anticipate happening in the long-term to the universal Medicare system you have here in Canada."

Dr. Brown nodded, chuckled slightly to herself, and was quiet for what seemed like a long while, although probably less than a minute in clock time. Then she said, "Well, in the past few minutes, as you walked with me through our neo-natal unit, and of course you would have no way of knowing this, the fact is that while many of the mothers present are on welfare, others are working professionals, and still others are what might be referred to as 'Rockcliffe matrons', or to give you a New York City reference, perhaps, 'Westchester socialites'. Our hospital deals with a very high proportion of distressed and problematic pregnancies of women who represent all socioeconomic sectors in the Ottawa area. Currently, of the patients on the unit you and I were just through, over forty percent are either on welfare, mother's assistance, or unemployment insurance. Another thirty percent are middle class, and the last thirty percent come from what you might call the ritzy areas of Ottawa, where many of the foreign embassies are and where most of this city's 'movers and shakers' reside."

Her voice, now rising in strength and brimming with pride, continued. "Yet, regardless of where they live, or their financial circumstances, they do not pay anything out of their own pockets for healthcare, aside from paying taxes on their income, if any. The idea that poor or economically disadvantaged persons should not get the very same high quality care as our more affluent citizens is, thankfully, a regressive, class-denoting idea to the majority of citizens in this country, regardless of what some in our media try to suggest. For instance, in our hospital this past year, over at the cardiac center, over 400 heart bypass operations were done. The direct cost to the men and women who had those operations was about $60 each for their four or five day stay, but only if they chose to have a telephone and privacy TV at their bedside. I believe that in your country many tens of thousands of individuals each year *don't* have possibly life-saving bypasses because they don't have private medical insurance."

"I am certain that you are right, Doctor Brown. But, not to put too fine a point on it, don't some of the wealthier patients resent the fact that poor people get the same quality of medical care that they do?"

Dr. Brown regarded him with curiosity, as if to determine if he was serious or being deliberately provocative. Then she said, with all the patience of a model 'special needs' teacher, "There are always some individuals who happen to be higher on the totem pole of economic life who do resent that less advantaged folks are able to get the same quality of medical care as they. But for heaven's sake, why should they? At least as far as most Canadians I have ever met are concerned, I think we have a great deal of trouble understanding the argument that rich people, or only people who can afford to pay out of their pocket for medical coverage, should have access to better–or more– healthcare than those who cannot. To us it is rather like education; you live in this country and therefore you are entitled to a publicly funded high school education. Likewise…"

"Excuse me, Doctor", interrupted Ken, " but the headlines in some of your major newspapers these past several years have been suggesting that there *already* is, here in Canada, what you call two-tier medicine, or at the least, that the more money people have, the more health services they use."

Dr. Brown said, "I am glad you brought those matters up, Mr. Simpson. I, for one, have always found those headlines very curious indeed, and in fact, they are grossly misleading. If you read the articles thoroughly, what they have usually said was that wealthier people tend to be more assertive in asking questions of their physicians, in seeking out medical advice, and in determining who might be the more experienced and able physicians in their area. And it is undoubtedly true that poorer people may tend to make less trouble, perhaps because they feel intimidated by persons in power or who have a much higher education, and especially those who have a 'Dr.' in front of their names. Or maybe they still can't believe their good fortune that they have the same right to seek and obtain the most suitable medical care, at no extra, out-of-pocket cost, or may not want to appear 'pushy' by asking to see Doctor A 'too often', or to see Dr. B instead of Dr. C." Ken nodded as he wrote. He had read that greater assertiveness often goes hand in hand with the more formal education and/or affluence the individual had.

"As to your other point, that there already exists a certain degree of two-tier medicine in this country, alas, you are quite correct. You see, while two-tier medicine is technically not allowed in Canada, certain key federal and provincial politicians have either simply turned a blind eye to the practice, or have created situations and circumstances, either by de-listing certain medical tests and procedures, or by allowing other practices such as psychotherapy by family doctors to continue on the books as paid-for procedures, so as to draw personnel and funds away from more appropriate practices. As to why these shenanigans are going on, perhaps we can discuss this subject more later on during our time together."

Ken got the message that Dr. Brown was not comfortable continuing further down that path just now, but since she clearly indicated they would come back to it again later, he put his additional questions about that area aside, for now.

They continued to sip their hot beverages in silence for several beats. And then Ken asked the main question he had come to Ottawa to have answered.

"Dr. Brown, what do *you* think has been happening to the Canadian Medicare system over the past number of years, and why do you think your various media seem to differ so widely in the opinions put forward, pro and con, about your system."

"Would you care to elaborate, Mr. Simpson?"

Ken said, respectfully, "Well, I had a search done of Canadian newspaper and magazine articles going back over the last few years, and there appear to be some extremely wide discrepancies, as far as I can tell, among the various major newspapers, say, for example, in regard to the causes of, and solutions for, the shortages of available hospital beds, nurses and doctors, and availability of adequate emergency and specialized services. In fact, your major newspapers often seem to disagree about the state of the entire Canadian Medicare system and how satisfied or dissatisfied Canadians are with it."

Dr. Brown could tell that Ken was not finished with his statements/questions, so she simply nodded and said, "Go on."

Ken said, "In our country, Dr. Brown, our news outlets gave some pretty major coverage a few years back to the apparent fact that some of your provincial governments were sending cancer patients south of the border for treatment in America. The stories said that was because you didn't have enough facilities available in this country, and because waiting lists had become so long, that patients' lives were being put in grave danger as they waited to see specialists."

Dr. Brown's gaze went to the pictures that were threatening to overflow the top of the credenza behind her desk. The photographs showed a multitude of people whom Ken took to be her extended family, including perhaps at least seven or eight great grandchildren.

In a respectful tone Ken pressed the question, "Why do we hear about some of your citizens not being able to get the tests and treatments they need for illnesses like…"

Interrupting him, she said, "Mr. Simpson, what do you say to a drive out in our beautiful Gatineau hills, just about fifteen minutes from here? It's a lovely day for a brisk walk." Dr. Brown's demeanor had instantly morphed from conversational to concerned, and then, if Ken's guess was correct, *scared*. Ken had the distinct message that Dr. Brown preferred to be beyond the walls of her clinic if they were going to continue this line of discussion. He wondered if she had any concerns that others might be listening in on their conversation.

He replied, "Of course." Ken understood and appreciated only too well how fear can permeate the offices of even the most prominent persons, but he hoped that the elderly doctor was wrong in what he surmised were her concerns.

CHAPTER 34

Ken got into the passenger seat of Dr. Brown's eight year old, dark blue, Buick Park Avenue. She drove across the Ottawa River and into what the approaching road sign referred to as the Gatineau Hills, which appeared to be just that, hills that seemed to range from 100 to 300 feet in height. As the large, cushy car followed the well-paved, curved road through the pristine park setting, Ken started to restate the question she had cut him off from asking in her office. Without looking away from the road she merely put the second digit of her right hand up to her lips to signify that she wanted Ken to delay going any further into that topic.

Eventually, after several more minutes of small talk and slow driving, Dr. Brown said, "Where we are going is one of my most favorite places to come and think." She turned right off the road at a sign that read "Prime Minister Mackenzie King estate." Within thirty seconds they came to a mostly vacant parking lot set back from the road, and Dr. Brown pulled into a spot near a marked pathway. They exited the car and began to walk along the path.

In a respectful tone Ken asked the question. "If I might ask, Dr. Brown, could you tell me why we in the U.S. hear about some of your citizens not being able to get tests and treatments they need for illnesses like cancer and heart disease in a timely manner? I am sure you have some insights that I would greatly appreciate hearing."

Dr. Brown replied, her voice starting to quiver with emotion, "When I was the Federal Minister of Health I was made intimately aware of certain elements at play that were, and I am certain still are, absolutely committed to destroying the viability of our Medicare facilities, including our ability to service patients expeditiously. Mr. Simpson, what I might choose to tell you from this point on may only be used as background at this time.

Without my explicit permission, you may not publish or otherwise communicate what I will tell you to anyone else, at your newspaper, or in your bed. Will you give me your assurance that you will comply with my request?"

Startled by her reference to his sleeping arrangements, Ken stopped writing, put down his pen, and looked up. "Yes, of course, Dr. Brown. But how did you...?"

Dr. Brown's raised eyebrow and teasing smile aborted his question. She said, "I still have my contacts, Mr. Simpson."

"I see."

"In any case, I am certainly prepared to tell you more, because my good friend, Dr. McTavish, told me that he believes you are a reporter of considerable integrity, and more importantly perhaps, because he also believes that you may actually be in an excellent position to be of help to those of us who believe in preserving and promoting accessible universal Medicare in our country."

Ken had the thought that she and Dr. McTavish would be a most formidable couple. He said, "Of course, I readily agree to your terms, Dr. Brown. Believe me, I very much want to understand your healthcare system's issues, including the forces that you suggest are operating to destroy it. I promise to not make any reference to what you may share with me, until and unless I receive your permission to do otherwise."

Brown smiled broadly, and her severe look melted away. She simply said, "Thank you."

Ken asked, "But would you mind telling me why it is that you believe that I may be able to be of some assistance to you in protecting your system?"

"Because your paper has considerable clout in *both* our countries, and so you are in a position to do both *your* and *our* citizens a service. We are well aware that your government recently passed into law medical services for Americans who are affected by acts of terrorism, largely because of the outpouring of support generated by your own articles in *The New York Era*.

"Meanwhile time is running short for effective action to be taken in this country. Mr. Simpson, let me share with you the fact that one of our most promising politicians, and one of my very closest associates, Dr. Trish Markridge, is shortly going to be introducing a private member's bill in the House of Commons that would, if passed as is, embed the Canadian universal Medicare system into our Charter of Rights and Freedoms. In addition, she has colleagues in all our provinces and territories who are prepared to file their own companion bills in their provincial legislatures, proposing making their respective provinces publicly accountable to their citizens via full disclosures, on at least a semi-annual basis, as to how they are distributing and utilizing their medical funds, personnel, equipment, and other resources."

Ken said, "You seem very delighted that Ms. Markridge is intending to take this action."

"I am, indeed. I am also very frightened for Trish. She has been my protégé since I taught her in med school, and it was I who helped induce her into political life. But I greatly fear that as soon as all the lobbyists, the privatization advocates, and the American companies who have been foaming at the mouth–*for years*–in anticipation of taking over our healthcare system, realize that they might not be able to succeed in their goal, that they may be inclined to take the most desperate of measures to prevent the proposed embedding from happening."

Even though it was sunny and the temperature was reasonably pleasant as they walked along the cleared pathway in the woods, Ken's body shivered as he recognized the extent to which TAMPRR was capable of going to protect their corporate clients' interests. *Would TAMPRR really kill again to prevent their goals from being blocked?*

Dr. Brown said, "So, now you understand why you must not prematurely reveal what I have told you. I am very much afraid for Trish's physical well-being until and after she introduces the proposed bill. She is about to begin a media blitz across the country to drum up support for her private member's bill and will announce that she intends to spearhead a grassroots movement to call for a so-called 'free vote' on the matter. I tell you all this so that you will know that the stakes are exceedingly high at this moment, and I fear all kinds of mischief once Trish makes her announcements."

Ken said, "I promise that I will keep your confidences and

will only refer to these matters or quote you if you give me permission to do so."

"Fine, then," said Dr. Brown. After a moment to seemingly sort out her thoughts, she continued, "When I was the Minister of Health I had access to information, some of it from our own police forces, which made it clear that at least one provincial premier was involved in direct meetings with the principals of certain American healthcare providers, insurance, and pharmaceutical companies, at which times agreements were reached, and 'down payments' in the form of trust fund campaign contributions, media support, and stock options were given over, on the verbal agreement that he would do all in his power to undercut the healthcare services in his province. *And he delivered–in spades!*

"The man is a known gross abuser of alcohol, and God knows what else some people had on him that we could not uncover. Whatever it was, I have it on very good authority that Linden decided during the course of those meetings, to sign on, big-time, as we used to say. He closed entire hospitals and closed down some outstanding specialized departments in some of the remaining hospitals, including–and this got my goat, I can tell you–a highly successful pediatric cardiac unit that was the only one for hundreds of miles around. All this he did in the name of 'fiscal responsibility'.

"Meanwhile, the premier and his Minister of Health outsourced into the private sector, health and safety inspection responsibilities for drinking water, livestock feed, pest control, and other regulatory and/or supervisory governmental responsibilities, which ultimately led to a series of entirely preventable disasters, and culminated in dozens of deaths among the citizens in their province. All of these problems, of course, put unprecedented pressures on the remaining healthcare system, at which point he and the other provincial premiers who were in cahoots with him and carried out similar tactics on their healthcare systems, turned around and said, in effect, "You see, the healthcare job is simply too big for our governments to handle alone. We must bring in the private sector to help resolve these matters." So they started to move increasingly towards what some refer to as the 'P3', private-public-partnership, model, which siphoned off some of the better talent from the lower-paying, publicly run, healthcare facilities.

"At the same time, monies transferred from my federal ministry that were specifically earmarked to extend the publicly run hospitals' hours of operation for certain diagnostic testing units, and also to permit the purchase of new imaging and radiation equipment, were instead used, literally, to build garbage dumps and four-lane highways in, among other places, the premier's own riding of Golfenbride. All this was carried out under the banner of, "Nobody is going to tell us provincial politicians what we are going to do with monies rightly ours according to federal-provincial money transfer agreements."

Ken asked, "Didn't the citizens of their provinces and/or their media raise hell?"

"Oh, a few 'private citizen' organizations, and a couple of small-town papers did, but too much of our media has become, in recent years, how shall I put it, 'very old-fashioned'. They are going through difficult financial times of their own, and need all the advertising money they could get. So provincial governments obliged by occasionally placing large ads in their papers extolling the virtues of one or other of their own party's policies, but only very selectively. As long as the specific media outlets played ball, they got those advertisements and the ones that the government placed for new positions in its civil service."

"Surely, though, Dr. Brown, your national healthcare system won't fall because of the actions of a few provincial premiers and their governments!" exclaimed Ken.

"Our national police force has identified a number of attempted 'points of entry', as they call these incursions, including several successes. The financial stakes are huge here, Mr. Simpson."

Dr. Brown sighed and paused. Ken was reluctant to press her further, yet anxious to find out whatever he could. "Do you have any first hand experience of such actions as you have suggested went on, doctor?"

Dr. Brown laughed, and nodded her head vigorously. "Of course, I do. Because *they* tried to get to *me*! There were offers of directorships of companies supposedly waiting for me after I left politics, plus some offshore stock portfolios, and very generous 'trust fund' contributions, just for starters. They were tenacious and outrageous. They even sought out and attempted to hire two of my grandchildren for jobs they were barely, or not at all, qualified to do, and then protested innocence when I confronted them about these reprehensible actions.

"After that, there were some hardly veiled threats that certain indiscretions I may have committed when I was much, much younger–while a med student, for Pete's sake–might somehow become known and publicized during the upcoming political campaign. And then, because I learned that their efforts had met with greater success amongst certain colleagues within my own and other political parties and I threatened to go public with this information, there were actions taken in cabinet aimed at interfering with my carrying out my ministerial duties.

"Mr. Simpson, please note that our party had only been in power for a little over two years when I left politics to look after my dear late husband during the last stages of his illness. I was in my position as Minister of Health for only that long. And yet, in that time, it was made clear to me by various senior people even within my own party, that if I did not cease and desist from issuing public statements pushing for additional funding for expanded and updated medical services, then my efforts could have what one of my colleagues termed 'most unfortunate repercussions'. I was later led to believe that what he meant by that term was that at nomination meetings for my riding for the next election, the Prime Minister would inject his own, competing nominee."

Judith Brown was becoming increasingly agitated during the retelling of what she had encountered during her tenure as a member of parliament. As they walked slowly along through the stand of blue spruces she paused, lifted her head upwards and took a succession of large in-breaths, inhaling their fresh scent. Ken realized that she was probably attempting to regain her composure before she went on. Finally, she said, "I was also told by the Minister of Finance that there wouldn't be enough money available to my ministry to expand pediatric research.

"And that was not all. My colleague, the Minister of

Immigration, intimated that it might become increasingly difficult to bring top medical researchers into the country. Meanwhile, it was, and remains, far easier for professional baseball and football players to be let in to play in Canada, than for medical researchers who might want to work here."

Dr. Brown paused, looking intensely at Ken as if to see whether he was 'getting' what she was saying or if she was wasting her time. Ken was obviously extremely attentive.

Relieved, she said, "Sometimes, Mr. Simpson, it is easier to fight from the *other side* of the barricades. On the inside there are political niceties such as not disagreeing openly with other politicians who belong to your own party, and especially not the big guns.

"I believed that the media would want to hear what I might want to say once I was out of parliament. But even *I* didn't realize how threatened or otherwise oriented much of the media in this country are. Indeed, some of our media are indirectly, if not directly, controlled by some of these same forces that have some of our politicians by their, eh… sensitive body parts.

"A good friend of mine from the old country is Commissioner of the RCMP. He told me in person, and even told the press, that there was a realistic danger of certain criminal forces unduly influencing members of parliament and senior bureaucrats. Only one of the major papers published what he said, and it only printed part of the story." Dr. Brown reached inside her coat, retrieved a piece of paper, and handed Ken a copy of a newspaper article. He quickly read it.

The article was from the January 25th, 2007 edition of *The National Times*. It read, "*Yesterday, RCMP Commissioner Denny MacDonald told the Standing Committee on Internal Security and Governmental Affairs that he believed certain major Canadian institutions, including even the Parliament of Canada, are at risk of being corrupted by certain unsavory forces, including organized crime. He added that some groups inside and outside of Canada have gathered so much money, power, and influence in this country that they now threaten our most precious democratic institutions.*

"Now, for the first time in our history," he said, "there exists in Canada criminal and other organizations that have infiltrated some provincial, as well as our federal, governments and bureaucratic circles. Furthermore, these forces are so sophisticated, dedicated, and cunning that they are unquestionably capable of destabilizing components of our democratic society's key structures. Some of these criminal organizations are even threatening to destabilize our Parliamentary system, and may have already begun."

"Jesus!" exclaimed Ken. "And what fallout has there been as a result of this story? He has made some very frightening charges. If the head of our FBI ever said that our Senate and House of Representatives were being undermined by organized crime groups, our guys would be all over this story."

Dr. Brown seemed less convinced. "So you say, and so one would sincerely hope, Mr. Simpson. However, these forces may also be attacking some of our other democratic institutions, such as the fifth estate, including newspapers and other media in our two countries. As far as I know, almost no other news organization has done or said anything further on the matters that the RCMP commissioner raised in that article, not even after several of our present and former federal politicians and bureaucrats were implicated in some very shady and expensive practices with certain lobbying organizations in the private sector. And I fear that there were some groups that the commissioner either didn't know about, or didn't choose to refer to outright, when he said 'crime groups'. I am of the opinion that he was not only referring to the Mafia and the other underworld types we civilians usually think of."

The former Minister of Health for Canada spoke quite softly even though, as far as Ken could tell, they were alone in the middle of a wooded park. She said, "Mr. Simpson, in our country, members of parliament are allowed to have and retain so-called 'trust funds'. These funds consist of contributions they have received that can be used for a variety of purposes, more than just election campaigns. They can be, and I have it on good authority that they have been, used to purchase cars, homes, cottages, clothes, in short, any damned thing they want. Or, they can simply keep the monies, period. Many members of our parliament have become almost instant millionaires by accepting such legal 'donations'."

Ken let out a low, long whistle. He said, "Sweet! Well, I can easily guess who some of the donors and some of the recipients have been over the past decade and a half, at least. And I suspect that we are talking about total amounts of millions of dollars *each* for certain key politicians."

Dr. Brown said, "That is what my own sources in government have told me in recent months. When *I* was Minister of Health, I was approached on numerous occasions by increasingly heavy-handed 'lobbyists', as they referred to themselves, to see if I would be amenable to 'being more open', I believe that was the phrase they used, to cutting back further on the federal government's payments to the provinces for purposes of healthcare, or at least to adopting a more laissez faire approach to what they labelled 'technical infractions' by privately operated medical services. They suggested that such an agreeable approach could be justified in the name of fiscal responsibility. And, after all, they pointed out, my predecessors were so inclined. When I refused to even consider such a thing but made inquiries regarding on exactly whose behalf they were asking, they gave me the names of 'shell' organizations and then disappeared into the Ottawa woodwork. Or at least, that is what I initially surmised.

"In fact, unfortunately, our current Prime Minister is employing a number of current and previous partners of the same lobbyist firm, supposedly to help guide his legislation through the various committees. What is questionable at best is who is guiding whom, if you get my drift."

Ken said, "Can you do anything about that collaboration?"

Dr. Brown replied, "I would dearly love to, but I am presently most definitely unwelcome in my old party's halls of influence. So my other avenue is to be of as much help as I can to Trish Markridge."

Ken asked, "What is your old party's official stance on the Canadian health care system?"

Dr. Brown laughed heartily. "Would it surprise you to learn that before each federal or provincial election, virtually *all* the leaders of *all* our political parties continually say that preserving and *improving* Medicare is their top priority? A few of them state from time to time that they are only interested in 'tinkering' with the healthcare system by means of some minor 're-tooling' in order to effect, as they say, 'cost-effective modifications'. Certainly my own party has some members who genuinely want to preserve and enhance what we consider to be one of the most successful universal Medicare programs anywhere in the world. However, there are others, many of whom have been carefully cultivating their positions of power for years, who I am certain are *ready*, *willing* and indeed are on the verge of being *able* to finally destroy our entire healthcare structure and then move quickly to replace it with an American-style system. Our national police force was keeping tabs on some of them and their only too regular comings and goings in and out of the U.S. embassy, among other places.

"In fact," Dr. Brown continued, "in anticipation of Trish Markridge's putting forward her private member's bill, some other members of parliament are planning to introduce bills of their own that will purport to do something similar to her's, but that will actually make ours ripe for the pickings by your country's 'health biz'. The devil, in this case, will be in the details. My understanding is that 'devil' will appear as a subsection of their bill that will be touted as improving Medicare. The subsection in question will make it not only permissible, but will actually make it mandatory that, unless certain facilities are able to provide X amount of service in Y amount of time, then privately built and run hospitals must be allowed to come into the country and provide these same services, as well as any others that will be deemed by their private investors to be necessary in order to make the new facilities 'fiscally viable'.

"Of course, by the time the for-profit 'managerial' and other costs are added on, those privately run institutions, in short order, will drain the government coffers so much that it will become necessary to curtail vital medical services in the publicly funded system to keep the overall costs of the Medicare budget from going through the roof. Before long, the for-profits will take over altogether. So, it is going to be imperative that Trish Markridge's bill cut them off at the pass by taking for-profit medical diagnoses and treatments off the table in this country–permanently."

Ken asked, "But won't your publicly-run healthcare system advocates easily spot the 'Trojan horse' subsection in their amendment to Dr. Markridge's bill and call them on it?"

"Unfortunately It will be a matter of too few doing too little much too late. So many members of this latest parliament have been either bought or scared off that they will not take any concrete actions to prevent the ultimate collapse of our system. Many others will not even bother to read the bill in its entirety–few seldom do. And before any meaningful opposition can be mounted, it will be a fait accompli. And meanwhile, most of our media watchdogs are either asleep or have fallen into a fiscally induced coma."

Dr Brown stopped talking, bit down on her lower lip in evident frustration, and looked off in the distance. As they were about to emerge from the trail loop they had been on and be back at the parking lot from which they started out, Dr. Brown suggested that they return to the hospital.

In less than ten minutes time they were back in the city, driving through Ottawa's lunch hour traffic on their way back to her working world. As she drove along the road that gracefully paralleled the Rideau Canal she pointed out the ice skaters and proudly informed Ken that in winter the canal formed the longest urban stating rink in the world. To Ken the entire scene of bright sun, white snow and ice on the canal, and the multi-layered and colorfully dressed skaters, looked very pretty indeed, but damned cold.

As they continued driving along, Ken gave his host and himself some quiet space and casually gazed at the lovely large houses and seemingly well-kept apartment buildings that graced the side of the winding road that paralleled the canal.

Ken asked, "Would you tell me more about Dr. Markridge?" Judith Brown's countenance brightened immediately at the mention of Trish Markridge's name. She beamed as she said, "More about Trish? Well, I should probably tell you that I am most certainly biased since she happens to be my goddaughter and, while this country may not know it yet, she is just possibly its god*send*! And she is probably the only member of the current Parliament with the guts to risk a potentially fabulous political future to save our Medicare system."

Ken asked, "Do you think I could get to interview her when she is back in town?"

Dr. Brown nodded and said, firmly, "She will be back tomorrow night and I will be delighted to ask that she give you an interview. I think that you will just love her; she is one of the few people in this town with an abundance of *both* conviction *and* courage. And she just happens to be a former beauty queen, to boot."

Ken enthusiastically nodded his appreciation and hoped that it covered his momentary ruminating about another, quite possibly less admirable, beauty of his acquaintance. He effortfully put Sylkeen out of his mind yet again.

Dr. Brown said, "I have taken the liberty of arranging for you to meet a couple of doctors back at the Center. I think you will find them very informative. They are a married American couple who worked for some years in your system before coming to Canada. They can give you some first-hand comparative information about our two systems. Do you think that would be useful to you?"

Ken expressed his appreciation of the opportunity to speak with physicians who had first-hand experience in working within both the American and Canadian healthcare systems.

Meanwhile, Ken again noticed in his side-view mirror the same black Ford Explorer with the tinted windshield that he thought he had spotted at least twice before on the way up to the former Prime Minister's country estate. That prompted another question.

He asked Dr. Brown, "Why do you think some parties in the U.S. might be dedicated to destroying the Canadian Medicare system? Is it for the additional ten percent profit that they are after by taking on another population one-tenth that in America?"

Dr. Brown cast a sideways glance at Ken, one that suggested he might be more naïve than she had thought. Then she smiled as if she suddenly realized he was probably just doing his reporter's type of probing.

She said, "Mr. Simpson, I am sure you will recall, before our government capitulated to influences from south of the border, when so many seniors in America were resorting to buying their prescription drugs from Canadian sources in order to save twenty, thirty, or even up to fifty percent or more, on each prescription renewal. Some of your pharmaceutical companies also lobbied your own government to come up with new, restrictive, legislation and tariffs in order to restrict their American customers to buying from U.S. suppliers. And that was for *drugs*, most of which had actually been manufactured by these same companies in the first place, either Stateside or in other countries under acceptable licensing agreements. The drugs we in Canada used usually even came from the same batches that were also delivered to the U.S.. Mostly, the Canadian online pharmacies were simply selling U.S.-made drugs to Americans, for a fraction of what they would have paid for them at home. Those drug manufacturing companies won that battle, but not before an awful lot of Americans began to get the picture that they were being unreasonably gouged. Now, various private citizens' organizations are banding together to press for limits to be placed upon the profiteering of those same drug companies. I suggest that the concerns of American healthcare companies are rather similar to those of their drug company compatriots."

Ken said, "Why do you think it is that Canada has developed such different ways of approaching the issues of healthcare and prescription drug sales?"

Dr. Brown said, "That is an excellent question. Goodness knows, we are so similar to you in so many ways, and yet we have somehow developed and maintained different traditions and sensibilities. It's actually rather miraculous, I would say, especially since we are so closely connected to you–geographically and economically. Our saving grace has probably been that we have established a truly different–that is to say, our own–national identity. In the past sixty years or so, in particular, we have been aided along the way by adoption of our own flag, and the existence of our own news magazines, our Canadian writers and publishers, our government-funded Canadian Broadcasting Corporation, and our still somewhat Canadian-owned and privately run media.

"Yes, I would have to say that it is undoubtedly through our print and electronic media that we have come to know who and what we are, and also how we are the same in some ways, and different in other ways, from Americans and other nationalities. Take our policies towards controlling the costs of prescription drug costs, towards the decriminalization of possession of small amounts of marijuana and providing for its use for medical purposes, and towards legalizing civil unions between homosexual couples–all of these progressive and humane measures have made us see ourselves as distinctly different from the citizens of many, perhaps most, other countries. And, of course, the very fact of our citizens having made different choices than those in your country, has forced people in your country, and therefore in your own government, to also change, or at least to *begin* to consider changing in those areas.

"I believe that certain American healthcare interests have become truly terrified of a successful Canadian Medicare system, because, if it does succeed, then just as with the prescription drug situation, more and more of your own citizens will demand that your government develop its own comparable system. But then the very continued existence of your healthcare companies will be threatened. And that is why I think there has been, and continues to be, a major effort to kill off our system.

"As Minister of Health, the huge offers that I received to help accomplish such a goal were obscene. Unfortunately, I have good reason to believe that since several of my federal and provincial colleagues had been much more receptive to their approaches, they just assumed that I could also be bought. And an indication of just how powerful they have become is the fact that it was *myself*, not them, who ended up losing influence and position in the halls of power.

"So now you can understand why I have been so willing to meet with you, and to set up a meeting for you with Trish

Markridge, and do just about anything else that might bring all that we have been talking about out into the open in both our countries.

Ken asked, "Dr. Brown, did you go to the press or the police about these matters?"

"I certainly went to our RCMP about it, but understand, Mr. Simpson, the people who are behind these coercions and manipulations are expert at keeping themselves in the shadows. Nevertheless, our police forces are continuing to look into all of this. At least, so I have been reassured on several occasions."

Ken nodded and changed the subject, asking Dr. Brown about security generally around Ottawa since 9/11, and then he inquired about security for former cabinet ministers such as herself. To his surprise, Dr. Brown laughed heartily.

"What did I say that was so funny, Dr. Brown?"

"Well, Mr. Simpson, there are *no* security details for almost any former politicians, and certainly not for former Ministers of Health. Former Ministers of Defence, maybe, and ex-Prime Ministers, definitely, but that's about it."

"Um-hum," said Ken lightly, glancing once again at his side view mirror.

The black Ford Explorer with darkened windows was definitely following their car, keeping a discreet distance but staying in step as they changed streets and directions. Ken thought, *The only question is, which of us is being tailed? Maybe Canada is not as different as their citizens would like to think.*

Ken said, "I think that I should point out, Dr. Brown, if I may do so without your making sudden changes to your very competent way of driving, that I believe we have been followed by the black SUV behind us, probably ever since we left the grounds of the hospital."

Dr. Brown physically shuddered as she glanced into her rear view mirror. "Damn." was her one-word response.

In addition to indignation, Ken thought he also sensed a deep fear gripping the elderly person riding beside him. He silently hoped that it was him in whom their shadow was most interested.

CHAPTER 35

After leaving the restaurant, Colonel Jake Marks walked around Fisherman's Wharf for about fifteen minutes before returning to his rental car. He drove back up Van Ness to the same hotel he had been favoring for so many years. He retrieved his own carry-on bag out of the trunk, handed the car key to the parking valet, and walked into the lobby. There were few seventy-nine year old men who still had his levels of vigor and presence.

As was his habit whenever he stayed at any hotel, he requested a last-minute room change from the one they had reserved for him. He also always chose a different floor from the one he had been assigned, and never requested the same floor two times in a row. He was fully willing to even change hotels if they ever refused his request, but of course, since he was on their 'very preferred' guest list and was well known by the management for providing the on-duty manager and front desk with 'a little extra' at the end of each stay, they had always complied with what they probably considered his eccentric requests.

He completed the room change negotiation and took the plastic key apologetically offered him by an initially resistant, but soon thereafter compliant, registration desk clerk trainee who had finally eyed the red-faced, fuming manager who was on the verge of intervening to assist one of his best tipping customers. Marks turned away as he happily repeated to himself his long-time, admittedly simple, mantra; *"Don't ever tamper with the head of TAMPRR."*

Marks unlocked the door to his suite on the eighteenth floor and smiled when he confirmed that it provided a breathtaking view of Sausalito and Angel Island across the bay. He unpacked, changed into his track outfit, and then went down to the mezzanine level recreation center, where he had a moderately brisk 45-minute workout. Marks admittedly enjoyed looking in the mirror at his still reasonably muscular frame, although he now felt mostly gratitude for good genes, rather than vanity for his efforts, when he examined the undeniably old man who kept staring back at him.

Back in his suite, Marks took a long hot-and-then-cold shower. He had deliberately set the upcoming meeting for five o'clock this afternoon so that his visitors' stomachs would want it to end within an hour or so. They would be physiologically impatient but would have to hear him out in order to get the whole picture. Then they would need to discuss his proposal with their respective companies' CEOs this very evening in order to reach a decision by nine o'clock, Pacific time. Marks would insist upon their deciding to sign onto his proposal by that time, which, after all, was only midnight back east

Jake had long since left the day-to-day running of TAMPRR to his handpicked successor. This project, however, and more specifically this particular meeting, was one that he wanted to handle himself. The stakes were enormous, the potential profit to be made, gargantuan. He had asked for the meeting only two days earlier, once he learned that things were going to be coming to a head in Canada much more quickly than anyone had anticipated. Certain monetary and other executive decisions would have to be made immediately if TAMPRR was going to have a chance of being successful in taking whatever drastic actions would be deemed necessary in order to stop that arrogant Canadian Prime Minister, Perry, and his protégé, Markridge, from carrying out their suddenly front-and-center, pre-emptive plans.

As usual, Marks had no intention whatever of informing those attending the meeting what those 'drastic actions' would be. Most of his guests would readily realize that they didn't want to know. As for any others who might dare to inquire, *this* Colonel's still withering glance had disarmed and sent running much more worthy combatants than this bunch of upper middle management suits with their limp pencils.

He made two calls–one to Ottawa and the other to his niece.

The call to Ottawa updated him as to the latest timetable of the one person he most needed to–but could not–control. He listened attentively to the senior operative who oversaw TAMPRR Inc.'s efforts in Canada. Wearing his tight grin as he listened to the most current update on the movements of Member of Parliament Markridge, Marks nodded but said little during the short briefing.

Finally, retired Colonel Jake Marks, President and CEO of TAMPRR, issued his orders: "All right. Good work. Now, don't make any of the moves yet that we have already discussed, but keep me informed daily about anything new that comes across your screen. We have to know exactly *what* she is planning, *where* and *when*! And take one last crack at seeing what else you can dig up about her background, even back to her high school or university days. ... That's right... Yes, promiscuity is good. Drugs are even better. ... We could perhaps use that."

The Colonel nodded some more, and then said, "Yes, the transfer has been arranged; you should find the additional funds appearing at your end by tomorrow noon your time. The amount may well be substantially larger than we discussed earlier, just in case there are any extra, eh, additional expenses. ... You're welcome. Your efforts are much appreciated. ... All right, then. Goodbye."

The second call was dicier but gave him information he needed and didn't particularly like. He listened to the answer to his question about the whereabouts of Ken Simpson, and frowned. If it were any other operative telling him that the quarry had gotten away, he would have torn a strip off the person on the other end of the line. But he just breathed deeply and then deliberately relaxed his tense body and worked mightily to soften his voice; his niece did not respond well to bullying.

He didn't think he let his disappointment show in the tone of his voice, which was almost kindly and parental. "I see. Well, couldn't be helped, I suppose, dear. The important thing is to get there as soon as you can. Make up any excuse. Say that you are there to follow up on information you have just come across. You used to live there, so tell him that you are there to meet friends if you have to... yes, that's fine. Maybe you can meet him for dinner? ... Whatever. ... Right. Call me from Ottawa and let me know as soon as you can. And, Sylvia," his voice momentarily becoming almost sweetly menacing, "do whatever it takes to find out what he is onto and what he plans to write about next. ... Yes, *whatever!* All right? ... Yes, I know those days were supposed to be past. But sometimes we have to dance with the party that first brought us. ... No, of course I am *not* pressuring you. Not at all. This is strictly business. You are a good girl, eh... woman. I know you will come through... Good. That's fine. ... Okay. Goodbye, dear."

After he ended the call he sat very still, his eyes boring into the pieces of the puzzle. He loved war games; hell, he loved war. This exercise was both. The enemy was clearly defined, the tactics– his favorite kinds–devious and dirty. Marquis of Queensbury rules were for patsies and pansies. If he had his way, any suspected enemies or their sympathizers should be broken by *any* means possible, including, if need be, turning them over to even semi-friendly third-world governments whose rules of dealing with those in their jails were much less stringent.

These guys' companies had found the geese that laid only platinum eggs. And he was about to take a sizable portion of their yearly production. All he wanted was a percentage of those eggs for TAMPRR Inc.–and, of course, himself. He would help them to keep their businesses going. That was certainly worth a great deal, say one percent of their industry's gross revenue for the last fiscal year would be quite satisfactory. *Fair's fair, after all.*

The phone beside his elbow rang.

Marks let it ring and only picked it up after the third ring; he believed in letting the other guy start worrying just a little bit, right off the top.

In what passed for his warm voice, he issued a quiet, "Marks here."

"Colonel Marks, good afternoon, sir. In which room will we be meeting, sir?"

Marks recognized the voice. He responded, giving the caller the room number and time of meeting.

"Right. Thank you, sir, we'll be there at five."

There would be five of them. Jake Marks placed his own high-back swivel chair at the head of the small conference table he had ordered sent to his suite. His chair would be positioned with the wide window immediately behind it. Now he opened the blinds so that his visitors would have to look at his face against the background of the bright outdoors. He was tired of this shit, but would just do it this one last time, and then hang up his sword, but with a record-setting fee that would be talked about in the bizwar world for decades to come. That is, if his guests and their masters didn't turn out to be incompetent wimps.

CHAPTER 36

As he waited for his guests to arrive, Marks sat in the easy chair by the window sipping his scotch. He was briefly reminiscing about how much times had changed in the past half-century, ever since he met in Los Angeles with Sam Brannigan and the heads of some of the then top military aircraft builders. Sam and Jake had offered them an opportunity to save themselves and their companies by killing off the Avro Arrow. Then, the top guys were usually the ones who had actually started and built their companies. *Those guys had balls!* Nowadays, the heads of the companies he dealt with were of a vastly different sort.

The present-day CEO was usually a self-interested hired gun who might not have even the slightest clue about the details of the industry his company was in. The man (or, yes, the woman) could be the head of a software company today, but a few months or years later, the same person might be the announced savior of a soap company. CEOs were now like movie stars: turn on the charisma, ask for millions, act as if you really are who you pretend to be, do your thing, make the company at least appear profitable, and then jump the hell off the stage using your golden parachute to ease your fall before the final credits, or nowadays' equivalent, the company's restated and negative annual reports were rolled out.

Even those CEOs who knew their companies' product lines, often didn't really have any major allegiance to the business. That was one thing that, all too often, the workers on the assembly lines had learned in the 1990s from the people at the top: *don't bother having any company loyalty, since it sure as hell won't pay.* You could be with the same company now for fifteen or even thirty years or more and they could, if things got too tough, let you go tomorrow, right after they had spent your company pension to help fatten their own compensation packages.

At 5:02 p.m. there was a properly assertive 'knock-knock' at the door. *All right. Here we go. It's Showtime!*

Colonel Marks, wearing his dark blue power suit and red tie, opened the door of his business suite and, with his infamous Cheshire cat grin, greeted his guests.

There were five of them arriving together, representing four of the larger companies in the healthcare and pharmaceutical fields, plus one vice-president from the accounting firm that currently did these same companies' books.

After less than five minutes of introductory chitchat bullshit (it had taken Jake less than half that time to size up the mostly less-than-half-his-age guests) over some pour-your-own poison, Marks decided that they were as primed and ready as they were likely to become. Jake silently complimented the TAMPRR researchers who had provided him with his guests' dossiers; the files were remarkably accurate from what he could tell by the initial behaviors of the people in his suite.

Josh Adams, whose cousin was one of the American president's inner circle, was a brilliant corporate lawyer V.P. for the newly amalgamated, now largest HMO in the U.S.A.. His colleague, Scott Redford, was a fast-tracked ivy leaguer MBA, senior V.P. type for Adams's company's competitor. *All right: these two are good little soldiers and will get the picture very quickly.*

The third person Marks greeted was more problematic. A hotshot with an obvious attitude problem towards authority that Marks sensed when his handshake was returned with one substantially more aggressive than his own–and caused him to wince internally, although he damned well didn't show it. From back in his military days, Jake had met more than his share of young lions with overpowering pissing-contest handshakes. This one belonged to Michael Bradley, undoubtedly a fitness fanatic who was also a V.P. for another recently merged company, this one a Preferred Provider Organization. *He might get a little testy. Fine.*

The other two guests who introduced themselves in a more collegial manner were Colin Pewter, a pleasant enough corporate accountant for a healthcare insurer, and chisel-jawed, former Olympian runner-up, James Pointer, vice-president of the recently amalgamated Pharma3000America, now one of the largest pharmaceutical companies in America.

Jake seldom personally dealt with second-stringers, but he also understood that this meeting could not be delegated to anyone else at TAMPRR. And he accepted that things were way too hot nowadays for most CEOs to risk attending this type of meeting, lest some hypercritical–and hypocritical–Senate sub-committee be authorized to delve into their companies' questionable competitive business practices. They couldn't *all* claim to have been out of the room at the same time that certain key matters were brought up.

"Shall we sit down, gentlemen?" Marks could never say those words without it sounding like a command. They all sat down, including hard-ass Bradley, but of course, only *after* the others had complied.

"Let's get right down to it, then" said Marks. A couple nodded. The others just stared at the living legend in the room, the diminished ex-superstar their bosses had told them about in preparation for this meeting.

Marks began with a little buttering, the better to…

He said, "Gentlemen, collectively you represent some of the most significant players in the healthcare, pharmaceutical, and accounting fields in America today. Of course, I need not remind you that, officially, this meeting is simply not happening. The fact that most of your competitors have not expressed an interest in joining this gathering will actually make your companies stronger by placing you in prime positions to profit from the achievement of our mutual goals.

"However, the reason I have requested this meeting on such short notice is because two days ago, one of my company's onsite staff got wind of the strong likelihood that the Prime Minister of Canada has rather suddenly decided to leave politics, and that he will be announcing that fact within a matter of days. His decision is related to the still closely held secret regarding his deteriorating health. Our source has confirmed that his stomach cancer has returned in a form that usually takes only a very few weeks to do its dirty work, and is nearly always terminal. The man now simply wants to spend as much time as he has left with his wife and family."

His guests looked at one another as if to say, "Is this what the old fart got us all here for? Who gives a shit about some other country's politician's health or career plans?"

Only Adams and Bradley didn't join in the eyeballing rendition of "Screw you, old man!" that zipped around the table. Instead, they kept their eyes locked on the Colonel's. They knew they had only heard the sound of only one shoe dropping. They were waiting for... *something*.

The *thing* landed a heartbeat later–full force.

Marks said, "The reason that this situation has warranted all of us coming together today is that the Prime Minister has intimated to a very few insiders that his choice of successor as interim Prime Minister is down to one of two of his cabinet ministers, at least until a leadership convention can be held, probably not for perhaps as much as a year or more away. The choice is probably going to be between our guy, who we have bought and paid for so many times over that he is like a popular whore after one of our aircraft carriers has left port, and his complete opposite, one Trish Markridge, the staunchest supporter in their whole bloody parliament, for Christ's sake, of their government-run public healthcare system. This woman has a mixture of John Kennedy's charisma and John McCain's guts, someone whose balls, if she had any, would be as big as her boobs. And, keeping in mind that she won a few beauty contests in her younger days, we are talking coconut-sized appendages here."

The guests mildly guffawed at Marks's imaginative commentary, and then quickly sobered as they contemplated the import of what he had said. From the wild-eyed looks they were now giving him and one another, it was evident to Marks that he had gotten through their bullshit bravado, and had succeeded in scaring the bejesus out of them.

Now he added the piece dé resistance. "Also, our sources have informed me, if she gets to be interim Prime Minister, she intends to use her bully pulpit to get her party to endorse a proposal to enshrine what they like to call up there *"free, accessible, timely, and accountable healthcare for all citizens of Canada"* into their Canadian Bill of Rights and Freedoms. She also will employ her more than ample powers of persuasion to get all their provinces and territories to adopt compatible legislation. And since she is a damn genuine hero and arguably the most popular politician in the country to boot, and seems to be seen as so damn caring about citizens in every part of the whole bloody country, she just might get the job done. Our latest unadvertised advanced polling, done just last week, indicates that her bill would already have support from a majority of Canadians in almost every province and territory.

"Up to now, we could always count on our provincial political friends in Canada to at least *pretend* to give a shit about their healthcare system, and to try and make out their federal government as the perennial 'bad guy', and vice versa, just so as to keep their population in a continual state of feeling frustrated and angry as hell with one or the other. But there are leaks in that boat, my friends. And now Markridge may well swamp our guys' positions if she is allowed to get up a head of steam from the position of interim Prime Minister.

"Lately she has even been using a line similar to that used by one of our own most liberal and dangerous politicians several years back. She has been repeatedly saying things like, *"There isn't a western Canada and an eastern Canada, a rich Canada and a poor Canada, a 'have' Canada and a 'have not' Canada; there is only 'one united, strong, compassionate, free and healthy Canada"*. If she continues mouthing that bullshit and manages to get enough of the citizens in her country to back her, then she might well get their government-run healthcare system locked up so that we will never be able to get at it."

It was hard to distinguish *which* of them had uttered *what* expletives. For a moment Jake had the distinct impression he was on a badly losing team's bench with almost no time left on the clock. He pressed the issue home.

"We believe that the lady has a hurry-up timetable. She is an ideologue who believes the crap she is spouting, that guaranteed, universal Medicare ranks up there with public education as a fundamental right of everybody. We also think that she will stake her run for the full-time leadership of her party on successfully driving through a so-called 'private member's bill' that would be the biggest threat to your businesses since that Clinton combo tried to strike your companies dead in your tracks.

Redford, asked in an almost deferential voice, "What do *you* think we can do about this, sir?"

Before Marks could respond, young Bradley got into his alpha male stance, banging his ham-sized fists onto the table and pronouncing in a belligerent tone, "What Redford means, Colonel, is what is *your company* going to do about it... *Sir!* After all, isn't that what our companies have been paying yours handsomely for, for the last many years? To keep us safe from this kind of threat? And why didn't you anticipate this happening before now and take actions to prevent it?"

Marks was much too old and far too experienced to rise to the bait and give Bradley either what he wanted or even what he undoubtedly deserved. Instead, he took the high road and responded in a strong but business-like manner. "The Prime Minister, up to and including three days ago, had never uttered a word in public, or in private for that matter, as far as we have been able to determine, that he was even contemplating such a move. He has fairly consistently moved his party to the right, and was, we had reason to believe, increasingly favorably disposed to bringing in an American-type healthcare system into his country, but didn't want to say so until after he had been re-elected.

"However, in the past year, his health has been a matter of some concern, he has appeared somewhat less energetic, and more recently he has been prone to canceling speeches at the last minute. His press secretary has been casually stating that Perry has had an unusually large number of colds and flu.

"We think that his intention is to not retire immediately, but to put Markridge in the job as temporary leader and acting Prime Minister first. That would be his way of giving a gigantic "Fuck You!" to his rivals in the party, several of whom he probably knows we have had on our payroll for years."

Bradley asked, only slightly less belligerently, "So how do we, *how are you* going to stop him? Can't the other politicians, who you say are on our side, influence him to not let that bitch Markridge in the door? Christ, if she gets the Canadian Medicare system embedded in their Charter of Rights and Freedoms, then we may never get it out of there, and the pressure is just going to keep building on *our* politicians to bring in a similar, across-the-board, government-run, Medicare program."

James Pointer of Pharma3000America, said, "Maybe we can try the same ploy we used a few years back, when we created a whole bunch of supposedly independent senior citizens' lobby groups that sounded legitimate enough to get a lot of our guys elected and to defeat most of the bills that were coming down the 'pike that would have given lower medical and pharmaceutical costs to seniors. It cost us hundreds of millions to buy the votes we needed in the House and Senate back then, but otherwise it was easy to accomplish."

Bradley countered with, "Oh, sure. And we know how well that paid off when the legitimate seniors' organizations uncovered the fact that they were really only front organizations paid for by some of our own companies."

Pointer responded, "Well, at least we got most of the mainstream media to either ignore the true facts altogether when they were exposed, or to bury those news items in the middle of their papers and broadcasts. Just like the defense department and their defense contractor buddies did when they leaned on the major television networks and print media to avoid publishing contrary pieces during the Iraq war. It's the same routine."

Bradley and Pointer were getting into a pissing contest with one another, one that the others seemed to be only mildly enjoying.

Marks stopped them both. "We are going to have to do something far more drastic, I believe. I am sure that the Prime Minister knows that his current Minister of Health, Timmy Cemente, has been in our pocket for years, from back when he was the Federal Minister of Immigration and made sure that Canada would lack a sufficient number of qualified technicians to run their newly purchased MRI and CT scans. And in the time he has been the federal Minister of Health, he has repeatedly winked as provincial premier Linden allowed the introduction of privately operated 'clinics' that do medical procedures that their patients have to pay out of pocket for, and that are actually outlawed by their Canada Health Act. Cemente is the man we have to back for the PM's job. But first, we have to stop Markridge, and she currently has a hell of a lot more clout with the PM and the Canadian public."

Adams inquired, "Didn't I read somewhere that Cemente is the guy who made sure that his buddy got grants to promote anti-drinking through an untendered grant after his own ministry had turned down the proposal as completely inadequate? And it turned out the guy also worked as a lobbyist for one of the biggest liquor companies in the country, and had been a major contributor to Cemente's election campaigns?"

Marks said, just slightly impatiently, "Look, you can't keep a pig from eating whatever shit he finds, *wherever* he finds it. We have been paying Cemente off for years. So how can you expect a corrupt politician to not act like one? Anyway, the Prime Minister knows damned well that Cemente is popular with some of the key backroom boys in his party as well as some of its wealthiest supporters–and that includes us. So, if the PM wants what is euphemistically referred to in their political circles as an "appropriate and acceptable exit strategy" with lots of statues, schools and bridges carrying his name, then he damn well better give *them* what they want, which is, of course, what *we* want. That way all of us will get richer. Unfortunately, he doesn't seem to see things that way any longer. The son-of-a-bitch now wants a 'more meaningful legacy', which he knows he will only have if he does something spectacular, like permanently protecting their Medicare system, not by building another pig farm near an already polluted river!"

The others said nothing for a couple of beats. Then Adams, in a conciliatory voice that was probably intended to insinuate his appreciation for Marks's resources having managed to find out about the Prime Minister's as yet unannounced plans, said, "Colonel Marks, I know that we very much appreciate everything you have done for our companies. We owe you big-time for making sure that so many Canadians are frustrated with the problems you helped create in their system. And it was brilliant to get Cemente to close down as many of their health facilities as they did, and so on, to the point that more and more Canadians have begun practically begging for our companies to come in and operate services that would reduce their waiting lists."

Marks said, meaning it, "Thank you, Mr. Adams, for the recognition of what we have been able to accomplish on your behalf to this point. It hasn't been easy but we've now gotten to enough people in their government to bleed so much out of their system that their citizens are beginning to crave a transfusion of good old American enterprise."

Most of those around the table nodded with conspiratorial camaraderie. However, pain-in-the-neck Bradley snidely said, "But, Colonel, I thought that what we have been paying your company was surely going to be sufficient to get the Canadians to come onside permanently. So why are we having a problem now?"

Marks responded in a superficially pleasant way to the little prick. "We *have* done a very great deal, and we have much to be proud of. Also, gentlemen, let me remind you how much effort and money it took to get some of the provinces to begin to organize their doctors into group practices. By arranging their group practices in the particular ways we did we were making sure that it would *not* be in their patients' best financial interests to seek out doctors outside of their doctors' group; nor in their doctors' best interests, for that matter. We also arranged to provide most of the doctors with virtually identical computers loaded with covert software packages that would, once unzipped by the appropriate passwords, convert all their patient files into a format immediately compatible with your own companies' admin packages. We did this even though we had faced more resistance than we had thought would be there, especially from some of the doctors who quickly realized that their autonomy to make doctor-patient decisions would be taken away from them, and that their own incomes would go down by twenty to forty percent while their insurance premiums would more than triple once we moved in, just like they have here."

"So?" queried Adams.

"*So,*" continued Marks, "our aim all along has been to make sure that we set in place the easiest possible transition of their systems to your own, once we got the green light. And until now, we had managed to postpone any Canadian government taking the kind of actions that we have just learned are now being contemplated by Markridge. She was the joker in the pack that we had no way of knowing about in advance. Keep in mind that, at the very least, our efforts have given your companies several additional years to make megabillions and to tie up millions of people in our own country as your clients."

Adams said, "We are grateful, Colonel, we are. Don't get us wrong. Only, what happens now? It sounds like you are now saying that all that good work is in jeopardy."

Marks looked around the room, pausing just long enough to make good eye contact with each one of them. Marks concluded that they were ready to get his main message.

"*What happens now* is that we have to take some virtually unprecedented and very costly steps to make sure that the Prime Minister doesn't appoint Markridge, or that if he does, that she never gets to see her announced dream of a constitutionally protected Medicare system, come into being. To counter this most serious and virtually immediate threat to your companies, and to achieve these goals without delay, will require immediate and massive additional funding, far in excess of what is covered under our current agreement. We will have to try and get to people who have thus far been unapproachable. But since nearly everyone has his–or her– price, we will have to meet it. And we will need to get through to someone in her security detail. Also, there may well be other measures that will need to be taken that you do not want to hear about–in advance, or ever. "

" How much, Colonel? How much will it cost?" It was Redford.

Bradley began to chime in with a similar question, but in a more accusatory tone.

Marks cut them both off. He said, "Markridge knows full well that she will have to move fast. And we also know that the Prime Minister has said he will campaign with whomever he chooses to succeed him as interim leader."

Bradley again: "Since you say he is seriously ill and leaving politics, so why would he do that?"

Marks said, "As I have said, Prime Minister Perry is obsessed with his legacy. What has apparently gotten to him are the lingering doubts about some questionable actions and financial programs that he and his party have carried out over the years and that, now that they have been exposed by some holier-than-thou whistleblowers and some of their more enterprising media, the whole mess threatens to reduce his legacy to the level of former Prime Minister, Bruce Malone, one of our very best catches, and the guy who is currently sitting on at least two of your companies' Boards of Directors.

"The very idea of being compared to Malone, well, Perry can't stomach that. For these reasons, we think that he might want to back Markridge's goal of a constitutionally guaranteed, publicly run Medicare, because if it can be brought in relatively quickly *it* will be seen, at least in part, as *his* legacy. If he and Markridge succeed, then *your* companies, gentlemen, would be sitting on top of a public relations time bomb that could eventually go off when some enterprising *American* reporter like that Ken Simpson guy, of *The New York Era*, starts writing syndicated articles on the subject in some of our own papers, about how the Canadians have 'solved' the healthcare problem in a way that most Americans are literally and figuratively dying for."

Now Marks played another one of his remaining aces. He said, in a voice that was deliberately terse, "And I am here to tell you today that Mr. Simpson is currently in Ottawa preparing to do *just that.* "

There was complete silence in the room. No one spoke; they were thunderstruck, as Marks had thought they would be. Marks could almost hear them chanting silently in unison, *"Please! Stop them."*

Jake Marks could almost hear his troops thinking as one. *Christ, a constitutionally guaranteed universal and free Canadian Medicare system. If that happened it would be virtually impossible, short of invading the whole goddamn country militarily, to ever get the Canadians to adopt the U.S. way of operating healthcare as a business. And then where would our companies be? What would my stock options be worth, if that happened?*

Bradley, like everyone else in the room, knew that his job and his stock options were now on the line. He was his company's point man in making sure that the Canadian system did not become 'an idea whose time had come' in America. If there was even a hint that that was about to happen, then he would be the first one to be cut loose. His face turned flaming red as he glared at Marks and asked, "How much, Colonel? *How goddamned much?"*

Jake appreciated Bradley's mind if not his manner. He said, "We have estimated the odds of Markridge succeeding, and they are disturbingly high. We have also calculated the cost of preventing her from ever doing so. The cost of guaranteeing that we can stop her is six hundred million dollars."

His guests alternately gasped and then swore. Bradley exploded. "Holy shit! Surely you're joking, Colonel."

Marks glared sweetly as he picked up some envelopes and started passing them out. "On the contrary. I am frigging *take-it-or-leave-it-by-midnight-tonight* serious. I must have your answers tonight, and your moneys, in the total amount of six hundred million dollars in total, by tomorrow at 3:00 p.m. east coast time, wired to the accounts specified in these letters." He passed out some envelopes. "In your letters you will also find the amount that your particular company is expected to contribute."

Over moderately protesting utterances Marks added, "Things are going to have to happen very quickly now. Keep in mind, gentlemen, that we have neither the time nor luxury to bicker over *how much* it is going to cost your companies to not get totally screwed if Canadians make universal Medicare an inalienable right. You and I know that if they succeed in doing that, then eventually, the pressure by enough Americans on our politicians for the same right, will beat the hell out of *all* the money *you* could ever throw at them. Just look at how our elected representatives, including the President, were forced to change their tune and vote to create the 9/11 commission after enough citizens had put enough pressure on them. And, after all, the amount you are being asked to deliver is much less than five percent of your companies' combined revenues for a single year. So now is surely not a time to be penny-pinching."

Jake Marks watched them open the envelopes with their respective companies' names on them. Gazing into their faces he saw frustration, fear, and just a dash of defiance from Bradley. The rest had observably surrendered.

Jake said, "Considering the massive amounts of media time and space we are going to need to get enough Canadian columnists and newspapers onside, *and* to make enough of the ruling party's members of parliament break ranks and vote *our* way, and to also do all the other things that you really *don't* want to know about, the total cost to your companies is very reasonable.

"Of course, you are all free to attempt to resolve these matters on your own." As he gazed around the table he saw that, bravado and bullshit aside, they were all too frightened to dare take matters into their own hands. Jake Marks was entirely in charge now. His quarry stared wide-eyed, frozen and caught in his headlights. Their looks and their circumstances reminded him of those aircraft manufacturers nearly fifty years earlier who had paid so handsomely in 1958 dollars to have the Avro Arrow killed off. They had similarly realized that they didn't have the wherewithal to accomplish that long ago goal on their own, either.

"My staff at TAMPRR have already sketched out radio and TV spots to be sponsored by your new group, 'Canadians for Free Medical Choice', and we have alerted our in-place operatives to be ready to act immediately and with overwhelming effect to inundate their media with commercials sponsored by your new group, and to get to as many politicians as needed with whatever funds are necessary."

Bradley, having regained control over his bodily functions, bellowed, *"But, really Colonel; you are asking for almost two-thirds of a billion dollars? That is outrageous!"*

Jake Marks refocused on Bradley. With forced patience in his voice he said, "The actions that will have to be taken to defeat, *permanently*, any attempt to protect the Canadian Medicare System behind the firewall of the Canadian Bill of Rights and Freedoms, must be both swift and decisive. I will only tell you that more than a hundred of our contracted people will be required to pull this off. And if we were to assist just one hundred members of parliament with two million dollars each for their ironically termed 'trust funds', that alone would eat up fully one-third of the total amount I have requested. And furthermore, some of the actions that may be required to accomplish our ultimate goal may put more several people–some of theirs *and* some of ours–in harm's way."

Bradley would not shut up. "And if you fail to stop this, do we get our money back?"

Marks wanted to squash the little shit. "There are only two things guaranteed in life, gentlemen, as we all know. And when was the last time any of *your* companies voluntarily repaid your shareholders when your projects or programs didn't work out? *Never is when!* Meanwhile, whenever your companies' stock prices went down the tubes, I will bet that each of you happily kept all of your incomes, bonuses, and privileges.

"So, does TAMPRR *guarantee* success? No more than your own companies do. All of us merely do our best. But as you well know, much more often than not, TAMPRR Inc. has succeeded magnificently, which is why most of you have relied upon us for so many years, to deal with all manner of obstacles to your companies' growth and increased revenues."

There was no comeback from anyone, including a now cowed Bradley.

Marks paused just long enough to let the full import of his last volley sink in. Then he said, "Some of you will recall that the cost of defeating the Clinton Medicare plan was almost as significant. Of course, we were helped then by the fact that most Americans have an aversion towards anything labeled as 'socialized' or 'liberal'. And thanks to our efforts over the years, we were able to plant so many articles, editorials, and successfully lobby so many politicians, that when push came to shove, Clinton's party didn't have the stomach or the resources to fight for universal health coverage. I will readily agree, of course, that we were fortunate that the man pissed where he swam. We got what we needed and used it to make sure that he and his bitch lost their fight. However, in comparison to what we are facing now, what we did to the Clintons' Medicare plan was about as difficult as stalking and shooting elephants in a playpen. TAMPRR Inc. saved your asses then, and we'll do it now."

Redford tried appeasing his host. "Colonel, I am sure that everyone here knows and appreciates the work you and your company did back then, but how do we justify these additional costs to our board members this time around?"

It was time to cut the crap. Marks said, "The cost is what it is. The amount, in each case, was arrived at by examining your companies' balance sheets going back over the past four years. The amounts are not equal, but proportionate–and more than fair."

Josh Adams tried a more soothing approach than Bradley had employed. "Colonel, can you give us any additional arguments that we can bring back to our people?"

That's it. The bullshit and the crying 'poor' stops here and now. Marks drew the blinds to cut the level of light streaming into the room. Before they arrived he had drawn down the screen against the wall to the left of the windows. Now he turned on the LED projector and began a piercing PowerPoint presentation.

His guests turned towards the screen as the first slide appeared, showing their companies' revenues for the previous years. In a cold, hard voice sans all the modulated niceness that Marks found a conscious effort to affect, he began to nail the phonies to the wall. "Mr. Adams, since your company amalgamated with AmerEastern Healthcare two years ago, your new company's annual revenues are higher than those of either Microsoft, Walt Disney, Lockheed Martin, Dow Chemical, or even Coca-Cola. In fact, your company's revenues were in excess of *thirty-six billion dollars* for last year alone."

Adams squirmed in his chair. The others were shifting as if they would rather be discussing another topic, *any other topic*, as Marks showed a succession of slides outlining their huge revenues. His commentary was searing. "And while Microsoft spent over a half-billion dollars on advertising last year, *all of your healthcare companies combined* were able to get away with spending a tiny fraction of that amount on radio, television, newspaper and magazine advertising. And you know full well that most of your customers, once you have them, won't or can't go anywhere else, either because yours is the company that their employer has a contract with, or because the older your customers get and the more illnesses they have, the more likely it is that other companies would charge either prohibitively higher premiums, or simply won't issue insurance to them at all. Every year your companies, in effect, *save billions of dollars on advertising alone*, compared to most other kinds of businesses your size. Furthermore, most of your advertising at this point is largely cosmetic and for purposes of flying the company flag and putting on a show of seeking more customers.

"Of course," Jake said while looking directly at James Pointer, "you and some of the other U.S. pharmaceutical companies are operating on a different business model, using an *immense* number of advertising dollars to get people to become users of your drugs. But if the Canadian model of price control for prescription drugs were to be adopted in this country, your annual revenue percentage increases would be reduced to mere single digits instead of the twenty to forty percent increases that you have been getting these past many years."

Most of his guests were looking somewhat sheepish. Only Bradley was again visibly bridling, willing to show how displeased he was with being lectured to as if he were a little schoolboy.

"Now, of course," Marks continued, "you men represent only a fraction of the HMOs, PPOs and pharmaceutical companies in this country. The rest either weren't approached to join your cadre or declined the opportunity, but alone in this room you represent some of the consistently biggest money making machines our country has ever seen."

Marks's voice began to increase in volume and intensity as each successive slide appeared on the screen. "In fact, last year alone, the top forty companies in healthcare in this country, made *over three hundred billion dollars in revenues!* Your industry had greater revenues than our aerospace and defense companies combined, and more than six times the revenues of hotels, resorts and casinos. Your revenues were more than two and one-half times what the beverage companies made. Hell, you guys made more than four times what the top computer software companies made. So please, don't cry poor to me, gentlemen. If it keeps your companies in business, I would say our proposed actions will make a mere single payment of six hundred million dollars one of the best bargains in your companies' histories!"

No one said anything for what seemed like a long time although, from the clock on the wall behind their backs, Marks could see that less than a minute had gone by. Then he began to close.

He ratcheted back his voice, and allowed an empathetic tone to couch his delivery. "Gentlemen, lets cut to the chase. The next interim Prime Minister of Canada, the Right Honorable Trish Markridge, intends to enshrine the principles of a not-for-profit, universal Medicare system in their Canadian Bill of Rights and Freedoms. Not since Pierre Elliot Trudeau has there been anyone in their country who could hold a candle to this woman's personal power and popularity. She is going to use her bully pulpit as interim PM to whip up the sentiments of the citizens of her country, and with their help, will strong-arm and shame the premiers of most of the provinces to introduce compatible legislations into their laws. Even premier George P. Linden, that hypocritical son-of-a-bitch who we have had on the payroll for so long and for so much that he should almost be able to *buy* his own province by now—even he is afraid of her."

Adams asked, "And what exactly are you and TAMPRR going to do about such an imminent threat to us all?"

Marks went into overdrive. "I will tell you what I *won't* do, and wouldn't suggest that you do, and that is sit on my hands while Markridge makes her moves. And please remember, more and more Americans travel to Canada for business or pleasure; they see that Canada is both a democracy *and* a capitalist country, with its own stock exchanges and large national and multinational companies—the latter are mostly ours, of course—but the country has a much more generous social support structure. *Dr.* Markridge is going to have her own mantra, telling Canadians that they receive at least as good quality healthcare as we do. She will point out, correctly, that Canada has some of the top medical researchers and surgeons in North America, and that nearly one hundred percent of the population is covered by their Medicare program, *at forty percent less cost per capita* than here in the U.S.A..

Jake's audience was certainly listening, uncomfortably. "And she will undoubtedly point out that the premiums *your* companies charge for relatively restrictive healthcare coverage, have been increasing by double digits every year since 2000, and so have the co-payments and restrictions that you have placed on what medical tests and procedures you actually *will* cover. Sooner than later, if the Canadian model continues to exist, I suggest that more and more Americans will become madder than hell and won't be willing to take what is happening to their healthcare much longer. At that point your companies may well soon become extinct. Have I made myself entirely clear, now?"

Again there were no comments from the men in front of him, nor were they looking at him or one another. They were either staring down at the table or up into space. Marks guessed that they were probably already preoccupied mentally constructing their telephone presentations to their bosses and, just possibly, also preparing their new resumes.

Marks said, "I think you all agree that TAMPRR is the only resource that has a chance of stopping Markridge's Medicare steamroller before it turns south and flattens your companies–and *your* lucrative jobs. Now, I don't want to detain you unnecessarily, as I am sure that you will want to speak to your bosses right away. The deadline for going ahead with this plan remains midnight tonight, and for wiring the money, by three o'clock tomorrow afternoon, New York City time. Any later, and the actions we may need to take may be too late to initiate because the Prime Minister's and Markridge's announcements will be out and their plans will be in the public domain. We want to use a pre-emptive strike in order to force them to rethink their strategies. I will know that we will be going ahead when I receive word that the moneys have been wired to the accounts mentioned in your documents. And if, for any reason, any one of your companies choose to not proceed, then the remaining companies will be so informed and will be expected to make up the deficiency within another twenty-four hours."

A decidedly somber and scared small gaggle quickly squawked their goodbyes, and flew away.

Less than ten minutes later, retired Colonel Jake Marks, the founder and CEO of TAMPRR, was sitting at the bar at the top of the hotel for a celebratory drink. *Scared little shits. You guys screw your customers out of their funds every chance you get: you deserve no better treatment yourselves.*

CHAPTER 37

When they arrived back at her office, Dr. Brown asked her secretary to page Drs. Diane and Brian Jones. Ken heard the public address system switching on as the secretary said in a clear voice into her telephone headset, "Dr Diane Jones, WR, Chief-of-Staff. Dr. Brian Jones, WR, Chief of Staff". He smiled as he realized that the clinic probably used the same 'WR' code, which meant *'Whenever Ready, But ASAP'*, as his editor employed. In the case of Rusty Elliot, however, everyone joked that WR actually stood for "Walk or Run–Now!"

While they were waiting, Dr. Brown told Ken that the Drs. Jones were two of finest physicians with whom she had ever worked. Brian Jones and his wife Diane were both pediatric cardiac surgeons who had been approached by several US hospitals to join their staffs, and for considerable amounts of money, both before and since they arrived at Dr. Brown's clinic. To date, however, they had declined such offers. Dr. Brown gave Ken a thumbnail on them both, including the academic and professional awards they had already received for the innovative surgery procedures they had developed to repair the hearts of fetuses and newborns.

Dr. Diane Jones arrived first, and if Ken had not already been impressed by her professional credentials, he would certainly have been by her presence. Dr. Diane Jones was in her late 40s, a tall, high-cheekboned natural blonde whose lovely figure suggested itself with every movement she made, even while covered by her doctor's lab coat. Her face was pretty, her smile relaxed, and her eyes lively and inquisitive. She extended her hand to Ken as they were being introduced. As Ken responded in kind to her warm "Hello," he flashed on former President Jimmy Carter's too-revealing comment, when he acknowledged to an interviewer that he had experienced lust in his heart. The only difference between Ken and Carter was where the source of the lust seemed to be located.

The door to Dr. Brown's office opened again and an athletically built male, about six-foot-three, with movie star looks and a successful quarterback's sure and charismatic presence, also wearing a doctor's smock, entered. Dr. Brian Jones shook Ken's hand in a firm, friendly manner, for which Ken was especially grateful, given his just interrupted fantasy.

Ken noticed that Brian had long, strong, and yet surprisingly sensitive-looking fingers, similar those that Ken had observed on some of the other top surgeons he had met. His sample was too small from which to generalize but Ken thought it would bear having some pup reporter on the 'human interest' beat investigate the subject.

In spite of his many years of 'political correctness' training and collected factual data, Ken caught himself thinking that Dr. Brian Jones was just too good-looking to be straight. Then he reminded himself that the two doctors were married. *So what? That doesn't necessarily mean anything.* Then, as they began speaking and Ken observed how these two 'tens' looked at one another, he reluctantly acknowledged that Dr. Brian was probably not only as brilliant and accomplished as Dr. Brown had said, but also, a very heterosexual male. Not that it mattered of course, in this time of equal acceptance. Still…

Ken shook his head, not at the thoughts and images his overactive mind was producing, but at the fact that even at his advanced age of sixty-three, his competitive and macho inclinations were such that he would be comparing himself with another man more than twenty years his junior. *Ah, vanity–and insecurity–thy name is Ken Simpson.*

Ken silently laughed at himself, and recalled a story that an even more senior fellow reporter, Barry Henderson, had told him recently. Apparently, Barry was heading to an interview that was conveniently located along the subway line several stops from *The New York Era*'s building. When he got into the very filled subway car he managed to grab an overhanging strap and stood there, still panting and out of breath from his short run to the subway stop. Glancing down, he saw that he was standing in front of a seated, vivacious twenty-something whom, he decided, was probably a soap opera actress or model. She looked up at him with what seemed to seventy-four year old Henderson to be an exceptionally warm and flirtatious smile. He smiled back in one of those making-your-day moments when one acknowledges the mutual attraction between oneself and a total stranger. Just then, somewhat abruptly, the voluptuous young thing stood up right in front of him, their bodies now not more than three or four inches apart and, almost whispering, said in an invitingly throaty voice, "Please, sir, take my seat. You seem a little tired."

When Henderson told Ken the story he added, "You know, Ken, that young lady not only gave me *her* place, but at the same time, put me in *mine!* I had been looking at her as a potential playmate; she was seeing me as a very old man. Take it from me, Ken. Growing old is the shits, I don't care what anyone says."

Dr. Brown interrupted his mini-reverie. Ken heard her say, "I was telling Mr. Simpson that I had asked the two of you if you would be willing to share your own personal experiences of our two countries' healthcare systems."

The Drs. Jones simultaneously said, "Of course."

Dr. Diane began. "Well, Mr. Simpson, Brian and I met when we were both training at the Miami HeartHealth Clinic, and also happened to both be volunteering our services at the same inner-city clinic in a poorer area not too far from the hospital. We both found that we loved working with those folks and their children, but we had little opportunity to do the work we had been trained to do, due to the very inadequate facilities available to us.

Dr. Brian continued the story. "After we'd finished our training in paediatric cardiovascular surgery we joined a medium-sized group practice, and also worked at a couple of the hospitals in nearby suburbs. It was all so frustrating, though, because the people who came to our clinics frequently could not afford the surgeries we believed were necessary. And while we did a moderate amount of pro bono work, the fact was that our own overhead costs, including our astronomical malpractice insurance of over $250,000 a year each, made it economic suicide to do more than one or two pro bono cases a month."

At this point Ken could see Diane Jones biting her lower lip as her tears welled up. She said, "Mr. Simpson, we both come from fortunate backgrounds. Our parents were immigrants who came to the U.S. west coast and established themselves in businesses in rather poor neighborhoods. My folks had a clothing store in San Diego; Brian's had a furniture store in west-central L.A.. They all worked hard and did rather well. They extended credit to people who couldn't get any elsewhere, and were almost always paid back, sooner or later. They understood that they were dealing with people who were good as gold, but who had to settle for stainless steel for a lot of years. Brian and I sometimes talk about those times and are amazed at how we both were taught similar values. Our entire families used to go and help out at the soup kitchens set up at various churches at Thanksgiving and Christmas; we kids helped serve the meals from the time we were in our teens. Our parents wanted us to learn about giving, and about giving thanks."

"Anyway," continued Brian, who had been gazing at his wife with unabashed pride and affection, "we realized that we both wanted to work with the disadvantaged as well as the more fortunate. We used to talk about the forty-six million Americans–that's over twelve percent of us–who have no health insurance whatever, and what that means to their families. It boggled our minds and nearly broke our hearts.

"Before we came here in 2003, many of the non-physician friends we had who were self-employed had to pay between $12,000 U.S. and $26,000 U.S. a year to acquire coverage for just themselves and their spouses." "Of course, the Canadian business people and media pushing for Canadians to adopt U.S.-style health care virtually never, ever, mention those facts in their articles."

Diane said, "Anyway, when we went to international medical conventions we spoke to doctors from many countries whose citizens had something approaching universal Medicare coverage, and where even poor kids and adults could get quality care, including major surgeries. Frequently the conversations would mention Canada as one of the best examples of where so-called 'universal Medicare coverage' meant just that."

Ken saw her countenance change, becoming shadowed and

somewhat sad. "When we would talk about what we had learned about alternative healthcare systems with our doctor friends in the U.S., a lot of them would become uncomfortable, tell us that we were naïve, or closet socialists, or worse, and they would usually want to change the subject."

"Which they did, quite often," added Brian, lightheartedly. "Meanwhile, we knew from firsthand experience what was happening to healthcare politics and business in the U.S.. More and more, when we wanted to treat our own patients, we had to fight to get permission from one of over dozens of HMOs and PPOs. We were in joint practice then, just Diane and myself. We had ten people working for us, including two clerks who just handled 'insurable referrals'. When a prospective patient contacted us, one of our clerks had to contact their particular insurer, fill out the required forms, and then follow up in order to get the go-ahead to provide the service. It was horrendous.

"Sometimes Diane or I would have to get on the phone and try to convince the 'case management person' at the other end of the line that a particular procedure was necessary. In some cases, it was even made clear to us that if we would only *not* proceed with our request to go ahead with particular diagnostic tests or surgeries, then we would get a 'good practice fee', in other words, a kind of kickback, at the end of the year. They preferred to pay us less to *not* do our jobs, rather than pay more for us to actually do the job we believed needed doing. A couple of them even told us, when we wouldn't go along with their covert bribes but insisted that they review the 'declined payment' cases, that they would probably lose their jobs if they were to give us the go-ahead."

Diane said, "So here were our patients who had paid good money to some insurance or Managed Care organization in order to get coverage for just such an eventuality as a major disease or needed surgery. And then there were these... these people... these case management gatekeepers who, as we later found out, were sometimes actually being paid bonuses themselves for *not* giving us permission to perform what we considered to be desirable medical procedures. The system in the U.S. too often allows the least competent, least knowledgeable people to tell the most competent, most highly trained professionals what they may or may not do. And underneath it all is the profit motive driving the system in the direction of providing the *least* service in order to make the *most* money for the executives and shareholders of these companies. In our view, for-profit health systems are pro-business and anti-people, and eventually we simply decided we had had enough."

Both Diane's and Brian's voices hardened during the telling, as they related more details of the 'hoops' that they had to jump through just to be able to perform the jobs they had been trained to do and believed to be appropriate.

Ken asked, "So is that why you ended up here in Ottawa?"

Diane nodded her head. "You know, Mr. Simpson, we used to hear some of the television and print 'pundits' declaring that Americans would never settle for a universal Medicare system because they have been brought up to expect the best treatment from the best doctors. What is amazing is that, in actual fact of course, ordinary middle and lower socioeconomic class Americans often could not afford to get *any* appropriate treatment from *any* doctors. A large percentage of Americans either don't have any medical insurance whatsoever, or they have insurance that binds them to their HMO's list of "preferred doctors", which too often means doctors who have agreed to take the lowest payments for their work. Is that really having the freedom to choose any doctor you want?

Brian added, "And yet, here in Canada *everyone* is pretty well able to seek out *any* doctor they think is the best, and that doctor can carry out whatever treatments he or she thinks is best, usually without having to ask for permission from any bureaucrat, glorified file clerk, or bean counter, which is all that most 'case managers' in the United States really are."

Dr. Diane chimed in. "Look. Many Americans actually believe that in Canada people are forced to see a particular doctor, and that they can't switch doctors or get second opinions. All of which is absolutely and totally false. In actual fact, of course, it is *Americans* who are restricted to doctors who are on the 'preferred doctor' lists of their HMOs, and it is Americans who, in practice, usually can't switch doctors or get second opinions without paying out of pocket for the privilege. Amazing, isn't it? Americans have been sold a bill of goods."

Her husband said, "Of course, there are ethical healthcare insurers in the USA, but Diane and I personally believe that too many of them have done a first rate job of lying to Americans about their own –and the Canadian–systems. Damn it, these guys are selling an inferior product to a gullible, ignorant population, and getting away with it.

"You know, I am reminded, when I think of how Americans have–so often–been sold an inferior product that has been wrapped up in a shiny, deceptive looking package, of the way that a small number of potato chips are often placed into a bulging, vacuum-sealed bag that doesn't let you see clearly how little you are actually getting."

Dr. Brian laughed, and added, "And when I hear these blatant distortions and outright lies and fabrications that are perpetrated by some of those in power and then 'sold' to us by the media, I am always reminded of something that happened before I went into medicine.

"At the time I had already finished all but one year of an architecture degree before I recognized that medicine was more my 'calling'. But I well recall what we learned in one of our architecture courses about building and then promoting high-rise condos. One day a prof gave us an assignment of going out, as if we were prospective buyers, and asking sales agents in some of the buildings that were nearing completion to show us what was available. We were to see what we could tell about the construction and layout of the condo units, and were then to report back on the quality of the buildings, how they were priced, and especially how the different suites were promoted. It was a fascinating exercise. Some of the stuff they tried to pass off onto buyers, you wouldn't believe. And I am talking about successful, often highly educated, intelligent, prospective buyers–including doctors, lawyers, professors, and business people.

"One building's sales agent, in particular, displayed the most chutzpah of all. Many large buildings have a 'runt' or 'remnant' apartment, the one that is designed last on any floor, after all the floor plans for the other units have been laid out. Many buildings are designed from the outside in; in other words, they know how they want the building to look from the outside, and so they design the end units and/or center units first and then gradually work they way towards the hub where the elevators are usually located. One of my friends, a professor of economics at NYU, was actually in the market for a new home and so I went along with her as a 'pretend couple' to look at some buildings."

Brian was in full story-telling mode now, and there was no holding him back. His wife was smiling broadly as she looked from her husband to Ken to Dr. Brown and back. She obviously knew the story well, and was anticipating their responses.

Brian continued with his parable. "It was awesome what this one particular company did. They had used the names of chess pieces in naming of different apartment units. The one they called the 'Queen's suite' and presumably one of the best suites, was naturally, the most expensive unit on each floor. The fact was, though, that the 'Queen' was actually the 'runt' unit. Hell, when we opened the front closet of the suite, and I kid you not, we found that fully half of it was unusable, since that was where the architects had placed the garbage chute for the whole floor. Not only that, but it turned out they didn't have room for a sink in the master bathroom, so they put it in the small hallway between the master bedroom and broom closet.

"*And* the apartment was right across from the elevator so that the suite's occupant, while in the bathroom, could be serenaded by the garbage chute's door being opened and closed, and by people talking to one another while waiting for the elevators. And for these wondrous pleasures the price of the 'Queen suite' was several thousand dollars *more* than the best designed suite on the entire floor, the one that they had called the 'Knight' and that had much more usable floor space, a far preferable view, and a full and proper bathroom—one that actually *included a sink!*"

Brian was roaring when he completed his tale. Ken had to admit that the man was remarkable; a surgeon, a nearly architect, great looking, and with a caring sense of humor. *All right, you can keep your wife. You guys really are a great fit for each other.*

"Anyway," said Brian, "that is how some people promote inferior products: call it 'the best', charge more money, wrap it up in the flag, and promote the hell out of it. And an awful lot of people, and I am including many of the brightest and the most educated folks, and especially those who 'want the very best' apartment, car, or whatever, will actually gladly pay more for a grossly inferior product, and say 'thank you', if only it is promoted shrewdly enough. And I think that is what is happening in America today, where the healthcare and pharmaceutical industries are selling inferior products with buzz words like 'freedom', 'choice', and 'no socialized medicine', printed all over them, and wrapped up in the flag.

Diane said, "A few months ago when we were in North Conway, New Hampshire visiting relatives, I was in a business supplies, 'big box' store late one evening buying some blank CDs for my laptop and I got to talking with the cashier, a woman in her sixties who was working part-time. It was one of those brief conversations, the kind that people sometimes have with total strangers at a bus stop or on the plane. When she saw the 'Dr' on my credit card she mentioned that she was working to get enough money to pay for her husband's needed cataract surgery. Apparently he had been laid off work a couple of years earlier and hadn't been able to find another job so they had no health insurance. She worked full-time as a check-out clerk in a grocery store, and was doing this other, part-time job four evenings a week, and had been working like that for over two years. Just another few months, she told me, and she would have made enough money to pay for his operation. It was obvious to me that she was exhausted from burning the candle at both ends–and in the middle, too. Then, when I mentioned the universal Medicare of the Canadian system, she said to me, 'Well, we don't want no socialized medicine in our country, where some government bureaucrat is going to tell us which doctor we are allowed to see.' I mean, where the hell did that nice woman get her erroneous information? That is how ill-informed and programmed a lot of Americans are."

Ken said, "I can tell you that 'socialized medicine' is the term that a lot of editors like their reporters to use when referring to the Canadian system."

Dr. Diane said, "Well, I tried to tell that woman that

Canadians were *not* told which doctors they could or could not see, and that it was actually we Americans who are usually restricted to seeing doctors who are on our particular HMO's roster of 'preferred physicians', unless we are prepared to pay out of our own pocket. But it was as if she hadn't heard me at all. She only repeated herself, like a programmed 'Manchurian candidate', saying, "Yes sir, we don't want no one telling us which doctor we have to see."

"It was amazing to me to realize that this reasonably bright woman had been so brainwashed that she couldn't or wouldn't handle any facts to the contrary, even when I then told her that I was an American, a doctor, and had worked in both countries. No matter; our politicians and media people have been drumming that term, 'socialized medicine', into American heads for decades now. It's like the word 'liberal'; to many Americans the terms seem inherently bad or 'wrong' or even 'un-American', whatever *that* is. Anyway, that is what has been going on in the U.S. for years in the healthcare field. Give people fewer choices and less service, but wrap it up in Old Glory and call it, 'the American way', and a substantial proportion of otherwise thinking people will mindlessly pay the price."

Ken began to ask a question, but Dr. Diane was not quite finished. "I mean, just look at tobacco sales. Tell Americans that some 'left-leaning-liberal-socialist' interest group is trying to take away their right to smoke cigarettes and give themselves, their children, and anyone else who happens to be around them, lung cancer, heart disease, emphysema, and God knows how many other lethal diseases, and an awful lot of red-blooded yahoos will fight to the death to preserve their right to die and kill others from the consequences of using these products. Every time I think of what is happening I get angry and then sad and then angry again. In every bloody case it's the consumers who lose, and the sellers who get to make more and more money, which is all they really care about. *Its madness!"*

Ken had been writing as fast as he could. Brian and Diane, both American doctors, had worked in both systems. From the point of view of his American readers, their comments would probably be given much more weight than any Canadian expert's comments.

At the same time, as impressed as he was with the Drs. Jones Ken decided to kick their tires a little. He said, "But surely you will agree that the American medical system has *some* advantages over the Canadian healthcare system."

The Joneses looked at one another, nodded their heads in the affirmative, and Brian said, "You go ahead, hon."

"Okay." responded Diane. "Sure, absolutely. At this point in time, I would say that Stateside we can justifiably claim to have some fabulous cancer and cardiac centers. And we are proud and grateful for all their accomplishments. Of course, Canada has similarly excellent physicians and facilities, as well. But for the moment we would certainly acknowledge the splendid programs at the Mayo Clinic, Cleveland Clinic, U.C.L.A., Mass General, Sloane-Kettering, and a number of other hospitals that are among the best in the world. But that is probably *not* the case because of the way healthcare is paid for in the U.S.

"At the same time, however, Brian and I have already discussed the matter in depth, and we are agreed that if either of us or our children needed *immediate* major surgery, then rather than sit on an deliberately, politically motivated, excessively long waitlist here, if urgent action was required, then we could get the services we need sooner in the U.S. or wherever else in the world the best and most readily available medical treatment was to be found. We also agreed that we would be willing to pay out of pocket for it. Of course, between the two of us we earn more than most folks. As well, we have contacts that could do the digging required to find out *who* and *where* to go for the best service. In many of those respects we have distinct advantages over most Canadians, and Americans for that matter."

Ken said, "So you do agree that we have many top doctors in the U.S.."

Diane Jones said, "Certainly. Of course, you have to keep in mind that a not insignificant number of neurosurgeons and OB/GYNs in America have given up their practices entirely because they couldn't afford to pay the upwards of two hundred thousand dollars a *year*–or more–in malpractice insurance, and where a single malpractice claim could bankrupt a lot of them.

"There are many fine doctors, even great doctors, practicing in the U.S., just as there are in Canada. It's just that we Americans tend to think *our* anything is the best anywhere. So, let me share with you that I had to have my own sternum cracked open last year, and thankfully, what turned out to be a benign, but grapefruit-sized, growth had to be removed from the middle of my chest."

Ken was shocked to learn that such a seemingly fit, fine young woman had needed to deal with such a gruesome-sounding medical problem. *We never know what anyone else has gone through– not really. Mr. And Mrs. America have not lived entirely charmed lives, after all.*

"Well, being from the U.S., Brian and I called and spoke to the heads of the thoracic centers at many of the finest hospitals Stateside. It turned out that the particular operation I required was pioneered by a surgeon here in Toronto, Dr. T Dodd, and he had actually trained several of the top doctors who now do the operation in the U.S.. So, of course, we had the surgery done here. And as you can guess, I am fine." She offered a glowing smile as the final punctuation to her story.

"You need to know," offered Dr. Brown, "that the waiting lists here in Canada are not so much an artefact of the system, but the way in which it has been–and still is–being manipulated. For example, a few years back Premier Linden restricted the use of certain cancer diagnostic and treatment equipment to regular business office hours, in other words, 9 to 5, five days a week only. One of my good friends in Toronto, a fine oncologist, told me that he and the others working on the unit–doctors, nurses, technicians, even clerical staff–had signed and couriered a letter to Linden and his provincial Minister of Health, my then provincial counterpart, in which they committed themselves to a economically viable schedule that would have kept their unit in that city operating 24/7.

"Well, guess what happened? Nothing. The letter was never even formally acknowledged. Instead, Linden's government put out a press release saying that their provincial healthcare system simply could not deal with the growing numbers of cancer patients who needed service.

"It had all been a politically manufactured problem. The result? Naturally, intolerably long waiting lists. *Well, no kidding!* The effects of the mandated limited services were a no-brainer, of course; the waiting lists grew exponentially.

"In the same press release, by the way, they announced that they were willing to consider proposals from the private sector to open and run facilities that would shorten the waiting lists. It was all a rather similar ploy to the brownouts and blackouts that California and some other states experienced at the start of this century. The electricity shortages had been artificially created, for the most part, but the effects were real enough. Afterwards, once the states had cleaned up the way in which electricity services were provided… abracadabra, like magic, fewer blackouts.

"Well, a couple of years ago, when the new provincial government in power hired back staff that had been let go previously, and then supplied their surgical units with more updated equipment, and kept their radiation units open twenty-four hours a day, seven days a week, voila! All of a sudden, the waiting lists shrunk drastically."

Ken said, "Those political ploys that you described definitely sound familiar. You would agree, though, wouldn't you, that we in the states do have *some* healthcare companies that are excellent in many respects; like say, American OnYourGuard Permanent HMO, which keeps getting rave reviews from its subscribers."

Brian and Diane nodded enthusiastically. Then Diane said, "In fact, to be fair, I will go one step further. There is even one area in which I would be prepared to say that the way our healthcare system operates Stateside is eminently more logical and appropriate than what happens here in Canada."

Ken was ready to hear it; he liked his articles to give credit where credit was due 'to the other side', so to speak. "Please, tell me about that."

Dr. Diane said, "Well, there is a huge loophole in the Canadian system that is almost impossible for Brian and I, or probably most American physicians, to understand. In Canada, I am told that because of the way in which the Medicare system was developed, room was made for family doctors to bill the government for doing what *they* refer to as psychotherapy. In the United States, of course, few, if any, insurers will pay family doctors to do psychotherapy, since most of them have had exceedingly little, if any, formal training in their medical school education in that discipline. I can only recall having attended a couple of classes in only one course that even referred to psychotherapy. I certainly would not refer to that two hours as psychotherapy 'training'."

Ken asked, "What would happen in the U.S. if a physician were to say that he or she was doing psychotherapy?"

Brian responded, saying, "Well, in many states it is considered professional misconduct to practice outside your sphere of expertise, except for very limited extraordinary circumstances. Most HMOs would never even consider paying a family doctor to do psychotherapy, unless, perhaps, they had at least taken a substantial number of academic courses and had appropriate, multi-year, intensive supervision and certification in that discipline."

Ken asked none of them in particular, "And in Canada?"

Diane said, "Believe it or not, in Canada, there are actually *thousands* of medical doctors in this country who claim to do psychotherapy either part-time or full-time, and they are allowed to bill their government's Medicare system for these services."

Ken inquired, "But isn't psychotherapy within the realm of psychiatrists?"

Diane said, "Of course. And, most of the Canadian psychiatrists I have spoken to are appalled by the notion that the government actually allows this to go on. After all, they went through the same med school program as the family docs, and only afterwards specialized in psychiatry. Their basic medical curriculum had almost no courses in human psychology, and certainly hardly any classes in 'psychotherapy'."

Dr. Brian added, "We all know the saying about 'too little knowledge...' Anyway, quite possibly due in large part to their lack of appropriate training, there have been, in the past few years, some spectacular cases in this country, of professional misconduct perpetrated by generally-trained physicians who were simply way out of their depth and area of expertise, and who became inappropriately involved with, and/or took advantage of their clients."

Ken asked, "And what about counseling and clinical psychologists in Canada? In the U.S. anyway, those professionals have had relatively extensive training in psychotherapy in their academic programs? Aren't *their* services covered under the government's universal Medicare system? Shouldn't *they* be delivering that kind of service?"

"Well, that is another bizarre thing," said Diane. "The professional services of psychologist-psychotherapists in private practice are entirely excluded from Medicare coverage in Canada."

Ken said, "Really? I seem to recall that in the U.S., politicians had it written into law several years back that the U.S. federal Medicare system could not discriminate against psychologists, but had to give patients the choice of being seen by either a psychologist or psychiatrist, and regardless, Medicare picked up the bill. Is that not correct?"

Dr. Brian said, "Absolutely correct. You see, we did get some things right, after all. Now, if only our Houses of Congress extended that logic to the rest of healthcare."

Dr. Brown, who until this point, had been mostly listening to the conversation that her two staff members were having with Ken, said, "Mr. Simpson, our system *is* far from perfect, and the lobbying that went on before–and since–the Canadian healthcare system was brought forward, was successful in leaving in that 'loophole', as you might call it. And it is true that in our country, we have a supposed shortage of medical doctors while many hundreds, if not thousands, of those who completed medical school in our universities–largely paid for by our taxpayers, I might add–*have* opted out of practicing physical medicine, and instead now claim to do psychotherapy.

"And, yes, it is also true that we have thousands of fully trained, registered psychologists in Canada who could or do function as psychotherapists, as that is what they have been trained to do. And no one would dispute the fact that their training and education qualifies them to perform psychotherapy. In fact, many Canadian universities' graduate programs in psychology have even been found by the *American Psychological Association* to be comparable to their own members' education and training."

Ken asked, "So who sees these psychologist-psychotherapists, if their services are not covered by your Medicare system?"

Dr. Brown answered, "I am afraid that only those who can afford to pay out of their own pockets or have some kind of extra insurance coverage are able to see them."

Ken shook his head. "So what I am hearing is that some of the *most* highly educated and specifically trained psychotherapists, these psychologists, are *not* covered under your Medicare system, while your family doctors who, in most cases, had little if any formal education or training while in medical school in psychotherapy, are actually permitted, to not only do it, or whatever it is they are doing that they are calling psychotherapy, but they also get *paid* for doing 'it' by the Canadian Medicare system. Is that right?"

Dr. Brown nodded, perhaps a touch embarrassed. "As I said, our system isn't perfect. And in certain respects, may not entirely make sense, except for paying physicians *something* for spending *some* time talking with patients, and this payment is usually requested and billed for under the terms 'psychiatric care' or 'psychotherapy'. But in some cases, as may happen when the doctor, for whatever reason, does not want to do physical medicine, they can legally set up a practice doing exclusively what they term 'psychotherapy', and the government will pay them for that.

"And it is true that our supposed 'shortage' of doctors in this country could be made up to a not insignificant extent, if only the loophole we have been talking about would be closed.

"Of course, some physicians would claim that they have picked up a lot of training in psychotherapy by taking a variety of weekend workshops and other short-term programs. But I am sure none of those doctors would claim that their 'training' is anywhere close to that received by those who have completed a doctorate in clinical or counseling psychology. And I am also sure that if the situation were reversed in a sense, that the majority of my medical colleagues would scream 'bloody blue murder' if psychologists were to be allowed to prescribe medication or perform other 'physical medicine' diagnostic assessments or treatments, and to get paid for doing so by Medicare, after merely having taken weekend workshops or short-term programs of similar lengths to those taken by physicians, in psychotherapy."

The four of them chatted a little more, the communication becoming more conversational. After about ten minutes, Ken thanked them all for their professional and personal observations, and for the generous offering of their time, and left with much more than he had hoped to gain from the morning.

Unfortunately, it was also more than certain others would have preferred that he had accomplished.

CHAPTER 38

In the taxi on the way back to the newspaper's apartment Ken reviewed his rough notes and reflected on what he had learned in the previous couple of hours.

He was beginning to understand the differing attitudes of the two countries' citizens–about what healthcare was, and what it should become. Americans viewed healthcare as a for-profit business that they bought. At the same time, Canadians, who had had Medicare in place for more than four decades, largely considered free healthcare to be a birthright.

Having now heard about the pros and cons of the two systems, from Canadians and informed Americans both, Ken thought he better understood why there were politically active groups in most of the states across the U.S. working very hard to turn their elected representatives and their President in the direction of creating an American version of the Canadian healthcare system. And, also, why corporate forces were at work to turn things in the opposite direction.

Ken quickly typed a first draft of a future article in his Toshiba notebook, summarizing and integrating his thoughts about the information sent the researcher Martha had contacted, with what he had been just told by Dr. Brown and the Drs. Jones.

Ken also reminded himself that he was also in Ottawa for another purpose–to somehow settle the score, at least to some extent, for a half-century old act of cowardice and murder. He recognized that he would have to work very hard to keep his private and professional goals separate; this was becoming increasingly difficult as he had concluded that the two travesties in which he was interested in uncovering and disclosing had been birthed by some of the very same cast of unholy characters.

CHAPTER 39

Once back at the newpaper's apartment Ken used his cellphone to check his voicemail messages; there were four: one each from his editor, Rusty, and from Martha, Sylkeen, and Lieutenant Colonel Stevens.

Rusty sounded distinctly ticked off and he firmly requested, or rather, demanded, a callback and an update, "A-S-A-bloody-P!" Ken would deal with that later. When Rusty heard what Ken had learned he was sure the guy would come around. At least, the old Rusty would.

The voicemail from Martha was more disturbing. Sounding like she was holding back tears, she said that Rusty had called her, too, earlier in the morning and "in a pissy mood", and said that he wanted her to follow Prime Minister Perry on his speaking swing out west *immediately*. He also wanted to know what she knew or even guessed might be up with Ken and his sudden traveling urge, days after she had been transferred to Ottawa, although he didn't quite put the matter that way. From the way he did put it, however, it was clear that he was intimating that Ken might have just gone to Ottawa to get laid. With difficulty she had held off telling Rusty where to go, partly because she feared that any backtalk from her might lead to him sending her to another bureau even further away from the U.S. and Ken. She ended the message by saying she was hurriedly packing to catch up with the PM, who was already in Manitoba, and about to head even further west. "Catch you later, Hon," were her signoff words, spoken with a touch of forced bravado.

The message from Sylkeen was very business-like, except for the fact that it was delivered with a sensual, throaty tone, and, at the end, an almost teasing laugh. She said that Rusty had decided that she should join Ken in Ottawa, get updated on whatever he had learned during his couple of days in Canada, and together they were to produce an article for the Sunday edition. The laugh came after she said that she hoped she wouldn't be interrupting any plans he might have made for the next day or so. *So she probably knows about Martha. Shit! Media businesses probably have more workplace gossip than any other kind of enterprise. And why not, since gossip, after all, is nothing more than 'grassroots news', delivered with malicious or sympathetic intent, and accurate or not, about what some people want to tell other people about people they know in common.*

At least Ken would not have to somehow stage-manage the presence of both Martha and Sylkeen in the newspaper's apartment at the same time. Ken's intuition was acting up again. Were the virtually simultaneous departure of Martha and appearance of Sylkeen merely coincidences, or did Rusty have method to his messing around? Ken would probably find out within the next several hours.

Ken listened to the final voicemail, the one from Stevens. The latter said, "Clearly, TAMPRR is now in the game," whatever that was supposed to mean. Ken was instructed to check his e-mail, which he did immediately using his laptop. He found one from Stevens, who had also sent along two attachments, which Ken opened immediately. The first appeared to be a directive, dated the day before, from the desk of the CEO of TAMPRR, *Colonel Jake Marks (Retired),* stating that it was absolutely imperative that all 'partners' in Canada put whatever else they were responsible for 'into a holding pattern', and give his new request "Mayday priority". All partners were to find out everything they could about the past and present life of Trish Markridge M.P., including especially her movements and contacts over the past several months as well as in the upcoming days and weeks ahead.

Marks's memo also stated that there had been, according to certain sources just in the previous 24 hours, "rumors of swift changes about to happen within the ruling political party and pertaining to the P.M., Markridge, and the Canadian Healthcare system."

The second attachment, according to the accompanying note, was a fifty-year old photo of Colonel Marks, evidently in his late twenties at the time, taken with a Canadian Admiral named

Franklin Dillard, sitting together at dinner at Bernie's Delicatessen in Ottawa. 'Bernie's', Stevens wrote, was then and remained today a favorite hangout for the movers and shakers in Ottawa. The snapshot showed a wiry, Cheshire cat-grinning Marks looking like he had just swallowed an entire aviary, his right hand extended towards Dillard, apparently congratulating the latter, who was dressed in his full military uniform. On the table between them was a newspaper with a picture of an Avro Arrow crossed out with a huge X. Above the Arrow was the headline, *"Avro's Arrow Shot Down–Permanently!"*

Stevens's note said that Dillard had played a key role in the closing down of the Avro Arrow program, and that he had become, over the decades since, one of TAMPRR Inc.'s most influential lobbyists in Canada's capital. After re-reading the e-mail, and using the telephone number provided, Ken called Dillard's home and spoke to an elderly woman who identified herself as Admiral Dillard's wife.

Ken explained that he was a reporter from *The New York Era* and that he was interested in the Admiral's comments on a story he had been working on about the Avro Arrow. He said that the article was essentially ready to go, but that he wanted, as a courtesy, to allow the Admiral an opportunity to correct or add to the part of the article that referred to his involvement in the Avro Arrow program. After having been put on hold for at least three minutes, the same woman returned and coolly told Ken to call back in one hour.

Ken guessed that perhaps the Admiral was phoning TAMPRR to get the lowdown on him and some direction as to how to handle the request for an interview. *So be it.*

Ken printed off Stevens's e-mail and attachments. An hour after he had called Dillard's residence the first time, Ken called again, and was told by the somewhat hesitant, even colder voice belonging to the protective Mrs. Dillard, that the Admiral, although somewhat under the weather, *was* willing to see him two hours hence for what would necessarily have to be a very brief interview. It must be understood, she also made clear, that the interview could be terminated straight away, and without further questioning, at the Admiral's pleasure. *Or displeasure,*

Ken thought. Ken agreed to the terms immediately and then set about preparing his notes and other materials for the interview.

The taxi had almost driven past the high-hedged property before Ken pointed out the small sign on the top of a post that said '22 The Bridle Road'. The cabbie backed up and turned onto the private lane. About seventy feet along they came to a closed gate. Through a small opening between adjacent bushes Ken was able to see that behind the tall hedge that ran parallel to the street, about ten feet further back, was a high brick wall topped by barbed razor wire. Attached to the iron gate in front of them was a sign at eye level with the words "*Absolutely* No Soliciting or Trespassing. Guard dogs on premises." Obviously the Admiral not only preferred, but insisted upon, his privacy and security.

The intercom was on a post to the left of the gate. When the driver pushed the TALK button, three banks of halogen lights, from in front and both sides of the car, shone in on the vehicle. Ken was sure that images of the people inside the taxi clearly appeared on television monitors located somewhere inside the mansion.

"State your purpose," demanded the military-sounding voice.

Ken lowered his window and said, "Ken Simpson of *The New York Era* here to see Admiral Dillard. I am expected."

After several seconds the box's voice said, "Exit the taxi, Mr. Simpson, proceed through the gate, and walk up to the front door. When the vehicle leaves, you will be admitted."

"Yes, sir." replied Ken, in his best 'fuck you, too' tone. He was not quite sure if he actually heard a human growl in response.

The cabbie and Ken did as they were told after they agreed that the taxi would wait, on the meter, on the other side of the street. Ken passed through the now slightly opened gate and it immediately closed behind him. He walked another fifty feet to the front door, which was opened by an extremely tall, wide, and powerfully built thirty-something, probably 'special forces' type, who said, not especially kindly, "Please step inside, sir."

Ken did.

"Now, please wait here, sir." With that, the man-mountain left.

Ken found himself standing (but not entirely alone, he sensed) in a seemingly empty foyer that looked more like the entrance to a jail. There were, he noted, all sorts of security measures, including a gussied-up version of an airport security scanning kiosk. Ken immediately pitied all delivery and courier types who had to service the place.

"Please place your briefcase on the counter," said the bulging quasi-butler who now reappeared from a different door.

Ken did as he was told. The 'counter' then folded itself around the briefcase, its sides and top coming together so that they entirely encapsulated their contents. 'James' watched a monitor that was hidden beneath the counter, and finally seemed satisfied that there weren't any lethal weapons or explosives hidden in the briefcase. While it was being subjected to the inspection, Ken glanced around the foyer. When he turned 180 degrees he noticed that the front door jamb probably doubled as a first-tier metal and explosives detector, as he saw two lights, one red and the other green, over the top of the door. If there were to be a shootout or a grenade attack at this point, probably only this small part of the house, and its sorry occupants, would suffer significant damage.

Given the post 9/11 life and times everyone was living in, Ken accepted that the admiral had an absolute right to protect himself against old, unforgiving enemies. The attitudes and behaviors of certain of his employees could, nevertheless, do with some further social skills training.

The guard handed back Ken's briefcase, and almost immediately a set of inner doors opened. The guard said in a slightly softer tone, "Follow me, *please*."

Ken walked through the doorway, then down a hallway, and soon found himself in a large, pristine den, filled with military-related books and paintings, a display case with various ancient firearms, and several battle-themed sculptures. Sitting in a wheelchair, legs covered with what Ken recognized as a Hudson's Bay blanket, and facing at a right angle to the door that Ken had walked through, was a mannequin-like waxen figure dressed in an admiral's jacket. He was gazing out at a bucolic lawn.

On closer inspection Ken saw a white-haired, sickly old man with tired, sunken face and shoulders. The Admiral's 'assistant' walked over and turned his boss's wheelchair towards Ken. Ken found himself looking into the fatigued yet defiant face of a nearly-dead man, with plastic tubing providing him with oxygen via the tank suspended on the back of his chair.

Ken was taken aback. He had expected to confront a powerhouse, a gung-ho, four-star Admiral who had, according to Stevens's note, first backed, and then back-stabbed, the Avro Arrow program. The remnant of a human being in front of him appeared to be struggling against pain to merely catch his next breath.

Well, at least you got to live almost five decades longer than my father, and to continue in your career and make a lot of money, apparently, enough to afford a very wealthy lifestyle–more wealthy than the average retired Admiral, surely.

"Good afternoon, Admiral; I am Ken Simpson of *The New York Era*." Ken walked over, shook a decidedly weak hand, and then offered it his business card. "Thank you very much for seeing me, sir."

The admiral glanced briefly at the card before dropping it on his lap. "How may I be of help to you, Mr. Simpson? I understand that you are looking for some kind of background information about a long-dead and nearly forgotten military project."

Ken said, "Well, sir, I understand that you were very active in the decision to develop, and later, to destroy the Avro Arrow program, and that later, after retiring from the military, you served as a member of parliament and as Minister of Health a few years back, during which period federal payments to the healthcare system were severely reduced."

The admiral said, "That is correct, although I take issue with your choice of the word 'destroy' in relation to the Arrow. We closed the project down, that was all. Now, why should those matters be of interest to you?"

Ken continued. "Admiral, I just wanted to ask you some questions to wrap up one of my upcoming articles for *The New York Era*."

"In regard to which matter, Mr. Simpson? The Avro Arrow or my political career?"

"Both actually, Admiral."

Admiral Dillard's eyes slitted, and Ken thought he saw the old man's neck muscles twitch and tighten a barely noticeable amount.

Dillard said, "*Both?* What in heaven's name do they have to do with one another?"

"That is where I thought you could help me, Admiral."

The coldest, most authoritative voice the Admiral could muster said, *"What exactly do you mean, fella?"*

Ken said, "Well, sir, my investigations indicate that similar, and even some of the same forces have been involved, first in relation to the Avro Arrow program and more recently in regard to the Canadian healthcare system. And since you were intimately involved in both matters I was hoping you could tell me more about why that was."

Ken had read in Stevens's notes that Dillard had an enlarged prostate and therefore may have had chronic difficulties urinating, but this reporter was having no trouble at all pissing the Admiral off. He said, *"How the hell should I know, for Christ's sake?* Just exactly what are you suggesting, Simpson? And do you have any evidence to back up whatever the hell it is you're implying?"

Ken said, "What I am more than suggesting, Admiral, what I am actually stating as fact, is that some of the same people involved in killing the Avro Arrow program have been working very hard, and in some of the same ways, for the past several years, to sabotage the Canadian healthcare system. I am intending to file a story within the next couple of days that says exactly that, and that also suggests strongly that certain highly placed Canadians–including yourself–acted in concert in regard to bringing down the Avro Arrow, and have also, in more recent years, furthered their own personal aims by conscientiously debilitating the Medicare system in this country."

The old man's face found its color. "Now just a goddamned minute, you insolent son-of-a-bitch. Who told you these lies? How dare you insinuate that... that... that I *ever* engaged in any inappropriate conduct in regard to the Avro Arrow, or that I was somehow involved in seeing to it that our shitty healthcare system goes down the drain."

The Admiral made a sudden movement as if to get up out of his chair. Ken flinched before he reminded himself that the old man was probably barely able to wipe his own nose, never mind punch somebody else's. According to Stevens's e-mail, the man had been confined to a wheelchair since he was in an automobile accident a few years back. He had undoubtedly benefited from receiving considerable and free medical care offered by the country's healthcare system.

Ken pressed on. "Admiral, I am interested in knowing just why it was that, in 1958, according to published reports I have read, right after its first and–by all accounts–very successful test flight, you changed positions entirely from supporting the Avro Arrow program, as you had right from the start, to recommending to the government that the whole program be cancelled?

Ken gave the older man full marks for recovering his demeanor, and for appearing and sounding almost nonchalant. He may have been old and, from the faint odor he was now detecting, perhaps incontinent, but he was by no means incompetent.

Dillard said softly, and almost sweetly, "*Mr.* Simpson, I was just one of *many* military and civilian personnel who had the foresight to see that the Avro Arrow was really a great failure in the making. Not that it couldn't reach its flight specs. No, it met or exceeded, or at least *would* have eventually met or exceeded its specs, given enough time and money. However, it would have required far *too much* time and money for a thinly populated country like Canada to invest in development and manufacture. And, besides, it no longer matched our or your country's military requirements. Many of us in the armed forces believed that what we really needed were nuclear-tipped missiles to protect North America, not additional aircraft. So we opted to acquire your Bomarc missiles to defend both us both. It is because of these reasons that I recommended the Arrow program be… eh, terminated."

Ken had an almost overwhelming desire to toss into the Admiral's lap the photo he had received of Dillard being congratulated by Colonel Jake Marks. Instead, he said, "But, Admiral, three years later, the Canadian government mothballed the Bomarc and purchased another, inferior American aircraft to replace the complement of Avro Arrows that weren't allowed to be built."

In a sarcastic and sneering, albeit slightly shaky, voice, the old man hissed, "Look, my friend. Our previous opinion about the lack of need of new fighter-interceptor aircraft was only determined to be somewhat faulty years later. And by then the Arrow program had already been closed down, so we *had* to buy American."

"You really mean *destroyed,* not 'closed down', don't you, Admiral? After all, all the initial aircraft, as well as the operational assembly line, were broken apart and the design and manufacturing blueprints and manuals were shredded, and whatever had been left of the blowtorched aircraft was literally sold for scrap!"

Dillard replied, "You don't understand. We couldn't afford to have those plans or those aircraft just lying around. They could have provided too much information that could have been used by the Soviets."

Ken said, "Or, for that matter, by Canadians. I put it to you, sir, that they were destroyed so that there was no way that any subsequent government would be in a position to allow Avro to get back on track with the Arrow."

Dillard's words narrowly escaped his clenched teeth. "What the hell would be the point of saving *anything* to do with the Avro Arrow? *The program was dead!*"

Ken felt only a twinge of guilt as he ratcheted up the rhetoric. "Well, *you* killed it, sir. You and your friends. You sabotaged the air supremacy that your country had developed on the very day that the first Arrow flew."

Ken paused and then added, emphasizing the word by uttering it very slowly, "It was your t-a-m-p-e-r-i-n-g that killed it."

Ken received the response he had anticipated; when he said the word "*tamper*", and in spite of the old man trying to shut down any telltale sign of recognition, Dillard double-blinked and his head flicked back somewhat, as if to avoid a glancing blow. At the same time his pupils became the size of black marbles, just as if someone had suddenly turned off most of the lights in the room. Ken was now sure that the man knew all about TAMPRR.

But Stevens had told him that the company's name –TAMPRR–wasn't coined until a few years after the Avro Arrow was shut down. So, obviously, Dillard had stayed in touch with his cohorts.

Ken pressed the old man some more. "You didn't really *want* it to be able to be resurrected by any *tamperers*, did you, sir? You didn't want anyone *tamper*ing with failure. Right?"

Ken noted that each time he used the word 'tamper', the Admiral seemed to startle, his eyeballs flaring. Now the Admiral's eyes narrowed again, and Ken guessed that Dillard realized that his repeated use of the word was not at all accidental.

From Stevens's e-mail, Ken learned that the Admiral had acquired most of his wealth by doing TAMPRR Inc.'s bidding. Now Dillard was an arrogant old man in his final days, with a desire to keep his public persona, such as it was, from being further tampered with, so to speak.

Ken watched as his host's demeanor transformed. Retired Admiral Franklin Dillard was beginning to have the same terrorized expression that some bone-weary, aged animals get, just before their escalating fear transmutes into a final–last stand– fury. He knew he had gotten to his subject's Achilles heel. While he, surprisingly, did feel some compassion for the old man, he also experienced his own hurt and anger at the man's actions and his association with those who had murdered his father. So he moved in for the admiral's close-up, using more of Stevens's ammunition.

"Admiral, I have reason to believe, according to certain sources, that your advice to close down the Avro Arrow program, and your recommendations in public speeches that the Canadian Medicare System be opened up to American-style HMOs or their equivalent, was based in large part on your first-hand involvement with, and remuneration from, certain interested American business sources." As he was uttering these words, Ken reached into his jacket's inside pocket, took out a photograph, and then, leaning forward, placed in the Admiral's lap the picture of Dillard eagerly shaking hands with Colonel Jake Marks, with the newspaper headline declaring the Avro

Arrow program dead, spread out in front of them.

Dillard gingerly picked up the photograph, put it close to his face and squinted, as if to try and place the time and place.

"Admiral, would you care to comment on these allegations, and describe the circumstances depicted in this photo, of your being at dinner with the man whose group led the campaign to kill the Avro Arrow, the very day after, according to the headline on the newspaper in front of you in the photograph, that the plug was pulled on that plane's program?"

"*You sonofabitch*!" exploded the Admiral, probably sounding like a remnant of his younger self. "How dare you? *How dare you! What kind of horseshit is this? If you and your newspaper dare print such a thing, or even imply it, then I will fucking crush you, Paulson prize or not! Now, get the hell out of here!*"

Although he had steeled himself, Ken was nevertheless startled by the intensity of the old man's fury. At the same time, he was impressed that Dillard could still manifest such a menacing countenance. The Admiral, in spite of his poor health, was still a warrior, and was not ever going to quietly fade away.

Ken said nothing but continued to watch as Dillard's colorful face slowly returned to its more usual pallor. The man was recovering his composure, and there was little more that Ken would be able to extract from him. However, he had gotten what he wanted, a first-hand confirmation that the man in front of him was indeed a part of the Avro Arrow conspiracy and, at least until his own health had made it impossible, probably was very much involved in lobbying and directing some key government people on the healthcare issue.

As Ken began to get out of his chair and prepared to excuse himself, the Admiral stopped him cold with his own question.

"Do you have any children, Mr. Simpson?"

Ken shivered. "One, Admiral. An eleven-year-old. Why?"

"Because I am certain that you will want the best for your child, and want to see the little tyke all grown up and married and so on, don't you?"

Ken glared at Dillard. "Are you actually threatening either me or my child, Admiral?"

Admiral Dillard said nothing, but with a menacing military

commander's arrogant grin made it perfectly clear that what he had just said was indeed a first, and probably last, warning shot across the bow of Ken's intentions. With a deadly cold voice, and his eyes mere slits once again, he then issued the words, "*Of course not*, Mr. Simpson. I am simply suggesting that you be *very* careful where you are going with this… this mischief. As they say, all is fair in love and war, *Mr*. Simpson. And I most definitely don't love you, *so I will not allow you to fuck me. Never! You need to know that.*"

Clearly the old sailor was prepared to fight for his reputation, or at least, what he believed it to be. So, thought Ken, perhaps that fact could be used to some effect. "All I am interested in, Admiral, is understanding more fully what happened to the Avro Arrow, and what has been, and is, happening to the Canadian Healthcare System."

"But why do you even care about that old bucket, the Arrow, let alone our so-called universal Medicare system?" asked the Admiral. "Why would a presumably patriotic *American* newspaper like *The New York Era* suddenly give a shit about what is happening in *Canada*? Most of your readers couldn't care less about us? We are irrelevant to you. So why bother to bring up this crap now?"

"Because, Admiral, when some*one* or some special interest group in America *tampers* with the truth, *tampers* with a friendly foreign country's citizens' lives, with that country's industries, institutions, and with that country's autonomy and economic life as if they were the sworn enemy of the U.S.A., that interests this investigative reporter, and I believe, will also interest a lot of my readers."

"But…" The Admiral started to respond but Ken cut him off, letting his next words out slowly and with a great deal of feeling, yet without raising his voice. The accompanying look on his face seemed to freeze the Admiral. He said, "When I learned, Admiral, that the same people who were behind the downing of the Avro Arrow program had also murdered my own father, then all of their activities, and all of their collaborators, became my business."

Ken got up out of his chair and began to take a step towards the Admiral, not certain why; no matter–at nearly the same moment the latter's special forces 'guardian' materialized between them, blocking Ken's way. The man's left hand drove firmly into the middle of Ken's chest while his right hand simultaneously reached inside his bulging sports jacket. Ken was propelled back into his chair. The bodyguard then moved to the side about a half a step so that the reporter and his subject could see one another, but from which position he could easily intercept any other untoward moves or, if he so chose, could fire his Glock G22 directly at Ken's heart.

The Admiral recovered his composure in the moment that it took for his bodyguard to disabuse Ken of the notion of moving closer to him.

Dillard asked," What do you mean, your father's murder?" As the words came out of his mouth a light went on inside the Admiral's skull. It appeared that the person he had been briefed by neglected to inform the Admiral about Ken's personal interest in the story he was researching.

"Simpson... Simpson. Are you related to a former U.S.A.F. pilot, Fred..., no. Eh, ... *Frank* Simpson? Are you..."

Ken spit out his response. *"I am his son!"*

"Ah. I see. I am sorry about that. I didn't know. I wasn't..."

"You weren't told?"

Dillard looked uncertain. His eyes moved about, and his voice softened slightly. "I simply was not aware, that's all. I am sorry for your loss. I recall that was a lot of years ago"

"Did you every meet my father, Admiral?"

The old man's defences snapped back in place once again. "I can't say that I recall us ever meeting. I just remember the story of an American pilot who was... killed, who had been somehow attached to the Avro Arrow program."

"What can you tell me about the connections between the demise of the Arrow program and what is happening to the healthcare system in Canada?"

Dillard became lost, entangled in his own thoughts. He mumbled, finally, "Nothing. Really. Nothing at all."

Ken said, "I understand that after you retired from politics in 2003, you were given an office across from Parliament Hill, with secretarial staff and security protection. Isn't that unusual, Admiral?"

"Unusual, yes, but not unheard of. You see, after I retired from politics I was appointed the voluntary chair of 'Our Families; Our Futures', a non-profit program whose mandate is to coordinate the bringing together a variety of agencies, corporations, and foundations to formulate ideas and programs that would further the health and well-being of Canadian families."

"So, in other words, Admiral, you were appointed to a position by the government in which your own party held a majority, a job that required you to meet with businesses and other organizations to look into issues such as healthcare."

"Not just healthcare, Mr. Simpson."

"Sure, but including healthcare, correct?"

"Of course. So what is your point?"

"Are you not just a lobbyist in non-profit clothing?"

"I deeply resent that. I am no longer a lobbyist."

"Are you being paid for your services as the 'voluntary chair'?"

"Only a single dollar a year."

"While you were the head of that organization, were you at the same time also receiving funds from any other agency, corporation, foundation or business such as The American Management Profit Recovery and Retention Company, or as it is known, TAMPRR Inc.?"

Dillard glared, angry again but this time, just possibly, scared. "*That* is none of *your* goddamned business, whatsoever!"

As the Admiral struggled to regain control, Ken knew that he had hit another bulls-eye. "Oh, but I am afraid that it *may well be* my business, *and* the business of your fellow Canadians."

The Admiral looked towards his bodyguard hard, and nodded once.

The hulk said, "This interview is now over, Mr. Simpson. Thank you for coming and thank you for leaving," as he reached under Ken's upper right arm and nearly pulled it out of its socket while encouraging the impudent reporter to very quickly move away from his charge. Ken decided to help the movement along, for the sake of saving himself the inconvenience of a dislocated shoulder, future osteoarthritis, or worse.

So this is what they do with some retired heavy hitters up here. Same as back home. Isn't the system comfy? If former politicians are appointed by the ruling party to certain quasi-governmental positions, then they aren't to be considered lobbyists. They can then operate as 'consultants' or whatever concocted term they may choose, and continue to do their dealings from the inside.

Ken now had an opening sentence for his next article: *The U.S.-Canada border has long been touted as the longest undefended border in the world. In actual fact, the word 'porous' is a more appropriate term, especially as it relates to the easy flow of undeclared political, military and business influences, and an endless variety of shenanigans.*

Ken was shaken but not stirred enough to be deterred from his quest to find the answers he had come to Canada to get. He decided to call his ex-wife, however, and recommend that Brad be watched very closely, possibly by hiring a legitimate security service. Unfortunately, he still didn't grasp the lengths to which a dying old military man and the American business people around him, would be willing to go in order to continue being able to exert massive influence over America's northern neighbor.

CHAPTER 40

Ken left Admiral Dillard's house via a JATO-assisted push out the front door that continued to accelerate him towards the once again slightly ajar front gate. A last shove assisted him to exit the gate. After he picked himself up off the dirt lane and brushed off his clothes, he ungracefully limped towards the street to the taxi that had waited for him on the soft shoulder of the road. Ken decided to head back to the *Era's* apartment to begin writing the next article that was already forming in his mind.

Once back in the empty apartment, however, he decided that he should first go for a run and sort out the ideas swirling about in his mind. Running did that for him, especially when he was able to use a path that was not interrupted by a lot of cross streets or stop signals.

The ex-cop concierge at the front desk told him that only a couple of blocks away was an entrance onto the four mile long walking and jogging path that paralleled the old Rideau Canal. Once Ken found the path he came upon a bronze plaque announcing that the Rideau canal had originally been a major waterway thoroughfare, and that Ottawa had been chosen as the country's capital in part because the previous nation's capital of Kingston, Ontario, had been determined to be "too close to the Americans" for comfort. Ken smiled.

Just because we attacked the British garrison at Kingston in 1812, the Canadians got nervous. Hell, they repelled us that time, so what were they worried about? Of course, if a company like TAMPRR had existed in 1812, we probably could have bought off one or more British officers who would have then mixed sand in with their gunpowder, thereby rendering it useless, and then they would have assisted in laying out the welcome mat and thanked us for taking Canada off England's hands.

Once Ken began his run he allowed his mind to turn to the matter at hand, specifically how he might further incorporate the information he had acquired since arriving in Canada into his series on healthcare in America.

To start with, of course, there was, according to Lieutenant Colonel Dan Stevens, a crucible of corruption, legislation-influencing, and outright vote-buying created and encouraged by The American Management Profit Recovery and Retention Company.

TAMPRR was apparently well organized in this country, so much so that it was very likely influencing the voting behavior of many members of the Canadian parliament. Granted this was 2009, but who knew for how long TAMPRR had been influencing legislation on Parliament Hill?

Ken was in the habit of interviewing himself, as a means of organizing the information he had gathered about whatever topic he was investigating. As he continued running along the six-foot wide paved path he went through his routine.

Question: Is it possible, or even likely, that TAMPRR is operational in other countries, including 'friendly' nations, doing the same kind of dirty government-influencing activities as it has been doing here in Canada?

The answer to that question is a no-brainer.

A follow-up question: "In what other countries was TAMPRR likely operating?

Answer: Don't know yet, but it is reasonable to assume that the list probably includes England, France, Italy, and Germany, for starters.

Supplementary question: What other U.S. interests are currently being covertly pushed in the hallways of power of America's other, supposedly close allies? And do these other countries do the same with us?

Answer: Don't know, but this kind of action probably does go on everywhere, and is probably carried out by most countries who can afford to do so.

Question: What are TAMPRR's next moves? Would it be possible to uncover one or more operatives, and perhaps even catch them 'in the act'?

Ken quickly realized that he had more good questions than firm answers. There was a lot of work still ahead to uncover more of what was going on here in Canada and the U.S, let alone in other countries.

It was close to 5:15 p.m. when Ken decided to turn around and run back towards the apartment.

The path was now sparsely occupied with walkers and runners, probably because it was dinnertime. Just as he turned, one of two well built, clean cut, CIA look-alikes, running *in three-piece suits,* veered into Ken's space. The man crosschecked Ken into the horizontal pipes that formed the fence-barrier next to the canal.

As he bounced off the pipes and began to crumple to the ground the second goon bent down low, got under Ken's chest and, by quickly and deftly lifting straight up, made Ken's body into an instantly airborne Raggedy Andy.

The very next thing Ken knew, he was upside down in mid-air and flying over the railing. During his descent he heard one of the thugs' dead cold, Brooklyn-born voice saying. "Simpson! This is our greeting card; so back off now, if you don't want you or your kid to…"

The rest of the threat disappeared at the same moment that Ken's head hit the ice, rendering him momentarily unconscious. He came to as he was being helped up onto his feet and off the frozen canal by a couple of surprised but cheery joggers. Unfortunately they had arrived on the scene too late to offer a description of the two men responsible for Ken's brief flight.

"Message received," said Ken under his breath, after he thanked his helpers and started to limp back to the *Era's* apartment. He could almost hear the old soldier who had probably precipitated the scare tactic he had just endured, saying, *"Alright, that's his first and last warning shot. The next time, sink him!"*

CHAPTER 41

When Ken finally arrived, limping, back at the *Era's* apartment, he was still very sore from both the bodycheck and hard landing. Soaking for a half-hour in the bathtub's soothing hot water, he tried to get some perspective on what the hell was going on.

In the few days that had passed since achieving what most of his peers viewed as the height of professional accomplishment, having been awarded the prestigious Paulson prize for Investigative Journalism, Ken had learned that his father had been murdered, his co-investigative reporter–and lover–had been shipped out of the country, and Ken found himself dealing with her substitute, a raven-haired and many years younger, beauty.

He had to admit that Sylkeen seemed sincere but was so damned young and sexy *and seemingly interested in him*, that it appeared distinctly likely that he was being deliberately set up for a trap of some sort.

From Lieutenant Colonel Stevens he had learned that there existed in the U.S.A. at least one company–and who knew how many others–whose sole mission was to service corporate clients by securing their pre-eminence in their particular areas of business by whatever tactics might accomplish their goals.

Ken had also learned a great deal about the Avro Arrow, and how the program had been sabotaged, and many of its key people acquired by certain U.S. aircraft companies.

He had also met some quite senior citizens, one of whom, Dr. Larson, was a physician-healer whose ethical commitment to serving his patients-citizens had probably cost him his job and, perhaps also, his health.

He had interviewed a Scottish psychiatrist and a retired historian, both of whom had formerly worked as engineers on the Arrow program. He had also met two elderly ex-military men, Lieutenant Colonel Dan Stevens and Admiral Dillard, who had sold out their respective countries for... *for what?* Power? Position? Profit? All of the above?

As he reflected upon the people he had seen over the past few days, it seemed to Ken that Canadians and Americans were very similar in most ways, with good guys and bad guys, and the whole gamut in-between. And given what he had learned about TAMPRR's existence and what it had been up to over the years, he was forced to consider that on both sides of the border there were those who would sell out their mothers and their children, if only the price was right.

At the same time it seemed that there was something different in the Canadian people's collective consciousness that had led–or forced–their successive governments to adopt very different attitudes from America in many important areas–towards matters such as gays' right to marriage, decriminalizing possession of small amounts of marijuana, and ways of resolving international issues without the use of excessive force. In the latter matter, and especially in more recent years, Canadians seemed to compulsively seek consultation and collaboration while Americans were keener to endorse confrontation.

Ken poured himself a fine single malt, possibly left behind by a bored, hard-drinking reporter of the old school, from the otherwise meagerly stocked liquor cabinet. He considered the likelihood that Stevens was not overstating the case when he suggested that Ken's own life, and possibly that of his son, were in jeopardy so long as he continued to investigate what was happening to the Canadian healthcare system, and the role that certain American businesses might be playing in its deterioration.

Of one thing he was sure: the stakes, whatever they were, must be damned high to have people carrying out such acts of intimidation as he had just experienced during his run along the Rideau Canal.

After another few minutes of contemplation, Ken reached for his cellphone, took a deep breath, and called his ex-wife. Her familiar–but emotionally distant–voice sounded quite surprised and somewhat suspicious of his call. Without going into any explanation, and not wanting to have her descend into an even more intense paranoia than he himself was now experiencing,

Ken simply told Nancy that he had received some veiled threats aimed at himself and his loved ones. He quickly added that they were likely the articulated gnashing of some garden variety nutcase that most major columnists receive from time to time. Hearing from his ex that their son was fine and was at that very moment downstairs playing on a computer, Ken felt his bodily tension ease markedly.

Ken asked to speak to Brad. After a thoroughly enjoyable twenty-minute conversation with his son, discussing a variety of topics, including his schooling, sports and music activities, and their planned upcoming spring break trip to Disneyland, Ken said goodbye to Brad and asked to speak to Nancy once again.

"Listen, Nanc, for the next few weeks anyways, it might just be a good idea to keep him close to home, or at least where there is going to be some responsible adult around whom you trust."

After taking one on the chin because it was "too bad you weren't ever one of those," Ken reiterated his concern, knowing that, no matter what she said in response, Nancy would watch over their son like a hawk for the next several weeks, or more likely, months. Hopefully his healthcare series and its fallout would be resolved long before that period of time had elapsed.

As he set his drink down on the kitchen counter he saw the folded-over note with his name on it, written in Martha's neat—especially for a reporter—handwriting. He unfolded the sheet of paper and read, *"Hi, Ken: the office called. Rusty said that all media outlets had received word from the Prime Minister's office that he is going to deliver a major speech the day after tomorrow. There is some speculation he might be going to say something about his own future and/or that of the Canadian healthcare system. The wonderful Trish Markridge, will apparently be with him when the announcement is made. By the way, I will miss you tonight. Martha. P.S. I hear that my 'replacement', the unbelievably ugly Sylkeen Bowry, is coming up to join you tomorrow. Be good... or... whatever. See ya."*

Ken thought, *So! In the couple of days everyone will know what the PM is planning regarding healthcare. Good. Wonder what TAMPRR will do when the PM lets everyone in on the scoop. Maybe Stevens can give me a heads up early enough so that I can begin to write...*

The phone rang with some of the information he wanted, but from a different source. The caller was Dr. Brown, saying that at the PM's press conference he would be taking some dramatic steps to move his healthcare plan forward. Perhaps as importantly, she had personally called Trish Markridge, and the latter was willing to meet with Ken, if he would agree to keep the meeting and its content off the record, at least until she might give him the go-ahead to print particular parts of what she might have to say to him.

"Would those terms be acceptable to you, Mr. Simpson?"

"Absolutely, Dr. Brown. When and where would she like..."

Dr. Brown cut him off. "You would have to meet her within the hour. She has to leave her home to catch a government plane right afterwards, in order to get out west to join the Prime Minister. And I am sorry to say that you will only have about forty minutes to..."

"That's fine. I could leave now, if you like."

"That's good. I will pick you up in front of your building in ten minutes. It is best if I drive you because the police and the press are quite used to seeing my old clunker pull into her driveway and park around the back of her house. Is that all right with you?"

'That's great,' said Ken.

"See you shortly, then, Mr. Simpson."

The news that Martha was out of town and that Sylkeen was coming to Ottawa was quite exciting, he had to admit, although he did feel some discomfort which he labeled, or at least heard his former therapist's voice label, as 'anticipatory guilt', that is, guilt about something wrong he had not yet even done.

After Dr. Brown's call Ken quickly turned on his laptop, and got onto the net through his privately-paid-for Internet service provider. Once online, he sent an e-mail to Lieutenant Colonel Dan Stevens, calling him "Uncle Dan" as they had agreed, saying that he was having a lovely time in Ottawa, how it was so clean and neat and so on, and using the special encrypted 'hidden comment' feature Stevens had given him as a download. He then filled him in on the highlights of what he had experienced and been subjected to during his time in Ottawa and pressed the 'send' button.

Less than five minutes later he received a "I wish I was there, too" e-mail, and 'selected' the word "there", which brought up a password query. Even when Ken responded correctly to the request for the password, the screen did not immediately respond. After several seconds during which time the screen offered a dancing mobile for him to amuse himself with, a deciphered e-mail revealed itself on the screen. He read the message with interest.

Hello, Ken:

I am very pleased and relieved to hear that you are all right. The messengers you met on your run almost certainly came from TAMPRR. Please, be careful.

Another thing. I have reason to believe that Trish Markridge is in much greater danger now that the word has gotten around that the PM is taking her out to western Canada where he is supposedly going to be making a major announcement about ensuring that the Canadian healthcare system's deterioration will stop.

Download the attached document now to get more of a sense of whom you are dealing with.

Stay in touch via e-mail and let me know what happens.

Signed,

D.S.

Ken downloaded the attachment and unencrypted it as instructed by Stevens. It was, apparently, a briefing note intended for newly hired employees of The American Management Profit Recovery and Retention Company. Stevens's accompanying note stated that it was never allowed to leave the room where it was shown to new employees, just once.

WELCOME TO *THE AMERICAN MANAGEMENT PROFIT RECOVERY AND RETENTION COMPANY [TAMPRR Inc.]*

Congratulations. You have been chosen to be one of our organization's new, crucially important operatives. Let us acquaint you with our in-house terminology and some key methods of operation.

<u>*First the words that will now become part of your daily thinking:*</u>

<u>BizWar:</u> the business of TAMPRR is civilized, preferably bloodless war-making on businesses, foreign governments, and power/media controllers, as per our contractual arrangements with our clients.

<u>BizBattle:</u> an action taken in the service of winning the BizWar.

<u>BizArmy:</u> Make no mistake; this is what you have joined. We have hired you, and are providing you with an excellent income, real adventure, and solid teamwork opportunities, as well as all necessary tools, including training and backup, to assist you in carrying out your responsibilities. Your previous experience in the CIA, Special Forces, or other specialized branches of our government and military have been your teachers. Now you are graduates about to enter full-time work.

Of course, there are a few other BizArmies who also offer their services to corporations, the military, and selected persons in the current administration. What makes TAMPRR unique is <u>you</u>... and <u>us</u>. WE WERE AMONG THE FIRST, AND WE ARE STILL THE BEST!

Our company's fees are scaled to the degree of difficulty of the project, and the estimated value of the success we... you... will achieve. Therefore, we usually only accept contracts where we are virtually certain of obtaining the results that our clients desire. Our 'bonus for success' formula has made us– and will make you– far wealthier than most of those who have served our country ever dared to dream. So welcome aboard.

One of the hallmarks of successful achievement is that while the results of our efforts can be measured, our presence and hands-on involvement must remain undetectable. Ours is a

Stealth Force. We don't show up on others' radar screens. Whenever possible, we operate in black-black configuration. If you are apprehended, charged or convicted for any action you undertake in the service of fulfilling the contract you have been assigned, you are never to reveal this organization's real goals. It will be increasingly worth your while to keep matters pertaining to TAMPRR confidential. Meanwhile, as your income continues, the Swiss bank account we hold for you (and into which your bonuses are also deposited) will grow and your ample retirement package will expand.

Of course, you will understand that if you commit any major action without authorization, or if you ever reveal the purpose or even the existence of us and our goals, other than those which we will provide you for 'public consumption' by your closest friends and relatives, then the consequences to you will undoubtedly be the most serious possible, and your monies will become unavailable to you–permanently.

Signed, Jake Marks, Colonel, U.S.A.F. (Retired)

CEO, The American Management Profit Recovery and Retention Company

This note must not be saved, printed or photographed; it will now dissolve without a trace anywhere on your computer's system."

Seconds later the words became fainter until they disappeared into the screen.

Ken sent an e-mail response back to Stevens, acknowledging having received and read his e-mail. He added a small note mentioning his new investigative reporting 'partner', Sylkeen Bowry, and the fact that, within hours, she was coming to Ottawa to join him. He also referred to his nagging sense that she might not be entirely trustworthy, although he had no definitive evidence for his impression. Stevens did not respond to this e-mail in the additional minutes Ken spent doing online searches on the Prime Minister.

As Ken was closing down the computer, the concierge called and told him that someone was waiting for him. Ken hurriedly left the apartment and took the elevator to the front lobby. He could see Dr. Brown's car at the entrance.

Ken had no way of knowing that the next few hours, days, and weeks would leave him re-evaluating his ways of viewing the worlds of politics and of business.

CHAPTER 42

With Ken laying across the back seat of her car, out of sight, Dr. Brown was waved through by the familiar security guard at the gate to Trish Markridge's home, and she parked in one of the several spaces at the back of the large stone house. She and Ken walked up the back steps and entered the house. Just inside the door, waiting for them with energized eyes and a lovely smile framed by long blond hair, was a tall and wholesomely beautiful woman in her forties. The extended hand that Ken shook was strong yet feminine.

The Honorable Trish Markridge, Member of Parliament, said in a firm, melodious voice, "Hello, Mr. Simpson. Judith has said such complimentary things about you. Would you care to come into the den where we can sit and talk comfortably?"

Ken said, "Thank you very much," already charmed by her down-to-earth manner.

Trish Markridge said, "Judith, dear, would you please excuse us for the next while? I made your favorite biscotti, so please make yourself at home. The decaf is freshly made, too. As you know, I have to leave within the hour so we won't be too long."

"That's fine, Trish. Go ahead. I will amuse myself here with the latest Scientific American that I spy on your breakfast table. But I warn you, I might also delve into your cookbooks and see if I can spot the recipe for that parchment-wrapped baked salmon you made the other night that was so divine."

Trish Markridge laughed, and said, "Try the book on the counter over there." She pointed out the one she meant, and added, "Although I must admit that having brought the just-caught salmon back with me when I came back from Halifax undoubtedly added a lot to the taste."

From their easy banter it was clear that the two women were very dear friends.

Ken followed the statuesque politician into the den, and when they sat down in two easy chairs that faced one another at an angle, he was given the answer to one of the questions that he had posed to himself earlier in the day. It wasn't simply that the woman was still 'mature beauty pageant' material; there was an energy that she manifested which made everything she said... well, *brighter*, somehow. The woman definitely had charisma–big time. Her captivating gaze signaled that she was giving him her full attention.

She said, "Judith called earlier today and told me of her meeting with you at her clinic. She has a keen nose for professional excellence and integrity, and she believes you have both in good measure. And at this point in time, Mr. Simpson, we are very much in need of both qualities, especially amongst members of the media as well as politicians."

Ken asked, "Why is that, Dr. Markridge?"

"Well, I will tell you. My country currently is standing on the brink of moving strongly forward in one of two directions–in politics, business, healthcare, and social consciousness. It would frankly be most helpful for our purposes to have an at-arms-length, interested, and prominent media person such as yourself, who is not just very much respected but would also be deeply informed on the subject of our healthcare system. But before I go on I would like to clarify that we must be agreed that our conversation is to stay 'off the record', until I release you from that obligation."

"You have my assurance that that will be the case, Dr. Markridge. For the sake of accuracy and clarity, though, do you mind if I make some notes?"

"Not at all."

Ken said, "Thank you." He took his notepad out of his jacket pocket. "Given our time limitations, might I suggest that we proceed to the direct reason you were willing to speak with me?"

Trish Markridge nodded, seemed thoughtful for a moment, and then said, "Mr. Simpson, I have a great deal of faith in people and institutions, especially those in the so-called democracies. I therefore choose to believe that most persons, including most of those in politics, business, the so-called helping professions, and the media, are basically honest and ethical in their working and private lives. I therefore think that most persons and organizations in my country and yours are what we can call good individual and corporate citizens. Do you think me naïve for holding these views?"

Ken was taken aback by being asked to comment on Markridge's views on such matters. However, he replied, "Not at all. I am also an optimist, and believe, as you do, that the majority of people are essentially good and usually do behave honorably, especially when they are given information in a full, understandable, and honest fashion. And this is in spite of the fact that, like you, I am also a realist, and being in the vocation I am in, I have seen more than my share of the opposite sort of behavior from individuals, as well as corporate, military, and other organizational entities. However, I have no doubt that the real bad apples are in the minority."

Markridge nodded her agreement. Then she said, "Let us speak, then, in confidence, about federal and provincial politicians in this country. Of course, most of them are fine and honorable women and men. However, our national and provincial police forces as well as our national security people have uncovered untoward contacts and liaisons involving certain individuals and organizations that suggest, among other things, that some politicians' elections were strongly supported, or not to put too fine a point on it, were essentially bought and paid for, Stateside.

"We have strong evidence, for example, that major elements in the current governments of our largest and wealthiest provinces has been compromised by certain American corporations whose primary goals are to influence specific Canadian governmental initiatives so that their own agendas would be inserted into this country, probably to reinforce their own positions back in America."

Ken was listening and writing, and wondering whether she was aware of TAMPRR. He also thought about whether to share Colonel Dan Stevens's concern for her safety.

Markridge continued. "For example, you are probably aware of the term 'P3', which means 'public-private partnership', and is frequently used to describe certain initiatives that some of our provincial governments enter into with private enterprise organizations. In this country P3s have been entered into in a variety of fields, including toll road building. Of course, some of these developments are entirely appropriate and serve the purposes and needs of our citizens in excellent ways. At the same time, and on the other hand, I have it on good authority that a few of these programs are probably 'Trojan horses'; in other words, they are intended to act as the thin edge of a wedge aimed at cracking open and eventually tearing apart our government-run Medicare system. And they have to be stopped."

Ken asked, "How can that be done?"

Trish Markridge replied, "To start with–and believe me that it is only a beginning–by entrenching our Medicare system in our Charter of Rights and Freedoms, and/or by creating a new Canadian Charter of Healthcare Rights and Freedoms. Those initiatives will be announced within a couple of days as the new goal of our Prime Minister, and that is my own goal as well–as a physician, as a politician, as a socially conscious individual, and as an unabashedly proud Canadian."

Ken nodded to signify that he was listening keenly. She went on for several more minutes, elaborating upon what plans she had in mind in order to achieve her goals. She referred to polls that repeatedly made it clear that Canadians wanted their provincial and federal governments to stop using healthcare as a political football, and get on with working together to provide this service to Canadians in an expert, efficient, and accountable manner. She even used some rather choice words to describe provincial premier George P. Linden who, she said, was already in the pockets of some HMOs.

Markridge said, "There is no way that that man will use federal funds that are given over to his province for their designated purposes within healthcare. Instead he blusters on and on about how no one is going to tell *him* and *his province* what to do with the healthcare money that is rightly theirs. And besides which, he continually says, his province, which incidentally is the wealthiest in our country, can't afford government-run and funded Medicare. What a crock that is. Why, his province is so rich it could fund Medicare at a *national* level! What he really means is that he will not allow publicly financed and run universal Medicare to succeed, no matter what. And we know that the man sold out years ago to American interests, for his own financial gain."

Now Markridge paused, shook her head, and laughed out loud at what she called, "The charade of the corrupt. It is up to the rest of us to not let bullies, stonewallers, and saboteurs like Linden get away with destroying one of the finest achievements of this country!"

Ken had been observing Trish Markridge very closely as she spoke. She was, of course, self-assured. But there was much more to her; she seemed… authentic. It was crystal clear that she would be an irresistible force in pursuit of her goal. He also knew now what he had to do, what he had to say.

'Dr. Markridge, I very much appreciate your telling me what problems you believe you are dealing with in this country and what you intend to do to pursue your goals of preserving the healthcare system in your country. As I promised, I will not share this information with anyone until and unless I have your permission."

Trish Markridge said, "Thank you. I appreciate you reiterating that." She then went on for several more minutes, laying out the details of some of her plans to encourage her fellow citizens and politicians to get behind her efforts.

Ken listened closely, only nodding occasionally as she articulated her audacious intentions. Then, employing a deliberately softened tone in his voice, he asked, "What about the possibility of your not being in a position to provide me with the go-ahead to write about what you have told me today? May I use this information, in that event?"

Markridge physically recoiled. Momentarily thrown off guard, she asked, "What did you mean when you say, "not being in a position to…" "?

Ken went for it. "Dr. Markridge, I truly regret to inform you that I have recently received undoubtedly reliable information that suggests that, at this very moment, you are in grave danger."

"What? How could you…?"

"I have my own sources, sources that your security forces

have apparently either not yet uncovered or disclosed to you. I have been told that you may never have the opportunity to do what you say you intend."

"I don't understand. Why would *you* have such a source...?"

"Dr. Markridge, the same source told me what you and the Prime Minister were planning to do even before you yourself told me. That same source has informed me that one of sort of shadowy companies that you referred to is The American Management Recovery and Retention Company, or TAMPRR Incorporated, headquartered in Miami Beach. TAMPRR has actually been working diligently, for over ten years, to help bring about the privatization of your Canadian healthcare system. And I am afraid that the principals of that company have concluded that *you* are currently the major remaining obstacle to the completion of their mission. And they already know what you and the Prime Minister have in mind. They intend to not let it happen."

Trish Markridge crumpled back into her chair, dumbfounded at what she was hearing. She asked, "May I ask Judith to join us, Mr. Simpson? I think I could use her mature wisdom at this moment."

Ken said, "Of course."

A moment after Trish Markridge called for her, Judith Brown entered the room like a mother hen who had just detected her offspring's voice signaling imminent danger. Markridge asked Ken to repeat what he had just told her. He did so, and saw fear overtake Brown's countenance. Dr. Brown asked a few questions, and then the two women talked directly to one another.

Ken had decided that he would tell them everything except for the name of his contact. However, he did explain to them that he was keeping a promise and that if what he was telling them was inappropriately disclosed, then there was a very high probability that his own life and that of his son, plus that of his sole prime contact, would all be in immediate jeopardy.

The three of them discussed plans that might thwart TAMPRR's possible actions. Trish Markridge decided, and the other two concurred, that her own security detail had to be informed about these matters. She pushed a button on the small black beeper-like device Ken had not earlier noticed on her belt. In a calm voice, she called the head of the detail.

While waiting for him to arrive, Trish Markridge briefly brought Ken up to speed about the embarrassing security problems that several RCMP security details had encountered years earlier, including the case of an intruder who was knocked unconscious by a previous PM's wife, after gaining entrance to their official residence undetected by officers stationed on the grounds. Since then, and a few of other 'keystone cops'-type faux pas, the force had tightened up its procedures, big-time.

Sergeant Delzatto arrived less than a minute later from his station in the guesthouse located near the back of the substantial property. His right hand was deep inside his suit jacket. A short but powerfully built, RCMP officer with a full head of graying hair, he was clearly initially off put by the presence of an unscreened individual at an unscheduled meeting at his charge's home that had evidently been discussing matters of his charge's security.

Markridge quickly got him calmed down and focused, however, when she revealed that it was Ken who had just provided information about a possible imminent threat on her life. Once he had heard Ken out, and had had at least some of his very pointed questions answered, it was difficult for Ken to assess whether Delzatto's bright red face was due more to embarrassment or anger at his own security force being oblivious to the very existence of, let alone the danger posed by, a covert, foreign organization called TAMPRR.

Before the officer could question Ken further about how he knew of the supposed threat, Markridge stopped Delzatto by saying that as a reporter, Ken was obliged to keep his source's identity confidential, and that any attempt to force the issue would have the most undesirable effect of closing off the only pipeline they now had to this previously unknown threat. From Delzatto's facial expression it was obvious to Ken that the sergeant might prefer to have Ken alone for a while to discuss the matter further in private.

Ken told the RCMP officer that, since the potential danger was possibly coming from ex-CIA and ex-special forces types, it was conceivable that, because of the close ties between the two countries' security establishments, Delzatto's own security detail's integrity may have even been breached.

Watching the senior national police force officer bristle was an intimidating spectacle. Delzatto was not the sort who would ever allow anything to happen to his charge, *not on his watch*. But bad apples were part of every police force, so he did not take offense at Ken's comment for longer than it took for him to decide that he would personally re-interview all of the men and women under his command, and have checks made on all their movements, contacts, e-mails, etc... He was too much of a professional to get personally defensive.

Sergeant Delzatto assured Trish Markridge and Dr. Brown that he would take all steps necessary to prevent anything untoward from occurring to either of them.

If only the sergeant were right!

CHAPTER 43

After their meeting with Trish Markridge, Dr. Brown drove Ken back to the paper's apartment. As they pulled up to the entrance of the building, she stopped the car, put it in neutral, undid her seatbelt, and then leaned over and planted a loud, motherly kiss on Ken's cheek.

She said, "Thank you, Ken, so much, for caring, and for *daring* to seek out the facts in your investigations, and for sharing the information that might well save my dear friend, Trish, from harm, to say nothing of the country from again being the victim of what you referred to earlier as a very dirty 'bizwar'. God knows those people have already done enough damage. The citizens of both our nations obviously need to become much more aware of the dangers that lurk out there, especially from individuals who care about making money and increasing their hold on power, than anything else."

Ken thanked her for her part in making his trip to Ottawa as informative and hopefully, as useful as they both wished. When they finished their goodbyes he got out of the car and waited until she pulled away and re-entered the late night street traffic flow. As he turned and walked into the building, however, he felt a cold shiver whose usual meaning he recognized only too well. He hoped he was wrong.

Riding up on the elevator, Ken mentally reviewed his visit to Trish Markridge. He was confident that he had done the right thing in telling her about the potential threat of TAMPRR to the future of the Canadian healthcare system and, perhaps as well, to herself. At ten-thirty in the evening, a half-hour after entering the apartment and getting ready for bed, Ken was in a deep, if fitful sleep.

The next morning, from 5:30 a.m. on, Ken lay in bed, wide awake, thinking. He stayed there until his wristwatch alarm went off at seven-thirty. After showering, dressing, having a small breakfast, and glancing at the morning editions of a local paper as well as *The New York Era* that had been delivered to the apartment door, Ken went to his computer and e-mailed Stevens, telling him what he had done the night before, including the fact that he had informed Trish Markridge about the existence of, and threat posed by, TAMPRR Inc. He added that now that it's existence was known to Canada's security forces he hoped that its influence might be on the wane. He didn't know how Stevens would respond to the news, but hoped that he would understand that Ken's actions were necessary.

In his e-mail's IN box was one that had been sent by Martha. She wrote that she had managed to arrange an interview with the current federal Minister of Health, Timmy Cemente for the next day, one that she had assumed she and Ken would be doing together. However, since she was now traveling with the Prime Minister, she hoped that Ken would be able to keep the appointment, "even if it means that you will be doing it with your newest little partner."

Ken suddenly realized that, if Rusty knew of the personal relationship between Martha and himself, then so might TAMPRR. In his reply to her e-mail, Ken told Martha to be especially on guard for any "bad guys", without elaborating. He wanted her to be wary, not worried.

Just as he was finishing sending the note, the apartment's concierge called up and informed him, in a rather snooty if not downright insinuating, tone, that a *very* young lady, *Ms.* Bowry had arrived. Ignoring the import of the tone he heard, Ken requested that the concierge let her in.

Less than a minute later, there was a knock at the door. Ken guessed that she had been informed that she could get her own key to the apartment by simply showing her *New York Era* identification, so the call up from security and the subsequent knock on the door were undoubtedly acts of courtesy, perhaps aimed at preventing an embarrassing situation. Ken opened the door and immediately experienced the feelings and sensations that had struck him when he had visited Sylkeen at her New York City apartment a few days earlier.

"Hello, Ken," said Sylkeen in her usual warm, sensual voice. She was wearing a parka open at the front, a smart white blouse, and a mid-length navy blue skirt. The friendly smile and flashing eyes were somewhat surprising yet particularly welcome, given that he had not bothered to inform her, two days earlier, that he planned to leave town and come to Ottawa.

"Hi." responded Ken, "How was your flight?"

"Just fine, thanks."

"Good. Listen, I was just getting ready to head out the door; I've got a meeting in about thirty minutes with the Canadian Minister of Health. Care to join me?" *Might as well try to make things up to her a little.*

In a somewhat playful yet pointed response, Sylkeen said, "Sure, great. I was beginning to think that perhaps you didn't need any help with the healthcare series."

Ken decided to not go there. He straightforwardly replied, "Of course I do. And this way we can get to know one another's interviewing style. We can get caught up on the way."

Her voice virtually purred when she responded, "Wonderful! I really want to learn as much as I can about you... and your style."

Ken saw her eyes widen innocently and noticed her lips part ever so slightly as her tongue peaked out from between them. *What the hell was she up to? Whatever it was, it was probably working.*

Then she said, "Just let me use the facilities for a minute and I will be right with you. Okay?"

"Fine. We can be there in about ten minutes. I'll go downstairs and hail a cab." Seeing her look past him and around at the apartment, Ken said, "The powder room is just down the hallway to the end, and then hang a right, second door."

She nodded, tossed her head back as she walked past him and said, "Back in a flash."

Ken watched her move down the hallway, brimming with youthful assurance. *Damn. I am turning into a dirty old man. Maybe looking at attractive women in their twenties, thirties, and forties is hardwired into the males of the species. Either that, or else I'm a pervert! Thank goodness we are getting the hell out of the quasi-intimacy of this apartment.*

Although he wasn't sure where they would go after the interview with the Minister of Health, Ken decided that it would probably be wise to not come back to the apartment too soon. So, he called out to Sylkeen that he was going downstairs and would meet her out in front of the building.

He heard her reply, "Fine. Be right down."

Ken quickly exited the apartment.

CHAPTER 44

Their appointment with the Canadian Minister of Health, the Honorable Timmy Cemente, was scheduled for 10:30 a.m.. As they sat beside one another in the back seat of the cab with a proper space of several inches separating their bodies, Ken retrieved out of his briefcase the file that Martha had prepared on their interviewee. He and Sylkeen read quickly though it.

The bio and photos in the file described Timmy Cemente as a 6' 6" tall, 290 pound, ex-professional football player. Now fifty-six years old, his handsome, if somewhat frightening, face could have easily given him an alternate career as a bit actor playing the role of a mafia hit-man.

Timmy Cemente, Minister of Health, according to his biography on the ruling party's oh-so-friendly website, was still the principal owner of a nation-wide fast-food chain called PlumpPizza, a company that had its own brand of chutzpah, having expanded (that being the operative word) across the country via its aggressive takeovers of its competitors' outlets. According to an accompanying article in his file, his company was known for using mucho saturated and trans fats in its tasty products; the writer had hypothesized that "the chain's unofficial mission statement seems to be that of providing *'the most efficient artery-clogging fat delivery systems'*, much as cigarettes were now known to be manufactured to operate as optimum nicotine and carcinogen delivery systems to the human body." The tattle-tale Citizen's Institute For The Employment Of Nutritional Health Science had awarded Cemente's company's products "5-clogged arteries plus a stroke," the highest, i.e., *worst*, rating they ever awarded, for its *eighty* grams of saturated plus trans fat *per slice!*

Just the kind of guy you want as Minister of Health. Incredible!

In another article Ken read aloud, one of Canada's most

prominent investigative reporters stated that, "Since taking over the health ministry portfolio Cemente has reportedly received a fifteen million dollar investment in his pizza company from a company owned by American interests, including a major HMO." Apparently, the deal included providing PlumpPizza with virtually free rental space in the food concourses of all of the HMO's hospitals across the U.S.. Ken read that a review of the matter by the government's own laughably termed 'independent ethics consultant' that followed the appearance of the article, concluded that Cemente's incorporated company, not himself personally, had received the admittedly "exceedingly generous lease arrangements" with the aforementioned hospitals.

Another five million dollars U.S. that he had personally received from the same HMO a few weeks before he had assumed his ministerial duties, the same ethics consultant had concluded, had appropriately been paid for Cemente's 'consultations' to the HMO for sharing his "expert knowledge of the potentially beneficial effects of nutritional food distribution systems on the general state of physical health and well-being of a nation's people". Ken and Sylkeen both laughed and shook their heads in amazement and disgust.

The cab dropped them off at the entrance to the grounds of the Canadian parliament buildings. Ken and Sylkeen walked up the driveway that led directly to the Peace Tower that fronted and bisected the main government building, the 'center block'.

A Kevlar-vested RCMP officer was waiting for them at the front entrance to the building when they arrived; at his request Ken and Sylkeen signed in and, after an intensive but courteous security screening, they followed along behind him towards Cemente's office. On the way they signaled to one another how impressed they each were with the old building's beautiful stonework and the paintings of prominent Canadian politicians and events that decorated the walls they walked past. Sylkeen whispered to Ken that the building seemed to have a much more British than American 'feel' to it. Ken indicated that he concurred.

When they reached the Minister of Health's office, the security guard knocked twice. Within seconds, the imposing wooden door with the minister's title and name on it swung open and as pseudo-suave and bordering-on-greasy a character as Ken would ever want to avoid meeting, emerged with his larger-than-life grin aimed in the direction of Sylkeen.

Ken introduced himself to the minister. The latter, without taking his eyes off Sylkeen, extended his hand in the general direction of Ken's voice. *Can't say as how I blame you, but a little less obviousness wouldn't be out of order.*

For the next few moments Ken sensed that he had ceased to exist. This fact may have helped him to shake off the minister's admittedly peculiar sort of charm somewhat more quickly than apparently did Sylkeen, perhaps partly because the Honorable Mr. Cemente hadn't kissed *his* hand, nor aimed any 'me-powerful-man-you-sexual-object' shtick at *him*! *Ah, lucky Sylkeen. Or, actually, come to think of it, luckier me!* Ken noticed that Sylkeen had turned on her own jets in return and Cemente responded by so very warmly inviting them both to *please* come into his private office where they could speak more comfortably. *Hell, if her charms work on the big guy and help us get somewhere useful, then great.*

Still without taking his eyes off Sylkeen for more than an instant, Cemente said, "Mr. Simpson and... *Miss* Bowry, is it? How very good of you and *The New York Era* to be taking an interest in our country and its healthcare system."

Ken couldn't think of how the man's tone of voice could have sounded less genuine.

The rounds of surface pleasantries lasted just long enough for the minister's assistant to appear carrying a tray with some bottled water and three glasses with ice and lime. The pleasant but otherwise nondescript helper exited immediately after setting the tray down on the coffee table.

The Honorable Timmy Cemente, M.P., Minister of Health, said, too warmly, "Now, what does *The New York Era*, and what do *you* (said to Sylkeen exclusively) want to know about?"

As prearranged as they walked up Parliament Hill, Sylkeen was prepared to speak first, in her best 'good cop' fashion.

"Well, firstly, thank you *so much* for seeing us, Mr. Cemente. Our paper is doing, or to be more precise, *Mr. Simpson and I* are doing a series on healthcare in various countries. Of course, with Canada being our closest neighbor, and with your health system being so often spoken of as a model for us to examine closely, if not emulate extensively, we had hoped to learn from you firsthand what state you believe the Canadian healthcare system to be in, and what initiatives and directions you might be promoting during your government's mandate."

Ken was impressed with the manner in which Sylkeen had succinctly summarized their supposed purpose in being there.

Cemente replied, "Well, of course, we intend to continue to grow what, to Canadians, is one of our most prized institutions. We are going to keep on expanding the available medical services, personnel, and equipment throughout the country. Those are our goals, and I can assure you that we are well on the way to accomplishing them in every way."

Now Ken horned in, although Clemente didn't even bother to look at him until he was halfway through his opening salvo. "Minister, would you care to comment on the rumor that, in fact, when your government came into power after the last election, your Prime Minister employed 'consultants' who, up to the time they were hired as such, had actually worked as lobbyists for some of *our* American HMOs and pharmaceutical companies?"

Ken thought the man might get severe whiplash from the manner in which he snapped his head in his direction and then recoiled it backwards so as to look down his long nose in Ken's obviously odious direction.

Before Clemente could get past "Now, listen here...," Ken said, "And what about other reports that some elements in your government are now pressing the Prime Minister to open wide the door to American-style health management organizations and insurance companies through some so-called P-3, 'public-private partnerships', free-standing medical clinics, and even full-fledged hospitals?"

Cemente's demeanor changed just a little as his gangster's eyes took aim at Ken. His initial reply, possibly due to having been temporarily knocked off balance by this American duo, had the right words but were set to decidedly limp music. Feigning a weak smile, Clemente said, "Now, look, I can assure you both that my government is committed to permitting no such thing. At the same time, of course, we *are* intent on exploring all possible avenues of improving our healthcare system."

Ken jumped on Cemente's last sentence. "I am sure you are well aware, Minister, of the artificially created crises in energy and energy distribution that some of those in business and government in my country created, in order to push through their agendas for more deregulation and market price setting competition in the energy field."

Cemente said coldly, "Of course. But what does that have to do with what we are discussing?"

Ken accepted the invitation. "Well, isn't it true that during your tenure as Minister of Health, you, together with some of your provincial counterparts, have in effect and in fact, restricted the number of qualified MRI and other technicians who could come into Canada? And haven't your respective governments precipitated other serious personnel and material shortages that threaten the very viability of your Medicare system?"

Cemente's red face looked as if it was about to explode in flames. Ken charged on, quickly.

"And isn't it also true that the medical and support staff at many of your hospitals that had very satisfactory MRI, CAT scan, and other specialized equipment, pleaded with your government to let them run the machines for sixteen or even twenty-four hours a day, seven days a week, in order to shrink their waitlists. And that you and your cohorts refused such permission, thereby creating unnecessary long waiting times?"

Ken could see Cemente's eyes narrowing into slits but that he was, for now, holding off until Ken had finished, and then he would likely want to squash the invasive and insolent journalist.

Ken charged on. "And after having *manufactured* these crises, didn't you then declare that privately-owned and operated clinics absolutely *had* to allowed to be set up and operated for the sake of those Canadians who needed such services but couldn't get them in a timely fashion at the publicly run hospitals?

"You son of a bitch. And *you...!*" he said in his most wounded affectation, glancing in Sylkeen's direction. Cemente really was beside himself. Although not an unattractive color if it were a shirt or sweater, the crimson-toned and very large head on the former professional football player's neck now appeared downright volcanic in its potential. Since the only kind of stroke he had been seeking in letting go both barrels so quickly was a stroke of *luck*, Ken almost felt sorry he had pushed so hard so fast. *But, this guy and his friends play far more lethally with their own people's lives, so to hell with them.*

Sylkeen was staring wide-eyed at Ken. He purposely had not given her any advance notice of his intention to try to shake Clemente out of his tree; he didn't know if she would approve, or maybe even go into a protective stance on behalf of the Minister of Health.

Maybe if I hadn't been tossed onto the Rideau Canal! Or if they hadn't threatened my son! Anyway, screw them!

Clemente said nothing but looked away as if he were considering whether to allow this arrogant American reporter-pimp and his whore to go on breathing. Ken had seen the look before. A recent American president had perfected the look. Ken knew he had only a limited amount of time and opportunity left, and after glancing at Sylkeen and seeing that she seemed stunned by his aggressive approach, he looked back at Cemente and went for it all.

Cemente started to say something banal that sounded like, "You two don't understand the nuances of political life..." but Ken cut him off, saying, "And isn't it also true, sir, that successive Canadian federal and provincial governments, as well as other interested parties, have been playing a kind of a shell game where various monies that could or should be earmarked for specific improvements, appear to move mysteriously in and out of various departmental pockets without ever landing anywhere in the healthcare system?"

Now Ken appreciated how opposing football players must have felt when this former defensive tackle had determined that the only way his team could win the game was if he was able to bring down the other team's key player, permanently.

The Canadian Minister of Health really looked like he wanted to hurt Ken–very badly. He said, his voice rising in loudness and energy as he spoke, "Before you both leave my office, which will be shortly, I want to assure *you*, Mr. Simpson, that what you have been spouting these last minutes–*all of it*–is pure bullshit. You have obviously been reading too many of our opponent's sympathetic newspapers, especially the scandalous Ottawa Star. Everything you have said could not be further from the truth. In actual fact, all of us in my party and among most of the premiers of the provincial governments have been doing our level best to save Medicare. It is just that some things simply can't be sav..."

The minister suddenly stopped talking. Seasoned politician that he was, he seldom allowed the press to piss him off to the point that he lost his cool. He tried to paste his cat-smile back in place, but it kept sliding off.

Ken had memorized the material Lieutenant Colonel Stevens had e-mailed him. He pressed on. "Well, could you tell me whether it is true that you are fighting in cabinet to get the go-ahead to place a piece of legislation before parliament that in fact not only allows, but encourages and in fact gives, tax incentives to private companies that want to establish privately run, for-profit clinics the size of medium-sized or even full-sized hospitals, to carry out medical procedures such as heart bypasses, organ transplants, and cancer treatments, and that these centers will be able to charge direct fees to their customers, er, ... patients, that will be above and beyond what the government would pay public facilities for identical procedures?"

Ken thought that Cemente was going to bodily throw them–or at least, Ken–out on his ear. Except that, if Ken's intuition was correct, underneath his adversary's obvious anger was something approaching fear, perhaps in regard to how Ken could possibly know what he appeared to, and how he might write about it. No matter how one sliced it, however, Ken was sure that Cemente was in up to his eyeballs in the sabotaging of the Medicare program that he had publicly sworn to protect.

"Who in hell told you that... that such a piece of legislation is under consideration?"

"A confidential source, sir. Can I take it by your response, though, that there is some validity to this notion?" inquired Ken, so very sweetly.

"Not at all. Not for one goddamn minute! Yes, we have some

new healthcare bills that we are going to put before the House of Commons, but they are merely meant to clean up some confusing language in previous pieces of legislation, and to improve the healthcare delivery system across the country. Now, is there anything else you wish to inquire about? Either of you?" He was not actually asking a question.

Sylkeen took advantage of his words, however, and asked, "Well, there is just one more thing, sir. Your wife, Cynthia, is an American citizen, is she not?"

The question surprised Cemente, who said, "As a matter of fact, yes. We happened to meet in the Caribbean on a junket about ten years ago, in fact. So what?

"Isn't she the daughter of the president and CEO of TomorrowsHealthUSA, one of the largest HMOs in the United States?"

This time it was Ken's jaw that dropped. *How the hell did she know that?*

Sylkeen then added quickly, "And didn't TomorrowsHealthUSA contribute heavily to your last two re-election campaigns through your trust fund? And hasn't the same company been actively lobbying to acquire licenses to build cancer treatment centers across Canada?"

Cemente shouted, "Now just a goddamn minute. What the hell are you insinuating, goddamnit? That has nothing whatsoever to do with *anything* that we have been discussing here today. How dare you suggest that it does! Contributors to my campaign get no preferential treatment. Never! And if either one of you print anything in *The New York Era* that suggests that they do, then I will sue both of you and your paper for so much that the whole frigging *New York Era* building will come down on your tiny heads. Now, I believe it is time that you two leave *my* place of work, so that I can get some genuine work done looking after the best interests of Canadians."

Timmy Cemente stood up, but did not extend his hand as he said, "Good day and goodbye!" The tone of voice he used intimated that "Go forth and die!" would seem less cold and final.

As they left the building, Ken and Sylkeen had difficulty concealing their excitement. The man was a sleaze, and he was undoubtedly buttering his bread on both sides *and* around the edges. He was touting the wonders of the Canadian healthcare system while at the same time working feverously to destroy it. His proposed legislation would allow American businesses, including his father-in-law's, to carve out a pre-eminent place in certain very expensive specialties, siphoning off some of the best available doctors and technicians for themselves, further debilitating the publicly funded and managed hospitals even further.

On the way back to the paper's apartment Ken asked Sylkeen how she knew about the Minister of Health's wife being connected so intimately to a huge HMO, since that information was not in the file they had reviewed on the way to the interview. She flashed her 'killer app' smile and said, "I made a phone call to an old girl friend here in Ottawa while I was in the 'powder room' at the apartment and got the more personal goods on him."

Ken said, "Well, that was a great job you did in there."

Sylkeen grinned widely, and replied, "Thanks. I know. I thought we made a great team actually, even though we have hardly even scrimmaged up until now."

They both laughed. They agreed that a rat had just received the shock of its life from within the confines of its own, supposedly secure cage. They also concurred that they could have pushed him even more.

In fact, they had already provoked him too much.

CHAPTER 45

After their interview with Timmy Cemente, Ken and Sylkeen walked around impressive Parliament Hill, and then had a light lunch at a restaurant near the *Era's* apartment, debriefing one another further on their impressions of the Minister of Health. They agreed he had shown major chutzpah by playing innocent about the conflict of interest he was in, given that his wife was the daughter of the CEO of a major HMO that had been given permission to begin setting up privately run clinics.

As they were walking back to the apartment Sylkeen shared with Ken the familial and business connections of several prominent American federal politicians to some of the major players in healthcare industry back home. While they were riding the elevator up to their floor, Sylkeen said that she was ready to go for a workout at the recreation center in their building. Ken offered that while she was working out he would take the time to write up the highlights of their interview with Cemente.

After Sylkeen had gone downstairs to work out, Ken used his cellphone to ring up Dr. McTavish at the home number that the doctor had provided him when they met in his office.

McTavish was very pleased to hear from him and listened very attentively to Ken's accounting of his visits with Drs. Brown and Markridge, his unscheduled dive onto the Rideau Canal, and, as well, the conversation with the Canadian Minister of Health.

Dr. McTavish told Ken that, coincidentally, he was going to be in Ottawa later that day for a conference of The Association Of Canadian Psychiatrists, at which he would be giving the keynote address. McTavish invited Ken to meet with him for a late lunch at the National University's faculty club. Ken readily agreed and they said goodbye. Ken sensed that McTavish wanted to tell him something in person.

Ken was not ready to divulge to Sylkeen that the elderly Scottish psychiatrist was one of his sources of information, so he left the apartment while Sylkeen was still working out, and hailed a cab. Before going, however, he left her a note saying that he had some additional research to do and would be back in the late afternoon. He suggested that she might want to begin writing her take on their visit to the Minister of Health. He also wrote that it would come out under their joint byline, hoping that such generosity would mitigate her disappointment and possible resentment towards him for having left her on her own after such an auspicious first interview collaboration.

Ken arrived exactly at 3:00 p.m. at the impressive old stone National University's Faculty Club building. Ken could see the elegant, Wedgwood blue and white painted, great dining room at the end of the dark wood-paneled hallway that led from the entrance foyer. A distinguished looking elderly gentleman standing patiently just inside the front entrance asked Ken whom he was there to see. Ken's response brought forth a small smile and nod in his questioner, who then led him proudly into the richly paneled library just to the right of the foyer. A huge old stone fireplace offered cheery warmth to three quite separate settings of couches and chairs that were placed around it in a semicircle.

Dr. McTavish was sitting in one of the weathered leather chairs, a well-worn briefcase resting against his right leg. The psychiatrist stood up, picked up his briefcase, and moved to greet Ken, extending a large right hand that the latter shook somewhat delicately. Ken had awoken that morning with the felt realization that during his flight onto the Rideau canal from the jogging path the previous day, he had probably reached out with his right arm in an attempt to control his landing, and his elbow had been severely jolted as a result.

They exchanged greetings and then Dr. McTavish led Ken out of the library towards the dining room where they were welcomed by the maitre d'. They were shown to a table somewhat discreetly set apart from its neighbors. As he quickly removed the 'Reserved' sign from the table he turned and said, "Enjoy your meals, gentlemen". With that, he was gone.

As they were being seated Dr. McTavish looked at Ken with what seemed to be a combination of professional scrutiny and fatherly compassion. McTavish started the conversation. "I appreciate the way in which you conducted your inquiries with my friend Judith. She found you very direct yet respectful in your questioning."

Ken said, "I am glad to hear that. She was very kind and an excellent resource for my investigative series."

"Excellent. So, how are you doing today, Kenneth, and what have you found out?"

Ken couldn't recall anyone having called him Kenneth for a very long time, but coming from Dr. McTavish, he found the use of his full name quite pleasant.

Ken replied to the question with a succinct summary of the recent happenings. He went into some detail about the meeting with the Minister of Health. After listening attentively to Ken's rendering of the interview Dr. McTavish uttered only a single word, quietly: "Asshole!"

Ken asked, "As a psychiatrist, can you explain to me why and how a person who may have started out in his political career sincerely devoting himself to serving his constituents, as I would like to assume Cemente had, could eventually make a mockery of responsibility and chuck morality for the sake of pure greed, even though by that time he was, as I understand it, quite wealthy in his own right, partly as a result of having married into money. I could understand it better if we are talking about ordinary thieves, but I have always found it astonishing when usually good and even exemplary people do reprehensible things?"

Dr. McTavish smiled and said somewhat sadly, "Well, unfortunately, such things do happen, more than many of us would like to believe. Let me tell you an illustrative story about entirely unnecessary greed. It may help you better appreciate the multifaceted nature of the human psyche, and how it is possible for a heretofore basically honest and successful person to have a shadow side that is nothing less than malevolent.

The story has to do with two brothers who grew up in a single parent home with a psychiatrically disturbed and occasionally violent mother and older sister. They survived it all somehow, and both went on to become medical doctors. Then the younger one, let us call him Gerald, who had to a large extent been 'fathered' by his older brother in the absence of their father, took a bad turn once their mother died. Up to that point the two brothers were evidently so close that even as adults in their thirties and forties they would frequently be seen by friends and colleagues, either playing tennis or throwing around a ball after work. They would do this at least a couple of times a week, after which they would often go out to dinner and discuss medicine, the world generally, and their own lives.

"The younger brother lived closer to their mother and was therefore the logical one to have power of attorney over their mother's heath and estate. Well, it turned out that he arranged over a period of years to steal the bulk of their mother's not unsubstantial estate, lying and deceiving his older brother the entire time. By the time he was caught out, he had absconded with over two million dollars."

As Dr. William McTavish was relating the tale his voice became progressively lower and perceptibly sadder. After a long pause during which he seemed momentarily lost in thought, McTavish continued.

"How can this happen, you ask? Well, some people do actually live dual lives, one in which they present themselves as highly responsible members of society while on the other hand, at the same time, they may also operate as bigamists, dope dealers, thieves, and/or chronic liars. Such individuals have a highly defended and compartmentalized self-centeredness that allows them to deceive not only others, but themselves as well. They have turned from an early tendency to learn and grow, towards an increasing inclination to selfishly hoard, and to hurt others. Such persons need help but will usually not acknowledge this fact, and they generally also have no interest or motivation to deal with their duplicity. And because they are frequently quite charming and intelligent, they can often get away with their dishonesty and duplicity for a long time. Few, if any others, including even their supposedly close friends, are aware of their darker nature until, perhaps, they invest and become entangled in their friend's schemes. As part of their dual nature, incidentally, they may carry on long-term or sequential extramarital relationships, as well."

Ken was very aware of the strain in McTavish's voice and face, and so he was hesitant to ask the obvious question. Dr. McTavish saved him the unpleasant task.

"Yes, Mr. Simpson, it is my own brother Gerald of whom I have been speaking. Sadly, his greed effectively destroyed his relationships with all the relatives from whom he stole. So, speaking not only as a mental health professional, but also from first hand personal experience, I can tell you that some people just turn, and it most often shows up graphically when money is involved. The underlying explanation? Some would say it has a lot to do with sibling rivalry; others suggest that it is displaced oedipal work; and still others would say that the older brother gets the brunt of the younger one's anger that really should have been directed to the absent father, whose role he took.

"There are far too many Geralds and Timmy Cementes in this world. They are like us, but also very different. They have no honest soul; they are oblivious to the idea, the original source of which escapes me at this moment that 'morality, like art, begins by simply and clearly drawing a line'. Many of those types are drawn towards teaching or politics, where their outward veneers of position, values, and virtue, camouflages their truer aim, which is to seize and hold power, and grab as much as they can for themselves while spouting platitudes about ethics and integrity. Sometimes, such as one of the FBI's most famous treasonous spies a few years back, they are also pillars of their religious communities."

Ken asked, "So, if they are so good at being so devious, how do folks find out about their underside and expose it?"

McTavish's deep eyes flashed fire. "Well, actually, I am going to help you do exactly that."

And so he did. Dr. McTavish leaned down and opened his briefcase. He took out a large thick envelope that he handed across the table to Ken. Its contents provided a dossier of documents about the various programs that Cemente had attempted to ram down the throats of provincial ministries of health and the physicians and pharmacists who operated within their jurisdictions.

Dr. McTavish said, "A physician and senior bureaucrat friend of mine who works at the deputy ministerial level in Cemente's department, was approached on several occasions by some of the same lobbyists who had Cemente's ear. Unlike his boss, he could not be bought. However, my friend pretended to go along with the attempts to involve him in wrecking Medicare so that he could, hopefully, accumulate and then turn over to the police evidence of these goings-on. He consulted with me on several occasions after he realized the lengths to which these people were willing to go to acquire effective political and bureaucratic control over Medicare. For security's sake, my friend also made me copies of the documents, video and audiotapes he accumulated during these attempts to gain his involvement.

"Once my friend had convinced the people involved that he was willing to go along with their plans, Cemente began meeting with him regularly to plot strategies. He was pressed by Clemente and his cronies to accept new policies that favored the lobbyists' clients but most certainly would not benefit Canadian taxpayers. When he had what he considered 'the goods on them', however, he then stopped appearing to cooperate with them and their rhetoric became increasingly threatening. A few months ago he had called me to say that he was FedExing me some crucial evidence, a copy of which you now have in your hands, Kenneth. He begged me to hold onto and protect the contents, "just in case." He also asked that, if something were to happen to him, then I should deliver the materials to someone who might actually be able to do something to stop what he referred to as "this corporate and political rape".

"Two days ago my friend apparently suffered a fatal heart attack, in spite of having bragged to me during our last conversation that he just passed his annual extensive checkup with flying colors. So I now feel obliged to divulge the information to you, since you may well be in the best position to make use of it." Dr. McTavish handed Ken a large package of materials that he took out of his briefcase.

Ken asked, "Why not just hand it over to the police?"

McTavish replied, "This morning I sent an identical packet to

RCMP headquarters in Ottawa. They will do their investigation; you can do your own. Hopefully, with the police looking into his charges and making use of this evidence, and your own publicizing of what has been going on, we may be able to stop this travesty-in-the-making."

CHAPTER 46

Ken returned to the *Era's* apartment after his meeting with McTavish and began following up on the material that had been provided to him. He knew the probability was that heads would roll over the revelations that he would publish in *The New York Era* within the next few weeks. He still had additional confirming sources to contact, and would make use of some of his discretionary investigative funds to hire Dean Dennison, his favorite New York City-based private investigator. Dennison was a unique, part-Elliot Ness, part-Bill Gates type of character who only took on jobs that were likely to be intellectually and physically challenging, and required relatively sophisticated, high-tech research, and only then, when he considered the purpose, admirable and the monetary reward, respectful.

Decades earlier Dean Dennison had been a U.S. Navy seal, and later, a senior computer analyst. Five years after leaving the military he had become a key manager of a commercial nuclear reactor manufacturing company. Once he was resident on the executive floor as vice-president in charge of quality control, however, he soon learned that the company had, for years, been deep-sixing internal reports detailing reactor manufacturing problems that had the potential to trigger a major catastrophe.

Dennison was unable to convince the other key people in the company that they should make public their disturbing reports or at least warn their customers of the potential problems and offer to speedily replace the faulty control mechanisms for free, a relatively straightforward but costly job. Finally, in frustration and out of a sense of accountability that he refused to relinquish, Dennison, without authorization, provided the said reports to a governmental subcommittee looking into problems in the nuclear industry, and was immediately fired for 'incompetence'. He then brought his story to a reporter whose writing he had come to respect, with the result that Ken Simpson's career as an investigative reporter was launched in headline-grabbing style around the country.

Dennison successfully sued his former employer for wrongful and malicious dismissal and was awarded several million dollars. His legal victory helped bring down the entire executive floor of one of the most powerful companies in the nuclear field, and led to sweeping changes in the ways in which that industry was regulated.

Dennison found that he thoroughly enjoyed the excitement and satisfaction inherent in bringing down some 'truly big, bad guys'. He was just the sort of individual who could do the kind of *undercover* investigation for which Ken had neither the training nor talent.

Ken phoned Dennison and briefly discussed what he was interested in having Dean look into; the latter readily accepted the assignment.

Ken walked into the kitchen to brew some coffee. On the dining room table he found a note from Sylkeen, saying that she would be gone for a few hours in order to conduct interviews with certain U.S. healthcare lobbyists she knew who had, for the past few years, dedicated themselves to ceaselessly cruising Parliament Hill "like vultures who had found themselves an exhausted, bloated behemoth". Ken would have liked to have been part of those interviews but realized that her solo efforts could be payback for his having gone out on his own to see McTavish.

Got to give her credit. She is an assertive woman with some potentially really useful contacts.

Ken opened his laptop and began writing his newspaper columns in earnest. It was time to begin to describe to his American readers a truer picture of the Canadian universal Medicare system and its problems, and to begin to suggest that many, if not most, of its difficulties were 'manufactured', and not inherent in the system. He also decided to make mention of the fact that in Canada, healthcare accounted for less than ten percent of GNP, and covered virtually all its citizens, while in sharp contrast, in the U.S., healthcare expenses accounted for over fourteen percent of GNP, and left over fifteen percent of its population, i.e., over forty-six million Americans, with no health insurance coverage. And while healthcare costs in Canada had been going up by single digits annually for the past several years, in the U.S. the health premiums of many of the major HMOs and PPOs had been escalating by double digits every year over the same period. The tentative title for his first article would be, *"What's Fundamentally Wrong With The American Way Of Providing Healthcare?"* That title would hopefully be sufficiently provocative to create curiosity in potential readers and infuriating enough to get TAMPRR's attention.

About twenty minutes later the phone rang, jangling him out of his concentration. *Any* interruption while he was writing tended to produce a mild to moderate shock-like response to Ken's mental concentration. For that reason, he had trained himself to *not* answer the telephone on the first ring, even if the phone was within arm's reach. He had learned through the feedback that his wife, some friends, and others had given him, that if he answered it after only one ring, his voice usually telegraphed his reflexive disapproval of the interruption by saying *"Hello!"* in a tone that made his greeting sound like, *"Who is this and why the hell are you bothering me?"*

Ken waited the self-imposed requisite two rings and then picked up the receiver and, as he had trained himself to do, said, *"Hel-lo!"* in a reasonable facsimile of welcoming pleasantness.

The unmistakable military presence in the voice at the other end snapped Ken's still partially pre-occupied mind to full attention. It was Lieutenant Colonel Dan Stevens. "Good afternoon, Ken; I am just around the corner at Starbucks. I want to see you. Now. We need to talk."

"What the...? How did you know where I was staying, and that I was actually here now?" asked Ken, undoubtedly sounding defensive. Truth be told, he really didn't like being tracked down, and the apartment was already too crowded.

"Remember the encrypting software we downloaded onto your phone and computer? Well, when you e-mailed me, you simultaneously transmitted your GPS location. It's a little perk from TAMPRR that I may have neglected to mention to you at the time." The man was chuckling.

Ken's stony silence signaled that he was not amused.

Now Stevens's voice became serious; "I would very much like to suggest, Ken, that you damn well leave the apartment by the main underground parking exit, pronto, and make your way to the Starbucks on the corner of O'Connor and Frank. Please make sure you are not followed, and I will be at the last table at the back."

"*Well...* all right!" said Ken, aware now of experiencing a stress hormone flow that typically accompanied his intuition's signaling of danger. "But I want you to know that I do not appreciate you spying on my location. And have you also downloaded my computer's contents, as well?"

"Only its location, my boy. I wouldn't want you to not trust me!" Stevens laughed again–alone.

Within less than five minutes Ken was out the door of the apartment. He took the stairs down to the parking garage, left the building via the underground exit, and then walked quickly to the Starbucks. He ordered a coffee at the service counter, which gave him an opportunity to look around. Stevens was partially hidden behind the current issue of *USA Today*. Ken picked up his coffee and walked over to Stevens as the latter casually glanced up at him.

"Would you like to sit down?" asked Stevens. Even when he was extending an invitation, Stevens was still unquestionably issuing commands.

Ken sat down and asked, "What are you doing here?"

"I'm here to save your ass, and just maybe your life as well." Stevens gave no hint of joking.

Ken was taken aback but tried to not show it. "What are you talking about?"

Stevens replied, "Ken, you are getting way too close to too many people who you are pissing off, big-time. They are currently considering doing you and/or one or more of your loved ones, major harm. Your interviews with that traitor, Dillard, and that pompous overgrown troll, Cemente, have really upset a lot of the friends they have in common. Fortunately, I am one of the people whom you are supposed to be upsetting. That is why I know."

"So it's TAMPRR again, isn't it?"

"Of course. Don't you get it? Now you are sticking your nose into not only the subject of the healthcare system in *this* country but in ours, as well. You are also dropping names like 'TAMPRR' and the Avro Arrow, and those folks are getting mighty nervous. Hell, you are stepping on more toes than a blind drunk in a men's club's communal shower. Your reputation and your Paulson give you both the clout that they fear, and their temporary hesitation to take you out."

"Why do they care so much?" asked Ken. "I am going to be writing mostly about *Canadian* healthcare; hell, most of my readers probably won't even bother scanning past the headline of the columns I am writing on the subject."

"So why bother writing them at all?"

Ken got hot. "You know why! Too many Americans are so damned programmed to think that anything *we* do is the right way, and whatever any other country does must almost certainly be wrong. And I did that to them; me and the other media people who have been feeding them that pseudopatriotic crap. If we and the people who pull our strings were genuine patriots then we would tell them the truth about the thousands of civilians, the women and children and old men, that we killed with our bombs in Iraq, for starters. It's like a variation of that old line a previous U.S. administration had used about Vietnam; only now it was that 'we had to destroy *entire cities* and their citizens in order to save them'. And about the real reasons why we went into that country in the first place? Thank God for Richard Clarke and the others who blew the whistle on what they knew, for all the good that it did. Anyway… anyway…" Ken slowed down his breathing to calm down; Stevens, who had let him riff, now spoke up.

"Look, Ken. Let's get back to the problem here. TAMPRR doesn't give a shit about little Canada and its one-tenth of our U.S. population. What TAMPRR and its corporate clients *do* care about, and this is the *only* thing, believe me, is that what happens up here may impact on their companies Stateside. I have warned you before; TAMPRR Inc.'s clients, these HMOs, PPOs and pharmaceutical companies, will do anything, and I do mean *anything*, in order to *not* allow the Canadian Medicare system to continue and to flourish. And by the way, while TAMPRR is the biggest, there are at least two other similar U.S. companies carrying out covert operations in Canada, and all of them are involved in bizwars here, in Europe, Australia, and South America as well. The guys who tossed you into the canal were probably contract agents hired by TAMPRR, but they could just as easily been working for some of our competitors. Regardless, the point is that your life really is in danger and I cannot protect you indefinitely, and certainly not if one of the other TAMPRR-type companies decide to take you out."

"What would you recommend I do, then? Fold up my tent and leave?" asked Ken, feeling more angry than frightened, at least for the moment.

"Well, for one thing, stop thinking about screwing the help", replied Lieutenant Colonel Stevens rather sharply.

Ken was not amused. He also didn't know if he meant Martha, who of course, he had, or Sylkeen, who he... well, anyway... Ken replied, "That is none of your damn business!"

Stevens calmly said, "No, but it is their's. Your friend Martha is at risk because they know about you two and figure if they were to threaten to harm *her* you might be persuaded to back off."

Ken felt relieved that he had only mentioned Martha. Possibly, Stevens was not yet aware of sultry Sylkeen. What would he say *then*, Ken wondered? But right this moment he was sickened by the thought that because of his actions and perhaps, his arrogance as well, Martha also might be in harm's way.

Ken asked, "Why you are telling me this? To protect me, or so that I'll back off? And maybe *you* are still part of TAMPRR's *mental* bizwar, and still very much on its side."

"Well, I am not. And you had better believe me when I tell you that you are now in grave danger. Somehow they know about what you might write about next. To TAMPRR, and especially to Jake Marks, your conduct is intolerable. He won't allow his company to be exposed.

"Your father was like you, Ken, just too much of a goddamn idealist. He was also a war hero who they couldn't easily discredit. So they took him out. And now they are having a nearly identical problem, fifty years later, with his son. And I am afraid that his son isn't going to listen, either! I am not bullshitting you, Ken, and I am not trying to stop you for TAMPRR's sake; I am trying to stop you for *your own sake!*"

The old man stopped talking, his breath labored, and his eyes filled with tears that threatened to fall. When he started speaking again, he was somber. "I *have* never and *will* never forgive myself for what I did and what I didn't do that contributed to your father's death. But I promise you, and I swear it on my own child's grave, that I will do everything I can to prevent harm from coming to you. And I don't even care any more what else is right or wrong. Harming you is wrong; *that I do know!"*

Ken looked into Stevens's sad eyes, and nodded a neutral acknowledgement that he had heard both the old man's mea culpa and his pledge. But Ken was not by any means yet ready to forgive.

"Ken, I will not lie to you nor will I try to get you to stop your investigations. You can trust me. *You have to trust me.* Now listen; the Prime Minister is about to resign, but before he does he will dump Timmy Cemente from the Federal cabinet and make Trish Markridge the government's new Minister of Health *and* deputy Prime Minister. Right now, therefore, she and you are the biggest political threats to our American healthcare corporate clients. For that reason, she is also in imminent danger."

While Stevens was speaking Ken regarded him with a mixture of so many conflicting feelings that he didn't know whether to hit the old man in the face *or* hug him and invite him to cry on his shoulder. *Or should I hit him first, then hug him and then let him cry on my shoulder?*

Stevens regained his composure and asked, "What do you know about your new partner, Miss Sylkeen Bowry?"

So Stevens did know about her. Ken could not hide his surprise at hearing the question. Maybe because he was feeling a little defensive, he responded with a scoop of bravado in his voice. "Well, what about her? She is young but has a solid background in journalism and has already shown me that she might well be a terrific asset as far as some of our investigations are concerned."

"Look, Ken. She may or may not be what she appears. "I

don't have any solid inside information yet but it is possible that she is a TAMPRR operative, so be very careful what information you choose to share with her. And for God's sake, don't disclose anything about me to her."

Ken spat out, *"You know I wouldn't do that.* But why would you even think to be concerned about her? "

"Well, I read something into a couple of e-mails that Marks sent to some of us, as well as a couple of comments he made at a partners' meeting. I had the impression that some of the others present were more informed than I was, and in the past that was almost never the case. They may have deliberately been keeping me out of the loop because of my former relationship to your father, and my stand on what was done to him. I don't know if she is a plant or not. But be careful. Jake Marks must not be underestimated. It is probably only a matter of time until he finds out about me being in contact with you.

"At that moment, I may cease to be of almost any value to you; or to myself, for that matter. So I have taken certain precautions. Here." said Stevens, as he reached into his jacket's inside pocket and passed an envelope across to Ken.

"What is this?"

"In the envelope is a safety deposit box key, and instructions where it can be found. I have made you the executor of my estate, Ken. Most of my assets are to go to you and your son. Being executor will also give you access to the box. Inside you will find a great many copied, and even some original, documents, enough to make Jake Marks and the rest of them at TAMPRR leave you alone forever. I only ask that you promise me that you will not open the envelope or the safety deposit box unless I either tell you to, or am no longer able to tell anyone anything."

Stevens slumped back in his chair, seemingly exhausted. Ken was reluctant to press him for further information at the moment. Hopefully there would be other occasions to do so, and Ken wanted to digest all the information he had just been given.

Stevens said, "Ken, when you started writing articles about our country's healthcare system you came right up on TAMPRR's corporate radar screen and you were tagged with the company's special WAREM designation, that stands for 'Watch

And Report Every Move'. Also, as soon as your name surfaced and we made the connection with your father, Marks called me into his office and asked if I would have trouble "working on this matter". Of course, I said, 'No', but I don't think he believed me entirely, so I am probably out of the loop as far as most plans going forward that might involve you. Each 'file' has its own password and after he and I met, the password on the 'Ken Simpson file' was changed. I have not yet been able to find out the current password."

Ken said, "Look, I do appreciate that you have come forward to try and help me. And I have to trust that you are not going to feed me a lot of crap in order to put me off the track. But I do want to tell you that if I get a whiff that you are setting me up, like you did with my father, then as long as I will be able to move and breathe, I assure you that I will settle *both* my father's score and my own."

Stevens nodded and said, "I understand, and if I were in your position, I would feel and do the same. And I am trusting *you* to not expose either me or my part in any activities past, present or future: at least not until our work together is done."

Ken scrutinized the old guy's face closely. Then he said, "All right, I think we understand each other. Now lets get back to the issue of TAMPRR's role in working to destroy the Canadian Medicare system."

Stevens said, "Agreed! Look, there have been over two hundred men and women in Canada functioning as TAMPRR's lobbyists or sleeper agents at different times during the past few years. Many of them work either in the media or in various businesses or government posts. Some others are working for supposedly non-profit–or at least, not yet profitable–healthcare related facilities. Many are Canadians but all are run by TAMPRR. In addition, some HMO clients are already operating here as organizations that provide medical information, supplemental healthcare insurance, and healthcare statistical polling firms.

"A few are already actually set up as facilities that perform day surgeries and other medical treatments that are not covered by the Canada healthcare system. Some of the more aggressive ones are functioning as P3 organizations, or 'public-private partnerships' running, in effect, full-fledged hospitals. Of course, some P3 facilities are run by the most honorable of business people who have no desire or intention whatever to undermine the country's Medicare system. On the other hand, there are some facilities built and run by a P3 group called *ONLY CANADIAN*, and it is actually a shell group of Canadian business people organized, financed and directed by TAMPRR. The clinic and hospital facilities run by *ONLY CANADIAN* are being run in such a way that they are ready, as soon as they get the word, to transform themselves overnight into full-fledged HMOs that can take over control of other already-in-place facilities that have been built and run by the government, which they will then run on a for-profit basis."

Ken was stunned by the brazenness of TAMPRR and some of its corporate clients. However, he now recalled that a few years earlier, a number of shell groups were set up in the U.S.A. that had names that sounded somewhat like A.A.R.P., the American Association of Retired Persons, but which were, in fact, entirely financed and run by–and on behalf of–certain U.S. pharmaceutical and healthcare corporations. The point of that exercise was to attempt to seem like legitimate groups lobbying on behalf of senior citizens while, in fact, they were actually carrying out a mandate that was virtually the complete opposite of A.A.R.P.. It was another 'Trojan horse' scam but it worked, at least to some extent. *'ONLY CANADIAN'*, indeed!

Ken asked a bull's-eye question. "Who are the highest positioned politicians that TAMPRR has in its pocket?"

Stevens looked at Ken, took a long breath, and said, "Well, for starters, how about at least one past Prime Minister of Canada, and of course, your friend, Timmy Cemente. In fact, TAMPRR wants Cemente to be the next Prime Minister. Or at the very least, regardless of who the next PM is going to be, TAMPRR would work hard to have him stay on as Minister of Health."

"Why so invested in Cemente?" asked Ken.

"Because Cemente has been working behind the scenes for a long time now with some of the other provinces' premiers and/or their provincial ministers of health, to insinuate U.S.-style alternative systems into the Canadian healthcare fabric. Whenever one of them carries out a U.S.-oriented innovation, Cemente has been paid to publicly huff and puff and *threaten* to close them down, but in fact to do nothing about them at all. Meanwhile he gets to spend his time counting the additional payments that have been deposited into his Swiss bank account.

"Hey, he is a pretty good actor. Actually, he used to be an actor on Canadian television and even had some bit parts in a couple of American movies before he got into politics. Different venues, same audiences."

Stevens added, "Ken, you and I can blow the whole lid off TAMPRR. Or, at least, we can just slow them down for a number of years, at least as far as they're taking over the Canadian Medicare System is concerned. Its probably too late for *our* healthcare system Stateside, but who knows? A defeat of TAMPRR here might just wake up our fellow Americans to how they are getting screwed."

"How do you figure that?"

Stevens responded, "Well, if every poor, or even middle class, person and his or her children were able to get free healthcare in America then there would be no need for HMOs, PPOs, or the rest. The government would handle the collection of payments through taxes, like they do up here, and then the government would pay the doctors and hospitals directly. Hell, the private health middleman would be cut out entirely. And that is where the money is to be made. Just like it is in the energy field. Just like it was with Enron. Get in between the supply and the consumer, and make your money on both sides."

Ken asked, "Given the obvious advantages of the Canadian Healthcare system over ours, why do *you* think that most of our press keeps giving a negative picture of the Canadian Medicare System? Is it because so much media in our country is tied into the healthcare business?"

"That's mostly it. But give TAMPRR a lot of credit, too." Every few months, for years, we have hired a polling agency to ask Canadians skewed questions such as, "Would you have any objection to a two-tier, or American-type, or other alternative system being set up along side the government's Medicare system, if it meant shorter waiting lists for you or your family?" And of course, we mostly ask middle and upper class citizens who could afford the costs and who, like everybody else, is scared shitless of long waiting lists for things like basic cancer screening tests. So naturally, those polls then show that middle and upper class Canadians would *love* to have a two-tier system and we would make sure that the poll's results were offered gratis to major media outlets, especially the most already favorably disposed ones.

"Furthermore, TAMPRR has worked on a lot of Canadian as well as American election campaigns. Hell, man, this is 2009, for Christ's sake; advertising is now a bloody science. That is why, other things being equal, most of the time the guy with the most advertising bucks to spend, wins. The same guys who sell aspirin can–and do–sell political candidates! The job of TAMPRR is to simply make sure that the targeted system is promoted or sabotaged, as the need may be.

"We first came onto the scene a little too late for the Avro Arrow. The Canadians had already built the plane. We couldn't deny its *potential* capabilities as completely as we would have liked. For example, we couldn't say that the Avro Arrow wouldn't ever meet specs, because it already had! So, instead, we said that it was just *too expensive* a project for little Canada to build on its own, and we put incredible pressure on certain individuals so that they would kill their own baby and then turn around and buy our clients' inferior products. Since the Canadian government of the day was not the government that had initiated the Avro Arrow program, they didn't even *want* to defend it as forcefully as the originating government might have; in fact, a lot of the people in the new government hated the Avro Arrow program. It wasn't their baby, so if they allowed it to become what it would no doubt have been, namely the pre-eminent warplane of its kind in the world, *they* wouldn't get any of the credit. The previous government would. No way would they allow that baby to grow up."

While Lieutenant Colonel Stevens was walking him through TAMPRR 101, Ken listened and shook his head occasionally at the craziness of it all. He asked, "How long has this sort of dirty business been going on then, that parties in the United States business or military have sabotaged our own allies' civilian and military projects?"

Stevens paused for a moment, as if he were considering which version of an answer to offer. He eventually chose the shortest one, and added a rider. "Forever. Ever since warring tribes first sent spies into the enemy's towns to ferment unrest, distrust, and chaos. Ever since greed came into existence, so that you could, for only a few shekels or gilders or greenbacks, buy off a few of your adversary's people. There is nothing whatsoever new here, Ken. However, TAMPRR has been in business since the Avro Arrow, and we have spent the last fifty years darn well nearly perfecting the tools of corporate, military, and political espionage and sabotage."

Ken protested mildly. "But Canada is not our enemy, for Christ's sake. Bribes, payoffs, blackmail, disinformation as regular fare with our friends? If this is really how we treat our friends, then God help our enemies."

The Lieutenant Colonel laughed as if he were a parent whose child was realizing for the first time that Santa Claus doesn't really exist. He said, "Actually, we often treat our enemies a lot better than our friends. At least they know we are out to take them down, and vice versa. We each know the rules of the game. When we catch one of their spies, or they get one of ours, no one is shocked. It's expected. Hell, they would be insulted if we didn't take them seriously enough to try and infiltrate, bribe, blackmail, or otherwise take them out."

"TAMPRR has always considered Canada to be our closest and dearest 'friendly enemy'. It is, however, a potential enemy of American enterprise and domination. All our friendly allies are potentially also our official enemies. But, hey, look. Canadians are not entirely blameless. They *like* to be hoodwinked; at least, a lot of them are hoping to be bought."

Ken asked, "How can you say that?"

Stevens asked, "Do you know what the Stockholm syndrome is?"

"Sure. When those at the mercy of their captors start to see the latter as 'good' and 'right'."

Stevens said, "Exactly. Well, with all of 10% of our population, Canadians are really being allowed to exist as a supposedly separate nation at our pleasure. If we wanted to, we could crush their tiny military and take them over in a second. So, big brother America says, "You know, little brother Canada, I don't think you should build those big, bad airplanes. You aren't *smart* enough, *rich* enough, *powerful* enough, … *whatever* enough. Instead, you should close down your aircraft company and let us take over your world-class product and people. Then, of course, our little brother, who doesn't dare get into a pissing match with his impossibly more powerful, big brother, shuts the fuck up and does what he is told. And that is all we did about the Avro Arrow program. And that is what TAMPRR is aiming to do now with the Canadian healthcare system."

Ken asked, "So why haven't you closed down their healthcare system long before now, if you have so many of their power people in your back pocket?"

Stevens replied, "Because our clients waited too long to hire us, and now there are too many people up here who know damn well that they have just about the best frigging healthcare system in the whole bloody world. So they are smarter this time around, and are holding on to their healthcare structure as if their lives depended on it–which, of course, may well be true, especially if they mind losing most of their life savings or going bankrupt to deal with their own, or their children's medical problems.

"Also, when we think that our handsomely paid media and politicians up here are going to be able to close the door on Canada's Medicare scheme, along comes something like the World Health Organization's 'Nations' Health Card Report' from 2007, that once again placed Canada's healthcare system way ahead of our own and many other countries, and so we have to back off for a while–again."

"We aren't talking about America's national security this time. So our government doesn't give too much of a shit, except for our paid-for members of Congress. But a lot of our business guys do, and so it is left up to the boys with the balls and the bullion to hire TAMPRR and let us try to get the job done for them."

Stevens was done. And looking at Ken's face he could read

the disgust in his younger friend's countenance.

"Remember our agreement, Ken. You may not use the name TAMPRR, or in any way identify TAMPRR, either in your articles or elsewhere, unless and until I tell you otherwise. If you do, there are several people whose lives will certainly be in great danger–including both of our's, your friend Martha's, and that of your own son."

Ken was afraid to lose contact with Stevens, who was a walking database about TAMPRR and the healthcare situation on both sides of the border. Suddenly he had one of his disturbing premonitions, that this might be the last face-to-face contact that he and Stevens would have for some time, or period. He had many more questions to ask, about TAMPRR, and especially about his father. He asked, "What more can you tell me about you three; you, Marks and my father?"

Stevens looked at Ken, then gazed far away into his own darkness. After a minute he gazed back at Ken. "All three of us were housed in the same cabin in the North Korean POW camp. In order to make it through the attempts at brainwashing and other experiments so atrocious you won't even find them in most of the history books on that period, we three 'bonded', as people like to say nowadays. Boy, did we *ever* bond! Every time one of us was put through the ringer by those bastards the other two would be waiting for him when he was finally delivered back to our compound. We nursed and deprogrammed the one that had been beaten or starved or subjected to their sensory deprivation experiments. We made up our own counter-torture treatment as we went along."

Ken had never heard his father talk about what he had been subjected to in the camps. He did remember that a few times, two air force 'intelligence personnel' (that is what his father called them) came to speak to his father in their family home shortly after Frank Simpson was repatriated back Stateside. Now Ken realized that those 'visitors' had probably been military deprogrammers of some sort. Ken recalled that each time they visited they always went into his father's den in the basement and put the radio on so loud that it was impossible to hear what was being said.

Ken remembered a couple of occasions when, for a moment, he had pressed his ear against the door to the basement, trying to hear what was going on. He heard what, at the time, sounded like muffled screams and sobbing, horrible noises that lasted several minutes before they were seemingly cut off. An hour later the two visitors came up from the basement and let themselves out the front door, but not before telling young Ken that he should not go into the basement because his father had told them that he wanted to spend some time alone.

Ken remembered wanting to immediately run to see if his father was all right. But something told him that doing so might somehow upset his dad. So he waited for his father to come upstairs. He did so about twenty minutes later, his eyes wide and reddened.

Young Ken asked, "Are you... are you okay, dad? Did those men... hur... bother you?"

"No, son. I am fine. Just fine,"

Ken couldn't help but notice that Frank Simpson's shirt and the crotch of his pants were all wet. Ken said nothing more, and focused instead on doing his best to not cry.

Stevens sat and waited until Ken's attention came back to the present. He could see that his story of the time in the POW camp had stirred up distressing memories. He also sensed that Ken believed him. "As I said, we bonded very, very tightly, Ken. And once, Jake Marks probably even saved your father's life by... by making sure that one of the guys in your father's squadron who had nearly been broken and was on the verge of revealing their true mission targets, was... silenced."

Ken, subdued after remembering the pitiful sounds he had heard from inside his father's den so long ago, asked in an empty voice: "*How* was he 'silenced'?"

Lieutenant Colonel Stevens said quietly, "Marks believed that the poor bastard was not going to make it but was going to take your father and some other pilots down with him, and so he made an executive decision. He decided that the rest of us would suffer a worse fate if the North Koreans ever found out that we knew about the secret tank they had under development at a large warehouse complex just outside of a major residential district of Pyongyang. So, he made it look like the guy had hung himself in the shower stall at night."

"How could you...?"

"Ken, there was no other way. I will only tell you that Jake didn't do it alone. Some others of us helped him."

"Did... did my father?"

"That I will *never* tell you. I will say that that act probably saved at least five good men. And that's all I will ever tell you about that. If you try to press me any further on that topic I will walk away from helping you in any way. Is that clear?"

As much as he wanted to know the rest of it, Ken also knew that he *didn't* want to know. And he believed the older man's warning so he let it go.

While he was thinking of his next question, in the periphery of his vision Ken sensed, more than saw, her standing at the corner waiting for the light to change so she could cross the busy street and walk towards the Starbucks. Stevens had started to speak again when Ken interrupted him, and nodded his head in her direction, over Lieutenant Colonel Dan Stevens's right shoulder. Ken said, "Here comes Sylkeen now. She's probably just coming to get an espresso. I didn't tell her that I was going to be here."

Stevens turned in his seat and scanned the faces of the people on the street who were crossing the street at the green light. There was only one relatively young female anywhere within about thirty feet of the direction that Ken was looking. She was an eye-catching thirty-something female whose face was partially hidden by the state trooper-type hats of a couple of large RCMP officers also crossing the street at that moment. But that stride, that manner of moving confidently along, aware of the head-turning looks she was getting from both men and women, comfortable with her beauty and its effect upon others... there was something familiar about that body language. Then the RCMP constables moved out of the way and Stevens got an unobstructed look at her beautiful face and long black hair.

"Oh, *shit!*" Stevens said, suddenly sitting bolt upright, as if he had been struck in his lower back by someone's fist. In a voice at once furious and frightened, Stevens said, "*Goddamn it! Fools! Both of us are goddamn fools!* For Christ's sake, Ken, that woman is from TAMPRR. You said her name is Sylkeen Bowry. It's not: it's Sylvia Best. And Best was her married name. Her maiden name was Sylvia Marks. She's Colonel Jake Marks's *niece*, for Christ's sake. *And she works for him!* She must have been sent in by him to get to you, and to find out whatever it is you've learned about the Canadian healthcare system and maybe even TAMPRR and its plans. *Shit!"*

Ken was speechless. His eyes kept darting from Sylkeen or Sylvia or whoever she was, and back to Stevens. Shock, embarrassment, fury charged through him. He asked, "Are you sur…?"

Stevens interrupted, immediately demanding to know, as he rose to leave the table, "What *exactly* have you told her about me?"

"Nothing!"

His voice the hardest yet, Stevens pressed him. "Are you sure? Have you told her *anything* about me? My name, or anything that I have told you about TAMPRR?"

Ken's mind quickly scanned his memory. "I told you. Nothing. I am certain. I haven't mentioned you at all."

"If you are wrong, or if you are lying right now, then I am as good as dead to you, and probably dead, period, if she tells Marks and he goes into one of his insane rages. If he goes ballistic he just might forget about the measures that he knows that I've taken to protect myself from any hostile action against me by TAMPRR."

After just an instant when Stevens seemed to be considering the ramifications of the entire situation, he added, "You must understand, Ken, you *must* believe, that she has been reporting everything back to Marks about every single bloody thing that you have said, every person she knows you have spoken to,. Do you hear me? Are you even listening to me, *goddamnit*?"

Ken nodded from another place. His common sense and intuition, both had let him down. He had been thinking too much with his little head instead of his big head about what he and… Sylkeen, … Sylvia… might get into with each other, right from the first time he saw her.

Stevens snapped him out of wherever he was, and said, "Count on her having told Marks everything she thinks she has learned about your work here, Ken. That may be why the two goons gave you that warning. Maybe it wasn't just because of how you spoke to Dillard. Or Cemente. TAMPRR may have also known that you spoke to Dr. Brown and Dr. McTavish. *Damn!* Are you certain that you didn't tell her anything about *them*?"

Ken was *not* certain. He had to give her *some* information or it would have been obvious that he was suspicious of her. Perhaps he *had* said something earlier today. He wasn't sure.

She was only about ten feet away from the entrance to the coffee shop now.

Ken said, "I didn't tell her about you, as we had agreed. She has asked from whom I was getting my leads. I said that I would only tell her if it was absolutely necessary, and only after I had spoken with my sources, and my sources had agreed. That was partly why I actually wanted you to meet her, so that you could gauge for yourself if I should tell her anything."

Stevens said in an exasperated voice, "*She knows me, Ken. I have known her from when she was a wild teenager. And I know…,*" here he paused and then decided to say it, to wake this supposedly prize-winning investigative reporter out of his self-induced hypnotic trance. He said, "*I also know about the butterfly tattoo on a very private part of her ass, too. Get it?*"

Ken's face reddened as a wave of understanding was followed by one of nausea. A microthought pierced his skull: *Why is it that no matter how experienced and knowledgeable one becomes, one can still be sucked in by one's desires?*"

The Lieutenant Colonel commanded Ken: "Lose her. Lose her now! Cut her off from your investigation and your sources. She will only put you and a lot of innocent people in grave danger. TAMPRR knows that it's crunch time–right now–as far as killing off the Canadian healthcare system is concerned. At this point TAMPRR will move against anyone, prize-winning reporter, obstinate politician, or whoever else might be in a position to sway a major segment of the Canadian voters to force their politicians to guarantee that their universal health care system is going to continue."

Ken nodded that he understood. Now, as if mesmerized, he simply watched Stevens and Sylvia simultaneously, as if he were an insect, with independently directed eyes on the sides of his head.

Stevens's harsh look told Ken to stay seated while he stood up. With that, he exited the side entrance just next to their table. Its close-by location was undoubtedly no coincidence. Having an emergency exit available was just a precaution Stevens had taken in selecting his table before Ken arrived, just in case of... *whatever*.

Ken glanced around the restaurant. He didn't see anyone who seemed to be paying him any mind, so after watching Stevens disappear, he sat back in his chair and pretended to sip his coffee. "Goddamn it, ... Sylvia." he said under his breath. It was all very distressing, to say nothing of ego deflating. *She had seemed genuinely interested in me back at her apartment, and since. Ah, vanity, thy real name is 'schmuck'!*

CHAPTER 47

About five seconds after Stevens left via the side door, Ken stood up and moved towards the front of the Starbucks. He was nearly there when Sylkeen/Sylvia entered. They exchanged seemingly warm greetings; she said she was just coming to get a takeout espresso and biscotti.

Ken decided to deal with her head on. He wanted to know more about what she was really up to as far as his investigations were concerned. He suggested that they get something to eat at one of the outdoor restaurants in the old Market area, just down from Parliament Hill. She was agreeable and they walked a few blocks to a local eatery.

After they had seated themselves at a table an obliging waitress came over and took their orders. While they waited they made medium talk, Ken speaking in generalities about his day, and 'Sylkeen' doing likewise, although she seemed more interested in Ken's day than relating her own. *What if Stevens was wrong?*

Ken didn't really feel like eating anything, but ordered a glass of white wine with his sandwich. Sylkeen ordered a glass of red, and a 'mixed greens' salad with a non-fat dressing. *Figures.*

Ken sat taking in his tablemate with a combination of fury and lust, which under other circumstances might portend an outstanding sexual experience. Watching her 'show' as she spoke and listened to him, he noted that her eyes and mouth continuously expressed the assurance of a vibrant, sexually confident and secure young woman, entirely aware that she could probably get almost any man she set her sights on. *That power can make her a millionaire. Although, come to think of it, it already has!"*

While they were talking, Ken's cellphone rang. Ken reached into his inside jacket pocket and retrieved the phone.

"Hello. Ken Simpson here."

The unmistakable Scottish brogue replied. "Mr. Simpson, are you and your colleague planning to go back to the paper's apartment after your meal?"

Ken instinctively began to look around the restaurant, trying to see where he was, surprised to be hearing from Dr. McTavish again so soon. He said, "Yes, actually."

"Then finish whatever the fuck you think you are doing within the next twenty minutes and get back to the *Era's* apartment. Both of you. I want to come up and speak to you." McTavish sounded very upset and/or just possibly, drunk.

Ken said, "Fine, but what do you have in mind?"

"I haven't quite worked that out in detail, but I will be at your paper's apartment in a half-hour. Be there."

Ken's anxiety meter's needle was trying to fly off the scale. Ken managed an "Okay, but, …", before his party hung up.

Ken needed to think. He pretended that he and the other party were still connected, muttering into the phone "Right," or "uh-hum, tell me more," while nodding his head in agreement and/or saying "Right," every several seconds. Meanwhile, his mind was racing to figure out what the hell McTavish was up to. Finally he pretended the call was over and said, "All right. Bye for now." as he put the phone back in his pocket.

Sylkeen asked, seemingly innocently, "Who was that?"

"Oh, that was, eh, Rusty, wanting to know if I was ready to send him any copy; he said that there was some pressure from upstairs to get something into print within the next day or so. He also said that since the paper has been spending a lot of advertising dollars promoting the healthcare series, it's time to start satisfying the built-up expection. So I guess we have our work cut out for us over the next day or two, Syl… Sylkeen. Maybe we should start right after we finish eating."

Sylvia Best said, "Sure," and chomped down on her lettuce with gusto.

Ken never enjoyed lying, and he knew he didn't do it very well, but he couldn't think of what to else to say. Ken changed the subject, more than once, until Sylkeen/Sylvia finally seemed to realize that she would not be finding out much more about what he had been doing this day. They finished the rest of their meals in a not uncomfortable silence, each seemingly enjoying the surprisingly good food. Sylkeen/Sylvia shared her biscotti with Ken while they had their coffees.

After the meal they walked back to the apartment, and once there went to their respective rooms to change into their leisure clothes. Ten minutes later they were in the den booting up their computers. Another couple of minutes later the apartment phone rang twice in succession. Ken buzzed the visitor in.

Here we go. Hold onto your hats, ladies and gentlemen. Whatever is bugging old McTavish, it's obviously important enough that he's tracked me down and knew that I was with Sylkeen... eh, Sylvia. Does he know who...

That was as far as Ken's thinking had gone before there was a knock at the door.

CHAPTER 48

Ken not so much opened the door as unlocked it and then was shoved back as Dr. McTavish forcefully pushed it open from the other side. The elderly psychiatrist was clearly upset, and Ken was shocked to see him slightly staggering and looking quite flushed; the man had been either crying or drinking, or both.

Dr. McTavish shuffled into the living room and slumped onto the nearest couch. Bending forward, he grabbed his head with his hands as if to get it to stop shaking. Ken sat down opposite him; Sylkeen sat in the companion chair, and both of them waited.

The psychiatrist said nothing. Ken awkwardly told Sylkeen (he decided to, temporarily at least, continue calling her by the name she had used when she had been introduced to him) that the distraught man in front of them was Dr. William McTavish, someone he had interviewed in Toronto two days earlier.

Before he could manage to say anything else, Dr. McTavish spoke out, in an anguished voice. Looking at Ken he said, "I asked you, Mr. Simpson, I *pleaded* with you, to not do anything that would hurt her, that sweet woman who finally had found some peace within herself, and some solace with me. You, they've... killed her. They've... they've murdered Judith."

Sylkeen nearly shouted, "What? What did you say?" She was trembling, her composure cracking.

McTavish said, "I said, they killed her! About three hours ago, as she was driving to an appointment, her car was forced off the road by a large SUV. It tumbled down an embankment and ended upside down in the bloody Ottawa River. She was dead before anyone could reach her, trapped in place by her seat belt and the airbag. Witnesses who were jogging by said it was not an accident. The people who did it were not teenagers, but two big guys in business suits. Right after they hit her car they stopped their SUV, backed it up, jumped out and looked to see where her car had landed. Then they apparently nodded to one another and ran back to their car, with revolvers in their hands in case anyone tried to stop them. Some brave, foolhardy driver tried to block off their car so they fired a shot at him and he backed his car off. Then they got away."

Ken was stunned. From everything he had learned about TAMPRR in the past few days and hours, he had no doubt that the elderly female physician he had met, *was it only yesterday*, was killed as punishment and to get a major adversary in the fight over Canada's healthcare system out of the way. Her death was also undoubtedly intended as a warning, possibly to Ken and, and... to whom else? Trish Markridge?

He uttered the utterly inadequate words, "I'm so sorry."

Ken glanced over at Sylkeen who looked like she was frozen in time and space. She wasn't moving. Didn't even seem to be listening or even breathing. *What the hell is it with her? Has she no conscience?*

Talking into his hands, Dr. McTavish said, "*You people*; you didn't protect your source as you had promised you would. Judith was left in the most vulnerable position. They knew she would give everything, *anything*, including her life if necessary, to fight for what she believed in. And they probably believed she had already given a great deal of potentially damaging information to you."

Dr. McTavish's voice grew stronger and more strident as he continued. "And God knows she had the ammunition with which to fight. She had sat in on the very earliest meetings, the ones with only a very few of the key players present, where they had started to talk, against her best arguments and advice, about doing things that she was sure would cripple the whole Canadian Medicare system. The people at those meetings discussed how they would put on this frigging charade at *both* the federal and provincial governmental levels, carrying out mock fights over minor issues, allowing a few photo-op friendly improvements to be made in the system, and all the while they were putting enough sand in the tank so that the entire engine would eventually seize up.

"The majority in her party agreed that the MRI machines and radiation therapy equipment wouldn't be allowed to operate more than eight hours a day, so that a lot of Canadians had to be shipped to the U.S. to get treated. That got plenty of publicity on both sides of the border, with headlines shouting that the Canadian healthcare system was defective. Hell, they had made damn sure it was defective. The message was received loud and clear in the U.S. that the Canadian system was not a good one to emulate. And it gave the right-wingers right here in Canada ammunition to use to try to convince our own citizens that we should adopt for-profit healthcare.

"Judith knew *who*, and *how* they were playing their shell games with their taxpayers' money, and that they were planning to *continue* to do so until they effectively killed the entire system. And she knew that she would not be able to stop them from *within* the government, because of how far up the food chain the corruption went. That is why she quit the political game. She was completely outnumbered. There were too many of them, with their drug and managed healthcare and health insurance lobbyist buddies, providing all kinds of lucrative stock and under-the-counter monetary offers to those who sang their tunes. Too many bureaucrats had been bought, too many politicians pressured, too many healthcare administrators compromised.

"And she told me that there was only one reason that all attempts to enshrine the Canadian healthcare system in the Charter of Rights and Freedoms or some other equally ironclad law had failed, and that was because once the government had done that, and the game had finally been lost by the HMOs and their friends, then they would stop supporting the various individual politicians with their trust funds and their parties with covert campaign contributions.

"Instead, they would simply pick up their marbles and their greenbacks and go back home. And none of those they paid off had the guts and decency to tell them to go screw themselves. They knew that as long as there was even the slightest chance that American companies could *eventually* operate in Canada, then they would just stay here, pitching and paying–all to protect their moneymaking machines back home. And their pharmaceutical buddies were involved up to their eyeballs as well, in order to push their symbiotic agendas."

McTavish's voice was shaking with fury. Looking plaintively at Ken and Sylkeen, he said with the voice of one who had experienced too much, "How could you, both of you... how could *we* have allowed this to happen?"

Sylkeen made a strange, soft sound and both Ken and McTavish turned towards her. She looked like she wanted to say something. Her mouth opened, her lips moved, but no more intelligible sounds emerged. Tears flowing, the noises she began to make sounded like an animal's keening. She was clutching her middle with both arms, hugging herself tightly, and began rocking quickly back and forth.

Later she would tell Ken that somewhere deep inside, at the level most people hardly ever touch, where they are rarely so honest with themselves, Sylvia suddenly felt as if she was witnessing, and complicit with, her own mother and father dying all over again, and feeling as if she had helped to kill them.

With tears running down her cheeks, she finally said, "Dr. McTavish, Ken had nothing to do with what happened to Dr. Brown. He didn't know anything about it. It... it... it was *my* doing."

Ken said, "What do you mean?"

McTavish said, "Young lady, what the hell are you talking about?"

Sylkeen began shaking violently. Finally, as if she had to push the words out from a stuck place deep inside, she said, sobbing openly, "I know... I knew... Dr. Brown. I used to live here in Ottawa. She was my ob/gyn when I was pregnant. Something went very wrong with the pregnancy... with the fetus. In the eighth month it... it... died. My baby died. And I had to carry her to full term. I thought I was going to go out of my mind. Every minute of every day and every night, I was aware that I was carrying my... my dead baby inside of me. Dr. Brown helped me. She stopped me from... from... hurting myself. She had my husband and me to her home a number of times. She shared with me some of her own story. She made me feel that I was not alone, that I was not responsible for what happened to the fetus merely because I had been promiscuous when I was younger. I didn't know if she was telling me the truth or not, but the fact that she said it made me hold onto her words for dear life.

"Dr. Brown delivered the dead fetus herself; she wouldn't let anyone else do it. It was as if she wanted to share some of the responsibility for giving birth to a dead child. She really cared; she always cared so much... maybe *too* much."

Sylkeen paused to get some more stuck words out. She looked from Ken to McTavish and back again. When she began to speak again her voice was different–stronger, somehow fuller, angry.

"Ken, I am so sorry. I have lied to you from the beginning. My married name is actually Sylvia Best, not Sylkeen Bowry. The name I was born with is Sylvia Marks. I am an operative for a company called TAMPRR. My Uncle Jake is its CEO. It functions partly as a covert company, and one of its current contracts–probably its biggest contract *ever*–has to do with bringing down the Canadian Medicare system. I thought this was just going to be another job for TAMPRR."

Looking now at Dr. McTavish she said, "The fact that they might want to destroy your healthcare system was never any of my concern. Not until now. I never, ever, was involved in anything that cost someone's life. Not since my baby died. But when the paper learned that Ken was here in Ottawa I arranged to come here.

"TAMPRR... my uncle... told me to report back to him whatever I found out. I know that other operatives were sent also; they found and followed you, Ken. When you saw Judith Brown they must have known, and probably feared what she may have told you. I am so very sorry." Her entire body was shaking.

Both men were looking at her, waiting, saying nothing. She continued, almost as if she were narrating, "I never thought they would resort to anything more than bribery or corporate sabotage. My own father, Jake Marks's brother, had worked for the CIA. He told me and my mother nothing directly, but from his strange behavior I learned almost everything there is to know about deceiving and gaining leverage. He was involved in our government's covert operations in Chile and Nicaragua. I would never have agreed to this assignment if I had truly believed that anyone would get hurt. Who the hell would ever kill over health care, anyway? Street drugs, sure. Gold, of course. *But healthcare?*"

Dr. McTavish snarled. "So it was all right with you if the company you were working for bribed politicians into unnecessarily postponing access to potentially life-saving tests and procedures, actions that could save children or their parents from dying needlessly of cancer, or heart disease. You didn't care about that!"

Sylvia Marks replied slowly, saying, "I was brought up to not care, to not feel anything deeply, about anything or anyone. My father was mostly away on assignment in other countries when I was growing up. And when he was home he usually had no time for us kids or my mother, at least not until I became about twelve years old. By then I started to blossom and I knew how to get his attention. I was a tomboy, but a sexy one. He could do things with me like go to football games or go fishing, and still enjoy the fact that I was female. We used to go camping together in Yellowstone. We went sea kayaking on the west coast for two weeks at a time. He was my father and he was hardly ever around and I missed him horribly, especially when my mother started drinking when she was left alone with us. So when he came home and offered to take me away for a skiing or kayaking or camping holiday, I *wanted* to go. Even when he took advantage of... when *he treated me like his wife*, part of me still wanted to be with him. I just learned to turn off my feelings so that no matter what he did to me, I didn't care. I wanted to be with him that badly."

Sylvia had been talking to the floor. She stopped speaking, and very slowly raised her eyes. She looked searchingly at Ken and Dr. McTavish though her curtain of tears.

Ken was dumbfounded, his emotions a mishmash of burning anger and surging warmth. He didn't know if he wanted to hurt her or hug her. He did nothing.

McTavish was gazing at her with what appeared to be a mixture of sorrow and compassion. He said softly, "So *you* learned that to have what time and attention and affection that you could from your father, you had to sacrifice your own self. Even if that meant..."

"Even if that meant that he used me, that he *abused* me? That's right. Then, when I was in my last year of high school, my mother and father's marriage was disintegrating. It was like he had suddenly awakened from a deep, drunken sleep; he seemed to be so ashamed, and so spent. He wouldn't look at me when he spoke. But his embarrassment made *me* feel ashamed and furious. And I felt as if everything I ever did when I was with him, even the innocent things, were somehow wrong, too. He resented my young teenaged friends coming over to our place, or me going to their home. He wouldn't come near me but he also wouldn't let me go."

"Then my parents apparently decided to try to make a go of things. They went to my Uncle Jake's cottage at Lake Tahoe for a week. Apparently there was a terrible propane heater accident. Carbon monoxide seeped into the cottage. Both of them died but weren't discovered for days. I had been away on a school-sponsored wilderness trip. When I came back home, my aunt Mary was waiting for me with the news.

"I used to see my Uncle Jake from time to time when I was growing up, especially in the last couple of years before my parents died. He and my father were quite close until they had some kind of falling out; I never really knew what about.

After my parents died I left home and went to New York City. A few months later my uncle tracked me down and brought me to stay with him at his house in Miami Beach where I finished my high school diploma. Then I left to go to university to take journalism. But I came back to Uncle Jake's home during Christmas vacations, mid-term break, and so on. "

Sylvia was transmuting back into a beautiful woman as she spoke through her tears. "I don't think I have really cared deeply for anyone except my uncle, not since my parents died. He took me in when I was a very rebellious teenager and he never physically touched me in any way that he shouldn't have, and for those things I will always be grateful He found me jobs, and because his company, TAMPRR, had such high-powered clients, he was able to introduce me to some very powerful and wealthy people. I used whatever tools I had to get what I wanted, and in return my uncle got what *he* needed.

"At the same time, however, as I got to know more about him and his business practices over time, it became increasingly obvious to me that he actually *enjoyed* being deceptive and unethical. Of course, I am not so sure that I am really much better at this point because, while I don't enjoy lying, I have done it so frequently that it has become almost second nature to me. But I know that I didn't ever intend that any harm should come to anyone, and most especially to Dr. Brown. When I took this assignment at the *Era*, Ken, I was told that if I could provide TAMPRR with inside information about what you were doing, then you were going to gradually be moved away from possibly causing any real damage to TAMPRR's clients. I hope you will believe me."

Ken just stared at her, at a loss for words to describe the extent of the betrayal he felt. Several deep breaths later, however, he was ready to pounce. He spat out his accusation. "So you've operated as a spy the whole time, and everything you did and said was calculated to find out who I was interviewing for the series, what I was thinking, and what I was going to be writing."

Sylvia resignedly nodded her acknowledgement as her tears continued to fall.

"And you reported everything that you heard back to your Uncle Jake?"

Sylvia nodded again. She said, "It has never happened before that anything other than a company's secrets were the target of what I was doing. That was the whole game, as far as I knew. I would be introduced to the CEO or some other senior executive of some high tech or old economy company and all the guy would see in me was some trophy to jet around with. I would often get involved with him, even if he was married at the time, and would sometimes accompany him to other cities where he had scheduled corporate functions. I would casually ask innocent questions and receive "There, there, you sweet thing, you couldn't possibly understand what I am talking about so I can afford to tell you a lot, just for the sake of bragging," kinds of answers. They never knew that I had often been given crash courses by some of our clients' scientists so that I was, at least in general terms, up to speed on the technology or advance that we wanted to know about."

Dr. McTavish responded, icily: "So you would gain access to

whatever companies, agencies, politicos you were sent to infiltrate, and if need be you would seduce the top guy, learn everything you could from him, and then funnel back whatever information you found out. And I presume it also paid very well."

Sylvia shivered in response to Dr. McTavish's witheringly correct description.

She said, "At first, when I was much younger I used to do it to please my uncle and, I suppose, just to see if I *could* do it. And yes, I would make a lot of money by working for a few days or weeks. But in recent years I didn't do it for those reasons any more. One of the CEOs I was to target was a charismatic forty-something who lived here in Ottawa whom I made the mistake of letting myself have feelings for. He had my father's looks, and my mother's kindness. We fell in love, had a whirlwind romance as he worked his way across this continent and Europe pushing the acceptance of his own company's software. We married after we had signed a very generous pre-nupt, and when we separated three years later, just before the Internet bubble burst, he was worth the better part of a half-billion dollars. The divorce was very amicable and the settlement gave me a several lifetimes' worth of financial security.

"Since then, I have simply worked for my uncle when it pleased me, just for the challenge, the adventure, and for something to do. It's been like the emotional and adrenalin high that some people get from doing 'extreme sports', only played for much higher stakes. Besides, '9 to 5' work and volunteer work bores me. So does the 4C way of life, the 'Country-Club-Coffee-Clutch' thing that I did for a year after the divorce until I thought I would go nuts like most of the wealthy women I met who were also bored out of their minds. All they did was occasional volunteer work. The rest of the time they would just sit around and drink, eat, occasionally play golf or tennis, shop, and 'manage' a household and the odd affair. Which really meant that they would tell the maid or nanny what to do, usually by cellphone, while they were at lunch with their vacuous friends or lovers. To hell with that kind of life!"

"But why *this* kind of life?" asked Ken. "Pardon my language, but why prostitute yourself at *this* point in your life?"

She flinched but said, "No offense taken. Look, I never took on an assignment where I didn't check out the target in advance and have my say about whether I would take it on. I was always provided a dossier on the individual. As I was in your case, Ken."

Ken was livid. He said, "You were what?"

Sylvia said, "That's right. They had an entire file on you, including complete medical information, a summary of your personal life, your military record, and your marital..." She deliberately hesitated for just a moment, and smiled malevolently, as if to pay him get back for his earlier 'prostitute' reference, and she then said "your marital situation as well as your 'screwing around' lifestyle when you were working overseas."

Ken said nothing but felt his face flush, whether with embarrassment or anger was not clear–even to himself.

Sylvia continued, "I even knew about that cute case of crabs that you had back in your thirties. And, of course, that you wisely had yourself tested for STDs after you left the Air Force, and again after you left your marriage and before you started up with Martha Harrison. You can't begin to imagine the sources TAMPRR has access to and who they have on their payroll, Ken, including even a couple of your colleagues at *The New York Era*. Be assured that TAMPRR's HMO clients had no trouble compiling an entire medical history on you that began even before your birth, starting with the false alarm about German measles when your mother was pregnant with you."

Ken exploded; *"Bastards! Them and you and..."*

Sylvia interrupted him, her voice changing to one that signaled her self-disgust. "Please, Ken. Dr. McTavish, I am unbearably sorry, most of all about what happened to Dr. Brown. It is about time that I stop playing at spy games and grow up. I need to somehow undo, or at least minimize, some of the damage I have been helping to bring about. I will do whatever you would like me to in order to stop what my uncle is trying to accomplish here. I owe at least that much to Dr. Brown."

Dr. McTavish thought for several beats and then said, with a vengeful flash in his eye, *"Well*, perhaps there is a way to use TAMPRR's–and your–talents for espionage and treachery."

Sylvia and Ken simultaneously turned towards Dr. McTavish, and then towards one another, as if suddenly the three were aligned. Sylvia said, "Please, tell me what I can do, and I will try my best to do it.

The engineer-turned-psychiatrist said, "I still have some friends in the scientific research facilities here in Ottawa. And I have a couple of ideas, actually. One of my best friends from back in my engineering days is doing some absolutely fabulous work with superminiaturization of digitized audio and video recorders that Canada's national intelligence service, CSIS, has started using as part of their undercover work. Sylvia, does your uncle wear glasses?"

She said, "Yes, he does. I have tried to get him to update them but he still prefers the old-fashioned ones, the kind with turtleshell plastic frames. Somewhat like yours, actually. ... Oh, sorry. I didn't mean to..."

McTavish said, "Yes, you probably did and that's fine. Look, let's meet back here in a few hours. Let me see if I can enlist my engineering friend in a 'field test' of some of the latest versions of the devices they have been working on."

Ken and Sylvia readily agreed to meet again later in the evening with McTavish. With that settled, and the psychiatrist seemingly sobered up, he was out the door and heading towards the elevator with a much more determined step.

Ken and Sylvia were left suddenly alone again, each evidently quite uncomfortable and at a loss for words. Finally, Ken said, "Look, I have to do some writing. And I need to think about what I am going to do with what you have just told us." With those words Ken turned and quickly walked out of the room and down the hall. She heard the door to his bedroom close quietly.

Sylvia sat still in the living room of the apartment, her own thoughts and feelings overwhelming her, sobbing silently. She kept saying to herself under her breath, over and over again. "Forgive me, Dr. Brown. Please. Forgive me."

True to his word, within less than three hours Dr. McTavish was back with both a plan and some most interesting high-tech miniaturized communication prototypes. The three of them discussed the doctor's plan in detail. If it worked, they would each have an essential role to play in the unraveling of TAMPRR.

Ken realized that Dan Stevens would also need to play a crucial role if their scheme were to have a possibility of success. He told neither Sylvia nor McTavish about the identity of his deep source, but said that he would need to be contacted and utilized within the next forty-eight hours if TAMPRR's intentions for Trish Markridge and the Canadian healthcare system were to be aborted.

At nine-thirty the following morning Sylvia used her encrypted cellphone to call Uncle Jake and tell him that she wanted to visit him at his home in Miami Beach. It was a highly appropriate place to do her penance.

CHAPTER 49

Jake Marks was at his luxurious Indian Creek Drive home in Miami Beach when the call came in to his 'master unit' cellphone, the one equipped with multiple lines that responded to a variety of incoming calls according to which encryption code was being used. The phone's screen could tell him many things, the least of which was whose cellphone was calling.

He was surprised to see that it was Sylvia's phone ringing him. Since the day that he called her to do a piece of work for TAMPRR by taking the job at *The New York Era* that he had prearranged for her with the new publisher, she had only called him three previous times: once to accept the assignment; the second time, after Ken Simpson had been to her apartment for dinner; and the third time when she phoned from Ottawa to tell him where they were staying and what Ken was up to, as much as she knew anyway. She hadn't yet been able to access the list of people that Ken had appointments with, and she told her uncle that Ken seemed very reluctant to share that information. She also said that she didn't want to appear to be pushing him, at least not until he had become more relaxed and hopefully more trusting of her.

"Hello, Sylkeen," Jake Marks said in what, in his personal universe, passed as a warm, gentle tone. "How are you, hon?"

Sylkeen said, "Hello, Uncle Jake. I'm fine."

Sylkeen's cellphone was, to all appearances, an off-the-shelf model, whose inner workings had been modified by the techies at TAMPRR to use an encryption coding that was unique to only her phone and her uncle's. By dialing his number, the phone's software had automatically kicked in the encryption software. Her phone had certain other features about which even she still did not know. It was loaded with a GPS program that told Jake where in the world the bearer of the phone was, exactly. Marks received the GPS information on his phone's screen automatically and so he knew very well that she was calling from *The New York Era*'s company apartment in Ottawa.

"What's up, Sylkeen?"

"Well, I am still in Ottawa."

He said in a surprised tone, "Really?"

"Yes. We, Ken and I, we have been seeing some of the key players in healthcare up here. I want to tell you all about what I have learned, but I would prefer to do that in person. I will tell Ken that I want to follow some leads I have gotten from people I have seen here by going down to Miami Beach, all in the name of 'deeper research'. There are also some other things, I would like to talk to you about, Uncle Jake."

Jake Marks hesitated a beat before asking, "Like what?"

Sylkeen said, "Well, nothing huge but I would just rather discuss them with you in person."

Marks thought he was picking up some anxiety in Sylkeen's voice, a quality that she seldom projected. So he hit a couple of keys on the phone pad.

Marks's phone was also equipped with the very latest 'voice anxiety and lie detection' software that TAMPRR had originally bought and later modified without bothering to tell the Israeli company that had developed it, so now their very useful program had some additional features. When he glanced at the phone's screen after activating the special filter, Jake saw the flashing words, *'probable deception'* and *'high anxiety'*. He decided that he had better get her to him as fast as he could and find out what the hell was really going on.

"Good idea, Sylkeen. Come on down. I will be here at the 'beach' for another few days. You have the keys and the codes. Just let yourself in if I'm not here. By the way, I have some healthcare business associates who you might like to meet coming over on the weekend."

"Great! Alright, Uncle Jake" she replied. "I'll get there as soon as I can; probably tomorrow sometime.

Jake Marks said, "Fine, dear. See you then." Better that she should be close by so that he could effect whatever actions might be required to determine and deal with whatever the hell her *'probable deception'* and *'high anxiety'* were all about.

CHAPTER 50

The next day Sylvia's Air Canada flight 735 from Ottawa was descending towards Miami International Airport on its way to an almost on-schedule ETA of 12:15 p.m.. As the plane was on final approach she gazed out of the Boeing 767's port-side window and saw the sun lighting the tips of whipped-up ocean waves that were crashing upon the almost unbroken stretch of Florida beaches extending all the way to her destination. The scene below reminded her of the bizarre occasion when she had walked along the beach near her uncle's home on a bright, cool, and windy late December 2000 morning, when she had to walk around seemingly hundreds of bloated bags that, at that time, were making landfall on the otherwise pristine beach. The translucent bags looked like large, economy-sized cereal containers made of sealed waxed paper that had somehow escaped their water-soaked cardboard packaging. Sylvia heard on the news later that day that the freighter that had been carrying the cereal and other foods to Haiti from Florida had gone down with all crew aboard during the previous night's storm, only a few miles east of the Florida coastline.

Now she was arriving on another deceptively beautiful southern Florida day, aware that she carried with her both the intention and the tools that might help sink her Uncle Jake's business, and his life as he knew it.

Aside from Carmella, her uncle's long-time housekeeper, Sylvia was probably the only other person who knew her uncle's home's security code, a privilege he gave to her when she first came to live with him after her parents died. She last visited less than a month earlier when she had been briefed for her current assignment. At that time Uncle Jake had provided her with the latest security code. She knew that he had the code changed very couple of months but since it had been changed just prior to her last visit it was likely still the same.

Sylvia walked off the plane with her carry-on bag, caught the Hertz shuttle, picked up her rental car and drove from the airport towards her uncle's home along highway 112, which became 195 as she approached the toll that would get her to Miami Beach. The skyline that greeted her, filled with medium and high rise hotels and condos, was one that she had some trouble relating to as beautiful, but she was told by her uncle that as she got older she would see the buildings more as communal refuge than concrete refuse. She wasn't nearly there yet, but admittedly she was now longing to get to the beach.

The Arthur Godfrey Expressway, which ended at famed Collins Avenue, the permanent or temporary home of the wealthy, the worried, and the weary, was crowded as usual at this time of day. She turned north onto Indian Creek Road, a street that ran for several miles, lined with gorgeous homes that on the east side backed onto the intracoastal waterway, and which in her uncle's case, held a private pier where both his yacht and cigarette boat were usually tied up.

When she arrived at Jake Marks's home she rolled down her window and, using the audio code that her uncle had programmed to recognize and accept her voice, she said in a computerized staccato, "This is Sylvia. Open, please." The voice recognition system acknowledged her identity, saying "Welcome, Sylvia." The iron gate opened; a motion-activated, closed circuit camera tracked her car as she drove up to the house. She knew that her uncle was notified over his cellphone whenever anyone buzzed the gate, and received the house's video cameras' images on his phone's screen. When she parked and got out of the car, she turned and faced the camera mounted discreetly over the door. Smiling broadly, she waved warmly while mouthing the words, "Hello, Uncle Jake." She then tapped in the code on the keypad next to the door and heard the same eerie electronic voice as at the gate saying, "Please, come in, Sylvia". She entered the mansion.

The home was magnificent, if distinctly cool in ambience. Black and white marble floors and pillars, and almost bare, cream-colored walls greeted her; she could see the pool through the one-way mirrored doors on the other side of the living-dining room. Putting down her bag in the hallway she walked into the kitchen as if to make some tea. This was the ritual that she always followed when first arriving at the mansion, at least whenever it was empty. And now, she knew, it was vital that she not do anything out of the ordinary. When the water had boiled she poured some into a teapot, and then made her way through the hallway and into the dining room, where she put down the pot of tea and pulled out a chair that allowed her to look out at the pool and its imitation jungle motif.

Sylvia knew what probably no one else did, aside from her uncle and the man who had installed his security system, namely that there were micro-miniature video cameras in every room, including *all* bathrooms and bedrooms, except for her uncle's and her own. At least, that is what she had been told. The last couple of times she had visited, however, she had felt uneasy, as if there were something somehow different, but she couldn't quite figure out what. However, she compensated for that intuitive hunch by not walking around her bedroom in her undergarments, as she always had previously.

Sylvia knew that turning out the lights in her bedroom, if she chose to change there, would be futile as a privacy countermeasure since her uncle had, on an earlier visit, proudly shown her that his latest zero-lux, night-vision video equipment automatically produced color-corrected images that were almost daylight-ish. The color-compensation software TAMPRR had refined, painted over the greenish shades initially standard fare for such equipment, and instead provided skin tone colors, whenever possible, based upon previous biometric identity recordings made of the same person in well-lighted conditions.

As she made her way from the kitchen to the dining room table, and then to the outdoor pool's seating area, she carried with her a couple of magazines and her purse. In a seemingly random fashion she stopped and read for a few minutes in each place, then got up and moved nonchalantly to another spot in the house–perfectly ordinary actions for a high energy, high strung, young woman.

Before leaving Ottawa, Sylvia had practiced in front of Ken and Dr. McTavish, looking in her purse or pockets for her makeup, lipstick, or whatever, and then sitting herself down while she applied her makeup or lipstick, or read or sipped tea, or whatever else she chose to do so while surreptitiously 'seeding' microminiaturized, voice-activated, digital 'memory sticky-strip recorders'–under tables, on book shelves, in potted plants, in the kitchen, living room, den, by the pool, and everywhere else that she thought might yield interesting data. Each transparent 'memory sticky-strip' came covered with easy-to-remove transparent tape, so she was able to remove these tapes, and thereby her fingerprints, even as she stealthily pressed the tiny recording sticky-strips to various surfaces. Each sticky-strip was capable of holding more than 72 hours of voice-activated recordings. She would retrieve them later, perhaps after her uncle's upcoming weekend business bash, and then download their contents onto the especially modified PDA she was given. She could then transmit them via Wi-Fi to Dr. McTavish's contact's e-mail address. At that point they would be downloaded onto CDs for further scrutiny.

Sylvia knew that her uncle preferred to have most of his crucial business meetings in his home where he could exercise maximum surveillance of his guests' verbal and non-verbal communications through his various surreptitious recording devices. After such meetings, he would have the significant portions of the audio and video recordings reviewed by TAMPRR personnel as well as by a special computer program that scanned for whatever keywords it had been programmed to identify, and then printed out transcripts that handily bracketed the spoken keywords.

Uncle Jake once roared hilariously while explaining to Sylvia how incredibly easy it was to ply information from supposedly experienced businessmen. Frequently all it took, he said, were several drinks and a few exotic South Beach party-type companions with whom his guests could 'commiserate' somewhere on the two acre property. These moments of commiseration were almost invariably taped; many a senior executive of TAMPRR's clients or targets had taken the liberty of poking or groping where he, or even she, shouldn't have, and had become surprisingly malleable after being made aware of the possibility that certain behaviors had been digitally recorded for posterity, or possibly, publication.

Sylvia had picked up her uncle's momentary hesitation when she called to say that she needed to consult with him in person. She would have to be very careful how she would speak with him over the next several days. Her own feelings of anger over Dr. Judith Brown's death had reached the level of what she once heard a psychology professor refer to as 'organismic disgust', the point at which individuals usually found they could truly no longer tolerate elements of a situation or relationship, and the point at which they were very likely to drastically change their thoughts, feelings, attitudes, or behavior in regard to the matter or the persons about which they were so repulsed. Sylvia now understood, at a visceral level, what the term 'organismic disgust' meant. She had reached that level in regard to her uncle, his company, and her own involvement with them both. Since no one had ever accused Jake Marks of being insensitive to nuances of changes in other persons' responses to him, she would have to be vigilant to not overly arouse his suspicions.

On innumerable occasions in the past he would get home after work to find his niece waiting for him with a gorgeous smile and sensual hug, which suited his preferences, and now her intentions, perfectly. This trip would hopefully begin to make some amends for some of what had transpired in Ottawa on account of her involvement with TAMPRR.

Corporate espionage was one thing; cold-blooded murder was quite another. The events of the last couple of days had turned her from one of her uncle's most valuable business assets into a primary tool of TAMPRR Inc.'s demise.

CHAPTER 51

Sylvia had been careful to appear laid-back as she wandered about the house planting the numerous memory sticky-sticks. About twenty minutes after she had planted the last one Jake Marks drove through the front gate of his home. As he was beginning to unlock the front door the action was completed for him from the inside; Sylvia opened the door and greeted her uncle with the familiar wide smile, dancing eyes, and a daughterish hug. "Hi, Uncle Jake! Its so good to see you!"

Jake Marks regarded his niece with a proud but somewhat guarded look; he was concerned that she had come home to ask for something that he would probably not want to give to her. He knew that she had no need at all for money; Mr. Dot-com made sure of that. Or, more accurately, she had done that for herself. *Hell, she's probably worth almost as much as I am, if not more.*

Jake recalled that when she married, her husband was merely a barely qualified millionaire. It was about two years after they married that he, and she, hit it big–really big. He sold his proprietary software to an already major search engine, and went right back to working fourteen hour days on his next 'killer app'. She told her uncle that she had had enough of sleeping, shopping, chatting with the other (as she referred to them) dot.knob wives. *She missed the action. That is what I provided her; she did it for the kicks, for the challenge, and to prove that she could still accomplish things on her own.*

All these thoughts, as well as a couple of impure and possibly illegal ones, raced through his mind as he felt this too young and too friggingly sexy young woman in his arms, giving him a surprisingly warm, long hug. *Christ, I need to get laid, soon.* He would arrange that over the next few days. Actually, the little helper he had in mind was younger than Sylvia.

As he hugged her back, probably just a little too tightly, he wondered to himself, "Now, what the hell does she want?" When he set up her current mission he had been very explicit in his instructions: get close to Ken Simpson–as close as need be, but find out what the hell he was up to. His damn Paulson had made him too hot a target to outright eliminate at this time. If there was a foul-up in any attempt to take him out, and if it could ever be traced back to TAMPRR, then the house that Jake built would come crashing down all around him. He wouldn't risk it; he didn't need the action.

TAMPRR's clients' problems almost never required such terminally extreme measures. Well, all right, a few had, like the Judith Brown business, but that was only because she couldn't be silenced in any other way, and she could give Simpson enough dirt to sink the mission. Besides, Markridge had to be warned of TAMPRR's seriousness in an entirely unambiguous way.

Boy scouts and girl guides like Ken Simpson and the late Dr. Brown pissed Jake Marks off, big time.

Initially, Marks hadn't wanted to use lethal force in this most recent instance. But that damn old bitch-doctor had known too much, had been nosing around through her contacts, and was on the verge of finding definitive proof that George P. Linden and some other provincial and federal politicians were on TAMPRR's payroll. Then she would have told that traitor's son, Ken Simpson, who would have gone public with the information, and that simply could not be allowed. TAMPRR's entire effort over fifteen years would come unraveled and Jake Marks would personally lose a huge amount of money, or worse.

Christ, people get killed for pocket change nowadays; for what I was going to lose I was willing to take out a whole regiment, if need be. Do whatever has to be done to take out the enemy. End of story. That is some of what we learned from the Avro Arrow assignment. When I issued the order to eliminate Frank Simpson, it wasn't that easy; after all, he was a friend.

I tried to get him to shut the fuck up about what we and our clients, really wanted. Hell, had to have! They couldn't afford to lose their businesses to that Canadian company. So when the son of a bitch wouldn't shut up, when he went and spoke to Ike, didn't he think we would find out? We bloody well couldn't let him give testimony to the Senate Subcommittee on Military Preparedness!

So we did what had to be done, and the guy died a flyboy hero, going down in flames. Hell, we should all be so lucky!

We wanted the Canadians to blow up those Soviet bombers over their territory, not over our own cities like New York, Boston, L.A., or Washington, for Christ's sake. And they agreed. Talk about being a good neighbor! The whole frigging country of Canada, the whole Canadian population, had signed on to 'take the nuclear bullet' to save our American hides. And if they were stupid enough or brave enough to agree to have nuclear warheads go off over their land, well, that was mighty neighborly. Of course, if the shoe had been on the other foot, would we Americans have agreed to have weapons go off over the U.S.A. in order to save Canada? Please!

That bastard, Simpson, was not satisfied that our country had preserved aircraft building supremacy for the corporations of the good old U.S. of A. Well, fuck him! So what if our pilots had inferior aircraft for a few years because we wouldn't buy the nearly operational Avro Arrows. Hell, a few years later they had aircraft that were almost as good, partly due, of course, to the fact that for most of the Avro Arrow engineers, there were no jobs for them left in Canada. So right after the Arrow program was closed down, our clients hired them.

Christ, why the hell do I still spend so much time presenting my side of this old story to myself? Is it guilt at killing a fellow POW from the Korean conflict? Hardly! Is it because, whenever I see Sylvia I remember that I also killed my own brother and his wife? Who knows? Who gives a shit? Forgetaboutit.

When Sylvia drew away from the inappropriately long physical greeting, Jake Marks felt a little flushed. He recovered quickly, asking, "How was your flight? Have you had a chance to take a swim yet?"

Sylvia forced a smile and replied, "The flight was just fine. I'll go swimming later. Want to join me, Uncle Jake?"

He replied, "Sure, maybe, later, but don't wait for me. Go ahead on your own whenever you feel like it."

A few minutes more of requisite chitchat was dispensed with over a light tuna salad meal that Sylvia prepared. They ate out by the pool, Jake Marks with a cold light beer that he rested on his belly and Sylvia with a glass of white wine that she placed on the nesting table next to her chair.

After they finished eating and Jake Marks had had another couple of beers, he got up and told his niece that he would be right back after he had made a business call. About fifteen minutes later he called for Sylvia to join him in his den. Sylvia prayed that he hadn't realized that this was her second time in there today.

When the house was being built her uncle had had his bedroom, living room, and home office enclosed in a special metal mesh so as to be electronic-eavesdropping proof from any external listening devices. After they sat down in facing easy chairs he inquired, "So what was it that you wanted to talk to me about, Sylvie, that couldn't be talked about over the phone?"

"Uncle Jake, one of the people that Ken Simpson talked to was killed a day later."

"Oh? Really? What happened to her, honey?"

As soon as the question was out of his mouth, Jake Marks knew he was in trouble.

Why did I have to say "her"? That damned third beer!

He searched for a sign that Sylvia caught it, but her head happened to be turned away from him and she was gazing towards the new sculpture she had admired when she was in the den earlier. She slowly turned back, appearing very composed and to have not noticed his slip.

"She was killed by a hit-and-run driver who forced her car off the road. The driver left the scene in an apparently stolen vehicle. But Uncle Jake, I need to know that he wasn't anyone who has anything to do with this job that you've asked me to do. I don't think I could take it, if I was involved in anything like that."

Jake Marks did not suffer impudence well. He said, with a steely smile, and a shatteringly cold, controlled voice, "You know better than anyone, Sylvia, that *we* don't talk about the details of *my* business. We don't *ever* do that. It would be... *unprofessional.* But I can assure you that TAMPRR had nothing to do with what happened to that person, Shit happens. *That's all.*"

Sylvia appeared to be relieved. "Thank you, Uncle Jake. I am so happy to hear that. You know that I have always found the work you have asked me to do... well... exciting and interesting, even a little dangerous. But it is important for me to know that we wouldn't do anything that would *physically* hurt anybody."

"Of course, I can promise you that, Sylvia. Now, look! You've have been doing great work on this assignment, but if you want to get out now, well, that's fine. I would prefer that you didn't, but your happiness is what is most important. That has been my attitude ever since I took you in after your parents died."

The last comment had virtually always worked in the past; it was a usually waterproofed guilt trip. This time, however, Sylvia's response sounded just slightly less than persuasive. "No, that's okay; I'll continue with the work. For a few weeks more, anyway, if that is what you would like."

"Are you sure?"

Sylvia said, "Yes, I'm sure."

Jake Marks said, "That's great, honey. Now, tell me what Ken Simpson has been up to, and then lets go into the kitchen and have some dessert."

Sylvia proceeded to tell her uncle a story, a rather good one that she, Ken, and McTavish had concocted. She made sure to mention some things that he would know were valid if he had any operatives in Canada checking up on her or Ken. At the same time, she said little that was of any practical use, and nothing at all about Dr. McTavish.

Jake Marks asked questions that seemed to indicate that he was buying her tales. At the same time, he did not want to seem to be pressing her. He would find out soon enough from the other contacts TAMPRR had embedded in various federal ministers' offices, as well as from some free-lancers, whether what she was telling him was true.

He impressed upon Sylvia that what he needed, most of all, was for her to get back to Ottawa, so that she could keep tabs on Simpson. He wanted to know whom Simpson interviewed and what he was told.

As he was trying to sell Sylvia on the importance of the role she was currently playing, Jake Marks was increasingly aware of how concerned he was about the progress of the current project. Some of his corporate clients had become more anxious than he had intended or expected when he had met with their representatives in San Francisco a couple days earlier. They all came through with the moneys he had asked for, but they made it clear that they expected results, meaning that nothing short of the final and complete destruction of the Canadian government-run healthcare system would satisfy. So *any* inside information that Sylvia could provide him about that snoopy reporter's activities would be welcome.

In order to reassure his niece that TAMPRR Inc. was strictly interested in bizwar and not conflicts that would take human lives, Jake decided to seem to bring Sylvia into his confidence. She had, after all, been involved in enough operations on behalf of TAMPRR Inc. to make her at least as informed as most of the company's other operatives, about its ways and means and goals. He especially wanted her to get past her upset over the death of Dr. Brown, at least insofar as the company's non-involvement was concerned, so that she could continue to work on Simpson. She was the ace up his sleeve.

He said, "You know, Sylvie, I always thought that I would want to leave TAMPRR to you." Acknowledging her surprised look with a nod of his head, he went on to elaborate about some of the means whereby TAMPRR had developed into the leading bizwar company in the country. And for the first time, he told her an almost unsanitized version of how TAMPRR was born, and that the demise of the Avro Arrow program was its first victory. He sounded like a proud father boasting about his child's accomplishments over the years.

"And never, never, I give you my word, was TAMPRR *ever* involved in the death of a person, in all the years we have been operating. I would never do that–to you, myself, or another human being."

As they left his den, Sylvia brushed against the front of his desk, and deftly removed the memory 'sticky-strip' that she had placed there earlier. She was now certain that her uncle and

TAMPRR were indeed behind the murder of Dr. Judith Brown. His use of the female pronoun before she had told him the name or gender of Dr. Brown, confirmed that to her. Colonel Jake Marks was such a chauvinist of the old school's first order that it was inconceivable that he would use the word "her" instead of "him" at that moment, unless he knew damned well whom Sylvia was talking about. And she now had the recorded evidence. It might not be sufficient in a court of law, but as far as she was concerned he was guilty as hell. And the other material that she had on the recording strip was probably enough, in the right reporter's hands, to help make the demise of TAMPRR quite likely.

CHAPTER 52

The next morning at 5:30 a.m. Sylvia was doing tai chi, having already finished her thirty minutes of meditation and forty minutes of yoga. Her uncle knew that tai chi had originated from oriental martial arts, and so he approved of these 'soft movements' exercises. As the mediation 'stuff', well that was another matter.

Jake came downstairs for breakfast shortly after his niece had finished her morning regimen. They chatted a while and he told her that he would be back in time to have a late dinner with her at 9:30 p.m. at Sam's Stone Crab restaurant. First, though, he had to go out of town for a few hours. If she needed him she should call his cellphone and not his office.

At the door, Marks and his niece said 'goodbye'. At the same time that she was helping him on with his suit jacket she managed to attach a recording sticky-strip to the inside of the right lapel. This device would be a backup for a more sophisticated one Sylvia had planted earlier that morning, while her uncle was taking a shower.

As she had on previous occasions, Sylvia had assisted her uncle to pick out frames for his most recent prescription glasses. After she decided to travel to Miami to see him, Sylvia, Ken, and Dr. McTavish brainstormed about the best ways to surreptitiously acquire information from her uncle. As they had agreed, first thing the following morning she called the Miami Beach optician's office where Jake had bought his glasses and obtained the make and model number of his 'turtleshell' frames, along with her uncle's prescription, all under the guise of Jake and her being out of town and his wanting to get another pair immediately after he had left his current pair behind in a cab on their way to a meeting.

The optician's secretary knew Jake Marks to be one of their

longstanding customers and expressed her regret that 'the Colonel' had lost his glasses. She added that it was unfortunate that he was not in town so that they could quickly get a new pair ready.

Sylkeen declined her kind offer to FedEx a new pair of glasses by overnight delivery, explaining that they were going to be leaving later that very day to head up to a remote hunting cabin in Canada's north. Sylvia said that she had been assured by a local optician she had just called that once they had the correct prescription and make and model of the frames, a virtually identical pair could probably be made in less than two hours.

Armed with the required information provided by the optician's office, Sylvia called McTavish's contact at 9:15 a.m. and faxed the required information to his office. The researcher called back shortly afterwards and said it would not be a problem to have the duplicate pair of especially modified glasses ready within three hours. The new glasses were dropped off at the apartment at the appointed time; as far as Sylvia could tell, they appeared identical to Jake Marks's own pair in looks and weight. From Dr. McTavish, however, she learned that the lenses functioned as transparent 'inverse' LCD screens, transforming the light that passed through them into electrical signals whose information was stored in over 500gigabytes of plasticized video memory located in one earpiece that, when triggered by a remote signal, could be downloaded via a microminiaturized transmitter in the other.

At her first opportunity, which came while her uncle was taking his morning shower, Sylvia replaced his glasses with the new pair, seemingly identical in every respect to the old pair, save their special modifications. Sylvia touched the frames with the dedicated 'electronic wand' she had brought along, and the 'glasses', which had been a development of Canada's ISD-COD, or Internal Security Department, covert ops division, began to record the first of at least 134 hours of images and sounds with videophone quality. When set in the 'transmit' mode by a remote controller the size and shape of a quarter, the recorded material could also be heard and seen by anyone within three hundred feet of Marks who was in possession of the specially developed microreceiver. If this receiver were attached to a 'booster-transmitter' it would be capable of providing near broadcast quality video to any interested parties.

After kissing Sylvia goodbye, Jake Marks left his home to begin his day's work at 7:15 a.m.. He arrived at his office less than ten minutes later and read over the documents that had been prepared for his trip. At 9:15 a.m. he would leave for MIA to catch the flight to Las Vegas.

The video data that his glasses captured would, when played back, show some intriguing internal company documents, the most important of which was entitled, *The Avro Arrow Manipulation Revisited: TAMPRR's Plans For The Dissolution Of The Canadian Universal Medicare System.* As Marks reviewed its provisions and timetables the pages were digitally stored onto the memory material in his replacement glasses. Around the corner from his building sat Sylvia in her rented car, downloading the visuals onto her especially programmed, PDA-sized receiver.

After reviewing the documents and nodding to himself approvingly, Colonel Jake Marks took off his glasses and rubbed his eyes. He next cleaned the anti-glare coated lenses, and might have been on the verge of noting something slightly different about the heft of his frames when his secretary rang. She said that the company limo was waiting and he was running short on time. He immediately replaced his glasses on his face, put the documents in question into his briefcase, grabbed his suit jacket, and made his way to the elevator with his 'Senior Master Of The Universe' swagger.

Retired U.S.A.F. Colonel Jake Marks reclined in his executive-class seat on the flight to Las Vegas. He was pleased to find that the seat beside him was empty; this was not a morning for small talk. He ordered a scotch with his snack and began to read the book he picked up at the airport bookstore, entitled *American CEOs And Their God Complex*, written by the founding president of a high-tech company who apparently had not only a degree in mechanical engineering from M.I.T. and an M.B.A. from Harvard, but also received his Ph.D. in Psychology after returning to university in his fifties. Marks respected authors who walked the talk, even though in this case a lot of what he read, while possibly accurate, was not particularly complementary to himself.

The book's author attributed a sort of mental rigidity and sense of omnipotence to some entrepreneurs, particularly those who assumed, because they had successfully launched a money-making company that now had anywhere from fifty to a hundred or so employees, that they could similarly manage a company that employed thousands. Another major failing that the author suggested these disasters-in-the-making CEOs had, was the belief that they could and should expand their businesses into areas in which they were not nearly as familiar without first seeking and heeding those business people who were much more cognizant of the problems associated with the proposed new areas of business.

Jake accepted that he was somewhat rigid in personality but not so much in his thinking. And since having made the mistake of trying to take TAMPRR into other fields such as personal surveillance for individual clients seeking the goods on cheating spouses and the like, he realized that he–and TAMPRR–were better off staying in the area of covert *corporate* work.

After his plane had landed and parked at the gate, Marks retrieved his belongings, disembarked quickly, and immediately located the limo driver who was holding a handwritten sign that said "Stuart Lever". He identified himself as the same, and took the fifteen-minute drive to the Jacket Club and Casino. He went up to his company's condo apartment, room 708, poured a drink, and watched the cable news while he waited for his guest.

The Las Vegas condo was, of course, an ideal perk for TAMPRR's executives as a getaway for themselves and as a venue in which to host corporate clients. Here they could find all the pleasures they might desire, delivered to their door or in their beds, at any time of day or night. Meanwhile TAMPRR could keep tabs of, and surreptitiously record, its guests' extracurricular activities. The chances were at least fair that at some time in the future this information would be of use.

The condo unit overlooked the magnificent Bellagio hotel and its justifiably famous dancing water fountains. The man-made lake that fronted the Bellagio became the reflective stage above which the spectacle took place many times a day, thrilling thousands of onlookers at a time. Marks nodded approvingly as he stood at the window watching the fountains do their magical thing to a song sung by Celine Dion.

Drink in hand and looking down at the frenetic scene below, Marks allowed that he loved Vegas. It offered all the pleasures that a man of his tastes enjoyed thoroughly, including the relief of 'no strings attached'. Occasionally, just to prove to himself that he still could, he availed himself of more than one of the 'platinum card level' prostitutes that TAMPRR kept on retainer. The fact that he sometimes used an ED-compensating drug to help him along hardly diminished his feelings of virility.

After watching the liquid sight-and-sound show for several minutes, Marks moved away from the window and sat down on the couch. He opened his briefcase and took out some papers he would want to reference to his guest.

In a few minutes, his very first TAMPRR employee, retired Lieutenant Colonel Dan Stevens, was scheduled to arrive. Marks was not certain what was going on with the man, but his suspicions had been aroused when Stevens had not checked in with him even once over the past three days, despite several attempts to make contact. Then, as if out of the blue, Stevens had called late the previous day from a number-blocked landline and asked that they meet today in Las Vegas to discuss aspects of the Canadian Medicare project.

While he waited, Jake Marks recalled their earliest days working together on what they had called 'the Arrow matter'. Together they had developed and employed a host of 'dirty tricks', including having quite convincing misinformation provided to President Eisenhower about the made-up deficiencies of the Avro Arrow program and the supposed advantages of the Bomarc missile. Their efforts helped get Ike to back the idea that the Canadians should drop their dreams of an

Allied sky filled with Arrows, and instead convinced them to buy the questionable Bomarcs.

There was a sharp knock on the door. Marks got up and opened it. "Hey, Dan, you old shit," he hissed, like a smiling python, in the trademark disingenuous way he had that unsettled younger employees of the company as well as his more gullible corporate clients.

As usual, Stevens regarded Marks with caution. "How the hell are you, Jake?" was his cheery mano a mano retort.

"Good, Dan. Really good." Here they were again, like two old sparring partners, getting back into the ring again for the umpteenth time for another few, friendly but bruising rounds.

"For Christ's sake, where the hell have you been the last few days, Dan? I tried to hail you a bunch of times. I wondered if you had lost your cellphone."

"I misplaced it, that's all, Jake. I'll find it when I get back home. I've just taken a few days off to visit some friends from the Avro Arrow days back in Ottawa."

Marks felt cautiously cold. "No shit? Which of the old farts did you see?"

Stevens mentioned the name of a retired former Canadian army buddy, a widower, who he knew was currently driving through Europe on a month-long vacation, did not have a cellphone, and was unlikely to be easily traced, at least for the next day or two. He said, "Mainly I went to look up old Bill Hutchison. Remember him?"

"Can't say I do," said Marks, making a mental note to check up on this bit of supposed information.

"Sure you do! Bill was one of their military brass we used to convince the Canadian government to drop the Avro Arr..."

"Oh, sure. Now I remember. Cost us a pretty penny to get *him* onside. He wouldn't bend right away, right? So we sent some hot young bitch to supposedly interview him for a military magazine's article. She was so hot and fit she could have fucked the entire Canadian chiefs of staff, given half of them fatal heart attacks in the heat of their passion, and not even broken out in a sweat. By the time she was through with old Bill, he hardly had

498

the strength to pick up the 'bonus' we gave him."

They both laughed.

After a beat, Marks said, "How the hell is old Bill?"

"Well, Jake, he had a mild heart attack a few weeks back and is probably going to be taking a while to get back to his old self."

"Ah, that's too bad. But listen, Dan, I've got a new project for you. Now that we have helped get the Canadians on board for the initial phases of our nuclear missile defence program, for which I might add your bonus should be coming through to your Swiss bank account any day now, some of the same clients want to expand the program by getting support for a brand new phase, what they are calling their 'Spy-'n-Fry' edition."

"What the hell is 'Spy-'n-Fry'?"

"What these same companies that are building the nuclear missile defence satellite shield have in mind is combining their laser missile-killing capability with ultra-telescopic spy satellites that use face-and-body recognition software to permit our guys to use the satellites to not only look around and watch for incoming missiles, but to 'Spy-'n-Fry' terrorists and/or their leaders back on the ground."

"Jake, are our clients really confident enough that we can get the American public on-side for this human 'Spy-'n-Fry' component? Won't that mean that the system could theoretically be programmed to locate and take out, say, political opponents Stateside, or to check out *which* guys in some paramilitary right wing or rabblerousing left wing group are *where*, and maybe to take *them* out as well?

"Hey, that's just a bonus, Dan. And besides, TAMPRR has already done some preliminary public opinion polling and it shows that the public *is* just about ready to let our government find *anyone* at *any* time. And that in itself is another indication of the great job we've done, *that you have done*, to get them to this point. The so-called 'war on terror' has been the best friend that our military and government hardliners and manufacturers have *ever* had. They've used that fear since 9/11 to gain megatrillions in contracts. And the fact that the former president has personal and business relationships with some of the bin Ladens and other Saudis has been helpful in ways I won't even begin to tell you."

Stevens nodded, seemingly reassured.

"What I can tell you, Dan, is that everybody with a price on his head is going to want to duck under cover any time he goes outside, even to take a piss. If the 'baddies' ever knew that with our new satellites we can now read the print on the books they are reading, to say nothing of the color of their eyeballs and other biometrics, it would scare the shit out of what our President is now calling the '*potential* evil doers'." Marks began laughing again. "Hell, Dan, 'Spy-'n-Fry' will terrify the bad guys so much that at least it will motivate them to avoid getting skin cancer. Covering up and wearing extra-wide brimmed baseball caps will be the new "in" style among your best dressed terrorists." Marks was roaring with laughter at the inner images he was creating.

Dan Stevens carried on the discussion with Marks of the new 'Spy-'n-Fry' satellite system as if he were actually enjoying the entire process. Which, truth be told, he was to some extent. He had no sympathy whatever for dictators or their soulmate buddies, terrorists.

"Jake, what are the odds that some of our enemies might hack into the system and use it against *us*?" While waiting for Marks's response Stevens casually put his left hand in his pants pocket and pressed the button on the car remote-like device that McTavish had given him.

Marks thought about Stevens's question for several seconds. Then he said, "Actually, pretty high if you ask me. So, we'll have to develop new counter-countermeasures to counter their countermeasures. It's the same old, same old, Dan; you know that!

"Christ, Dan, its just a game. We both know that the most serious threat to the U.S.A. is some single frigging suicide terrorist carrying anthrax or some other biological disease in a single vial, and who will decide to release the stuff into our air or water. But that problem is almost impossible to protect against. And besides, that is the kind of problem that only a very few, highly specialized companies have the wherewithal to tackle. And their work is lab-intensive and therefore not at all sexy. Also, only a few people will actually get rich if they actually succeed in developing a SuperSniffer or other device that will be able to locate the anthrax or other toxin in time. So the administration is not exactly going overboard to support solving that problem. Instead, frankly, the White House will probably continue to pretend to fight 21st century wars while using a 20th century mindset 'cause that's where the money is; in missiles, in planes, and in space. And besides, they're sexy.

"Hey, TAMPRR stands to make a whole lot of money pushing the 'spy in the sky' stuff, and you and I will become even richer.

"Anyway, enough of this horseshit. The question we need to address today is, what the hell are we going to do about this guy Simpson? If he keeps sticking his nose into what TAMPRR has been doing, then we are all going to be in some serious shit. And we can't afford to let that happen."

Stevens stiffened just a little. He had to let out the line slowly. He asked, "Are you really so concerned about him and the whole Canadian healthcare business, given what you have just been saying about our defense contractor-clients?

Marks said, "Just look at the latest numbers, for Christ's sake, Dan! You take the top aerospace and defense companies, and they had less than eighty percent of the revenues of the top healthcare companies. And less than one-half the profits! And the top healthcare companies had over two hundred and fifty *billion* dollars in revenue *last year alone!* Hell, even the top pharmaceutical companies made more than most aerospace and defense companies. Healthcare and pharmaceuticals, Dan; they're the 'sweet spot' in our company's racket."

Marks wasn't done. "And furthermore, you know damn well that the whole game is tied up in perception–and that means propaganda. Population-Control, via radio, TV, magazines, newspapers, opp-ed pieces, and controlled press releases; they constitute the K-Y jelly that we have to keep applying through the media to make screwing with the public mindset a smooth slam-dunk."

Stevens said, "And so?"

"And so, this guy Simpson is a loose cannon who makes a loud bang. And now that he won the Paulson, he can't be ignored any longer. The gloves have to come off – now."

"I thought you had some people assigned to keep his articles from getting too close for comfort, Jake?"

"I did that and I even sent a couple of 'contractors' to physically scare the shit out of him. They even tossed him onto a frozen canal in Ottawa a couple of days ago, just to make sure that he got the message that he was sticking his nose in where he shouldn't have. Right now, I have someone on his tail 24/7."

Stevens caught himself in mid-flinch. Hopefully they had not spotted him talking to Ken. If they had, however, he would likely already be dead instead of here in Las Vegas.

He honestly inquired, "So what now, Jake?"

Marks said, "Well, that is what you and I have to talk about. To be honest with you, Dan, I was beginning to worry about you. At least I was until you called and said you wanted us to meet here.

Stevens said, "Well, I knew that one of our main Canadian contacts, that ex-Prime Minister, was here with his wife the last couple of days, getting some R & R."

"Yeah, as soon as you told me that, I got our staff to have some clients meet with him at his hotel last night. Greedy bastard, though. He wanted a serious piss-pot full of money just to sit on the board of directors of an HMO that wants to move into Canada as soon as we get their current federal government onside. Well, he got his price because that company wants to move into his home province right away and start building a couple of full service, for-profit hospitals, and so they wanted the ex-PM to be right there, sitting on their board of directors to give them legitimacy and hopefully to signal that U.S. healthcare is an 'irresistible wave' that is bound to sweep across their country."

"Did the guys give him some cash in plain brown envelopes when they met? I recall that he prefers that."

"I really don't know; probably they gave him an 'advance' on his Board of Directors' stipend."

Stevens said, "Yeh, some stipend. The slime can probably buy a penthouse condo apartment at the Trump Casino with the advance they gave him."

Marks said, "Screw him. He isn't our problem; he is part of our solution. The real issue is this guy, Ken Simpson."

Stevens asked, "And what do you want to do about him?"

Marks matter-of-factly said, "I think we have to kill him."

Stevens feigned shock. "Why?"

"Because the guy just won't quit."

Stevens responded, "Let me try some things first."

Marks said, "Alright. I was hoping you would say that, Dan. Look, I thought after what we did to his father, you might be feeling some reluctance to move on this. I mean, I remember you were real close with the guy."

Stevens kept his voice level. "I thought we both were, during and after Korea. Anyway, I can handle it."

Marks smiled. "You sure? Because if it is a problem for you then I will give the assignment to one of our younger guys."

It was now Stevens's turn to smile at his old comrade. "Trust me, Jake."

A momentary quizzical microexpression crossed Stevens's face. Marks caught it, but wasn't sure what it meant. He said, "All right. But we also have another problem, just as serious as this Simpson guy."

"What is that?"

Marks said, "Well, this morning, before I came here, I received this report."

Marks handed over a file folder that Stevens took and opened. As he began to read it, he looked up momentarily with an expression of shock, and then finished reading the report.

Stevens asked, "Do we know that this operative is right, that their Prime Minister is really going to resign soon, and that he actually intends to support embedding their country's universal Medicare system within their Charter of Rights and Freedoms?"

Marks said, "Well, some of their recent Prime Ministers have made sounds like that, but usually only just before elections. And, naturally, after they got re-elected they forgot that they ever said such a thing. Or they claimed unforeseen financial problems in their budgets. But, yes. The sonofabitch is apparently serious this time."

Still reading the report, Stevens looked up and, feigning astonishment, said, "And is he really going to name this doctor, this Member of Parliament, Trish Markridge, as the new interim Prime Minister? And is she actually going to go on the record as being willing to put it all on the line, politically speaking, in order to also create this Federal-Provincial Health Council Recording and Reporting Committee with actual teeth, to make sure that both the federal and provincial governments really do fulfill their agreed-upon respective healthcare policies and goals?"

"Yeah, we are virtually certain that the report is accurate. And if she can get *that* done, who knows what else she could accomplish from her bully pulpit."

"Whew. So, what are we going to do about her?"

In a frigid monotone Marks said, "We have to get rid of her, too, one way or another! If we can't buy her or dig up something with which to discredit her, then we will make something up, like questioning the accuracy of her supposed accomplishments in Afghanistan, or even spreading a rumor that she was screwing the Prime Minister. Whatever it takes. And if nothing works, then we will have eliminate her along with this guy, Ken Simpson, if you can't get him to stop poking his nose around healthcare issues on both sides of the border."

Stevens started to speak, but Marks interrupted, going back to the topic of Ken's father. "Now, I know he and you were best buddies. I mean, shit, we were all 'best friends' in the POW camps, weren't we? *Had to be!* But, Christ, Dan, an immovable obstacle can't be tolerated. We didn't do it in the camps, and I sure as hell won't stand for it now, not with everything we have to lose."

Stevens began to protest. "But, damn it, Jake…"

"Don't you get it, Dan? We are still at war, Goddamn it! This bizwar is every bit as serious, as far as I am concerned, as the Arrow problem and the Korean conflict were. And it might have to become every bit as deadly as the military kind. Hell, there isn't that much difference, anyway. The military uses brute force; where possible, we prefer to use persuasion. They use missiles; we use hit-and-run 'accidents', or supposed suicides. They use bombs; we use fires of unknown origin that destroy the homes and buildings of our clients' competitors. Big bloody differences! When I ordered our people to kill Simpson's father, we knocked him out of the sky for $5,000. That was a damn lot of money at the time, just to get the right technician in to totally sabotage his aircraft. So do you have a problem with what we did, and are about to do? If so, my friend, then you and I will have to deal with this difference of opinion in some way."

Stevens didn't say anything in response. He merely gazed at Marks, and more specifically, at the micro-recorder/transmitter glasses that Jake was wearing, hoping that the transmission of their conversation, which he had begun by pressing the remote key several minutes ago, was providing a reasonable quality sound-and-picture show to his colleagues at the hotel across the way.

Marks regarded Stevens's silence as an immediate problem. He decided to raise the ante. "Come on, Dan! When our healthcare clients finish paying us for our work you can buy your own bloody island in the Caribbean and get out of this business. But you will never again have as much fun as we have had over the years. Admit it, man; think back to what we did, what with the Avro Arrow, and then, a decade later, when we helped put the kibosh on that other Canadian aircraft manufacturer's ahead-of-its-time, Osprey-like hybrid aircraft, the Convert CL-209. Remember? They had gone and built the first practical military plane ever whose wings rotated from vertical for takeoff, to horizontal for level flight, and back again to vertical landings. You know I saw one of them in the National Flight Museum of Canada in Ottawa a few years back? That was another sweet piece of work we did then, wasn't it? And we even did it on our own hook, almost gratis, as a sort of bonus for some of our former clients, though not the ones involved in building the Osprey. *That is what I call being a patriotic American.* And now, decades later, the same sort of aircraft that the Canucks were developing is being built and flown Stateside. Damn but we've been good at our job, haven't we?"

Dan Stevens said, "Yes *we* were, and *you* are!"

Marks caught the curious choice of words and asked, "What do you mean by that?"

Stevens said nothing, but got up and turned on the television, tuning in AWNN, the American World News Network. On the screen was a picture of the same television they were now looking at, with Dan Stevens standing beside it, smiling.

"What the hell…!?" bellowed Marks. As he moved his head the picture on the screen changed somewhat, showing more of Dan Stevens and less of the wall unit on the other side of the television set. The mirrored wall behind Stevens took in the rest of the room, and prominently showed Marks standing and beginning to literally shake with fury. In the instant he saw himself on the screen Jake fully realized the image's significance. Less than thirty seconds later, there was a knock at the door, accompanied by someone shouting, "Open up. This is the FBI. Open up the damned door *right now*."

Marks was rooted to his spot, looking from Dan Stevens to the television set and back again, and again.

Someone used a portable battering ram to force the door open. Marks surrendered without a struggle. Only his mouth was moving, hurling expletives. Its target turned and smiling sadly, walked out the door beside a large FBI agent.

CHAPTER 53

Two hours before Marks's flight arrived in Las Vegas, Dr. William McTavish moved into a hotel room on the fifth floor room of the hotel next to the Jacket Club. The previous evening the same former engineering colleague who supplied the spying prescription glasses that Sylvia substituted for her uncle's own, had shown McTavish how to use the companion suitcase-sized, all-in-one receiving, recording, and transmitting studio.

A single tantalizing phone call that Ken made to a news editor at the AWNN network less than fifteen minutes before Dan Stevens knocked on the door of suite 708 at the Jacket Club, led to his news department leaping at the prospect of broadcasting live the unedited takedown of an American company that had been involved in numerous illegal activities, including even murder.

The live feed from room 708 was soon broadcast nationwide over the entire AWNN network. Ken Simpson, speaking from a television studio in Ottawa, provided a brief lead-in to the live broadcast, informing the audience that there existed in America shadow companies devoted to carrying out the most serious breaches of business ethics on behalf of some major corporate clients who were themselves reluctant to be more directly involved in such activities.

After phoning his AWNN contact, Ken next called his editor. Rusty was thankful to finally be hearing signs of major progress on the healthcare series, even though he was initially put off by the fact that AWNN was going to have the scoop 'live'. After giving Ken hell for not having contacted him sooner, Rusty got with the program after he accepted the fact that the newspaper could not do live breaking news, and that this was the only way to go.

As Ken and Rusty agreed, less than five minutes before the beginning of the broadcast emanating from room 708, Rusty called an FBI agent with whom he had had dealings previously, and asked him to turn on the nearest television set and tune in his local CWNN station. A subsequent call by the agent to the local Vegas FBI bureau resulted in a team being stationing themselves outside the door to TAMPRR's suite within minutes. Almost immediately after retired Colonel Jake Marks realized that his conversation with Stevens was being videoed–by himself–the FBI agents broke in the door of TAMPRR's apartment.

Taking into account that he had voluntarily come forward as a whistleblower, Lieutenant Colonel Dan Stevens was offered, and accepted, immunity from prosecution by the FBI in return for his full revelations about TAMPRR spanning a period of nearly fifty years, and for his subsequent testimony at the trial of Jake Marks and some other principals and senior operatives.

It was with poignant pleasure that, along with Martha, Ken covered Marks's trial for *The New York Era*. He experienced a profound sense of closure as Marks's own recorded words and images were used to convict him of arranging the murder of Frank Simpson, some forty-seven years earlier. Given the nature of his company's covert activities and the damage that was inflicted upon the businesses and populations of some of America's closest allies, it was determined that the rest of Jake Marks's days would be spent in federal custody.

After considering her personal history as well as her assistance in ensuring the undoing of her uncle's company, Sylkeen/Sylvia was sentenced to eighteen months probation for various illegal activities, including that of being a co-conspirator. After she served her time, and with Ken's personal recommendation, she obtained a good job with a prominent, medium-sized independent paper that offered her the opportunity to write investigative pieces on a wide variety of state, as well as local, issues.

As for Timmy Cemente, the federal Minister of Health, after thoroughly investigating and corroborating the information that

Dr. McTavish provided him, in one of his syndicated articles Ken exposed Cemente's incestuous relationships with the lobbyists for various American pharmaceutical and healthcare firms. Ken revealed that these companies had funneled moneys into the trust funds and offshore coffers of Cemente and a number of his federal and provincial political colleagues. Even the government's own appointed so-called 'ethics commissioner' was not able to condone or excuse their conduct, and they were forced to resign their positions in what turned out to be one of the most sweeping scandals in Canadian history.

Several of their corporate cohorts in the U.S., together with a few politicians on both sides of the 49th parallel, were convicted of either bribery or accepting bribes and were given the usual slap-on-the-wrist sentences that persons with ample funds and able lawyers usually received. Still, it was a symbolic victory for those like Ken who were fighting hard to clean up the world they lived in.

Trish Markridge received beefed-up protection from the RCMP, became interim Prime Minister, and was relentless in her fight to enshrine her country's universal Medicare system in Canada's Charter of Rights and Freedoms. She also fought to introduce legislation that would make both the Canadian federal government and its provincial and territorial counterparts, jointly accountable for ensuring the efficient and effective operation of the healthcare system. She repeatedly made a point of saying that the changes she was seeking were more than merely cosmetic actions or theoretical constitutional statements. She said that she was going to push for the establishment of agreed upon–and enforceable–medical standards, including a medically acceptable 'maximum time' to be spent on waiting lists, the maximum number of patients that on-duty nurses in hospitals would have to care for, and 24/7 use of major technological diagnostic and treatment tools like MRIs. She also stated that she was prepared to fight to include those with doctoral degrees in clinical and counseling psychology among the groups of professionals who would be paid by the Medicare system. Physicians would continue to be covered by the healthcare system to the extent that they were involved in the delivery of *physical* medicine services, for which they were unquestionably the best educated and trained–psychiatrists, of course, would continue to be paid to treat the most seriously mentally disturbed.

With her already large and exponentially growing popularity, the likes of which had not been witnessed in Canada since so-called 'Trudeaumania' had taken hold decades earlier, and with her ability to appeal to both lay persons and professionals in both official languages, the prospects for success appeared better than they had ever been. Markridge said that she would introduce *all* of these changes into law *before* she called a new election, but not before she had ordered a national referendum on the proposed changes. She stated that she would then run for re-election on the basis of accomplishments and not mere promises.

Because none of the few HMOs and pharmaceuticals involved in sponsoring TAMPRR Inc.'s shenanigans were willing to leave their destiny in the hands of just one group, in addition to TAMPRR they had, of course, hired other bizwar companies with comparable credentials and credos. The demise of TAMPRR made these other companies even more aggressive, and they pressed ahead, albeit more cautiously, to make the challenge Trish Markridge faced almost as difficult as it had been before the cover was blown off of Jake Marks's creation.

This time, however, the Canadian public was much better informed by at least some of their media, including some of Ken's syndicated articles that warned his readers on both sides of the border of some individuals and groups who were masquerading as patriots and defenders of the 'little people' but who, in fact, continued to push for more expensive, for-profit healthcare.

The American HMOs, PPOs, and pharmaceutical companies that had pushed so hard for so long for the destruction of the Canadian government-run Medicare system, now faced the serious prospect that the next U.S. presidential election would be fought primarily over the proposed introduction of an American version of the Canadian system.

CHAPTER 54

In an extensive series of syndicated columns Ken described TAMPRR's activities as they were revealed in court, including that organization's first project, the shutting down of the Avro Arrow program. With Dan Stevens's assistance, he went on to describe TAMPRR's efforts, over the previous fifteen years, to sabotage the Canadian Medicare system.

In one article Ken revealed what he had learned about his own father's death, and referred to a signed and notarized statement made by a *"former U.S. military person and major TAMPRR Inc. figure, Lieutenant Colonel Dan Stevens, U.S.A.F. Retired."* Ken revealed that Stevens was his main source that assisted in uncovering the covert and largely illegal activities of TAMPRR Inc..

Ken also wrote that Stevens had signed and delivered a 250-page deposition, with Ken present as witness, to the FBI, the Canadian RCMP, and Britain's MI-5. The latter's interest had increased when it was revealed that TAMPRR had spearheaded a similar operation in England, in an attempt to sabotage the British healthcare system and acquire a beachhead into Europe for some American HMOs.

Ken's articles described the dossier as providing great detail, including the names of many other targets in several other countries that had been attacked over the years, and in many instances compromised, and included the times, places, means, and names of TAMPRR personnel who had been involved in these activities.

In his deposition Stevens mentioned that, as more and more corporate clients had paid increasingly larger figures for the services that TAMPRR offered, two of Jake Marks's long-time acquaintances (university roommates, Stevens believed), a New England-based investment banker by the name of Chuck Mallard, and his Russian colleague, one Boris Sebastyenovitch, had convinced TAMPRR's principals to allow them to invest a substantial portion of their earnings in some supposedly legitimate and failsafe ventures. The partners had agreed, at Marks's strong urgings, and they handed over many millions to Mallard and Sebastyenovitch. Unfortunately, the investment bankers reported back several months later, after stalling for many weeks in delivering upon their investors' supposedly significant profits, that unfortunately, all the money had been lost through completely unforeseeable circumstances.

Perhaps because Marks's then wife was a close friend of Mallard's spouse, and in an attempt to re-establish some semblance of harmony in his own house of considerable discord, Marks and the others allowed the two swindlers or incompetents (nobody believed the latter, except Marks's wife) to get away with their story–and their money.

Marks eventually repaid all of the contributions of his partners out of his own pocket, with interest, and never again spoke to either Mallard or Sebastyenovitch. As far as Stevens knew via his own privately conducted investigation, Mallard was continuing to work part-time while enjoying his home on Martha's Vineyard to which he frequently invited potential new investors to take part in some new deals he supposedly had going on in Asia. Apparently he and his partner decided to utilize their love of boats by sailing around the countries of Asia while continuing to reel in as many wealthy Vietnamese and other south Asians as they could con into their fraudulent ventures.

From that point on, having learned first-hand that even one's supposedly closest friends might turn, if only the price was right, the five members of TAMPRR's executive agreed unanimously to extend their mutual security compact by accepting the concept that if any of them were found to have been the source of leaks pertaining to any of TAMPRR's dealings or their parts in such, then not only *their* lives, but also those of their family members, would be put in grave danger. This compact was not agreed to in writing for obvious reasons, but each man present, in turn, had to verbally state to what he had agreed, until all had taken the same oath.

The appendices accompanying the deposition that Stevens

handed over to the FBI, RCMP, and MI-5, included forty discrete sections, each of which referred to a separate TAMPRR project, and included numerous internal memos and e-mails, notes of executive meetings, and contracts with clients that had been deliberately kept short and vague, but had been required because of the very large fees for which the companies' CEOs would have to account.

Also, in his final column in the series, Ken described the attempts to subvert his and *The New York Era's* reputations. It was one of the most difficult pieces that he ever had to write. In the column Ken mentioned one specific TAMPRR operative, a beautiful, intelligent, and gifted investigative reporter who happened to be the niece of the founder and head of TAMPRR, retired Colonel Jake Marks. Ken described her insertion into the newspaper staff, and her attempts to discover Ken's sources and what he was going to be writing next.

That column appeared on the opp-ed page, opposite a long editorial that spoke about the measures that the paper had taken since to ensure that the likelihood of such an event happening again would be minimized. Ken's column revealed that the junior reporter had, in fact, been his investigative assistant over a period of less than two weeks, and that she had been injected into *The New York Era* through TAMPRR's direct influence over a recently hired managing editor. The editorial went on to say that this executive was fired by the management of the *Era* after admitting to the authorities, with the paper's owners present, that he had been paid over $40,000 for his actions on behalf of TAMPRR to that point, and that these activities had included the deliberate removal of a highly competent reporter, Martha Harrison, who had previously been working with Ken, and the injection of the junior reporter in her place. Ken wrote a relatively sympathetic portrayal of his recent assistant, all things considered, pointing out that she had voluntarily revealed the nature and the extent of the plot TAMPRR had laid out and nearly executed in its effort to seriously influence the editorial direction of the *Era.* Those efforts would have included the termination of Ken 'for cause', and the end of his investigations of the healthcare situations in the U.S.A. and Canada.

Ken learned from Dan Stevens that the latter had told Sylvia the truth about her parents' deaths. Apparently, in a tormented, drunken rage one night many years earlier, Marks actually bragged to Stevens that he had had an affair with his brother's wife. It had been a brief liaison that she insisted on breaking off, saying that she could not emotionally handle having intimate relations with her husband's brother. She also told Jake that as she had learned more about him through their encounters, she had grown to actually despise and pity him, saying that his sadism and narcissism was beyond anything she had ever witnessed or heard of before, or that she ever wanted to be exposed to again.

Marks became livid, but asked her to restart their sexual encounters. She rebuffed him several times, and then told him that she had disclosed her infidelity to her husband, Bill. She had not, however, told Bill the identity of the man with whom she had been involved. She had pleaded for his forgiveness, but he became so distraught about her extramarital affair that he withdrew from both her and their young daughter, Sylvia, and sank into a very deep depression.

A few weeks later Bill confided to his brother, Jake, what his wife had disclosed to him. Because of his own anger toward his sister-in-law, Jake had contemplated telling Bill the true identity of his wife's lover. However, her previous comments about what she called his "sadism and cruelty" had been very insulting to Jake, and he would be damned if he would give her any additional 'evidence' of the validity of her opinion. Instead, Jake suggested that Bill take himself away from everything for a week or two, to think things over. He even offered his own cabin near Lake Tahoe.

Jake told Stevens that he had known there were problems with the natural gas-fed heating system at the cabin, something to do with insufficient burning of the fuel. As a former fighter pilot himself, Marks had known enough physics and chemistry to recognize the potentially lethal danger of the problem. He told Stevens that he was certain he had intended to phone the local utility service department and have the problem dealt with before his brother arrived. However, he had been particularly busy that week and it simply slipped his mind.

Jake said that he also thought that perhaps while Bill was away commiserating with nature at Tahoe, he might yet persuade his brother's wife to have another go at their liaison. What he had not counted on was Suzanne becoming so desperately frightened about what her husband might do to himself holed up in a cabin in the woods in the middle of winter, alone and depressed, that at the last moment she was able to finally convince him to let her come with him to try and work things out. She brought their young daughter to her parents' home to be looked after and then flew out to join her husband.

After they had been at the cabin for two days, Jake 'remembered' to call the gas company to check out that the furnace and a few other things were in working order, saying that his brother might be up at the cabin, even now. It was the serviceman who found Bill and his wife, in bed, dead of carbon monoxide poisoning.

Jake felt not so much remorse as cheated. He acknowledged that he did have fantasies of eliminating Bill, marrying his brother's wife, and raising little Sylvia as his own daughter. He decided that at least he could do the latter, in a manner of speaking. And so, after her parents' untimely deaths, her 'Uncle Jake' took Sylvia under his wing while she grew into womanhood. He paid for her university education, and played the 'uncle' role as best he could.

In certain corporate, military and political quarters around the country the crap was really hitting the fan with increasing frequency during the weeks of Ken's revelations. The media was filled with denials of wrongdoings by some of the healthcare-related companies that had been named by Stevens. Protestations of innocence and promises to thoroughly investigate and clean up any unfair influence-peddling and covert actions were flowing like crocodile tears at a liars' convention. A seemingly endless stream of press releases were issued about being falsely accused and looking forward to defending themselves before various Senate and House subcommittees that were presently being formed.

The New York Era and Ken were rumored to be in line for more journalistic rewards as a result of his latest series of articles. Ken agreed to a new five-year contract with the paper on the conditions that Martha be given her old job back and that they were each provided their own full-time research assistants. The paper rapidly agreed.

Ken and his son, Brad, made a pilgrimage to the mountain where Frank Simpson's aircraft crashed. Once at the crash-site, Ken dug a foot-deep hole nearby and there he buried his Paulson medal. *The Paulson belongs to us both.*

In his last article in the series on TAMPRR Inc. and the state of uncovered corruption at the corporate and governmental levels in both America and its northern neighbor, Ken disclosed that the next area he wanted to focus his investigations upon was the entire matter of how American democracy might become more openly citizen-based. He would soon learn that this announcement had far greater impact than he ever anticipated upon some of the very people who were actually in a position to help make and direct such changes.

CHAPTER 55

One Month Later

The entirely unexpected phone call came from the senior senator about four weeks after Ken's column–announcing his intention to examine the future possible direction of democracy in America–had appeared in the pages of *The New York Era* and in hundreds of other newspapers across the USA and Canada. After their conversation, and with the senator's permission, Ken wrote in his column for the paper's next edition that he had been contacted by a major, unnamed political figure and had been informed that some important announcements on that very subject might be made soon, and that they might well be of vital interest to most Americans.

These announcements, he wrote, would deal with some innovative proposals regarding the ways in which governmental decisions could be arrived at in the future, including decisions regarding major matters such as the means of healthcare delivery in America.

Complying with his caller's request, Ken refused to tell anyone, even Rusty, the name of the political figure who had contacted him. Not surprisingly, Rusty let him know, in his own colorful terms, that he was not at all pleased about this latest excursion into secrecy. The expression of utter resignation on Rusty's face, however, suggested that he was more likely thinking, *Ah, well, the more things change, the more they…*

Ken was told that one announcement to be made in a matter of weeks would be about an intention of some very prominent U.S. politicians of various affiliations, together with a few internationally known business leaders, to introduce a new mechanism for nation-wide discussion and referendum-making in America. The first step in this collaborative effort would probably involve a series of nationally televised 'town hall meetings' to be broadcast live over a period of successive weeks and hosted by one of America's most popular and trusted media personalities. Ken was asked to keep this more detailed information to himself for the time being and he agreed. He was also told that a proposal would be likely put forward during these town hall meetings to inject into the American Bill of Rights the notion of affordable access to healthcare as one of the inalienable rights of every permanent resident of the United States, and that it would be similar to the bill that had recently been put forward by the interim Prime Minister of Canada for insertion into their own Canadian Charter of Rights and Freedoms. The senator said that the tentative, light-hearted working motto of the advocates for taking this action was at least as old as many Americans' grandparents and great-grandparents; "If you have your health, you have almost everything; if you don't, then you are missing out on too much!"

The other announcement, Ken was told, would be of even greater import. His caller said that it would involve a proposed profound shakeup in the corridors of power in America. "The impact of these recommendations," the senator said, "would be to hopefully alter forever the future roles of lobbyists, campaign contributions, and voting procedures that had been deliberately kept in place for far too long."

Ken had his source's permission to publish a few specific sentences that would give some hint of what was to come.

Suffice to say that the senior executives of many healthcare-related corporations, their lobbyists, and their purchased politicians had difficulty sleeping the night after Ken's succinct comments were published. More than a few corporate CEOs had their security personnel double-check whether any breaches had recently occurred, especially involving information (read 'evidence') of any questionable corporate practices.

Near the end of their phone call, the senator made a mighty appealing proposal to Ken, one that included an opportunity to meet with the senator and the others who were behind the proposals and developments he had mentioned.

Ken thought for less than a semi-beat before saying, "Sure; where and when?"

"How about tomorrow morning at seven, at Kennedy, Executive Gate 57?"

"Fine. Is someone arriving, or am I going someplace?" Ken asked, expecting he would might be catching a flight to another city in the U.S.A..

"Just bring your passport, Ken, along with clothes for at least three days in the sun. And by all means bring your bathing suit. We will all be working hard but playing, as well."

CHAPTER 56

The 12-passenger Lear Jet, with its single passenger on board, began its descent into Dominican Republic airspace, aiming for touchdown at a private airstrip in cloudless Punta Cana, the easternmost province of the Dominican Republic. Looking out the window, Ken Simpson thought again about the phone call he had received from Senator Tom Cassidy the previous day.

Cassidy's smooth New England accent made his generous words of thanks to Ken all the more charming. He said that, first of all, he wanted to let Ken know that his articles had elicited in the senator a profound degree of disgust with 'dirty-politics-as-usual' as practiced in current-day America by certain parties in business and government, and a resolution to attempt to make things better. The senator said that informal conversations between himself and a few of his political colleagues and business acquaintances regarding the import of Ken's revelations had already spawned some remarkable and innovative ideas and proposals. Furthermore, for the previous couple of days, and indeed at this very moment, the senator and his associates were debating these notions at the private estate of one of the participants. He then casually mentioned that the estate was located in the Dominican Republic. Senator Cassidy was calling to invite Ken to fly down to the D.R. as their guest, and was prepared to provide the host's corporate jet for the flight.

When Ken replied that it was against company policy to accept such a 'gift', Cassidy pointed out that the plane would be flying directly to a very small, private airfield just a short distance away from the isolated retreat where they were staying. Unfortunately, the property was located in an area inaccessible by commercial airlines or most other means of transportation.

Senator Cassidy assured Ken that he would find the trip most worthwhile, and said that it would provide him unprecedented interviewing access to some exceptional Americans and

Canadians who had, incidentally, voted unanimously to request his input–on what matters, the senator preferred not to discuss in further detail over the phone.

Ken was surprised by the call and honored by the invitation. Truth be told, even with all his years in the trenches of various political, military, and business intrigues, Ken felt slightly intimidated by Cassidy's summons. What, he wondered, could *he* possibly offer as a *participant* of such a gathering, rather than in his usual–and much more comfortable–role of 'fair witness' reporter.

Tom Cassidy was a man Ken had long admired for his social conscience and political courage. Like millions of Americans, Ken also felt compassion for the man, especially in more recent years as the aging lion lumbered on, bearing his great personal burden of a script left forever unfinished, cut short by more tragedies than a single man, brother, and uncle should ever have to bear. He persevered regardless, bent under the weight of heaping measures of dedication, sorrow, and guilt, even after so many decades.

Truth be told, Ken was more than happy to get out of New York City, and out of the country for that matter. Things had been quite tense around the paper generally, and for Ken in particular. His relationship with his editor was slowly repairing, especially since Ken learned that Rusty hadn't had any choice in the decisions to bring Sylkeen/Sylvia onto the scene and simultaneously banish Martha to another country. Also, the newly established managing editor, a tough ex-reporter of the old school, let it be known that Ken's columns on healthcare, TAMPRR, and the Avro Arrow business were generating more legal threats than usual against the paper while at the same time markedly increasing daily circulation.

While the paper's board members were confident in the veracity of Ken's reporting, the fact that an unprecedented number of threats were also being made against Ken's own person meant that the paper was not willing to take chances with his safety. Management had hired the same security company that usually protected UN dignitaries and visiting celebrities to the Big Apple. This company had been told to guard Ken *24/7 and tight*, until further notice: Ken was to inform them, in advance, of all of his movements.

Ken accepted the security detail only because the paper said that it could not risk publishing any more of Ken's "obviously inflammatory (to some)" columns unless he allowed for the however inconvenient security detail that the paper and its consultants deemed prudent at this time.

Ken realized that he had no real choice in the matter, not if he wanted to continue working at *The New York Era*. However, his acceptance of the bodyguards was made on the condition that the individuals involved, mostly ex-FBI and ex-Special Forces types, would not, unless it was absolutely necessary, disclose their or Ken's whereabouts, not even to their own fellow employees at the security service, nor to Ken's bosses at the paper. Also, they had to agree to stay no closer than hundred feet to whomever Ken might be meeting. The last thing Ken needed was to have any prospective sources get antsy when he showed up with at two obvious 'heavies' in tow.

Fortunately, Ken discovered that the same company that had been hired to protect him, had also been providing security for Senator Cassidy for over two decades. As a result, Ken's detail willingly handed him over to the one looking after the senator.

The logo on the Lear's fuselage signaled that it was the corporate jet of a hugely successful 'new economy' billionaire, at whose Caribbean retreat the meeting was evidently being held. As the aircraft's flaps were applied, signaling imminent touchdown, Ken became increasingly excited at having been invited to whatever confab was going on. Over the telephone Senator Cassidy had only said that he was getting together with a few very high profile friends and colleagues, and that they would greatly appreciate his joining them towards the end of their time together, and would tomorrow be too soon?

As the aircraft was completing its landing approach, Ken's mind flitted over several topics, including wondering what the hell the meeting he was going to be attending shortly was really about. Ken appreciated the problem with unsecured telephone lines, and so he did not ask, nor did the senator offer many details whatever about *why* he was asking Ken to fly more than 2500

The Avro Arrow Manipulation: Murdering Medicare

miles to another country for a few days? Senator Cassidy had only said that he was being asked to join "us" *(whoever 'us' was)* primarily for background only at this point, but also those present were genuinely interested in obtaining Ken's opinions about the actions they were considering taking.

The chief carrot that led him to take the flight was that he had been assured that when 'they' were ready to go public, he would have unprecedented access to whomever he desired to interview from among those in attendance, and that the interviews could most likely be *on* the record. *That was more than enough reason to fly to the Dominican Republic on a private jet, or for that matter, personally paddle a canoe across the Caribbean, if need be!*

Ken's monkeymind jumped about, recalling the events of the past few days; his series on the myriad problems associated with treating healthcare as a commercial commodity; the attempts by so many healthcare providers to limit the use of, and payment for, tests and procedures; the lack of coverage for over 46,000,000 Americans; the earlier age of mortality for both males and females in the U.S. compared to Canada and many European countries, and so on. These facts, as he had gathered and then stated them in his columns, had struck a nerve with a large number of readers on both sides of the debate, way beyond what even he had anticipated.

Moments later the Lear touched down, slowed, and then turned and taxied to a small airport building. Ken exited the aircraft to be greeted by an exceedingly friendly D.R. customs official who made quick work of his entrance into the country. The official then turned and walked back to his glassed-in station at the entrance to the building.

Next, Ken shook the hand offered to him by the local on the tarmac who had been sent to greet him by Senator Cassidy. "Hello, Mr. Simpson, my friend." said the broad, smiling face of a towering black man probably about half Ken's age but looking considerably older. The man took Ken's carry-on and lifted it as if it were weightless. The tone of the man's voice was warm and welcoming.

"Over here, my friend," the man gestured. "My name is

Donaldo. This way, please. Now we take helicopter. It is only ten-minute ride. Very fast, very smooth."

"Thank you," replied Ken, as he felt the humid, thankfully warm Caribbean air bathe him. His tense muscles eased as he involuntarily sighed. *It is one of the blessings of air travel, that we can be transported, in less than four hours, from frigid, snowbound New York City, to this… this as yet mostly unpolluted, blessedly warm, sunny, summer weather.*

As the helicopter lifted off Ken's mind jumped again; this time he thought about Senator Cassidy's Cape Sole summer retreat area. Ken had been to East Deansport on several occasions; it had been a favorite vacationing spot for him, his wife, and their son, when Brad was only four or five. The quiet Cape Sole cottages and mansions, manicured lawns and laid-back, northeastern oceanside lifestyle, were a respite from the harried intensity of '*Mad*-hattan', as his wife referred to New York City.

After a week at the beach of East Deansport, walking, sailing, and just kicking back, whenever Ken first returned to New York City he would sometimes stand completely still on the sidewalk near his paper's building, just off Times Square. There, for a few seconds, he would close his eyes and physically sense what seemed to be the actual vibrations of thousands of buildings, hundreds of thousands of vehicles, and millions of people, all teeming with kinetic energy. The shock of traveling from East Deansport to Times Square was always palpable.

East Deansport was known all around the world, of course, as the summer home of the senator and his famous, and too often ill-fated family. People still came in droves to the Cassidy museum at East Deansport to pay their respects, to somehow get closer to and momentarily experience the proximity of greatness, almost as much as they came to any of the bucolic towns along the Cape for the tonic peace and perfumes of the ocean beaches.

Ken looked out the four-seater chopper's bubble at what the American pilot pointed out was "the 20-mile long Bavaro beach". The broad strip of sand at the edge of the ocean seemed to go on forever towards the horizon.

A momentary feeling of melancholy swept through Ken as his

memories of his only previous visit to the D.R. bubbled up from his deep databank and momentarily flooded his 'mindscreen'. It was probably on this island that Brad was conceived, when he and Nancy had stayed at the Celebration Prince All Suites hotel, an extremely large resort that they had hoped would provide some relief from the increased frequency of fighting of the previous few weeks that had left them both emotionally drained. She had insisted that he take time off from his job, which now that he thought of it, was almost humorous, considering the demands being made on Nancy by her law firm for a minimum of 2500 docketed hours a year.

Well, as she had pointed out to Ken on numerous occasions, at least she was *in* town most of the time. She contrasted that fact with the movements of her husband, who was usually immersed in one or other of the world's war zones, witnessing and trying to describe men's inhumanity to one another, while at the same time presumably trying not to get killed. When Daniel Pearl, the Wall Street investigative reporter, was beheaded in Pakistan in 2002–that was the last straw. Nancy could not handle Ken risking his son's father's life any longer. So, at her almost hysterical insistence, Ken had agreed to stop working as a war correspondent and returned home within two weeks.

Three weeks later they came to magnificent Bavaro beach in an attempt to rekindle their closeness. The fact that the weather was perfect and the locals were almost always polite and helpful, made their stay extremely pleasant. Ken recalled that they made love several times that week; angry sex at first, probably because they were both dealing with pent-up frustrations and resentments towards one another. Later the sex was sweeter, but, as it turned out, not curative enough to save their marriage for much longer.

The chopper touched down on the back lawn of the estate less than ten minutes after they had left the airfield. Ken's memories and thoughts had preoccupied him much of the short journey. As soon as the rotors stopped turning another attendant arrived, greeted Ken, and quickly led him to his suite in one of the smaller buildings within the fenced-in, multi-acre compound. Ken found he had access to the beach and ocean less than fifty feet from the apartment's sliding glass doors. After being given about fifteen minutes to 'freshen up', he was accompanied by the same attendant to the "big house". A huge, two-story, white mansion, probably about twenty-five thousand square feet, with three wings that met at the two-story tall front foyer, it was painted all brilliant white and bright yellow on the outside. In the foyer was a soaring, futuristic silver and gold sculpture of what appeared to be representations of different generations of spacecraft traveling around and between various celestial bodies.

The tall attendant recaptured Ken's attention with a respectful tap on his shoulder and proceeded to lead him towards what appeared to be an extremely large room at the ocean end of the middle wing of the house. As Ken got closer, an increasingly wide expanse of floor-to-ceiling windows revealed a panoramic view of the turquoise water and very light beige, sandy beach that seemed to stretch towards the far reaches of what must have been a three-mile wide bay.

If ever I win the lottery... Ken began to muse, before another inner voice said, *Forget it!*

After walking along the gradually widening hallway for at least seventy-five feet, Ken finally reached the formal entry to the great room, announced by elegant three-story tall, marble pillars set some twenty feet apart on either side at the end of the hallway. Even more breathtaking than the architecture and the view, if that were possible, were the other twenty or so guests who were present, and who at this moment were all turning towards Ken, and smiling, waving and saying, "Hello.". Every one of them, with the exception of the two attractive, significantly younger adults present, he immediately recognized, of course, as major business, political, or media mavens.

The two forty-somethings, he now recognized, were the adult children of former political leaders in the U.S. and Canada. Ken felt quite embarrassed, as all had stopped talking among themselves when he entered and were now *standing* as one and *applauding* the newcomer.

The heavy-set Senator Cassidy walked directly over to Ken, shook his hand vigorously and warmly thanked him in his New England accent "for being so good as to come and join us on such short notice." In turn, the others present also greeted him, congratulating him for winning the Paulson and/or saying that they were regular readers of his columns and/or that they admired his work greatly. Among the first to greet him were Fred Tunney, the repeatedly retired media tycoon; Phil Tate, the software legend and supposedly now the richest man in the world; Michael Teller and Stefen Hobbs, who together helped revolutionize the development, marketing and distribution of computers for home and business. The most pleasant surprise for Ken was seeing the statuesque interim Prime Minister of Canada, Trish Markridge, who smiled warmly and said loudly enough for all present to hear, "Hello, again, Ken."

The other media-related person present was Zelda Leighter, or 'Z' as she was known to her millions of daily viewers who helped her become a household name and billionaire. Z, as everyone knew, ran her own television, radio, magazine, Internet, and clothing empire. She had gained even greater prominence and respect by choosing to *not* take her company, Z Productions, public during the 'new economy' Internet boom, because, as she famously said to a reporter, she was told that the stock market bubble was going to burst sooner than later and she cared too much about her mostly lower and middle socioeconomic audience to take their money and then watch them fall into a bottomless abyss when the bubble finally burst.

Everyone in the room took turns personally greeting Ken.

Ken muttered a simple "thank you" in response to their congratulations and greetings, rather than daring to respond by saying, "And thank *you* Steven, for helping to invent the personal computer," and "thank *you,* Phil, for developing the software that made you far wealthier than many of the *countries* in the world, and *you,* Morgan, for providing less expensive computers by direct 'built to your specs and delivered to your door' efficiency, and you over there, Fred, for developing a 24-hour television news channel with worldwide reporting capabilities, and you, Mr. ex-President, congratulations to *you* for winning the Nobel."

The continuing congratulatory greetings were becoming excruciatingly embarrassing; Ken felt like a waiter at a Mensa meeting who had been momentarily mistaken for one of the members.

Not to say that waiters can't also be bright. But please! The brainpower, financial resources and, yes, the egos of some of the people in the room, have enough energy and influence to almost move the entire continental United States around the ocean as easily as a toy tugboat could push a bar of soap around a bathtub.

After several minutes of such pleasantries the conversation began to slacken as the more goal-oriented, which is to say, all those present, seemingly simultaneously grew weary of the small talk. Sensitive to his guests' limited tolerance for chit-chat, the senator invited the entire group to repair to the 'den', which turned out to be a large board room, where they proceeded to sit at the huge, black walnut, elliptical-shaped table, at the places marked by hand-printed place-cards that seemed to signal an undoubtedly desired sense of informality.

Ken counted twenty-one people at the table, including himself, and it seemed clear from their banter and first-name ease with one another that they had likely been at their deliberations for some time, possibly, Ken mused, with time off for the bonding that could come with sailing on the sixty foot-long schooner he had admired that was moored at the dock. Or perhaps they had commiserated while floating or swimming in the huge pool or the always perfect-temperature ocean that he remembered from his previous time in the D.R..

Ken noted that there were two thick leather-bound folders on the table in front of each Herman Miller High Back chair, along with fresh fruit, soft drinks and bottled water, current-edition cellphone-equipped PDAs, plus a wide variety of laptops or PC tablets that were laid out in a seemingly chaotic fashion. Clearly none of the security-vetted support staff dared to touch, never mind rearrange, these leaders' twenty-first century weaponry whenever they took breaks from their deliberations.

Ken noted that no one brought any alcoholic drinks to the table, and no one smoked. His host was a notoriously vocal anti-smoking advocate and he had heard that the senator was on the wagon again. Ken was happy that no one was smoking but wouldn't have minded the latter crutch at the moment. Before he could give that thought much mind-time he was personally directed by Cassidy to a chair to the immediate right of the senator's, who was seated at the head of the table. Ken's position had obviously been reserved for him; on the table in front of his chair were one leather-bound folder, two bottles of Perrier, and a caffeine-free, diet 7-UP. *How did they know?*

Once everyone was seated, Senator Cassidy did the more formal introductions, giving Ken time to look directly at the person being introduced to him, and for them to exchange brief greetings. Then, swiveling his chair so that he was looking directly at Ken, and speaking loudly enough for everyone to hear, Cassidy said, "I want to thank you again, Ken, for agreeing to join us on such short notice. What you see here is a 'working group' of exemplary American and Canadian men and women that has completed its deliberations far more quickly than I had even dared hope. What you don't realize is that this group was actually spawned in response to *your* articles over the past many months.

"From initial one-on-one conversations amongst some of us, Ken, what has been developed over the past weeks is this group of concerned, eminent citizens who, with the help of a few constitutional authorities who we flew in for the specific purpose, have now spent the last seven days reviewing and discussing our two countries', America's and Canada's, voting procedures and representational processes, which we now believe are more different in appearance than in operation. And we are now well on the way to conceptualizing and fleshing out entirely new tools for our citizens to make use of, in the service of moving our countries towards becoming more truly representative and participatory democracies.

"To put the matter simply, it is this working group's intention to take advantage of the truly fantastic capabilities our societies' technologies have created and/or could easily develop, in order to permit, provide, and promote more genuinely participatory democratic processes for the United States, Canada, and any other countries along the way who will be interested in pursuing such a path."

The others around the table nodded and amen'd in unison,

seconding Senator Cassidy's comments.

Cassidy continued. "All of the people here are agreed that there are only sinners at this table. We have all been to one kind of contaminated trough or another, more than a few times. In the past we acknowledge that we have sometimes taken advantage of our positions, our financial resources, our overt or covert political and/or business contacts, to get what we desired, sometimes by highly questionable means. And while we may or may not apologize for what we have done in the past, all of us here recognize that these ways of operating have not ultimately not usually been in our countries' or our fellow citizens' best interests."

Ken had seldom heard a politician or a businessperson voluntarily issue a mea culpa unless he or she had been exposed for wrongdoing. Ken began to wonder if he had perhaps been invited to a high end, 'born again' confessional.

Cassidy said, "But that is the point that I want–that *we* want–to make. We know first hand that most people who have power over anything or anyone will not, readily or willingly, give up those means or power. And that goes for people who are in position to influence or control any level of government.

"The problem is, as we see it, that now matters have reached such a crucial point in our countries that, if we do not act to counter the ways in which government in particular operates, it may well be too late. And what we at this table have concluded is that we now have, or can soon develop, the technological capability to change forever the way our governments function by making them truly more democratic and participatory. But as citizens we cannot, must not, wait for governing bodies to offer these means to our citizenry; they never will. The changes that need to be introduced will have to be driven from the bottom up, from ordinary citizens who will force their governments to change.

"Without a doubt, Ken, it was your articles about the travesties visited upon the victims of 9/11 and the other terrorist actions that followed, that created a groundswell for change that forced the congress to pass, and the President to sign into law, the *War Against Terrorism Heroes-And-Their-Families Guaranteed Medical Benefits And Financial Support Act*. Well, now we need your help to promote action by our government to change the way America is governed so as to again make it more truly a democracy.

"Now, it has been pointed out to me, Ken, and I agree, that I have undoubtedly been spending far too much time in various committees trying to get things done with my political colleagues alone, many of whom—and I have to admit that I myself have been rightly accused of the very same fault—don't seem to be able to ask the way to the can, eh, bathroom, without launching into a speech about water purity and preserving America's glorious rivers." Many of those present, including the former American president, laughed aloud at the senator's description of too many politicians.

"Perhaps I also forgot that it should not necessarily be required that a politician agree to sell his or her first born every time we wish to accomplish something of value, and that sometimes one shouldn't need to get something in exchange merely for doing the right thing. I… we, have also been reminded of this by the truly remarkable interim Prime Minister of Canada, Trish Markridge, who we are so fortunate to have had with us these past four days."

This comment was met with enthusiastic head-nodding and spontaneous applause from the others around the table. Markridge smiled her appreciation.

"The fact is, Ken, we have been commiserating for several days straight by now, and have agreed upon certain intentions and plans unanimously. We are very much in need, right now, of someone with your keen investigative mind, established integrity, and healthy professional skepticism. We want to run some of our ideas past you and would sincerely welcome your open and honest responses to the results of our deliberations."

Ken responded, "I am flattered and honored, Senator, but I am certain that you and," Ken looked around the table as he then added, "the others of you here have such people, either amongst your staff or otherwise accessible to you. So, why ask me for my opinion?"

Cassidy's eyes instinctively narrowed for just a moment; then he appeared to relax and issued a broad smile that gently expanded across his large, square-shaped face. He replied, "Excellent question, Ken. Let me say that inviting you here was a group decision, one arrived at unanimously and in short order. We did so, I believe, for at least three excellent reasons.

"First and foremost, like most of the rest of us, you are at the pinnacle of your profession, and are, shall we say, part of the same 'age range of maturity' as most of the rest of us, myself being just a *touch* older," he added, smiling broadly again. "We are also convinced of your integrity as well as your repeatedly demonstrated willingness to take risks, to put your reputation on the line, if such was required, for the greater good of finding out, and then informing your readers, just what the hell has been going on in our countries. And, as I shall explain shortly, that is *exactly* what everyone *here* is prepared to continue doing in the weeks and months ahead.

"Secondly, your recent Paulson, which all of us were delighted that you received (a burst of enthusiastic applause from everyone at the table immediately accompanied his words), has given you and your writing even greater cachet. At last count, we were informed, your column has been syndicated in every part of this country and Canada, in over four hundred newspapers. We know, therefore, that more than any other reporter in North America, you reach a very sizable proportion of our citizens with your views. Also, your guest appearances on major radio and television talk shows clearly show that you can present whatever you have to say in a clear, concise manner via a variety of media, in ways that lay persons can usually comprehend.

"Thirdly," the senator continued, "once you have heard our ideas and read the materials that we are prepared to share with you, *then*, if what we have been discussing is a matter that interests you and if you agree with its basic tenets, we will be prepared to invite you to consider doing a series of columns detailing, to whatever depth you think appropriate, just what we are proposing and intending to do. And if you are interested in doing such a series, then everyone here has already agreed to make himself or herself available to you for further, in-depth, one-on-one follow-up interviews where you would be free to ask for our individual thoughts and feelings on these matters, asking whatever questions you may have related to the subjects we are here to discuss–on the record."

Ken looked around the table and saw the other power heads bobbing and smiling in agreement. Whatever the subject matter was going to be, it was hard to resist saying "yes" immediately, but he managed to hold off. It would be fascinating and exciting to have the opportunity, and in many cases, the *rare* privilege of sitting down for individual interviews with the people now sitting at the table. Ken knew that a few of them had reputations of being notoriously media-shy, especially when they could not entirely control the agenda, or might be asked questions about their personal (as opposed to professional or business) opinions. He himself had previously been refused requests for interviews with at least five of these movers and shakers in the not too distant past.

Did somebody just say, "Eureka, I've hit the motherlode?"

The senator said to Ken, "I, as an elected representative of the citizens of my state, and Shawn over there (Cassidy looked and nodded in the direction of Shawn McArthur, the respected maverick Republican senator from the southwest), are both prepared to implement our group's proposals within our own constituencies as soon as feasible, which we estimate will be within twelve to twenty months."

Senator McArthur issued a broad smile in Ken's direction, and said in his trademark straight shooter voice, "We are committed to this action, Ken, and we hope to convince at least some of our fellow senators and congressmen and women to join us in our groundbreaking endeavor."

Whatever they have up their collective sleeves, it must be a humdinger, to get these two old warhorses on the same side in what they evidently anticipate will be a highly provocative venture.

Cassidy said, "Ken, let me start by sharing the name of our proposal. Phil came up with it; well, actually, it was his second title. The first one somehow ended up with the name of his company written into it."

This time all of those present laughed heartily. Phil's nerdy persona had a tough, take-no-prisoners underside yet he also joined in the laughter, although perhaps a touch self-consciously and in a slightly forced manner.

None of these dudes probably really enjoy being the butt of anyone else's humor, however lightly delivered.

"Anyway," continued the senator, "we have come up with what we think is a descriptive, if not what you folks in the media would call a 'sexy' title. In fact, you may be able to come up with a better title. Meanwhile, we are referring to our proposal as, 'Technologically-Enabled, Real-Time, Participatory Democratization'."

"At the risk of giving offence," Ken said lightly, "perhaps the name does need a *little* work."

Everyone laughed, including Phil, who seemed to appreciate Ken's gentleness. Ken was relieved; it wouldn't pay to piss off the richest person in the universe. Out of habit, Ken took his reporter's yellow notepad out of his briefcase, preferring to use it to the pad of paper provided inside the leather-bound folder.

Now Cassidy's amiable demeanor changed ever so slightly, and that deep New England voice became a touch more senatorial, and perhaps even a little conspiratorial. "Ken, all of us in this room have come together with one unified concern. Because of the huge geographical size of our countries and because of the tremendous growth of our populations over the past two hundred years, with the influx of so many millions of folks who have come from every part of the world, the mechanism of governing has become increasingly unwieldy and certainly a far more complicated problem than our founding fathers could ever have imagined."

Ken noted that everyone at the table nodded or voiced their agreement on this point.

"Furthermore, and perhaps of even greater concern, all of us present know full well that the distribution of wealth and power in our countries has come to rest in a relatively few hands, including, we are prepared to admit, our own. You will find no apologists here. We, *I*, have played the game as well as nearly anyone. And most of us have profited mightily, largely in legal, if not always philosophically or morally, justifiable ways. Furthermore, the inequitable distribution of power that we have all been a part of, and have profited by, has led to the disproportionate representation in our government of lobbyists over logic, of wealth over welfare, of greed over need, and of the privileged few over the vast majority. As a result, many groups of less well-connected individuals have been–and I don't know another way to put the matter succinctly–royally screwed!"

Hearing a senior politician saying what nearly everyone knew but most politicians repeatedly denied, was refreshing–and promising. *Or, was Cassidy simply paying lip service?*

The senator continued; "For example, Shawn and I co-sponsored an election reform bill a few years back that got watered down so much that little has really changed since whatever was left of it finally passed."

Most of Cassidy's comments to this point, while valid, were hardly news. Surely, this was not what Ken had been invited to travel over two thousand miles to respond to; it reminded him of the first President Bush, who seemed to marvel at having suddenly discovered what everyone else in America was well aware of, namely a supermarket check-out scanner.

It was Cassidy's next comments that made the 2500 mile schlep-by-jet worthwhile.

The senator said, "Ken, by using the technology, power, and accessibility of personal computers, PDAs and the Internet, we are proposing to give participatory democracy back to the people and where, ever since the days people began to live in large cities, it has never, until now, been possible to fully implement. But it is now, and we intend to begin to provide individual American citizens with the means whereby each one will be able to have a much greater say about the political goings-on in our country than presently."

An enthusiastic round of applause accompanied by supportive comments echoed from around the table.

In his more than thirty years as a reporter Ken had never heard a politician say–*and actually mean*–such words. But the old silver-headed fox seemed to mean what he was saying and as he gazed into the approving faces of the others around the table he sensed that this group was really serious about the matter.

Former President Barney Chambers spoke up in his soft

Southern drawl. "Ken, when our country was formed our population was less than 4 million persons, or merely about one and one-half percent of what it is now. In other words, our population has grown by more than seventy times what it was then. Over two hundred years ago our founding fathers spoke of a government "*of* the people, *for* the people, and *by* the people. Well, right now we are hardly delivering one-third of what was promised; government is still *by* the people, of course, by virtue of the fact that citizens can vote for their representatives, but all too often it is not *for* the people who did the voting.

"Our voting structure in America is more like what happens when the entire student body of a large university get the opportunity to vote for prom queen. *They* don't actually get to take her to the dances. It is the 'heavy hitters', the 'in-crowd' or, in the situations we are talking about, the company executives and even the unions that have contributed mightily to the candidates' campaigns, who get to 'dance' around the floor of the Senate, the Congress and even the White House. And that is simply no longer good enough, especially because now we can have the means to deliver on the original, three-part promise originally made to the citizens of this country well over two centuries ago."

Ken asked, "But is it really feasible to do this, to have every adult citizen who wishes to, be able to contribute to the debate on issues of their concern, or even to exercise an actual *vote* of some sort on any, let alone *every*, issue that comes before the federal legislative bodies of this country?"

The software tycoon, Phil Tate, responded in his excited, and now even higher-pitched-than-usual voice. "Mr. Simpson, we can create new dedicated devices with secure software programs that will allow exactly that!"

President Chambers, a former engineer, added, "I think it is useful to remind ourselves and the American people that, after all, we are the country that is known around the world for conceiving, designing, and building all sorts of awesome technological devices. We built the incredibly complicated technology that put men on the moon and robotic devices on Mars. We already have personal computers of every type, PDAs, and multi-functional, e-mail sending and receiving cellphones. If we want to, we can certainly develop the technology required to provide voters with better tools to participate directly, *daily if they so desire*, in the actual governing process of these United States of America. In fact, according to my friends here at this very table, compared to the time taken to conceive and then create some of the other devices I have mentioned, we are nearly already there. We just have to put the needed functionality for the tools we are speaking of into a single device. And with new variations of some of the software that Phil Tate's company already provides, with the added encryption and other security functions similar to that which our military uses, and with the research and product development personnel that Morgan's company and some of the others here have available now, we are only a matter of a couple of years away from being able to provide virtually every voter in America with a portable device that will allow that person to take part in a genuine participatory democracy. That is, if we have the will to do it."

Senator McArthur added, "Ken, all of us at this table have committed ourselves to delivering on the promise made by our forefathers more than two centuries ago. We also are, truth be told, either at the apex or in the twilight of our own years of public service or private enterprise. And both individually and collectively, we have given this entire matter a great deal of thought. We can't wait; in fact, we refuse to wait any longer, for the younger men and women who are just coming into politics to somehow do the job for us. They are much closer to the beginning than to the end of their careers. And like students who have finally graduated from college and are out working, they have the equivalent of student loans to pay off, only some of *their* loans are actually IOUs to the individuals, unions, and corporations who bankrolled and supported them, and got them to the 'dance'. In other words, the reason they have been elected is due, to a large extent, to the old guard and the longstanding use of political and corporate influence and money. For these reasons, I am sad to say, most of them may even *want* to continue being part of the old power system. Too many of them may be vulnerable to being more focused on their own progress up the party ranks than the actual personal needs and wants of their constituents.

"Unfortunately," McArthur continued, "while they may *want* to do some good, they are political party members and that is the only game they've ever learned. And they know that they damn well better mind their p's & q's, and toe the party line–that is, if they want to stay around long enough and build up enough brownie points, to be able to *ever* think of acting mildly independently. And if they *don't* continue to play the game they were taught and brought up on, then their days in the House or Senate will probably be short-lived. That is what too many of *us* did for too long, myself included. *This* revolution, if it is going to happen, will have to be led by us *seniors!* Now isn't that a hoot?"

Senator Cassidy added, "My father once said that the only person who can afford to tell the whole truth and then act on it, is someone who either is prepared to be martyred, or has his bags packed. Well, all of us around this table have our bags ready, if it comes to that. And we are close enough to the end of our working lives that if we are martyred, i.e., drummed out of our parties, so be it. The more crucial question is whether other folks like yourself and some of our senior colleagues will be prepared to risk *their* positions by advocating *real* political change, change that will forever alter the ways that things will be done. For far too long, decisions have been done in the dark stairwells and backrooms of power in these United States."

Trish Markridge added, "Truth be told, Ken, virtually everything Tom has been saying about America also applies to Canadian politics. I intend to work to change that."

Phil Tate said, "I have been very blessed, Ken, as have most of us here, beyond my wildest dreams. And now, we all believe that it is now time to 'give something back'. All of us at this table who are in business *started* our companies. And we still have the clout and the energy, we hope, to move the organizations that we founded in the directions that we think are crucial, not merely for our companies' success, but our nation's future."

Ken now found that famous high-pitched, nerdy voice almost as endearing as it was grating.

Tate continued. "All the company founders at this table have agreed to pledge sizable portions of our own personal wealth, and measurable proportions of our companies' R&D and manufacturing resources, to develop products and facilities through which Americans can more easily participate in setting and directing the agendas and actions of our government.

"Specifically, Ken, my company will help develop the software required to give citizens with voting rights the ability to easily research and comment upon, via the Internet, any non-classified issue that their elected officials have under consideration. And more than that, they will be able to express their opinions via the most advanced and secure e-mail voting and two-way communication delivery systems that we can create. Eventually the new system will allow our citizens to actually *pre-vote and pre-comment* on proposed bills scheduled to appear before our legislatures. The prototypes of these systems will first be offered to the voters in the jurisdictions of Senators Cassidy and McArthur. And they have agreed to cast their votes, not with their own parties necessarily, but rather, in the direction that their constituents will indicate by their 'pre-votes' that they want their elected representatives' votes to go."

Senator McArthur quickly added, "That does not necessarily mean that we *must* vote the way the majority of our voting constituents will have 'pre-voted'; it does mean, however, that we will agree to vote that way if the number of pre-votes cast exceed a yet to be determined percentage of eligible voters, *unless* our consciences suggest otherwise. In that case, we will provide all of our constituent-voters with our detailed, written rationales for doing so. So our accountability will be to the individual voters in our districts, not to our political parties."

Senator Cassidy picked up on the last points. "We are fortunate to have in my state, Ken, a relatively high proportion of homes with computer access. I am going to announce next month that all those individuals eligible to vote in my state will be able to pre-vote on each and every bill that will pass across my desk, and that, depending upon the relative proportions of Yeas and Nays I receive, and assuming that a sufficient proportion of voters actually take advantage of the opportunity to vote, I will commit myself publicly to be guided by them, and will cast my own vote in the Senate in a manner that reflects the wishes of the majority of my pre-voting constituents."

Ken was listening, spellbound, afraid to interrupt lest the entire conversation vanish. He realized he was holding his breath, as if waiting for a 'but' to erase the import of all that he was hearing. He was awestruck by the audacity of the ideas being put forward, and by the courage of the speakers, who surely realized the forces that would soon be unleashed against them. *I am sitting here, present at the founding meeting of a profound evolution, if not a revolution, of our democracy. Washington lobbyists and the groups that give them billions and billions will immediately freak out. They will unleash hell upon everyone in this whole group. And me, if I take them up on their offer to interview and report upon their views about this incredible proposal.*

Cassidy said, "And by the way, on the real-time websites that we will have up and running in conjunction with these developments, voters will be able to confidentially check that their own votes were actually received and counted, and they will see the same tabulated results that I will. Each voter's social security number will be the key to unlock his or her own voting tool. There will also be an additional password that only they will know. Plus, we will use a new fingerprint identification keypad on their equipment that will verify that it was indeed the registered user who has done the voting."

Zelda, the most prominent talk show host in America, had been listening to the conversation and acutely assessing Ken's non-verbal reactions to what he had been hearing. Spotting what she thought was some healthy skepticism in Ken's visage, she said, "All of us here recognize the importance of preserving the privacy of a person's opinions, as well as the sensitivity some may have to having their fingerprint on file in the bowels of governmental bureaucracy. For those reasons, the servers that will house the fingerprint and other data provided by each voter will be located in a secure, non-governmental location by a nonpartisan National Trust organization which we have code-named the Participatory Democracy Trust, or PDT, whose mandate will be the housing and preserving of personal identifier information and voting records."

Cassidy added, "I will get the contents of the voters' e-mails but not their e-mail address or any other identifiers, unless the individual voter chooses to override the default settings to allow me to know who he or she is and I or at least people in my office can perhaps respond personally. Alternatively, an e-mail responding to the voter's own, will go through an intermediary web address so that the voter will get our response but we won't know who that person is, or their usual e-mail address."

Cassidy paused and caught his breath. Ken was momentarily concerned for the man's physical well-being, until the senator smiled and said, "My breathing, … hell, my heart, is not what it used to be. Pay it no mind. It just takes me a moment to get it back in line."

Ken was not very reassured, and for the first time he had an inkling that this high drama was taking its toll on the man.

Cassidy continued talking, however. "This entire enterprise is going to take a lot of fine-tuning, Ken, *of course*, and we all know that. But at this point I am prepared to say publicly that if a majority of the voters in my state who are eligible to vote, will be willing to do so via the voting devices that are being created for them, *then*, except in the case of a bona fide national emergency, when there might not be sufficient time to have a meaningful public dialogue about an issue–and in which case I will vote according to my own dictates–if more than 50% of all eligible voters cast their vote in one particular direction, then I will cast my vote in the Senate in that direction. The only exception to that guideline will be in instances where I may personally disagree strongly with the voters' majority opinion. In such a case I will choose to vote in accordance with my own conscience. In that event, however, I will immediately e-mail all voters and state the reasons for my having done so. At election time, if my health allows it, I will run again so that voters can have the opportunity to vote me out of office, if enough of them so wish."

With his New England accent underlining his words, he said, "Let me take a specific issue. It is my belief, and it has been for many years now, that most Americans want to be covered by a government-run universal Medicare plan. Or at least, they *would* want it, if they were presented with the entire truth on the matter.

For example, as you well know, the truth is that our medical system is, in effect or in fact, bankrupting hundreds of thousands of our citizens and their families *every year*, because they can't otherwise afford necessary surgeries or medications

"The truth is that most workers are, in effect, being kept hostage by the companies they work for, because if they were to change jobs, they risk losing the medical coverage that they may currently have. And if one of the members of their families has developed a chronic condition of some kind, then gaining coverage elsewhere might be exceptionally difficult and costly, if they could get it at all.

"The truth is that if, for some reason, they become unemployed, in most cases they would become uninsured as well.

"The truth is that most other countries in the world, including most of our closest allies, have already put into place various kinds of universal Medicare programs.

"And the truth is that our people are stressed out about what will happen to them if they or their loved ones get sick because of the tremendous individual out-of-pocket expenses they could be forced to pay."

The senator was at full oratorical throttle. "I want to show Americans that, given a real opportunity to cast a vote *directly* for a particular bill, that they would force our legislators to pay heed, that is, if they were to dare to do what Shawn and I will be doing, and give their constituents more control over how they cast their votes."

Ken was transfixed. Cassidy was not kidding; he really was serious about what he was saying: imagine, giving constituents a day-to-day and bill-to-bill individual voice and vote, not just a once-every-two-or-four-year carte blanche ticket. The concepts being presented were breathtaking. He was imagining voters expressing their opinions directly on issues and upcoming bills in the House and Senate, not via pollsters hired by one side or the other of an issue and perhaps using questionable, skewed questions on a sample of only a very few hundred or thousand voters. What the people around the table were proposing certainly sounded like an attempt at providing a truer form of representational, participatory democracy, which was possible now because of the tremendous advances in electronic personal communication.

Ken had a great many questions as well as some doubts running through his mind. He also recognized immediately that Cassidy had been correct when he said that if the proposed changes were to become the norm it would only be because the citizenry had demanded it. Very few political or business leaders outside of this room would likely voluntarily give up their current positions to influence and effect changes in the laws of the land. Not without a fight; not without a grass roots-inspired groundswell.

Senator Cassidy realized that a lot of ideas had been fired in Ken's direction in the past several minutes, and he picked up on their guest's increasingly contemplative expression. He decided to give him the opportunity to come up for air.

"Ken, we have thrown quite a lot at you in a short time. Thank you for your tolerance and patience. Now, we would be more than pleased, I am sure, to get your initial responses to our proposals, and answer any questions you might have to this point."

After several beats Ken said, "You all have taken my breath away. I have already pinched myself more than once to make certain that I was not dreaming. While I may not have yet heard your proposal in its entirety, what you have told me to this point has certainly raised several questions in my mind and also elicited some responses that I think might also play on the minds of many Americans, once they hear of your plans. I would appreciate being able to raise some of these matters before you go on any further, and while they are still fresh in my mind."

"By all means. Go ahead," said Senator Cassidy.

Ken began by offering a caveat. "The way I might pose some questions may seem impudent or even downright offensive to some of you; let me apologize for that up front. But let me also add that the tone and manner with which I will be asking these questions might accurately reflect the mindset of a significant number of Americans. Some of them, for instance, might feel quite uncomfortable by the changes you are proposing, if for no other reason than the fact that it is such a radical shift from the way things have been done in this country for literally hundreds of years."

Ex-President Chambers responded, saying, "Well, Mr. Simpson, that is what you and we are here for. I recall a friend telling me about a talk he attended a long time ago by some motivational speaker. Apparently he told a story, a parable really, about when President John Kennedy announced that Americans were going to send a man to the moon within a decade, it was as if this country had built a huge and almost empty warehouse, with a sign hanging over the front door that proclaimed, "A MAN ON THE MOON IN TEN YEARS!"

"At the very front of the building, just inside the front door, he said, was the office of "IT CAN'T BE DONE." Inside that office were all the skeptics and doubters who basically said, with seemingly great pleasure, "No way can this be done. Why, don't you realize that in order to get a man on the moon you would have to build a lunar landing device with such-and-such capabilities and associated equipment, and that you would also need a booster rocket with this much thrust that would have to reach this exact speed at that specific angle to the earth's surface in order for you to be able to do all that?"

President Chambers went on, obviously enjoying telling the story. "Well, those guys in the office of 'It can't be done', through their unremitting criticism, pretty well told us nearly all the things we needed to know and do in order to accomplish our mission. What they didn't appreciate is that they were actually working *inside* the building, and that they were an essential element in helping us to figure out how to get a man on the moon in ten years.

"And that, Ken, is your job here. By all means critique and criticize and tell us what you've heard that sounds impossible or unlikely or questionable or even crazy. And by doing so, sir, you will have done us an invaluable service."

Ken said, "Your story is a good one, and probably very apt on this occasion. I'll do my best, Mr. President, but let me say at the beginning that I do not for one moment belong to the group of 'It can't be done'. I would more happily see myself having a desk in the office of 'Let's look at the problems that may need to be faced."

Chambers responded, "Excellent response, sir. And by the way, in the story I just told you the only other office in the whole otherwise empty building that was also occupied at the time of the announcement, was the office of the 'True Believers', who knew that the job should be done, could be done, and that America was just the country to do the job. Well, Ken, you see before you the optimistic occupants of the office of the 'true believers'. So please, take your best shots. No matter what you might say, you will be working *with* us, aiming at achieving the same end goal."

Ken said, "Assuming that the technology you have mentioned will be accessible and easy enough to be used by most Americans, which is a big assumption that I would want to come back to at a later time, let me ask you all, what makes you think that the average American is capable of, let alone interested in, making well-thought-out judgments about what new bills should or should not come into being?"

Senator McArthur jumped in on that one. "Ken, that is the same line of doubtful thinking that was applied in the past to women and that kept them from having the vote for an obscenely long time. They were told that 'making laws isn't women's work', that they weren't sufficiently politically minded, and other such baloney. To take another example, as you well know, many whites, especially but not only in the south, said for a long time that African Americans shouldn't get the vote because they weren't smart enough, or knowledgeable enough, or whatever. Thank goodness, and no small thanks to the women and the blacks who refused to take such prejudices laying down, women and blacks now have the vote. So, already in our own history in America, we *have* made some major changes in the way voting has been carried out in our country. And we are all better off for it."

Phil Tate added, "At the start of the first Internet revolution some people said that children were too undisciplined and television-glued, that seniors were just too old to learn to use the net, and that many men and women of working age wouldn't want to be bothered using the net when they could just sit back and watch television. Now, of course, all of us are aware that children and seniors are among the main users of the Internet, and that more and more working folks are going online for everything from news and sports to books and buying."

"Agreed," replied Ken. "I am simply raising the issues that I think some may use in an attempt to kill or at least stall your proposal, and that you have to be prepared to answer—as you have done so very eloquently in this first instance.

"Now, however, let me raise another issue. I could suggest that your ideas run counter to the way politics has been—and always will be—done in this country. You may still be an idealist, Senator Cassidy. After all, most representatives in both houses simply vote the party line, not necessarily their own views. So why would these representatives even be *interested* in having greater voter participation? If they were to actually learn the way in which the majority of their voter-respondents were leaning and that was not the same direction that their party was leaning, then to put it bluntly, going along with the expressed wishes of the majority of their voters could mightily tick off a large percentage of colleagues in their own parties, to the point that they might not be re-nominated to run again in the next election. And if the lobbyists supporting them couldn't count on their votes then surely they will take their money and influence off the table, and leave. So why would they want to risk that? "

"Not only that," chimed in Senator Cassidy, "but you know, I am sure, that many, if not most, members of the House and Senate don't even actually read the entire bills either, and so they don't know everything that is in each and every piece of legislation. Well, our voters may be similarly inclined to not be bothered. But if and when issues that really matter to them arise, such as healthcare or going to war, for example, then I believe that many of them, especially if they think they can actually influence such singular issues by their personal vote, *will* read and investigate the issues and then *will* indicate their votes, yea or nay, for the proposed legislation. As much material as possible will be posted on our interactive websites so that voters can ask and get their questions answered, and both questions and answers will be posted on our website. Then, by golly, their elected representatives will really have to do their *own* homework to stay up with their constituents. And if elected officials are not prepared to read up on proposed legislation and take their voters' wishes into account, then they probably *shouldn't* be re-elected the next time around."

Many of those present laughed heartily, perhaps as they thought of hundreds of legislators actually having to thoroughly read what they were now going to be queried about by their constituents.

"Good riddance to them," said one unidentified voice from the other end of the table.

Ken asked, "And what about the people who don't have, or don't know how to use, computers?"

Morgan Teller took on that question with relish. "Ken, two weeks ago I personally placed one billion dollars of my own into the bank account of a newly-formed foundation whose existence will be announced next week, and whose sole aim will be to provide disadvantaged voters with their own dedicated voters' computers, or where that is impractical because they have no fixed address, close-by 24/7 access to a voting computer, probably to be located at schools, libraries, and places of worship throughout the country. The device, which by the way, we have tentatively called the 'Voter's Vector' is already being designed by teams of our engineers. The device will use the software that Phil's company is now developing and will be provided *for free* to all those who request one, take a three-hour course that will show them how to use them and who will be willing to register their thumbprint. Also, self-learning CDs and videos, plus in-class teaching support will be made available at these same libraries, schools, and houses of worship in both the senators' states."

Senator Cassidy added, "Ken, we are in this for the long run. Shawn and I have discussed these proposals long and hard. We have agreed to seek assurances from our respective state education officials, who are almost always reiterating how they do not have a sufficient number of computers, that in return for providing every school, college and university with some of the very latest and fastest personal computers that Steve's and

Morgan's companies make, they will need to introduce into their curriculums a series of classes that we have tentatively called "Citizens' Voting Rights and Responsibilities: Ways and Means of Using the 'Voter's Vector' Technology". These steps will help prepare our future voters to be comfortable and confident with the technology as well as with the idea of how important the individual can–and should–be in a true participatory democracy.

"Also, on the date of their age of maturity, when they can first cast a vote, high school students who have completed the required course will be eligible to receive their own Voters' Vectors–for free–if they simply request one in writing on the form that will be provided at the end of the course they have taken."

Phil said, "And my company will make available, for free of course, CD-ROMs and DVDs that will allow those persons who would prefer, to have all their Voter Vectors' features right on the desktop or laptop computers they already have. Since the basic versions of the voting devices will have somewhat limited features, they are not meant to replace reasonably current models of personal computers, and therefore won't interfere with the continued sales of new personal computers, PDAs, etc..."

Ken asked, "Well, what about costs? Won't providing these new devices, these Voters' Vectors, be astronomical? Do you really think that this tool can eventually be provided, for free, to voters across the entire country? Wouldn't that cost be in the billions?"

Senator McArthur was one of the many around the table who nodded and chuckled in response to Ken's question, as if they had already discussed and dealt with that subject themselves. McArthur said, "Ken, another excellent question. But, now think about the debacles of the past few years, including Enron, WorldCom, Arthur Anderson, and so on. Those travesties were perhaps, to some extent, *allowed* to happen because of the cozy relationships of some private companies to certain government officials and departments whose regulatory agencies, if not complicit, were at best, passive insofar as making sure that citizens were protected from those companies' unscrupulous activities. The lack of political involvement to make sure that

Americans and their investments and pensions were protected, cost our fellow Americans *hundreds of billions* of dollars. And the last Iraq war cost us *thousands* of times what the Voter's Vector technology will cost to bring it to every single voting citizen in this country."

The senator from the Southwest had a head of steam up now. His usually set mouth and chin, the result of severe injuries he suffered in Vietnam, were held even tighter than usual as he spat out the next words; "Furthermore, Ken, if our citizens had a more direct vote on an issue-by-issue basis, then I believe that strengthened regulations would include much stiffer penalties for any future corporate misdeeds, making it far less likely that these types of financial fiascos would occur again."

Senator Cassidy piggybacked on McArthur's comments. "We understand, Ken, that what we are proposing here is just the beginning. We are intending to use my state, and Shawn's, *as test states*, so that we can work out the wrinkles and get a truly viable 'one person-one vote', mechanism into place. What with all the cozy relationships amongst sympathetic politicians with their favorite lobbyists, corporations, and unions, it is unlikely that many *currently* sitting Senate or House member will vote to change the system. And what we are planning to put in place in our two states will surely scare the bejesus out of most of them, because our proposed system will take a lot of their power away and put it back in the hands of the people, where it belongs.

"And with the Voters' Vectors in the hands of our citizens, anything that an administration or that our two main political parties do, from passing weak legislation that allows companies to continue to pump out pollution that is sickening our air, earth and water, all the way to waging war, the so-called 'representatives of the people' will no longer be able to use dubious polls that select a meager sampling of the voting public. The entire voting public itself will be able to speak, in real time, on specific issues. Do you think the powers that be, in and out of government, will allow such changes to happen without a hell of a fight? Not bloody likely!"

Ken conceded silently that was indeed likely to be the scenario that would play out.

"But," Senator Cassidy continued, "when the citizens of the other forty-eight states hear about what we two are doing in our states, then we believe they will begin clamoring for similar rights, demanding to have *their* say, and my party and Shawn's also, will have to get on board, and help bring America's ways and means of governing into the twenty-first century, or get the hell out of the way. And by the way, we are thinking and talking about modernizing state and municipal governments using Voters' Vectors, as well."

Zelda Leighter spoke up. She said, "I grew up on a lot of Bob Dylan's songs. When he sang about the "Masters of War", his was one of the few publicly heard voices of the time warning of our country's involvement in Vietnam, and he influenced my generation, thankfully, a lot. He warned the old guard to get out of the way if they were not going to help change and improve things in our country. Well, a half-century later, here we are. And his words were never more relevant than they are now. And *my* intention is to have each and every one of the people around this table who are willing, including you, Ken, appear on my television show to talk about what we have been discussing here."

Ken suddenly remembered when, as a boy, he and his father also listened to Bob Dylan's records; Frank seemed to display some kind of uncomfortable acknowledgement whenever he heard Dylan's raspy voice, harmonica and guitar pressing his musical arguments.

Zelda continued speaking with passion. She said, "I call the Voter's Vector, 'The Equalizer', the tool that will make sure that black people in the southern states, in Florida, in Mississippi and Arkansas and all the other places where they have kept from voting by hooks and by crooks, *do* get to vote at election time *and all the rest of the time*, whenever *they* want to, about issues that matter to them. No more roadblocks, inadequately staffed polling stations, or other shenanigans like overly complicated voting directions or inefficient or defective 'black box' voting machines will keep them from voting. Not ever again." The lady was lit up with commitment and conviction.

Ken found 'Z' as impressive an individual in person as she

was on television, perhaps even more so. She was physically smaller in person than he had thought, but her forceful personality took up a lot of space. Her warmth and sincerity were front and center whenever she spoke.

"Ken," Z continued, "you and I are the only 'out front' media professionals at this table. We are the ones who can begin to let America know what this plan is really about. CNWN used to do that; their call sign used to stand for the Cable News World Network. Now–sorry to say this, Fred–too often they have become the Cable Nuanced Wuss Network for the you-know-which party.

Fred responded, saying, "No need to say 'sorry' to *me*, Zelda. *I* am the one sorry enough for the whole country, that instead of insightful, reasonably unbiased news, viewers of the network that I started are now getting party line commercials 24/7. Hell, we used to do real investigative reporting. But that was 'too costly' said the bean counters, and it ruffled feathers whenever we uncovered deceit or corruption or unfair practices. "So what?", I said. But the current owners hear from their accountants that 'too vigorous' reporting can cost the network sponsors and so-called 'exclusive' interviews with top officials and so they back off. They would rather kiss someone else's ass than get off their own."

Fred suddenly stopped talking, as if realizing that he had changed the tone of the discussion from reasoned to rabid. Slightly chagrined, his face turned crimson red. He said, "Look, the sad fact is that I turned over the keys to a Rolls Royce to those folks and now it runs around like a scared little rabbit."

The former President spoke up, possibly partly to take the attention away from a deeply wounded man. "I believe that by taking some of the steps we have talked about over the last few days we are weaving a new fabric for governing this nation. I have been an election observer in more than fifteen countries over the years, and am always delighted and proud to see the progress that so many nations have made–including our own. But coming from the south I am keenly aware of the continuing failure of the execution of our own people's voting rights. The last few presidential elections, in particular, have seen so many efforts to keep African Americans and other citizens from exercising their votes. By providing too few voting stations and booths, the result has been blocks-long waiting lines that have discouraged many hundreds of thousands, and maybe even millions of our people from voting. People should not have to be required to stand in line for hours in order to be able to finally cast their votes. I fully endorse the actions being considered by this group to develop these Voters' Vectors devices, for that reason alone. And as a former engineer, I believe that the foolproofing measures being contemplated will protect the integrity of individual citizens' votes far better than any so-called mass voting machines that do not provide a record of a person's vote being counted the way that individual intended.

"As well, Ken, I believe that those persons who will seek out the jobs of being senators and congressmen and women, will be more committed to genuinely servicing their constituents than in sucking up to the big power groups, or grabbing a lot of money and power for themselves, if they are held accountable to their constituents' recorded desires on specific issues. We can, we must, and we will develop the technology to put power back where it belongs, into the hands of the people, and by doing so *they* will get to decide a heck of a lot more than merely which party the large power groups will get to dance with for the next four years. Lobbying will have to change from attempts to buy specific members of the two houses behind closed doors towards efforts to capture voters' hearts and minds by making their cases to the public."

Senator Cassidy added, "And the first series of questions that Shawn and I are committed to putting before our voters will have to do with healthcare. We want to know whether voters would like a universal, publicly-funded healthcare system similar to what they still have in Canada, or some other model that would be very different from the profit-driven, self-serving corporate version that has dominated the field in recent years."

Fred Tunney added, "Look, we all know that many advertisers are now using neuropsychologists to learn how to get people to buy their product by digitally altering messages in order to make them more palatable to viewers and listeners. Now that the term of my non-competition agreement with the buyers of CNWN is up, I intend to go ahead with creating an all-politics news network and companion Internet web site, *where each and every view*, as long as it does not proselytize prejudice or genocide, or the physical harming of another identifiable group, will have an opportunity to air its views.

"My new network will avoid becoming a cheering section for the then-current federal or state governments and the elected representatives. And it will not either dumb down or exclude dissenting views. What the present owners of the network I founded have done is an anathema to me. They are numbing and dumbing their viewers, at least the ones they have left. Which is partly why they are so busy kissing the current administrations' ass. And war is, by far, their best seller; they do calamity and war best. The next time I get ready to retire, I will work damn hard to make sure that the same thing does not happen to my *new* network, which by the way, will be called the American Citizens' Political and Social Network, ACPSN."

Tunney went on, a touch less angrily but no less energetically. "We are going to have programs dealing with the state of healthcare in America. We will have people from all stripes on the shows, but we will encourage them to be very clear as to on whose behalf they are speaking. We will have televised 'town meetings' where we will disclose how the people who formed the presenters and the audiences were chosen. Also, the panelists and guests that we will invite to be on our shows will have to agree to the public disclosure of their relevant financial holdings and/or working relationships to the people and organizations related to the issues they will talking about. Of course, many people will be discouraged from participating because they will know in advance that they will have to inform the audience where their personal, political, or business investments are positioned. So be it: we are certain that there are many others who would be willing to state any potential conflicts of interest or allegiances right up front, for the privilege and potential value of presenting their comments to millions of viewers.

"Also, our own program hosts, reporters, and interviewers will also have to agree to publicly disclose *their* political affiliation and financial investments and involvements–if they are going to be talking about business or politically or socially relevant issues–and whether they have had any financial dealings or other agreements with any guests or the organizations that they represent, and they must state those to us before they are hired, and at the top of each reporting segment, and on the webpages devoted to their programs. I know that that will raise heck with a lot of the people who might want to work at our network, but I want a transparency in our programming and I will start it off by posting my own list of assets and political and social affiliations, and those of the other owners and major investors in our network, right on the web. Viewers deserve nothing less. I am damn tired of the covert bias and bullshitting that goes on by the supposedly objective media."

Senator Cassidy shifted the tone even as his smile and nod told Tunney that he respected his position and understood his frustration. "Fred and myself, indeed all of us around this table, are talking about a work still very much in process, Ken. We are not offering today the end-product solution to returning genuine participatory democracy to the American people. Our ideas, however enthusiastically stated–and no one can match Fred for enthusiasm–(some laughter, including from Fred) are still being outlined and filled in; but, at least, we are offering a *beginning* towards helping to solve the problems we have been talking about.

"Furthermore, President Chambers has agreed to have a new Participatory Democracy Research and Education Center attached to his presidential library. This new center will aim to provide post-graduate and post-doctoral level research into improving and enhancing democratic processes at all levels of government, and many of us here have pledged substantial sums to fund the appropriate fellowships as well as the requisite buildings and faculty."

While Senator Cassidy was speaking, Ken became increasingly aware of the two youngest people present, both of whom were listening attentively to the senator while vigorously nodding their heads in agreement and in near unison. The young woman was tall and slender; her bright, wide eyes seemingly simultaneously expressing sadness and positive energy. She reminded Ken of her father, a fallen American leader.

The young man beside her, Ken recalled from news broadcasts several years earlier, had spoken movingly at the funeral of his own father, a former political leader in Canada. The funeral service, attended by dignitaries from many countries, had been broadcast in an abbreviated version on American television. When the grieving son finished his eulogy Ken realized that he was crying, also. In that instant he had joined with this young man, and once again felt the gigantic loss of his own father.

Noticing the direction of Ken's attention, the senator said, "Before asking you for any more of your initial impressions, Ken, let me introduce you again to my niece, Charlene, and our Canadian friend, Marc-Louis Tremblay."

Ken instantly realized, of course, at least some of the bonds that Charlene and Marc-Louis shared. Both had lost siblings in tragic circumstances. Both belonged to families that were considered the closest things to royalty or nobility in their respective countries. And both were recognized as having pure political blood in their veins and public service in their hearts and minds.

Marc-Louis Tremblay spoke in a clear voice with a charming French tinge to his English, looking at Ken with direct, intense, yet soft eyes. "Mr. Simpson, I am very grateful to Senator Cassidy and the others for including me in these deliberations and for making me feel so welcome." As he spoke, Marc-Louis looked briefly at the people to whom he was referring, and Ken noted that they all were gazing back with kind and respectful acknowledgement.

This young man definitely has his own large measure of charisma.

"Charlene and I are the evidence," the young man continued, "that the proposals being put forward at this table are not *entirely* those of the 'senior' generation. I have, for many reasons, always been interested in the process of moving society forward, an interest I am sure that I acquired in large part from my childhood circumstances. But until the last few days I had not known of a way that I might help bring something new and valuable to the political process in my country, something that will give Canadians a more meaningful part to play in the future directions and decisions of our country. Growing up, and as an adult, too often I have seen politics being pursued by persons whose focus seemed mostly centered on their own and certain vested interests' agendas; for that reason I have always resisted taking an active part in politics. Now, however, as a result of these deliberations and the developments we have been discussing, I see a way to bring a new energy and empowering innovation to our political landscape."

The young man's eyes shone with enthusiasm. "Over the years I have been pulled, or more accurately perhaps, I should say I have been *pushed* in the direction of becoming more directly politically involved. It is now my intention to consider taking up the offer of many in my father's party to do so, on condition that they will agree to my introducing the use of the sorts of technology we have been discussing here. I would want to be a true representative of my constituents and the Voters' Vector and accompanying technology would allow me to have meaningful, continuous communication with, and feedback from, my constituents, about issues that matter to them. And I would certainly be prepared to represent the voting majority's view in parliament, unless of course, it strongly conflicted with my own personal ethics or beliefs."

Tremblay continued, "Like Senators Cassidy and McArthur, but for different reasons, I too have little to lose in bringing these tools of a more participatory democracy to the table. If the party I would be most inclined to join were *not* to be amenable to the approaches we have been discussing, then I might well choose to run as an independent. And I strongly believe that there are others of my generation who would also be interested in contributing to real and meaningful changes in the ways our government works. For these reasons I am prepared to pursue a political course for at least the next few years of my life."

The young man stopped talking but kept his liquid gaze in contact with Ken. Ken's intuition informed him that he was perhaps looking at a potential Prime Minister of Canada.

Ken noticed that Trish Markridge had been keenly listening

to Marc-Louis and smiling broadly. She said, "Marc-Louis and I have already begun discussing his ideas for introducing Voters' Vectors and the accompanying technology into our country's politics. I have assured him that as long as I function in the role of Prime Minister he will be free to employ such an approach within our party, even if that means that he might end up voting against bills that, as the governing party, we will be introducing to Parliament. And I will offer the same opportunity to any other members of our party who might wish to make use of similar technologies."

Charlene Cassidy, who had been nodding her agreement the entire time Marc-Louis was speaking, said, "I think and feel very similarly to Marc-Louis. As you know, Mr. Simpson, politics has been a very mixed blessing for both of us. I have watched my uncle fight the good fight, even within his own party, to try and get the policymakers to accept positions that he sincerely believes are in the best interest of his constituents. That part of politics has never appealed to me. Why should an elected representative not represent more directly and accurately the needs and desires of those he or she is *supposed* to represent, rather than those to whom he or she has become beholden for fundraising and favors, past and future?

"I am so excited about the prospects that we have been discussing that, like Marc-Louis, I truly believe that an entirely new generation of politicians will be willing to work towards changing the ways in which our countries are run, and that we can help make participatory democracy a reality in ways that even we in this room have not thought of yet, simply because we are also the products of our own pasts.

Senator Cassidy was beaming with pride listening to his niece. He now happily chimed in, with, "So, you see, Ken, not all of us are senile old fogies who have come up with a cockamamie scheme as part of our dementia." Most everyone around the table joined in the laughter.

He continued. "And I have decided to take one more run at securing publicly funded healthcare in our country. I expect it will be at least a year before people in my state will be provided with their own Voters' Vectors. In the meanwhile I will be holding electronic town meetings on the subject, and will invite suggestions as to how we might make these tools and new ways of operating more effective. After receiving such input, if I have the numbers–and I am confident that I will–I will propose that our country move towards a government-run, publicly funded, universal healthcare system that will put an end to the travesty of bankruptcies and unperformed operations for so many Americans who are in need of medical services."

A burst of applause greeted both Senator Cassidy's resolve and his resolution.

"Ken, I know you will want to examine the dossier you have in front of you on your own. But before you get to do that, is there anything, right now, that you would like to offer us in the form of suggestions or criticisms? Whichever, or both, we will give your comments serious consideration."

When Ken began to speak the words would not emerge. Instead, his own and his father's tears welled up, and in a barely audible voice, he merely said, "I wish all of you... I wish you all... Godspeed."

CHAPTER 57

By the time the Lear began its descent into LaGuardia three days later, Ken had written the first two of his new series of articles on the challenges and opportunities for real 21st century-style participatory democracy in America.

When he said his goodbyes to Senator Cassidy and the others Ken had gazed in awe at the mostly graying participants at the meeting. Here were sinners and philanderers, people whose fortitude and motivations had been questioned time and again over the years, not entirely without some justification. In the course of his more than three decades as a journalist Ken had met and interviewed thousands of people–the rich, the middle class and the poor; famous, infamous, and neither. He had only ever found a few who might have been destined for official or unofficial sainthood. He agreed with those who said that all people are wanderers and sinners. Yet amongst the fallen, the fallible, the egotists, and those afflicted with other kinds of less than exemplary qualities, it nevertheless did happen that some eventually found ways, perhaps at last, to redeem themselves in their own–if not others'–eyes. And in the Dominican Republic twenty men and women, in this age of terror, trauma, self-interest, and downright greed, had come together to forge new vehicles with which to advance the governing of cities, states, and countries.

In the course of the three days that Ken was part of their deliberations it became abundantly clear that no one present thought for a moment that they had discovered the final or complete answer to the problems of how to better govern a country. But in the course of their deliberations they had developed a series of proposals and became very specific as to what each of them could and would be doing to further their joint aims. Ken felt certain that this group of ultra-achievers, utilizing all the means at their disposal, were incubating what could eventually provide the next evolution in democratic, participatory governing.

It had been a long time since, as a teenager, Ken heard America's president utter the words, "Ask not what your country can do for you; ask what *you* can do for your country." The people around the table in the D.R. had taken John F. Kennedy's provocative challenge to heart, and were ready to respond at some considerable risk, not so much monetarily, but in terms of how they would be viewed by their business, political, and social peers, as well as by their friends and family.

They fully grasped the fact that it would not be an easy ride over the next few years, because too many of those already drenched in political power would surely want to hold onto their positions into the future, and therefore would not voluntarily give up control. The media that was already in the pockets of vested interests would be merciless; Ken was not even certain that *The New York Era* would be supportive of his part in the proposed process, although the exclusive interviews he was assured of getting would give him a great deal of leverage. He was sure, however, that the battle to pursue America's founding fathers' promise of government "for the people, of the people, and by the people," had begun anew.

Ken had thought of his own father many times while in the Dominican Republic. Like Frank Simpson, the people present at the meeting were ultra-high achievers who were willing to fight–perhaps late in the game, but much better late than never–and risk position, power, and prestige for the sake of their fellow citizens and for 21st century innovations that they truly believed were in their countries' best interests. Ken was determined to do all he could to report fairly and in depth upon the proposals from the D.R. meeting that would soon be forthcoming. If brought to fruition, they would have a seismic impact upon the ways in which government and business would operate in America, Canada, and possibly beyond. Putting power back more directly into the hands of the people had been an ideal for hundreds of years. Now, it was realizable, due to the highly do-able developments in electronic technology that would soon be birthed by that group of remarkable men and women. And Ken was determined to do his part to bring the entire story to his readers.

The next few months would be exciting times. There were so many interviews to be held with the folks from the meeting in the D.R., and so many articles to be written. Ken would surely need all the assistance he could get from Martha to help carry the load.

As the jet touched down Ken felt exquisitely aware of all he had been through recently, both the highs and the lows, including being the recipient of the Paulson Prize for Investigative Journalism, revisiting the life, death, and personally meaningful loss of his father, and learning about–and bringing justice to–the people behind his father's murder.

As the aircraft taxied to the hanger, Ken felt excitement at the thought of sharing his recent experiences and upcoming writing series with Martha. And just then he had a mini-revelation, that he wanted to communicate to Martha not just the *facts* of what he had been witness to, but his personal thoughts and emotional reactions as well. Even in the short time that she was stationed in Ottawa, Ken had missed her more than he would have anticipated, and not only their writing collaborations or their physical relationship. Those were important, of course, yet there was something more… As the realization hit him, Ken shook his head in amazement; it shouldn't have required a prize-winning investigative reporter's musings to finally conclude that he was, in fact, in love.

The End

REFERENCES (partial list of books and videos)

BOOKS:

Campagna, Palmiro *Storms of Controversy: The Secret Avro Arrow Files Revealed*, Toronto: Stoddart Publishing Co. Ltd., 1992, 1997

Campagna, Palmiro *Requiem For A Giant: A.V. Roe and the Avro Arrow,* Dundurn Press, 2003

Shaw, E. Ken *There Never Was An Arrow*. Toronto: Steel Rail Educational Publishing. 1979

Stewart, Greig *Shutting down the National Dream: A V Roe and the Tragedy of the Avro Arrow*. Scarborough: McGraw-Hill Ryerson Ltd., 1988

Whitcomb, Randall *Avro Aircraft & Cold War Aviation.* Vanwell Publishing Ltd., St.Catherines, Ontario, 2002.

Wood, Derek, editor *Janes All the World's Aircraft*. London: Janes Publishing , various years

VIDEOS
Arrow–From Dream to Destruction: The Story of the Plane, the Politics, and a Legend, by James Lloyd, Aviation Videos Limited, 2214 Courtland Drive, Burlington, Ontario L7R 1S4

... also, from *Aviation Videos*, numerous other important videos, comprising many hours of archival records of the Avro Arrow being designed, built and flown.

DEDICATION

This novel is dedicated to those individuals who dared to dream, and then create, one of the finest technological achievements in flight–of their time *and* ours–and whose only fault, perhaps, was that they succeeded *too* well. The Canadian designed and built CF-105 Avro Arrow was the finest fighter-interceptor in the world. It first flew in March 25, 1958, and likely would have achieved and maintained its true destiny for years and perhaps decades thereafter, had the entire program not been shut down by the then Canadian federal government's ruling Conservative party headed by Prime Minister John Deifenbaker, on February 20, 1959.

To those who fought mightily in an effort to prevent the travesty of the destruction of the Avro Arrow program, and to those other writers and workers who, even today, have refused to allow either the *fact* or the *meaning* of the Avro Arrow to be forgotten, this novel is also sincerely dedicated.

The Canadian Medicare system, at the time of this novel's final completion in early 2005, is still one of the finest such programs in the world. This book is also dedicated to its founding father, Tommy Douglas, and to its other conscientious guardians who are continuing to do their best–against mighty and moneyed odds–to preserve, protect, and enhance the Canadian government-run and publicly funded Medicare system, lest it meet the same fate as the Avro Arrow, perhaps by similar means and political and business interests, and perhaps even by some of the same individuals, and their philosophical clones.

About The Author

Will Cupchik entered engineering at McGill University in 1956, when the Avro Arrow program was still in its infancy. When he graduated with a Bachelor's degree in electrical engineering, the Avro Arrow had already been dead for two years. In 1961 Will was employed as a 'Navigation Systems Design engineer' for one of Canada's most innovative companies in the aeronautical field–where he designed navigational guidance systems for the then-next generation of military aircraft.

For the past four decades-plus, including the past quarter-century since obtaining his Ph.D. in counseling psychology from the University of Toronto, Will has worked in the mental health field. He was on staff of the forensic service of the Clarke Institute of Psychiatry in Toronto for twelve years (1984-86), including a period during which he held the position of *Psychologist-in-Charge, Forensic Outpatient Psychological Services.* Since 1986 he has been in full-time private practice in Toronto. He has also taught courses to graduate students at the University of Toronto.

Will Cupchik is a recognized authority in the forensic psychology area of usually honest adults who steal, and regularly assesses and treats both Canadian and American clients. He is the author of the *non-fiction* book, **Why Honest People Shoplift Or Commit Other Acts Of Theft.** Will has appeared on most American and Canadian television networks, including such shows as ABC's <u>Good Morning America</u>, CBS's <u>Early Show</u>, NBC's <u>48 Hours</u>, <u>MSNBC Investigates</u>, CBC <u>News</u> and <u>Venture</u>, CTV <u>National News</u>, and Global <u>National News</u>. He has also been quoted in The New York Times, The Globe and Mail, National Post, as well as PEOPLE, HEALTH, SELF, and CHATELAINE magazines.

For further information, visit *www.DrWillCupchik.com*